Linda Fairstein is a former prosecutor and America's foremost expert on sex crimes. Her first novel, *Final Jeopardy*, introducing Alexandra Cooper, was published in 1996. She lives in New York and Martha's Vineyard.

LINDA FAIRSTEIN OMNIBUS

Cold Hit
The Deadhouse

LINDA FAIRSTEIN

sphere

SPHERE

This omnibus edition first published in Great Britain in 2009 by Sphere

Cold Hit

I am spellbound by the mystery of murder.

—Weegee (Arthur Fellig)

1

It was after eight o'clock, and all I could see of the sun was its gleaming crown as it slipped behind the row of steep cliffs, giving off an iridescent pink haze that signaled the end of a long August day. Brackish gray water swirled and broke against the large rocks that edged the mound of dirt on which I stood, spitting up at my ankles as I stared out to the west at the Palisades. The pleats of my white linen skirt, which had seemed so cool and weightless as I moved about the air-conditioned courtroom all afternoon, were plastered against my thighs by the humidity, and I swatted off the mosquitoes as they searched for a place to land on my forearms.

I turned away from the striking vista across the Hudson

River and glanced down at the body of the woman that had snagged on the boulders less than an hour earlier.

The detective from the Crime Scene Unit reloaded his camera and took another dozen shots. "Want a couple of Polaroids to work from till I get you a full set of blowups?" I nodded to him as he changed equipment, leaned in above the head of his partially clothed subject, and set off the flash attachment.

The old guy with the fishing rod who had made the grim discovery was twitching nervously while he answered questions hurled at him in Spanish by a young uniformed cop from the Thirty-fourth Precinct. The officer pointed at something bulging in the man's pocket, and the fisherman's free hand shook uncontrollably as he pulled out a small flask of red wine.

"Tell him to relax, Carrera," Detective Mike Chapman called over to the rookie. "Tell him this one's a keeper. Catch of the day. Haven't seen anything this clean pulled out of these waters since Rip Van Winkle used it as a bathtub."

Chapman and his good friend Mercer Wallace had been talking with each other from the time Mercer and I reached the site ten minutes earlier. They had walked away from me so that Lieutenant Peterson could fill Mercer in on what he and Mike had learned since being called to the scene, while I stood at the woman's feet, staring down at her from time to time, half hoping she would open her eyes and speak to us. We were all waiting for one of the medical examiners to arrive and take a look at the body so it could be bagged and removed from this desolate strip of earth on Manhattan's northernmost tip before onlookers began to gather.

Hal Sherman rested his camera on top of the evidence collection bag and wiped the rivulets of sweat off his neck. "How'd you get here so fast?" he asked me.

"Mike was reaching out for Mercer to help him on this one

and got me in the deal. Mercer was down in court with me for pretrial hearings in an old case when Mike beeped him. Said he had a floater with a possible sexual assault, and he wanted Mercer to look at her."

"Tell the truth, kid. You couldn't resist a night on the town with the big guys, could you, blondie?" Chapman asked, after coming over to check whether Sherman had finished the photography. "Hey, Hal, who's the guy seems like he's about to lose his lunch over there?"

We all turned to look at the man, not more than twenty-five years old, who was leaning against a large boulder, taking in deep breaths of air and cupping one hand over his mouth. "Reporter for the *Times*, fresh out of journalism school. This is his third assignment, tailing me around to see how we process a crime scene. Two burglaries in the diamond district, one arson in a high school, and now—Ophelia."

Chapman went into a squat next to the right side of the woman's head, impatient with the presence of amateurs as he set to work on what was clearly the start of a homicide investigation. "Tell him he ought to look into getting the gig for restaurant reviews, Hal. Much easier on the gut."

I stepped closer to watch Chapman go over the corpse again, this time as he concentrated on details that he had observed before our arrival and explained them to Mercer Wallace. The two had been partners for several years in Manhattan North's Homicide Squad, where Chapman still worked, until Mercer had transferred over to Special Victims to handle rape cases. Despite the differences in their backgrounds and manner, they came together seamlessly to work at a crime scene or on a murder investigation.

Mercer, at forty, was five years older than Mike and I. He was one of a handful of African American detectives who had made first grade in the department, a detail man whom every senior prosecutor liked to count on, in the field and on the witness stand, to build a meticulous case. He was as solid as a linebacker but had passed up a football scholarship at Michigan to join the NYPD. Slower to smile than Mike Chapman, Mercer was intense and steady, with a sweetness of disposition that was, for those shattered victims who encountered him, their first lifeline back to a world of normalcy.

Mike Chapman was just over six feet tall, a bit shorter than Mercer. His jet black hair framed his lean face, momentarily somber as he reviewed the dead woman in front of him. A graduate of Fordham College, where he worked his way through school as a waiter and bartender, Mike had never wavered in his determination to follow the career path of his adored father, who had been a cop for more than a quarter of a century. He had a grin that could coax me out of almost any mood, and an encyclopedic knowledge of American history and military affairs, which had been his major concentration while in school.

"Four-point restraint," Chapman began, focusing his pen like a pointer in a college classroom. The slender body was resting on a wooden ladder about eight feet long. The victim's ankles and wrists were bound to narrow rungs above her head and below her feet. The cord used to hold the woman in place was firmly knotted and secured. Longer pieces of a thicker rope dangled from parts of the frame, and two of them still had rocks attached to their tips.

Mercer was bending over now, looking at the extremities from every angle. "Somebody went to an awful lot of trouble to make sure this body didn't come to the surface anytime before Christmas, wouldn't you say?"

He tugged at one of the loose lengths of rope, holding up the ragged end, from which it appeared a weight—perhaps another rock—had torn free.

Over the top of his head I could see Craig Fleisher, the on-call medical examiner, walking toward us. He waved a greeting and added, "Better move quickly, the vultures are gathering." Next to his parked car the satellite dish sitting above a Fox 5 television truck was suddenly visible. The first field reporter had already picked up word of the unusual find from a police scanner, and it would take only minutes before other camera crews joined him to try to get the most salacious shot of the corpse.

"What have you got, Mike? A drowning?" Fleisher asked.

"No way, Doc. Throwing her overboard was just a means of disposing of the body." We all leaned in closer as Chapman placed his hand on the crown of the woman's head and moved it slightly to the side. He slipped his pen beneath her matted black hair, which was still wet and splayed against the wooden crosspieces of the ladder, then lifted it gently to expose the scalp. "Skull was bashed in back here, maybe with a gun butt or hammer. I'd bet you'll find a fracture or two when you get in there tomorrow."

Fleisher studied the gaping wound. He was stone-faced and calm, running his fingers over the rest of the rear of the head. "Well, she wasn't in the water very long. Only a day or two at best."

He repeated what Chapman had told us when Mercer and I arrived. There was no putrefaction or decomposition, and the bruises he noted on her body were probably antemortem. "Fish and crabs usually get to work on the soft tissue pretty quickly," he explained, "but the face is completely intact here. Seems like they didn't have much of a chance."

Fleisher had trained in San Diego, so although he was a recent hire in New York, he was quite familiar with marine deaths.

"Could be our lucky break, Doc," Chapman said. "The killer—or killers—couldn't have picked a worse place to dump a body if they expected to keep it from surfacing."

The doctor straightened up and scanned the area—a

barren headland, just thirty feet long, that sat at the end of a city street, nestled between Columbia University's Baker Field and below the toll bridge leading north out of Manhattan, to the Bronx. "That water sure looks angry, doesn't it?"

"Spuyten Duyvil," said Chapman. "Welcome to the neighborhood. It's an old Dutch name for this tidal strait that connects the Harlem and Hudson Rivers, separates us from the mainland."

Mike knew the background as well as I did. Settlers in New Amsterdam had called it that in the early 1600s. *In spite of the devil,* they said, because the waters were so very rough, rocked by the tides in both directions. Passage through it had been impossible for centuries, until the government cut a canal almost one hundred years ago.

"Not that you'll see any Dutchmen around here now, Doc. Rice and beans replaced Heinekens a few years back, if you know what I mean. But they named it well."

The kid reporter had gotten to his feet and come up behind me, out of direct view of the body but close enough to listen to the conversation and jot down what we were saying.

"You mind not putting anything on paper for the time being?" Chapman asked, in a voice that was more of an order than a question. "You'd be required to give your scribbled musings to Miss Cooper here. It would become discovery material for the trial and she'd have to turn your notes over to the defense, once we catch the prick who did this."

"But, but I'm—uh—there's a privil—"

"You want to wait in the car while we do this, or you want to stand here quietly like a good scout and count on your memory to get this right? The local history you can find in a book, the current events are off the record. Start with the fact that she's got a crater the size of a teacup in the back of her head and that nobody planned on her doing any laps once she hit the water. Now keep out of my way. Understood?"

Chapman turned back to our small group, which was huddled around the body. Only the police divers, dressed in their scuba gear and holding for directions, stood off to the side as the rest of us waited for Fleisher to finish his inspection. Wallace had sent Officer Carrera up to his radio car to get a blanket, and he and another cop were holding it open as a shield between the dead woman and the curious busybodies who were gathering on 207th Street. He opened his cell phone and called the local precinct for crowd control backup as the news crew moved up within feet of our operation.

"Who's the blonde?" I heard the Fox 5 news reporter ask his cameraman.

"Alexandra Cooper. District Attorney's Office. Runs the Sex Crimes Unit for the D.A., Paul Battaglia. Probably means the cops think the deceased was raped. They always bring her in on those cases."

I wanted to hear what else the cameraman was going to say about our work, but Fleisher was talking again and I focused back on his remarks.

"You've got a female Caucasian who I'd guess to be in her late thirties." I had recently turned thirty-five, and I peered down at the frozen gaze of the woman, wondering what had brought her to this violent end, so prematurely. "I'm not going to turn her over or do any more work here, gentlemen. Too many eyes. But I'm certain the cause will be blunt force trauma—that blow to the head which Chapman located for us. I don't think we'll find any signs at autopsy that she was alive when she was submerged."

Fleisher went on. "Possible sexual assault. We'll be checking the vaginal vault for abrasions. I would doubt there'll be seminal fluid of value, once the seawater invaded. Hard to tell whether the missing clothes suggest rape or the rough current ripping them out of place."

The well-toned body of the young woman still had a beige

silk shell covering her bra, and a skirt of the same material. Both had tears and rips in the fine fabric. But there were no underpants, and I noticed what appeared to be finger marks embedded in the skin of her inner thighs.

"Doesn't look like a local girl, does she, Mercer?" Chapman remarked. The Thirty-fourth Precinct still housed some elegant old apartment buildings, but it was not one of the tonier neighborhoods of the city. "Check out the fingernails and pedicure. From the shape she's in, I'd bet she spent a lot of time on the StairMaster."

The vermilion polish on her toes and nails had been slightly chipped by her struggle with her assailant or by the tides. It was clear that she had taken good care of herself, until this week.

The Eyewitness News truck had joined the posse. "Hey, Mike," I heard a voice call out from the far side of the blanket Carrera was holding, "got anything for us?"

"Gimme a break, Pablo. Have a little respect for the dead. C'mon, Doc. Can we get her out of here now?"

Fleisher told him to cover the body, move the waiting ambulance in, and load up the ladder as it was, its cargo still lashed to the wood. "Need anything else from me?"

Chapman shook his head and said he'd be at the morgue for the autopsy proceeding the next day. He bent over and noted the name of the manufacturer on the underside of the ladder before an attendant loaded it onto the van.

"Summer backlog," Fleisher said. "I won't get to this one until two P.M., and that's with jumping her over a few unclaimed souls I've got in the cooler."

Four new arrivals from the precinct formed a human chain to separate the growing crowd from the diminishing group of us who were standing where the lady on the ladder had been.

Chapman walked over to talk with the lieutenant, who was watching the scuba team members tether themselves to huge pieces of equipment that Emergency Services had ferried to the scene. They were going to attempt to crawl around the border of the whirling passage in the unlikely possibility that they could feel for any evidence or weapon. It was obvious that there would be nothing to see along the silt-lined sides and bottom of the treacherous waterway gap.

"Don't waste their time or energy, Loo," Chapman urged Peterson, using the informal nickname that rank evoked from all detectives. "She didn't go into the drink anywhere near here. Could have been Yonkers, could have been the Bronx. It's just my good fortune that she stubbed her toe and washed up on a little piece of Manhattan North. I haven't picked up anything except drug shoot-outs in weeks."

Only Mike Chapman would consider this discovery to be his good fortune. I looked around the neglected plot that had become this woman's temporary graveyard, its surface littered with broken beer bottles, empty crack vials, scores of spots of pigeon droppings, and a few dozen used condoms.

Mercer Wallace came up beside me, grasping my elbow in his enormous black hand and guiding me out to the street, running interference for me through the rows of news teams and the neighborhood cronies who were looking for excitement now that darkness had fallen. He unlocked the passenger door of his car and I ducked into the seat.

People moved back to the sidewalk as Mercer made a U-turn on the narrow road, and we drove off. He turned in and out of a maze of one-way streets, accelerating when he reached Broadway, taking me downtown and across Central Park to my apartment, on the Upper East Side. I was silent for blocks.

"Where are you, Alex? Talk to me. I can't let you go upstairs alone just thinking about that body. She'll be with you all night. You'll never close your eyes."

I knew that without being told. But I was deeply distressed and much too wired to sleep after what we had just seen, despite my exhaustion from a couple of weeks of hard-fought courtroom battle in front of a demanding judge. "Thanks, Mercer. Just wondering about the obvious, knowing that there aren't any logical answers. I'll be fine."

"We'll get him, Alex. It doesn't seem very likely tonight. But Chapman and me, we'll get him. In spite of the devil, Miss Cooper. In spite of the devil."

2

A cold blast hit me as I opened my apartment door. Thank God I had forgotten to turn down the air conditioner. The coolness felt good as I moved into the bedroom to take off my wilted suit.

The green light flashed on my answering machine. I smiled at the thought of hearing a friendly voice or two, someone who would ease my transition from a scene of violence to the peace of my home, secure and comforting, on the twentieth floor of a high-rise apartment. I pressed the playback button as I began to undress.

I was on my way to the shower when I heard the voice that I had been waiting for, so I walked back and sat on the side of my bed. "Alex? . . . Alex? . . . It's Jake . . ." The telephone connection sizzled and faded. Before I could move, it started again. "Don't know if you can hear me . . . still in China . . . and . . . must be about nine o'clock your time. Sorry I missed you . . . I'll see you . . . and just wanted to tell you that . . ." I pushed the replay button. The machine hadn't captured any more words than I had heard, but it was Jacob Tyler's voice that I wanted to listen to over and over. We had been dating for only a couple of months and the newness of the relationship still got me tingling when I heard him speak. I pushed the save button and went in to shower.

I lifted my face up to the steaming water that poured out at me and drizzled down the length of my legs. I reached for the bar of soap and stared at my fingernail, noticing the chip of polish at its tip. My eyes closed and all I could see was the bright red on the nails of the dead woman's hand. I opened my eyes and shook my head, willing myself not to call up other memories of that body on the ladder. There would be all night for such visions, as I knew too well from past experience. I scrubbed the day's grime off my face and body, then dried and wrapped myself tightly in a warm, thick terry robe.

I toweled my hair as I played Jake's message once more. I was smiling again, imagining what he might have said in between the snatches of words that were actually recorded and not gobbled up by the satellites. I'd have to phone my best friend, Nina, and tell her about Jake's call. I could guess what her response would be: "What good is it to have a guy half a world away when you need him to put his arms around you right now?"

Maybe I'd wait and call her tomorrow. She wasn't wrong about my needing Jake, but I had been dealing with images of victims for more than ten years. Most of the time, my work was with women who survived their assailants and who would triumph in the courtroom. But very little could soften the shock of seeing firsthand the destruction of a human life—a life as young as my own, as full of promise and hope as I dreamed mine would be.

I shook the dampness off my hair and looked at my watch. It would be morning in China. I had no idea where Jake was at the moment and no office number abroad at which to call him back. I wished he were here with me now. This was not a night to be alone.

My head ached and my stomach was making noises, demanding to be fed. I pressed the telephone button to speed-dial the deli on the next corner and order a turkey sandwich. I could nourish the body if not the soul.

"Sorry, Alex: It's almost ten o'clock," said Clare at P. J. Bernstein's delicatessen. "We're just closing up."

I never cooked at home, so I knew there would be nothing in the refrigerator. I had cans of soup in the cabinet, but it was too warm out to entertain the thought of hot soup. I put some ice cubes in a glass, moving on to the den to fix myself a stiff Dewar's. A mystery novel waited for me next to my bed, but there was nothing like the sight of a real corpse to alienate me from the genre for a couple of weeks. Jake had left a dog-eared Henry James on my dresser. Perhaps I'd start that instead of trying to go to sleep.

I hadn't bothered to turn on the lights before I sat on the sofa, drink in hand, and gazed out over the city. Soft music from my CD system distracted me until Linda Ronstadt began to sing about the hungry women down on Rue Morgue Avenue. I flashed again to the body on the ladder and visualized the setting where it rested tonight.

The sharp buzz of the phone startled me. I caught it on the third ring.

"You almost sound happy to hear from me for a change."

"Mike?" I asked, having hoped it would be Jake.

"Wrong voice, huh? Don't go getting dejected 'cause it's me.

It's not like I'm the Unabomber or Ted Bundy calling you for a quick squeeze. The lieutenant asked me to get hold of you. Says he'd really like you to be at Compstat in the morning."

Compstat—comparative computer statistics—the NYPD's hot new demonstration for leadership accountability. Meetings held at headquarters several times a month, in the War Room, to show off the commissioner's ability to identify and solve the city's crime problems.

"What time do I have to be there?"

"Seven o'clock sharp. Seems the brass went berserk over this one tonight—it screws up all the mayor's statistics for the month. The commish may even call on you if he gets frisky and wants answers for all his questions, or wants to blame your boss for refusing to prosecute some of the quality-of-life cases."

"Thanks for the warning."

"You sound really flat, kid. You okay?"

"My head's still back at Spuyten Duyvil, if you know what I mean. Want to grab a pizza and come on up here for supper?"

"Sorry, Coop. It's almost eleven o'clock. We'll be working most of the night, trying to figure out who this broad is and when she got popped in the river. See you at reveille. Better sleep with the night-light on."

It wasn't the dark that frightened me. It was the fact that moving around out there, below my window, were creatures capable of splitting open the head of a young woman and throwing her body into the water. I stared out at the lights of Manhattan for the next hour, watching them gradually go off as people went to sleep. And all the time, as I sat awake, I thought about the monsters who walk among us.

3

There were still a few cars parked on Hogan Place near my office, most of which belonged to the lawyers working the midnight shift in night court, when I pulled my Jeep into a reserved slot behind the district attorney's space at six forty-five on Friday morning. I took the shortcut over to One Police Plaza, cutting behind the Metropolitan Correctional Center and alongside the staggeringly expensive new federal court-house, which made our digs, complete with oversized rodents and roaches that obviously thrived on Combat, look like judicial facilities in some third-world country. I stopped at a cart being wheeled into place by one of the regular street vendors and bought two cups of black coffee, remembering that the brew served in the hallway outside the meeting room was too weak to start me up for the day.

One by one, black Crown Vics with red flashers mounted on each dashboard pulled into the tightly secured parking garage beneath Police Headquarters, marking the arrival of bosses from all the commands in Manhattan North, the upper half of the island. I continued past that underground entrance and jogged up the two tiers of granite steps, walking around in front of the building to display my identification to the cop at the door and run my shoulder bag through the metal detector.

"Eighth floor," the guard said. "Elevator's behind the wall to the back."

I knew the way well. In over ten years as a prosecutor, I had come to this building more times than I cared to count. Some days I was sent to sit in at meetings called by the commissioner in which the district attorney himself had no interest; on other occasions I came to brainstorm on investigative strategies in cases the department was struggling to solve; frequently I was there to plead for manpower in a matter that was not getting appropriate police attention; and every now and then—under this administration's budget-driven oversight—I walked over to attend the promotion of a friend to a higher-ranking post.

Compstat had revolutionized the accountability of precinct commanders when it was introduced to the department in the early nineties. Several times a month, at seven o'clock in the morning, bosses from one of the city's geographic divisions were summoned to appear at One Police Plaza, to spend the next three hours being grilled by the chief of operations and two of his trusted henchmen. There was only one direction in which this mayor wanted the crime rate to move, and each man was called upon to answer for the evil that crossed his borderlines and played havoc with the numbers regularly released to the press by the Public Information deputy.

When the elevator doors opened on eight, I was facing a wall of blue-uniformed backs of the commanding officers, pressing ahead against each other as the invited guests who were not members of the department turned the corner to enter the Operations Room and take their seats in anticipation of the arrival of Chief Lunetta.

Chapman called out to me before I noticed him, wedged between two full inspectors who were laughing at whatever tale he was spinning. "Hey, Coop! Meet Lenny McNab. Just been transferred over to clean up the Three-three. Take a good look at him now, because after this meeting I doubt he'll be able to sit down for a week."

McNab shook his head and my hand at the same time. The newspapers had been full of stories about the string of bodega burglaries in McNab's territory. If he couldn't account for progress in the investigation by this morning, he'd be made to look like a fool by the three grand inquisitors.

Lunetta's voice boomed out at us from the stairwell door. "Let's get it going, guys. We've got a lot to cover this morning." His entourage brushed past us and we dutifully followed.

Room 802 was a cavernous space, with double-height ceilings and state-of-the-art electronic equipment, that had been designed to become Command Central in case of any terrorist takeover or natural disaster in New York City. Three gigantic media screens filled the front wall of the room, which was lined on one length with concealed booths—to hold the crisis solvers at more critical points in time, and observers on more benign occasions—while the other wall was decorated with police shields and murals featuring flags of various law enforcement agencies. Two tables ran through the center of the room from forward to rear, around which the commanders seated themselves with the personnel who ran their investigative and uniformed forces, as well as a few detectives who might be called upon to explain the status of a particular case that had attracted media attention.

Directly beneath the huge screens was the podium, to which speakers would be called at the whim of the chief of operations. Lunetta would tell the computer programmer who sat beside him which graphics to display over their heads on the three screens—usually starting with a map of the precinct, a chart of the previous month's crime statistics, and a graph plotting the most recent week's violent crime activity, with robberies flagged in red, rapes in blue, and burglaries in green.

Lunetta and his superchiefs sat in the rear at a table perpendicular to the array of well-decorated men spread down the center of the room. He was tall and lean, with angled features and black hair that was drawn sleekly back and trimmed at the neck in military fashion. He looked great in the dark navy blue uniform, and knew it.

My seat was in one of the three rows of folding chairs behind the chief's position, which were reserved for non-NYPD spectators. Each chair was labeled with a scrap of paper torn from a legal pad. Excusing myself, I tried to slither into place, passing over two lawyers from the United States Attorney's Office and four guys from upstate police departments, before sitting down next to a woman who introduced herself as a trend researcher from the Department of Justice. I opened the lid of my coffee cup and took a slug as Lunetta called the first group of officers to the podium.

Frank Guffey moved forward to the mike, flanked by his supervising staff. He was smart and well liked by police and prosecutors, a tough boss who had been moved from the East Harlem area a year earlier down to the cushy confines of Wall Street, and now back to the high-crime neighborhood of the Twenty-eighth Precinct.

"G'morning, Chief. I'm reporting on the period that closed July thirty-first." Guffey smiled and paused briefly, weighing whether to add a personal pleasantry. "Nice to be here again in the North, after a brief visit to Manhattan South, sir."

Lunetta shot back, "I hope you can say as much *after* the meeting."

"First of all, the decrease in overall crime continues." Clearly, Guffey knew the drill. That's what these guys wanted to hear, right out of the box. "Now, we do show an increase in robberies, but—"

Forget the "buts," buddy. I watched as Lunetta turned his head ninety degrees and gave a command to the computer programmer sitting at his right shoulder. Seconds later, the three overhead graphics changed. A map of the Twenty-eighth Precinct's territory dominated the middle screen.

Lunetta barked, "Break them down for me, Inspector. I want them by day of the week, and then by the time of day of the tour."

Before Guffey could lift his papers and find the correct answers, we could all see the numbers in the projections that the chief's team had prepared for this attack.

"I want to get right into these spikes, Guffey. Take us through them. Give me reasons."

I could see the color rise in Frank's cheeks, as most of the bosses around the tables seemed to squirm in sympathy.

Guffey started to respond. "Several of them seem to be the work of the same team, Chief. The numbers started to spike when a pair of male Hispanics began to hit a couple of apartments on Broadway, just north of McDonald's. Same M.O. Gain entry with a ruse—female knocking on the door for the perps and asking for her sister. Then she disappears while the guys tie up everyone inside with speaker wire—"

"Drug related?"

"Probably. Only, the one last week, on the twenty-ninth—"

"You mean the restaurant manager they burned with an iron?" Lunetta thrived on displaying to the crowd how well he could learn the detail of hundreds of these cases, outlined for him in his briefing books, and talk about them as familiarly as if he were working on them himself.

"Yeah. We figure that was a mistake. They went to the wrong apartment. I got Louis Robertson here. They're his cases, if you'd like to hear from him."

"Not unless he's got answers for me, Guffey. Excuses I got plenty of. It's answers I want. You guys doing the obvious? Running fingerprints through Safis?" The new, automated fingerprint-matching system was solving scores of cases that used to require tedious hand searches. "Checking with surrounding precincts to see if they got anything like this going? Parole—probation—informants? I assume you'll study these charts and decide how to redeploy your manpower to address the situation more aggressively."

Guffey said his men had been doing all of the above and that he would certainly make use of the time charts. He got through the other crime categories fairly gracefully and back to his seat without a great deal of damage.

Inspector Jaffer was next up. A real breath of fresh air for the department. As I ran my eyes around the table, Joanne Jaffer and Jane Pearl were the only two women inspectors I noted in the room. They were both young, bright, and attractive, and were changing a lot of opinions about female bosses in the department, held by too many of the hairbags, those dyed-in-the-wool old-timers who were petrified in their traditions.

Jaffer's numbers in the Twentieth Precinct were excellent. The Upper West Side had always been one of the safest residential areas in Manhattan. Robberies, burglaries, and car thefts continued to be lower than ever. No homicides in over six months. Her only problem was a serial rapist who had been operating for more than two years—hitting sporadically, and not even linked to a pattern until DNA tests on the rape kits had confirmed that the most recent attack was committed by the same assailant as the first one, which had occurred more than twenty months ago. Battaglia had been asked to address a community meeting about the case in a few days and would be pleased if I could come back to him after this morning with a sense about the chief's role in the investigation.

Jaffer gave her report and began to answer Lunetta's questions about the rapist.

"How many cases you up to now, Inspector?"

Jaffer answered sharply. "Eight, sir. That we know of. Eight with an identical M.O., and two of those have been linked to each other by DNA. Serology is working on two others this week."

"What took you so long to put this pattern together? Somebody asleep in the station house?"

She started to answer, as a hand went up on the right side of the room. Sergeant Pridgen, who was assigned to Special Victims, was responsible for the task force handling the investigation. He had been running the cases long before Jaffer became involved and was trying to jump in to take some of the heat.

Lunetta ignored Pridgen's waving arm. I knew he'd like to see Jaffer sweat, and I kept my fingers crossed that he would fail to make it happen.

"Serology finally came up with a cold hit, Chief. That's what broke it for us."

Her answers were clipped, to the point, and good. The investigation had floundered until the Medical Examiner's Office made a computer match—known in the still-evolving language of genetic fingerprinting as a "cold hit"—between DNA samples left by the rapist in his victims' bodies more than two years ago and those found in the most recent case. Cops who had argued about whether or not the older attacks bore any connection to the current crimes were silenced by the stunning ability of the database to definitively link an assailant's targets to one another.

"Why can't serology match it to a perp in their data bank?" Lunetta asked.

"Because the bank is just up and running in New York. It's only been in operation since last year, and they've got fewer than a hundred samples from convicted rapists and murderers."

Legislation created genetic data banks in most states across the country during the late nineties, but few of their labs were equipped to process the information collected from inmates and create the pools from which to search for repeat offenders, until quite recently. It would be unlikely to get a hit on this serial rapist, who had been operating on the streets of Manhattan since the days before the law enabled the collection of blood samples from incarcerated prisoners.

Jaffer continued to describe the team's approach. Last week the department sketch artist, working with several of the victims, had completed a composite that was being distributed to stores and residences throughout the precinct—the "generic male black," as Mercer liked to describe the suspect. Medium complexion, average height, average build, between twenty-five and thirty-five years old, possible mustache, close-cropped hair, no distinguishing features, scars, or marks. Before too long, every African American adult male who set foot north of Sixtieth Street and south of Eighty-sixth Street, between Central Park West and Riverside Drive, would be stopped and questioned. Neighbors would be turning in their deliverymen or elevator operators, and good citizens would be frisked by anxious and weary cops, each one hoping to get a lucky break and catch the compulsive rapist.

"Stop dancing around, Pridgen. I'm getting to you. What else is your crew doing about this one?"

The sergeant stood to answer. "We've got Traffic giving out summonses on the midnight tour, tagging all the unregistered and uninsured plates. Mounted's working the area on week-ends, which is mostly when he hits."

I could see Lunetta rolling his eyes even as I stared at the rear of his head. Mounted cops riding up and down West End Avenue at midnight on a Saturday. Not the most subtle way to patrol the neighborhood. Even the rapist might catch on and change his movements.

Pridgen continued. "We've called in the Profiling Unit at Quantico and—"

Say the magic word and the duck comes down, hitting Lunetta square on the head. "Feds? *Feds?* Whose stupid idea is that? Aren't you guys up to handling this one yourself? Answer me, Pridgen. Whose idea was it?"

Lunetta saw Pridgen flash a glance in my direction. "District attorney calling the shots on this one, Sarge? You just sit back and let them take right over and run the show, huh? Maybe you're moonlighting on the side, too busy to do major investigations? We got an opening over at the auto pound, looking after towed vehicles, if you think this is too tough for you. What does Cooper use on you guys anyway, a nose ring? Just leads you around on a leash all day? Let me know if you start rolling over on your back or baying at the moon."

The woman researcher from Justice bit into her lip and looked at me for a reaction. I didn't know whether I was blushing for Pridgen or for myself. I ripped some paper from my legal pad and dashed off a note to Lunetta, passing it forward, in which I asked his permission to explain where we were going with the investigation. By the time it reached him, was opened and read, he had continued to pepper the sergeant with questions and then kept on going at Pridgen even harder, choosing to ignore my offer. If he had intended to call on me before I asked to speak, I had just sealed my fate by assuring him that I wanted to give him answers to these questions.

"Last week's attack—was this girl coming from one of those Columbus Avenue bars, too?"

"No sir," Pridgen answered.

"Where from, then?"

"Actually, her boyfriend drove her home, just before two in the morning. Let her out of the car about half a block from her apartment, up at the corner. She walked to the front of the building alone. The rapist pushed in behind her, after she unlocked the vestibule door."

"So much for the boyfriend. I guess chivalry's dead, wouldn't you say, Sergeant? I want some progress on this one before the next time you come back here. Take your seats. I want the Three-four up now. Let's hear about last night's homicide."

Chairs pushed back and the podium assembly changed over, with Lieutenant Peterson and Chapman accompanying the CO up to the stand.

The general precinct figures were good. Lunetta was pleased that the deputy inspector in charge had taken the story of one of his burglary patterns to a local cable TV program, ¿Que Pasa NY?, which resulted in an informant breaking the case. He liked that kind of creative policing, as he would call it. What he never had liked was wisecracking, not even back when he had been Chapman's boss in the Street Crime Unit, almost a decade earlier.

"Who's going to bring me up to speed on the new case?"

Peterson pointed at Chapman and stepped aside. Mike rested his notes on the podium and ran his fingers through his thick dark hair. He dug one hand into the pocket of his blazer, then started his description of how he was summoned to the scene. He was thorough, detailed, and professional—the best homicide cop in the business—but I fidgeted and recrossed my legs when he got to the end of the narrative and closed his description with Dr. Fleisher's directive to load "Gert" into the EMS van.

" 'Gert'? I didn't know she'd been identified." Lunetta was annoyed. His head whipped from side to side as he checked with each of his aides to see if they had failed to give him the morning update on the city's most visible crime of the moment. The case was on the cover of both daily tabloids, and he should have had the newest information about the unfortunate victim before the public did.

"She hasn't been identified yet, Chief."

"Well, *is* her name Gert, or isn't it?"

Don't go there, Chief, I urged quietly from the peanut gallery. All of us who worked with Mike knew that he named his victims in every case. Always did it, and often stuck with his nickname, no matter what the eventual I.D.—his own perverse way of personalizing his cases.

"I call her that, Chief, so she's not just some number, some cold statistic for the mayor to get off on. I named this one in honor of Gertrude Ederle—three Olympic medals and the English Channel. I figure, given the way somebody tried to send her to sleep with the fishes for keeps, she must have had the soul of a great swimmer to stay afloat."

There were a few snickers around the room, but most of the group knew it wasn't the safest direction to follow.

Lunetta wouldn't bite twice. He moved away to the next questions. "What are you looking at here?"

Chapman went on. "After the autopsy results today, we'll work on a press release and sketch."

"Can't you give the papers a photo from the scene—a close-up? Get an I.D. more quickly?"

"I don't think the way she looked coming out of the water is the way any of her loved ones would want to see her featured. We're working with Missing Persons and each of the precincts."

"You checking every area that borders the creek? May turn out to be a Bronx homicide after all, Chapman. The numbers

33

get tallied in the precinct where the crime occurred, you know."

"I don't care where she dove in, Chief. *We* got her now."

Fat chance, Lunetta. Count it as an outer-borough murder so we keep the Manhattan numbers down? Nope, I'm with Chapman. She landed here, and no matter where she was killed, that gives us jurisdiction.

"I see from the newspapers that you had Miss Cooper up at the scene last night. You throwing in the towel, too, Detective? Ready to call in the Feds? I can't help but wonder what it is you need a pet D.A. for at all these crime scenes and station houses. D'you carry her lipstick case for her, or her hairbrush?" The chief smirked at his put-down, jabbing the detective and me in the same thrust.

But trying to embarrass Chapman that way wouldn't quite work. He'd simply use the opportunity to get more laughs, even if they would be at my expense. "No, no, sir. She never lets me near the makeup. You know me, Chief—I'm strictly a leg man. I'm in charge of her spare panty hose. Each time there's a run in one of those suckers, I pull out a replacement pair. Best I can do at the moment."

A couple of my friends around the room raised their eyes cautiously to meet mine, to make sure I was rolling with the flow. Not a problem. Battaglia had trained me well. I could control my short fuse with the knowledge I'd get some shots back at the chief eventually. The district attorney might even take them on my behalf.

Lunetta's number-two man leaned over and whispered something to him, flipping through the briefing book to an earlier page. He scanned it and looked up. "Is that case of the body that came out of the East River last month related to this one, you think? That's still open, isn't it?"

"Yeah, but no connection. That one, a homeless man was fishing, hooked up and pulled an arm out of the water. Right out of its socket, actually. Scuba went in and found the rest of the body, weighted down with concrete blocks. She'd been in the water more than half a year. Feet bound, ligature round the neck. That's a mob case—got a good snitch who's working with us. We know who we're looking for, just haven't been able to find him yet."

Great restraint, Mikey. He had resisted the temptation to tell Lunetta that he had christened that victim "Venus." A one-armed Italian woman in a cement overcoat didn't lend herself to any appellation except Venus de Milo.

The aide whispered to Lunetta again. "We had Bronx South here on Wednesday of last week. They've got a rape pattern as well in a couple of the housing projects. You might check over there to see if there are any similarities."

Chapman looked less than interested. The likelihood that the well-groomed, silk-clad woman he had dubbed Gert had anything to do with ghetto dwellings in a run-down neighborhood that wasn't his official territory didn't engage him very seriously.

Lunetta listed off a punch list of places to go and things to do that would have been elementary for a rookie homicide detective. Mike listened patiently and assured the chief that as soon as they figured out who the deceased was, he'd be off and running. "I assume we'll know who she is by the end of the day."

"That's great, Chapman. Then I'll expect an arrest within the week. Maybe next time you'll do a better job keeping the shutterbugs away from the scene you're working. No reason for a case like this to be front-page news, except for the photo opportunity you gave them. Now it'll take a couple of days to make these headlines go away."

Lunetta finished snapping at Chapman, looked around the room, and announced to the bosses, "I think you gentlemen realize how much the commissioner hates it when this kind of thing happens. Tourists aren't scared away by drug dealers killing each other off on their own turf or gang members shooting other gang members to death. But if this woman turns out to be an innocent victim of violence, I don't think I have to tell you what it means to the city. Last night, at a fundraiser, the mayor was just telling his supporters that murders in New York had dropped to their lowest numbers in more than a quarter of a century—when he got word of this mess." Lunetta scanned the brass arrayed in front of him. "That's the point of all these exercises—in case it's slipped your minds. Letting everyone know how safe this city has become. Our homicide rate hasn't been this good since nineteen sixty-one."

Chapman made sure he muttered into the microphone as he picked up his notes and pocketed them. "I hate to burst Hizzoner's bubble, but I gotta tell you his numbers are small comfort to the broad who's laid out in a refrigerator up at the morgue, waiting for her last physical."

4

Mike spent most of the short walk over to my office, three blocks north of One Police Plaza, trying to worm his way back into my good graces. I was used to being the butt of Chapman's humor and had long ago stopped letting it get to me. It was not even ten thirty and I was already more bothered by the oppressive heat that had blanketed the ugly stretch of asphalt that ran in front of the city and state buildings along Centre Street.

"Aren't you going to be late for court?" he asked me as we rounded the corner and I stopped at the cart to buy us each another round of coffee. Mike called up to the vendor to throw in a cruller for him, too. "Couldn't eat a thing last night. Kept looking into that hole in the back of Gert's head every time I closed my eyes."

"No court on Friday. The defendant's a Muslim. Today's his holy day," I answered, hanging my identification tag on a chain around my neck as we approached the entrance to the District Attorney's Office.

"Reggie Bramwell's a Muslim? I collared him on a gun case five years ago, and he was a full-press Baptist then. I'm sure of it."

"Jailhouse conversion, Mike," I said, pushing through the revolving doors and holding the security gate open for one of my colleagues who was on her way out of the building, headed toward the other courthouse, pushing a shopping cart loaded with evidence. "A week ago Thursday, in fact. Must have been a deeply religious experience. Someone at Rikers Island convinced him of the joys of the three-day workweek. The judge uses Wednesday as a calendar day, and the prisoner—Reggie Bramwell, now also known to the court as Reggie X—gets to worship on Friday. Just prolongs my agony for a few days. In fact, I think he's just doing this because he knows I wanted some vacation time this month—and if he can't go to the beach, why should I?"

We waited for one of the three elevators to return to the lobby floor, while a small commotion started behind us. "Alex, tell this jerk who I am, will you please?" a familiar voice called out.

My colleague Pat McKinney was standing in front of the security counter dressed in his running clothes, which were drenched with sweat, arguing with the officer on duty. Pat's already reddened complexion was deepening and appeared to be spreading to the tips of his ears and down his neck.

"I'm telling you I left my I.D. on top of that pad next to the telephone before I went out at nine thirty. Now, if somebody moved it or walked off with it, that's *your* problem and not mine."

The cop, obviously a summer replacement who was stuck with this security detail, didn't recognize the deputy chief of the Trial Division. Most of us who jogged from time to time during our lunch hours had taken to leaving our photo identification tags at the entrance desk and picking them up on our way back in. The officers from the Fifth Precinct who regularly worked the desk knew most of us by sight and held the tags in a pile on the corner of the counter, behind the bank of telephones. I had no time for running these days, because of my hearings, and no inclination either, because of the intense heat. McKinney, who liked to take his daily jog earlier than the lunch hour break during the hot summer months, was probably more aggravated by the fact that this police officer didn't recognize him than that the officer had misplaced his only means of official access to the building.

I held the bucking elevator door open with my left arm and started to explain to the officer that I would vouch for McKinney, despite the fact that he hated my guts.

Chapman nudged me out of the way by bumping his hip up against mine and clamping his hand on the button that said *Close.* He was also calling out to the cop as the doors came together in front of my face. "Hey, Officer. Don't let that guy in. He's a whack job—comes around here all the time, looking to get in. The real McKinney has a huge wart on the tip of his nose and foams at the mouth a lot."

"That'll do wonders to break the ice between me and my supervisor, don't you think?" I asked as I pressed the button for the eighth floor and replaced my sunglasses in their case.

"What's the difference? McKinney hasn't had a decent word to say about you in the entire time you've been here. Screw him. Who's going to miss him for the next half hour, his girlfriend?"

"What girlfriend? You mean Ellen? She just works for him, she's not his girlfriend."

We got off the elevator and headed for my office.

"Don't tell me you're as gullible as his wife, Coop. All that platonic crap? 'Beep me, darling, I'm working on a gun bust tonight with the cops. Field assignment. Midnight grand jury.' You know anybody else in the Trial Division who gets the kind of close supervision Ellen does? One on one, behind closed doors? Trust me. Next time he gives you any trouble, I'll run interference for you."

My secretary, Laura, had a smile on her face by the time we came into view, no doubt hearing Mike's voice as we made our way down the hall together. He broke into his best Smokey Robinson imitation as she began to go through the morning's messages with me. She sailed through the first six, all of which could be returned later, accompanied by Mike's humming and finger snapping. When he broke out in his modified lyrics— "And in case you go to court, then a lawyer is the one you want to see . . . but in case you want love, Laura . . . call on me"—I gave up the battle and went in to my desk to see what else awaited me.

I opened the desk drawer and took three extra-strength Tylenols. The fatigue of the trial schedule on top of my usual duties supervising the Sex Crimes Prosecution Unit had been wearing me down. Sarah Brenner, my close friend and second in command, had been ordered by her obstetrician to stay at home, since she was already three days overdue with her second child. I had all weekend to complete the legal memorandum the judge in the Reggie X case expected from me on Monday, so I decided to focus first on the queries from the other lawyers in the unit.

"Who sounded more critical?" I called out to Laura.

"If I were you, I'd get Patti down here first. Want me to call her?"

"Yeah. Then back her up with Ryan, please."

Mike took off his navy blazer and hung it on the back of

one of the chairs before picking up the pile of morning news-papers that had been delivered to my desk. He was looking to see whether any clever reporter had scooped him on some aspect of the Gert murder that he might have missed.

Patti Rinaldi was one of my favorite young assistants—a solid lawyer with sound judgment and dogged courtroom style. Her enthusiasm for her work, and for resolving the plight of her victims, seemed to emanate from her when she entered my small office carrying the case file of her latest problem.

"A vision in lavender, Ms. Rinaldi," Chapman said, eyeing the tall, thin brunette carefully over the top of his *New York Post*. "You look ravishing today. You're not cheating on me, are you?"

"Cooper doesn't leave me any time to even think about it, Mike. I worked the four-to-twelve shift on intake last night. Thought you'd want to know about this one, Alex. Have you had any cases at a sleep disorder clinic yet?"

"Not so far."

"I think we got our first."

Mike's interest was piqued. "What's a sleep disorder clinic?"

"Latest psychobabble moneymaker. Almost every medical center has one at this point. Patients who have trouble with sleep—insomniacs, sleepwalkers, snorers, you name it—come in to be 'examined' while they sleep. Idea is to find a cure for the problem."

Patti added to my description. "And they pay dearly—a thousand, fifteen hundred dollars per visit—just to spend the night on a cot and let somebody 'watch' them sleep, measure their dream time and the intervals between dream segments."

"Are there job openings?" Mike asked. "I suppose by now someone's come up with my time-tested solution. Two cock-tails, get laid, roll over, and smoke a cigarette—guaranteed to put you out for hours. Maybe I could be a consultant."

"Is this one of the legitimate operations, Patti?"

"Yes, Alex. It's affiliated with Saint Peter's Hospital. It's located in a large office building which houses all their clinics up on Amsterdam Avenue. This is actually run by the head of their Department of Psychiatry, so they treat the whole thing very seriously."

"Your victim?"

"Her name is Flora. Very fragile twenty-two-year-old who lives with her mother in Flatbush. Met the defendant a couple of years ago when he was her psychology professor at Brooklyn College. She began to see him for therapy after the school year, but was smart enough to stop the sessions when he started coming on to her sexually.

"Now, almost two years have gone by and she was suffering from depression. Found his number in the book, called him, and he made an appointment for her to come in to the clinic, where he told her he's currently working. Said he still did therapy on the side."

I was taking notes as Patti continued the narrative.

"Flora got to the office at eight o'clock on Tuesday night. Paid the therapist—his name is Ronald—for the session, and at the end he advised her that she needed to get a job, to engage herself in something serious. He offered her a position as a computer analyst at the clinic. Took out a contract for one year's employment from his desk, signed it, and had her do the same."

I had dozens of questions to ask, but rather than punctuate Patti's story, I would let her tell it and assume she would cover most of what I needed to know.

"Finally, Ronald took the contract back and told Flora that he wouldn't make his boss, the chief physician, enforce it unless she thanked him right now by performing oral sex."

"I am definitely in the wrong line of work," Chapman mumbled.

Patti went on. "Ronald waved the contract back and forth in front of her and kept repeating, 'No blow job, no job.' He reduced Flora to tears in about five minutes, and she complied with the condition. Meanwhile, in a few of the cubicles attached to Ronald's module, people were sleeping—naked, of course, with monitors attached to measure their breathing, their blood pressure, their REMs, and so on. So when Ronald handed her back her half of the contract, he told her this was better than usual. He said that most of the time he stood there and masturbated while he watched the struggling sleepers try to find the Land of Nod."

Chapman was on his feet. "You mean these idiots are paying big bucks to have this frigging pervert get his rocks off watching them toss and turn? That'd cure my insomnia instantly. I'd like to tie him to a chair by his testicles and make him listen to lullabies for twenty-four hours. See how he sleeps. I don't get it, Coop. This stuff you people work on makes murder look comprehensible."

"How'd she come forward, Patti?"

"When Flora called Ronald yesterday to ask when she could start to work, he told her that there was no job because he really didn't have any power to hire or fire employees. She stormed right into the clinic and showed the contract to the physician in charge, who said it was bogus. So she went directly to a pay phone on the corner and called the cops. I thought you ought to know about it before I did anything on the case."

"Good thinking." Brownnosing worked with me almost every time. Patti knew that if we, as prosecutors, could direct the course of an investigation prearrest, we could usually build a stronger case for trial.

"What's to think about?" Chapman asked. "Cuff him and put him in the can, now."

"What's the crime, Mikey? What does Patti charge him

43

with?" I stood with my back to the air conditioner, trying to cool down as we talked.

"Sodomy in the first," Mike suggested.

"I didn't hear you describe any force, did I?" Patti shook her head in the negative in response to my question.

"Public lewdness," Mike spat out at me.

"It's not a public place. Ronald's sitting right in his own office when he's playing with himself. Expectation of privacy and all that," I countered.

"I told you murder is easy. You got a dead body, an unnatural cause of death, and it's one kind of homicide or another. You girls gotta sit here and play Find the Crime."

"Here's what you do," I suggested to Patti. "Bring Flora in and get all the facts. See if you can make out a coercion charge. Try section 135.60 of the Penal Law, sub 9—compelling her to perform an act which might be harmful to health, safety, reputation, et cetera.

"Also, there's a good chance he's been holding himself out as a doctor or some other licensed position at the clinic. Figure on next Wednesday—that's my calendar day, so I'm free to go with you. You can have a search warrant prepared and ready by then. We'll have a couple of guys from the squad take us up to the clinic, and we'll go in that morning with the warrant. That way we can seize all his personnel records, Flora's files, his appointment book, any documents he has on his walls—with credentials that can be checked out—and any other information you can develop during your interview with Flora. No one will be on notice that we're coming, so none of the records will be destroyed. Let's keep this one quiet. No need to embarrass the legitimate part of this operation at Saint Peter's, okay?"

Patti picked up her folder and was gone. I found my list of topics I needed to update Battaglia about and added this one to it. I had to remember to ask his executive assistant, Rose

44

Malone, whether he had accepted the invitation I heard he had received to be Saint Peter's Hospital Humanitarian of the Year, for his charitable work on behalf of underprivileged kids.

"Don't you have anything to do?" I asked Chapman after I reminded Laura to get Ryan Blackmer over to see me. Mike was lifting things up from the piles on top of my desk and reading them. Some were complaint reports and investigation updates, others were personal notes and messages.

"Nothing till the autopsy this afternoon. I was hoping you'd come with me to Forlini's and grab a bite to eat. I'm always more content in the morgue when I've got a full stomach."

"I don't have time to go out for lunch today. Call Kindler or Holmes—just get out of my hair for a while so I can catch up on everything here."

"Have you returned yesterday's call to Jacob Tyler yet?" Chapman asked, fanning out a handful of messages from Laura's telephone pad. "And does that one have anything to do with the fact that the white lace camisole you ordered is out of stock but will be shipped by FedEx as soon as—"

I lurched across the desk and ripped the papers from Mike's hand as Ryan entered the office.

"Well, I can't imagine that the underwear delivery would upset you, so there must be something about the call from the newscaster that has you jumping, Ms. Cooper. Go easy on her, Ryan, it's been a long morning." Mike always liked to tease me about my social life, but I hadn't yet told him that I had been dating Jake and knew this wasn't the right moment to explain the relationship to him.

Ryan was as good-natured as he was competent, and for every serious case that he indicted, five or six more bizarre situations wound up on his desk. "You got any time next week to help me with an interview?" he asked me. "I'd really like your opinion."

"Sure, which one?"

"Remember the Cruise to Nowhere you assigned to me? Four girls from Jersey celebrated their high school graduation by taking a weekend cruise," Ryan reminded me. "Boarded the ship in New York harbor, then it sails out past Long Island for three days. I didn't know there was anything that could float capable of holding the amount of liquor on board this thing. Or that any land-roving mammal could imbibe as much as these kids did and still be alive."

"I don't remember any of the facts. Sorry, but I've been pre-occupied with my hearings."

"The girls started drinking mimosas at breakfast Saturday morning. Stacey, the victim—and I am using that word loosely, Alex—got seasick and went down to their cabin to throw up for a couple of hours. Bounced back in the afternoon for some Bloody Marys and beer. Wine and champagne with dinner. Doesn't remember anything after ten P.M. She was a bit surprised to find the ship's magician in her bunk with her—starkers—when the ship pulled into the dock on Sunday morning. She's screaming rape. And by the way, suing the cruise ship."

"The *Love Boat*," said Mike.

"Well, that's what her bunk mates say, but she's insisting she would never have done anything like that if she were sober. Personally, I don't even think we have jurisdiction if this happened more than three miles out of the harbor, but I know you believe in seeing everybody who makes a complaint."

For far too long, when rape laws prevented prosecutions and the system was not open to its survivors, women had no place to turn for justice or advocacy. One of our goals in setting up a special unit was to see all those women who wanted to report cases, and give them the appropriate guidance—whether their matter belonged in the criminal court or elsewhere.

"Make an appointment with her for the Friday after next

46

and have Laura put it on my calendar. Just give me all your witness interview notes before then, so I know where the inconsistencies are when we start talking to Stacey. Be sure you check with Laura on Thursday, 'cause if I'm still tied up with this new homicide, I'll have to move you back a couple of days. And Ryan, what are you doing for lunch?"

He brightened and looked back at me, waiting for the offer. "Take Chapman across the street and feed him. Stick it on my tab. I've got work to do."

"I'll give you a call when we've taken care of Gertie, Ms. Cooper. Personally, I'm a little bit worried about *you*, though. I think your father's right—listening to stories about all this sex and violence day in and day out can't be very good for you. C'mon, Ryan." Mike was almost out the door when he turned back and threw me the last question. "Whatever happened to romance? Doesn't anybody believe in dinner and a movie anymore?"

5

Alex Trebek told the noisy crowd of prosecutors and cops packing "Part F"—the name affectionately given to the bar at Forlini's, since at many points on a Friday afternoon it was likely to have more office personnel in it than most of the dozens of court parts across the street—that the Final Jeopardy category would be New York State History.

I could see Chapman's dark head positioned beneath the television that was hung in the far corner of the room, surrounded by six of the guys from Trial Bureau 50, celebrating the end of another workweek.

"Get it up, blondie!" Mike shouted down the bar at me as I squeezed through friendly packs of coworkers who were reliving their cross-examinations and telling one another about their latest triumphs and travails. "How are you on the Empire State?"

"I'll go the usual ten," I said, sliding into the space cleared for me by Ed Broderick and Kevin Guadagno. Dempsey had seen me arrive, too, and my Dewar's on the rocks was already on the countertop.

"All right, then," Trebek continued, fighting for our attention over the noise of the jukebox and the banter of more than a hundred of law enforcement's thirstiest troops. "The answer is: City that was the site of the largest Confederate prison camp during the Civil War."

I shook my head and rested it in my right hand, ready to acknowledge defeat, while I sipped my scotch with the left. Chapman was writing furiously on the back of a cocktail napkin. "I've been had. This isn't a New York question—it's military history," I moaned.

Mike Chapman had majored in history at Fordham College and amassed a limitless knowledge of battles, gunboats, warriors, and even the names of the stallions on which they rode. Our long-standing habit of betting on the Final Jeopardy questions—whether in the middle of a crime scene, a good meal, or a round of cocktails—had taught each of us to stay away from the categories that were the other's strong points, and I was about to be taken down in front of my colleagues on Chapman's principal strength—much to his delight.

As the timer ticked and the theme music jingled on, my mind sped through lists of upstate names, but all I could think of were prisons to which my convicted rapists had been sent over the last decade—Green Haven, Ossining, Clinton, Auburn, and so on. Nothing conjured up the Civil War. Mike was singing an Irish ballad in my ear, confusing me further, and substituting the name of one of the grimmest institutions for the town in the classic song. "How are things in Dannemora?" he crooned as I tried to brush him away from me.

Trebek picked up the card lying on the podium in front of the septuagenarian wallpaper hanger from Minnesota, saw that it was empty, and commented that it was too bad he hadn't ventured a guess.

"Take your best shot, Cooper?" Mike said.

"What is Attica?" I asked, stirring the ice cubes with my finger.

"*Bzzzzzzzz.*" Mike imitated the penalty buzzer as the show's second contestant bombed with her answer, too. "What is Elmira?" he said, loud enough for everyone at our end to hear.

The Stanford professor who had won on the show four days this week also had the correct answer, and was beaming no less proudly than Chapman as Trebek congratulated him and announced that his five-day total was $38,000.

"Cooper's got the next round, Dempsey. For me and everybody in Trial Bureau 50. Elmira, the flower of Chemung County. Treaty of Painted Post proposed there in seventeen ninety-one, to end the settlers' war with the Iroquois. Wouldn't expect you to know that, kid. But three thousand Confederate soldiers are buried there. Actually, called it 'Hellmira' during the war, 'cause the conditions were so bad. What'd you think they were going to ask, Coop—where's Niagara Falls? Who's buried in Grant's Tomb? Too much time wasted at Wellesley with those Elizabethan poets and that Chaucerian crap you're so full of."

"I'm going back to the office, Mike. You want to talk autopsy before I go?"

"You gotta be kidding. We got a table in the back room— we're all having dinner together. Aren't you going to stay for that?"

"I'm taking a salad back with me. Honestly, I'll be in the library all weekend. Just tell me what happened this afternoon."

Chapman and I walked out of the bar toward the rear of the restaurant and sat at an empty table for two. "Still no I.D. Dr. Fleisher makes her out to be about forty years old, and in very good health—except for that crater in the back of her head. No kids—never given birth. He was also right about the cause. Blunt force injury—dead long before she hit the water."

"Does he know what's responsible for the laceration?" I asked.

"You can start with the fact that this wasn't a 'slip and fall.' Whatever she was hit with was hard enough to cause a skull fracture. Could have been a gun butt, a brick, a rock. Doubtful that it was a bottle or anything like that—no residue or fragments in the wound," Mike went on. "The impact was probably a glancing blow, but it was so deep that the subcutaneous tissue separated from the underlying muscle fascia."

"And the internal exam?" I asked.

"Fleisher didn't find anything remarkable. Sexually active adult female. Only thing that will interest you is that there were abrasions on her upper thighs, close to the vaginal area."

"Nobody mentioned them last night at the scene," I commented.

"Doc said it's typical with a body that's been immersed in water. That kind of injury—scraping of the skin and removal of superficial layers—only becomes noticeable after the body has dried out," Mike said.

"Were those actually finger marks I saw?" I asked, wondering if the abrasions had been caused during an attempt at a sexual assault.

"Looks consistent with that. They took lots of close-ups, so you can study them."

"How about rope burns from the ligature marks?"

Chapman described the autopsy proceeding, in which Fleisher cut the skin directly under the wrist and ankle restraints, looking for that answer. "Not enough hemorrhaging to suggest she was alive when they tied her up," he answered. "It was probably just the means of securing her body to the ladder, for the purpose of disposing of her. That's it, except for the toxicological workups, which won't be ready for another week."

"Any reason to think there'll be findings of significance?" I wondered.

"Yeah, Fleisher thinks she's had some problems with cocaine. He didn't like the looks of her nasal septum. Could be just one more of those uptown drug deals gone sour," Mike said. "She looked classy, but she undoubtedly liked to stick that sugar up her nose."

"What's next?"

"Gert just stays tucked in her fridge until somebody figures out who she is. Tomorrow morning, she's out of the newspapers, and I start looking for who-done-it."

"Give me a call over the weekend if anything develops, will you?" I asked. "I'll be down here most of the time, either in the library or at my desk."

"Don't you want a ride home later?"

"Thanks, no. I've got the Jeep right in front of the office. Ciao." I said my "Good nights" around the bar, picked up my take-out salad, and walked the quiet block back to the office.

It was after midnight when I locked up my files, rode the elevator down to the lobby, and drove home to park in the garage and drag myself upstairs to go to sleep. I played the messages left by friends on my answering machine throughout the day and evening, and made a list of calls to return at some point on Saturday. Most of my pals got out of the city on the steaming summer weekends—to beach houses they owned or rented, borrowed or shared—and I was just as anxious to get this court proceeding behind me so I could disappear to my home on Martha's Vineyard for some rest.

I bathed, ignored the usually appealing pile of magazines next to the bed, and read a chapter of *The Ambassadors* before falling off into a sound sleep. On Saturday morning I went over to the west sixties, where I took a two-hour ballet class with my instructor, William, who tried to remove all the knots that several weeks of courtroom tension had worked into my shoulders, back, and thighs. When I left the dance studio I headed directly downtown to the office, to continue researching and crafting my arguments for the complicated presentation I had to make on Monday.

It was close to eight o'clock when I realized that my eyes were bleary and my thought process was getting fuzzy. As I neared home on the FDR Drive, I was trying to decide whether there was anyone in town I could call on such short notice to meet me for a light supper. The beeper went off while I was still a few blocks away from my apartment, and when I glanced down and noted that the number on the lighted display was unfamiliar, I decided to wait until I got upstairs to return the call.

"Hello?" I said tentatively.

The accented voice of an older woman spoke into the telephone. "One moment," she said, and I heard her say something inaudible while passing the receiver to someone.

"Yeah?" It was Mike Chapman's voice.

"Hi. Got your beep on my way home."

"Hey, Coop. We got an I.D., just an hour ago. Housekeeper came back from vacation. Says the lady of the house was supposed to be here all week but nobody's seen her. Noticed the sketch in yesterday's news, then she put it together with the fact that 'Madam' is not around. Called the precinct, and they notified us. I grabbed one of the guys and we ran down here with a couple of the head shots from the M.E.'s Office, and the housekeeper breaks up on us as soon as she sees the photos."

"Who is—"

"Lady's name is Denise Caxton. Lives—well, lived—at 890 Fifth Avenue. Ever hear of her?" Chapman wanted to know.

"No. Why?"

"She and the husband own an art gallery, same place where you get your roots done."

"The Fuller Building?" I asked. Madison Avenue at Fifty-seventh Street—the crossroads of the art world, as the owner of my salon liked to call it.

"Yeah, the Caxton Gallery occupies the entire top floor."

I could hear the background conversation between Mike's partner and the tearful woman as Mike whispered into the phone. "You wouldn't believe this apartment—five-bedroom duplex, with a modern art collection that most museums would kill for."

"So, *did* they? And where's Mr. Caxton?"

"The housekeeper doesn't know. Denise split with him—Lowell Caxton—a few months back. They both still share the apartment—separate entrances and living quarters—but there's no sign that he's in town. And she says there's nothing to suggest any foul play in the apartment, either."

"Want me to come over and—"

"Forget about it. Valerie's giving us the boot. Won't let us look around or touch anything. Not till she gets her orders from Monsieur Caxton."

"Any date book, calendar—to trace back the deceased's movements?"

"All on computer, Coop, and she's not letting us anywhere near that room or any of the equipment."

"Can you secure the apartment until I can get a warrant to search it?" I asked.

"You bet your ass we'll have to. Any of this stuff disappears, we'll all be nailed to the wall. I've sent for some uniformed guys to watch each of the entrances, just to keep the place buttoned up tight.

"And get your beauty sleep, blondie. I have the distinct feeling that you and I will be dancing together on this one. If there's one motive for every million hanging on these walls, we're gonna be busy."

6

"Think about it for a minute," Chapman urged me. "*Rebecca*? Domestic violence. *Notorious*? Domestic violence. *Gaslight*? Domestic violence. *Dial M for Murder*? Domestic violence. *Niagara*? Domestic violence. Every one of your favorite movies has some kind of spousal abuse in it, you know? What does that say about you, blondie?"

I was staring at a Monet hanging in the Caxton living room. I had never seen any painting from the water lily series in private hands, and here was a glorious canvas, practically as large as the triptych that hangs in the Museum of Modern Art, stretching the length of the wall.

"*The Postman Always Rings Twice*? Domestic violence. *Double Indemnity*? Domes—"

"Yeah, now you're getting to the good ones. The ladies strike back, Mikey. Those are the ones I *really* enjoy." I walked over to Mercer, who was studying the signature in the corner of the painting.

"Is this for real?" he asked me.

I smiled and shrugged my shoulders. "I assume so. I played around on the Internet for a couple of hours last night after Mike called me with the I.D., and it seems the Caxton collection is world famous. A lot of it has been in the family for generations."

Mercer and I were moving around the forty-foot-long room like it was a gallery in the Louvre. Each painting and object was museum quality, and I was fascinated by their beauty and number.

Chapman was sitting on a sofa facing the stunning view of Central Park, watching as the housekeeper delivered coffee and English muffins to the table in front of him, pouring from a Georgian server that was worth our collective salaries for at least the next couple of years.

"Thanks, Valerie. I was starving." Chapman gave the red-eyed woman his best grin and began slathering butter on the toasted morsel he had picked up from the plate. "Valerie makes these from scratch, Coop. Got her own nooks and crannies—better than Thomas'. You oughta take a lesson from her."

Mercer shook his head and walked over, spreading a napkin across the knee of Chapman's jeans. The dripping butter would have been an unwelcome accent to the delicate design of golden Napoleonic bees on the peach silk fabric of the sofa. "How'd you get Valerie to let us in?"

"We bonded last night over a bit of Mr. Caxton's Irish

whiskey. I've frequently found it helpful in periods of bereavement. Basically I told her I wasn't going anywhere until she located him for me."

Chapman had called me again at midnight to tell me that Valerie had reached Lowell Caxton at his home in Paris and that he would be taking the Concorde back to New York. It was Mike's idea that the three of us await him in his home, to deny him the opportunity to alter or destroy any evidence before we could interview him.

Air France flight 002 from Paris had been due in at 8:44 A.M. on Sunday. Chapman had returned to the building at six, and Mercer had picked me up at home two hours later. "Why'd she let you back in today?" I asked. "The boss won't be too happy about this, I'm sure."

"Let's just say she was encouraged by the doormen. One thing they frown on in these snooty buildings, Miss Cooper, is scenes. The sight of me alone in the lobby wasn't all that upsetting to them at first, but it was probably when I asked Frick and Frack if they thought it was gonna be necessary for me to get the Emergency Services Unit over here with battering rams that they called and suggested to Valerie that I might be more comfortable waiting in Caxton's salon. I'm telling you—doormen despise scenes."

So much for any evidence that we might be lucky enough to come up with in the apartment. The kind of pressure that Mike liked to apply to get his way more often resulted in a consent under threat than the freely given consent necessary for a lawful entry or search.

Valerie returned to the room with another ornate tray and porcelain cups for Mercer and me. Her hand trembled slightly as she poured the coffee, and I wondered whether it was because of grief over her mistress's death, the effects of a hangover, or fear of Caxton's reaction when he found us settled in and enjoying his hospitality. She replaced the silver pot on a small table beside a large ormolu clock that bore an engraved seal depicting a royal crest I couldn't identify.

"Hitchcock had it right, Coop. Think of how many movies it's the husband or wife who offs the other spouse. Just because this guy was in Paris all week doesn't mean he isn't a prime suspect. Shit, we don't even know exactly how many days she's been dead. Besides that, someone with this kind of dough could hire a killer with his pocket change."

"Well, what did you get out of Valerie during your fireside chat last night?"

"Precious little. Seemed to genuinely like the late Mrs. C., who hired her personally and relied on her for all kinds of intimate service. But the husband pays the bills, and she's not about to throw that out the window so fast." Mike was almost finished with his second muffin, the buttered topping covered over with some kind of strawberry preserve. "Hey, Mercer, might as well lift the lids on those little—Coop, what does your mother call useless little dust catchers like that stuff over there? Tchotchkes? Maybe Denise stored her coke in one of those."

Chapman pointed at a gilt-trimmed *bureau plat,* only half in jest. It was completely covered by miniature porcelain snuffboxes. Half a dozen of them would have fit at once in the palm of Mercer's hand, but he lifted the lids of several of them individually. I sipped on my coffee as I walked beside him, noticing that each box was hand painted with portraits of cavalier King Charles spaniels in a variety of regal backgrounds.

Above the table was a Degas, familiar to me from my Wellesley introductory art course and close enough in detail to the famous *Foyer of the Dance* that it had to be the study for the great painting that hangs in Paris.

Chapman was on his feet, wiping his hands with the heavy damask napkin. He was standing in front of a Picasso about four feet by six, his head cocked as he tried to make some sense of the Cubist representations. "I just don't get it. Why would somebody pay millions of dollars for something like this, which isn't supposed to look like anything anyway? I must have spent too much time in church. I haven't liked any artists since Michelangelo and Leonardo da Vinci. Just give me a Madonna—I mean, the old Madonna—and I'm happy."

I had circled the room and was back in front of the lilies. "You'd like Monet. Impressionism got its name from one of his paintings—*Impression of a Sunrise*." Chapman joined me to look at the vast canvas, one of the endless images of the same subject portrayed at different hours of the day in different variations of light.

"That one you're looking at was painted at Giverny, just before his death. He was nearly blind." Caxton's voice startled us as we turned to look toward the entryway of the long room.

"Looks to me like most of the stuff painted in this century could have been done by a blind man. Mike Chapman, Homicide," Mike said, advancing to shake Lowell Caxton's hand and show his identification. "These are my colleagues—Detective Mercer Wallace, and Alexandra Cooper from the District Attorney's Office."

Caxton extended a hand to each of us. "I hope Valerie has made you comfortable. Perhaps you'll allow me to step inside and freshen up for a moment before we get on with what you need to do."

It was a reasonable request after a trans-Atlantic trip, and although Chapman would have liked to tail him into the private quarters of the apartment, we had no choice but to let Caxton disappear to his suite of rooms.

Fifteen or twenty minutes later he returned to the living room, opened a set of sliding pocket doors, and gestured the three of us into the library. The walls were lacquered in a rich shade of Chinese red, strikingly showcasing another Picasso, this time from the artist's Rose Period. Bookcases were lined with sets of leather-bound volumes, valuable and rare, and assuredly untouched and unread. Some decorator's idea of a complement to the art.

Lowell Caxton seated himself in the largest chair in the room as we took our places around him. "It's a bit more intimate in here," he said to no one in particular.

As he looked each of us over to size us up, waiting for Valerie to bring him the tea he had requested, we examined him as well. The articles I had seen in Lexis-Nexis gave his age as seventy-four. But he was trim and vigorous, with a full head of thick gray hair, and I would have guessed him to be no older than sixty-five. He remained in the clothes in which he had traveled—gray slacks, loafers without socks, a tennis shirt, and a pink cashmere sweater looped around his shoulders. The solid gold Cartier Pasha on his wrist was the only jewelry he wore.

Valerie delivered the tea on yet another small silver tray. "Close the doors after you, will you, Valerie?" Caxton asked. Her hands were still shaking as she backed out of the room, sliding the doors together by pulling the brass knob on each of the sections.

"Am I supposed to open this session by telling you how distraught I am by Deni's demise?" he went on. "Or have you already found ample fodder in the tabloids to know that it wouldn't be a very sincere way for me to begin? The flight home—even with the abbreviated flying time of a supersonic transport—was more than enough for me to shed whatever tears I had left. I didn't kill her, although there'll be plenty of her friends to suggest as much to you. But I certainly didn't love her any longer, so you might as well know that from the outset."

"You want to ask us anything, before I get started?" Chapman queried.

"I know everything about how and where she was found, Detective. After Valerie reached me with the news last night, I had my assistant make all the inquiries he could. I'm sure you'll tell me whatever else you think it's necessary for me to know."

I had worked with Mike often enough to get inside his head. You couldn't look at a situation like this without thinking you could easily find a motive for the husband to want the wife dead—money, business, infidelity, and in this instance, even more money. A contract hit in this kind of marriage would be cheaper than any alimony decision made by a judge or jury. But it was also so obvious that we were each thinking that it was too easy. Now the guy plays right into the theory by not even expressing interest in how his estranged wife was killed. He probably had more channels of access to whatever information he wanted than I had pairs of shoes.

Mike had two short-term goals. He needed to get as much information about both Caxtons, personal and professional, as he could, and he wanted to shove open the pocket doors so he could see whether anyone was coming or going into the private rooms of the apartment.

"It's warm in here, Mr. Caxton," Mike said, taking out his notepad and loosening his tie as he rose and walked toward the doors. "Mind if I open these for a little air?"

Caxton lifted a remote control panel from the table beside him. "Not necessary, Detective. I'll simply adjust the room temperature. It stays much cooler in here without the summer sun beating through those glass windows off the park. Carry on. Tell me what you need to know."

Whether we needed it all or not, the Caxton family history and the building of the art fortune had to be explored, in case they proved to be links to the murder.

Lowell Caxton III was the grandson of the Pittsburgh steel baron whose name he bore. The grandfather had been born in

1840 and was one of those great American success stories—a poor kid from a large family who rose from menial mill jobs to running a production plant before he was thirty. When he recognized the growing demand for steel, needed to build the railroads across the country, he borrowed all of his working-class relatives' money and purchased a factory. In 1873, when another young fellow, named Andrew Carnegie, came along and began his acquisition of businesses which he later consolidated into the Carnegie Steel Company, Lowell Caxton never had to work again. He became an investor and speculator, and thereafter a philanthropist responsible for helping Carnegie build libraries and art museums all over the Northeast.

In the mid-1880s, Caxton became enamored of the bohemian lifestyle of many of the young artists living and working in Paris. He bought several apartments in Montmartre and let some of the struggling upstarts live there rent-free, in exchange for paintings that he took to America.

On one of his trips, drinking in the nightclubs with Toulouse-Lautrec, Caxton took up with a dancer, whom he married and brought back to the States. Their son, Lowell II, inherited the entire fortune—the money and the art—when both of his parents died in the sinking of the *Lusitania,* in 1915. He was thirty years old at the time.

As though the passion for art had been genetically transmitted, the junior Caxton carried on his father's interests, patronizing the creators and expanding the family collection. He was a popular figure at Mabel Dodge's "evenings" in her home at 23 Fifth Avenue, where he championed the Post-impressionists to Lincoln Steffens, Margaret Sanger, John Reed, and the other intellectuals who gathered to exchange ideas while Dodge puffed on her gold-tipped cigarettes. It was at one of those soirees that he met his wife, a guest of Gertrude Stein's named Marie-Hélène de Neuilly, who was a well-known patron of avant-garde art before the First World

War. Our host, Lowell III—or Three, as his father liked to call him as a boy—also had the love of art in his blood.

"The first artist I ever met was Picasso," Caxton continued, "at our home in Paris, before he went off to Spain to fight. He was having an affair with my mother at the time, although I was much too young to pick up on that. And in case you're wondering, it was perfectly all right with my father. Got him some stunning paintings for his collection. You might like to see them someday. They're in my bedroom—never been shown publicly."

"Do you mind if we talk about your wife, Mr. Caxton?" Chapman asked.

"I've had three, Detective. I assume you mean Deni?"

"Well, actually, why don't you tell me about the other two first? Then, yes, I'd like to know as much about Denise as possible."

"Not much to say about them. Rest in peace." Caxton looked over at me, daring a smile. "I married Lisette in France at the beginning of the war. She died in childbirth. Tragic, really. I adored her. My second wife was from Italy. She raised Lisette's child and then two more daughters of our own. Killed in a boating accident in Venice."

"Aha!" Chapman said under his breath, shifting in his chair and leaning across to me. "*Rebecca*. I told you so."

I ignored the crack and went on. "Where are your daughters now?"

"All grown, married, living in Europe. And if you want to know whether or not they liked Deni, they didn't. She was younger than all of them, and they never got along very well. But they've had absolutely nothing to do with her for years."

"I understand," Chapman said. "We will, of course, need to get in touch with them at some point."

"I'll have someone from my office get you all their information."

"Back to Denise, if we may."

"Certainly, Detective. I met Deni nearly twenty years ago, in Firenze. She was—"

"You were widowed at the time, Mr. Caxton?" Mercer asked.

"Widowed once, Mr. Wallace. My second wife was alive and quite well. Her mishap occurred several years thereafter. In any event, I had flown over to look at a Bernini sculpture that I wanted to bid on. It was at the gallery that I first saw Denise, and I was more infatuated with her than with the statue. That hadn't happened to me in years."

"And she was there to bid on the same piece for the Tate?" I ventured, having found that item of her biography on-line the previous night in an old magazine clipping about a museum opening.

Caxton smiled. "I should think you'd know better than to believe everything you read in the newspapers, young lady. Deni was just off her year as Miss Oklahoma, and a very-distant-second runner-up in the Miss America Pageant. You were probably too busy with your nose in your schoolbooks," Caxton said, with a nod in my direction, "to be watching that year, but she was the kid from Idabel with great looks and no talent to speak of—traded in baton twirling in favor of reading a soliloquy from *As You Like It*. Not exactly a crowd pleaser. She took her ten-thousand-dollar scholarship prize and escaped. Worked her way over to Florence to study art, which she didn't know the first thing about at the time. Figured if Andy Warhol could fool the world with what he was selling, she could catch on and find a niche.

"I decided to follow my grandfather's route, Miss Cooper. What Denise lacked in breeding, she made up for in—shall we say?—élan. She was a marvelously quick study and I enjoyed teaching. All she needed from me was to create a provenance for her, no different than a clever forger would do for a fine painting.

"I gave Deni a vague and somewhat mysterious background—orphaned as a young child, with a trust fund. Raised abroad in a series of boarding schools. Moved her from the *pensione* she was living in to the Excelsior, where I was staying when I came to town. Had her tutored in French and Italian—she was adequate in the former and tolerable in the latter. Most of the men who met her were intrigued and forgave her the minor incongruities. She didn't care much about what the women thought of her. Denise was never a contender for Miss Congeniality."

"What did your second wife think of her, Mr. Caxton?" Mike clearly was fascinated by the circumstance of the thrice-widowed husband.

"I'm not sure she ever knew about Deni, to tell the truth. She was riding in a cigarette speedboat when it flipped, killing her instantly. I had only known Deni a few years at that point. The whole arrangement was working perfectly for me. And yes, Mr. Chapman, there was an inquest when my wife died. Accidental death. I'm sure Maurizio, my assistant, can get you all the records that you need."

"How long have you had the gallery in the Fuller Building?" Mercer wanted to bring this story up to the present.

"Deni and I moved back to New York twelve years ago. We bought this apartment so that she could open our gallery. For me, the satisfaction has always been in finding and collecting the great pieces—more than a century of Caxton taste that I can surround myself with in the privacy of my own homes. Not entirely selfish, mind you. We frequently exhibit portions of the holdings, whenever asked, and many of my mistakes have wound up permanently on the walls of museums all over America and most of Europe.

"But Denise also liked the game itself. It wasn't enough to gift her with unique art or jewels, which worked very well at the beginning. She had come from nothing—her father was a soybean farmer—and she really needed to prove she was as smart as any of the rest of us out there. She liked the hustle of the art world. She adored being a tastemaker, if you will. But I suppose your research has revealed all of that."

Now I was doubly sorry that I had suggested I knew anything about either of the Caxtons. "Not at all, Mr. Caxton. Forgive me, but I only tried to acquaint myself with information about Mrs. Caxton's business when I learned that it was she who had been killed. It's always helpful to me if I can get as close to the victim as possible—to try and understand why she might be a target for someone. That is, if her loved ones allow me that kind of access."

"Anything you'd like, Miss Cooper. Perhaps it would help if we took a walk into Deni's quarters, to give you an idea of how she lived. Would you like that?"

Chapman was on his feet before I could answer. Caxton moved to the double doors as Mike leaned in behind me and whispered, "Very smoothly done, blondie. Keep batting those eyelashes and you could be the fourth late Mrs. Lowell Caxton. A very temporary position, from the looks of it."

As the doors slid apart I could see the back of a man carrying a black leather suitcase as he walked out of the entryway that led from the living room to the elevator. Mercer nudged Chapman. "There goes Kardashian with Simpson's bloody clothes."

"Mr. Caxton," Chapman said, "I'd appreciate it if you could hold that gentleman before he leaves here with any property that we might need to look at."

"Is it safe for me to assume, Detective, that you don't have a warrant to search my luggage?"

Mike and Mercer were silent. Caxton continued. "That

was Maurizio. He simply unpacked the bag I returned with this morning and is taking it down to the storage area in the basement of the building. Sorry to disappoint you." We heard the heavy door swing closed.

He led us past the Picasso and pointed at three doors across the room. "That far exit goes to the kitchen and the servants' quarters. Unless you think the butler did it, Mr. Chapman, that portion of the household needn't take up your time. These other two are—rather, were—our separate apartments. Nothing new about that. Even when we were getting along very well, we always had distinct living spaces. Different lifestyles, different tastes in art.

"I didn't approve of the drugs, and I didn't much care for Deni's current passion for modern painting—some of the very abstract, jarring works she'd developed an interest in recently." We followed Caxton as he opened the door to Denise's wing.

"You know, gentlemen, this may sound a bit peevish in light of the fact that I'm standing here with you while my wife is being fitted for a coffin, but if your department had taken *my* shooting a bit more seriously, perhaps this wouldn't have happened to Deni."

Mercer, Mike, and I couldn't conceal our puzzlement as we exchanged looks.

"Are any of you with the Nineteenth Precinct? That's the unit that's handling the investigation," Caxton explained.

"No, we're not. Could you tell us what happened?" Chapman was plainly annoyed that we had come here without such an important piece of information.

"Just crossing Madison Avenue, six weeks ago, on my way home from the Whitney. Holding a Styrofoam coffee cup in my hand. A car driving past slowed down, and the man in the passenger seat pointed at me—it was happening so quickly that all I saw was his hand—then I heard the sound of a gunshot and felt a stinging on my scalp. I found myself sitting on the curb, people running over to help me. Never even dropped the coffee."

Caxton bowed his head and parted his silver hair with his hands. "I'm sure you can still see the scar, like a seam across my scalp. At that moment I was quite sure I was dead. This must be what it's like to die, I thought to myself. No pain at all. It took me a few seconds to realize, as the blood dripped onto my face, that I had been grazed by the bullet and not seriously injured at all. If someone had actually tried to kill me, they'd hired the gang that couldn't shoot straight.

"I trust you'll be able to figure out whether Deni's death had anything to do with that, won't you?"

He pivoted away and walked on ahead of us to turn on the lights in the dim hallway. "The only thing I trust," said Chapman, "is that some ass-kissing lieutenant in the Nineteenth was trying to make his numbers look better for the commissioner. When I call over for the case report on the assault on Lowell Caxton, I'll probably find out that they're carrying the investigation as disorderly conduct instead of attempted murder. Heaven forbid you alarm the good citizens of the Upper East Side by suggesting a violent crime could happen here— they might confuse the place with Harlem."

7

"Here's another Degas," Caxton said to me, stopping in front of a painting. "Perhaps you remember from your college days that after the Napoleonic wars, it was presumed of firstborn sons of a certain class that they would become lawyers. Edgar dutifully followed his father's wishes and enrolled at the Faculté de Droit. Fortunately for the rest of the world—if not his parents—he dropped out in favor of doing something more creative than litigation after only a month."

He walked on. "Cézanne spent almost three years at law school in Aix, replete with boredom. And Matisse actually clerked for a lawyer for quite a while, drafting briefs and keeping files. It was only when he was forced to stay at home with appendicitis that he was given his first paint set by his mother. A decade later, he changed the history of the art world with the birth of Fauvism—exuberant colors and wildly distorted shapes. Imagine our loss if any of these giants had become mired in the law. You don't paint by any chance, do you, Miss Cooper?"

Lowell Caxton managed to summarize a bit of art history while making clear his disdain for the legal profession. I got the point.

So far, the hallway lined with Impressionist paintings was as breathtaking as any gallery in the finest museums. Caxton opened the last door, which had been Denise's bedroom. The contrast was stunning.

"A bit self-involved, would you say?" he asked rather facetiously.

The room was like a shrine to its former occupant, with almost every painting in it a portrait of Denise. "Gifts from the artists, of course. Thankful for her ability to turn their talents into gold, in some instances. Quite like alchemy. The Warhol is the great irony, in that he started this whole odyssey for her, without his ever knowing it."

Displayed above the headboard of the king-size bed, covered in an exquisite set of antique linens with countless throw pillows layered on top, were the four-colored Warhol images of a younger Denise Caxton. The youthful bride with a swan-like neck and beauty queen smile was deserving of a few portraits, I conceded, but this accumulation was a bit frightening.

The three of us circled the space, looking at signatures and taking in the variety of styles. I recognized some of the names—Richard Sussman, Emilio Gomes, and Aneas McKiever among them—but Caxton pointed out the rest of those I had never encountered. There were Deni Caxtons fully clothed and bejeweled, and there were Deni Caxtons completely nude and erotically posed. There were torsos without heads and limbs, and there were heads without body parts.

"How'd she let this one slip in?" Chapman asked. He pointed at a yellow canvas, three feet square, with a small pink rectangle in the upper right corner.

Caxton laughed. "That *is* Denise, Detective. According to Alain Levinsky. Even she had a sense of humor about it. She managed to sell about a dozen Levinsky 'portraits,' Mr. Chapman. One each to Bardot, Trump, and Ted Turner—can't remember who sat for the others. A few rectangles, a few oblongs, a few squares. *Et voilà,* a portrait."

"This is all like 'The Emperor's New Clothes,' if you ask me," Chapman said.

"Precisely," Caxton responded. "I couldn't agree with you more. Denise mocked me for my traditional views—too representational, she used to argue, too old-fashioned. I wish P. T. Barnum had lived long enough to encounter this trend. Nowadays there are two or three suckers born every minute, if you ask me. He might have gone into partnership with Deni."

Mercer was scouring the surfaces of the furniture—bedside tables, dresser top, lingerie chest—for any signs of notes or papers, names or phone numbers. But there was nothing loose and nothing casually laid about. Either Mrs. Caxton lived that neatly or Valerie had removed every jotting or message pad before we arrived.

"Would you—or the housekeeper—know whether any belongings are missing?" Mercer asked. "Jewelry, clothing, anything like—"

"I couldn't begin to guess," said Caxton. He stepped to the only other door in the room and pulled the handles back to reveal a walk-in closet, which was probably larger than half of the studio apartments in Manhattan. Clothes were assembled by category—dresses, slacks, suits, evening gowns—and then again by colors within those groupings. "The lesser jewels are kept in that safe at the rear. The more important things, from my mother and *grand-mère,* are all safeguarded in a vault. We'll certainly check for you during the week.

"If you've seen enough here, we'll go inside to Deni's office."

I wasn't sure that I was ready to leave the boudoir, but we were given no choice, and the three of us dutifully followed Caxton, retracing our steps back up the corridor and into the next room.

Denise had constructed a thronelike encampment for herself at one end of this huge home office, centered around a fifteenth-century table that Lowell told us he had found in an Umbrian monastery. The table had become her desk and was ornamented only by a Fabergé clock. There were two chairs placed opposite Denise's high-backed leather seat, and four more scattered around the room that matched that pair. Here the walls were decorated with paintings that were completely unfamiliar to me—all contemporary and none bearing signatures that I recognized.

Caxton walked behind the table and lowered himself into Denise's chair, looking around the room as if for the first time from that perspective, and invited us to sit down and ask him whatever questions we wanted to pose about her.

"When do we reach the point at which you ask me who her enemies were, gentlemen?"

"We're ready anytime you are. How long's the list?" Chapman said.

"Depends on where you are in the art community, I would think. A disgruntled 'artiste' who thinks his dealer has taken too great a commission for his work. Just glance at the walls and see how many of those there might be. Then you've got the clients, who've found they've paid too much for a painting, on the dealer's advice, that they neither like nor will be able to resell for anything remotely near the price they put out.

"There isn't anyone in the business," he went on, "who hasn't been accused of selling a forged piece, by accident or design, over the years. And then there's the current brouhaha in the auction houses, with the government charging sellers with rigging the bids to knock up the prices. On the surface, gentlemen, it's a world of exquisite beauty and refinement. But it's every bit as filthy and cutthroat as any other commercial enterprise, as soon as you get beneath the top layer of gouache."

Mercer was leaning forward, balancing his pad on his knee while he reviewed subjects he wanted to ask Caxton about. "We'll need a client list, then, as well as contact information for the painters she represented."

"You'll have to talk to her partner about that tomorrow at his office."

"I thought you were her partner," Mike said.

"As I mentioned, I set her up in the gallery in the Fuller Building originally. Without the Caxton name, I doubt she would have been able to sell the *Mona Lisa,* had it come on the market. I was the entrée to the uptown world in Manhattan— old money, large walls, deep pockets. But once she got involved in the New York scene, she had her own separate business—a thriving one at that—with a silent partner who mirrored her taste much more directly. Perhaps you've heard of him—Bryan Daughtry? They called their business Galleria Caxton Due."

Mercer and I certainly knew Daughtry's name. He had been a suspect in a very bizarre murder case in a neighboring county—beyond our jurisdiction but right up our alley. Chapman went for the bait. "Dead girl in the leather mask? *That* Daughtry?"

"Indeed, Mr. Chapman. That's why I was so grateful that

he was a silent partner. The scandal didn't alarm Deni at all. Might even have helped, with her type of clientele. But none of the stigma ever stuck on Bryan. I haven't spoken with him yet today, but he knows all the players in their professional life."

"Does he have any part of your Fifty-seventh Street business?" I asked.

"Not a dime. Not a speck of paint."

"Where was their operation? SoHo?"

"You're not keeping up with the trends, Detective Wallace. SoHo is dead. It's a commercial mall these days, not a creative zone any longer."

The area south of Houston Street and north of Canal had been claimed by the avant-garde art community in the sixties and seventies. Abandoned lofts and warehouses, uninhabitable and overrun with rodents, had been renovated, populated, and gentrified by the struggling artists who were unable to afford midtown rents and needed the cavernous space to house their oversized canvases. The old meat district known as Washington Market became chic with its new infusion of hip locals and its redesignation as "Tribeca," the triangle below Canal. By the late eighties, galleries there were being displaced by designer boutiques, chain store branches, and bed-and-bath shops with their ubiquitous supply of votive candles.

Caxton described the exodus. "In the mid-nineties, Paula Cooper moved her business up to Chelsea, the west twenties between Tenth and Eleventh Avenues. Have you been over there lately?"

"You won't be asking Alex questions like that after you get to know her a little better, Mr. Caxton," Chapman said. "She doesn't eat, shop, or sleep outside of her zip code. Makes her skin crawl soon as you say the words 'West Side,' doesn't it, Coop?"

"We have a lot in common," Caxton replied, smiling back at me. "Paula Cooper—no relation, I take it?"

"No, I know her only by reputation." And because my father had bought some paintings from her, I thought to myself, remembering a Jennifer Bartlett I particularly loved.

"Well," he continued, "she's the real class of this business. And its bellwether. I don't actually know the reason she moved, but it's a safe guess to say that it's because of what happened in SoHo. This district in Chelsea was full of enormous warehouses. Fifty years ago, when the ocean liners docked on the piers all along the Hudson and connected to the railways there, it was a commercial hub. Lately, the warehouses have been used for auto repair shops and taxi dispatch centers—vast and utilitarian, but not terribly attractive.

"Paula found a fabulous space on Twenty-first Street. Cleaned it up, put in some skylights, whitewashed the interior, and everyone who thought she'd been out of her mind realized what a genius she was. Deni and Bryan started buying up land on those blocks a couple of years ago, planning to open a new venture together. Real estate's gone through the roof over there. Kind of sorry I ignored them in the beginning. I could have made a killing on the property alone." Caxton paused. "Bad choice of words today, isn't it?"

Remorse wasn't his strong suit.

"And the cocaine? What were her sources for that?"

"The problem only started four or five years ago. About the time that her taste in art changed so radically. Deni knew how strongly I disapproved of her drug use. I could only joke that one had to be stoned to appreciate the work she was trying to hawk to the great unwashed."

"Do you know who her dealer was?" Mercer asked.

"I think she used to get it from the kids who hung around the galleries. Then, as she got hooked, she'd just beep whoever wasn't in jail at the moment, and a delivery would arrive, brought up to our home by the white-gloved doormen. Usually camouflaged in potpourri or packaged in a bag with assorted foodstuffs from Dean & Deluca."

"Did she owe money to anybody? Any suppliers?"

"No reason to. More than enough money to support all her habits."

Mercer was working the drug angle with good reason. Deni's body had been found at the tip of the Thirty-fourth Precinct, which was the heart of Manhattan's illegal drug operations. Colombians, Dominicans, and African American street gangs—Santiago's Sinners, Latin Kings, and Wild High-tops—mixed it up with one another night and day as they pumped the streets of the city full of heroin, cocaine, and all their derivative forms. Even if Deni had been thrown in the water from the Bronx side of the creek, the odds were over-whelming that the site of the dumping was heavily infested with users and sellers of every kind of controlled substance.

"Had either of you started divorce proceedings, Mr. Caxton?" I wanted to know.

"Yes, yes, I had. More than a year ago. No rush about it, and not that I had any plans to go to the altar again, but the marriage was over and I wanted to be sure that I got out of it with most of the treasures I came in with, you see. The money was irrelevant to me, but I needed to protect the collection and keep it intact, as well as I could."

"What was the status of the legal action?"

"Our lawyers were negotiating, Miss Cooper. I'm sure you know what that means. Trying to run up their bills at hourly rates with endless phone calls and meetings and suggestions—and general nonsense."

"I assume there was a prenup—"

"Certainly there was. But most of its contingencies were useless after the marriage survived ten years. You must realize how much older I was than Deni. I thought a decade with her would be bliss. It's like the salesmen who try to sell a man my age a watch with a lifetime guarantee," the septuagenarian went on. "I always tell them that I'd be interested in a similar piece, but for a lower price and with simply a ten-year guarantee."

"So what was she fighting about?"

"It wasn't money, Detective Chapman. I've offered plenty of that, and she made quite a lot of it on her own projects. But she wanted more of the art, some of *my* pieces. Claiming an entitlement for many of the things I'd bought since we'd been together. As though I needed her judgment to lead me to a Titian or Tintoretto. Perhaps next time you're here," Caxton said, making it obvious that we were coming to the end of his hospitality, "you might like to see what it is I want to hold on to.

"Unlike that mishmash of styles my wife favored, I've hung my favorites each in its own salon. My bedroom is devoted to van Gogh—Deni thought they were minor, but they're quite wonderful, really. My office is the Poussin room, and my—"

Chapman had just about had it with the self-importance of Caxton and the arrogant cataloguing of his wealth. "How about your inamorata's bedroom, sir? How'd you decorate that one?"

"Not a stupid guess at all, Detective. Yes, I've been seeing someone. She's in Paris, and quite content to be there. And if you think it bothered Denise at all, you'd be wrong. We've been leading separate lives for a long time."

"Do you know who she's been seeing?" I asked.

"Perhaps the help would know that, Miss Cooper. They change the linens here—I don't."

That last exchange brought him to his feet, as he ushered us out of his wife's office and back to the living room.

Chapman wasn't quite done. "When was it, exactly, that you left for Paris?"

"Maurizio will give you all that infor—"

"I'm sure Maurizio would give me oral sex if you told him

to, Mr. Caxton. I'm not talking ancient history, here. This is Sunday—what day did you leave New York to go to Paris on your last trip? I'd like to hear it from *you*."

Caxton's veneer had worn thin, and Mike's patience even finer. "It was Tuesday, Tuesday evening at seven o'clock."

"Any other homes that you and Denise owned? Any place that she might have gone if she left this apartment for a few days and you were holed up in Paris?"

"Well, we've got a house in Saint Bart's, but it's not the season there, of course. I doubt it's even opened up this time of year."

Chapman couldn't resist the cheap shot. "Yeah, I know you two wouldn't be caught you-know-what there off-season, would you?"

Caxton ignored him.

I knew the small Caribbean paradise well. My parents had bought a home and begun spending winters there after my father retired from the practice of medicine. The Cooper-Hoffman valve, which he and his partner had invented as young physicians, had revolutionized the then-new field of open heart surgery and made possible a lifestyle that allowed him to live in that French-owned resort while continuing to travel for his lectures and conferences all over the world. It would be easy for me to get information about the Caxtons from my connections on the island.

"I'd suggest that when you speak with Bryan Daughtry you ask him about the truckload of paintings—mostly Della Spigas, I think, and quite ghastly—that was hijacked at the end of June. I don't know if the art was ever recovered, but the hijacking had Deni completely crazed when it happened."

Mercer added the truck incident to his list.

"May we spend a few minutes with Valerie?" I asked, hoping to get a closer handle on personal life in Denise's wing of the house.

"I'm so sorry I didn't think of it before I excused her for the day. I told Maurizio to let her go after she prepared my tea. She'll grieve enough for all of us, Miss Cooper. I'll let her know you'll be contacting her, of course.

"Now I've got to ask you to leave so I can get ready for tomorrow. I must arrange for the services at Frank Campbell. Find a minister. Suggest an appropriate psalm. That sort of thing. I'm afraid the closest Deni ever got to a church was her frantic scrambling to buy that incredible Velázquez of Innocent the Tenth."

Caxton opened the door to the landing that put us at the elevator. "You know, Miss Cooper, there's a poignant fact about values in the world in which Deni and I lived that very few people realize. More than ninety percent of the art sold in America will never again fetch anywhere near the same price when the buyers attempt to resell it." He paused, not quite ready to turn his back on us. "It was like that with Deni, too, and I think that fact was even beginning to dawn on her. She had invented herself once—brilliantly—and sold the stunning result at the very top of the market. I'm not sure she could have done as well—repeated her success, if you will—the second time around. Very sad, that, don't you think?"

This time he closed the door behind him without waiting for us to be gone.

It wasn't even noon when we emerged from the lobby of Caxton's building onto the pavement in front of the Fifth Avenue co-op. The temperature was already over ninety degrees and the humidity was best measured by the tiny ringlets that formed instantly at the nape of my neck.

"Hate to say it," Mike remarked, "but even this feels like fresh air after an hour with that pompous jerk. Where to?"

"I've got to spend the day at my office. I'm supposed to finish up the hearing tomorrow, and I need to put the finishing touches on the brief I'm submitting after the argument."

"Is P. J. Bernstein's air-conditioned?"

"Yeah." The delicatessen near my apartment was my morning hangout on weekends.

"Let's grab some breakfast while we break up my to-do list. Then one of us can shoot you down to your office, okay?"

I rode the short distance to Third Avenue with Mercer, who parked at a meter in front of the deli, a feat that could be accomplished only in August. Midtown Manhattan was a ghost town on summer weekends, between vacationing New Yorkers, others who commuted to beach houses and shared rentals in the Hamptons or on the Jersey shore, and day-trippers who made their way to Jones Beach or the suburban pool of a friend or relative.

The three of us sat at a table in the rear, near the kitchen, each of us taking out a pad to make lists and notes for the next week's work.

"Any point in my gracing the funeral?" Mike asked, after we ordered.

"The best reason to go," Mercer offered, "is to try and get a look at—maybe even a copy of—the list of attendees. See if you can scope the sign-in book. They've always got one of those at Campbell's. Might give us a jump start on some of the people in her business, beside what we hope we'll get from her friend Bryan Daughtry."

"Already thought of that. There's always some sweet old mick used to drink at my father's bar who runs the show at that funeral home. If I spread a little cash around, I'm sure they'll make a copy of the guest list."

The beeper attached to my waistband went off just as the waitress returned with my iced coffee. Mercer saw me slip it off the belt of my slacks and lift it to check the callback number. "Trouble for us?" he asked.

I laughed when I read the dial. "It's Joan Stafford, and she even added a nine-one-one after Jim's number." Joan, one of my closest friends, was vacationing with her fiancé on the

Outer Banks off the coast of North Carolina. "Either of you want to guess what she thinks is so urgent she's got to talk to me immediately?"

Mike grabbed the cell phone from my hand after I dialed and heard it ringing. "Get your skinny ass out of bed with that foreign policy wonk and c'mon home to me. It's lonely here without you—just the Cooperwoman to give me orders all the time. What's with the emergency beep, kid—half-price sale at Schlumberger you gotta tell her about?"

Chapman looked up at Mercer and me as he repeated Joan's answer. "You wanna dish about a dead woman? Well, now that it's been on CNN this morning, I guess all you art mavens will be calling in with useless information." He paused to listen to something Joan was telling him, then glanced back at us as he said good-bye and turned off the phone.

"It's not enough we gotta deal with *you*. Nancy Drew's on board, too. Joan just gave me the names of three of Deni's clients and a couple of her lovers," he said, writing in his notepad as he talked, "and also has the story about why Caxton was no longer welcome at Sotheby's. She'll be up this week—dinner on Tuesday. Y'think this is some of her fiction, or should we run with it?"

Joan was a playwright, just back from London, where her latest satire had opened to brilliant reviews and full houses. "Go to the bank with her on this one. It's the world she was raised in. It wouldn't surprise me at all if she knew most of the players in the gallery scene—she's got a marvelous collection herself, plus she's been shopping the auctions to redecorate Jim's place in Washington."

I looked at the list on my pad. "I need to do a search warrant for some of Deni's things and have it ready in case you connect with her partner by tomorrow. The appointment book and calendar, records of sales and purchases—"

Mercer interrupted me. "We've got to assume a lot of this stuff is on computers. Be sure you draft the warrant so we can walk out of there with the hard drives, disks, and anything else in the office. The guys can download the data and get information that way, too. We'll search the gallery first to let you know what's there."

"I can always amend the warrant if you see more than we've thought of by the time you go in," I said.

"I'll reach out for Daughtry," he continued, "and call the funeral home for details on the memorial service."

I finished my Raisin Bran while Mike worked his way through an omelette, home fries, a side order of bacon, and toast and Mercer picked at a bagel with cream cheese. "Who's going to check out Lowell Caxton's shooting incident in the Nineteenth?"

"I'll swing by there later tonight," Chapman said, barely coming up for air between bites of his breakfast. "I'll also take care of the ladder manufacturer—see how common the brand is and who sells it." He aimed his fork at Mercer. "You see if you can run raps on all the employees at both galleries, and work on the art hijacking in June. What was it—Della Spigas? Who's Della Spiga, Coop?"

"I've got to go back to the books for that one. Ask me again at the end of the day."

"What's your schedule like this week?"

"Once I knock off the brief on Reggie X this afternoon and argue it tomorrow, I'm free. It'll take the judge a couple of weeks to make a decision and write his opinion. The sooner I get downtown, the faster I get it out of the way."

Mercer pushed off from the table and took the check from the waitress, while Mike dredged the last few fries through the ketchup.

"No point in you taking me," I said. "My car is right up the street. Just keep me posted." I waved good-bye and walked to my garage. I pulled the Jeep out and made my way over to the FDR Drive, while the all-news radio station wedged the story of Denise Caxton's identification as the murder victim between the Yankees' doubleheader victory last night and reviews of the Spice Girls' concert in Central Park. Maybe Chapman wasn't entirely crazy—live fast, die young, and be a good-looking corpse. Deni's fortune hadn't seemed to offer her very much more.

I escaped the rest of the hot afternoon and evening by immersing myself in completing the court papers I had to submit on Monday morning. The case was an old arrest of Mercer's, and my adversary had used his skills to challenge every aspect of the police procedures used in the investigation. The hearings we had just ended included the propriety of the arrest tactics, the legality of the search and seizure of evidence linking the perp—Reggie Bramwell—to the beating and rape of his estranged lover, and the admissibility of statements that Bramwell made to Mercer in the hours after he was taken into custody.

The case was pending in front of Harry Marklis, a jurist from the old school who didn't get domestic abuse at all. My last pretrial motion was an effort to convince the judge to allow my victim, Mariana Catano, to testify to two earlier episodes that involved the same defendant. One was an attempted assault that he had pleaded guilty to a year before, and the other was a confrontation in which he had threatened to set fire to her so that she'd look ugly enough that no other man would want her.

I had argued myself blue in the face, but Marklis was clueless. "So, why didn't she just leave him, Miss Cooper? What the hell'd she take him back for?" If I hadn't been able to explain the complex dynamic of a relationship of battering to a justice of the Supreme Court of the State of New York, I could only imagine how the average juror would respond to the same issue. Yet over and over again, my colleagues and I would see the cycle of violence escalate in these cases, and attempt to understand the complicated panoply of emotional, familial, and economic binds that kept the partners in place.

Mercer Wallace joined me in my office at nine o'clock on Monday morning. He was keenly interested in the outcome of Mariana's matter and wanted to hear my argument on this final pretrial issue. Marklis had directed our appearances for 10 A.M., although he was known for taking the bench late in the morning and quitting early in the afternoon.

"Anything develop last night?"

"Nope. Wasn't able to reach Daughtry anywhere. Gallery's closed on Sunday and Monday all through the summer, and his answering service just kept telling me they'd given him my message several times. Trying to get his home address so we can pay him a visit, but I'll wait till you're done upstairs. All-nighter?"

"Not too bad. I was home before midnight. Polished this off and started a rough draft of a warrant on the word processor, ready to go when you guys come up with something."

"All work and no play . . ."

"Don't go there, Mercer. You're as bad as Mike." I gathered up my file folders and motioned to him to move so we could head upstairs to Marklis's court part. "I'm fine. Got stood up for the weekend 'cause this guy I've been seeing was sent out of town on assignment. But thanks for asking."

The only people in Part 59 were the three court officers and Rich Velosi, the court clerk. I placed my files on the counsel table and asked if there was any word from the judge.

"Yeah, Ms. Konigsberg just called," Rich answered, referring to the judge's law secretary. "He's working in chambers, she says, so he won't get up here for another half hour."

The court officers all laughed, knowing that "working in chambers" was just a euphemism for "The judge hasn't arrived yet." But neither had my adversary. "Prisoner produced?"

"He's in the pens."

Mercer began to schmooze with the officers while I reviewed my notes. From baseball they went to golf, from golf to the first pro football exhibition games, and from the games to the Bramwell case. "Y'think Cooper's got a chance to get a decision on this motion before Labor Day?"

"Marklis make a decision? Listen, he's got two toilets in the robing room and it usually takes him twenty minutes to figure out which one he wants to use. All depends on the troll factor."

Mercer and I both smiled. The officers referred to the petite law secretary, Ilse Konigsberg, as "the Troll." Whatever she whispered in Marklis's ear was bound to be the law of the case.

It was exactly eleven twenty-eight on my watch when Marklis, short and stout, waddled through the door and took his seat at the bench as the clerk called us to order and asked everyone in the courtroom to rise. The defendant had been brought out from the pens minutes earlier, when his lawyer had entered the well.

"Good morning, gentlemen. Miss Cooper. Why don't you all state your appearances for the record, and then we'll get started."

"Alexandra Cooper, for the People." I spoke aloud and remained standing while the defense attorney, Danny Wistenson, spelled his name for the stenographer.

"It's now nine thirty-five, and we're going to resume argument in the Bramwell case."

I glanced over my shoulder at Mercer and rolled my eyes in disgust. Marklis had long protected himself by making a phony record of the time of the proceedings. My colleagues and I had challenged him on any number of occasions, but I knew that if I tried it today, it would seal my fate in the argument I was about to make. His arrogant grin confirmed that he knew he had me.

"I have the papers you submitted in support of your *Molineux* application, Ms. Cooper. Do you have anything to add this morning?" It was clear that he was hoping I did not.

"I do, Your Honor." I rose to my feet, but before I started to lay out the law that supported my position, Marklis went on.

"You know, evidence of a defendant's prior crime can't be admitted at a trial for the sole purpose of showing that he has the propensity to commit the crimes he's now charged with."

"I do know that, Judge Marklis." He'd obviously done the minimum amount of homework necessary to get through this process. "But *Molineux* makes it quite clear that it's admissible when it's probative of his motive, his intent, and a common scheme or plan.

"In the instant case, Bramwell's prior threats and assaults on Ms. Catano are 'inextricably interwoven,' using the language in the *Vails* opinion, and—"

"You got that cite, Counselor?" Marklis swung his chair around and pointed at Wistenson.

"It's in Ms. Cooper's brief, but I'd like to be heard on this, Your Honor."

"I'm not finished, Judge."

"Yeah, well, I've got about all I need on this point, dear."

I turned away from the bench, steaming at Marklis's laziness and choice of appellation. At some point during the argument, Chapman had slipped into the courtroom and joined Mercer in the front row on the far side of the rail. I read his lips as he mouthed to me, "I love it when you're angry."

As I walked toward the detectives, I asked over my shoulder, "Judge, may I have a few minutes?" and kept moving without waiting for a response.

"When you put your hands on your hips, blondie, it's a dead giveaway. Temper, temper."

The diminutive judge stepped down from his seat and walked over to whisper to Ms. Konigsberg. Chapman couldn't resist another crack, looking at the huddle of two small figures, like conspiring Munchkins. "What's going on, Coop? Looks like a wrap party for *The Wizard of Oz*."

"Don't get me in any more trouble with Marklis. How come you're down here so early?"

"Caxton played cute with the memorial service. Ten o'clock this morning. Invitation only—just a handful of friends, and Daughtry wasn't among them. My guy inside says the husband wants to wait until the fall, when everyone is back from summer vacation, before he holds a real memorial. Wouldn't want to slight all the artists and clients who couldn't get here on short notice. But you better cut this exercise in futility short, 'cause we need some help."

"With what?"

"Looks like we found the car Deni's body was transported in. Need you to do a warrant."

"Great. How'd you get it?"

"Uniform cop in the Bronx noticed an abandoned station wagon this morning. Not far from the water. K-9 Unit took a dog up there a little while ago and got a positive hit. Looks like there's blood on a canvas tarp in the back, too."

"Any plates? Whose is it?"

"Stripped clean. VIN number's been scratched out a bit, but the computer still came up with a list of possibilities."

"And?"

"One of them comes back to an employee who works in Deni's Chelsea gallery. Bingo."

I stepped back and smiled at the judge. "That's it, Your Honor. No further argument. We'll rest on our papers." I grabbed my files off the table and followed Mercer and Mike out of the courtroom.

9

Laura tried to pass the telephone to me as I swept through her alcove. "It's Rose. She just wants to warn you that Battaglia said he'd like an update on the Caxton investigation."

"Tell her that he'll have it by the end of the day."

Mike was at my desk, using the private line. "It's a girl!" This time I grabbed the receiver out of his hand. Sarah's baby had been born during the night, and she was calling to tell us about it, urging us to come visit Janine as soon as possible.

"You okay?"

"Much easier this time. When are you coming up to the hospital? I'll only be here until Wednesday."

"Don't worry. We'll come see her tonight or tomorrow.

Give her a kiss and tell her we'll all be up the first break we get." I placed the phone back in its cradle.

"See, Alex, that's what you should be doing with your life instead of chasing around after scumbags like we do all day."

"You're beginning to sound like my grandmother." I turned to Mike as I sat down at my desk. "Have you ever done one of these before? I mean, a search warrant based on a *dog* as the informant?"

"No, but I got the officer right outside who knows how." He walked to the door of my office and signaled to a plainclothes cop who was reading the *Daily News* on a chair in the hallway. "This is Detective Loquesto," he said, introducing me to a sandy-haired man with a crooked smile that seemed to align with his long, hooked nose. "Armando, meet Alex Cooper."

"Good to meet you. Thanks for the break."

"Don't thank me," he said. "Tego did it. Latin word for 'I protect.' I'm just the handler; the dog does the heavy lifting."

"Can you walk me through the affidavit?"

"No problem—do it all the time."

I pulled up my standard search warrant application form on the computer, quickly punching in the information Chapman fed me about the target automobile, a '91 light blue Chevy wagon, partial vehicle identification number 6683493, registered to Omar Sheffield.

"How'd you connect Sheffield to one of the Caxton galleries?" I asked.

Mercer spoke up. "Caxton's aide, Maurizio, faxed me a list of all the employees. It was on my desk when I walked in today. Also had the names of some of Denise's clients—said we'd have to get the rest of them from Daughtry."

I fleshed out the paragraph delineating that there is reasonable cause to believe that we might find blood, hair, fibers, fingerprints, and other evidence of the presence of the body of

Denise Caxton. Then I added in the "moreover" clause, asking the judge to believe that this property was used to commit or conceal the commission of a crime.

It was essential to explain to the court how, when, and where the body of the deceased had been found, and that her death was the result of a homicide. When I finished that paragraph, I looked up at Armando for help. "Now what?"

"You gotta throw in some background about me and Tego."

I typed in his name and shield. "Your command?"

"NYPD Emergency Services, K-9 Unit." He told me how many years he'd been on the force and what his training had been to qualify him for this special duty. "Tego's got four years on the job—specializing in cadaver duty."

"What?" I knew German shepherds were used to great advantage in police work, trained to identify the scents of bomb materials and controlled substances. This one was new to me.

"True. He's like Chapman—death is his specialty. Sniffs it out and loves it."

"How do you train them for that?"

"There are a couple of chemicals that simulate cadaver odors—"

"Yeah, Coop, and Chanel doesn't make 'em," Mike cut in. "So don't try and seduce me by dousing yourself in 'em."

Armando continued. "They're called Cadaverine and Pseudocorpse—both are artificial commercial scents. The dogs practice by smelling body parts, corpses, crime scene areas. Then we sprinkle some of the fake stuff on items like you'd find at a scene and let them go to work."

"Tell her what you give them when they come up with a body."

"Three treats and a rawhide pull toy, just like if he'd brought home your missing slipper."

I improvised a few paragraphs about Tego's training and the fact that he had completed more than sixty tests in the company of Detective Loquesto.

"What else do I need?"

"You gotta say what the dog did when he got to the target. The Chevy was parked in a row of nine cars. In training we call it a 'marked reaction,' which—"

"What'd he do, exactly?"

Chapman was impatient and anxious for me to complete the warrant. "He went ape, like you do when you see Alex Trebek. Drooling, panting—"

"Pretty close," Loquesto said. "He sniffed next to the right rear passenger door, then ran around to the back of the wagon. He jumped up against it and began pawing at it, whining and scratching like it'd get him inside. I looked in—window was slightly tinted—and there's a dark stain on a canvas-colored matting. Then I pulled Tego away and took him one at a time to the doors of each other car. No reaction at all."

I finished the application with the routine language, respectfully asking the court for a warrant and order of seizure. "As soon as the lunch break is over, we'll go down and get the judge who's sitting in the arraignment part to sign it, okay? Anybody want me to call in something to eat?"

"Nah, we'll grab a bite on our way to the Bronx."

"Okay. I'll open a grand jury investigation this afternoon so I can start some phone company subpoenas for muds and luds on the Caxton telephones—home and galleries." Contrary to what most people thought, prosecutors have no power to subpoena people or evidence to their offices. It was only the authority of the grand jury in New York, not the district attorneys, that enabled the request for a witness to produce documentary evidence. "Who's looking for Omar?"

"*My* job," Mercer said. "Since the gallery's closed today,

there's no activity at all. The address on the Motor Vehicles Bureau records—for Omar's residence—is in Brooklyn."

"Before I came up to the courtroom," Mike went on, "I called the boss at the Eighty-fourth Precinct and asked them to do a drive-by of that address. Desk sergeant beeped me back and said it's a burned-out building. Mercer'll be working on it this afternoon."

My paralegal, Maxine, came into the room and greeted the trio of cops. "This looks like the wrong time to ask, but what do I do with a walk-in who just arrived now for her ten-thirty appointment?"

"Who is she?" I looked at my watch, noting that the woman was more than three hours late.

"Her name's Unique Matthews. Says she's here to see Janice O'Riley, but Janice has to do a preliminary hearing all afternoon."

"This one's the prostitute who was raped at gunpoint by the trucker on Houston Street, right?"

"Yep." Maxine smiled and motioned discreetly with her thumb for me to look out the doorway to Laura's desk. A young woman was towering over my secretary, balancing on four-inch platform sandals with straps that wrapped up to her knees. The cheeks of her buttocks were hanging well below the bottom of her shorts, and her cleavage strained against the skimpy cut of her fuchsia cotton tank T-shirt, exposing a tattoo of Mickey Mouse on her inner left breast, outlined against her dark skin. Unique was chewing a wad of gum and sipping from a large bottle of Yoo-Hoo.

I called out to the witness, knowing that there would be no particularly good reason for her tardiness. "Unique, how come you're so late today? You were supposed to testify this morning."

She took the straw out of her mouth and sneered at me, certain that I could not understand how hard it had been to rouse herself for something as relatively unimportant as her court appearance. "I overslept."

"Why don't you take her across the street to Catherine's office?" I said to Max. This was going to take more experience and a firmer hand than Janice had with these cases. "Let her work with Unique for a couple of hours."

Chapman patted Max on the back. "Remind O'Riley of Cooper's basic commands. Never make a morning appointment for a hooker. Like vampires, they don't thrive in daylight. C'mon, blondie. Let Mercer get on his way. Me and Armando'll come down to court with you to get the warrant signed."

"Armando and I."

"What else do you do in your spare time besides give grammar lessons? Wellesley meets the NYPD. Now *that's* an exercise in futility."

I stopped at Laura's desk and asked her to check the docket assignment sheet. "Who's sitting in arraignments this week?"

"You've got Roger Hayes in AR1 and John Reick in AR2."

Mercer chided me. "Judge shopping, Alex? My money's on AR1. I'll check in with both of you as soon as I get back from Brooklyn."

Mike, Armando, and I took the circuitous route to the first-floor arraignment parts, down the interior stairway one flight and over to the elevator bank that serviced the courtrooms and stopped on only a single floor of the District Attorney's Office, as a security measure. As usual the wait for a functioning elevator going in the right direction seemed interminable. And walking the hallways with Chapman was more of a social occasion than a business trip. He had worked with and partied with every senior assistant in the office at one time or another. He was a legendary storyteller, a great foil for people's jokes, and the best investigator that most of us would ever encounter in the NYPD.

The double swinging doors of AR1 pushed open as I

entered behind Mike. Families and friends of prisoners arrested within the last twenty-four hours and awaiting their first appearances before the judge filled rows of benches on both sides of the room. Some mothers looked tearful and anxious, waiting for word from the Legal Aid attorneys that their sons would be coming home today, while other relatives slept soundly despite the noise and activity, clearly accustomed to the routine of this process.

We made our way down to the front row, saved for attorneys and police officers, and I scooted into the only available seat, between two uniformed cops who were dozing until their cases were called. Mike and Armando sat behind me, scrunched between an elderly Hasidic Jew dressed in his traditional black overcoat and an obese Latina woman who was whining some kind of prayer over and over again under her breath.

The air-conditioning wasn't working and the windows were so tall in the two-story room that there was no way for the crew to open them for fresh air. Everyone in the well of the courtroom—lawyers, stenographer, officers, and clerks—was fanning with different files or sheaves of papers. The stench was unbearable.

As soon as Judge Hayes made eye contact with me, he waved me up to the bench. As I rose, Chapman grabbed my shoulder. "I'm coming with you. This place smells like a broad I used to date."

"May we approach, Your Honor?" I asked as I closed the swinging gate that separated the benches from the counsel tables.

"Absolutely, Ms. Cooper. We'll take a ten-minute recess, folks," Hayes announced, eliciting groans from almost everyone in the gallery. "Why don't we all go into the robing room? Will we need a reporter?"

"Yes sir."

Hayes had been one of my first supervisors in the District

Attorney's Office when I started there, more than ten years ago. I respected his judgment and valued his guidance and friendship enormously.

Mike, Armando, and I followed Hayes out of the court-room and into the small chambers behind it that served the arraignment part. He normally sat as a trial jurist in Supreme Court but was serving a week's rotation in this duty since so many of the judges took vacation time during July and August. Hayes greeted Mike and me warmly, and we intro-duced him to Armando.

"I'd tell you to make yourselves comfortable, but that's obviously not possible."

The small room was bare except for an old wooden desk, three chairs, and a black rotary telephone that hung on the wall. It was painted the institutional green that must have been bought in vatloads by the city of New York fifty years ago and was now chipped and peeling from every corner and molding. Next to the phone, written on the wall in ink, were the num-bers of most of the delis and pizza joints within a mile's radius, jotted there by lazy court officers who called out for deliveries during the meal break of night court.

I explained our visit to the judge, and we went on the record with the stenographer so that he could make the appro-priate inquiries before signing the warrant.

"Everything seems to be in order, Alex." He initialed the papers and chatted with Mike while I went back to the clerk to have the official seal put on the documents. As the court offi-cer gaveled the crowd back into order and Hayes resumed his position on the bench, we left the courtroom with exactly what we needed to move the investigation forward.

The rear entrance of the immense Criminal Courts Build-ing was adjacent to AR1. Mike took his copy of the paper-work from me, and he and Armando headed for the door while I started to retrace my steps back up to my office.

"I'll call you as soon as we're done checking out the wagon. Wanna meet Mercer and me for dinner?"

"Sure. Cocktails and *Jeopardy!* at my place, then we'll go somewhere in the neighborhood."

Upstairs on the eighth floor, Laura greeted me with word that Patrick McKinney, deputy chief of the Trial Division, wanted to see me. The chief, Rod Squires, was on summer vacation and McKinney would use all the muscle he could to make me answer to him and try to micromanage my case. I thanked Laura for the message, then did my best to ignore that she had given it to me. I knew I could deal directly with Battaglia on something as major as the Caxton murder.

I called my friend Rose Malone, in the D.A.'s suite, and told her that I was ready to update the boss whenever it was convenient for him. Things looked good, I assured her, since the cops had already found a critical link to the deceased's disappearance. I was optimistic enough to think this early break would signal a speedy conclusion to the investigation. Battaglia was on his way to Albany for a meeting with the governor on the legislative agenda, so I knew I was off the hook for the rest of the day.

The intercom buzzed. Laura reported there was a woman on the line who refused to give her name and would speak only to me. She said she had some things to tell me about Denise Caxton.

"Put the call through on my private line and close the door so no one interrupts me." I pressed the flashing light on my dial pad. "This is Alexandra Cooper."

"Thank you for taking the call. I thought you might be interested in some personal information I have about Deni Caxton."

"Yes, but it would also help me if you would tell me with whom I'm speaking."

My request was met by silence.

"Hello?" I asked, getting no response. At least she hadn't hung up, so I didn't want to push her too hard. "I hope you can understand that we get an awful lot of crank calls whenever our names appear in the paper on a sensational case. It just helps me to know that I'm dealing with someone who really has something useful to say." And who isn't wasting my time.

Still a pause. Then, "I'll give you my name, but I'd like a few assurances first."

"That's not unreasonable. May I ask what they are?"

"I can't have my name connected with this case in the papers. Not in any way. Can you promise me that?"

Impossible. "All I can promise is that no one will get your name from *us*. You have my word that it is not the kind of thing we would ever give to the press. But obviously, since I have no idea what your connection is—either to Denise or to the investigation—I simply have no idea how you figure in the matter at all. Perhaps reporters already know who you are."

I was clearly fishing now, and she was just as clearly getting agitated. "I have nothing to do with the case. I'm a friend of Deni's, that's all. One of her oldest friends. I know things about her that I doubt anyone else knows. Very intimate things. Perhaps they'll be useful to you, perhaps they won't. But I thought I'd be more comfortable talking with you than with a bunch of detectives."

"And your other requests?"

"Just one other, really. Lowell Caxton must never know I've spoken with you."

"That's easy. He's a witness in this matter. We'd have no business telling him where or from whom we get our information."

"He's terribly well connected, Ms. Cooper. I'm afraid it's more difficult to keep secrets from him than you might think. That was one of Deni's biggest problems."

"Would you be willing to meet with me this afternoon?" I glanced at the clock on the wall, and it was already after three. "Or this evening?"

"I'm coming into New York late tonight. I can meet with you tomorrow."

"Let me give you the address of my office—"

"No, I won't come there. I don't want some tabloid photographer camped out on your doorstep snapping witnesses as they go in and out of the building."

Rivera Live, Burden of Proof, and Court TV had been real wake-up calls to the public about the way high-profile cases frequently spin out of control.

"We're closer to a solution than you might think," I said to ease her concerns, sure in my own mind that Omar Sheffield would be the key to Deni's disappearance. "But I'll be happy to meet you at your home, if you prefer."

"My hotel, if you don't mind. I'll call you during the day, and perhaps you can meet with me by late afternoon. The name is Seven. Marilyn Seven."

"Thank you for that, Ms. Seven. I appreciate it. Where will you be staying?"

The click on the other end of the phone reminded me that she didn't trust me or the system all that much. I went back into our office E-mail and sent one of my regular messages to my colleague who ran the computer section's Investigative Support Services, Jim Winright.

CooperA to WinrightJ: Can you please run me a background check on a woman named Marilyn Seven? Sorry, I've got no date of birth, no social security, no residential address. Nothing but a name. It's a long shot, but could you see if you can come up with anything before I meet with her tomorrow? Thanks, as always.

With Jim's skills and a bit of luck, the not-so-common-name search might call up something on his database, whether out-of-state driver's registration records, licensed professional information (if her occupation required some kind of government control), property ownership records, or even a Dun & Bradstreet report. It would help me not to go to the meeting blind, so that I could better evaluate whatever it was that Marilyn Seven had to barter.

When I finished drafting the subpoenas, which Laura could format and print, I ran upstairs to the ninth-floor grand jury room, to open an investigation into the death of Denise Caxton. Several of the jurors whispered to one another as I spoke, recognizing the deceased's name from the newspaper accounts. I was out of the chamber as quickly as I had entered it, and on my way back to my desk.

"Call Catherine or Marisa," Laura told me. "They want to make arrangements to go to the hospital tomorrow to see Sarah and the baby. And Kim McFadden, from the U.S. Attorney's Office, called. Here's her extension."

I took the slip of paper from Laura and dialed the number immediately. I hadn't seen Kim, who was a federal prosecutor, in months. Our offices often tangled when investigations crossed jurisdictional lines and our bosses became territorial, but she and I had been friends since she started to date one of my colleagues, several years ago.

"Sorry I've been so out of touch," I began our conversation. "Can we make a lunch date for later in the month, when things slow down here?"

"That'd be good, Alex, but it's not the reason I'm calling. Got the clearance from the top to give you a heads-up on this, once I saw you were handling the Caxton case."

"Just when I was beginning to think this was a ground ball, don't tell me it's going to get muddier. My guys think it's a disgruntled employee—raped and dumped her in the water.

Probably just hired the wrong guy. I'm waiting for the results on his rap sheet now, with a team of detectives out looking for the subject."

"That's probably what you've got, then. Just thought that you should know—and I'd appreciate it if you didn't tell anyone other than Battaglia—that we've had a major investigation under way with Justice. Price-fixing by auction houses and art dealers. We've had subpoenas out for months—you may have seen the story in the *Times*."

"Well, if I did, I didn't pay any attention to it. I don't remember a thing about it."

"We're looking at it as an antitrust matter. Know what bid rigging is?"

"Not in the art world. Bring me up to speed, Kim, and the next time you get a sexual assault on federal property, I'll walk you through it." I said it only half in jest, since once every few years their office actually claimed jurisdiction for a rape in a Veterans Administration hospital or on a military base.

"The claim has been that some of the biggest art dealers in the city have formed a ring agreeing not to bid against each other on paintings in which they all have an interest. That collusion keeps the price down at auctions—an illegal restraint, really. Then the participating dealers hold what's called a 'knockout.'"

"Which is . . . ?"

"That's a second auction—but a secret one. The dealer who got the piece at the public auction sells it off for a much higher price, and then the members of the ring all split the profits. The agents who've been investigating this for years can lay out the whole thing for your team."

"Any direct connection to Denise Caxton?"

"Nothing certain yet. But records have been subpoenaed from both Lowell and Denise Caxton, Bryan Daughtry, and quite honestly, a cast of thousands. All the big dealers are being called down here—Leo Castelli, Knoedler, Pace Wildenstein. They're all in the contemporary field. David Findlay and Acquavella in modern and Impressionist works. Even Sotheby's and Christie's have gotten those unfriendly little slips of paper. I'm not saying any of these places are targets—there's no allegation they did anything wrong or participated in the knock-outs—but we're trying to get a handle on the nature and extent of the scam."

"Any results yet?"

"We're getting buried in an avalanche. Travel logs, phone records, invoices from business transactions, correspondence between the auction houses and some of the dealers."

"Can I bring my detectives over later in the week if we don't settle everything in the next twenty-four hours?"

"That's why I called. No reason for you to reinvent the wheel. If you're going to have the legal authority to request the same kind of documentation, maybe we can shortcut some of this for you."

"Thanks a million, Kim. I'll call you in a day or two."

There was enough to keep me busy at my desk until after six, so I successfully avoided contact with McKinney through the end of the day. I drove home, went upstairs, turned on all my air conditioners, and filled the ice bucket in anticipation of the arrival of Mercer and Mike. I called Lumi, who owned the wonderful Italian restaurant over on Lexington Avenue, and made a reservation for the three of us at eight o'clock, after confirming that she had Mercer's favorite pasta on the menu tonight—cavatelli with peas and prosciutto. I settled in to watch the end of the evening news, knowing that very little would keep Mike from missing the Final Jeopardy question at seven twenty-five.

I had told the doormen that they didn't need to announce either of the detectives, who were well known to the staff in the building. Mercer was the first to come through my front door, and we decided there was no reason at all to wait for Mike before we poured our first drink. I fixed him a Ketel One with two olives and lots of ice before filling my own glass with Dewar's.

"What'd you find out in Brooklyn?"

"I found out that the last time anyone lived at the address given on Omar Sheffield's automobile registration, he wasn't even a glimmer in his momma's eye. The whole block is a wreck. The Eight-four squad had some informants in the 'hood that they rousted for me, but nobody ever heard of Omar. I spent three hours pounding that hot pavement and every minute of it was wasted time. Hope Chapman did better than I did. Zip, zero, nada."

He sipped on his vodka while I started to tell him about my phone calls from Marilyn Seven and Kim McFadden.

Mike came in minutes later and walked straight to the den, checking the screen and pouring himself a drink before he took over the conversation with the results of their search.

"I think I'm asking for a new partner. Gimme one of those four-legged sniffers any day. Man, I've worked with detectives so bad they couldn't find dog shit at the pound."

Mercer smiled over at me. "I guess this means Tego was on the money."

"Emergency Services broke into the car. No question about it—there was definitely a body in there. Backseat is down, and there's a big piece of sailcloth laid out full length, with a bloodstain on top. It was folded over, so we opened it up—you know what I mean? It was like the body had been sandwiched in between. Huge bloodstain, kinda matching the hole in Denise's head. Even some hair. And a pair of lace panties—beige, size four."

"What did you do with them?"

"Everything's vouchered. Going directly over to the lab. They'll run the DNA tests at the M.E.'s Office. We could have preliminary results within forty-eight hours."

In the mid-1980s, when the lawyers in my office had first been introduced to DNA technology and the science of genetic fingerprinting, it took three or four months to obtain results from the private labs to which materials were sent for testing. Now the city had established its own laboratory, and the methodology had changed so dramatically that we could include or eliminate suspects and match samples to victims or defendants in a matter of several days.

"Tonight's Final Jeopardy category is Bob Dylan's Music," announced Alex Trebek as he led into a commercial break and Mike *sssshush*ed us into silence.

"I'm out. I do not know anything about this one," Mercer said, standing to freshen his drink.

"I'll go twenty," I offered, comfortable with the category.

"Let's keep it at ten," Mike said. That was a sure sign that he didn't have a clue.

"Nope, it's twenty or I'm not betting."

He reluctantly put his money on the table.

"Let's show our contestants the answer, ladies and gentlemen." Trebek read along with the words that were revealed on the screen: "Famous rock musician who plays the organ on Dylan's 'Like a Rolling Stone.' Ooh, that's a tough one, folks."

The theme music played as Chapman cursed, noticing the smile on my face. "Double or nothing?" I asked.

"Talk about obscure, how could you possibly know this? No way."

The bioethics professor from Oregon shook his head and didn't even attempt an answer. The mother of eleven from Nevada and the crab farmer from Delaware both guessed wrong, as Trebek was sorry to tell them.

Mike's beeper gave off with a loud series of noises as I put my response in the appropriate question form. "Who is Al Kooper?" I asked. "Impossible for me to forget, right?"

"A Jewish organist, no doubt," he said, squinting at the number after he took the device off his waistband. "Turn to Comedy Central. Let's watch *Win Ben Stein's Money* before we go eat."

We had a new quiz show favorite in the seven thirty time slot, so I switched channels and passed Mike the portable phone. "Who's the beep from?"

"It's the lieutenant's line," he said, dialing the number at the squad. "Hey, Loo, what's up?"

"*What?* How certain are they?"

I muted the television sound while Mercer and I waited to hear what seemed so surprising to Mike.

"Mercer Wallace is with me. We'll get over there right away. No, no—we're just ten minutes away." He hung up the phone and handed it back to me.

"I'll start with the good news. They found Omar Sheffield."

"Where?" Mercer and I spoke at once.

"In the culvert next to the railroad tracks, between Tenth and Eleventh near Thirty-sixth Street. Dead. Very, very dead. Run over by a freight train."

10

"Death Avenue," Chapman said flatly.

"Seems like an appropriate name after last night."

Mike and I were standing on Eleventh Avenue at the edge of the Thirtieth Street rail yards at eight thirty in the morning. He had called to suggest that I meet him there on my way into the office so he could show me where Sheffield's body had been found.

"Forget last night. That's what this stretch was called a hundred years ago." His sweeping arm gesture took in all the property north and south of the tracks that had once been owned by the New York Central Railroad. "My old man grew up here—Hell's Kitchen. Used to tell us stories about this neighborhood all the time."

After the Civil War, when a large area of Manhattan's West Side was thick with slaughterhouses, factories, lumberyards, and tenements, it housed one of the worst slums in the city. Cops who covered its beat called it Hell's Kitchen, from Thirtieth Street north to Fifty-ninth Street, and from Eighth Avenue west to the Hudson River.

"Freight trains rolled through here every day and night. The place was notorious—for its filth and for the dangerous gangs that controlled its everyday life. The kids who weren't killed by disease or driven out by dust and noise were just as likely to be flattened by one of the trains. Big Mike was around long before they elevated the tracks, after nineteen thirty, to get them off the street." Mike grinned as he thought of his father's stories. "Used to fascinate me, 'cause he said that every time a train came through, there was a 'cowboy'— a guy who actually rode on a horse ahead of the engine, waving a flag to get people out of the way. Can you imagine that—in the middle of Manhattan, in the twentieth century? When he was four or five, my dad dreamed about being that cowboy when he grew up. By that time the trains were raised above street level. But Death Avenue is what they called it, even then."

"Here's Mercer," I said, pointing to the corner of the next block, where I saw him parking his car. "What's the plan?"

"We're meeting Daughtry at the gallery in a few minutes. Thought you'd want to be along for the interview."

Mercer greeted us with, "What's the word from the morgue?"

"I was just telling Coop. Train messed up Sheffield's body pretty well. But there's no way he just happened to be crossing these tracks. Fleisher says it'll take a few days for the toxicology reports to come in. My guess is somebody probably filled him up with dope or tranquilizers and left him here in the dark to make it look accidental. And by the way, it didn't happen last night. Omar was lying here a couple of days—out of sight, out of mind."

Mercer held up a roll of papers he was clutching in his left hand. "Let me tell you about Mr. Sheffield. Forty-six years old, three felony convictions—worked his way up from burglary to gun possession to armed robbery. Released on parole about eight months ago. Needless to say, he reported faithfully to his parole officer, who didn't have a clue that Omar's residential address simply didn't exist."

"You think Deni Caxton knew that when she hired him?" I asked.

"Let's hope we're about to find out. Daughtry returned my call late last night. He's waiting for us at the downtown gallery. Ready for this?"

Mike and I left our cars parked near the rail yards and rode down to Twenty-second Street between Tenth and Eleventh Avenues in Mercer's department car. I had never met Bryan Daughtry but knew well the story of his involvement in a murder in Westchester County almost ten years earlier, even though he had never been charged or prosecuted.

In the late eighties Daughtry had a gallery in the Fuller Building, where Lowell Caxton still maintained an upscale presence. Daughtry was forty years old at the time and had worked his way up quite rapidly from apprenticing with another successful dealer to owning his own business, once he became the personal business associate of the wealthy Japanese collector Yoshio Tsukamoto.

Daughtry was buying and selling major works—Jackson Pollocks and Franz Klines—and living a lifestyle that matched his newfound ability to afford it. A town house in the east sixties and a grand Victorian country place south of the highway in East Hampton. He was intensely private about his personal relationships, but rumor had it that he preferred teenaged girls—young, lean, fond of drugs, and dressed in leather.

By 1992 his professional life seemed to be unraveling just as quickly as it had taken off. Creditors had trouble collecting money from him—even small amounts—and auction houses as well as other prominent dealers began to sue because of misrepresentations Daughtry had made about ownership of some of the works he sold. Then the IRS piled in after a disgruntled accountant whom Daughtry had fired reported that Daughtry had withheld tax payments on more than $5 million of income. Informants told the Feds that he was buying almost fifty grams of cocaine a week, at $100 a gram. His lawyers were working on a deal to get him out of his legal problems.

And then, the body of a fifteen-year-old Swedish girl, a would-be model, was found in a wooded area surrounded by enormous private estates in a suburban town north of Manhattan. The bird-watchers who stumbled on the carcass were stunned to find that the only part of the remains that had not been consumed by rodents was the stunning head of the child, her faded blue eyes staring out from a black leather mask that tightly covered her skull.

I reminded Mike and Mercer of the rest of the story. Posters of Ilse Lunen had been plastered all over the Village, where she had last been seen at a leather bar, one frequented by Daughtry and his crowd. Although no one had placed the dealer there the evening of the girl's disappearance, his closest personal assistant, Bertrand Gloster, had been at the bar for hours and was known to pimp for his boss when Daughtry was too wrecked to appear on his own.

In fact, it was rare for Bryan to come on to his subjects face-to-face. His preferred mode of pickup was to sit in a private room on the third floor of the building in which Cuir de Russie ("Russian leather"), as the bar was called, was situated. He'd stare out the window for hours, doing an occasional line of coke. When he saw a girl who was young and nubile enough standing on the sidewalk for a chat with a friend or a smoke, he would call the number of the pay phone outside the bar, talk to his target, and invite her up to the owner's lair.

Long after the death of the Lunen girl, people in the art world told stories of visiting Daughtry in his office, where he often had sex toys casually displayed on his desk and cabinet tops—handcuffs, collars, studded bands, and even leather masks like the one found on the corpse. In those same encounters he would refer to the ever-subservient Bertrand as "my executioner," the enforcer who had been brought in to serve as a bodyguard against the rough characters Daughtry encountered in this underside of his life. No one took his words seriously at the time.

Also later, acquaintances admitted hearing stories of the sadomasochistic games that Bryan and his pals had favored, wild evenings of drugs and sex, complete with whips and chains, during which Daughtry increasingly lost his self-control.

Bertrand Gloster was picked up within days of the discovery of Ilse Lunen's body. He had once been employed as a caretaker on one of the neighboring estates, and his borderline intelligence level made him an easy subject for police interrogators. He admitted killing the young girl, who had gingerly agreed to participate in the S&M activities in return for Daughtry's promise of an airline ticket home to Sweden.

In Gloster's chilling confession, he described Ilse Lunen putting on the leather mask and zipping its mouthpiece shut before Daughtry handcuffed her behind her back and directed her to kneel behind a large boulder in the woods. Then, Gloster said, the already floating art dealer snorted a few more lines and leaned over to whisper to Ilse, "You'll be going home, all right—in a wooden box," before he ordered Gloster to shoot her in the back of the head.

"End of story?" Chapman asked.

"Not exactly. Gloster's doing twenty-five to life for murder, and the Westchester D.A. has never been able to nail Daughtry." The testimony of an accomplice has to be corroborated by some other evidence—it's not sufficient in and of itself to charge the coconspirator with the crime of murder. "There has never been a single other thing to link Daughtry to the child's death."

"So this friggin' lunatic did eighteen months for tax evasion and now he's back in business like he's a normal guy, right? Man, I'd like just five minutes alone with him while you wait in the car. Whaddaya think, Coop? No loss to society, I promise."

Mercer parked in front of Galleria Caxton Due, the newest Chelsea outpost, which Deni and Bryan had just been setting up for a fall premiere at the time of her death. It was too early in the day for the galleries to be open, so there were few other cars and little pedestrian activity on the street.

Mike paused briefly to read the sign that was posted below the bell: "*Service entrance in rear on Twenty-third Street.* Hope that doesn't mean us."

The front door was unlocked, so Mike pushed it open and we followed him in. The cavernous first-floor space of the former auto repair shop had been completely whitewashed and gutted of all signs of its earlier life. New Age music played on speakers tucked up high in corners of the room.

"Guess they're not set up for the exhibition yet."

"You're about to step on a masterpiece, Mikey. Read the sign." I pointed to a piece of gray string, about twelve feet long, that extended out from the wall to form a triangle and was tacked to a point on the floor near my left shoe. He ignored me, looking around, instead, at similar strands of colorless yarn spread across sections of the gallery like giant cat's-cradle forms. I called out the words written on the placard describing the display: "*In these string sculptures, the* space takes on an incorporeal palpability, concentrating on the planar or volumetric components. Illusion and fact are interwoven, with overlapping linear trajectories."

"This is *art*?" Mike responded. "You think some horse's ass is going to pay money for these things? I never saw anything so useless in my entire life."

Bryan Daughtry's voice called down to us from a high balcony area off to the side of the airy room. "Don't be so quick to declare this one the most absurd, Detective. There are several more floors above you might like to see. Why don't you take the lift up here to my office?"

"Can I make it up there without hanging myself on any of this string crap you call art?" Mike said to Daughtry, rolling his eyes at the bizarre exhibit of yarn sculptures that stretched across the mostly bare space on the ground floor. Then he turned to me. "Let's head up, blondie. Maybe if I dangle my handcuffs in front of him he'll get a hard-on. You're certainly much too old for his taste."

There was a small lift in the far corner of the wide room. When the doors of the elevator opened on the sixth floor, I was struck in the eye by a blaze of light. The southern exposure of the building was a wall of glass, which let the bright midday sun flood into this most unexpected setting.

From this point, with no tall buildings in the immediate area, I could see over the rooftops of nearby galleries and garages and out to the Hudson River, which curved in toward the east just a few blocks below us.

The most striking surprise was that about three floors beneath where we stood, running from the north end to the south side of the airy atrium, was an actual stretch of railroad track. It was heavy, thick, covered with rust, and overgrown with weeds.

I stared down at it. "Is that real?"

Chapman was rapt. "I wish my old man could see *this*. Sure

it's real. Look," he said, pointing to an opening where the track ran out of the glass-sided building and across the street, directly into a warehouse facing the Galleria Caxton Due.

I leaned against the railing to see that in similar fashion, the grass-filled ties also ran back out of the converted garage, crossing over the double width of Twenty-third Street and rolling on between two buildings on its north corner.

"What is it?" Mercer asked.

"The old Hi-Line Railroad. Another Hell's Kitchen special. When they raised the tracks off Death Avenue north of the rail yards, they still needed trains to get down to the meat markets in the Fourteenth Street area. So, south of Thirtieth Street, this became the elevated line. Haven't you ever noticed the old tracks?"

Mercer and I looked at Mike blankly and shook our heads.

"Just drive uptown on Tenth Avenue and look to your left. The air rights over the railroad tracks were sold off, so all these warehouses were allowed to build above and surrounding the actual path of the Hi-Line. Between every block in the twenties and even below that, till you hit the old Gansevoort Market, you can see the great tracks right from the street."

Daughtry stepped out of his office, on the southwest corner of the floor, and looked across at us. "Amazing space, isn't it? We're the only gallery in the city smart enough to incorporate this bit of history into our design. Glad you appreciate that much."

He invited us into his chilled office, and despite the temperature in the climate-controlled gallery, I was surprised to see that beads of sweat were pooled on Daughtry's forehead. He repeatedly dabbed at the streaks running down the side of his neck.

Mike, Mercer, and I introduced ourselves, and he invited us to sit opposite his desk. There were no signs of his former indiscretions here, and although he resembled the photos I had seen in the press during the Gloster trial, Daughtry was paunchier now, and jowls had replaced the even line of his pointed chin.

"I'm sure you know all about my background, Detective," he began tentatively, as his eyes darted back and forth between us, trying to measure our level of hostility or the extent of our familiarity with his past. His fingers trembled when they were at rest on the desktop, so he kept wiping at his head and neck, even before it was necessary. "But you need to know that I adored Deni Caxton, and I'll be glad to help you in any way that I can."

Chapman was unmoved by Daughtry's effort to set a cooperative tone, so I sat back quietly, like a guest privileged to be at the interrogation but not encouraged to participate. Mike was aware of his witness's vulnerability, so, in contrast to his meeting with Lowell Caxton, he knew he could control the conversation.

Mike let Daughtry think that if he bared his soul about the tax fraud matter, we'd get off the old case and move on to the mystery of Deni's death. It seemed to calm him to tell us what we already knew about the tax matter, as though we would think better of him for admitting his wrongdoing aloud.

Then Mike moved his chair directly across from his target. "Now, Bryan," he said, knowing the use of his first name would bring Daughtry down one more notch, "tell us about *her*."

Daughtry seemed relieved to be off the subject of himself and onto his friend. "Oh, Deni. She's the only reason I'm still in business today, after getting out of—"

"No, no, no, Bryan. Not Deni. I want to know about the *girl*—about Ilse Lunen."

The moisture gathered again on his pasty skin, and now he

looked from me to Mercer and back again, hoping one of us would intercede with Chapman and call him off.

"I had nothing, nothing to do with that girl, Detective. I've never been charged with any crime. That sick little bastard should have been strung up and—"

"And stringing *you* up would probably have given you more pleasure than any pervert like you deserves, Bryan. Just keep in mind that there's no statute of limitations on murder. You play with us on this case, you tell me even one little white lie about you or Denise Caxton or Omar Sheffield, and—"

"Omar? What does he have to do with any of this?"

The collar of his hunter green sport shirt was soaked through, and the underarms matched it. His surprise about Sheffield seemed genuine to me.

Chapman continued. "The slightest misstep with us, and I'll go to the ends of the earth to find the nails for your coffin, the evidence that'll stick you in a jail cell right next door to Bertrand Gloster. So, now—you tell me, Bryan. What's this operation all about? And sit on your hands while you're at it— you're making me crazy with all your mopping and dabbing. Take a shower after I leave—you need it anyway."

Bryan responded like a three-year-old child and literally put his hands under his thighs. He explained how he and Deni had met in 1990, when both of them had galleries in the Fuller Building. They discovered their similarities early on—both from poor families and with invented histories, each with an untrained eye but great instincts. Deni and Bryan delighted in the big sale to a famous client, and both would do almost any- thing—testing the boundaries in a fairly sedate business—to stumble upon a sleeper, a lost masterpiece that had suddenly come back on the market, and then find a Streisand or a Nicholson to buy it.

"Don't forget the candy. You still sniffing, Bryan?"

"Not really."

"No such thing as 'not really' when it comes to cocaine addiction. You and Deni had that in common, too, didn't you?"

"May I wipe my mouth, Detective?" Chapman nodded and Daughtry lifted one of his hands and wiped his face and neck with the sleeve of his shirt. "We got high together occasionally."

"Who's your source?"

"Actually, Deni was. With my felony conviction I couldn't take chances buying off the street. I relied on my—well— friends to give me coke. Artists, dealers, even the guys who work in the warehouse. There's no shortage of the white stuff on the streets. You know that."

Chapman stood and looked out through the glass wall of Daughtry's office, down over the tracks to the string-lined display that we had seen on entering. "Did Denise really go for this garbage? I mean, you've seen the paintings in her home, and in Lowell's gallery, haven't you? They've got an amazing collection."

"Detective, van Gogh only sold five of his paintings in his lifetime. Relatively speaking, merely a handful of artists have ever been recognized by their contemporaries. Deni wanted to get in on the next wave, pick the giants of the future, take some chances. What Lowell does with his collection of masters takes no brains at all, no imagination. Just money."

"Let's talk about your business."

"It's Deni's business, not mine. I've put some money into it, but she couldn't risk attaching my name to a venture like this. Too many people seem to remember too much."

"D'you know she was having problems? Legal ones?"

"Of course I did." Daughtry looked down at his desk. "I mentioned van Gogh a moment ago. I'm sure you knew about the controversy over *Vase with Eight Sunflowers*."

"Let's say we know *our* version of it," Mike bluffed. "Why don't you tell us yours?"

"There's a bit of a storm in the market these days. Vincent van Gogh only painted during the last ten years of his life. He's been credited with completing 879 oils, 1,245 drawings, and a single etching." Daughtry was talking to me now, as though Mercer and Mike wouldn't be able to understand the story.

I glared back at him. "Talk to the detectives, Mr. Daughtry. They're much better at this work than I am. They're really quite intelligent."

"The brouhaha is that a great many experts now believe that some of the most famous paintings, and even the one etching, are fakes. In fact, they suspect that many of van Gogh's contemporaries created them and others passed them off as the real thing. Since his work is fetching higher prices than almost anyone else's, it's a rather hot debate these days."

"And Deni?"

"Well, Deni recently sold *Eight Sunflowers* to a client in Japan. I don't know his name offhand, but it's a matter of public record. He's now made a claim with the United States government—"

I broke in. "I don't get it. There are supposedly fake van Goghs everywhere from the Musée d'Orsay to the Metropolitan."

"Yes, Ms. Cooper, but the gentleman's claim is that Deni sold it *after* she had sent it to Amsterdam to be authenticated by the curators there, and after they'd told her its value was questionable."

"So, after she'd been told it was a copy?"

"An opinion she fought vigorously with the Dutch Ministry of the Arts."

"But rather than waiting for the outcome," Chapman said, "she stiffed the client anyway. How much?"

"Four-point-six million."

Chapman let out a whistle. "Not a bad day's work, Bryan.

What's your cut of that? And what do you know about the bid-rigging investigation the Feds are doing?"

Daughtry was shaking his head. "I didn't have a piece of the van Gogh. I'm only involved in buying the contemporary works."

Chapman was pacing the small room, looking through the glass panel at the space below. "Phew. You musta had that leather mask wrapped too tight around your brain. This junk'll never bring you a nickel."

"Deni wasn't the least bit worried about the auction investigation. She was above all that—it never occurred to me to even mention it. And about your eye, Mr. Chapman," Daughtry said, "if what you're referring to as junk is that single oblique line of string you saw downstairs, I just sold the artist's last piece—*Red Yarn as an Octagon Half*—for a quarter of a million dollars."

"To some yupster Cooper went to school with, no doubt. When's the last time you saw Denise Caxton?"

"I think it was Wednesday of last week, before I went to the Hamptons. Things were very slow here—there's really nothing that goes on in August in our business. I invited Deni to come out to the house with me, but she said she had errands to get done in town. I left her here late in the afternoon, and we never talked again."

Daughtry was more emotional about Deni's death than her husband had been, but this reaction could just as easily have been a function of his nervousness and discomfort.

"Alex, you got a couple of subpoenas for Bryan? Why don't you give 'em to him now?" Mike turned back to Daughtry. "We'll give you a few days to get this stuff together. Two other things. I assume you were printed when you went in the can, right? We'll be pulling those out for comparisons with some of the evidence we've found. And you'll also notice that there'll be two cops parked in front of the gallery in a patrol car for the next few days. Nothing—and I mean nothing—goes in or out of here until we've been through the place with a fine-tooth comb. Ms. Cooper here will draft one hell of a warrant that'll cover my ass in court, and I'll expect your complete cooperation while we execute it."

Daughtry stood up. "But, Detective, there'll be art shipments coming in and out all the—"

"I don't think so, Mr. Daughtry. From what I read in the newspapers, I take it you liked to be the top in your little S&M games. Well, I'd like nothing better than to make you the bottom—for me and for some eight-foot-tall, three-hundred-pound convicted rapist waiting for you in a very crowded cell upstate, if I can get you there. So don't misbehave too badly, 'cause you may go back into prison a tight end, but I know you'll come out a wide receiver."

I turned to face Mercer, biting my lip to suppress a laugh. "Get me out of here, will you?"

"Mr. Daughtry," Mercer said, standing up and towering over the rest of us, "when's the last time you saw Omar Sheffield?"

He looked up at the ceiling. "I'd guess sometime that same afternoon, last Wednesday, almost a week ago."

"Who hired him to work here, and what'd he do for you?"

"Deni did all the hiring—and firing. Omar's a sort of handyman—moves exhibits, hangs the artwork. Painted the gallery with a couple of his friends. Ask him yourself. He'll be here within the hour."

"Don't count on it, Bryan. Omar's feeling a little sluggish this morning."

Mercer said, "Did you know that Omar had a record? That he was on parole?"

Daughtry hesitated, and I sensed that he was starting to filter his responses to us.

"I'm not sure. I may have heard something about that, but didn't pay any attention."

"Didn't pay attention?" asked Chapman incredulously. "What was this place, one-stop shopping for the parole board? You know that there are restrictions about who you do business with, don't you? What if I tell you that you gotta hire a new whipping boy—oops, damn it, there I go again with that dominatrix crap. Omar Sheffield is the latest casualty in the Caxton-Daughtry partnership. He's as dead as Deni. What do you think of *that*?"

Daughtry drew in a deep breath, and his hands started trembling again, uncontrollably. "I think, actually, that it's not such a bad thing, Mr. Chapman. Would you like to know why Deni hired Omar to work for her?"

"Let me guess. A direct pipeline to a cocaine source, right?"

"Well, that was just a lucky coincidence. Denise actually had a special job for Omar," Daughtry went on, clearly banking on his betrayal of his dear friend and partner to get Mike Chapman off his own back. "She put him on the payroll for a single purpose. And now that she's gone, I don't suppose there's any harm in telling you.

"The sole reason she employed Omar Sheffield was to kill Lowell Caxton."

11

The three of us settled into a booth at the Empire Diner, the sleek-looking chrome-fitted slice of a Deco eatery on the northeast corner of Tenth Avenue and Twenty-second Street, to regroup over a late-morning cup of coffee.

"I'll take a mushroom-and-cheese omelette, too," Chapman told the waitress.

"How many breakfasts have you had today?" I asked.

"I try to fortify myself in advance whenever I know I'll be hanging out with *you*. And throw in an order of crisp bacon and some sausage, okay?"

Mercer was doodling on his napkin, connecting stick figures with arrows and seemingly going around in circles.

"Someone killed Denise Caxton. I assumed it was Omar Sheffield. Someone probably kills Sheffield—I don't think he just walked under a boxcar after forty-six years of careful living, but we'll know for certain in a day or two. Denise had hired Sheffield to kill her husband—so maybe Omar's the guy who screwed up the job and caused Lowell's scalp wound. Deni seems to have all the money in the world, but keeps scamming for more. Plus, she's got a class A dirtball pervert for a business partner. Where are we going here?"

"Nowhere, fast. I'll feel better after some more caffeine," I said.

I called Laura on my cellular phone. "I hope you picked up the voice mail I left at seven this morning, telling you I wouldn't be in till we finished uptown. Any messages for me?"

"Jim Winright found nothing on the Internet about the woman you asked about in your E-mail. He doubts it's her real name," Laura said. "And someone called Marilyn Seven phoned to say she could meet with you at noon in the restaurant at the Four Seasons Hotel, on Fifty-seventh Street. Then the M.E.'s Office wanted you to know that there was indeed seminal fluid on the canvas piece taken from the Chevy, and they'd probably have DNA results by the end of the day tomorrow. Last one is from Jacob Tyler. He expects to be back from China by the weekend, and hopes you can get away to the Vineyard."

I repeated the first three messages to my companions, omitting Jake's call and my hope that we might find Deni's killer so I could be with him by Friday.

"Good," Chapman said. "I already told the M.E. we'd need a comparison DNA print for Omar, so he should have that one under way, too. One of us oughta take that meeting with Marilyn Seven and you."

"It doesn't sound like she wants to have this conversation with police around. I think the Four Seasons is still a pretty safe place to be."

"Let Mike get on with what he's got to do, Alex. I'll take my car up there and sit in front of the hotel, in case you need me for anything."

Mike took us back to where we had parked earlier in the morning, and I drove uptown, throwing my parking permit in the windshield and leaving the Jeep near the entrance to the building.

The only woman in the lounge was a slight, serious-looking brunette whose long hair was wound into a French braid. Her tortoiseshell eyeglass frames held tinted lenses, and as I stood in the entrance to the room she dipped an ivory cigarette holder in my direction.

A bit dramatic for my taste, but I approached her and introduced myself. She stood and shook my hand, smiling openly and inviting me to join her. "Sorry for the dark glasses. I've had some vision problems lately, and even the softest light bothers my eyes. And I also apologize for being so mysterious. With all of Deni's problems, I just don't know where to turn and whom to trust. I called the lawyer who handles all my business affairs here in New York yesterday—Justin Feldman—and he assured me that I could rely on your judgment and your discretion."

"If he's your lawyer, then you're in very secure hands. Justin's the best in the business." Although I had been put off by her phone call, I liked this woman immediately. "Are you also an art dealer?"

"No, but my late husband was a collector. I live in Santa Fe now, but we bought a lot of our paintings from Lowell in the old days."

She was wearing a dark blue sweater, probably silk, with a dark blue skirt that extended to midcalf, showing a bit of her thin ankle above the tops of her delicate blue sandals.

"Like Deni, I was married to a much older man, and a very rich one. Unlike her, I had inherited a lot of money, too—an automobile fortune—well, automobile parts, actually." She smiled at me. "And Lowell had sort of put Deni in my hands, to help polish her up a bit. I was ten years older than she—I'm forty-nine now—but we became friends, best friends. I'm sure you know how important that is to a woman."

"I can't imagine going through life without one," I said. Nina Baum, my Wellesley roommate, had taught me everything there was to know about friendship and loyalty. And even though she lived in Los Angeles and Joan Stafford was spending more and more time in Washington, I counted on the intimacy of our relationships to bolster me through the sometimes dark days and nights of my chosen work. "May I ask you to tell me about Deni—what you know, as well as what you think was going on recently?"

"Certainly. Would you care for something to drink?"

"No, thanks." I watched as she sipped at a glass of white wine.

"At the very beginning, it was as though Deni had walked into the pages of a fairy tale. Lowell was amazingly seductive, and Denise was like a magnificent jewel that he wanted to place in the center of his crown. His dinner parties were legendary—has anyone told you about them?"

I shook my head in the negative.

"Not that it was *his* idea, really, but he copied a page out of Gertrude Stein's ingenious recipe for entertaining. The living room—perhaps you've seen it—was hung with old masters and works from many of the greatest artists who ever lived. Then, with a handful of the richest collectors at the ready, he'd sprinkle the guest list with whoever was hottest in the art world—and seat the artist opposite his own paintings. Brilliant, wasn't it? Those often surly and sullen personalities couldn't help but smile as they were reflected in their own canvases and assured of almost immediate sales.

"Imagine at one table having Ellsworth Kelly, Keith Haring,

David Hockney—all sitting amidst their creations while they debated with each other about style and talent as well. Those were the days that Deni loved."

"How long did life at the Caxtons' go on like that?"

"Quite a good while, actually. Beyond Deni's youth and exuberance, Lowell seemed to love everything about her, not least of all how eager she was to learn everything there was to know about his life's passion. She was a tireless student, and though she had an untrained eye, her hunches could be brilliant. Lowell called her 'my budding alchemist.' First, he tempted her with really fine paintings that he'd search out in the châteaux of Bordeaux and the palaces of the once-rich in Venice. She'd a gift for knowing there was something lurking beneath the crusted dust and oil, and she would coax Lowell to take the gamble.

"More often than not she was right. They came home with a Canaletto and two amazing Delacroix that way. Stole them, in a sense. Paid practically nothing for the works, then turned around and sold them for a fortune to several of the Caxton stable—Lowell's devoted followers. He was less amused when she turned the same talent on the current art scene. He thought she was wasting her time."

"Chicken or egg, Ms. Seven, which came first? Do you know how the marriage began to unravel or come apart?"

"That's a bit too quaint a description. I'd say it came to a screeching halt.

"It was when Lowell had gone to Bath, a year ago this past June. There was to be an auction for the estate of Gwendolyn, Lady Wenbotham. She was the ninety-four-year-old dowager who'd owned a fabulous collection of portraits—lots of minor royalty and major military figures. Lowell and Deni were feuding, rather mildly, because she was too busy to go with him on the trip. Not only did he value her eye, but he wanted her there to show off at all the social events—Ascot, if they could get away early enough, staying on for Wimbledon, dinners, and balls. Kind of thing she usually loved to do."

"What kept her away?"

"I'm not sure, really." Ms. Seven stopped, as though considering whether or not to tell me what she guessed had been the reason. "She was vague even with me at the time."

"Another man?"

"No, up to then she'd been quite faithful to Lowell. So he left for England—did the tennis and the horse races—and Deni was quite aloof for those weeks. Finally, she called and said that if I would go along with her, she'd surprise Lowell in Bath. We packed our trunks and off we went. I had a driver pick us up at Heathrow the morning of the auction and take us directly to the Royal Crescent. Do you know it?"

"Yes, I do." I had stayed at the charming old hotel when one of Joan Stafford's first plays was staged there before opening at the Lyric Theatre in London.

"Denise went to the desk and announced that she was Mrs. Caxton and would like the key to the room. I had one of those suites facing the crescent, but to get to Lowell's room she had to pass through that quiet little garden, where half of the guests were having high tea.

"Five minutes later I heard Deni yelling as though she were standing in my very room. Language I doubt many of the hotel guests had heard before. Lowell, as I later learned in exquisite detail from Deni, was in the middle of some kind of acrobatic sexual maneuver with Gwendolyn's great-granddaughter, a twenty-five-year-old local beauty who was no doubt trying to up the ante on the family fortune. She had captured Lowell's attention and was hoping to keep his bids high that evening."

"Any point in asking what happened next?"

"Deni used more four-letter words than I thought I'd ever find in Webster's. The young lady came downstairs wearing a hotel bathrobe, and Deni tossed her underwear out the window, probably landing it on someone's scones and crumpets. Gwendolyn's eighty-nine-year-old sister, Althea, watched the whole episode unfold from her wheelchair in the middle of the courtyard.

"When Lowell stormed through there, fully dressed, about fifteen minutes later, Althea lifted herself up with her cane, reached it out to stop him in his path, and announced for all the family friends to hear, 'I applaud your courage, Mr. Caxton. Must have been something like trying to fit an oyster into a parking meter, having your way with my great-grandniece? Lovely to have met you. Sorry you can't stay for the evening.'"

"He didn't go to the sale, after all that?"

"No. In fact, he had our driver take him directly to the airport for a flight back to New York."

"And Deni?"

"She and I went to the auction. She was furious, and determined to do something to show what he had taught her professionally. Everyone in the room, of course, was impressed that she showed up at all. To them it was pure American moxie. She dressed elegantly, beamed at everyone—flirting with the men and being unusually courteous to the women—and focused her attention on every item in the sale."

"How'd she do?" I asked.

"Like a dream. She bought a portrait of the Marchesa Cecchi for sixty-seven thousand dollars. It had been unattributed in the catalogue. But Deni brought it back to her restorer, Marco Varelli—have you encountered him yet? He's a genius. And after he cleaned it up, they actually found Sir Joshua Reynolds' signature under a couple of centuries of grime. She sold that piece for more than a million and a half. And just for fun, she bought a small piece of garden statuary, some kind of wood nymph if I remember correctly. I don't think it cost her two thousand dollars."

Marilyn Seven took a breath, put out one cigarette and lit another, and reminded the waiter to bring her another glass of Saint-Véran.

"I'll tell you, Miss Cooper, I was sitting in the same room, looking at the same objects. I thought the sculpture was too kitschy to put in my own backyard. Turned out to be an original by Giambologna, the great Florentine artist. Worth close to ten million. Deni refused to sell it. Just shipped it home and installed it in Lowell's bathroom. She wanted to remind him of the entire experience. Make it indelible."

"I take it that was the beginning of the end?"

"*Basta. Finito. Terminato.* Neither one of them was willing to forgive the other, and for Lowell it was a confirmation that they had been moving in separate directions for a couple of years. Deni had no idea if that was his first indiscretion—although I really doubt it. He'd finished the Pygmalion thing with Deni. He was ready to take on someone new."

"Why didn't she just walk away from him? Certainly she'd made enough money to go out on her own."

"I suppose when you come from a background like Deni's, there's never quite enough to erase the fears that you're going to find yourself back on the farm sowing soybeans in the dirt for the rest of your life."

"With what she was sitting on? I can't believe that."

"It wasn't a very attractive side of my friend, but she also wanted to take Lowell to the cleaners. Deni wanted some of the Caxton treasures as well, and she had no plans to walk away without them."

"But she had no right to them, Ms. Seven. They're clearly Lowell's, aren't they, except for some of the works acquired during the marriage?"

She looked at me as though I were an absolute idiot. "I'm not talking about the art in their home or in the gallery. Don't you know anything about the Caxton operation? Because if not, you've got a lot of catching up to do.

"The Caxtons have been at this now for three generations. Lowell has such a tight grip on the collection that not even his employees know the extent of what he owns, or more importantly, where all the art is. Deni knew there were paintings stashed in Swiss vaults and even in an old Cold War bunker on a hillside in Pennsylvania. He moves his pieces in armored cars and by private jet."

Deni's friend was certainly devoted to her. I could see she was going to go on bashing Lowell as long as I'd listen.

"Are you aware that Three—you probably know it was his childhood name, and it made him crazy when Deni called him that—was never invited to join the Art Dealers Association of America?"

Again, I shook my head to tell her that I was not.

"In seventy-five, I think it was, and certainly before Deni, he was caught bugging the telephones of the most prestigious galleries in New York, long before hi-tech spying became a tool of the business world. He was checking on their inventory, as well as trying to get an idea of what their customers were searching for on the market. Lowell's father had used a lot of his money to pay scholars to write catalogues raisonnés."

"Sorry, you've lost me. I don't know what they are."

"They're the key to individual artists and their works. Good ones are well researched and documented, and by controlling the catalogues of a particular artist, you control the price and value of his work. Many experts think there's an aura of questionability about the Caxton catalogues, that histories and pedigrees have been altered for the family's private gain. Several art historians have denounced the works publicly, which made Lowell furious. It threw into question his Vermeers, his Légers, his Davids."

"But Deni thought she could get her hands on those paintings?"

"Well, yes—in part. She was also terribly frightened that she knew too much about them for Lowell to let her go. His first two wives had never really participated in his professional world. But once Deni learned it and loved it, he let her in. She knew things about Caxton and his father, and their manner of doing business, that Lowell regretted having told her once the bottom fell out. Her greatest fear—and she spoke of it to me often—was that he'd never let her walk away from him, knowing what she did about his dealings. She couldn't stay with him, Ms. Cooper, but he wouldn't let her go."

I wondered if Marilyn Seven knew anything about Deni's partnership with the late Omar Sheffield. "Do you have any idea how desperate your friend was to get rid of her husband?"

"About as anxious as you or I would be, if your life had been threatened like hers had."

"How and when was *she* threatened?"

"Well, that answers that. I didn't suppose Lowell told you about the letters Deni got last year, which practically drove her insane."

"No, so far he hasn't mentioned any letters to us at all."

"I've brought you a copy of one of them, if you'd like to see it."

Marilyn Seven withdrew a xeroxed paper from her slim purse and passed it across to me. The copy was a page of lined white paper, covered with neatly printed handwriting and addressed to Denise Caxton. I scanned it quickly.

My name is Jennsen, and I live in Brooklyn. I know you don't know me, but I have been watching you since you got home from England. I know how you look like, and I know how to find you. Listen, if you go to the police about this, I will hurt you bad, or go back to Oklahoma and kill someone you really love. I know when you leave your house and go to W. 22nd St., so I could follow you. I know you get your hair cut at La Coupe and you eat dinner twice a week at Fresco on 52nd St. Your husband pays you $125,000 a month for your expenses. Are you getting this yet? I know where you buy your underpants and how much you pay for your wine. Now here's what I want. Listen close. I want you to send $1,000 to my friend, who is in jail, and who's address is on this letter. This is to show you that I am not kidding, by two ways. One is that I know every move you make, and the other is to show you that my best friends are locked up doing time, so you know I am not playing games. We know how to hurt people very bad. Lowell also told me who the five men are who are your lovers. Now you think I'm jiving? Send a check or money order to my friend Omar Sheffield, 96B-1911, Box 968, Coxsackie Correctional Facility, Coxsackie, New York 12051.

REMEMBER NO POLICE. If you don't send my friend the money, I will take charge by getting you in the near future. Include your phone number so we can talk.

I looked up at Marilyn Seven. "What did she do about this?"

"Certainly not call the police."

"Did she do what this guy wanted?"

"What would *you* have done?"

"Look," I said, my impatience growing. "It's not a contest about us trying to match wits. *I* didn't get this letter."

"These letters, Ms. Cooper. A shoe box full of them. It was obvious to her that this man could only have gotten the detail about her from Lowell, and that Lowell had hired him to kill her. She knew she was being scammed, but of course she did as he told her."

"She sent money up to the state prison?"

"You bet she did. Early and often. The faster she sent it, the faster the ante was raised. By the time the guy finally called her, she must have already sent him twenty thousand dollars. She was terrified, and asked him point-blank whether her husband had hired him to kill her. He confirmed it for Deni. Told her that Lowell was trying to torture her first, mentally, and that's why he'd given this guy Jennsen so much information about her movements and whereabouts. They were planning a way for the hit to happen sometime when Lowell was abroad and Deni wasn't in her apartment—almost exactly the way it *did* happen—so it couldn't be traced back to Lowell."

"But she kept the correspondence going, of course," I said.

"To stay alive, and to turn the tables on her beloved husband. It was her idea to outbid Lowell on this deal, too—and to get the Jennsen fellow to kill Lowell before he murdered her." Marilyn Seven leaned in and put her hand on top of mine. "I told her over and over again that she was insane, and that it would be a deadly mistake for her to play with fire. She wouldn't listen to me, of course, and my insistence that she abandon her plan took her further and further away from me. I don't think, in the end, that she really had anyone left that she could trust."

"Bryan Daughtry?" I ventured.

"You'll forgive me if I don't dignify that question with a response."

"Do you have any of the other letters that she received?"

"No, I never saw them. And I have no idea where she would have kept them. The first one was the only one she sent to me, when she wanted my advice. I don't know if they're at her home, or office, or in a safe deposit box. I felt you should know about them."

She removed a fifty-dollar bill from her pocket and summoned the waiter to bring a check. "I'll be at the hotel for a few days before going back home, if you need me for anything."

"Under the name 'Seven'?" I asked.

"Yes, of course." She smiled. "Why, I suppose you tried to check up on me before we met, Ms. Cooper. It's close enough to my real name—the Italian word for 'seven.' I used it briefly, almost thirty years ago, when I attempted a career on the stage. Did I stump you?" she asked, seemingly pleased by the idea.

"In fact, you did. We came up blank. Much too blank for someone of your means."

"That *is* my name, in a fashion. I was actually born Marina Sette, in Venezia. My mother abandoned me when I was eighteen months old. Left my father and ran off with a very dashing American—Lowell Caxton."

I suppose that I was unable to stifle a slight gasp.

"My father left Italy and came to the States, where his parents raised me while my mother raised her stepchild and had two more of her own with Lowell. She never glanced over her shoulder, not even to stop from being run over in that boating accident."

I had grown up with the most loving mother on the face of the earth and could not comprehend how any woman could leave a child to take off with another man.

Marina Sette went on. "My father turned his automotive parts factory in Michigan into an integral part of the Ford Motor Company—Sette Moto—by the time I was six. If you can measure wealth in material ways—and believe me, I can't—money has never been an issue."

"But Lowell Caxton—surely he knew who you were."

"Perhaps he'd have recognized me if I were as breathtaking as my mother must have been. But he never caught on. Not for a moment. Then, after the fireworks in England, when Deni was looking for every conceivable way to hurt him, she couldn't resist telling him exactly who I was."

"And his reaction?"

"I wanted it to be rage, of course. I wanted it to cause him to agonize over me—or at least, if he didn't care about my feelings, he should regret the loss of my husband as a rather substantial client. As I should have expected, all I got was indifference.

"Surely you can understand why I thought Deni was on such a treacherous course with her pen pal. After all, there was no need to go outside the family." Marina Sette removed her cigarette from the holder and crushed it in the ashtray on the table. "I could have killed Lowell Caxton myself."

12

Laura stopped me on my way back to my desk, half an hour after I had left Mercer in front of the Four Seasons Hotel. It was almost three and I was making my first appearance of the day at the office. "McKinney was looking for you. He's assigned someone to the investigation of the dead guy they found in the rail yards last night."

"Tell him to listen to his voice mail. I called him this morning to tell him it's part of my case. As nicely as you can say it, Laura, tell him to keep his hands off my corpses, okay? Boss back from Albany yet?"

"Rose said not to worry. He's in a meeting all afternoon with some of the lawyers on that foreign bank scandal.

They're offering millions of dollars of forfeitures—Battaglia hasn't even asked about your case since he returned. But you've got an unexpected visitor, Alex. Mrs. Braverman is back. I've had her in the waiting area since lunchtime, but she won't leave and she won't talk to anyone else. You're the only one who can help her."

"Tell Max to bring her in. I don't think I've seen her in six months, have I?"

"Got that search warrant ready for me yet?" Chapman asked. I knew he'd come down to meet me when he had finished at the M.E.'s Office, but I hadn't expected him to walk through my door quite so soon.

I lowered myself into my chair and groaned. "Slow down. I just walked in and I've got some social work to do. Just stand by for a few minutes. You're about to meet my favorite witness."

"Do not ever go to an autopsy of someone run over by a freight train. I've seen some pretty gruesome sights, but this was like chopped—"

"Spare me the details. The photographs will be more than I need to know." It was mandatory for one of the assigned detectives to be present during the medical examiner's autopsy proceedings on a possible homicide victim.

Max walked in, leading a very obese elderly woman on her arm. Mrs. Braverman was wearing a garishly colored sundress and a chartreuse straw hat with an enormous brim.

"Alexandra, darling, I'm so glad you got down here in time to see me." The octogenarian dropped Max's hand and waddled across the room to embrace me as I came out from behind the desk. "And who's this handsome young man?"

"Michael Patrick Chapman, ma'am, Miss Cooper's favorite detective," he replied, giving her his best and brightest grin.

"Is he on *my* investigation now?" she asked me.

"He's the man. I brought him in specially for you. He's solved hundreds of these cases. What's been going on since the last time you were here?"

She plopped into one of the leather armchairs opposite me, while Mike leaned against a file cabinet and listened to her story. "You were right about Christmas and New Year's, Alexandra. They must have gone away for the holidays because I didn't have any problems after I saw you. Then, of course, I went to Boca to be with my son and grandchildren for a few months. Now, ever since I'm back, they're making life miserable for me."

"Tell Detective Chapman who they are, Mrs. Braverman."

"Extraterrestrials, son. In my day we used to call them Martians. But I've done a lot of reading up on this, and now I know they could be from anywhere out there."

Mike kneeled by her side and looked her directly in the eye. "What are they up to this time?"

"They've moved into the apartment upstairs, where old Mr. Rubenstein used to live before his daughter shipped him off to a home," she said, now slipping into a whisper as she talked to Chapman. "They've been flashing signals at me, beaming them through the ceilings and the walls. They're trying to control my brain waves."

"Are they doing it through the toaster and the television set, too?" he asked, with the same degree of intensity that I had seen him question murder suspects.

"Exactly!" she replied emphatically.

"I told you he was good, didn't I?"

"Nobody in my family believed me, Mike—I could call you Mike, couldn't I, sweetheart? The precinct wouldn't do nothing about it. They sent me down here to see Alexandra after I told them about the time one of them fondled my breasts while I was napping. She's been wonderful to me, really. I feel better every time I see her." She cocked her head and looked over at me. "I try not to be a nuisance to her. Then, as soon as I saw her picture in the paper with this lady in the water, the rays became even stronger. I got worried that maybe the same people are after you, sweetheart."

"We're gonna solve this for you, Mrs. B.," Mike said, rising up and pointing to my top desk drawer. "Coop, gimme a couple of boxes of clips, right away."

"Clips, of course," I repeated, sliding it open and removing two boxes of paper clips.

"Not those, the giant-size ones. Those ordinary ones don't work with E.T.'s."

I took two boxes of large clips out and Mike ordered me to make it four.

"Now, here's what you do. When you get home, take a couple of dozen out of the box, make yourself comfortable, and start to string them together, know what I mean?"

Mrs. Braverman's eyes were gleaming with delight at the attention she was getting. "Sure, sure. This I can do." She nodded as Mike looped the metal pieces together to demonstrate to her.

"Then, you take the top one and you attach it to the belt on your dress. You gotta have enough clips to make the chain reach to the floor. Then—you're grounded. You're completely safe because the signals run right through the chain and onto the carpet, missing you completely. Who lives beneath you?"

"Mrs. Villanueva. Dominican, but very nice."

"No problem. Sometimes the waves go through to the apartment below, but Dominicans are immune to extraterrestrial interference. She'll be fine."

Mrs. Braverman got up from her chair while I put the four boxes of clips in a plastic bag and handed them to her. "Costs the city a dollar forty-five, but it's worth every penny for your peace of mind. Just call Coop if you need a refill."

"I'm gonna kiss you for this, Mike." She puckered her lips

and reached out for his face, planting herself firmly on his mouth. "Could I make a *shiddach* with you and Alexandra here?" I recognized the Yiddish expression for a brokered marriage.

"Hey, Mrs. B., you'll excuse me, but I don't have the balls to take on a broad as tough as this one. Don't you have a daughter for me?"

"Three sons. An oral surgeon, an accountant, and one we don't talk about. Plays the horses, best I can tell. I'll leave you two to your business now. And you, don't use that kind of language in front of my girl here," she said laughingly. "Someday she's gonna meet a nice man who'll take her away from all this, right, Alexandra?"

"Right, Mrs. Braverman." I walked with her and Max to the door so that I could accept another hug and sent her off to the elevator.

"Wouldn't it be great if we could solve two percent of our cases that simply?" Chapman asked. I came back to my desk and waved him out of the way so I could get to the word processor to work on the search warrant for the Galleria Caxton Due. I told him about Marina Sette and showed him the letter she had given me.

"Looks like we need another visit with Lowell Caxton. And you'd better do a subpoena for Omar Sheffield's prison records. Be sure and include the visitors' log. Let's check to see when Deni made her appearance there."

"Make yourself useful," I said, as I filled in the facts to establish probable cause for a search of Daughtry's gallery, from all of Deni's property through the contents of Omar Sheffield's locker. "Go tell Laura what you want and she can type up the subpoenas for me to sign. And ask her to hold all my calls for an hour so I can knock this thing out. That way you can execute it tomorrow."

I had almost finished the application when Chapman came

back in the room and reached across the desk to pick up the blinking phone line of a call that Laura had put on hold.

"She assured me you'd want to be interrupted for this one. Jake Tyler, with an overseas operator patching him through."

I took the receiver from Mike's hand and spoke into it. "Hello? . . . Hello?" I waited for a response but there was none.

"I thought this technology worked all over the world."

"So did I. My luck, he's in the one little village in the middle of nowhere that can't pick up the signals." I held on for several more seconds and then hung up the phone.

"So, what's all the secrecy about this romance with Jacob Tyler, blondie?"

"For one thing, I only met him last month—Fourth of July weekend, at a clambake on the Vineyard. It's still very new. And for another, you know what a gossip mill this place is."

"Jeez, you'd think Mercer or me was gonna slit our wrists if you were getting laid."

The next look I flashed at him wasn't so pleasant.

"Mercer or *I*?" he asked.

"It's not the grammar I'm so worried about this time, it's the sentiment."

Mike's feet were up on my desktop now. "What do you hear from your friend Drew? I felt kinda sorry for that guy."

"He just wasn't ready for anything that intense yet. As much as we liked to be together, he was still getting over the death of his wife. When Milbank offered him a transfer to their new law office in Moscow, he took it."

"Like my pal Scanlon says, 'The camel shits. The caravan moves on.' I agree with little old Mrs. B. You need to get a life before this job sucks everything out of you, kid."

"Don't start with me, Mike. It's everyone else I know outside these doors who can't understand why I love what I do and who just doesn't get it. From my pals, I at least expect that you agree that this is the most fascinating job in the world. How many people get up in the morning and look forward to going to work? You and I have never had two days that have been at all predictable in our entire careers, and no two that have been even remotely alike. And on top of it, you do a little bit of good for somebody else in the mix." I knew I was preaching to the choir, but Mike was just in one of those moods that swept over each of us from time to time.

"Jacob Tyler. Isn't he the guy who's like a baby Brian Williams?"

"I don't think that's quite the description he'd favor."

"But he's the one who sits in for Brian Williams when Williams sits in for Tom Brokaw, right? Anchorman-to-be. Deep voice, lots of hair, best-looking striped shirts on the air-waves."

"When you're ready to tell all about *your* love life, I'll buy the drinks and we'll compare notes for an entire night, if you'd like."

"All I need is half a minute. The story of my love life'd fit on a matchbook cover. C'mon, let's get this thing signed so I can rattle Bryan's cage tomorrow morning."

As we returned to the office from the courtroom, Catherine Dashfer and Marisa Bourges, the two senior members of the Sex Crime Unit, were waiting for me. "Did you forget that Rich was on trial?" Marisa asked, referring to one of our colleagues, who was in court with his first date-rape prosecution.

"Damn it, I forgot completely. I'm so wound up in this that I'm not paying attention to the daily routine."

"That's okay. When he heard you weren't in, he called and we went over to help him. The medical testimony was on today, and his witness handled it extremely well."

In more than 70 percent of reported sexual assaults, the victim suffers no gross physical injury. And even though physical injury is not an element of the crime of rape, most jurors expect that they'll hear evidence of bruises and lacerations. Frequently we need an expert physician to explain the absence of visible trauma, as well as the elasticity of the vaginal vault.

"Thanks for covering for me. Michael Warner is such a prick, I thought he'd make mincemeat of Rich's doctor." The defendant's attorney was a mean-spirited character as well as a screamer, and though the physician who had examined the victim was an experienced practitioner in an emergency room setting, he had never testified in a courtroom before.

"I think Rich has a lock. Dr. Hayakawa held up beautifully. Every time Warner went back at him, he held his ground, described his findings, and concluded that they were consistent with the victim's version of the events. Finally, Warner was halfway across the room and yelled out at the doctor at the top of his lungs, mocking him for dramatic effect. 'I want you to tell the jury why it is, Doctor, that you did not expect to find any lesions or tears, even though this woman had described to you an absolutely brutal and life-threatening encounter.'

"Dr. Hayakawa never lost his cool. He just looked straight at the jury and said, 'Because actually, penis not so awesome weapon, ladies and gentlemen.'"

Catherine broke in. "The foreman cracked up and the rest of the jurors followed. I never saw anyone run for his seat as fast as Warner. Rich is going to sum up tomorrow. We took him through it when we got out of court tonight and he's going to do fine. You still have time to go to the hospital to visit Sarah and the baby?"

It was after six. "Sure. I told Nan Toth to be downstairs at my Jeep at six fifteen."

"You two ride with me," Chapman said to Catherine and Marisa. "They can meet us up there."

I finished returning phone calls before going out to meet Nan. We headed up First Avenue to New York University Medical Center and parked the car on Thirty-fourth Street, stopping to buy flowers before going in. Keith Raskin was getting off the elevator as we waited for it on the ground floor. A brilliant orthopedic surgeon, he had painstakingly reconstructed the bones in my right hand after they were shattered in a horseback riding accident several years earlier. I flexed my fingers and made a fist to demonstrate how successful the operation had been.

"After that Dogen murder case you worked on this spring, I never thought I'd see you inside a hospital again," Keith remarked, referring to the tragic slaughter of a neurosurgeon inside one of the city's largest medical centers.

"Just a visit to the obstetrical floor, Doctor. In and out as fast as I can make it." We caught up with each other briefly, and Nan and I continued on our way to Sarah's room.

We arrived in time to join Catherine, Marisa, and Mike in admiring the baby as she squinted up at us through teeny brown eyes. The room was well stocked with bouquets, Beanie Babies, and oversized stuffed animals, and the phone rang constantly while we each took turns holding Janine in our arms.

When the aide came to take her back to the nursery, Sarah put on her slippers and padded down the hall for a few laps of exercise around the maternity floor. Mike grabbed the clicker and turned the television on to *Jeopardy!*, having timed his visit to be sure to get in for the final question. The screen lit up just as Trebek displayed the category for the night, which was Famous Quotations.

We looked at each other and I shrugged my shoulders, knowing this could go any which way, depending on the subject of the quotation. "You guys in for ten?" Chapman asked all four of us.

Marisa, Catherine, Nan, and I each dug in our pocketbooks to match the ten-dollar bill that Mike had thrown on Sarah's bed.

"And tonight's answer is: John Hay referred to it as 'a splendid little war.'"

"So much for all your fancy degrees and the twelve years of law school among you. This is the quickest fifty bucks I ever made," Chapman said, scooping up the money and fanning it in our faces.

There was not much about American history—and nothing about military history—that Mike Chapman didn't know. I looked at the other women and told them I conceded defeat. Not one of us had a serious guess.

Before any of the contestants revealed their answers, Mike announced, "The Final Jeopardy question is: What was the Spanish-American War?"

"That's exactly right," Alex Trebek said, remarking on the answer given by the poultry inspector from Lumberton, North Carolina, which earned him $8,700 and the evening's championship.

"Eighteen ninety-eight was the year. And John Hay, ladies," Chapman continued, "was our ambassador to Great Britain during that conflict. Later he was secretary of state. His comment may have seemed appropriate at the time, since it was a very short and one-sided war. Now, more than a hundred years later, we're still dealing with the fallout—Cuba, Puerto Rico, Guam, and the Philippines.

"A little less time shopping at the Escada sample sales and a bit more with your noses in the books—and I don't mean Dorothy L. Sayers or Anthony Trollope, Mrs. Toth—and you'll be able to hold on to your husbands' well-earned money. C'mon, blondie, we got work to do."

"We're meeting my friend Joan Stafford for dinner. She claims to have some inside poop about the deceased. See you in the morning."

We said good night to Sarah and the others near the nursery. It was a quick ride up to Forty-sixth Street and the quiet elegance of the best steak house in Manhattan, Patroon.

Mercer and Joan were already seated at the front corner table when we entered. I kissed the top of her head before sliding into the banquette and told her how much I missed having her in town, now that she was spending all her time in Washington with her fiancé. Ken Aretsky, the owner, sent a round of drinks over to the table.

Mike was already buried in the menu and banking on Joan's inimitable generosity. "I'm starting with a dozen oysters. Then the veal chop with the garlic mashed potatoes. Let's order so we can talk business." He raised his glass in Joan's direction. "Cheers. So whaddaya know that we don't?"

"Here's the thing. I never knew Deni personally, but a lot of my friends did. And I've met Lowell more times than I can remember—at his gallery, at auctions, and even dinner parties. But there have been stories floating around town for years, for whatever they're worth."

"You gave Mike the names of two of her lovers when you called. Any significance to that?" I asked.

"I ran rap sheets on both of 'em," Mike broke in. "Came up clean. Look like legit businessmen."

"There's Preston Mattox, who's an architect," said Joan. "Not much talk about him. The other one nobody really gets. He's Frank Wrenley, an antiques expert and dealer. Scratch a bit below the surface on him and I'm not quite sure the kind of guy you'll find. Maybe it's just that he's such new money. Sprang up on the art scene out of nowhere, and suddenly he's in the big leagues, running side by side with Deni Caxton."

"I'm telling you, Coop. This case has everything for an art

151

caper except Nazis," Mike said, eschewing the dainty shellfish fork in favor of slurping up an oyster.

Joan Stafford picked at her warm foie gras. "So it's Nazis you vant, Herr Chapman? Then it's Nazis I shall give you."

13

"Have you ever heard of the Amber Room?"

The three of us shook our heads in the negative.

"I'm sure I don't have to remind you about all of the art that was seized and stolen by the Nazis during the Second World War," Joan said.

My father had insisted that my brothers and I learn about the Holocaust from our childhood on, both to understand the magnitude of its atrocities and to know its historical and cultural importance. As a Jew, and also as an art collector, he had followed the stories of families fleeing Europe before the war, and those sent to the death camps, whose personal treasures became the property of their conquerors. Recent years had seen a series of legal wrangles to reclaim such confiscated art-works and restore them to the survivors or the rightful heirs of their owners. I knew of many of the cases that had been brought in the courts as paintings surfaced at auctions or institutions after half a century of being secretly held, but I had never heard of something described as a room.

"In seventeen seventeen, King Wilhelm I of Prussia gave the tsar—Peter the Great—a unique gift. It was a set of gilded oak panels that were decorated with more than six tons of amber, elaborately carved and inset with Florentine mosaics and Venetian glass mirrors. The walls were installed in the Catherine Palace in Tsarskoye Selo, and had actually been dubbed the 'eighth wonder of the world' by the British ambassador. So far as I'm aware, only a single photograph of this breathtaking creation was ever known to have been taken in its two-hundred-year history.

"When Nazi troops invaded Russia in nineteen forty-one, they brought their own art experts along to aid in the plundering of the Soviet bounty. The priceless Amber Room was taken apart and shipped off to a town called Königsberg, which is on the Baltic coast. But by the end of the war, as some of the treasures began to appear, there was not a sign of this enormous chamber."

"Any theories about it?" I asked.

"Dozens. I researched it carefully because I intended to write a play about it." She glanced across at me, knowing that I always chided her about her abandoned efforts. "Had to stick it in a drawer once your DNA buddies matched the Romanovs' bodies. I had it all set to be reconstructed for Anastasia, who was found alive and well in—never mind.

"I take it you want the leading theories and not the obscure ones. Some professional treasure hunter showed up a few years ago with Xeroxes of documents signed by Himmler, claiming he could prove that the room had been redirected to Quedlinburg but that the general transporting it had made an independent decision to change the route in the face of the Allied advance."

"Quedlinburg," Mike said. "That was a major Nazi stash, wasn't it?"

He reminded us that in 1996 the Feds tried to prosecute two Texans for the return of several hundred million dollars' worth of medieval reliquaries, stolen by their brother—an American soldier—at the end of World War II. German troops had looted the religious treasure—everything from ninth-century prayer books and lavishly painted manuscripts to gem-encrusted vases and figures. And in the process of the American liberation of Europe, lowlifes in our own army had made off with the already stolen cache of goods.

"So, one school has the amber buried in the quarry beside a seventh-century castle, while the latest claim is that the son of a German military intelligence officer who helped with the actual logistics of the move has used his father's papers to establish that the stuff never even got to Germany, but is still buried in the Russian system of underground tunnels and mine shafts."

Mercer had been unusually quiet throughout the meal. "Connect this to Denise Caxton for me, will you?"

"This all goes back to the Second World War. Lowell Caxton's father lived in France, as you may already know by now."

"Yes," I said. "He made some reference about how his parents met, and his being raised in an apartment in Paris."

"Although the senior Caxton spent the war years in the States, he never severed his ties with a guy called Roger Dequoy, who was later identified as one of the worst collaborators in the art world. Dequoy was selling paintings to all the Nazi leaders, and they in turn were trying to dump the Impressionist works they had stolen. Thought it was all too degenerate, if you can imagine that.

"The French government considered bringing charges against Caxton's father for selling to the Nazis, but they were never able to build a case. What *is* quite clear is that the Caxtons were positioned—both financially and politically—to have had access to an unbelievable number of the pillaged works. What they also had was the ability to move them around Europe pretty well, too."

"It seems to me," Mike said, "that with all the wealth they had already accumulated, the old man could afford to sit on the stuff until the millennium. No need to try to sell it and show his hand, like most of the others who got caught."

"The Caxton thing has never been about selling or making any more of a profit. That's just sport for them, father and son. It's all in the possession—sheer, unadulterated greed. You've been to the apartment, right?"

"Yeah. We were there over the weekend."

"Lowell has suites, as you may know, each done in a favorite painter or period. Of course, I've never seen it myself, but rumor has it that somewhere, in one of his properties, he has rebuilt the Amber Room. It's not complete—some of the wood was warped when the mine shaft was flooded. But he got most of the jeweled pieces out of Europe somehow, and found craftsmen to regild the mirrors and panels in separate units, so none of them had reason to suppose that he had actually found a whole room. It must be as close as anyone in the world is going to come to feeling like a tsar."

"And Deni?" I asked.

"She certainly knew about it. Each of his wives did. That's what Liz Smith was alluding to in her column this morning."

"You'll forgive me if I tell you I didn't have a moment, between autopsies, to read the friggin' society pages, won't you?" asked Chapman.

"Sorry. Liz wrote something about how getting to Caxton's inner sanctum was certainly the kiss of death for each of his three lovely wives. You know, like Bluebeard's castle. Once he got them in his secret lair and made love to them there, he had to kill them."

"Don't lose me here, Joanie. Are you suggesting that Lowell was trying to shut her up about the Amber Room, or that someone else was trying to use Deni to get to it? And please don't tell me that your personal trainer is the source for this." I knew that half of Joan's best gossip came from the guy who worked her out at home every morning when she was in Manhattan, where she still kept an apartment. He had a fantastic client list, and something about lifting weights and doing inversions seemed to cause these well-toned, tight-lipped women to reveal their deepest secrets to him.

"The way I heard it, the Russian mob was pushing its way into the Chelsea art scene, hoping to put pressure on Deni to lead them to the amber so they could return it to the palace, which has been under restoration for twenty years. They've got a patron, a Soviet businessman who hit it big in the telecommunications industry, willing to pay the tab for what they assumed she could lead them to."

"Ever been to Brighton?" Chapman asked Joan.

"Sure, my play had tryouts there and in Bath before it opened in London."

"Not Brighton, England. Brighton *Beach*. Home of the Russian mafia."

"You think *I* don't do the West Side, Mikey? Well, Joan doesn't do the outer boroughs. Forget Brooklyn, Queens, the Bronx. They're just places she has to drive through to get where she wants to go."

"So she's not coming with us when we go poking around for double agents looking for Nazis looking for stolen art, huh?" Mike asked me.

Mercer picked up the thread. "What do you know about Bryan Daughtry?"

Joan laughed. "More than anyone needs to know, that's for certain. Denise Caxton didn't create that monster, but she was certainly feeding him."

"Why was she so attached to him, do you think?"

"She was the classic underdog, Alex, and there was something in her that must have made her reach out to characters with the same background. I'm sure you remember that I used to buy from Daughtry, in the old days, before any of us knew about the dark side with the leather and young girls. Like Deni, he's basically a dreamer, trying to create a fantastic life out of whole cloth. His business was riskier than anything that Lowell did, and she apparently liked that. I mean, it doesn't take much skill to sell a Picasso, right?"

"Got any suggestions for who we talk to about their commercial enterprise?" Mike asked.

Joan thought for a moment. "Marco Varelli, perhaps."

"I just heard that name today, but where?" I was tired, and confused as well.

"Sweetest little old guy you'd ever want to meet. He's a restorer, perhaps the most respected in the field."

Now it came to me. Marina Sette had mentioned him to me during our conversation at the Four Seasons this afternoon.

"I mean, if I tripped over something like the Amber Room, Varelli's the person I'd go see to make sure whatever the treasure might be is not a fake. He looks like a gnome—must be well over eighty by now. Varelli might have known some of Deni's secrets. You'll find him in a small atelier he keeps in the Village."

"We expect to be getting as many of the gallery records as we can. With a little luck, maybe she kept notes about her love life, too," Mercer said.

Joan shook her head. " 'Good girls keep diaries; bad girls don't have the time.' Tallulah Bankhead, by the way. I don't think that's very likely."

"You said you were going to tell us why Lowell Caxton wasn't welcome at the legitimate houses any longer," I reminded Joan.

"The Gardner Museum heist, almost ten years ago. Has that come up in any of your interviews yet?"

"You should stick to your fiction, Joan," Mike said. "Wanna pour me another glass of that red wine?"

I knew that around the turn of the century Boston socialite Isabella Stewart Gardner had built a Venetian-style palazzo to house one of the country's most spectacular art collections, which she had put together with the aid of her close friend Bernard Berenson. I had been to the museum many times when I was in college, and even once last year on my way through the Fenway section of the city.

"I remember the break-in, but it was years ago. Hasn't that ever been solved?" I asked.

"Never. Listen, guys," said Joan, telling the story of what remains to this day the costliest art theft in United States history, "this is where Lowell may have gotten his hands even deeper in the dirt.

"In March of nineteen ninety, two men disguised as Boston cops presented themselves to the museum's security officers at the side door of the building, and were let in. The robbers locked up the guards, disabled the unsophisticated alarm system, and made off with about ten paintings. Estimated value? Almost *three hundred million dollars.*"

"Are you serious? What was in the place?" Mercer asked.

"A few Impressionists—I think a Manet and a Degas—an ancient Chinese bronze work, a finial from a Napoleonic flagstaff, a Vermeer, and most importantly, the masterpiece that all the fuss has been about. It's a three-hundred-and-sixty-year-old Rembrandt that hung in the Gardner's famous Dutch Room. The title of it is *The Storm on the Sea of Galilee,* and it was the only seascape that he ever painted.

"Nothing from the heist has ever been found. Not a trace. The Gardner had so little insurance at the time of the theft that the reward they offered was only a million dollars. Just a year or two ago, the FBI upped it to five million. There have been rumors in the art world for years, but not a clue to follow up on. Except the chips."

"What chips?"

"I'm just being dramatic, Alex. Paint chips, of course. Most of the works were small enough to be taken frame and all. But—maybe because of the way the Rembrandt was fastened to its mountings—the robbers actually *cut* it out of the frame. Isn't that awful? Anyway, the varnish on it—and its great age—must have made it so stiff that literally dozens of paint chips fell onto the floor, and that's all that was left behind."

"Get me from there to Caxton," Mike said, licking the chocolate sauce from the profiteroles off the side of his mouth.

"Everyone knows the painting is too hot to handle. Over the years, several mobsters who've turned up dead in the Boston area have been linked to the robbery. And each time there's been a buzz in the galleries and auction houses that the Rembrandt's at the heart of it. If anyone could hide this kind of booty, or better still, transport it anywhere in the world, it could only be an individual with the means of a Lowell Caxton, or someone who flirted with danger as freely as Deni.

"There was an opening at Lowell's gallery in the Fuller Building a few months ago. Deni had left before I arrived. Everyone said she was high and kind of mouthing off about this astounding coup she was about to make that would turn the art world on its ear. Be sure and ask Lowell about it when you see him again."

This time it was Mercer's beeper that went off before the end of the meal. He rejected my offer of a cell phone and stepped away to return the call from a booth at the top of the staircase.

When he came back down the flight of stairs, he approached the table and tapped on it with his knuckles. "Off to Chelsea, m'man."

Mike threw back his head and chugged down the La Tâche '86 as though it were a Budweiser. "More string sculptures at this hour of the night?"

"Nope. Denise Caxton's car."

"Where?"

"Right under our noses the whole time. In a chop shop one block away from her gallery. About to be dissected and shipped overseas, from Chelsea Road Repairs, Ltd."

"Anything in it?"

"Crime Scene's going over it now for fingerprints. And it looks like there's blood. Could be she was abducted from her car and then finished off in Omar's wagon."

Mike stood up from the table and thanked Joan for the meal. "How about we pick you up in the morning and drop in on Lowell at the Fuller Building?" he asked me. "Be downstairs at nine."

"Don't rush off before I finish with the news from the Medical Examiner's Office," Mercer said, putting a hand on Mike's shoulder. "DNA isn't in yet, but they did a basic ABO typing from the sperm sample found on the canvas where the body had been. We got a new ball game, ladies and gentleman. Omar Sheffield did *not* rape Denise Caxton."

14

"'Lovers,' Mr. Chapman? It's not the term of art I would have chosen," Lowell Caxton said, standing behind the desk in his office in the Fuller Building and seemingly looking out at the view northward on Madison Avenue. "Personally, I referred to them as Deni's 'shareholders.' Each had a piece of her at some point in time. But it was a very volatile market."

"You're not suggesting they were interested in Deni because of her money, are you?" Mike reeled off the names of the men Joan had told us about—Mattox, the architect, and Wrenley, the antiques dealer.

"Come, come, Mr. Chapman. You're brighter than that. Not her money, certainly. *My* money. The Caxton fortune has attracted all kinds of maggots to Deni as well as to me." He turned back to face us. "Something I've had to deal with all my life. And no, as I've told you, I was spared a proper introduction to either of those gentlemen you've mentioned."

Morning sunlight was beaming in and hitting Caxton directly in the eye, so he came out from behind his desk and gestured for us to sit in the overstuffed leather chairs grouped beneath a pair of Boudin beach scenes.

"How come you didn't tell us anything about the letters Deni had gotten? The threatening ones, the blackmail?" Mike asked.

"Ah, do I sense the presence of a little guttersnipe?" Caxton groaned.

"What?"

"*La povera Signorina Sette,* am I right? Poor little Miss Sette, still peddling the same nonsense at the drop of a hat. Let me guess, gentlemen—when you sell the movie rights to your ridiculous fantasy here, you'll be played by Arnold Schwarzenegger," Caxton said, grinning at Mike. "You'll be Denzel Washington, Marina Sette will be some two-bit Shirley Temple look-alike, and as for me—if only they could bring Bela Lugosi or Vincent Price back to life. I'm always to be cast as the villain, am I not? At least, it's usually such a richly textured role."

There was a knock on the door and an assistant entered with a tray holding a Baroque silver coffee service and a mound of croissants and Danish. Caxton was silent as she put the heavy load on the table in front of us and walked out of the room.

"Why don't you help yourselves, Detectives?"

"Nah, I'll just let Sharon Stone over here pour for me. That's why I bring her along. Not very useful, but sometimes decorative." Mike jerked his thumb in my direction as I was leaning forward to pour the coffee.

"What made you connect Marina Sette to the letters Deni received?" I asked.

"This isn't the first time she's tried to bring me down, Ms. Cooper. Did she take the trouble to come all the way here just to stir the same old pot again? You know why she hates me, don't you?"

There wasn't much of a way to protect Sette in all this. "I know what she told me."

"Her story is nonsense, of course. There's no way for her to prove it, but sadly, there's no way for me to *dis*prove it, either." I remembered that the woman Marina claimed was her mother, Lowell's second wife, was killed in a boating accident. "Buried at sea, as it were."

Caxton flashed one of his more loathsome smiles at me as he said that, and went on. "Even these latest scientific techniques of yours—genetic fingerprinting—are useless in this instance. I can't convince anyone that this waif was not the child of my wife."

"So, why does she hate you so much?" I didn't bother to tell him that the DNA of Marina's half sister could indeed prove the claim that she was his stepchild.

"I think it has more to do with her husband. He was a substantial client of mine until we had a falling-out over a serious acquisition I made. Richard tried to claim a piece of the profits, but he wasn't successful. Soon they were coming at me from all directions."

"But the letters were real, weren't they? I've seen one of them."

"Quite real. I can give you copies of all of them, if you like." Caxton removed a microrecorder smaller than a matchbook from his shirt pocket and spoke into it, reminding himself to ask his lawyer for a set of the correspondence.

"They played quite a dramatic role in the matrimonial

sparring. Deni's lawyer tried to use them to show that I had hired someone to take a hit on her life."

With good reason, I thought to myself. "In the letter I saw, the information was strictly private in nature, Mr. Caxton. It had to come from someone who knew Deni intimately. If not you, then can you suggest who it might have been?"

He looked through me as though I were a complete idiot. "I guess when my attorney charges me four hundred fifty dollars an hour, it's worth the results. *He* got to the bottom of it rather quickly. Once you check this fellow out, this—what was his name?"

"Omar Sheffield," Mercer offered.

"Yes, Omar. You'll find, as my lawyer did, that Omar had developed quite a scheme for himself in state prison. He's got a file six inches thick, just up at the jail, blackmailing women the same way. Every single one of them in the middle of a divorce."

"I know I'm only a dumb cop, but where'd he get his information?"

"The library, gentlemen. The law library. Would you believe, our pen pal Omar is a regular little scholar, though you'd not know it from his crude language."

We still didn't get it.

"When the divorce proceedings began, Deni applied for temporary alimony. I don't know if you're familiar with these civil actions, but they tend to involve a lot of mudslinging. I was prepared to be more than generous with Deni. After all, she'd given me a great deal of happiness for ten years.

"Either she or her lawyer got greedy. Suddenly her bills for hairdressing and entertaining escalated to ridiculous numbers. She claimed more for facials and massages during the last year than most people in this city spend to eat."

"So, what book did Omar find in the prison library?" Mercer asked.

"It wasn't a book at all. It wasn't even the tabloids. Su͏͏ you can guess by now, Miss Cooper, can't you?"

I was dumbfounded.

"What's it called?" Caxton went on. "The *Law Journal*? Have I got it straight?"

All three men looked at me, and finally the lightbulb went on in my head. "Of course, the judge's opinion in the matrimonial case. It would have everything—details and facts—in it."

"Thank you. Vindicated at last."

The *New York Law Journal* was printed every weekday and subscribed to by most law firms and libraries in the state. It was my daily tool for keeping up with case law in the criminal field; I clipped and filed articles about court decisions and issues related to my work. It rarely interested me to read write-ups of divorce matters, but I had seen enough of them to know that every detail mentioned in Omar Sheffield's letter was likely to have been referenced by the judge in reaching conclusions about the case at hand.

Caxton continued. "My lawyer was furious—even took it up with the editor. After all, there's no reason not to have redacted some of the confidential information, because of precisely this kind of escapade."

Mercer had never read any of the decisions. "So, how did Sheffield get your address?"

Caxton seemed almost exasperated by our collective density at this point. "My dear fellow, the judge practically spoon-fed the whole scam to him. You'll read it for yourself, but I can pretty much paraphrase it for you. 'The couple live in separate apartments in the matrimonial residence, which is located at 890 Fifth Avenue.' And so on down the line, chapter and verse, hairdresser, masseuse, pedicurist, and psychic all included.

"Go visit the warden, as my lawyer did. Omar Sheffield is a more prolific letter writer than Winston Churchill. The

...ad done this operation a dozen times. Check with ...ne was quite candid with my lawyer."

"Omar ran out of ink not too long ago," Mike said.

Our intentions of putting Caxton on edge by confronting him with the threats against Deni that we had assumed would be linked back to him had failed dismally.

Mike was noshing on a cheese Danish and took a swallow as he looked over at Caxton. "So, is there really an Amber Room?"

"You don't look the gullible type, Detective. Have they suckered you in with all this nonsense, too? Is this another Marina Sette story?" He was looking back and forth at each of us, to see if one of us would make a telltale slip. "Willing to sacrifice one nubile young prosecutor? Legend has it, I think, that once I let a seductress in that secret chamber with me and make love to her, I have to kill her."

It did sound a lot sillier than it had when Joan told us about it last evening, and I absorbed it on one Dewar's and two glasses of superb red wine.

"Keep them coming, gentlemen. Your questions get easier to answer all the time."

"Why didn't Deni go to England with you in June of last year? What was so important to her that she needed to stay behind, until you went on to Bath?" I asked.

Caxton stiffened noticeably, perhaps because the reminder of the scene in Bath rankled him. "Well, *you're* the ones they pay to do the investigation, aren't you? Suppose you get on about your business and get an answer to that for me. It's puzzled me for quite some time now."

He tried to bring the meeting to a close now, but Mike and Mercer weren't entirely ready.

"Got any Rembrandts in stock, Mr. Caxton?" Mike was on his feet, walking to the far side of the room to study the portrait hanging on the opposite wall. "A little something with water in it, for a change?"

"No, Detective, not on hand. But I'd love to buy one from you, should you come across it. The Caxtons, going back a couple of generations, have been known to squeeze every penny worth of value out of a fine painting, but we simply don't do armed robberies. Not my style.

"*The Storm on the Sea of Galilee,* painted in sixteen thirty-three. Probably the most famous missing artwork in the world, Mr. Chapman. And I would be delighted to get my hands on it."

"Did Mrs. Caxton ever talk to you about it, or about the theft at the Gardner?"

"Everyone in my business talked about it at some time or other. Quite frankly, it fascinated all of us. Such a bold under-taking, and then to be stuck with a treasure that no museum would dare touch, despite the fact that eighty percent of the things you see in European collections have been stolen or looted over the centuries.

"Once a year thieves pull off a caper at some institution or other—even the Louvre has had its share of embarrassments. Deni was a free spirit. Not exactly, shall we say, to the manner born. Would it intrigue her to be the one to find the lost Rembrandt and make her mark on the world? No question in my mind. Would she sleep with the enemy to do that? Two years ago I would have been confident in saying no. Now I'm really not sure."

"Tell us about the opening you gave here a few months back. The party that Deni came to—she might have been high that night."

"There haven't been any shows this summer—not enough of my clients stay in town to make it worthwhile. Perhaps you're referring to the eighteenth-century Italian landscape collection that was installed here in May? Yes, Deni showed up. No problem with that."

"People have told us she was talking openly about some great thing she was onto, some kind of coup that she was going to have."

"Nothing I heard. But after all, I was hosting the party and there was a rather large crowd around."

Mike was expressing his skepticism that Caxton hadn't observed or heard what Deni was up to. "So busy that you didn't notice what your estranged wife was saying to your clients?"

Again a snide look. "Well, Detective, I wasn't out in the kitchen with the Ritz cracker box open, making the appetizers by myself. I simply had no interest in anything she had to say at that point."

"We located Mrs. Caxton's car last night," Mercer said. "She might have been attacked while she was in it. We still haven't found a witness who knows where she was or what she did from last Thursday on. I realize you were away, but have you heard from anyone who saw Deni?"

"Not a soul."

"She have any trouble with the car, that you know of? Any reason to bring it in the shop?"

"The car was a dream. Never a moment's worry. I gave it to her several years back. Mercedes 500—E Class. A collector's item. Only about a thousand of them in total. Benz body with a Porsche engine. Deni could fly in that car.

"It only had one dangerous feature. Got her in trouble once before."

"What's that?"

"The lid on the gas tank was controlled by the door locks. To fill it with gas, you had to unlock the car doors. In case you haven't noticed, most gas stations in Manhattan are in fairly unsavory parts of town. One time, over on Eleventh Avenue late at night, Deni had to unlock the doors. After the attendant stepped away from the tank, a man with a pistol opened the rear door and got into the car. Held the gun to her head and took her a few blocks away, where he robbed her. Took her cash, her jewelry, the Chopard watch I'd just given her for our tenth anniversary—none of it insured. Cost me a bloody fortune. Tried to make her get rid of the car after that, but she refused.

"Anything further?" Caxton asked. "I'm sure you'll excuse me. I've got a condolence call to pay this morning. One of the most respected figures in our business, and a dear friend both to me and to Deni, passed away yesterday." He stood up, walked to his desk to retrieve a pair of sunglasses. "I've really got to be going."

"They're dropping like flies around you, Mr. Caxton. Hope it isn't contagious," Mike cracked. "Anyone I knew?"

"I sincerely doubt it, Mr. Chapman." Caxton lifted the *Times* off his desk and passed it to Mike. "A lovely gentleman. A very distinguished art restorer called Marco Varelli. Read the obituary page if you think I'm deceiving you yet again."

"Marco Varelli?" My lips moved as Mercer said the name aloud with disbelief.

"How'd he die?"

"A heart attack, in his studio. Eighty-four years old. I'm off to console his widow."

15

Battaglia was drinking apple cider and puffing on a cigar as he waved me into his office an hour after I left Lowell Caxton on Wednesday morning. I could tell there was no urgency to the district attorney's questioning of me by the fact that he removed neither the cigar from the corner of his mouth nor his feet from the edge of the desk.

"Any progress in this art dealer's murder?"

"Developments, yes. Progress, no."

"I've got to give a speech at the Department of Justice next week on the significance of the drop in the crime rate in New York. Rose is typing it up today. Any figures you can give me to throw in on sex crimes?"

"Nothing that will help you. Rape is the only crime in which the rate of reporting has increased in the last three years. Stay away from those numbers, unless you think Justice will give us more money if we can show how the volume has gone up."

"Suppose they ask me why it hasn't dropped like the other violent crime categories?"

"Not complicated at all. A lot of the credit for the reduction goes to aggressive community-policing policies, right? Most people don't realize that almost *eighty percent* of reported rapes occur between people who know each other. The stranger rapist—the guy who jumps out from behind trees in the park or breaks into homes—he's only responsible for about twenty percent of the cases. But he's the guy most women fear.

"So, while violent street crime is way down, the acquaintance-rape victims aren't at all affected by the presence of the cop on the beat. They trust their assailant—so they walk right past the officer into the apartment or dorm or hotel room of the man they're with—and then the attack occurs."

Battaglia went back to the report he was reading. "Get me a memo on that before the end of the day, will you? Flush it out a bit so I can use it in Washington."

I was almost out the door. "Hey," he called after me, "what's with you and this news guy, Jacob Tyler? I'd like to meet him. Maybe we could get him to do a story on the new Welfare Fraud Unit we're setting up."

It was impossible to keep a secret from Paul Battaglia. He never even had to leave his spacious office on the eighth floor of the building to get the most complete intelligence—professional and personal—from a cadre of loyal and talented men and women who served him in his distinguished career in public service.

"I'll be sure to let him know, Paul. May I ask how—"

The cigar was parked squarely in the middle of his gritted teeth now. "Tell him I said I never divulge my sources. He'll appreciate that, as a good reporter."

I stopped at Rose's desk, knowing that I could learn from her what Battaglia had been told about the status of my new romance, but she had stepped away, so I went back to my office.

"Mike's on hold. I tried to transfer him over to Battaglia's wing but they said you were on your way back," Laura said.

I went into my room and picked up the phone.

"Just checked with the morgue," he said. "No autopsy done on Marco Varelli. Didn't have to. He was eighty-four, with a serious heart condition, and under a doctor's care. Once his own physician signed off on the death certificate, that's it. By the end of the day he'll be resting at a funeral parlor down on Sullivan Street. We'll go over for tonight's visiting hours and see if we can turn up some employees or friends.

"Also," he continued, "spoke to the Feds on the auction-bid-rigging investigation. Can you meet us at Kim McFadden's office at five? They'll fill us in on that, and update us on the Gardner Museum heist, too."

The United States Attorney's Office for the Southern District was a four-block walk from my office, set back behind the old federal courthouse, near Police Headquarters, and the New York City offices of the F.B.I. "Fine, that gives me the rest of the day to catch up on the things I need to do. See you at five."

"Is this a bad time?" Carol Rizer asked as she stood in the doorway. She was new to the unit, and although her skills were good, it was important that she be supervised on complicated matters.

"If I told you to wait for a good time, your witness is likely to die of old age. What do you need?"

"I'm having a lot of trouble with a victim in a case I picked up last night. The defendant's got a really bad record—three felony convictions—but there's something wrong with the victim's story and I just can't break her on it. Can I bring her in for you to talk to?"

"Yes. Give me the background."

"Her name is Ruth Harwind, and she's nineteen years old. Lives in Queens with her mother. Has a boyfriend named Wakim Wakefield—he's waiting up in my office. The defendant is Wakim's roommate, and his name is Bruce Johnson. Ruth claims that she stayed in their apartment one day after Wakim left for work. She says Bruce forced her bedroom door open with a knife and dragged her into his room. That's where she says he raped her."

Carol knew how I handled these interviews. She had written out a list for me identifying all the inconsistencies in the story Ruth had told, first to the police and then to her. She had also highlighted for me the facts that didn't make much sense.

"What do you find troubling?"

"Start with the point that in the middle of the rape, the boyfriend came back to the apartment, knocked on Bruce's bedroom door, and asked where Ruth was. Bruce said he didn't know, and Wakim left. My first problem is why she just didn't scream out for help when Wakim was right there in the next room.

"Now, if she'd told me it was because he'd threatened her again with the knife, it might have been credible. But all she says is that it didn't occur to her."

"What else?"

"The cop examined the door that she claims was pried open with a knife. There's no sign of any disturbance on the paint or to the wood. Also, there's no immediate outcry. When she left the apartment and went outside on the street, she ran into Wakim. She went back upstairs with him, showered, and made love. Nobody mentioned the word 'rape' until Bruce's girlfriend came home and told Wakim that Ruth had been cheating on him. He's the one who challenged her to go to the police if the story was true."

Frequently the motive in a false report can be gleaned from the circumstances of how and why a sexual assault gets related to the police. In many cases like this, an angry boyfriend dares the victim to prosecute if the crime really happened.

"Did Bruce make any statements?"

One of my favorite bureau chiefs, Warren Murtagh, had a list of training rules, and Murtagh's Rule #3 was a good one. "No defendant ever says absolutely nothing." Everyone arrested makes some comments to the cops, spontaneously or in response to questioning, which is usually useful in sorting out the facts.

Often the perp's remarks can be discarded as self-serving and of no value, but just as often there are kernels of truth that can be used to shed light on the victim's version of events. Every now and then, the real story lies somewhere right in between.

Carol answered, "Johnson says it was consensual. Says he gave her ten dollars to come in his bedroom and have sex with him. Even told us they watched a porno movie together. And that he used a condom, 'cause she asked him to.

"Also, Alex, she's lied about some of the basic stuff. Said she worked at the Victoria's Secret store in the World Trade Center for six months. I called over there and got the woman who's been the manager for two years. She's never heard of Ruth."

"Bring her in." Once a witness has lied about facts that are *not* essential to the case and that can be easily verified or disproved, there is reason to be suspicious about the underlying allegations in the criminal complaint. Until caught in a direct lie, every witness who walked in the door was presumed to be telling us the truth.

Ruth Harwind was not happy to be ushered into my office. At five foot eleven she was a couple of inches taller than I, dressed in jeans and a T-shirt and directing her defiant pout toward the floor.

I began with a series of pedigree questions to get as much background knowledge about the young woman as I could. "Why you need to know all this business about me?" she asked, balking at the personal information for which I was probing.

"Because I need to know as much about *you* as Bruce Johnson knows, as much about you as he's going to tell his lawyer to use against you. It may be the only way that Carol and I can protect you when you go to court.

"Who do you live with in Queens?"

"My mother."

"What's her name?"

Ruth's annoyance level was growing. "What's that got to do with me being raped?"

"Like everyone else who's been the victim of a crime, you walk through my door and tell a story that could keep Bruce Johnson in jail for the next twenty-five years of his life. That's longer than you've been alive. And that's what he deserves, if everything you told the police about him is true.

"But Carol doesn't know you and I don't know you, so I'm going to ask you a series of questions that are really simple to answer and that are a very easy way for us to be able to prove that things you tell us are true. So, let's start over. Would you please tell me your mother's name?"

"No, I won't." Ruth had dug her heels in. Slouched down in the chair, she stared at a small vase of flowers on my desk, refusing to make eye contact with me.

"Why won't you tell me?" I asked. "Look at me when I'm speaking to you, please."

" 'Cause I don't want my mother to know I'm here, that's why."

"That's fair. I can accept that." Since Ruth was nineteen, there was no legal requirement that her parents be notified. "Why don't you tell me what you do? Do you go to school? Do you have a job?"

"Like I told her," Ruth said, jerking her head in Carol's direction, "that's nobody's business but mines. This is about me and Bruce. Why don't y'all ask me questions about that, huh?"

"You're not going to be able to give the answers you're giving me to the judge, when he asks the same things in the courtroom. He's going to insist on a little respect and make you respond to whatever he needs to know."

"Well, let's just drop the whole thing and lemme outta here." Ruth slammed her hand on my desk and stood up. "Wakim can take care of Bruce."

"Sit down, Ruth. You're not going anywhere. There's a man who's been held in jail since last night, and based on what you tell me today, the judge is going to decide whether to keep him in on high bail any longer."

We glared at each other for a couple of seconds before she took her seat again. The questioning continued at the same pace and with similar results. When we got to the part at which Bruce forced Ruth into his bedroom, I asked whether he had turned on the television or a movie.

"Yeah, he put on the VCR, but I wasn't watching."

"That's not what he says."

"Well, who you gonna believe, him or me? Whose side are you on, anyway?"

"What kind of movie was it?" I asked, ignoring her questions to me.

"I seen it before, at Wakim's. Some kind of dirty movie

with two girls sucking on each other. I only looked at it from time to time."

Great. Already Bruce's version was making more sense than Ruth's.

My intercom buzzer went off and Laura asked me to step out to her desk. "If there's anything else about your story that you remember now that's different than what you told the police, this is the time to tell Carol. Once we put you under oath and you swear to the judge about something, if it turns out not to be true, then it will be too late for Carol and me to help you." I excused myself and said I'd be right back.

"Alex, this is Mrs. Harwind, Ruth's mother. One of Ruth's friends told Mrs. Harwind that her daughter was coming down here today, and she's asked to talk to you."

The middle-aged woman in the hallway outside Laura's cubicle was agitated and tearful. I introduced myself and took her into the conference room to explain what was going on. Since Ruth had asked me not to tell her mother about the case, I was avoiding the fact that her daughter was fifteen feet away, inside my office.

"Miss Cooper, you've got to help me find my child. I've got a warrant for her in Queens Family Court, 'cause she ran away from the group home they put her in."

"How long ago was that?" I was confused, since Ruth was too old to be a candidate for court placement in a group home.

"Just back two weeks. This guy Wakim, he's got her hid in his apartment. My girl *looks* big, but she's only fifteen."

"Fifteen?"

I sat Mrs. Harwind down and explained that Ruth was with me. Since there was a warrant issued in her case, I was legally obliged to return her to court.

"Laura, call the D.A.'s Squad. Ask for Sergeant Maron, and

tell him I need a detective down here immediately. Get two, and tell him to make sure that one is a female."

This would not go down easily, and I expected that the girl would get confrontational. With Ruth and Carol in my office, and Mrs. Harwind in the conference room, I waited at the foot of the staircase for the detectives from the squad to come downstairs. Before they appeared, a man who seemed to be forty years old got off the elevator holding two cans of soda and headed straight for Laura's door. I heard him ask for Ruth.

"Excuse me, are you Wakim? I'm Alex Cooper, one of the D.A.'s working on Ruth's case. We're almost done, but I'm going to need you to go back to Carol's office until we finish the interview, okay?" Without protest, he handed me a soda and asked me to give it to Ruth, and walked back to the elevators. I didn't want him anywhere around when I explained to Ruth that she wasn't going home with her boyfriend.

Sergeant Maron and Detective Kerry Schrager arrived within minutes. "This could get ugly. I've got a very unhappy teenager here who needs to make a court appearance in Queens. Just stand by while we break it to her, okay? And then you can help me get transportation for her."

I opened my office door to walk in. Maron and Schrager stayed in the doorway, and Ruth immediately sensed this was trouble.

"Why don't we go back to a couple of basic questions, Ruth. What's your date of birth?"

"I told you, I'm nineteen," she said, glancing back over her shoulder at the cops. "Why are these people here?"

"I didn't ask how old you were, Ruth. Tell me the year you were born."

She was smart, but like many of us, lousy at math. The subtraction was off, and the year she gave would have made her sixteen.

"Your mother tells me that you're only fifteen. Is that true?"

Ruth picked up a copy of the Penal Law from the top of my desk and threw it toward the window, missing my right ear by a couple of inches. "I *hate* my mother. All right, y'all, is this what you want to hear? Bruce Johnson didn't rape me, okay. Bruce Johnson gave me ten bucks to get him off, and you know what? I did it. And you know what else? It wasn't the first time."

The tears began to flow. "Wakim woulda killed me if he caught me in that room with Bruce. And Wakim don't ever give me nothing. No money, no clothes, no presents. You woulda made up a story, too, if it was your ass that woulda got broke."

I spoke softly to Ruth as I tried to give her some tissues. "You just can't go into a court of law, swear to tell the truth, and then lie about something. I realize Bruce is a bad guy, but you can't put him in jail to save yourself. How old does Wakim think you are?"

She was sniffling. "He know the truth. He know I'm fifteen."

"You understand that *he* can be arrested for having sex with you, because you're underage? When you try to act like a big girl, Ruth, you're gonna get stuck with the consequences." I paused. "Your mother's down the hall."

She got up from her chair, shouting curses at the top of her lungs and trying to push past the detectives. I told Kerry to stop her. I made her sit down and explained that she had to go before the judge in Family Court, since she had absconded from the program and was wanted, AWOL.

"You can do this the easy way, like a young lady. I'll let you leave here with your mother, and put you in a taxi to go to Queens. Or you can do this the hard way. That means the detectives would have to handcuff you and take you there like a prisoner."

"Well, you can all go screw yourselves, 'cause I'm not going anywhere with her or with any of you." She was screaming again and kicking the side of my desk. "I don't care what you do with me, 'cause I'll just run away again and Wakim'll take me home."

Sergeant Maron raised a pair of handcuffs and looked at me questioningly. "I guess that's the way our customer wants to go."

Ruth looked me straight in the eye and spat across the desk, hitting an old indictment on top of a pile of papers. "And you, you bitch, I hope you get what's coming to you. I hope you—"

"Attitude," I said. "Attitude from a fifteen-year-old. Save your breath, Ruth. You know how lucky you are to have a mother who cares about you and who—"

"Where's Wakim?" She was screaming now, at full pitch. "I wanna go home with Wakim."

While Kerry Schrager cuffed Ruth behind her back, I called Witness Aid to make sure that Margaret Feerick, one of our social workers, could go with the detectives and Mrs. Harwind to Family Court. Pat McKinney came to my doorway and started yelling over Ruth's wail. "What the hell is going on in here? This is an office, Cooper, and the rest of us are trying to get some work done."

I asked Sergeant Maron to go to Carol's waiting area, find Wakim, read him the riot act about hanging out with a minor, and send him on his way.

Eventually, the miserable troupe of characters was ready to leave the office, with Ruth Harwind in tow. By the time I got them off to court, contacted Bruce Johnson's parole officer to find out if we could have his parole revoked for statutory rape—the sexual acts with an underage teen—wolfed down a light yogurt, and dealt with the stack of messages on Laura's desk, it was a quarter of five and time to go to the U.S. Attorney's Office.

With summer vacations in full swing, the elevators were practically empty as I rode down to the lobby. I chatted with some of the secretaries who were walking out onto Hogan Place with me, then made the left turn onto Centre Street for the short walk to McFadden's office.

The area in front of the Supreme Court, Civil Division, had been under renovation for almost a year in an effort to convert a cement triangle into a small green park.

I crossed with the light and had just passed in front of the plywood frame of the construction area when a dilapidated livery cab with tinted windows veered across the sparse line of cars moving north on Centre Street. Brakes squealed and horns blasted, so I picked up my head to see what was happening.

The gypsy cab was coming directly at the sidewalk, where I was trapped between a parked police car and the wooden fencing behind me. The driver slammed into the patrol car, which jumped the curb and was catapulted toward me, as I flattened myself against the plywood boards. The marked police vehicle caught its right fender on the fire hydrant in its path, but as the left fender made contact with the lumber, the fencing gave way and I fell backward into a small ditch.

My embarrassment was greater than my discomfort as I lay on the ground in the dirt, my heart racing and my lip quivering. Three court officers had seen the accident from the steps of the courthouse and came running down to check if I was all right.

"Are you a juror, ma'am? You're gonna have some great lawsuit against the city," the first one to my side remarked.

"I'll be fine," I said as they helped me to my feet. I wiped pebbles out of my hair and brushed the soot off the rear of my pale aqua suit. There were long scratches on my calves and one of my elbows was bleeding.

"Did you get a license off that car?" one of the men asked

me, as onlookers gathered to see what the disturbance was about. "We'll help you make out the police report."

"No, thanks. I couldn't see the plate at all." But I had no trouble making out the face of the driver.

"Must've been a madman," the second guy said. "Did you hear him?"

I shook my head to indicate I had not. But as I thanked the officers and continued on my way to Kim's building, the driver's words—"You're dead meat, bitch"—were still reverberating in my ears.

16

I walked into the conference room after clearing security on the ground floor. Mike and Mercer were exchanging war stories with four very buttoned-down federal agents while they waited for me to arrive. I didn't need a mirror to tell me what was obvious from the expression on Mike's face as he looked up to see me.

"Mother of—jeez, what the hell happened to you? That picture's got 'line of duty' written all over it. Someone messes *me* up like that and I could go out on three-quarters disability pay tomorrow."

Mercer came over to examine the scrapes on my arm and ask whether I was all right.

"Yeah, I tripped into a hole on my way over from the courthouse."

"All those years of ballet lessons and you're a regular twinkletoes. You got four city blocks to walk here, what kinda hole we talking about?"

"I'll explain later. Let's get going here."

"You'll explain now, blondie."

"Ran into somebody who doesn't like me. Wakim Wakefield, a forty-something ex-con. Took his fifteen-year-old plaything away from him this afternoon and he didn't appreciate it." I told them a short version of the story.

"Just another friggin' Ponce de Léon looking for his fountain of youth," Mike said. "Let's call in a police report on your hit-and-run attempt."

"No," I said firmly. "Just leave it alone. I'm not hurt. And this'll blow over by the time he goes out tonight and finds himself another teen angel. It couldn't have been anything more than chance that he saw me on the street as I was leaving and took out his frustration on me. I hate to tell you, but some cop's going to walk out of Central Booking later tonight and find a radio car that got bashed up worse than my pride. Point me to the ladies' room and give me a little time to make myself presentable."

Special Agent Rainieri chose not to delay the discussion until my return, since I had already kept the group waiting an extra twenty minutes. He seemed to be speaking in answer to a question one of the detectives had asked. "Yeah, we had a turncoat. That's what started the whole investigation. Seems he got cheated out of a very big sale and decided to rat out some of the other dealers in the pack.

"The point of these rings, you know, is to keep the prices of the artworks at auctions way down. One of them buys the painting at the public sale, then resells it at a vastly greater price—usually to a private client—and splits the big profit with his—or her—small clan of coconspirators."

"Denise Caxton?"

"She was a player all right. Don't forget, not only do we have ordinary business receipts and phone records, but we've got tapes of all the telephone bidding that goes on during an auction house sale. And the expense statements and each gallery's credit agreements."

I had to remind Mike that beyond the social cachet and great expense connected with the grand auctions, art was one of the only objects in the world that could be purchased in any currency and from any location.

"Do you know who her cohorts were in these deals?"

The only female agent present, Estelle Grayson, answered. "She moved in and out of a few partnerships. Lowell Caxton didn't mess much with auctions, and didn't run with the pack. He has always had his own sources and paid dearly for them. Doesn't leave much of a paper trail, and didn't mix well in the sandbox with the other kids."

"Bryan Daughtry?" I asked.

"He's everywhere in this. Not up front, not sitting there with a paddle in the air. But he was pumping cash into her operation and trying to guide her into play with some of this very contemporary art inventory."

"Any names you can give us connected with the auction investigation?"

"Denise Caxton spent a lot of time at events this year. Sometimes she was with a personal client, a big collector." Rainieri referred to his file and gave us a list of names, none of which sounded at all familiar. "Often she brought a friend or escort, and it's hard to tell if there's any business purpose instead of a social one. Chapman says you've been talking to Mrs. Caxton's friend Marina Sette. She's a figure at these things. Could be she's just a big spender.

"Two of the men Denise had been socializing with also show up—Frank Wrenley and Preston Mattox. Again, one's an antiques dealer and one's an architect, so we've got sub-poenas out for their records, too. Nothing in on them yet. We just don't know if they're around for the fun or the profit."

"Well, do they buy anything?"

"Wrenley does. But that's a new twist, new buzzword in the auction world. It's called 'cross-marketing.' So, when Sotheby's has a sale of Impressionists, for example, they don't start the program off with a Monet. Last spring at their big show, the first piece sold was a pair of silver soup tureens made by a French silversmith in the eighteenth century. Used to belong to J. P. Morgan. Went for more than seven million bucks. The houses are trying to lure art collectors into new passions."

"Wrenley bought those tureens?"

"No, no. But he's shown up often and bought a lot of silver pieces—old French royalty. And Denise Caxton had Preston Mattox bidding on a set of murals out of an old Scottish estate. So we haven't reached a point of figuring whether this was business or romance.

"Anyway, Kim asked us to start making connections between Mrs. Caxton and anyone who'd have a reason to do her in. We're looking, and a few months down the road, when we have all the paper we need, something might leap out at us. In the meantime, if you guys have subpoenaed some of the same phone and business records that we did, we can cut through a lot of this and give you our copies. Maybe you'll find things that wouldn't mean anything to us."

I fished through my overstuffed pocketbook to pull out copies of the file folders with the subpoenas inside. The bag had turned upside down in my fall and was even more disas-trously messed up than usual.

"I don't know how she finds anything in there," Chapman said as I clasped lipstick, a compact, a handkerchief, Tic Tacs, four pens, and a wallet in my left hand, trying to free up the folder with my right. "What do you know about the Gardner Museum heist?"

"Not our turf. We've talked to the team who've worked it for practically ten years, just 'cause they're figuring the stolen items have got to surface somewhere before too long. So they're watching the auction houses pretty closely, too. D'y'all know about Youngworth and Connor?"

More than anything, Mike hated telling a Fed that there was something about which he was ignorant. He wouldn't say no to them, so I did.

"There are two guys in Boston, William Youngworth and Myles Connor. Youngworth's an antiques dealer—been in and out of the can on minor things—and Connor's a master art thief. Both of these men were in jail when the Gardner job was pulled, but word is, if they weren't the brains behind the theft, they certainly knew about it.

"Last year Youngworth claimed that he could broker the return of the missing Rembrandt for the five-million-dollar reward the FBI put up, along with immunity for him and his pal. You know about the chips?"

Another thumbs-up for Joan Stafford. "Sure," said Chapman, puffing. "Know all about the chips. Those assholes cut the painting right out of the frame."

"Yeah, well, Youngworth gave some Boston news reporter a few chips to support his claim that he could produce the goods. Our experts looked them over. Not authentic, not from the missing painting. That's the latest on the Gardner case."

"Who was your expert? Got a name for us?"

"No idea who it is. We'll get it for you tomorrow."

We spent the next half hour sorting through documents to see which ones I was legally entitled to examine at this point. At six fifteen, Mercer suggested we close up. "Let's get over to the funeral parlor before the seven o'clock visiting hours. Maybe we can chat up some of Marco Varelli's friends and family."

Varelli's wake was in a small, dark funeral home on Sullivan Street, in the narrow block just north of Houston. I had been in the neighborhood before, which had been home to Vincent "the Chin" Gigante, whom I had often seen there walking up and down the street in his bathrobe, feigning insanity, before his recent conviction and trip to federal prison.

I stepped out of Mercer's air-conditioned car and onto the steamy pavement in front of Zuppelo's funeral parlor. "You think they got a TV in there?" Mike asked.

"You are *not* watching *Jeopardy!* in front of the mourners," I said. "Call your mother when we leave here and ask her what the question was, okay? Live without it for one night."

The three of us presented ourselves to the manager of the mortuary. "The only one here at the moment is Mrs. Varelli. You're a little early. Are you friends?"

"Distant relatives," Chapman answered.

Mr. Zuppelo looked skeptically from Chapman to me, then frowned at Mercer Wallace's dark skin.

"Northern Italian," Mike said. "With a trace of Sicilian."

He flashed his badge at Zuppelo, who led us into a dingy sitting area. The odor of more than thirty flower arrangements—mostly orange gladioluses and yellow carnations—was especially stifling in the intense late-summer heat. The open casket was in an alcove at the far end of the room, and Mrs. Varelli sat beside it, clutching a set of rosary beads. The jacket of her gray suit seemed to overwhelm her delicate shoulders, and she looked as if she had cried all the tears she was capable of shedding in the past twenty-four hours.

Mike nudged me and told me to introduce myself. "See if you can get her outta this hothouse and away from her husband's body. Bond with her, Coop. Be sensitive—if you still remember how to do that."

I left Mike and Mercer at the doorway and approached the widow. "Mrs. Varelli, I'm Alexandra Cooper. I'm—"

"So nice to meet you, Miss Cooper. You were, perhaps, a friend of Marco's?"

"Actually, no, Mrs. Varelli. Would you like to come inside with me, to another room, and I'll explain why I'm here?"

"Sixty-two years, Miss Cooper. Never apart for one night in sixty-two years. What am I going to do without him?" She grabbed the side of the coffin and started to talk to her husband. "I'm just going to be a few minutes, Marco. I go with this young lady to see what she's going to try to sell me."

She extended her hand, and I grasped the white cotton glove and braced her elbow, helping her to her feet. "Everyone thinks I just got off the boat from Napoli. Do I want a mausoleum, do I want a condominium, do I want a ticket back to the old country? I was born in Newark, New Jersey. Lived here all my life. These people think I'm stupid. Think I'm going to give away Marco's paintings or turn his studio into the YMCA.

"All I want is for Marco to get up and walk around the corner with me to have our dinner at Da Silvano, sitting on the sidewalk, like we did almost every evening in the warm weather. Artists would look at Marco with respect, Marco would look at the young ladies with longing, I'd have a couple of glasses of wine, and together we'd go home very happy. It's awfully lonely after sixty-two years, Miss Cooper. You want to sell me something, or you want to buy?"

As she talked, I walked her past Mike and Mercer and into an empty room decorated in somber, waiting-for-the-next-body tones of neutral palettes. There was an elegance to the old woman, with her perfectly erect carriage, fragile body, and very keen mind.

"I'm an assistant district attorney, Mrs. Varelli. A prosecutor."

"Somebody make a crime here?"

"I'm working on another case, a murder case. A woman who was killed last week. I understand that Mr. Varelli had done work with her. We—the detectives and I—had planned to come see him later this week. Then we learned about his death. I'm so sorry for your great loss. I don't mean to burden you now, but maybe you could give me the name of your husband's assistant, who could tell—"

Her back was straight as a rod as she poked herself in the chest. "I am the only one he trusted with his work, Miss Cooper. He had several workmen who helped him with the physical labor, the movement of large pieces, the arrangement of supplies, and from time to time he had an apprentice. But there is nothing I didn't know about his business. Who is this lady who was killed?"

"Caxton. Denise Caxton."

Mrs. Varelli turned her face ninety degrees, away from me. She was silent.

"You knew her, then?"

"It's not good to speak ill of the dead, is it?"

"What kind of business did she have with your husband?"

"The same as everyone, Miss Cooper. You know about Marco?"

"I have to admit that I had never heard his name until this week. But all the people I've talked to say what a wonderful man he was."

"A genius. Did they say that, too? Mostly, he was a genius."

I nodded to her.

"As a boy, in Firenze, he studied art at the Accademia. Paint is what he loved—not the canvas, but the substance that made color—and he had even more passion for that than for beautiful women. But he never did it so well himself—the drawing or the creation. What he did brilliantly was to find the beauty in the paintings of others who had gone before him.

"Marco could stand in his atelier for hours, some eager dealer at his heels watching, working on what appeared to be a dirty old piece of burlap. He'd fasten his binocular headset on—that was the only thing that even looked like it connected him to this century. Gently, ever so gently, he would swab at the tired colors with a little touch of cotton.

"Behind him, some greedy collector or dealer would be urging him on. 'What do you see, Marco? Who do you think it is, Marco?' You have no idea what treasures he has found over the years. Even so recently, his eyes saw things through the filth of centuries that no one else could dream possible."

"And his illness—he was still working until recently, even with his heart condition?"

Mrs. Varelli snapped at me. "Illness what?"

"I, uh, I knew that a doctor had come when he collapsed."

"A touch of arthritis, that's what the doctor was for. Marco's skill depended on two things, his eye and his hand. Neither one of us—no pills, no machines, no medicines. He only had a doctor to help him when his hand ached from the arthritis and it hurt him to hold a scalpel for so long. *Un po' di vino,* Marco believed in. The medicine from the grapes."

"It was his heart that gave out," I said, hoping it was gentle enough a reminder of what the doctor had told the M.E.'s pathologist.

"There was nothing wrong with Marco's heart. His heart was so good, so very strong." Mrs. Varelli became tearful.

"Were you always in the studio with your husband?"

"No, I was rarely there. We have an apartment in the same building. We had our coffee together in the morning, then he would go upstairs to work. Back home for lunch and a nap. Then more work, always. Sometimes into the evening, if he found himself in the middle of a surprise or a painting he had come to adore. Then he would come home to bathe himself, to get rid of the oil and varnish and streaks. Together we would go off for dinner, alone or with friends. A simple life, Miss Cooper, but a very rich one."

"Had you ever met Denise Caxton?"

"It was her husband I met first. I can hardly remember when, it was so long ago. He was not a warm man, but he was very good to Marco. Lowell Caxton bought a portrait at an auction house in London, maybe thirty years ago. It had been miscatalogued in England and sold as an unidentified portrait of a young girl. Lowell bought it only because he said it reminded him of his wife, whichever one that happened to be at the time. He didn't believe it had any value, and he brought it to Marco simply to clean it up to be hung.

"But Marco thought she was a beauty, too. 'Overpainted,' he complained to me every time he came downstairs. He didn't use many words, Marco. He didn't need to with me. Days and nights he worked on it, until there was life in the child's face and her petite blue dress had texture and the warm glow of silk. One afternoon, Marco came down for lunch. I give him his soup and he looks across the table. 'Gainsborough,' he said to me, 'it's a Gainsborough.' Every museum in England wanted to buy it back.

"Many people would just have paid Marco the price he asked for the restoration, and still my husband would have been happy. Lowell Caxton did that. But then he came back the next week, when Marco had come home for his lunch. I let him in the house—that's when I met him. He had under his arm a small package wrapped in brown paper. It was a Titian—very small, very beautiful. We have it still. You come to my home, you'll see it."

"In your apartment? A Titian?"

"But so very little. It's a study, just a piece of one of his great works. You know *The Rape of Europa*?"

Of course I knew it. Everyone who had ever taken an art course in college had studied it. Rubens had called it the greatest painting in the world. And I had seen it many times because it was part of the collection at the Gardner Museum. Was this just another coincidence? "When did you say Mr. Caxton gave you the Titian?"

Mrs. Varelli thought for a moment. "Thirty, thirty-five years ago."

Before Denise, before the Gardner Museum theft.

"And Denise Caxton, was she a client of Mr. Varelli's?"

"First she came many times with her husband. Then alone. Then with other people—maybe dealers, maybe buyers. I never met them in the studio. Sometimes Marco would tell stories about them."

"Did he feel the same way you did about Mrs. Caxton?"

Mrs. Varelli tossed back her head and laughed. "Of course not. She was young, she was quite beautiful, and she knew how to make an old man feel wonderful. She'd practice her Italian on Marco. She'd flatter him and tease him and bring him fascinating paintings to examine. Always looking for gold where there was none. Wasting Marco's time, if you ask me."

"Do you know who the men were that she brought recently?"

"No, no. For this, I give you the names of my husband's workmen. Maybe they were introduced or can tell you what these men looked like. You give me your card, and next week I call you with their telephone numbers."

"Is that the only reason you didn't like Denise?"

"I don't need many reasons. She was trouble. Even Marco thought she was trouble."

"How, Mrs. Varelli? What did he tell you about her?"

"Like I said, Miss Cooper, Marco didn't use a lot of words. But these past few months, on the days that Mrs. Caxton came to see him, he didn't come home smiling like he used to. She was trying to get him to work on something that upset him, gave him *agita*. That he did say. 'At this age, I don't need any *agita*.'"

"But didn't he get any more specific than that?"

"Not with me. I was just glad he didn't want to work with her any longer. He didn't seem to like the people she was bringing around."

"Did Mr. Varelli talk about Rembrandt ever?"

"How could one make his life in this world and not talk about Rembrandt?"

I was grateful that she had not responded by saying what a stupid question I had asked. "I mean recently, and in connection with Denise Caxton."

"You don't know, then, that Marco is"—her chest heaved visibly as she breathed deeply and changed the wording. "Marco was the world's leading expert on Rembrandt, no? Perhaps you're too young to know the story."

Mrs. Varelli went on. "Rembrandt's most famous group portrait is called *The Night Watch*. Have you ever seen it?"

"Yes, I have. It's in Amsterdam, at the Rijksmuseum."

"Exactly. Then maybe you know that originally, more than three hundred years ago, it had a different name."

"No, I've only heard it called by this one."

"When he painted it, it was entitled *The Shooting Company of Captain Frans Banning Cocq*. Over the decades, it became so covered with grime that people assumed that the setting was at nighttime—the name you know it by. Well, after World War Two was ended—in about nineteen forty-seven—when Marco was just getting a reputation as a restorer, he was part of the team of experts put together to restore the enormous painting. During the cleaning, it lightened brilliantly. That's the first time anyone in the twentieth century realized that it wasn't a night scene at all.

"Marco was the only member of that restoration group still alive fifty years later. When anyone—and I mean *anyone*, Miss Cooper—has a question about the attribution of a Rembrandt today, it was only my Marco who knew the truth.

Monarchs, presidents, millionaires—they all came to see Marco Varelli about their paintings."

"Denise Caxton, did she ever bring him a Rembrandt?"

"This I don't know."

"Did your husband ever say that she or anyone else asked him to look at paint chips recently?"

Again Mrs. Varelli looked at me as though I had no brain at all.

"That's what my husband did every day of his life. Paint, paint chips, paint streaks, paint fragments. From this, Miss Cooper, come masterpieces."

"Excuse me, Alex. Could I see you a minute?" Mercer was speaking to me from the hallway.

"May I go back to Marco now?"

"If you'd give us another few minutes, Mrs. Varelli, we'll be out of your way," he said to her.

I thanked her for her graciousness at such a terrible time and walked back to the room in which the coffin rested. Mike was standing next to the dead man's head.

"I hope by paying your respects to the deceased you got more than I did from the widow," I said to them as I reentered the room. "A bit of art history and a hunch that Denise Caxton was nothing but trouble."

"Then I'd say Mrs. Varelli's got great instincts. Remember that case I had a few years back in Spanish Harlem? The Argentinian dancer, Augusto Mango, who died prematurely during a sexual encounter with a rabid fan?"

"Very well."

"You know how we found out it was murder and not a bad heart?"

"No."

"Some doctor declared him dead at the scene. I think he must have been a podiatrist. Then, at the funeral parlor, while they were combing his hair into place, the mortician found a bullet hole in the back of his head. Small caliber, barely the trace of an entry. The fan's husband was the killer. *Post* headline was *Don't Tango with Mango.*

"Well, Mr. Zuppelo wouldn't make such a good barber."

Mike carefully turned Marco Varelli's head away from us and smoothed the thick white hair back from his left ear, much as he had done at Spuyten Duyvil when we first saw the body of Denise Caxton. There was the unmistakable mark that a bullet had pierced the skull of the gentle old man.

17

"Criminal court press room—where every crime's a story and every story's a crime. Mickey Diamond here." The veteran *New York Post* reporter had covered the courthouse for longer than anyone could remember, and answered the phone with his usual élan on Thursday morning.

"What did you think you were doing by running that story this morning?" I asked when I called, trying to control my temper.

Pat McKinney had left a copy of the page-three clipping on my desk, quoting me in an article about the Caxton murder investigation. Battaglia had an inviolable policy about assistants talking to the press. He enforced it rigidly, and he was right to do so. With more than six hundred lawyers in the office and three hundred thousand matters a year coming through our complaint room, it would have been insane to let prosecutors comment on cases they handled. First I had called Rose Malone, urging her to let Battaglia know that Mickey's feature was pure fiction, and then I had dialed the newsroom.

"Slow news day, Alex. My editor was begging me for a story."

I looked at the lead paragraph in the piece, in which Diamond attributed to me a statement about a major break in the case.

"If we're close to a solution, as you say I say, then it truly is news to me," I told him. The story reported that, working closely with detectives from the Manhattan North Homicide Squad, I had discovered the motive in the Caxton killing and an arrest was imminent. "Battaglia will be furious when he reads this. It's bullshit, but now he'll get pressure from the mayor to make an arrest, and we don't even have a suspect yet."

"The truth is so rare, Alex. I like to use it sparingly." He laughed at his own joke, knowing that I wouldn't. "Straighten me out. Give me some real scoop to go with. Maybe this'll make the killer show his hand—he'll think you know more about him than you do."

"Thanks for the help, Mickey. When he turns himself in because of your story, I'll make sure you get the reward money." If nothing else, I confirmed that word of Marco Varelli's murder had not yet leaked to the press. Diamond would have been all over me if he'd heard what we had discovered last night.

We had broken the news to Varelli's widow just as mourners had gathered for the evening visit to the funeral home. Her initial shock at the fact that her husband had been assassinated was replaced with her proud resolve that she had known he had not died of natural causes. Bravely, she composed herself and greeted their friends and associates for more than two hours, while we mingled with the small crowd in the room.

She had finally thanked Chapman warmly and then turned to tell me good night. "You see, Miss Cooper, I was sure that Marco Varelli would never have chosen to leave me. Such was his love, such was his life."

The funeral was to be on Friday, after the second night of the wake, and she invited us to come to her nearby apartment the next week.

Mike had gotten her permission to seal Marco's atelier last night and secure it with patrolmen. He would go back later today to process it with the detectives from the Crime Scene Unit. We needed her, or one of Varelli's workmen, to help discover whether any artworks or valuables were missing. That might have to wait until after the burial.

Finally, when everyone left the dingy funeral home, Mike and Mercer had arranged for the Medical Examiner's Office to pick up the body of Marco Varelli for an autopsy.

I had come downtown to work, busying myself in the review of new cases till I could meet Mike or Mercer in Chelsea. We were going back to Galleria Caxton Due to talk to Bryan Daughtry again, as well as to oversee the execution of the search warrant.

It was Mercer who phoned at eleven thirty to tell me he was leaving his office to go to West Twenty-second Street. Mike had witnessed the proceeding on Varelli at the morgue, which had validated his discovery at the funeral parlor, and would join up with us in Chelsea.

I drove my Jeep up to the gallery thinking about Denise Caxton, Omar Sheffield, and Marco Varelli. What common factor in their lives so closely linked them in death?

I parked right in front and walked to the Empire Diner, where I sipped another cup of coffee until the guys arrived a few minutes later.

"You got the warrants?" Mike asked, slipping into the booth along with Mercer, who had met him at the front door.

"Everything we need."

We walked across the street and down the block, where the entrance to the gallery's garage was blocked by a radio car. One of the uniformed officers saw us coming, recognized Mike, and got out to say hello.

"Hey, Chapman, how's it going? Been a long time. I thought you did steady midnights?"

"Used to be, Jack. Now I'm afraid of the dark—doing day tours. Any action here?"

"He ain't givin' us any trouble. A little pedestrian traffic around, but no packages going without gettin' searched, and no trucks in or out. Same report from yesterday."

A receptionist met us inside the front door. "Mr. Daughtry thought you might be coming in sometime this afternoon. He's upstairs with a client. I can make you comfortable down here, if you'd—"

"No thanks," Mike said, ignoring the young woman and leading us to the elevator in the far corner. When we reached the top floor and stepped out onto the landing, there was no sign of Daughtry on the walkway. Mercer headed over to see whether he was in his corner office, while Mike and I looked out at the old railroad tracks again.

"My father used to tell me the stories about the gangs from Hell's Kitchen who terrorized the train lines—the Hudson Dusters, the Gophers. When he was a kid, he hung out in a saloon right up the street here, running errands for a guy named Mallet Murphy. Called him that 'cause he'd crack disorderly customers over the head with a meat hammer."

Mike leaned back against the waist-high iron rail as he

looked out at this view of Chelsea. He couldn't have been any happier if you'd sat him at the top of the Eiffel Tower. This was his father's home turf, and the neighborhood held his family roots.

"This view could change my whole opinion of both Denise Caxton and Bryan Daughtry. It's really cool that they left the old tracks in place." He turned and noted the Plexiglas doorway that led out of the gallery onto the tracks.

"Hey, Coop, someday after me and Daughtry have put our differences aside, I'll walk you and Mercer out that very door, onto the tracks, and take you as far downtown as it goes. Tell you stories about real gangsters and show you where the bones are buried."

"We're down here, Mr. Chapman. As long as you've made yourselves at home, why don't you come tell me what you need?" Daughtry called up to us from somewhere a level or two below. I couldn't see him from where I was standing, but he had obviously been alerted to our arrival.

The catwalk around the edge of the upper floor was about four feet wide. The three of us walked around its perimeter until we came to a metal staircase that led down a level.

Here the space extended out over the track below, and there were couches and sitting areas that faced various exhibits on the vast walls that ringed the gallery.

Bryan Daughtry and another man were seated facing each other in brown leather armchairs. Daughtry stood to reach for Chapman's hand.

"Let me guess," Mike said, looking at two yellow columns positioned next to each other and representing some sort of sculpture. "*The Cat in the Hat?*"

"Shall I read to you from our brochure, Detective? 'A minimal freestanding work, this kinetic fiberglass piece conveys a charming, vertiginous uncertainty.' Like it? Or do you prefer the one behind me? A very creative new fellow—uses beeswax, hazelnut pollen, marble, and rice to make sculptures, as we say, 'of mute yet implacable force.'"

"Come to think of it, my apartment looks fine with a couple of NFL posters, a slightly used baseball signed by Bernie Williams, and an eight-by-ten glossy of Tina Turner that Miss Cooper gave me. Your stuff makes me wanna puke."

"Shall we go back up to my office?" Daughtry asked.

Mercer and I started to follow him. Mike stretched out his arm to Daughtry's companion, who remained seated as I started to walk away.

"Hi. Sorry to break this up. I'm Mike Chapman. Homicide. You are . . . ?"

The attractive dark-haired man, who I guessed to be about forty years old, stood up and smiled, returning the handshake. "I'm Frank Wrenley. How do you do?"

"Well, well, well—Mr. Wrenley. And how do *you* do? Tell you what—c'mon upstairs with us. I got a few questions for you when we're done with Mr. Daughtry."

"Of course. I assumed you'd want to talk to me about Deni. I'm happy to try to help."

Mercer whispered to me as we walked to the narrow staircase, "You and Mike go at Daughtry. I'll baby-sit Wrenley till you're done, so he doesn't make any calls while he's waiting. This is a rare opportunity to get him when he wasn't expecting us."

Mike and I settled into the dealer's office with him. "Like I told you, we got a warrant to go through your gallery and warehouse. A team of detectives will be here shortly to do that. You can make this real easy on yourself if you wanna give us most of what we ask for, which are Deni's business records and belongings, access to the contents of Omar's locker, and things like—well, look at the papers for yourself.

"We'd also like to look through some of the paintings you've got stored here."

"Anything in particular you're looking for? Your taste in art, Mr. Chapman, is so hard for me to define."

"Got any Rembrandts on hand?"

"So you're joining the search for the mythical Holy Grail, too? Everybody's looking for the big score. You've got a better chance of winning the lottery than finding that missing painting."

"Then you won't mind if we look, will you?"

"Certainly not."

"Had you and Deni talked about it? I mean, about *The Storm on the Sea of Galilee*?"

"Many, many times. But so did everyone else in our business."

"Seems to me," Mike said, "that if I were an ex-con sitting on a hot item, my best bet would be to contact somebody else in the same shoes. I wouldn't be likely to walk into a classy operation where they might give me up to the Feds just for talkin' to them, but I'd sure be likely to sniff out some creep who'd done time and was completely amoral."

"What do you want me to say, Detective? 'Sticks and stones'?"

"Look, we know someone offered Deni the Rembrandt. And we even know about her meetings with Marco Varelli, to authenticate the chips."

Daughtry met Mike's stare head-on. "That's the oldest trick in the book, Mr. Chapman. Varelli is dead. Don't expect me to believe he summoned you to his bedside just before he had the big one. I doubt you ever spoke to him. Not much of a talker, that man. Try me again, harder this time."

"Lowell Caxton told us about the hijacking of the Della Spiga paintings last June. Said to ask you why it made Deni so crazy."

"Well, I assume the disappearance of a truckload of any artist's work would make his dealer berserk. Caxton Due represented Della Spiga. The whole thing was rather odd. Nobody ever saw who stole the truck, so we don't even know whether or not the thieves were armed. Deni had actually rented an eighteen-wheeler from a soda delivery company so the truck would be inconspicuous on the highway. After the drivers made a stop for coffee on the thruway, they came out of McDonald's and the truck had disappeared."

"Never found it?"

"To the contrary. It was found the next day, abandoned behind an old factory upstate. Not a thing missing. Either the thieves didn't like Della Spiga or they were looking for cola and not art."

"What did Deni think?"

"That first night? She was wild. Figured it had to be an inside job, someone who knew she was shipping fine art but disguising the delivery truck. When every painting was found intact, she calmed down and assumed the hijacking was just a coincidence. Amateur soda swipers foiled again."

"So maybe somebody did think she had the Rembrandt and was slipping the stolen painting in with the transport of the Della Spigas?"

"One might have thought that to see how upset she got. But of course, Detective Chapman, the police who found the truck went through it and listed every item on it. No Rembrandt recovered. And Deni was far, far too relieved the next day to have been missing one great masterpiece."

Mike jumped back a year in his next question.

"That trip to England that Lowell made alone the June before—the one that broke the marriage apart. What were you and Deni up to that kept her away, that kept her so busy here?"

"Try as you might, Chapman, you won't mix me in this soup. Whatever it was, Deni never let me in on it. But you're right, it was serious. Whoever called her, whoever contacted her—someone made an offer she couldn't refuse. She withdrew from me completely and was very secretive. It bothered me at the time, but after a few days she changed her mind and went off to join Lowell. You obviously know the rest. I didn't think any more of it. Figured she'd been onto a deal and that it must have fallen through. Happens all the time in this business."

The receptionist buzzed on Daughtry's intercom to tell him that more detectives had arrived.

Chapman stood up. "Why don't you show my guys around?" Then he bent over the desk, the top of his fists pressed against the leather blotter. "Remember, it ain't just me you gotta worry about, Mr. Daughtry. Mess with the cops and you've still got the boys on Eleventh Avenue to deal with—Knuckles Knox, Stumpy Malarkey, One-Lung Curran. They got ways I couldn't get past the Supreme Court in six lifetimes."

When Daughtry left the room, I turned to Mike. I was steaming. "Who the hell are you talking about? Bad enough I don't know what you do when I'm *not* standing next to you. You can't threaten people like that, and I can't stand by and let you do it."

"Not even once? I've waited a lifetime to say that to somebody. 'Battle Row,' this block used to be called. Those guys, Knuckles and Stumpy? Real hoodlums—used to scare my old man to death when he was a schoolboy. Relax, blondie. That gang broke up around nineteen thirty-two. Six feet under, all of 'em. Did I sound like Cagney? Did I scare you?"

Mike stepped to the doorway and motioned to Wrenley to come into the office and sit down. I introduced myself.

He was dressed in black from head to foot—collared polo shirt, linen slacks, tasseled loafers—and his jet-colored hair was slicked back, every strand in perfect placement. I guessed it was his style, not an expression of mourning.

"Hope you don't mind some questions about Denise

Caxton," Mike began. "We understand you and she were quite close." The edge in his voice with which he had addressed Daughtry was gone. It was clear to me that he was hoping to get Wrenley's help with more personal information about the past year.

"Not a secret, Detective. I'd met Deni two or three years ago. After she and Lowell had their blowup last year, our relationship became more intimate."

"You didn't mind the competition?"

"Her husband, or do you mean Preston Mattox? I understood what it was about. Deni was just a kid when she hooked up with Lowell Caxton. She'd been faithful to him throughout the marriage, and don't think there weren't lots of opportunities for her to have a fling. After he embarrassed her with that episode in Bath, she was more than ready to spread her wings.

"And besides, she was still married to Lowell. She wasn't very anxious to tie herself down permanently so quickly. We both seemed to get all the pleasure we needed out of each other's company, professionally and personally."

"I take it you're single?"

"Always have been," Wrenley answered.

"How'd you and Mrs. Caxton meet?"

"When I moved most of my business interests to New York—"

"What's the business?"

"Antiques. High end. Furniture, silver, nineteenth-century for the most part."

"Where'd you move here from?"

"Palm Beach, Detective. Grew up in Florida, in the Keys. Set up shop there, but I was always on the road. Auctions in England, France, Italy, and of course, New York. I still keep a place on the water down there, but I live here now.

"I saw Deni long before I met her. She was hard to miss—

not just her looks but her spirit and energy. Always in the chase for a great find, and in those days, something to show Lowell how much she had learned from him."

Mike tried the man-to-man thing. "Never came on to her before she split with him? Never asked her out, called her, till after the Bath scandal?"

"I never called her then, Mike. It was Deni who called *me*. We'd been to auctions together and gotten to know each other a bit. I'd asked her for advice about paintings when I was making acquisitions for particular clients. Nothing social. After she flew home from England that time, she was determined to make a statement to her friends back here. Called me and invited me to go to a couple of dinner parties with her. It almost began as a game, for both of us. I never imagined I'd fall in love with her, nor she with me."

"What was the story with the other guys?"

"There were lots of men pursuing Deni. I'd have been an idiot not to think that would happen. I suppose my most serious rival was Preston Mattox. Had an airtight way of getting under my skin."

"Why Mattox more than anyone else?"

"Ever hear of something called the Amber Room?"

"Yeah," Mike answered. "Know all about it."

"Mattox was convinced that Lowell Caxton had smuggled some of the panels out of Europe and had them hidden somewhere. He's an architect, world-class. Deni said he had this dream—you ought to talk to him about it—of creating his *chef d'oeuvre* with remnants of the room. I don't know whether he was interested in *her* or in what she could lead him to. But that possibility made her furious whenever I suggested it.

"Look, I'm on the road a lot of the time. I never expected her to sit home doing her needlepoint, waiting for me to come back to town. She knows—sorry, she knew—that I dated other women when I was in Europe, and that was fine with her. She'd been tied down too long to care about that kind of thing right now."

"So, what brings you here?" I asked. There was nothing in Daughtry's world that seemed remotely connected to the nineteenth century.

"I wasn't invited to Deni's funeral, as you probably already know. Bryan and I are old friends, and he knows how devastated I was by her death. I just wanted to talk, reminisce, try to make some sense of it. May I call you Alex? When you catch the bastard who did this, Alex—" Wrenley paused, then dropped his head and shook his hand back and forth, as though asking us to wait a few moments before he spoke. "No point in my going on. There's nothing you can do to him in a court of law that would resemble any kind of justice.

"The newspapers said the police thought she was sexually assaulted. Is that true?"

"Probably," Chapman answered.

He lowered his head again. "She was so loving, so—God, I can't bear to think of any animal touching her, hurting her." Again he paused. "There must be something I can do to be useful."

"Let me have your numbers," Mike said, taking his notepad out of his pocket. "There's a lot more I'm gonna need to talk to you about as this thing unravels. As soon as we sort through some of the business records and evidence that's developing, I'll give you a call and set up an appointment, okay?"

Wrenley removed a business card from his wallet, added his home telephone to the number on it, and passed it to Chapman.

"Want me out of the way here? Sounds like you've got things to do with Bryan."

"D'you know that Mrs. Caxton was being blackmailed? Threatened by a man in prison?"

"Sure I did. It terrified her. She was convinced Lowell was behind it."

"Got any idea why she hired that guy Omar and had him working here with her?"

"It made me furious, actually. Bryan can tell you. I had dozens of arguments with Deni about Omar. And I wasn't sorry to see him turn up in a ditch, Mike. But she thought it was her best protection against Lowell, sort of an insurance policy."

"She'd have been a very rich widow if Lowell had died first, wouldn't she, Mr. Wrenley?"

"Take a trip with me to Palm Beach, Mike. You want rich widows? I didn't have to come to New York to catch myself one of those, if that's your implication. They're as thick as palmetto bugs down there."

"Sorry about Denise, Mr. Wrenley." I offered my hand as he stood up to leave.

For the rest of the afternoon, Bryan Daughtry led the detectives through the beginnings of a painstaking search of the art inventory in the gallery and adjacent warehouse. I sat in his office as he produced much of the documentation requested in the subpoena, reading and xeroxing stacks of bills and papers, the endless figures blurring my vision by the close of the day.

"You guys need me for anything?" I asked Mercer at six fifteen. "I'm supposed to go to dinner and the ballet tonight, if you can carry on without me."

"Scat. We'll grab some chow when we leave here, and see if we can catch up with the Crime Scene guys at Varelli's studio. I'll leave a message on your machine if we find anything interesting. You around tomorrow?"

I was tired, dismayed by the dead ends we kept meeting in this case, and glad the following day was Friday. "I'll be in all day. I've got a ticket on the seven-thirty evening flight for the weekend, but I feel guilty leaving you with all this hanging."

"Nothing you can do, Coop, till we give you a perp. Be on that plane. We'll be talking to you before that."

I went out to my car, squared the block, and fought the tunnel traffic of Jersey commuters going north on Tenth Avenue to begin their ride home. After I passed the entrance, I continued up to Sixty-fourth Street, turning to park in the cavernous garage below the Lincoln Center complex. Although the Metropolitan Opera House was usually dark during the month of August, there was a gala performance this evening, with pieces that the ballet company was staging for an international tour that was about to begin.

There were tiered sections in the underground lot, each identifiable by an enormous band of colored paint that wound around the walls of that area. In my fatigued state, I kept trying to think of a memory device to help me recall that I was directed up the ramp to the red-striped portion of the garage, and parked in the fifth row away from the door, behind a column boldly labeled 5.

I joined the line of patrons to prepay the parking ticket and took the escalator upstairs. Natalie Moody and her party of friends had already been seated in the Grand Tier Restaurant, below the immense Chagall mural looking out over the plaza. The group was ordering their dinners as I arrived, so I chose the grilled salmon and we chatted and ate before moving downstairs to take our seats in the orchestra.

Few things are as capable of transporting me from the images of violence that permeate my working days as is ballet. I have studied dance for almost as long as I have walked, and have continued to take lessons as both a form of regular exercise and a medium of escape from some of the seamy underside of life that I encounter on the street. Had I had the talent, I would rather have been a prima ballerina with American Ballet Theatre than almost anything else in the world.

So I sat back in my seat, ready to take refuge in this fantasy world, as the crystal chandeliers rose into the ceiling of the opera house and the curtain went up on the first piece. Victor Barbee made a rare appearance to partner the exquisite Julie Kent in a pas de deux from *Swan Lake*. The audience responded wildly with more than six curtain calls, and for half an hour I forgot about Denise Caxton. The second act featured Alessandra Ferri with the dazzling Julio Bocca in the balcony scene from *Romeo and Juliet*, and I lost myself completely in the perfection of their pairing.

There was a sparkling *Rodeo* with Kathleen Moore and Gil Boggs, and a final intermission before the corps was going to perform the "Kingdom of the Shades" from *La Bayadère*. It was after ten thirty, and I told Natalie I needed to get a jump on the crowd and head for home. I was afraid the Minkus music and the endless line of white-tutu'd Shadows would lull me to sleep in my seat.

I dug into my seemingly bottomless pocketbook for the Jeep keys, reminding myself that I had to relocate the red-striped parking area, behind column 5. The walk back to the car seemed farther than it had on the way in, but it was four hours later and I was really dragging. There were plenty of gaping spaces between the automobiles, I noted to myself, and it usually displeased me that so many suburban ticket holders walked out of the theater before the end of the event. Tonight I was one of the guilty leave-takers.

I started the engine, flipped on the headlights, and backed out of the space, heading over to the end of the row toward the ramp down to the exit. As I made the wide turn, a sport utility vehicle larger than my own careened around the adjacent line of cars and came racing at me, head-on.

My foot jammed the gas pedal to the floor and I swerved to the left, speeding down lane Red 4 as the chase car followed closely on my tail. I saw an opening midrow, where two spaces had been created side by side as well as back-to-back, and I barely braked as I nosed the Jeep into a curve and an immediate second left turn.

The dark car in pursuit took the long way around, and I could see that it was skipping two rows to try to cut me off at the top of the ramp.

I was pressing on the horn with my left hand as I steered with my right, hoping that someone would be annoyed by the blaring honk. A Jaguar with two couples in it pulled out in front of whoever was trying to cut me off, and I lurched ahead, hoping to see a security guard at the foot of the incline, where the giant red arrow merged with the equally wide yellow and blue stripes.

Instinctively, my foot hit the brake as a caution, and I immediately recognized that even a second's delay could be a costly mistake. But I had hesitated as I always did when leaving that garage, choosing between the exits on the north and south sides of the building, depending on which one was open at a given hour.

Just as I decided to make the right turn and go out onto Sixty-fourth Street, where there was a bus stop and, always, a posttheater crowd, the dark chase car came roaring down the steep rise of the garage behind me. Its driver passed me on the left side and cut me off. His engine still running, a male figure with a stocking cap over his head opened the door and got out, running toward me with the gleam of something metallic in his hand.

The empty sport utility vehicle was between me and the mechanical arm of the barrier that would have been my escape. As he slammed his left hand on the hood of the Jeep, I juiced the gas again and jumped the curb of the divider that separates the entrance from the exit gate. My Jeep kept going, smashing against the retractable arm of the entry blockade and cruising up the hill to the wide flat pavement of Sixty-fourth Street.

My repeated pounding on the horn cleared the crossing of pedestrians who were out for a summer stroll on Broadway. I paused to make sure the traffic light was with me, then goosed the car across the busy intersection, never stopping for a moment as I raced through the Central Park transverse and reached the East Side.

18

"You're not going home alone tonight, Coop. End of story."

It was midnight, and I was sitting at the corner table in the front of Primola with Mike and Mercer. The third Dewar's had failed to calm me.

After I had driven through Central Park, I headed directly across Sixty-fifth Street to my second home, the Italian restaurant where I frequently entertained my companions for dinner. I knew that even at eleven o'clock, Primola would be full of people, so I parked at a fire hydrant in front and ran inside to find Giuliano, the owner. He was my friend, and just as important, he was a soccer player who had competed on a World

Cup team several years earlier. If he was between me and the door, I'd be perfectly safe until reinforcements arrived.

I told him that someone crazy was following me, so he sat down at my table, asked Adolfo to get me a drink and Peter to bring over the phone. I dialed Mercer's beeper number and inhaled the scotch as I waited for a callback. He and Mike had just left Varelli's studio and were sitting in a bar in SoHo, eating dinner and enjoying their first cocktail. It took them half an hour to get uptown to meet me. Once they arrived, Giuliano left us alone to talk, and Fenton, the bartender, kept sending rounds over to the table.

"Obviously, I didn't want to go home alone. That's why I called to tell you what happened. But if you two deposit me there and lock me inside, I'll be fine." I live on the twentieth floor of a high-rise building with two doormen, and pay dearly for a great sense of security once inside.

"Why didn't you just go right to the station house, instead of coming here?"

"Because then there'd be a police report, and then somebody would call the tabloids, and then Battaglia would have me under lock and key for the next month."

"You don't even know who you're looking for, blondie. I've had blind victims who've given me a better scrip than you have."

"It's awfully hard to give you a description when the guy's wearing a mask and gloves."

"I think it's time for a slumber party. One of us is gonna hang with you overnight."

Mercer took it a step further. "And besides that, you are on the very first plane to the Vineyard in the morning. That is, if you're not going to be by yourself up there this weekend."

"Clark Kent's booked in for a visit, Mercer. Ace reporter for the *Daily Planet*. She's dumping us for some news jock, m'man. What time of day do they start flying those tin cans?"

Either the liquor or the scare I had just experienced made the idea of a weekend in the country even more attractive than it had seemed earlier in the day. I had completely neglected matters like the sleep clinic investigation for the more pressing problems of the Caxton murder, but I'd push that one back another week as well. "There's an eight A.M. out of LaGuardia. Probably over-booked this time of year. I'm not sure I'll get on."

"Know how much pleasure it would give me to officially bump some investment banker off that flight?" Mike asked. "I'll take you out there myself."

I looked at my watch. "Make you a deal. Let me call David Mitchell. If he and Renee are home," I said, referring to my next-door neighbors, "I can sleep on their sofa, and they can drop me at the airport on their way to the Hamptons in the morning. You two have better things to do, okay? Try solving this mess before anyone else is killed."

My call awakened David, as we knew it would, but he was more than gracious. Renee made up the sofa bed while Mike parked my Jeep in my garage and Mercer escorted me up to my own apartment so I could grab my robe as well as a shirt and pair of leggings to wear in the morning.

"Want me to wait while you pack things to take with you to the country?"

"I've got everything I need up there," I said, as I gave him a hug and opened the door to David's apartment with his spare key, which I kept in my dresser drawer. "Thanks. Call me if anything happens before I see you on Monday."

I undressed, took a steaming hot shower, and wrapped the terry robe around me. I was too jumpy to sleep, but I turned out the light and rested, with their dog, Prozac, curled up by my side.

We left the apartment at seven, and David walked me in to the gate to make sure I got on the flight. There were the usual number of no-shows, and ten minutes before takeoff I boarded the thirty-seat Dash 8 and fell asleep for the short flight to the Vineyard.

I had a monthly parking spot at the airport. It was a brilliantly clear day and a good ten degrees cooler than it had been in the city all week. I put the top down on my little red Miata and drove up-island to Chilmark, to the house.

Once I passed the crest of the drive, where my friend Isabella Lascar had been killed, the gray-shingled farmhouse came into sight and, beyond it, the stunning view of Vineyard Sound, which never failed to take my breath away. This is the one place on earth where every tension I have dissolves, and where I have spent the happiest hours of my life.

My caretaker had unlocked and prepared the house for me, and I went inside to open the windows, settle in, and see what messages were on the answering machine.

The first was from Nina Baum, calling late last night from California. Chapman had phoned to tell her about the incident in the garage, and she was checking on me as well as urging me to get on a plane and come out to Malibu until the investigation was over. Nina, by luck of the draw, had been my college roommate during freshman year at Wellesley. She remained my closest friend, and she and her husband were often my refuge when I wanted to hang out away from the problems that my job presented.

The message I'd been waiting for was next, the voice of Jacob Tyler calling from an airport phone booth. "It's Jake here. Can't find you anywhere—all I get are machines. It's Friday morning and I'm on my way to the Vineyard, if that's still the plan. I've gone from China to California, then an overnight in Chicago. I'm due into Boston before noon. And if there's no fog, should be on a Cape Air hop that gets me there at one thirty. I'll try your office in a bit. If you're not at the airport, I'll just take a cab up to the house. Miss you."

I took the portable out onto the deck and dialed Laura's number.

"Alex? Are you okay? Mercer left a message on my voice mail telling me not to expect you today. Is everything all right?"

"It's fine. I'm just whipped. We worked late last night, so I'm taking a long weekend. If people are looking for me, you can reach me on the Vineyard. Anything interesting yet?"

"Jacob Tyler called first thing. He didn't leave a message, 'cause I couldn't tell him what your plans were. And Robert Scott, from University of Virginia Law School. Wants to know if you can do a lecture about public service this fall."

"I'll take care of Tyler. Would you call Bob Scott back and tell him I'd be glad to, if he can suggest some dates?" Maybe I would tell the students about last night's encounter. What the D.A.'s Office lacks in financial rewards, it makes up for in drama and intrigue.

I changed into shorts and a T-shirt, set the dining room table for two, went out to the barn to get birdseed to fill the feeders, and sat back down on the deck to read the *New York Times* and the *Vineyard Gazette*. The osprey nest at the foot of my hilltop, on the side of Nashaquitsa Pond, had a nestful of babies, being hovered over by their mother. Goldfinches and cardinals fought for the seed I had just put out, and my wildflower field teemed with the pink, lavender, and white heads of cosmos and the cobalt blue of Oriental poppies.

This was the place that I considered my home. Professionally, I thrived and flourished in the fast-paced life I led in New York City. Most of my friends were there, and I had been born and raised in a suburban village in nearby Westchester County, so my parents and brothers were frequently in and out of town. But this island, especially the quiet rural end on which my house was sited, was where I came to relax and to restore the tranquillity that eluded me in the midst of an intense investigation.

Most of my life had been a charmed one. I was one of three children—the only daughter—of loving parents whose marriage was still not only a sound one, but a great romance as well. The trust fund endowed by my father's invention, the Cooper-Hoffman valve, had been used to give me a first-class education, first at Wellesley and then at the University of Virginia School of Law. It permitted me to indulge my dream of working in the public sector without the enormous burden of student loans that forced so many of my colleagues to leave the prosecutor's office for more lucrative careers. And for frivolous interests like travel and my collections of first-edition books and antique jewelry, it was a route to some indulgences that I would never otherwise have been able to afford at this stage in life.

While the Vineyard had offered me some of the most spectacular days of my life, it also held for me my most difficult memories. Adam Nyman, the physician I had fallen madly in love with while I was at law school, had summered here all of his life. When we became engaged the year that I graduated, we bought this house together. It had belonged to the widow of a fisherman whose family was one of the original group of settlers in the seventeenth century. I had delighted in having it redecorated in celebration of our wedding. A local artist had stenciled the walls in pastel designs she had copied from a set of antique hand-painted Limoges plates my mother had given us as an engagement gift. The evocative landscapes by island artists that Adam had collected over the years had been reframed and hung throughout the cheerful rooms.

Our families and friends had been assembled in the homes of friends and country inns around the island for the wedding weekend. The house and its gardens had never looked more beautiful than during that lush summer after an unusually rainy spring.

And then came the morning phone call that ripped my

spirit and heart to pieces. Adam had completed his last rounds in Charlottesville and had set off late in the day to drive all night for the trip to the island. It was my mother who took the call from the state police, and it was she and Nina who sat me down on my bed to tell me that Adam's car had been knocked off a bridge in Connecticut by another driver and demolished on the rocks in the river below.

Everything sealed up inside me for years, or so it seemed at the time. I had been afraid to let myself get close to anyone else for fear that something I loved would be seized from me when I was happiest. I went aimlessly from room to room in the house on those rare weekends I could bring myself to come up here, imagining how Adam would have adored what I had turned it into for us.

The ten years that had passed did nothing to lessen the pain of his loss or to make less vivid the depth of our passion for each other. But I had learned to love again, without ever forgetting that I would have sacrificed all the other pleasures and triumphs of my life to have had this time with him.

I had made changes in the house, too. Something had nagged at me to create a different feel, a sense of another phase of my relationships. So the previous winter I added an addition with a larger living room, a huge slate-trimmed hearth, and tall windows open to the handsome sweep of sea and sky. And with Nina's urging, for her upcoming Labor Day weekend visit, I had the architect build a new bathroom, decadently luxurious, with a steam shower and whirlpool tub. Slowly it had become possible for me to be here without any longer feeling that I was betraying Adam's love for me.

Now I found myself looking at my watch every ten minutes, filled with anticipation about the arrival of Jacob Tyler, with whom I had serendipitously become entangled in early July. Less than two months later, I sat here daydreaming about seeing him again this afternoon, excited by the pleasure he gave me, emotionally and physically, and still palpitating from the newness of the romance.

I read the papers, knocked off the Friday crossword puzzle, and called the office to make sure everything was still quiet. I wasn't a cook, but there was an easy trick to serve an elegant Vineyard dinner with no effort at all, and I set about making it happen before Jake arrived. A phone call to the fish market to order a late-afternoon pickup, a stop at the Chilmark store for island corn and tomatoes—at the peak of perfection at this point in the summer—and I was off for the twenty-minute ride to the airport to meet Jake's plane.

Cape Air's one o'clock from Boston was the only flight due in when I arrived. As usual, not many people were leaving the island on a Friday in summer, and several locals waited with me for the nine-seater to come into range. The tiny plane first appeared as a small dot in the cloudless blue sky, and circled out over the south shore before coming in for a landing. I could see the crown of Jake's thick brown hair emerge from the door first as he bent down to get out onto the steps that the pilot had lowered. He picked up his head to look for me behind the arrival gate and broke into a wide smile when he saw me standing on a bench against the chain-link fence, waving at him with both arms. His suit jacket was slung over his shoulder and hooked by the finger of his left hand, and he blew a kiss to me with his right hand when he touched ground.

When he reached where I stood in the waiting area, next to the luggage rack, he dropped his briefcase, took me by my shoulders as he said, "Hello, angel," and kissed me for what seemed like three minutes. My head nestled in the crook of his elbow, and I closed my eyes and stood still to savor the feeling of his embrace.

"Got room in that little car for a duffel full of dirty clothes? It's hard to travel light for ten days in China." Jake had covered the presidential summit in Beijing for NBC and had been traveling for almost two weeks on his way there and back. We had spent a weekend on the Vineyard before he took off, and our communications had been frustratingly erratic since then, between time differences and our unpredictable schedules.

"I'm thinking of giving up prosecution and taking in laundry. I'd be delighted to start with yours, Mr. Tyler."

"Bad week? I couldn't seem to catch you anywhere, no matter when I called."

The suitcases were off-loaded to the luggage rack, and Jake lifted his bag out so we could walk to the car. I carried his jacket and briefcase under one arm, taking hold of his left hand with my right. "You'll get a full report this evening. I've been ordered to take today off, so if you don't talk to me about the gross national product or global warming or the Japanese commodities market, I won't bore you with the twists and turns in my murder case."

"There's nothing boring about it. What's been happening?" he asked, as I opened the trunk to put the bag inside.

I put my index finger up to my lips, whispered "*Ssssss-sssssssshhh,*" and slipped behind the wheel of the Miata. "I'm taking you for a ride. Just relax and enjoy the scenery."

We left the airport and started up-island. After about a ten-minute ride on the South Road, I turned the car off onto a wide-mouthed dirt drive, unmarked and unpaved and full of rutted holes that threatened to devour the small car.

"Am I being kidnapped?" Jake asked, tousling my hair. "Nobody at the network will ransom me, you know. Take me away now and you'll be stuck with me forever."

The brush was thick on both sides of the way, and we bounced along the winding path for more than a mile until we came to a fence attached to two wooden posts, which seemed to be standing on guard in the middle of nowhere. I took a key from the glove compartment, got out of the car to unlock the gate, drove through, and locked it again behind us.

"Where the hell are you taking me?" he asked with a laugh. "I'm exhausted. Quite frankly, I was hoping for a long, hot shower in your fancy new digs, and then—well, something in the way of a warm welcome stateside."

"I promise you'll feel like a new man after this. You've got to trust me."

After a few more seconds I went around a bend, and ahead of us we saw the flat stretch of the dusty long green grass of the wetlands, and a pond populated only by a handful of swans. Beyond that were the rolling dunes of South Beach, merging into the wide-open expanse of the Atlantic Ocean.

There were a couple of other cars parked at the entrance to Black Point Beach, on one of the most exquisite summer days. "What's with the gate and key? Where is everybody?"

There are only two states in the country, Maine and Massachusetts, in which you can own beachfront property to the mean low-water mark. As a result, the Vineyard was dotted by vast lengths of ocean beaches that were privately held and not accessible to the general public. This was one of them—more than a mile in length—and I had bought a piece of it when I purchased the house, more than a decade ago.

"Better than a shower. Let's go for a swim."

I parked the car, grabbed two towels from my tote, and ran to the footpath that led over the dunes, kicking off my moccasins and telling Jake to do the same with his loafers. We reached the peak together and stood looking out at the wide belt of white sand and the white-capped blue water that seemed to go on forever.

"Great, Alex. You think I didn't see enough of the Pacific, that I needed this today?"

"Don't be such a grouch. Get those rags off you—c'mon, hurry up."

"There are people—"

I lifted my sunglasses and peered down the beach. "It looks like there are maybe four stick figures between here and Edgartown," I said, turning to Jake and unbuttoning the business shirt that he had worn on the plane, while he stood with his hands on his hips. I reached for his waistband, drew off his belt, and unzipped his pants.

"Well, I guess if they won't recognize that you're the sex crimes prosecutor from the big city, they won't have a clue that the tired, naked guy you're molesting is a newscaster." Jake finished taking off his clothes while I lifted my T-shirt over my head and dropped my shorts on the sand. I ran down to the water's edge, hesitated for a moment as the cold surf dashed against my feet, then dove into the sixty-eight-degree water and started swimming straight out, away from shore.

By the time I picked my head up and turned back to look for Jake, he had overtaken me with a strong crawl stroke.

"Isn't this glorious?" I asked. I swam to him, wrapped my arms around his neck, and we played our mouths against each other as we bobbed in the endless roll of waves.

"I feel like I'm about fifteen years old—and I like it."

There was nothing quite like the sensation of the brisk salty water against bare skin. Swimming naked in the ocean ranks among the world's best pastimes. I set myself a course parallel to the beach and swam back and forth until I had done almost fifty laps. The undertow was getting more fierce as the tide started going out, so I reluctantly dove under a big breaker and went up on the sand to join Jake, who thought the water was too cold for a long swim.

"I'm exhausted just watching you."

"Harrison High School swim team. Hundred-meter crawl and anchor of the relay. Don't ever try to get away from me by taking a water route." I stood behind him, steadying myself on his shoulder as I put my shorts back on.

"I'm not going anywhere anytime soon," he said, grabbing my knee and kissing the still-damp back of my calf. He pulled on his trousers and we walked slowly over to the car, arms entangled, drying in the breeze as the early afternoon wind shifted and kicked up a bit.

Once on the main road again, I was conscious of driving too fast and tried to slow myself down. The outdoor shower was behind the house, its oversized head curtained only by a couple of old lilac bushes. I soaped up and washed off all the sand before going into my bedroom through the sliding door off the rear deck.

Jake did the same, following me in and pulling me toward him, onto the pale blue cotton sheets that covered the bed. "If dreaming counts, then I've made love to you over and over again all these last two weeks—in hotel rooms, on airplanes, every time I closed my eyes."

"It doesn't count at all," I said teasingly. "I didn't feel a thing." I reached an arm across his chest and he raised my face to his, his tongue reaching in to taste mine. He ran his hands up and down the length of my thighs as I wrapped my leg inside his. We kissed and rolled and laughed and touched for as long as we could both stand to, and then Jake entered me and told me that he loved me.

For the next hour we rested on the cool sheets while I explored the surfaces of his body, which seemed so pale next to my own.

"Aren't you going to answer your phone?" he asked me when it rang.

"Let the machine get it."

"Coop? It's me. Are you okay? Nothing urgent, but I wanted to make sure you got up there without any trouble. I started beeping you an hour ago but—"

It was Chapman's voice speaking into the recorder, so I

grabbed the receiver from beside the bed. "Hi, Mike. Sorry. Yeah, I'm fine." For some reason that I didn't understand, it made me feel uneasy to be lying in bed with Jake while I was talking to Mike, with whom I had had such a close and complicated relationship for so long.

"For chrissakes, why didn't you call us back? Me and Mercer have been worried about you after last night. Whaddaya trying to scare us for?"

I glanced over at Jake. I hadn't yet told him the story about the week's events. "I apologize. Actually, I never even heard the beep. I stopped off at the beach for a swim and left the beeper in the car. My fault—I won't do it again."

"Don't tell me, Coop. Your new man's into that *From Here to Eternity* crap. Burt Lancaster and Deborah Kerr on the beach, waves washing up over them as they make love on the shore. That it? Too much sand in the crotch for me, kid. I'd rather—"

"Grow up," I snapped into the phone as I slammed it down on the table.

"Friend of yours?" Jake asked jokingly.

"A very good one, actually. One of the detectives on the Denise Caxton case."

"Remind me not to cross you. Why did you hang up on him?"

"Some other time," I said, leaning back and caressing Jake as I did.

"Have you made a reservation for dinner? I'd love to grab a nap before we go out."

"Even better. I thought you might enjoy a good home-cooked meal."

Jake looked over at me and raised an eyebrow. "Now I'm really confused. What time zone am I in? Who *are* you?"

"While you're resting I'm going to sneak out for half an

hour, and by about eight thirty tonight we'll have a candlelit dinner for two." I wasn't proud of the fact that I couldn't cook, but it was the truth.

"A little more exercise, and then you might lose me for a few hours," Jake said, pulling me over on top of him and starting to arouse me again. "Put every one of those bad guys out of your mind, Alexandra Cooper. This weekend you're all mine."

When I finally rested in his arms, half an hour later, we both fell sound asleep. Shortly before six o'clock I showered and dressed and headed down the road. In the little village of Menemsha, less than ten minutes away, I could forage for an entire gourmet meal with no more effort than a few phone calls and a quick ride.

My first stop was the Bite, where I picked up a steaming quart of clam chowder and a side order of the world's best fried clams. True to form, the Flynn sisters had the most-up-to-the-moment island gossip. "Heard you got a real looker with you for the weekend. Is it really that guy on the evening news?" Karen asked.

"He hasn't even been out of my house yet. Who's spreading this one?"

She pointed at her sister. "Jackie's best friend works at the Cape Air counter. She called as soon as you picked him up. Bringing him for lunch tomorrow?"

"What, and lose him to one of you two? See you."

A quarter of a mile farther, I pulled into the narrow space beside Larsen's Fish Market. One of the best services on the island was provided by Betsy and Chris. You could call in the morning, place an order for lobsters, and pick them up at the appointed hour—all cooked, split, and cracked—ready to serve and eat. I could place them in the oven to keep warm, and then serve up the two-pounders anytime I wanted. I went next door, to Poole's, for a few fresh oysters from Tisbury

Great Pond. Last stop was the Homeport Restaurant, right on the edge of the harbor, where I stopped at the back door and bought a Key lime pie from Will for dessert.

When I returned home, I shucked the corn and put the water up to boil, poured the chowder into a pot to reheat it later on, and tucked the pie into the refrigerator to keep it chilled.

It was almost eight o'clock when Jake woke up, shaved and showered, and dressed for dinner. The red ball of the sun was setting off to the west as we sat on the deck and sipped our drinks. I listened to the details of the China trip and Jake's descriptions of the meetings he'd had, the personalities he had met, and the opinions he had formed during his travels. For me it was fascinating to get inside a world so foreign to my own, and to contrast the problems of the witnesses' lives in a single criminal case to the global problems he studied every day.

I disappeared into the kitchen to stir the pot, lit the candles in the dining room, and opened a bottle of '91 Puligny-Montrachet. "Why don't you come in and sit down?" I asked, dishing up the thick chowder and carrying it to the table.

With Smokey Robinson singing in the background, we feasted on the delicacies of a Chilmark summer, talking and laughing as we devoured the food. As best as I could I tried to explain the events of the week since Deni Caxton's death, walking Jake through the steps of the investigation to date. "No more of this tonight or you'll have bad dreams," I said, pouring decaf with a serving of the pie.

"Have you made any plans? Outing us to any of your pals this weekend?"

"Everyone, Jake. It's August on the Vineyard—I don't have much choice, do I?" The usually tranquil island more than quadrupled in population with summer people, and it was an opportunity for me to be with friends from all over the country—some of whom I rarely saw all winter—when I came for a weekend or vacation.

"What's the drill?"

"We're teeing off with Janice and Richard at Farm Neck, eight A.M. Louise Liberman and Maureen White are giving a cocktail party in the evening, and we're invited to stay on for dinner." It had amazed me, when Jake and I first met, to discover how many people we knew in common. Those with whom I had social relationships of long standing, he had gotten to know through his position in the media. Somehow it made us seem even more connected than the short months we had known each other would indicate. I looked forward to letting everyone see how happy I was to be with him.

"Will the president and Mrs. Clinton be there tomorrow night?"

"Not sure, but I know they're invited. I hope so."

"Let's clean up this mess and go to sleep."

I held his face and kissed him on the forehead. "Go inside. This is the part I do really efficiently. I'll join you in ten minutes."

By the time I cleared the table, loaded the dishwasher, and straightened up the kitchen, Jake was spread-eagled, face down on the bed. I folded my clothes and placed them in my armoire, slipping in beside him and raising the comforter over us against the soft night wind that always makes my hilltop such an easy place for sleeping. I don't remember any tossing and turning after my head came to rest on the pillow.

I was startled by the sharp ring of the telephone. Light was just appearing on the horizon as I picked it up and spoke softly into it. It could not have been much later than 6 A.M. "Hello?" I asked somewhat disoriented, perhaps by the hour, perhaps because of too much wine with my dinner.

"Alex, it's Mercer. The lieutenant insisted on me calling you. Said you raised a stink last time you read it in the newspaper without a heads-up from us."

"Don't worry, he's right. What is it?" I sat up as Jake raised his head and rested it on his elbow, massaging his eyelids with his thumb and middle finger.

"West Side—Eighty-sixth Street. Our man just hit again early this morning, about an hour after midnight. Got a twenty-year-old kid going into her building. Raped her, beat her up pretty bad when she tried to resist. I hate to do this, but can you come on back into town?"

19

I got out of bed, made the coffee, dressed in jeans and a blazer, and sat on the deck while Jake unpacked his golf clothes from his duffel and got ready to leave the house.

"You sure you don't want me to go back with you?"

"Of course not. It's a sin to leave anything as beautiful as all this unless you have to. You've got a lot of friends on the Vineyard," I said, "and tonight, when I finally crawl into my bed at home, it will give me enormous pleasure to close my eyes and think of you being right here, wrapped in my sheets and looking out at this view.

"I'm the one who feels guilty, promising you a weekend together and then flying off-island to go to work." I was worried that the unpredictability of my job and its all-consuming nature when I was working a big case or a complex trial would put Jacob Tyler off, as it had done other men.

"Hey, if a guy with *my* schedule and lifestyle can't relate to this, then you'd have something to worry about."

The airport was on the way to the golf course, so he dropped me at the terminal, kissed me good-bye, and I promised to be careful and stay in touch. There was no direct service to New York on Saturday morning, so I took the next Cape Air flight to Boston and called the Special Victims office to tell Mercer that I'd be on the ten-thirty shuttle.

With runway delays and air traffic, it was after eleven thirty when I got through the gate at the Marine Air Terminal.

"Sorry, Alex. Sounds like you were planning a nice couple of days. Hate like hell to pull you away from it."

"You know that's never a problem. How's she doing?"

"She'll be okay. She's got a lot of guts. Tried her damndest to fight him off. She saw the gun but didn't think it was real, so—"

"That's some chance to take," I said.

"You're not kidding. She grew up in Florida, around handguns. So she felt pretty comfortable with her guess. Maybe she was right. The guy stuck it back in his waistband and started to pummel her with his fists."

"Completed rape?"

"Legally, yes. He penetrated but he didn't ejaculate. So there'll be no DNA on this one."

The elements of the crime required penetration of the victim's vagina, however slight, for the charge to be rape. Most victims had no reason to be aware of this technicality, so many would tell us that the assailant "tried" to rape them but hadn't completed the assault. In fact, the insertion of the defendant's penis, whether or not he completed an act of intercourse, was all that was needed, by law, to accomplish the act.

"Where are we going?"

"She's down at headquarters now, working on a sketch. The lieutenant figured you'd want to get as detailed an interview as soon as possible, so that's where we'll do it."

"What time did she leave the hospital?"

"I got called at home and went over to Roosevelt Hospital at three. Treated and released. Had a head-to-toe exam, and one of the advocates stayed with her the whole time." The Rape Crisis Intervention Program run by the hospital was one of the best in the city. Like most others, it was underfunded and staffed by volunteers, but the quality of the care and service was superb.

"I took her home so she could clean up and rest for a while, then picked her up at nine this morning to take her to One Police Plaza."

The NYPD had a unit of detectives whose specialty was the artistic re-creation of likenesses of defendants, the police sketches that were made into Wanted posters and distributed throughout the neighborhood at risk or the city at large. Some preferred to work freehand, and others used computer-generated programs that assigned a particular feature from a description provided by a witness or victim. Every nuance, each subtle distinction, led to a thickening of facial hair or a change in shape of an eyelid. The results in many cases eventually proved to be almost photographic reproductions of the attacker's face.

In this instance, with a serial rapist, the artists had already produced several composites. And although each one resembled the others, there were variations that were reflective of the circumstances under which each woman saw the man who committed the crime. This witness would add her own detail to the pictures that had already been circulated.

"You think it's too much for her if I go back over everything with her today? Can she handle it now?" I asked Mercer, trusting his judgment and knowing the sensitivity that he brought to this work.

"I didn't push her. Thought if you and I did the questioning together at once, we'd get whatever we need, and she'd have to explain it all one less time. She's game, Alex. Determined to get this guy and put him behind bars forever." He had pulled away from the curb and we were headed for the Brooklyn-Queens Expressway and the bridge to Manhattan. "I promised her I'd find him and that you'd make sure he never sees daylight again. She's really eager to talk to you."

So much had changed in this business, just in my professional lifetime. Women, who had traditionally been reluctant to report cases of sexual violence, were now far more likely to come forward, as society lifted the age-old stigma on victims who cried rape, and began placing the blame where it belonged: on the offender. Still, those who were attacked by strangers and not acquaintances were believed more readily and were far more likely to be victorious in the courtroom. Paul Battaglia, who was passionate about this issue, had devoted resources to prosecuting these cases that no other office in the country could match. Whether the assailant was a date, a relative, a spouse, or a professional colleague of the victim, we had a mandate to vigorously investigate and take to trial the case of any credible witness who deserved her day in court.

"Guess you didn't get much rest last night," I said. Mercer looked exhausted. He had worked all week on the Caxton case, which relieved him of other duties at the Special Victims Squad. So he had not caught new cases, but he was still the one they beeped when the West Side rapist struck. He had been assigned to that task force from the outset, and the lieutenant counted on his skill in relating to victims, as well as his ability to remember the similarity in modus operandi—language, actions, order of the sexual acts—that would help coordinate all the cases in the pattern.

He laughed. "First night in weeks I had some companionship in the form of a warm body, other than Chapman. I don't think I'd been home an hour when I got the call." He took his eye off the road for a moment to look over at me. "This job can't do much for your love life either, can it?"

"I'm in no position to complain after you gave me the day off yesterday." I spent the rest of the ride telling Mercer about my evening with Jake and how relaxing a single day away from the city had been.

"Did anything important develop on Caxton?" I asked, as we parked behind headquarters and walked up the long sets of steps from Park Row to the front of the building.

"Bits and pieces. The manufacturer of the ladder found the lot number of the one that was attached to the deceased. Sold last spring to a hardware store on lower Broadway. We got them checking receipts now. Not going to be any kind of surprise if it came from her own gallery. Wouldn't have been unusual for Omar to have one accessible to him. You'd need to use them to install all the art and exhibits.

"And we located Preston Mattox, the architect boyfriend of Deni's. He was abroad on business all week. Gets back here today. Said he'd give me a call so we could speak to him about her this weekend."

"What did Crime Scene come up with on Varelli?"

"The studio was clean as a whistle. Someone got in and out without leaving a print, or else they polished the place up before they left. Nothing appeared to be disturbed. Only thing that looked out of place was a pair of sunglasses."

"Prescription?" I asked optimistically.

"Not so lucky. Could belong to anybody, but they're just a bit too mod for the old man. And there is a young apprentice who worked for Varelli. He's been home in California all month, visiting his family. He wasn't due back here until after Labor Day. But he's apparently distraught, so he's coming in tonight to see the widow. We can interview him on Monday.

"Also, Caxton's lawyer came up with more of the letters that Denise had received from her blackmailer. Mike didn't see any point in taking them to the lab for fingerprints. They'd already been handled by too many people for us to get anything off them. He copied them for the case folder. Said he'd take a set home to read this weekend."

We had gone through the security checkpoint and were in the elevator heading upstairs to the artists' unit.

Josie Malendez was sitting with two plainclothes detectives, eating a roast beef sandwich and drinking a can of soda. She smiled as she saw Mercer enter the room, and I struggled to show no reaction as I looked at the large purple bruise that had swelled and caused the closing of her left eye. She squinted at me from the good one and held out a hand. "You must be Alex Cooper."

Mercer and I let her finish her lunch. We examined the sketch that resulted from her session with the detectives. "She gives him a rounder face than the last two. Thinner mustache, same eyes, same nose. And she's adamant about the lisp. Slight, but it's there. She's the first one to mention anything significant about his speech."

"She's the first one to engage him in as much conversation, trying to talk him down, talk him out of it, isn't she?" I asked, relying on Mercer's knowledge of the details. "And she was stone sober—unlike the last two—which makes me want to trust her observations even more. They giving this one to the press?"

"Yeah. The commissioner and the mayor want it for the six o'clock news. Any objections?"

"Nope. Ask them to use the same quote from Battaglia's

comment, the one he gave last time the guy struck. It got lost in the coverage of the bomb scare story that broke the same night."

We knew that for a rapist to be operating in the same geographic area for more than two years, it had to be, for him, a comfort zone. Clearly he was someone who lived or worked in the neighborhood and could move about it easily without seeming to be suspicious. If the police and scientific techniques did not break the case, our best hope was that a neighbor or coworker would notice a resemblance to the sketch and call the hot line with a tip. The most difficult thing to overcome was the stereotypical reaction of most of the public— that the guy who lives next door couldn't possibly be a rapist.

When it appeared that Josie had finished eating and had a few minutes to rest quietly, I went over to sit with her and began to talk, to explain the process. The detectives who had worked with her on the drawing excused themselves, and Mercer replaced them at the table, ready to take notes of our conversation.

Our questions had to be more specific than those that had yet been asked. While the physician who had conducted the physical needed answers to what kind of contact had occurred and what Josie had experienced at her attacker's hands, and the uniformed cop who responded to her home had asked for the broad outlines of the criminal event, Mercer and I began our probe in microscopic detail. Things that frequently seemed insignificant to the victim were crucial to our ability to put the puzzle together, and often to link one case to another. I always started the process by explaining to the witness why such seemingly irrelevant minutiae could be useful to us.

And so we went on, asking Josie to explain her whereabouts all throughout the previous afternoon and early evening. While her actions may have had nothing to do with what happened on her front doorstep, we could not eliminate the possibility that she and her assailant had crossed paths earlier that night, or that he had followed her from one location to another.

The original police report, as in most cases, had summed up Josie's assault in a single sentence: "At the time and place of occurrence, the defendant displayed a pistol, beat the complaining witness about the face with his fists, causing physical injury, and thereby forcibly engaged her in an act of sexual intercourse."

Almost four hours after we began to talk with our victim, Mercer and I were ready to wrap up the interview. We knew exactly how the rapist's approach had been made, where Josie was in regard to him when she was first aware of his presence, the precise language he had used when he accosted her in the vestibule of the building, and how she had responded to him. We knew in which hand he had held the weapon, and what about its design and appearance had allowed her to assume that it was an imitation.

The process was inordinately draining on the witness, and we were keenly aware of that.

"Can you think of anything else that we *haven't* asked you that you think we should know?"

"Not a thing." Josie's fatigue was obvious.

"Are you going home tonight?" I asked. It was almost six o'clock.

"No, no. I'm not ready to go back there alone. My sister lives in Brooklyn Heights. I'm going to spend some time with her till I figure out what I want to do."

"That's smart. I'm sure the counselor at the hospital told you, but these first few nights are going to be hard."

"I know. The doctor gave me something to help me sleep."

"Yeah, but even sleeping doesn't always provide an escape. You may have dreams—nightmares, actually—and flashbacks.

You'll see people on the streets who will remind you physically of your attacker, and you may have a visceral reaction—tremble, recoil, cry. All of these things are normal in light of your experience. And believe it or not, time will truly make it better."

"And finding this son of a bitch will be the best of all," Mercer assured her.

One of the detectives who had done the sketch was driving home to Bay Ridge and said he would deliver Josie to her sister's apartment. I walked with her to the restrooms down the quiet hallway, and waited while she went inside. In a few minutes, from where I stood, I could hear her sobs coming from within. I opened the door and found the young woman leaning against the sink, running a finger over the discolored portion of her thin face as she stared at her almost unrecognizable image in the mirror.

I walked to her side and placed my arm around her shoulder. She turned and pressed the unharmed side of her face against me, her chest heaving as she tried to speak but couldn't catch her breath to do so.

"Don't try to talk. Let it go, Josie."

Her body became deadweight in my arms as she cried for several minutes. She pulled away from me and washed her face again in the sink. "Whew. I hadn't shed a tear until now. I was so intent on following everyone's directions and being cooperative, but there's nothing left in me to give. It's like he took everything away from me."

"You're alive, Josie, and that's the most important thing. Whatever you did last night was the right thing, because you walked away from him in one piece. You'll triumph in the end. The hard part is catching him—that's Mercer's job. Convicting him, with a witness like you, won't be difficult at all. We won't let you down—I can promise you that."

I led her back to the detectives' office. Mercer told Josie

that he'd be in touch with her on Monday to set up an appointment to look through mug shots of sex offenders, and we said good-bye to her.

"We've got to figure out what to do about *you* for the rest of the weekend. Battaglia thinks you're safely tucked away in the country."

"Drive me home and I swear to you I'll stay at the apartment all day tomorrow. Sleep in, read books, watch old movies. Nobody knows I'm in town. It'll be heaven."

Mercer called his office to see if there were any messages, but there were none. Then he checked the Homicide Squad to see if any of the witnesses expected in town had phoned to leave word for Mike Chapman.

The civilian worker who answered the phones at Manhattan North said there were two calls during the afternoon. Mercer listened to her relay the messages and asked her to let the lieutenant know he was on top of both situations. Then he repeated the news to me. "Preston Mattox is available to come into the office on Monday afternoon to meet with Mike and me.

"And Marina Sette called. Didn't leave a number, because she said she'd had to check out of her hotel after receiving some threatening phone calls. She didn't know how to get in touch with A.D.A. Cooper, so she asked if Mike or I could meet her tomorrow morning."

"Where? In your office?"

He looked down at the notes he had scribbled in his pad. "Said she's staying with an artist she knows in Chelsea. There's an exhibit being set up for an opening later this week in a brand-new gallery called Focus. It's in a renovated warehouse on Twenty-first Street, a block away from Deni's place. She'll be waiting in the office at the back of the exhibit, Sunday morning at nine. And she wants me or Mike—whoever keeps the meet—to bring you along."

"Why me?" I didn't mean it seriously. But my visions of languishing in bed with the Sunday *Times* crossword puzzle were dissipating quickly.

Mercer looked up from his pad. "Ms. Sette says you're the only one she's comfortable talking to, the only one she trusts. Says she's come up with information about Denise Caxton's murder that she thinks you'd really like to hear."

20

I called the Four Seasons Hotel and the front desk confirmed that Marilyn Seven had checked out first thing this morning.

"You want me to invite Chapman to go with us tomorrow?" Mercer asked.

"Let him take his mother to Mass. I think we got on each other's nerves yesterday. If you don't mind doing this without him, I'm game."

"Why the mystery from Ms. Sette, do you think?"

"I don't know. She was very secretive about Lowell Caxton not knowing she was in town. He had no trouble guessing correctly that she was the source of some of our information. Anyway, she seemed to like creating a little suspense. Told me she used to be an actress, and I think she still has a flair for the dramatic. Hey, a little culture on a Sunday morning can't be too bad for either of us."

"On one condition. You let me sleep on the couch in your den tonight—consider it that you're saving me a long ride home, not that I'm baby-sitting. It'll make Battaglia and the lieutenant happy, and give us a jump start in the morning."

"You're in charge, Detective Wallace. Do I get dinner before you lock me in for the night?"

"Seems to me I haven't had Chinese food in weeks. I could go for some Peking duck at Shun Lee Palace. How about you?"

"My mouth is watering. Give me a few minutes, I've got to make a call." I dialed my house on the Vineyard and Jake answered on the first ring. "How's the sunset tonight?"

"I'm sitting on the deck with my drink, ready to drive to Louise's for cocktails and dinner. How's your day been?"

"Long. We're just about to leave headquarters now. Mercer and I are going to have dinner together, and he's going to spend the night at the apartment. We've got a date in the morning with a skittish witness on the homicide."

"I'm glad he's going to stay with you. It's smart, till somebody knows what's going on. Tell him I'm insanely jealous, will you? I'll call you when I get home tonight."

"Give my love to everyone."

Mercer and I drove uptown and spent a quiet evening enjoying a good meal and the ambiance of the handsome dining room. We parked in the driveway in front of my building and Mercer left his police plate in the windshield so the car would not be disturbed overnight. We went upstairs and settled in, flipping channels on the television looking for something to watch and settling on CNN, until Jake called to give me a rundown on the party. I watched a bit more TV until I got drowsy enough to say good night and go inside.

When I awakened, shortly after seven, Mercer had already

brought the newspaper inside and brewed a pot of coffee. "Slim pickings," he said to me as he surveyed the near-empty shelves of the refrigerator.

"Check the freezer. I've always got a package of English muffins in there."

While I showered, he nuked the muffins and put them in the toaster. We sat at the dining room table like a married couple, each coming out of the night's slumber at our own speed, buried in our favorite piece of the Sunday news. Mercer had his head completely immersed in the Sports section. I skimmed the book review, reading the "Crime" column to scout for new mystery writers, and checked the best-seller lists.

"You're not drinking your coffee," I said.

"I hate this flavored stuff. It's really a girl thing."

"It's Colombian cinnamon. I think it's delicious." I picked up the Arts and Leisure section and riffled through to find the write-ups on galleries and exhibits. "Here's a piece about Focus—the place we're going to this morning."

"What does it say?" Mercer was dumping the dregs of his cup into the sink and looking in my kitchen cabinets for a different coffee blend. "Mind if I make another pot of dark French roast?"

"Go ahead. Focus is described as a 'stunning new exhibition space dedicated to long-term installations of works of art that are unlikely to be accommodated by existing museums because of their scale and substance.' Apparently, like everything else in that neighborhood, the place used to be a warehouse building. It's massive—forty-four thousand square feet."

"Is it open yet?"

"Doesn't seem to be. There's a scheduled premiere the first week of September."

"Who owns it?"

I continued to scan the article. "Doesn't mention. This is

mostly a description of what it's going to have, why it was built, how unusual it is." I paused to read on. "Hey, we're in luck. Ever hear of Richard Serra?"

Mercer shook his head in the negative.

"He's probably the greatest sculptor alive. Had a superb show at the Museum of Modern Art not too long ago. His work is set up now for the opening. Sounds extraordinary. Want me to read it to you?"

"Sure." Mercer was seated again, waiting for the new pot of coffee to be ready. He picked up the Sports section once more as I tried to describe the show at the gallery.

"It's called *Torqued Ellipses VI*. The concept grew out of Serra's fascination with ships and with steel. Are you imitating Mike Chapman, or are you going to listen to this?"

Mercer put down the paper and I showed him the photograph of the massive steel plates, more than a dozen feet high and several inches thick.

He was impressed. The pieces looked formidably strong, resembling curved hulls of three ocean liners split into a handful of pieces and laid out on the floor of the renovated space like a giant maze, covering more than eight thousand square feet.

"I thought you were talking about tiny little sculptures. These things look like the base of the *Titanic*. How does he do it?"

"The article says Serra contacted every mill in the world, until he found a machine that had been used in World War Two, at a shipyard near Baltimore called Beth Ship, that could roll and bend these huge pieces of steel plate. Each one of them weighs twenty tons."

"So I guess Ms. Sette picked a good spot to hold this conversation. She can tell us about the people running the place. Must be a friend who's letting her use it."

I went inside, ran a brush through my hair, and put on

some lipstick. I had on a linen pants suit with ballet flats, casual but professional. The morning was overcast and the air-conditioning in the car and in the gallery was likely to be cool.

It was shortly before nine when Mercer drove into the quiet street. There were no residential buildings, a scattering of still-used warehouses, and four galleries that probably wouldn't open on a summer Sunday until after one o'clock, if at all. As Mercer parked, I pointed out the Hi-Line tracks that sliced through the middle of Twenty-second Street, north to south, rife with weeds, just as they had looked when they passed through the Caxton Due gallery and ran on downtown. It still surprised me that neither one of us had ever been aware of the tracks till we saw them when we were here with Mike the week before.

The entrance to the new gallery was quite discreet, a rect-angular white sign with very small letters printed in jet black ink: *Focus.*

Mercer put his hand on the doorknob to test it, expecting to find it locked. It gave at once and opened into the dimly lit space. A young woman came forward and invited us in. "Good morning," she said. "I've been expecting you."

I recognized her immediately as the receptionist who had been at Bryan Daughtry's office on Thursday, when the three of us had gone there with the subpoenas. The face was less distinctive than the four silver studs in her right ear, the three in her left, and the small ring piercing one of her eyebrows.

I followed Mercer inside. "Is Ms. Sette here yet?" he asked.

"I'm not sure who's coming, exactly, but you're the first ones to arrive. I was told to be here to open the gallery and let the police officers in. You're welcome to look around. I'll be up front at the door if you need anything. Hope you don't get seasick," she said to me, smiling. "It's a really weird feeling inside those things."

Mercer and I stood at the prow of the first sculpture, which loomed over us like the hull of a great oil tanker. I rounded the corner and stood in the space between two ends of the first ellipse. When I looked back at Mercer, I couldn't help but laugh. It was so unusual to see any physical thing that dwarfed him so completely.

"What's it like inside?"

I stepped between the enormous curved surfaces and started to walk to the far end. It was immediately confusing and disorienting to the senses. I knew I was standing still on a flat surface, but the arrangement of the pieces made the entire thing feel out of proportion and dizzying. To my left, the structure bowed outward and was wider at the top, more than ten feet above my head. The one to my right sloped inward, and when I raised my eyes to see its top, I had a claustrophobic reaction, as though the entire steel frame might fall on me if I so much as brushed against it.

"Whoa, c'mon in, Mercer. It's almost like a brilliantly artistic fun house. I see what she was talking about—it's a very bizarre spatial illusion."

Mercer paused in the entry while I kept walking, about to exit the first ellipse and trail around its outer side to get to the second one, in which the side shapes were set up in reverse. Each of the five forms was angled in a dramatic fashion, different from the others. He caught up to me inside the third figure, bracing himself against a wall the reverse in shape from the last one, which surprised him so radically.

"Don't lean on it," I said, half jokingly. "Doesn't it seem like it would fall over and crush us instantly?"

Mercer was fascinated with the composition of the colossal steel plates, and stopped to bend and rub his hands up and down against the skin of the sculpture. "This mother isn't going anywhere, Alex. It must have been like moving a bunch of battleships to get it in here. Man's a genius."

He straightened up at a sound coming from the front of the warehouse space. "D'you hear that?"

"Sounded like the door closing. Let's go meet her." I moved to find my way out of the ellipse and toward the front of the gallery.

"Hold it. That noise *after* the door closed, that's what I'm talking about."

"I didn't hear it. I must have been speaking to you."

"Wait here, Alex. Let me see who came in."

Mercer passed by me, motioning me to stay put as he walked out of my line of sight.

I could distinguish the sound of the hard-soled bottoms of his loafers clicking on the concrete floor, moving away from me. I heard him call out "Hello," then pause and call it out again, but the words only echoed in the cavernous expanse of the room without eliciting a response.

"Oh, shit!" he exploded. "Hold still, Alex, stay there. I'm coming to get you."

I heard his first exclamation and started to run, screaming, "What?" as I did, until I heard his command for me to stop.

I was turned around inside this torqued ellipse, not certain where the front or back of the gallery would be when I emerged. I could make out the sound of what I thought was Mercer's shoes pounding toward me, and then something softer, perhaps rubber-bottomed, coming at me from another direction. There was nothing to hide behind or duck under within the shell of the sculpture, and I didn't have the least idea about whether there actually was an office in the rear of the exhibition space, and if so, whether it would be locked or open.

I was frozen in the same spot, accustomed now to the obscure lighting and the lack of contrast between the gray steel mammoths and the interior walls and ceiling. My yellow linen suit stood out against the dark colors like the bull's-eye on a target, and my head whipped back and forth, not knowing from which direction my friend would appear.

At the same moment as I saw Mercer's hand grab the end of the ellipse, I heard him yell, "Alex, DOWN! Now!" The discharge of his gun resounded like a cannon in the open space between the sculptures as he fired at someone I could not see.

I squatted on my haunches as though I were on the starting blocks of a relay, fingertips poised to lift me up and out the moment Mercer gave the next order. His single shot was met by a return salvo of two or three bullets, which pinged off the side of the steel almost even with the level of my head as I crouched and cowered.

Mercer's left hand reached around for me, and I moved to meet it. Without more than a glance, he grabbed me by the wrist and we started to jog in the direction of one of the other structures, Mercer's large frame running interference for me as we searched in vain for something that would provide a shield.

"It's your stocking-mask guy from the garage," he whispered, trying to catch his breath and check the gun that he usually kept holstered on his ankle.

"The girl?" I knew the answer before I asked the question.

"Dead." He stopped to listen for noise and heard none. "At some point I'm gonna signal you to run, and you're gonna move like a gazelle to get to that front door and call in a ten-thirteen."

Word on a police radio that an officer needed assistance was the universal beacon to summon cops to any emergency situation in which another cop's life was at risk.

"Not without—"

"That's movie bullshit, Coop. When I send you, you fly."

There was no point arguing. It was a decision I would have to make if an opportunity even presented itself to us.

Mercer stepped in front of me, practically flattening me against the side of one of the exteriors. He must have heard a sound that I had not picked up. He cocked his ear in the direction of its source and moved in a 180-degree arc as he turned to fire off another round. He swung back in front of me and waited for the return fire, ~~as~~ my sweaty palms pressed an imprint on top of the dark steel.

Now the padded footsteps had drawn closer, and I could actually hear them running across the floor on the far side of this ellipse, toward our position.

"We're moving," Mercer mouthed to me as he briefly turned his head to face mine. Again he took me by the wrist, and we dashed around into the sculpture we had stood behind, and through its far end, bullets chasing us and bouncing off the cylindrical walls as we zigged and zagged together.

I trusted that Mercer was trying to find his way to the front door. Despite the variety in shape and curve, every one of the steel walls looked identical to me. Their height and their solidity had become oppressive, and I tried to steady myself as I ran behind him, praying that he had maintained some idea of the relationship between these gigantic barriers to our freedom.

Pure silence again. Mercer bent his head to peer around the edge, then looked back at me and winked. His lips formed the word "now," and he tugged on my jacket sleeve to try to propel me out in front of him. With blind faith in his instincts, I broke into a trot and sped through the length of one more sculpture. At its far end, I thought I made out the doorway that led to the street and an escape. I looked over my shoulder to make sure that Mercer was coming along with me, and as I did I could see the expression of horror cross his face.

"Down!" he screamed at me again as he saw the gunman run into place behind my back, aiming at me from a site between me and the gallery exit.

Shots were fired from both guns, and someone shrieked in pain. I couldn't tell whose voice had cried out, but in the split second after hearing the noise, I bolted in Mercer's direction.

"Stay right here, Alex. I got him." Mercer's gun was in his

hand as he overtook me and raced toward the masked figure, who was bent over from the waist and trying to run to the door. He seemed to be dragging his left leg.

I ignored Mercer's order and chased after him as he let himself out the door. When I was within ten feet of the front wall, I could see the body of the receptionist slumped over in a leather armchair, blood oozing from her forehead a fraction of an inch away from her pierced eyebrow. I stopped in my tracks, turning to kneel and check her for a pulse.

As I dropped to my knees, Mercer was edging himself to the long metal bar that pushed out onto the street. Suddenly daylight flooded into the huge space of the gallery as the door was pulled by someone on the outside. A burst of light exploded close to where I saw Mercer standing, at about the same time as I heard the noise of the discharge. The gunman had swung the heavy entrance open from the sidewalk and let off three more shots into the gallery.

Mercer Wallace collapsed to the floor without uttering a sound.

21

I picked up Mercer's hand and spoke his name with an urgency I had never known before. His eyes opened, and he tried to talk but could not.

"Thank God," I said. "Stay with me, Mercer. I'm getting help."

The doorway gave against my push and I was on the street. Three teenage boys were Rollerblading, heading westward to the piers. I had no idea where in the gallery I had dropped my tote and the cell phone I kept inside it. "Call nine-one-one," I shouted at them. "Please call nine-one-one—tell them a cop is shot. Please!"

One of the kids held his index finger and thumb together in

an "okay" sign and skated off, I assumed, to a telephone on the corner. The other two came to the sidewalk and were only seconds behind me as I scrambled back to Mercer's side.

I sat on the floor next to his motionless body and tried to find where he was hit. His eyes flickered open and he attempted to follow the movements of my hands.

"Oh, shit," I said, both to myself and to the boys, who stood dumbfounded at my back, not knowing what to make of the dead girl and the dying cop. "Are you sure your friend's going to call nine-one-one? One of you should stand in front of this place so you can point it out when the police car comes." I was barking commands like a general. "Get out to Tenth Avenue. Flag down anyone you can find to get in here to help."

One kid took off but the other watched with fascination as I folded back the lapels of Mercer's jacket and saw the bullet hole that had torn through his clothes and perforated the left side of his chest, terribly close to his heart.

"Bad," Mercer mumbled as I held my ear over his mouth to better hear him. He opened his lips to say more. No sound came out as he turned his head away from me and his eyelids shut.

"Don't close your eyes, Mercer. Don't close your eyes, please." I could hear sirens in the distance and I kept on praying that he wouldn't lose consciousness, that I wouldn't see his eyes roll back into his head. I held one of his strong hands in my own, stroking his face and head, trying to keep him with me by talking at him ceaselessly.

"Listen to me, Mercer," I begged him. "I can hear a siren. They're on the way. We'll get you to Vinny's in three minutes. Stay with me, Mercer. You got that son of a bitch, now stay with me, please." Saint Vincent's Hospital was less than ten blocks away, with an emergency room well equipped to handle trauma like gunshot wounds.

I watched his chest move up and down, his labored breathing giving off a low, rumbling noise from his throat. "Keep looking at me, Mercer. I'm gonna be with you through everything, just give me a chance. Breathe for me." I was wiping sweat off his forehead with my fingers as it dripped down both sides of his neck and into his eyes.

The smallest blader skated back in the door. "We got a fire truck, okay?"

"That's great, that's excellent. Hear that, Mercer? We got a truck coming in." I turned back to the kid. "Tell them we need an ambulance." He was gone again.

Mercer's mouth curled up on one side, as though he was trying to smile. I pressed the palm of his hand to my lips. Again I started babbling anything I could think of to keep him alert. I talked about Mike and about food and about the department and about how he could go to my house on the Vineyard for his recovery, and as I was rambling on to the next topic, four firemen in all their gear tore into the room and surrounded us.

I got up and stepped back, telling them that Mercer was a detective and that he had been shot at close range in the chest. Before I could finish the explanation, an ambulance had pulled up next to the hook and ladder parked in front of the gallery. I got lost in the commotion as the EMS team started an IV drip in Mercer's arm and loaded him onto a stretcher. As I stood on the sidewalk, five radio cars pulled into the block from both directions, responding to the call for assistance that each cop dreads most of all, for himself and for everyone else in blue.

Now I was just a hanger-on at the fringe of the growing crowd. None of the officers who arrived knew me, and my identification and badge were somewhere in my bag on the floor of the gallery. I pushed the kids who had helped me out of the way, trying to explain to the cops who Mercer was and what had happened.

The EMS workers lifted the stretcher onto the rear of the ambulance, and as it tilted, I could see that Mercer's eyes were closed shut. "I'm going with you," I shouted over the heads of the firemen who were clustered around the wagon.

"Sorry, lady. You'll have to meet us at the hospital—Seventh Avenue and Eleventh Street." One of the men was getting into the driver's seat and the other was closing the first side of the double rear doors.

I squeezed ahead and climbed up onto the back running board. There was no point telling them I was an assistant district attorney. That fact, without any supporting identification, didn't buy me a ride on the ambulance. "I'm his wife!" I screamed at them. "I'm going with him." I ducked into the van, and the medical technician came in behind me and slammed the door.

I held Mercer's hand for the short ride, ambulance sirens blaring, as we were escorted to Saint Vincent's by three police cars leading the charge downtown.

I couldn't tell if the moisture on the crease near Mercer's left eye was perspiration or a tear, but a big drop formed and hung there until the shifting of the stretcher dislodged it as his body was removed and carried toward the entrance of the emergency room. He didn't open his eyes, not even for a moment.

22

"Stop beating yourself up over it, kid. He's a cop and you're not. Aren't we supposed to take bullets for the rest of you ungrateful assholes who delight in calling us pigs? *You* didn't shoot him. Some friggin' mutt who I should have alone in my office for maybe fifteen minutes . . ."

I had beeped Chapman even before I called the lieutenant and the district attorney. "It's my fault we kept the meet without telling you about it."

"Great, blondie. You wanted *me* pumped full of lead too, huh?" Mike had raced to the hospital, arriving within an hour of my call, and was waiting with me for word from Mercer's surgeon. He was white with fear about his friend's medical condition, and his fingers combed through his hair constantly—a sure sign of his agitation.

"What did you tell Spencer?" Mercer's father was a widower, retired from his job as a mechanic at Delta Air Lines. Mike had stopped by his home in Queens on his way to the hospital, to tell Spencer Wallace about the shooting.

"Man, that sucked. Better me than seeing some chaplain on your doorstep, like it was normal for him to drop in every week to pray for Mercer's well-being. I just didn't want his pop to hear it on the news later without some personal contact first. Might be the toughest thing I've ever done." Mike stopped pacing long enough to sit down on one of the institutional beige vinyl chairs in the waiting lounge and rest his head back against the neck cushion.

"Did he want to come here with you?" I knew Spencer had already suffered a mild stroke earlier in the year and had not yet fully recovered. But Mercer was the light of his life, and it tore me apart to think of how the impact of this event would pain him.

"Yeah, but I told him absolutely not. He just looks so weak to begin with, Alex, and I knocked whatever remained right out of his guts. His sister lives down the block, so I called her to come in to sit with him for the afternoon." Mercer had two ex-wives and no current steady. "Spencer was worried about you, too. He just looked at me and said that you and I are Mercer's family now. We're the ones to be with him today."

Mike was on his feet again, first circling the room, then walking out the doorway.

"Where are you going?"

"I got some calls to make. Sit tight."

"There's a phone right here. We can use my credit card number to get an outside line."

Mike ignored me and walked off. I understood the dynamic and knew that, as close as the three of us were, I was an outsider in these circumstances. The fraternity of police officers who put their lives on the line every day for the rest of us circles the wagons pretty tightly when one of their own is harmed. I had been there today with Mercer, but I had escaped injury. Most cops swear they would rather have given their own life than to have failed to protect a partner. I didn't carry a gun and would not have been expected to play the role that a police officer would play in this situation. But my heart was heavy with guilt knowing that I had drawn Mercer into a situation that had, perhaps, cost him his life.

"Are you Miss Cooper?"

The halls were swarming with cops—some of whom had responded to the news of a downed colleague, others of whom Mercer had worked with and had heard of the shooting through the department grapevine. The commissioner was coming back by helicopter from a weekend upstate, and the mayor was expected to arrive at the hospital within the next hour to visit Mercer's bedside.

"Yes, I am."

"Lieutenant Gibbons asked me to bring these to you. Thought you might need 'em." The young patrolman handed me a brown paper bag. Inside were my identification badge, wallet, keys, and cell phone. "Said to tell you that he had to keep the pocketbook and the rest of the contents to send over to Latent to be processed for prints."

I couldn't remember when I had dropped the bag from my shoulder, and even though I doubted the gunman had stopped to touch my belongings, I knew the routine investigation of a police officer's shooting would include the most painstaking details. This gunman would be found.

"Tell him thanks."

Chapman reentered the room. "Man, you don't want to set foot out in the lobby of this place. The hospital is crawling with reporters. Last thing they need to see is a bloodstained prosecutor, and Battaglia'll have you begging for a job with the Legal Aid Society's Baghdad branch office." I glanced down at the pale yellow suit now covered with blood from Mercer's wound.

"Maybe Mickey Diamond was right. Maybe his fictitious story saying we were close to a solution and an arrest made the killer nervous and drove him to the surface."

"Did you call the other emergency rooms?" I asked, pretty certain that the shooter had fled only because Mercer had nailed him in the thigh with at least one shot, and that the wound was serious enough to need treatment.

"That's a waste of time. He ain't walking into that kind of trap, if he's been this smart."

"Just do it. Remember the Trenta story?" I had handled a case a year before in which a burglar had surprised a woman in her apartment and, after stealing her money, demanded that she perform oral sex on him. As she kneeled on the cold linoleum floor in her kitchen and placed her mouth on the defendant's penis, she noticed that he put his knife down on the counter. So instead of acceding to his request, she bit him as hard as she could and kept biting as the defendant howled in pain.

An hour later, Harry Trenta walked into Roosevelt Hospital and asked to be treated for an injury to his private parts that occurred, he told the nurse, when he fell out of bed. She examined what she described in her notes as a "shredded penis"—a condition completely inconsistent with a fall—and contacted the local precinct to ask whether anyone had reported a recent attempt at a sexual assault.

As is often the case, we count on the stupidity of the perpetrators to make our jobs easier. In this instance, that kind of slip had not yet occurred. Mike didn't expect us to get lucky now.

"Someone else can take care of that end of it. I did check

out Santa Fe. Marina Sette got back there yesterday afternoon. The airline can probably confirm that for us. In any event, my guess is that she was airborne when that call was made to the squad asking us to come to the gallery. So either she's a part of this—phoned from the plane or had someone else place the call for her—or whoever set it up knew she was unreachable all afternoon and that's why her name was used."

In the hours since Mike had arrived at the hospital, I had also brought him up to date on the contacts Mercer had told me about yesterday. Mike had made appointments to see Preston Mattox and Varelli's apprentice, Don Cannon, on Monday, but I also knew that he would not step outside the doors of Saint Vincent's—no matter how long it took—until he could see Mercer.

Again Mike was pacing. "Your faithful pal Mickey Diamond has a new one for his Wall of Shame." The *Post* reporter papered the small pressroom in the courthouse with his front-page stories. "News radio's already calling this one 'Slaughter off Tenth Avenue.' No doubt they're gonna run that poor girl's puss all over the tabloids. What a waste of a life—she was just in the wrong place at exactly the wrong time. This guy is a monster."

Mercer had been in surgery for more than four hours at this point. Mike and I were running out of things to distract us. Every half hour brought a new wave of detectives who came by—to console, to pray, to offer blood or whatever aid was needed. The mayor and police commissioner had given their sound bites from the hospital lobby, urged all the citizens of New York to keep Mercer in their prayers, and moved on.

When two men in green scrubs that were stained like my suit entered the room smiling, Mike embraced me before they could speak. "Your partner's going to make it," one surgeon said. "We've just—"

"Well, what the hell took you so damn long to let us

know?" Chapman asked. "We'd like to be with him." He was walking to the door while the surgeon was still talking, and I knew he was fighting back tears that he didn't want me to see.

"Mr. Wallace is still in the recovery room. Give him another couple of hours there, and when he gets to intensive care, one or two of you can be with him briefly."

Mike did not turn his face to me but said that he was going down the hall to call Mercer's father and give him the good news.

"I'm Alex Cooper. I was with the detective when he was shot. What was—"

"The bullet missed his heart by less than half an inch. Lodged in a bone just above it. But there was a huge amount of internal bleeding that posed an even greater danger. I think we've got it all taken care of, but the next few hours will be rough." He looked at his watch. "It's almost four o'clock. Why don't you go out and grab some lunch? Give the nurses a little time to get your friend settled in."

"We'll be here for a while, Doctor. I think we'd like to see Mercer before we do anything else." Mike and I weren't moving until we could be with him.

I thanked them for their work and they left me alone in the small room. I lowered myself onto a chair, put my head in my hands, and thought of all the promises I had made to God in these past few hours of things I would do differently and better if only Mercer came out of this okay. Every part of me ached, and I tried to relive the day, thinking of what might have happened had the two of us not gone to the gallery. The throbbing in my head was now a constant, and when it intensified, it reminded me of the sound of the morning's gunshots. I could not even imagine the physical pain that Mercer experienced when the shot ripped through his chest.

I reached into the paper bag and removed the cell phone,

dialing Battaglia's home number. I was relieved to get the machine and not the person. I didn't need another rap on the knuckles, and I just left him the good news about Mercer and told him I'd be staying with a friend overnight.

Jake was booked on a seven-fifteen evening flight back to LaGuardia, the same reservation that I originally had. I couldn't find him on the Vineyard, so I left a message on my machine there and one at his apartment, telling him about the shooting and asking if I could stay with him for a couple of days.

Mike came back about fifteen minutes later with coffee for both of us and a deli sandwich. "Wanna split this?"

"No, thanks." My stomach was still roiling. "I need to apologize for snapping at you on the phone on Friday."

Mike's appetite was directly related to his spirit. He opened his mouth wide to get around the hero, which was stuffed with ham and provolone, lettuce, tomato, and onions. He garbled a "Never mind" through the food. "I know you're full of crap, blondie," he said when the first three mouthfuls had been thoroughly chewed. "Hey, you think I haven't been through this before? You just spent half a day praying over Mercer's soul, probably had to swear you were even gonna be tolerant of *me* in the bargain." He winked at me and shoved the sandwich back in his mouth.

"So, I spent yesterday reading Omar Sheffield's file." He was able to concentrate again. "He was really a pro at that scam. Whole bunch of complaints against him to the prison warden. Lowell Caxton may have been right. Looks like Omar hung with the jailhouse lawyers. Pulled a lot of the divorce cases directly out of the *Law Journal*. One opinion, the judge even wrote which private school the two kids attended. Omar lifts the name of the school from the judge's decision, threatening that he could have the kids picked off on the sidewalk as they came down the steps after class. Wife went nuts, blaming the husband. All along it was Omar, with the aid of the honorable jurist."

"Didn't anybody arrest him for aggravated harassment?"

"Nope. Worst I can see is that he got box time." Put in solitary confinement for twenty-three hours a day, denied use of the library and any mail service. "Added a few months against an early parole.

"But the warden told me there's an even bigger problem now, with the Freedom of Information Act. Prisoners write to agencies like the Board of Elections, and because of the law they can ask for and get the home addresses of anyone they want. One guy just used it to get the new address of the ex-girlfriend he's been stalking for six years. I'm telling you, the lunatics are really running the asylum when it comes to the criminal courts." The last sentence was muffled by the remains of the sandwich and by Mike licking the mustard off his fingers before wiping them with a napkin.

"Any record of Denise Caxton in the visitor log?"

"Not that they've found yet. But I gotta go through it myself. Maybe she didn't even use her own name. Meanwhile, you given any thought to where you're gonna be spending the next few weeks, when you're not at work?"

I nodded my head. "I'll stay at Jake Tyler's apartment. Maybe you can swing me by my place so I can pick up some clothes."

"I'll get somebody to do it. I'm not leaving here tonight."

There was no point in suggesting that Mike do otherwise. He would be at Mercer's side throughout the critical hours, no matter how long they turned out to be.

It was almost six o'clock when a nurse came to tell us that she would take us to the intensive care unit. "He's sleeping now," she said. "Doctor said you wanted to see him. Then I'll take you to a place where you can be more comfortable."

Mercer had been placed in a cubicle directly opposite the nurses' station. I could hear a gaggle of monitors beeping before we reached the entrance to his room, which was guarded by two plainclothes detectives. I stood in the doorway and looked at his long frame, which filled the hospital bed completely. There were tubes coming out of his nose and intravenous lines attached to his forearm. He didn't move or respond at all to the sound of Mike's voice saying, "Hey, buddy," as he lifted the sheet that covered Mercer's chest to expose the bandaging there and stroked him gently on the blade of his shoulder.

"That's a lot of anesthesia he's got to sleep off," the nurse said. "I'll come get you in a bit. There's a room right over here."

She led us down the hallway and we resumed our vigil with the families of several other critically ill patients. Mike couldn't stand the company and the prattle of the anxious people. "I'll be in with Mercer."

"But there's no room——"

"I'll make room. I wanna talk to him." He shot me a look that had the same effect as adding the word "alone" to his statement and walked away.

It was impossible to drag my thoughts away from the day's events. I was trying to ignore my pounding headache, and as I covered my eyes with my hands, I didn't notice the approach of the two men who planted themselves in front of me.

"Alexandra Cooper?"

I looked up as they palmed their gold shields and identified themselves. "Sean Iverson and Tom Bellman, Major Case Squad," one of them said, pointing first to himself and then to his companion. "We'd like you to come downstairs with us. Hospital director's given us a room to do interviews in. Just need to go over everything with you."

I stood up, gesturing toward the hallway. "But I'd like to be here with Mercer. We're waiting for him to——"

"We're not going very far, Alex. We'll get you right back up here when he comes around."

"Why isn't Homicide working on this?" I hadn't moved at all, and both men appeared to be annoyed. I knew I was getting paranoid, but I wanted detectives who knew me and loved Mercer to be working on this shooting.

"C'mon," Iverson said, turning his back on me. "They're not gonna give something like this to one of your pals. Chief of detectives brought us in on it." He looked over his shoulder and smiled at me. "He even mentioned that you might be difficult."

"I'd like to have Detective Chapman with me, if that's all—"

"And we'd rather *not* have him, if it's all right with you. He wasn't there, it's not his case, and we'd like to handle this our way, okay, Miss D.A.?"

Clutching my paper bag, I obediently followed the pair down the quiet hallway to the elevator bank and downstairs to a small office with a plaque on the door that read *Security*.

For almost three hours, Iverson and Bellman grilled me about everything that had gone on since my return to Manhattan from the Vineyard the previous morning. I had done this myself to thousands of witnesses in my ten years as a prosecutor, and I was as impressed as I was exacerbated by their demand for precision and detail. Over and over again they pushed me to recall every physical twist, movement, footstep, direction, and sound that had been made or taken in the gallery that morning with Mercer. I strained every one of my senses to re-create the scene exactly, certain from their implacable expressions that I was failing some kind of test that they were giving me.

When Iverson closed his notepad and stood up, I looked at each of them the way witnesses had looked at me so many times, wanting to know if the answers supplied had been good or correct. And I kept my mouth shut, knowing that neither man could give me that assurance.

"Tommy'll take you back up to intensive care, Alex. That's it for now, but later in the week we'll have to get you over to Twenty-first Street with us. Walk us through the place, okay?"

"Sure. Anything you need."

Detective Bellman and I had nothing to say to each other on the way upstairs. He escorted me around to Mercer's cubicle and shook my hand as he said good-bye. Mike had pulled a desk chair from the nurses' station into the niche next to the bed, with his back to the door. He was leaning forward, his hand on one of Mercer's, and he was speaking in a low voice. I could hear him naming friends they had worked with and knew that Mike was telling war stories and reminiscing, just chatting at his silent partner. The position of Mercer's body had not changed at all since I had first seen him several hours ago.

"Hey, Mercer," Mike said, "Coop's back." Now addressing me, "Where you been, blondie?"

I told him about the interrogation. "These dicks must've worked her over pretty good, Mercer. She looks like shit. I just wish you could open your eyes right now and take a look at her. I oughta borrow one of your intravenous tubes, man—run a little Dewar's through it and give her some juice. Who's the team?"

"Iverson and Bellman."

"Dammit, Mercer. Get your ass outta that bed. I wouldn't let those two lightweights handle a bad check. They treat you okay, Coop?"

I shook my head up and down.

At about midnight, a policewoman from the Sixth Precinct came up to the nurses' station with a few containers of hot soup for Mike and me.

I walked it back over to Mercer's room. Mike was standing now, and I could hear him saying something about an administration.

"What are you talking about now?" I asked. "Can I spell you for a while?"

"Know how they say people in a coma can hear you? Well, if that's true and he's only sleeping off some gas, I'll be getting through to him before too long. I just want mine to be the first voice he hears. Remember my dictionary? I'm going through it with him now. Used to make Mercer so mad—especially if all the other guys were laughing when I did it—he'd be ready to punch me in the face."

Chapman always joked that he was going to sell a reference book to compete with the *O.E.D.*—the *Oxford English Dictionary*. He called it the *C.P.D.*—*Chapman's Perpetrators' Dictionary*—and he thought it should be printed and issued to every rookie in the department.

He took his seat by Mercer's side. "I'm only halfway through the *A*'s. 'Administration'—that's when a woman gets her period." Then he launched into an imitation of the high-pitched voice of a female witness. "'But Detective Wallace, I couldn't let him do the nasty to me. I was on my administration last week.'

" 'Athaletic.' Used interchangeably with the word 'epileptic.' 'Officer Chapman, you can't go arresting my brother. He be having an athaletic fit right now.'

" 'Ax.' What you do uptown with a question. 'Officer, let me ax you this . . .' You ever know anybody Irish or Jewish or Italian who axes questions, do you?"

"Alex, are you in here?"

Mercer's frail voice came at us from the other side of the bed, his eyes still closed, his head still facing toward the wall, and his words barely audible. Mike bounced up from his chair, grabbed Mercer's left ankle—which seemed to be the only part of him not hooked to any kind of medical device—and started kissing the sole of his foot. I answered "Yes," and we both bent over to get close enough to hear Mercer speak.

His lips pulled together to form a smile. "Will you get that racist son of a bitch out of this room?"

23

"Cold hit, Coop." I had just stepped out of the shower a few minutes after seven o'clock on Monday morning, and Jake handed me the telephone to take Mike Chapman's call.

"On what?"

"Bob Thaler just called. He said they got a match on the semen found on the canvas tarp that was in the back of Omar Sheffield's station wagon—the one that Denise Caxton's body had been wrapped in. Did it through the data bank."

"Cold hit" was the slang term that scientists used to describe what occurred when a computer made a successful comparison between DNA samples, linking a piece of forensic evidence to an actual human being.

The detectives did not have to submit names, latent prints, mug shots, or vouchers for hours of overtime legwork in order for this technology to work. The computer's ability to make a cold hit took only an instant.

Thaler was the chief serologist at the Medical Examiner's Office and had helped to pioneer this technology. The data bank had been established by the New York State legislature, and there were data banks in almost every state by the late 1990s. New York's was slowly being filled with the genetic fingerprints—DNA developed from a single vial of blood— taken from every prisoner in the state convicted of sexual assault or homicide. Like their latent print counterparts, these unique codes were becoming an invaluable tool in the solution of cases of rape and murder.

"Who's the match?" I asked.

"Anton Bailey. Convicted of larceny three years ago up in Buffalo. Did half of a four-year sentence and was released to parole eight months back."

"Then why was he in the data bank?" His blood would not have been taken for a crime like larceny, a nonviolent theft.

"That's just it. He wasn't in the New York base. Thaler had the Feds run it interstate and, sure enough, got a hit in the Florida data bank." The Sunshine State had passed the legislation before most other parts of the country. "Seems like Mr. Bailey had gone by a different name down South—Anthony Bailor. And Mr. Bailor did some hard time back in Gainesville. Put away at eighteen, for almost twenty years. Rape in the first degree.

"So it looks like Anton Bailey is the man who sexually assaulted Denise Caxton."

"And killed her."

"Talk about cold hits," Mike said. "If this isn't a straight-out sexual assault gone bad, then someone must have hired old Anton to do Deni in. That could be the coldest hit of all."

"Now all we need to do is figure how and where he came into this picture."

"Thaler's the only government guy whose office opens up at seven A.M. I'll get on the horn to State Correction after nine. Just thought you'd like to know first thing."

"How's your patient?"

"Restless night. He was in a lot of pain. But they're taking some of the tubes out today and hope to get him moved into a private room."

"Battaglia arranged a full security crew for me until this thing is over. I told him I already feel like I have a human strait-jacket wrapped around me. They're driving me down to the office. Are you doing any interviews today?"

"If they have Mercer set up by the early afternoon, I'll call you so you can come up to the office with me. I'm beginning to think it's safer to let our interviewees drop by our place."

"What did you do about sleeping?"

"Not as cozy as you. Nurses let me curl up on a gurney in the hallway."

"Anybody I.D. the girl yet?" I asked, assuming the receptionist who opened the door for Mercer and me yesterday, whom I had first seen at Deni's gallery, could be a link to the killer.

"Yeah. Name was Cynthia Greeley. Twenty-three years old, from Saint Louis. Bryan Daughtry claims that most of the time she freelanced. He insists that it was Deni who hired the kid, not him. And that Deni met her when she was working for Lowell, on Fifty-seventh Street. Lowell thought Cynthia had too many pierced body parts to be working the uptown scene, so he was glad to let her go."

One more twisted path to unravel. "I'll get down to work and wait to hear from you. Give Mercer's hand a squeeze for me. Tell him I'll come over with you tonight. Need a place to clean up this morning?"

"Nah. I can shower at the squad. Change of clothes in my locker. See you later."

Battaglia had assigned two detectives from the D.A.'s Squad to accompany me from place to place for the duration of the investigation. I didn't like the restrictions it imposed or the waste of taxpayers' money. But he had given me no choice and had sent them to the hospital last evening. They had driven me to my apartment so I could pack a suitcase of belongings that would get me through the week, and then on to Jake's home, not too far from my own. Front-door-to-front-door service.

I had reached there in time to find Jake watching the news on CNN. It was after one o'clock in the morning. "Turn it off and I promise not to tell anyone at NBC that you were checking out the competition," I said to him when he embraced me at the door. "I don't want to hear anyone else's spin on the day, okay?"

I stripped my blood-soaked clothes off right there in the hallway and stood naked, offering them to him with both hands. "Take these to the incinerator and just throw them down the chute, would you please? I'm going to take a bath. I don't suppose you have anything that passes for bubbles here, do you?"

"No, but the bar's still open," he said, kissing the tip of my nose. "If I can see through the steam, I'll bring you in a drink as soon as I've dumped these."

I soaked in the tub while Jake sat on the floor beside me, sipping his drink while I tasted mine. I told him how Mercer and I had walked into the trap that had been so carefully laid for us at the exhibit, and how terrified I had been at the thought of losing Mercer. Jake didn't interrupt at all as I went on and on, stepping from the tub into the bath sheet that he wrapped around me; then I shivered for the first time in days as I tied the belt of his white terry robe on my waist and sat on the edge of the bed to call my mother and let her know that I was okay.

I stared into the masked face of our gunman—seeing nothing—for what seemed like hours, until I finally fell asleep on my side, with Jake's arm resting on my shoulder.

At seven forty-five I was ready to leave for the office. "What's your day like today?" I asked Jake, watching him knot his tie and ready himself for the crosstown ride to the NBC offices at Rockefeller Center.

"Kind of like yours, in the sense that I won't really know until I get there. I'm supposed to be covering the secretary of state's speech at the U.N. Do I have to worry about *you* as well, or just nuclear warheads, civil wars, and an erupting volcano in the Antilles?" he said jokingly.

"Battaglia has me under lock and key. So, your beeper will call my beeper?"

"Count on it. See you tonight."

I was out the door and down the FDR Drive with my armed escorts. The early arrival gave me time to catch up on the matters that had come in on Friday, when I had stolen the day to get away to the Vineyard. I checked my appointment book. One of the assistants had asked me to pencil in a re-interview at ten with her witness in a domestic violence case.

That gave me a couple of hours to return phone messages and speak with friends. As my colleagues began to arrive, many dropped by my office to see how I was, express their concern, and ask about Mercer, having heard accounts of the shooting on last evening's news. I finally shut my door to avoid a visit from Pat McKinney. There was enough salt in my emotional wounds without his venom added.

At ten fifteen I called Maggie to check whether her witness had arrived.

"She just called to cancel. Her husband offered to take her on a cruise over Labor Day weekend. She'd like to come see you when she gets back in two weeks. Guess she isn't quite as frightened of him as I thought."

That freed up another hour of the morning, or so I thought until Laura buzzed to say that one of the young lawyers from Trial Bureau 60 had been sent to discuss a new case with me. I opened my door and found Craig Tompkins waiting outside.

"Something different, at least for me. The intake supervisor thought you might have some ideas about how to charge this."

"What have you got?"

"The security guards over at the Javits Center are holding a guy, but I'm not sure they've got a crime to arrest him for."

"What did he do?" The Javits building was the city's convention hall and regularly the scene of large group meetings, trade association gatherings, and exhibitions.

"He signed up to attend this week's Trekkies reunion. Seems to have spent all day yesterday riding up and down the escalators, from floor to floor. Kind of got the guards' attention 'cause he was sort of goofy looking, carrying around a big gym bag the whole time, but never actually went into any of the lectures or conference rooms. When he came back in this morning, the head of security took a few rides up the escalator, right behind the guy.

"This jerk's got a video camera hidden in the bag. What he does is wait for a girl in a short dress to get on in front of him, then he rides up behind her, holding the camera so it shoots the view up her skirt. A thrill a minute, I guess."

"So what did they do with him?"

"Arrested him for harassment. Confiscated the gym bag and the video camera."

"Sounds right to me. What's the problem?"

"Well, they don't have any victims."

"What about the women he was filming?" In order to make out the charge of harassment, there would have to be people who would claim that the amateur moviemaker's conduct had annoyed or alarmed them.

"None of them ever realized what he was doing. They each just stepped off the escalator at the end of the ride, unaware that they had been immortalized on film. Then the security guys played back the videotape. Thighs, knees, lots of underwear—but nobody is recognizable from the angle of the shots. No way to figure out who they are."

I thought for a minute. "How about trespass? That he was unauthorized to be in the center."

"Won't work either. He paid full price for admission and that entitles him to be in the facility."

"Did he make any statements? Admissions?"

"Yeah, he gave it all right up. Married businessman from Connecticut, works for a public utility company there. Started doing this a year ago, just 'cause it turns him on."

"Talk about arrested development. Guess he never got past the sixth grade."

"Now he says he can sell them to a Web site. It's called U.S. Videos—only, the initials stand for 'Up-Skirt.' Lots of videocam voyeurs, he claims. Cops checked it out. Each tape sells for forty bucks."

"And that's exactly what's on 'em?" I asked incredulously. "I'm not sure there's anything criminal to charge him with. Let me call Mark." The usual response for any of us in the Trial Division when we were stuck on legal issues a lot thornier than this was to reach out for the head of the Appeals Bureau, our in-house lawman. We waited for his callback, which confirmed that there was no recourse in the criminal justice system for the Trekkie's actions. Craig used my phone to tell the Javits security force to let the guy go. The Internet was creating more opportunities for perverts than most of us had imagined, and law enforcement agencies were less aggressive than the cyber-geeks in coming up with solutions.

Mike called from Mercer's room at eleven thirty. "Forget those surgeons you saw yesterday. There's a lady doc here today, and a posse of very attentive nurses, and I think Mercer Wallace is really on the mend.

"I'm gonna scoot up to the squad at one. The pain medication makes Mercer pretty sleepy. His father wants to sit with him this afternoon. Varelli's assistant is going to come in for an interview. Wanna be there?"

"Absolutely."

"I'll swing by and pick you up, since I'm so close to your office," Mike said. "Then I can bring you back here to the hospital tonight. The D.A.'s Squad can take over your chauffeuring duties from that point on."

I called the Special Victims Unit to see who would inherit the day-to-day work on the West Side rapist matter and was relieved to hear it was in the capable hands of two veteran detectives who had worked with Mercer for years.

Then I stopped at Rose Malone's desk so that she could see that I was physically unharmed and tell Battaglia that Mercer's shooting had not unhinged me completely. Now that I was an eyewitness to the attempted murder of a police officer, I knew that the district attorney would assign another prosecutor to take over at least that part of the inquiry, just in case the crime was unrelated to our probe of Denise Caxton's killing.

"Would you ask Paul to let me have a say in who McKinney assigns to Mercer's shooting?" I asked Rose when she told me that Battaglia had just gone to lunch.

"Sure. I know he won't get to it today. He's got to polish up a speech he's giving tonight, and I don't think he'll have time to speak to Pat McKinney," she said, looking through the crammed schedule sheet that she kept on top of her desk.

"Great. If he wants me for anything, I'll be up at Manhattan North."

When I reached Laura's office to pick up my case folder and wait for Chapman, she told me to call Marjie Fishman, my counterpart in the Queens District Attorney's Office.

"Are you okay?" Marjie began the conversation.

I assured her that I was and gave her the update on Mercer's condition.

"You don't have any racetracks in Manhattan, do you?"

"No." I waved Mike in when I saw him standing with Laura outside my room.

"Well, we've finally got a situation that you haven't seen yet."

"Try me." There were days when my colleagues and I were sure there was nothing left that one human being could do to another that could shock us. And then, without fail, something else came along to prove us wrong.

"Last Monday, out at Aqueduct, a cop patrolling the stables in the middle of the night came upon, shall we say, an intimate encounter between one of the grooms and a horse. The defendant's name is Angel Garcia. The officer heard a loud thud, which was the sound made by the naked Garcia falling off the plastic bucket he'd been standing on."

"How's the horse?"

"The vet says she's fine. If you pass an OTB office on your way uptown, tell Mike to put some money on Saratoga Capers. Last Friday, after a thorough examination and clean bill of health, our horse came in third. That's her best start in weeks."

I hung up shaking my head in amusement, although I couldn't help feeling sorry for the poor creature. Fortunately, there were laws against inhumane treatment of animals, and Marjie's Special Victims Unit was prosecuting Garcia for abusing Saratoga Capers. Mike laughed out loud when he heard the story.

"Just feature sharing a jail cell with Angel Garcia," Mike said. "Every other prisoner has pictures of Cindy Crawford or Julia Roberts or *Penthouse* centerfolds on the wall. Meanwhile, Angel's got giant-size pinups of Trigger and Mr. Ed. Go figure. C'mon, blondie. Let's blow this joint."

"Wait a minute. Has anybody explored that part of Omar Sheffield's background?"

"Whaddaya mean? Horseplay?" Mike asked.

"Cell mates—just what you were joking about. When Omar was in the can doing time upstate, who did he share a cell with? Do we have any names?"

Mike stopped and double-backed to my desk to use the phone. "I don't think I asked that question. I'm not sure anybody did." He dialed the squad and reached Jimmy Halloran, a baby-faced cop who'd been on the Homicide Squad for more than a decade but looked like he was still in high school. Jimmy had been added to the Caxton team last night, after Mercer was injured. He bristled every time Mike called him by the nickname he'd been given by his team—Kid Detective.

"Hey, K.D.," Chapman said. "Squirrel around on the lieutenant's desk. See if you can find the paperwork on Omar Sheffield. You know, the bad boy who forgot his mother told him not to play on the tracks. See if anyone checked the names of his roommates in state prison. Coop and I are on our way uptown. If you don't find anything in the file, call up to the warden at Coxsackie and get some answers. And if they need a subpoena, call Cooper's secretary and she'll crank one out for us and fax it up for her signature. Make yourself useful." He hung up the phone.

"Where are you parked?" I asked.

"Behind the courthouse, on Baxter Street."

"Good. Let's slide out the back door. The fewer people I have to talk to about yesterday's events, the better off I'll be." We went downstairs and took the elevator from the seventh floor to the lobby, walking past the arraignment parts and the roach coach, as the building's snack bar was affectionately dubbed. It was half an hour before the courts recessed for the afternoon lunch break, so we navigated the hallways and went out onto the street without much delay.

As we walked into the squad office, Jimmy Halloran took his feet off the desk and stood to greet us, pointing out a young man who was reading a newspaper at a desk across the room. "That's your one o'clock. The guy from Varelli's studio.

"And those names you wanted from the warden? He said Omar Sheffield spent some of his time in solitary." Halloran looked down at his notes. "Had three cell mates while he was upstate. Kevin McGuire, who's done mostly burglaries, and Jeremy Fuller, who sold heroin to an undercover cop. They're both still in jail."

Again, he glanced at his notepad. "Third one is named Anton Bailey. Does this stuff mean anything to you?"

24

The Manhattan North Homicide Squad office was virtually empty. Every man and woman, whether on duty or off, had come in to try to crack the attempt on Mercer's life. Those who were not officially in the field were pounding the pavement, leaning on informants to try to get a lead on which to follow up. The rest were filling the lobby at Saint Vincent's, even though it was far too soon for all but the closest friends and family to visit with him.

"Cooper and I are gonna use the lieutenant's office for this interview. Call Albany, call whoever you've got to, but get every single sheet of paper that exists in this state on Anton Bailey," Chapman told Jimmy Halloran. "And when you're done with that, call the Gainesville, Florida, P.D. and start all over again. Use both names, Bailey and Anthony Bailor."

"Hey, Alex, how'd he get into the system up here without them picking up the Florida case?" Halloran asked me. "How come nobody figured out that Anton Bailey and Anthony Bailor were one and the same before today, huh?"

"Just lucky, I guess." No one could be arraigned for a felony in New York State without a fingerprint check. But every now and then, all of the automated techniques failed. In some cases, if the interstate computer system was down and the perp used an alias, the fingerprint comparison was never actually made. The fine type at the bottom of the rap sheet, if the prosecutor or judge stopped to read it, said that the results were based on a name check and not a verified latent exam.

If the prior rape conviction had been reflected on Bailey's record, then the larceny case would have drawn a mandatory prison sentence longer than the time he served. He would not have been free to have sexually assaulted Denise Caxton and to have set in motion the chain of deaths that followed.

"You must be Don Cannon," Mike said, shaking hands with the man sitting in the squad room. "I'm Detective Chapman, Mike Chapman. And this is Alexandra Cooper, from the Manhattan District Attorney's Office. Thanks for coming in."

I guessed Cannon to be younger than I am, in his late twenties, perhaps. He was a bit shorter than I, with a serious mien and horn-rimmed glasses. He seemed no more at ease than do most civilians who find themselves in the middle of a homicide case but express a willingness to cooperate, which few mean as sincerely as he seemed to.

"Why don't you have a seat and tell us a bit about yourself?" Chapman asked. "I'd like to know what you did for Mr. Varelli in his business. That kind of thing."

"You probably know by now that Marco was the master, the most meticulous workman in his field. Just about every important restoration project in the last fifty years has been offered to him. Those that excited him most, he worked on himself.

"I'm from Sacramento originally. Went to UCLA, have a graduate degree in fine arts. That the kind of thing you want to know?" He looked from Mike's face to mine, tentatively, to see whether he was proceeding in the right direction. We both nodded.

"One of my professors had worked with Varelli on *Guernica*, back in the eighties. Do you remember, that was the Picasso that was defaced at the Museum of Modern Art by some deranged fanatic?"

"Yes, of course. Our office handled the case."

"The professor knew that I wanted to work in restoration, that I hoped to develop a career, go back to the West Coast, and set up shop at the Getty or one of the other museums. To apprentice to Marco Varelli, well, there's simply nothing better to prepare to learn this business, and no finer credential on a résumé."

"When did you start to work for him?" I asked.

Cannon hesitated. "Nobody worked *for* Varelli. I mean, technical people did—laborers who picked up and delivered the paintings or arranged the studio. But he was quite a loner. Once he had established himself as the virtuoso, more than forty years ago, he was insistent on working alone. If you were fortunate enough to get his attention, and he agreed to work on your project, then he wanted the result to be only *his* handiwork."

"What do you mean, 'he agreed'? Didn't people just pay him?" Chapman wanted to know.

The serious Mr. Cannon smiled wryly. "No, no, no. Mr. Varelli had more than enough to live on. He was paid handsomely for his craft. So, at a certain point in his life, it was easy for him to turn down whomever he pleased. If the painting or the artist was not one he deemed worthy of his effort, no matter what the price offered, he wouldn't touch it."

"How about if the ownership was cloudy?"

"Well then, Miss Cooper, there was simply no way to engage him. I can recall an instance when a collector showed up in the atelier with a Léger. The particular painting had been classified in the Pompidou Center as an R2P, which means that it had been seized by the Nazis during the war and later returned to France. To date, no one had been able to connect it to the original owner or his descendants. Signor Varelli refused to become involved until an effort was made to trace the lineage and try to find the owners. The more money that was offered to retain him, the more offended he became. I'm sure it's a lot like that in the legal profession, don't you think? I mean, with all the ethical dilemmas defense attorneys have?"

He looked over at me for an answer, which came instead from Chapman. "You're watching too much *Geraldo*. I never met a defense attorney with an ethical dilemma—if the check clears, his client's not guilty."

"You said that no one worked for Varelli. Didn't *you*?"

"I had the privilege of being apprenticed to him, Detective. An expensive privilege."

"You had to pay to help him?"

"I had a grant, actually, from a private family foundation. That's what made the experience possible for me. I certainly wouldn't have had the means to do it otherwise. Consider it like going to the best school in the world. For close to three years I was tutored by a genius. The skills he has given me are qualities I could never have learned anywhere else." Cannon bowed his head. "I still can't believe he's gone. And worst of all, murdered." He looked up at us. "He was such a quiet, benign man. There's not a reason I can think of for someone to hurt him."

"Let me run some names by you. Tell us if you know any of these people, okay?"

Cannon cleared his throat and said it would be fine.

"Start with Lowell Caxton. Ever meet him?"

"Many, many times. I'd guess Marco had known him for as long as I've been alive. I think he was one of the few collectors whose taste Mr. Varelli admired. I've never been to any of Caxton's homes, but I understand there were several generations of a great genetic eye for art. Mr. Caxton used to come by for an opinion every now and then. Do you know about the Titian—the one he gave to Marco?"

"Yes. We spent a few minutes with Mrs. Varelli at the funeral home. We expect to see her in the apartment later this week."

"Marco adored that gift, a real jewel of a little drawing. I think his acceptance of Lowell Caxton had a lot to do with that gesture. It would be hard to dislike someone who had done such a generous thing."

"Any conflict between them, ever?"

Cannon shrugged his shoulders. "Not that I ever witnessed. Keep in mind, I wasn't there all the time. Mostly I was with Marco when he was actually doing the work on his projects, not when he was talking with his clients or when they dropped in for a glass of grappa and some advice about what to bid on a particular piece.

"He was very good at dismissing me. 'Thank you so much, Mr. Cannon. And now, *per piacere,* I think we are finished for the moment.' He'd kind of flutter his hand in my direction, and I'd know it was time to take off."

"To . . . ?"

"The grant covered the expenses of my study, but not an apartment in Manhattan. My girlfriend and I sublet a room in a loft in SoHo. She's here in graduate school at NYU. When I was free to leave I'd head for the library, an art show, or a movie. But I'd get out of his hair, that much was clear."

Chapman checked off Caxton's name on the list he had started and went down to the next line. "Bryan Daughtry. Ever run into him?"

"Yes, he was another visitor. Not so much anymore, with the contemporary work he was trying to sell. But Marco had done ventures with him before I arrived here, which was before Daughtry went to jail. On that tax fraud, not that other thing." Cannon looked at me to see whether I registered any reaction to his reference to the girl in the leather mask.

"What do you know about his background?"

"I don't mean to make light of the story about Bryan Daughtry's involvement in that old case, but it kind of fascinated Mr. Varelli. He never saw the cruel side of Bryan. Met him as a young man who had a rather good eye for art, albeit untrained. I was a bit shocked to meet him myself when Bryan first came to the studio. Marco told me all about him that first day."

Cannon moved in his chair, put the fingertips of his right hand together, and shook them easily in front of his face, imitating the old man's accent. " 'But can you tell me why, Mr. Cannon, *why* a young man wants to tie up a beautiful young girl and cause her pain? This I don't understand at all. From a body like this you should get only pleasure, only sweetness, only—*come si dice in inglese?*—rapture. But maybe I am too old to understand.'

"Quite frankly, I used to think when Daughtry was here to visit and Mr. Varelli kicked me out, it was to ask him questions about his sexual proclivities. Marco was much more curious about that than he was about contemporary art."

Cannon talked for a while about Bryan Daughtry's more recent business focus, but again could think of no incident that unnerved him in regard to Varelli.

"How about Marina Sette?"

Cannon seemed to draw a blank.

"Marilyn Seven?" I asked, adding a physical description as well as telling him where she lived.

"It's quite possible she had been to see Marco, of course. It's just not a name I recognize."

"Frank Wrenley?"

Again, not familiar. Neither was Preston Mattox. Cannon knew the names of some of the workmen, but Omar Sheffield and Anton Bailey were not among them.

Chapman put down his pen and clasped his hands on the desktop.

"Talk to me about Denise Caxton. Everything you know. When you met her, what she was like, what Marco thought about her. Things that don't seem important to you may be exactly what we're looking for, so give it all to me, okay?"

"This one's a bit complicated, Detective. There was Denise Caxton the woman, and there was Denise Caxton the collector. Marco Varelli's eye was unerring. He admired great beauty, on a canvas or in human form. Nothing inappropriate, nothing unusual. But he would look at a handsome woman's face as though it had been sculpted by Michelangelo. Didn't matter if she were a waitress in a diner or a client with millions. Mrs. Caxton had a real head start with Marco, from the old days. He had met her when she was a kid, just married to Lowell.

"If I'm not mistaken—you might have to check her apartment for this—I think Mr. Varelli once painted her portrait, a full-length nude. He was very proud of it. Told me it was hung in her room at home. I believe she had a collection of self-portraits, right?" He chuckled at the vanity of that idea, it seemed to me.

Cannon continued, "She was a real flirt—Mrs. Caxton, I mean. Knew exactly how to play the old guy, with words. When I first met her, almost three years ago, she could light him up like a flare when he knew she was coming. She would always bring his favorite chocolates, if she had been to Paris, or a chilled bottle of wine to sip with him in the afternoon. She loved to listen to his stories, wanted to know every painting he'd ever worked on—who owned them, what he did to them, what became of them. Marco used to complain that his wife didn't want to hear the old tales over again. Denise Caxton hung on his every word, or at least she let him think that she did."

"Did you ever work on any of the paintings she brought into the gallery?"

"Yes. She had a knack for picking up sleepers, bidding on some incredibly lifeless old canvas that she'd either had a good tip on or had followed with her gut instincts. 'Who is it, Marco? Tell me who's hiding underneath there, *mi amore*.' She'd tease him into playing with almost anything she brought in. And what was funny about it was that most of the time, he wanted me there to watch this game she played with him. As if he wanted me to see that a magnificent young woman doted on him, that it wasn't just happening in his imagination."

"When did his feelings for Deni change?"

Cannon paused. "Is that what Mrs. Varelli said?"

"Yeah. Said she didn't make him quite so happy anymore."

"I can't recall exactly when the change occurred, but she's right. Mrs. Caxton's visits were fewer and farther apart. She rarely came alone anymore, and the games were over."

"Who'd she bring with her, if she wasn't alone?"

"Friends, clients—I don't know. Varelli would shoo me out of the studio. There was no longer any verbal foreplay, so he didn't need me around."

Chapman was annoyed. "You must know who some of them were, don't you? Start somewhere—women? men? young or old?"

"Occasionally she came with people I knew, like Bryan Daughtry. Once or twice she might have been with a woman—

maybe even that lady you described earlier, with the French braid. Seven or Sette, whatever you called her. But most of the time it was men, two or three different ones in the past few months, since she split up with her husband."

"Can you describe any of them for us? Would you recognize them if you saw them today?"

Again Cannon shrugged, not attaching any importance to these visitors. "There wasn't anything remarkable about any of them. Sure, maybe I'd know them if I ran into them again, maybe not. You have to understand, Detective, that if Marco Varelli wasn't working on a canvas, I was just as happy to be out of there. It was as much an education for me to spend a free afternoon at a museum as to be a fly on the wall when he was chatting up rich collectors. I didn't need the small talk."

Chapman stood now, walking behind Cannon's back. "In the last three years, is there anybody else who spent as much time with Marco Varelli as you did?"

Cannon thought and then told us, "No. Except for his wife."

"Anybody who knew what he thought about everything and everybody?"

"No, probably not."

"They have any kids?"

"No."

"I bet you were sort of like a son to him, weren't you?"

"Not exactly. But he was very good to me."

"What was the most important thing in the world to him, Don? Leave his wife out of it for the moment. Tell us."

"You know the answer. He lived for great art—for looking at it, touching it, smelling it, dreaming about it."

"And he trusted *you* with his legacy."

"Well, I'm not the only one who ever apprenticed with him. There are dozens of experts in museums around the world who—"

"But *now,* Mr. Cannon. You've spent these last three years joined to him at the hip. I find it really kinda hard to believe that he had many secrets from you." Mike's fist pounded down on the top of the lieutenant's desk. "I'd like you to tell me why he and Denise Caxton had a falling-out."

Cannon started at Chapman's change in mood. "I wasn't his confidant, Mr. Chapman. I was merely his student."

"And you're too damn smart, too good a student, not to have been aware of what was happening in that little garret every day, that's what I think. If you've got a special talent, Mr. Cannon, it's your powers of observation, isn't it? Tell me what you saw up there, what you heard."

Mike's voice bellowed in the small room as Cannon looked at me to call off the angry detective. "She's on *my* side in this, buddy. If I let Cooper cross-examine you for fifteen minutes, you'll forget you ever walked into this room with a set of balls." Chapman was shouting now, and red in the face. "Three people are dead and my partner's lying in a hospital bed with a hole in his chest. Stop wasting my time!"

"Do I need a lawyer?" Cannon spoke quietly and again directed the question to me.

I began to answer but was interrupted by Chapman. "If you're gonna tell me you killed someone, we'll call you a lawyer. Somehow, I doubt that's the problem. Just tell me what's on your mind and worry about that later."

"Well, what if I have information about a crime?"

Mike's open palm slammed the desktop another time. "Whaddaya think I've been asking you to tell me about for the last hour?"

25

Cannon had stalled for about as long as Mike was going to let him, and he knew that. "I suppose there are two things that changed the relationship between Mrs. Caxton and Marco. The first problem began about a year ago."

"When, exactly? 'About' doesn't help me all that much."

"I can't give you a specific date. I'm pretty sure it was before she and her husband began to have problems in their marriage. I remember that because I thought it was strange she had come to see Marco about a matter so important but that it was something she wanted to be sure he wouldn't tell Lowell."

"That's a start. Coop, make a list for me. First thing, try to put a date on that visit, okay? What happened that day?"

"Denise was exuberant. It must have been spring or summer, 'cause she wasn't wearing a coat. She was dressed to the nines when she came in, and she looked spectacular. They began the usual flirtation, and Marco made sure that I took it all in. She handed me a bottle of wine—a very special one, she made sure to tell me—and asked me to open it. I did, and Marco invited me to pour for all three of us."

"Had you known she was coming?"

"Yes, she'd called the day before and told Marco she'd found a surprise. A painting, that is. Asked if he would look at it for her. Of course he agreed."

Cannon took a breath before going on. He rubbed his hands together and talked slowly, as though uncertain he should talk at all. "After half an hour of cajoling Marco, she got up from the chaise and picked up the bag she'd come in with—one of those large canvas sail bags. She removed something from it, and all I could see was a small mound of plastic bubble wrapping. She unwound several layers of it and lifted out a painting. Then she walked to one of the easels and rested it on the stand. 'Come, Marcolino—come play with me.' Mrs. Caxton took him by the hand and stood him before the canvas."

"Did you know what it was?"

"I certainly didn't. It was dark, really covered with dirt, and hard to make out."

"Did Varelli say anything?"

"Then? No. It would have been unusual for him to speak until after he'd gotten to work and made up his mind that he knew what he was looking at."

"What'd he do?"

"What he did best, Detective. He put the glass of wine down next to him, strapped his headset on—sort of like small binoculars—and steadied himself in place to look at every inch of the canvas with the aid of the light from the glasses. You want to know the details?"

"All of them."

"It was obvious that not only was there soot on this one, and varnish, but something had been painted over the original work. That happens frequently with oils, you know, sometimes just because the artist changed his mind about what he wanted to portray. But in this case it looked like it had been put on top to disguise an earlier version of whatever was depicted.

"So Marco got out his acetone, soaked a cotton swab in it, and went about dabbing at a corner of the canvas, sort of the top right quadrant."

"And you, what were you doing?"

"I stood behind him to watch, to be there to assist him should he have needed me to."

"And Deni?"

"Practically breathing down his neck. Not that he minded that, from her."

"How long does this take, what he was doing?"

"Depends. On what's there, how many layers, how easily—or not—it picks up. I would say Marco worked for close to an hour before he said very much. He stopped to tell us that he thought he had gotten through the primary layer. He stood up to stretch, and to have me take a look, which I did."

"What did you see?"

Cannon smiled for the first time in ten minutes. "You sound just as anxious as Denise. 'What do you see, Marco? What can you tell me?' He poured himself another glass and asked me a few questions, ignoring Deni completely.

"'What century, boy, do you see now? What school, what artist?' He did that with me all the time, delighting in those rare occasions when I could pinpoint a good answer as rapidly as he was able to do."

"Did you recognize anything?"

"Only that Marco had gone back several centuries, between

removing the new paint and the grime that had so discolored the original canvas. Wherever this piece had come from, it had been terribly, terribly neglected."

"What then?"

"He went back to work, this time adding some ammonia to the acetone and patiently dabbing away. It's a very slow business. After a while, Marco's touch exposed some bright blue paint trimmed with a very pearly sort of highlight. He almost gasped when he saw the contrast of the two colors next to each other."

"Excuse my ignorance," Mike said, "but why?"

"I didn't know myself, but now I assume that was the point at which he thought he had recognized the artist, perhaps even the painting."

"And Deni?"

"She had seen him do this enough times to know he was reacting to something serious." Again, Cannon slipped into one of his imitations. " 'Go in deeper, Marco,' she urged him. I remember that he hesitated for a bit, then picked up one of his pointed tools, almost like a scalpel, and began to dig at the thick varnish in another part of the painting. More of the picture came into view, near its center, revealing a clear yellow tint that had been almost brown in color in the layer above.

"That's when I was banished."

"By Denise Caxton?"

"By Marco Varelli. That familiar little gesture I told you about earlier, sweeping me away with his hand like you might do to a pet dog you wanted to get out from underfoot? That's exactly what I got from him. 'That's all I'm going to do for today,' he told me. 'You may go home now.' "

"And did you?"

"I left the studio, certainly. But my curiosity had been aroused. I went straight to the library at NYU to do a bit of art research. At that point I was fairly confident that we had been looking at something from the seventeenth century, probably Dutch."

"A Rembrandt?" Mike asked.

"Not bad, Detective. It was an interior scene by a great colorist. I was guessing Vermeer, who was known for his pearl-colored reflections and the fantastically luminous shades of blue and yellow. I pored over textbooks until I found what I was looking for. Have you ever heard of a painting called *The Concert*?"

Neither one of us had.

"You know about the break-in at the Gardner Museum?"

Mike was following the story intently. "Yeah, we do. Why?"

"Along with the great Rembrandt that was taken," Cannon said, acknowledging Chapman as he went on, "which you clearly seem to be aware of, there was one Vermeer stolen that has never been found either. It's called *The Concert,* and it depicts a young woman playing a pianoforte for two others. I believe I'm one of the very few people in the world who has seen that painting—at least, any portion of it—in the last ten years. The other two who saw it with me that day—Mrs. Caxton and Mr. Varelli—are dead. Maybe now you can understand why I'm reluctant to speak about it."

Mike had no sympathy for Cannon's fear. "What's its value?"

"Not as great as the Rembrandt, but still in the multimillions. Vermeer is known to have painted only thirty-five works in his lifetime."

"Was it still at Varelli's studio when you got there the next day?"

"No. I never saw it again. Nor did he mention it to me. We went right back to work on the portrait we had been commissioned to restore for the Tate, the one we were immersed in before Denise Caxton asked to drop by. I came in that next morning eager to hear what he and Mrs. Caxton had found after he had dismissed me. Not a word. But then, the texts I had consulted were written before the Gardner theft, so I had no idea the Vermeer had been stolen. I thought that perhaps the museum was deaccessioning the painting, and it made sense to me that the Caxtons were among the few collectors with the means to acquire it—legitimately.

"It wasn't unusual for Marco to work in silence. Finally, when we broke for lunch, I thought I'd impress him with my knowledge. I'd be the perfect pupil and answer the questions he had asked me when he had started to uncover the picture in my presence."

"Did it work?"

"It backfired colossally. Marco almost took my head off. I told him that not only did I think I knew the century and the school to which the painting could be attributed, but that I also knew the artist and the work itself. He looked surprised and challenged me." Cannon looked up at us rather sheepishly. "When I said the words aloud, he became furious at me.

"'But why?' I asked him. 'Why are you so angry?' 'You have never, *never* seen that Vermeer, do you understand, my boy? It has *never* been in the studio of Marco Varelli.' He went on to rant and rave about the fact that Denise had brought him a fraud, some lousy copyist's effort to re-create a Dutch domestic scene, that Denise was a rank amateur who had occasionally been lucky but had made a bad guess. He practically made me swear that the event I witnessed had never taken place."

"Have you ever told anyone about it?"

"My girlfriend, sure. No one else. I had gone right back to the library and searched the periodicals. That's when I realized that it must have been the stolen Vermeer, and that Varelli wanted no part of it. I respected him for that, and thought that would be the end of it."

"You mean it wasn't? Did Deni come back?"

"Of course she did. Several times, not too long after, just trying to regain favor, I guess. Lots of good wine, charming coquettishness, gifts. Marco wasn't at all materialistic, but she'd find wonderfully whimsical things—small sculptures, paintings, objets d'art that he couldn't resist—and bring them by to appease him."

"Any talk of the Vermeer?"

"None. And again Marco wanted me around when she showed up and made a fuss over him. So they weren't alone very much those next few visits. Then," Cannon said, rubbing his eyes with his hand, "there was another tempest. Perhaps, if I hadn't been such a coward, I'd have done something about it at the time. Deni came in one day very excited, very flustered."

"When was this, do you remember?"

"Not off the top of my head."

"Months later, Don?"

"No, no. Three or four weeks at most. But I'm pretty sure she had been away, out of the country, in the meantime. I think it was shortly after she and her husband had some kind of huge fight and split up. Anyway, I knew immediately that something different was going on."

"How?"

"As soon as she arrived, it was Denise who asked me to leave. Even Marco looked puzzled, because she dispensed with the usual flirtation. 'You don't mind, do you? I've got some personal matters to discuss with Signor Varelli. It's the middle of the afternoon, Marco—let him have the rest of the day off, okay?'

"For once he seemed reluctant to let me walk out. I think, at that point, he didn't quite trust her anymore. But she was insistent, and he gave me the back of his hand."

"Do you have any idea what she wanted? Was she carrying the same bag?"

"She wasn't carrying any sail bag this time. Just her pocket-book. I took off my work shirt, said good-bye, and closed the door behind me."

"Didn't Varelli ever tell you what it was about?"

"He didn't have to, Detective." Cannon pursed his lips and looked away from us before speaking again. "I'm not proud of this, but I really couldn't help myself. Instead of leaving, I ran down the steps from the atelier door, then I slipped off my sandals and walked back up, sitting on the top of the stoop, so that I could listen against the door.

"It was Denise Caxton at her best, pulling out all the stops. She was pleading with Marco to look at what she had brought with her—coaxing and cajoling him with her limited vocabulary of Italian platitudes. 'My little gems,' she kept repeating. Then I heard her tell him that he was the only person in the world who could know the truth. That this adventure would crown his illustrious career and be his great heritage—to restore a priceless painting to the world."

"Little gems?" Chapman asked. "Could you see what they were talking about?"

"I never saw them, but it became quite obvious. She had a small pouch, which she opened, and placed the contents on Marco's workbench. Chips, a dozen tiny pieces of paint chips."

"From the stolen Rembrandt?"

"That's precisely what she wanted to know."

"I realize Varelli's expertise," I said, "but is that the kind of thing that a restorer would be able to determine with any certainty?"

"I guess you both know that when *The Storm on the Sea of Galilee* was taken in that theft, the burglars were unusually sloppy, just slicing it out of the frame with a knife and leaving behind a dustpan full of chips. That probably means that slivers continued to flake off the edges of the actual painting itself, so whoever possessed the painting would have more pieces like the ones collected by the police. A science lab would have to make the ultimate determination of the authenticity of the age of the chips. They can do it with electron and polarized-light microscopes, like the F.B.I. uses. Specialists have uncovered frauds, for example, by proving that minuscule amounts of chalk in a paint primer were made twenty years ago, not three hundred. That's technology.

"But Marco wasn't a bad place to start, to get a first opinion. What lab technicians do with their tools or their scopes, he did with his nose and his fingers and his infallible eye. It was the trait that made him a genius at restoration. Besides that, Ms. Cooper, Denise Caxton could hardly walk into an F.B.I. office and ask whether the fragments she was holding actually matched the ones that had fallen behind at the Gardner during an unsolved theft, could she?"

"Did Varelli look at the chips?"

"I never found out. When I left, he was still being obstinate and refusing to entertain Mrs. Caxton's request."

"Why didn't you wait?"

"Believe me, I wanted to stay there. But a couple of the workmen were coming back with some large frames that Marco had sent out to be regilded. We had been expecting them earlier in the afternoon. When I heard the buzzer ring from downstairs, I was afraid Mr. Varelli would open the door and find me hiding there. So I left.

"The next day, he carried on as usual. And after what had occurred with the Vermeer, I didn't dare ask him about these paint chips. I don't think I ever mentioned Rembrandt's name to him for a couple of months."

"Didn't he talk about Deni anymore? Didn't she still come to visit?"

"Less frequently, so far as I know. But whenever she showed up, he insisted I stay to help him or have a glass of wine with them. And he was much too discreet to talk about her. After she'd leave, he'd shake his head and say she was crazy. '*Bella pazza,*' my beautiful crazy one. That's what he called her more recently."

"And when she was killed, what did he have to say about her then?"

Don Cannon shook his head at us. "Don't know. I was on vacation with my girlfriend, camping out in Yosemite. My family couldn't even find me to tell me that Marco had died. But those scenes with the Vermeer and then the paint chips were the cause of the breach that developed between him and Deni, I'm sure of it. The other thing," he said, stretching a bit and arching his back, "the other thing was also a bit odd, at least to me."

"What other? I thought you said there were two things that estranged them—meaning the Vermeer and the chips."

"To me," the young man replied, "those two were part of the same headache—the Gardner Museum heist. The other one was something else again."

Mike was jotting notes on his pad, while I added points to my list of questions. "A bit later on, Denise came back to the studio. It was well after she and her husband had separated, I know that. She had another man with her and—"

"Who?"

"Sorry, I can't help you with that. I never got much of a look. He was standing quietly off to the side, and like Varelli, all my attention was on Mrs. Caxton. It wasn't unusual for her to have men with her who were clients. They rarely entered into her conversation with Mr. Varelli and I never paid them much mind. Anyway, she was telling Marco about the breakup, and she said she had brought a gift, this time for Gina—for Mrs. Varelli. It was a necklace of beads—very large amber beads—and a carved figurine that matched them. 'Come look, Dan,' she said to me. She'd met me a few dozen times, but she was a bit too self-centered to bother to learn my name. Always called me Dan instead of Don. 'Come look, you'll never see anything like these. They're quite rare. Lowell gave them to me, and I really don't want to wear them anymore. Might give him too much satisfaction. Gina will adore them, don't you think, Marco? You don't have to tell her they're from me.'

"Mrs. Caxton reached over with both hands to pass them to Varelli, but he recoiled instantly and the strand fell onto the floor. 'Not in my house, *signora,* not under my roof. Too many people have been killed for these trifles with which you amuse yourself.'"

"And she left?"

"She got down on her knees to pick up the beads. One end of the strand had broken and they were rolling across the floor like golf balls. I helped her gather them up and put them back in her purse. Then she and her friend left.

"But they left behind the little amber statue. By accident, I would think. Mr. Varelli didn't even notice it. But when Gina came upstairs the next morning to bring us some tea, she saw it there. She spotted it immediately and admired it. Just picked it up with her and took it down to the apartment."

"Didn't he say anything then?"

"Only to himself, under his breath. He rarely said no to Gina—about anything. But when she carried off her little treasure, Marco muttered something about Nazis. It meant nothing to me then, but a few more hours at the library, and the computer research came up with stories about the Amber Room. I even found a few articles that connected the lost room to Lowell Caxton."

Chapman was holding his notepad in his right hand, tapping it against his other fist. "There must be some way to reconstruct the dates that these things happened, no? You keep any kind of appointment book or calendars?"

"No reason to, Detective. I went to work at the same place every day at the same time. I keep journals about exhibits I've gone to see and I keep loads of sketchbooks, but they don't have any engagements in them."

"How about Varelli?" I asked. "People made appointments with him, there were deliveries, someone paid the bills—"

"Gina Varelli, of course. She was the only one who Marco let control his business."

"The widow, right?"

"Yes. She made most of the arrangements. Marco didn't like to be bothered by telephone calls and mundane things." Cannon laughed. "Like money. Didn't she give you that book when you spoke with her? It's got everything in it—every visitor, client, bill, receipt. I'm sure it would be a great help to you in your investigation."

"No. We'll get it from her when we see her this week," I said, adding to my list and nodding at Mike. "Perhaps we can get her to talk about the amber piece, too. Maybe Marco and she spoke about it at home, privately."

"Yeah. I'll call her tonight and see if I can go over in the morning and pick up the journal and the statue, okay, Coop?"

I didn't have to answer.

Don Cannon spoke. "Not tomorrow, Detective. About two hours before the funeral that had been scheduled for last Friday, Gina got a call from the mayor of Florence. It's where Marco was born. The Italian government offered to fly the body home for burial in the family's church, somewhere up north, in the mountains, alongside all his ancestors. Kind of like a national hero—which shows the respect they have for artists over there.

"Gina Varelli left for Italy last evening. Some little town in Tuscany. I don't even know how to reach her."

26

"Your to-do list is getting to be a mile long," Chapman said after Don Cannon left the office and we were eating our sandwiches at the lieutenant's desk.

"I'll call down to my paralegal now and see whether she can get a number for the mayor of Florence. You double-check with the guys from Crime Scene to see whether they took any kind of book when they processed Varelli's studio."

"I'm telling you, Mercer and I were there with them. No such thing anywhere we looked. The only evidence they vouchered was the pair of sunglasses. Whatever this appointment journal or calendar is, it's probably in his apartment, not the studio."

"Well, if we can find the niece who took Gina Varelli home the other night, maybe we can convince her to let us do a consent search. If not, I'll draft another warrant in the morning." I looked at my watch. "It's already almost four o'clock."

The shifts had changed, and detectives working the day tour were signing out while those doing four-to-twelves were coming on. Even the teams that had finished their official tours were working overtime, without pay, because of Mercer.

Jimmy Halloran opened the door. "Your secretary's on line two. Wanna pick up?"

"Sure. Laura? Everything okay?"

"Just a couple of things you need to know about. Pat McKinney is having a meeting at ten tomorrow with a few of the senior trial counsel. Catherine said to tell you that he hasn't given them any specific agenda yet, but she assumes he's planning to pick someone from the group to assign to prosecute Mercer's case."

"Thank her for letting me know. I'll be there."

"You're not invited, Alex. That's the point. That's what Catherine wanted me to get across to you."

Damn it. McKinney would do everything in his power, as deputy chief of the Trial Division, to make me uncomfortable as a witness to Mercer's shooting. I wanted to have a say in who would prosecute the gunman when he was caught. "Can you find a number for Rod Squires? Scout around for me, will you?" The chief of the division, my friend and ally, was also on summer vacation. If I could enlist his aid before morning, I'd have some control over the selection process.

"Let me call Rose Malone. I'm sure she'll know how to find him. And you also need to know that the man who tried to run you down last week, Wakim Wakefield? Well, he was back here at the building today, trying to get upstairs to file a complaint with Battaglia about you."

"Did security let him through?" That's a bit too close for comfort.

"No. His name was on their daily chart." The security crew in the lobby at 1 Hogan Place kept a roster of names of people not welcome in our office—an ever-expanding list of psychos, malcontents, and cranks who were expert at creating disturbances once they got inside.

"Was he arrested?" I asked with some hesitancy.

"No. The guard called up to the squad to get some detectives to come talk to him, but there's only one elevator working today, and by the time somebody got downstairs, Wakefield was already gone. Mr. Battaglia himself called about it. Made me promise to ask you if you were using your bodyguards."

"Don't mention to him that I groaned when I told you yes," I answered. "I'm smack in the middle of a police station right now, and unless Chapman goes ballistic 'cause I tell him to wipe the mustard off the side of his mouth, I'll be perfectly safe. I'll stay with him a few more hours, and then he'll pass me back off to the D.A.'s Squad. Tell the boss I'm being a very good soldier, okay? And please see if you can get a number for any government officials in Florence. We need to find Marco Varelli's widow."

"Alex, it's after ten at night over there. I'll see what I can do, but I doubt I'll have anything for you until tomorrow. And one last thing."

"Some good news, right?"

"Not exactly. Pat McKinney dropped by. He told me to remind you that you are to stay away from the hospital. No visits to Mercer, no talking about the case. He doesn't want you comparing notes and conforming your stories to fit each other's recollections. Sorry, Alex."

"Don't worry, Laura. I know you're just the messenger."

I hung up and Chapman asked what the news was, so I told him about Wakefield.

"Jeez, blondie, if it wasn't for me you'd have no friends at all. Let's take off. Preston Mattox will see us at his office whenever we get there."

"I thought you said everyone else would have to be interviewed *here*."

"What happened to your sense of humor, kid? D'you lose it yesterday? This guy's got his architectural offices in a penthouse suite on Fifth Avenue, overlooking Saint Patrick's Cathedral, with about fifty employees in the surrounding rooms. I'll get you home in one piece tonight."

Mike called the hospital and spoke with Mercer's dad, who told him that Mercer had been sitting up for a few hours in the early afternoon and now was sleeping again. We gathered our things to leave the squad. Jimmy Halloran had been kept over to do back-to-back tours, to man the phone and hot line, since City Hall had announced a reward for information leading to the arrest of the shooter.

"Hey, K.D., give me a beep if anything comes in on Bailey before your shift is done. We've got an interview to do before we stop off at the hospital."

With that we were on our way to the offices of Mattox Partners, and our first introduction to another one of Deni's suitors, Preston Mattox. His secretary announced us and we were led into the stark glass-enclosed headquarters of the prominent architect, which looked south toward the spires of the great church below.

My first reaction was surprise. He appeared to be about fifty years old. He was in good shape and dressed in a navy suit, exuding a much more businesslike air than the art-world denizens we had encountered throughout the last week. But what struck me most about Mattox was that he looked truly distraught, and as though he had been crying for days on end.

There was a hollow contour around his eyes and a lifelessness emanating from within, which hit a chord in the core of me that wanted someone to be mourning for Denise Caxton.

Once more Chapman and I made our introductions.

"Why don't you have a seat?" he said, coming out from behind his desk and pulling three chairs around in a circle. "Sorry I didn't get back to you sooner. I really had to get away from here after Deni was killed. Lowell made it clear that I wasn't welcome at the service, and I just needed to be somewhere else."

Mattox was cordial, but he seemed distracted and unable even to muster a smile.

"Have you made any progress in solving Deni's case?"

"Not as much as we'd like," I answered.

"I've stopped reading newspaper accounts, so I don't know what you're up to. The stories about her all made her sound so vacuous and unpleasant. She was a most unusual creature— clever, funny, warm. She craved affection, and I loved giving it to her."

Mike showed unusual restraint in not mentioning Deni's other liaisons. He let Mattox do it for us. "You've probably talked with some of Deni's other friends. Obviously, I wasn't the only man in her life, but I was fighting hard for that slot." He stood up and walked to the window, looking out and not speaking for several seconds. "I had asked Denise to marry me."

"But she wasn't even divorced yet," Mike said.

Mattox rested against the ledge of the windowsill. "No, but I was urging her to speed up the process. Stop fighting with Lowell and walk away from him. Frankly, it made me sick just to think of them living under the same roof. I don't quite have the art collection that her husband does, but short of that, there wasn't anything she wanted that I would not have given her."

"Do you know why she didn't leave?"

"Really why? Probably I don't know. None of the reasons she ever gave me made much sense. 'Just wait,' she used to say. 'Don't rush me.' She was obstinate about it and I was madly in love, so I didn't push her. It was the only thing we ever fought over. And she could fight," Mattox said, almost amused at the memory of it.

"What do you mean?"

"Deni was a battler. She looked so soft, so fragile. But she had an iron will, and if something got under her skin, she'd go to the mats for it. It was one of her best traits as a friend—a tenacious loyalty that endeared her to anyone who got close enough." He took a handkerchief from his pants pocket and held it over his mouth as he cleared his throat, and then tamped the cloth against his eyes. "I keep thinking of how she must have died. I know it wouldn't have been without a struggle."

So many victims of sexual assault had described to me their reactions to the assailant. The greatest number submitted to life-threatening words or display of a weapon. Others chose to attempt to fight back. Some were successful and became survivors. For many, the resistance served only to aggravate the attacker and caused him to use more force, which resulted sometimes in serious injury to the woman, and often in her death. No one could second-guess the decisions each victim had to make in the seconds when she was confronted by a rapist.

Mike tried to direct the conversation back to the areas that interested him.

"Did you have any kind of relationship with Lowell Caxton?"

"A casual one. I'd known him for years—never did any work for him, but we traveled in the same social circles here in town. Always been a perfect gentleman to me."

"How about to Deni?"

"I think I understood him a lot better than she did, to tell you the truth. I don't think she had any business trying to make him let go of some of the artwork that had been in his family for decades. It wasn't the prettiest side of Deni, as you probably know by now."

"What about her concerns that he was trying to have her killed?"

Mattox frowned at that suggestion. "I ridiculed the idea at the time. Sort of makes me crazy to think about that now. It could just as easily be Lowell behind all this as it could be anyone, I guess." He looked up at Mike. "I don't envy your job, Detective. Saw an article in the paper not long ago. Said there are more murderers in the United States than there are medical doctors. More murderers than college professors. It's mind-boggling, really." He talked on about the Caxtons' marriage for more than fifteen minutes, until Mike changed the questions to ask about Bryan Daughtry.

"Never had any use for him, Mr. Chapman. It was a major point of contention between Deni and me. Whenever we talked seriously about the future, I made it clear that there was no room in it for Daughtry. He's a despicable piece of— well, human garbage." Mattox walked along the window on the far side of the room, dragging his finger along the sill. "Why you people never nailed him for the murder of that Scandinavian girl upstate escapes me completely. Whatever he does, he somehow lands on his feet each time. Makes me sick just to think about it."

"Did you spend any time at Caxton Due, their new gallery?" I asked.

"Not when Bryan was around. I'd gone there on several occasions with Deni, when she went to check on shipments that were being unloaded. She found all that very exciting— loved to watch the men break down the packing boxes and lift some painting or sculpture out of them. She was like a little kid on Christmas morning, poring over every inch of the canvas, examining the artist's signature, checking out the condition of the frame.

"I'd go just to see her reaction. Frankly, the art she and Daughtry were interested in did nothing for me. I'm rather a classicist, as you can see from my work." He pointed at the office walls, which displayed the plans and finished results of some of his buildings. There was an elegance of line and style that didn't mesh with the contemporary works we had seen in Chelsea.

"Do you know Varelli? Marco Varelli?"

"Certainly. I'd actually met Marco many times."

"With Deni?"

"I'd met him through clients long before I started to date Deni. But I'd never been to his atelier until she took me there. He was a genius—a lovely man."

"When were you there—at his studio, I mean?"

"A couple of times this spring. I don't remember exactly, but once or twice, probably in June or July."

"Why did Deni take you there?"

"She usually went when she had a painting that she wanted Varelli to look at."

"Like a Vermeer?" Mike asked.

I wanted to slow him down. I could see Preston Mattox stiffen when Mike mentioned the artist's name. If he jumped into the territory of stolen artworks too quickly, I was afraid he'd lose his cooperative subject.

"So, you two have bought into all the gossip on the circuit. Denise Caxton and the masterpieces from the Gardner heist. When you find the goods, be sure and let me know," he said, scowling at Chapman as though he had made a terrible mistake.

"Deni ever talk to you about the Vermeer? Or the Rembrandt?"

Mattox was angry now. "She wasn't a thief, Detective. Deni made more than her share of enemies, but she was an awfully decent woman when you gave her a chance to be. There was no way she was involved with the scum who've been peddling stolen property. She didn't need that kind of trouble. Between the life that Lowell had built for her and what I was willing to provide when she married me, there wasn't any reason to debase herself with something that would land her in jail."

While Mattox was hot, Mike decided it was a good moment to offer him up the name of his rival. "And Frank Wrenley? Where did he fit in Deni's life?"

"As far out of the picture as I could move him, Detective."

"Why? What did you know about him?"

"Not enough, clearly. But that's because whatever I saw I didn't like."

"More than just jealousy?"

"Yes, Mr. Chapman. Far more than that. Frank moved in on Deni like a vulture right after she and Lowell split. I mean, they had known each other before around the auction houses, but he pounced on her like a panther when her wounds were still quite raw."

"But she loved him, too, didn't she?"

"She certainly liked what he offered her as an immediate alternative when Lowell Caxton brought their marriage to a crashing halt. Wrenley was a vehicle to get back at her husband. First of all, he was young, and youth was something Lowell couldn't buy for himself with all his millions. Wrenley was slick—too slick for my taste."

"Was he a real player in the antiques business?"

Mattox was slow to answer. "He's been making quite a name for himself. Not necessarily someone I'd bring in on a project, but he seems to know what he's doing."

"Would you say that you were closer to Deni in recent months than Wrenley was?" I asked.

Preston Mattox crossed his arms and leaned against the sill. Something he thought of brought a smile to his face. "I almost gave up on Deni before I got started. For a while it wasn't Lowell's shadow that got in the way, it was Wrenley's. Everywhere we went, he'd been there with Deni first. Just your mention of Marco Varelli reminded me how unreasonable I'd been about it. I'd been introduced to the man any number of times, but that last afternoon we were up in his studio, Deni and I walked in with a bottle of wine and some *biscotti* and he embraced me in a bear hug, calling me 'Franco.' Instead of correcting *him,* I took it out on Deni as soon as we left, asking her what the hell she'd been doing there with Frank."

"What'd she tell you?"

"I'm not sure she ever gave me an answer, Mr. Chapman. As with most of our arguments, she got me over them by taking me home to make love. I knew she and Wrenley had been doing the auction scene together, so it made sense that they had taken some work to Varelli to be cleaned up or restored. I just didn't like following in his footsteps wherever we went. But I didn't answer the question you asked, did I, Miss Cooper?

"Yes," he went on, "I was confident that I'd be spending the rest of my life with Deni. I can't tell you how extraordinarily happy that made me."

"Why had you gone to see Varelli that day?"

"Because Deni asked me to. Simple as that. He'd been mad at her about something, she wouldn't tell me what. So she wanted to take him a gift for his wife, smoke the peace pipe together—that sort of thing. I suppose I was an intermediary. She knew he liked to talk to me about my work—and that I could hold my own, whether it was about the architectural principles of Leonardo da Vinci and Thomas Jefferson or about drawings and art."

Chapman didn't care about the dome on the Rotunda. "What was the gift that Deni took for Mrs. Varelli?"

Again Mattox hesitated before lifting his head to meet Chapman's stare. "It was a necklace, Detective. An amber necklace. But I suppose you knew that already. I imagine you found the small figurine that Deni left behind, and that Mrs. Varelli told you the story."

Neither of us responded to his statement.

"I take it the peace offering didn't go very well, did it?"

"Varelli was furious." Mattox seemed to be open with us, having convinced himself that Varelli had told the story of the encounter to his wife. I guessed that he did not even recall that the soft-spoken young apprentice, Don Cannon, had been in the room when the beads were presented. "He assumed that the amber was part of Lowell's secret cache of looted Nazi riches. The old guy didn't even want to hold the necklace in his hands."

"Isn't that the truth, though? Isn't that the source of the amber?"

"Hardly, Mr. Chapman. All of us who've been looking for the Amber Room have combed the Baltic coast for years. In Lowell's case, for half a century, if you can imagine that. We've each come back with bits and pieces—the area is rich with amber. There are places along the coast where you can pick up chunks of it right on the beach. But no one really knows whether the great room was destroyed in some wartime bombing or is buried in one of the quarries that treasure seekers are constantly drilling."

"How about the rumors that Lowell Caxton has smuggled half the remains out of Europe and re-created the palace room in some hideaway in the Pennsylvania countryside?"

"And that's why I had latched on to Mrs. Caxton, Mr. Chapman? I've heard that one, too. If you could have seen

Deni throw back her head and roar at those stories—and the nonsense that she and Lowell had used this mini Amber Room for their trysts—well, then you would have seen the woman I adored. She liked to fuel those absurd tales when she heard they were circulating. The more bold and bizarre, the more it pleased her. She loved outrage, Detective, and if she was at the center of it she loved it even more."

"Were those the only jewels from Lowell that Deni wanted to give away?" I asked, referring to the amber beads.

"Lowell?" Mattox said with some surprise. "I don't think she was parting with anything *he* gave her. His gifts to her were pretty substantial."

"Then why the amber?"

"Those pieces weren't from Lowell."

I was sure Don Cannon had repeated that as part of Deni's explanation when she tried to hand Varelli the necklace.

Mattox thought for a moment. "You know, you're right, though. She told Marco they had been given to her by Lowell." Now he looked up at me. "But you see, that was part of the game she liked to play. By implication she'd let people assume they were part of Lowell's collection. Knowing Deni, she thought it would titillate old Marco to think there really was an Amber Room and that she and Lowell had cavorted in it. She and Varelli may have talked about it on other occasions—I simply don't know that."

"But she wouldn't take anything fake to give Varelli," I said. "I realize that his specialty was paint and artworks, but he had such a great eye. People tell us he had a unique sense of touch, and could identify the age of artworks so precisely. She wouldn't pass off something to him as an antique or a valuable if she was trying to appease him, would she?"

"The necklace and figurine were genuine, Miss Cooper. Very old and very fine amber. The Baltic region is full of great pieces. It's just that these things had absolutely nothing to do with the mysterious Russian palace and its amber. Deni may have tried to create that impression, but she knew damn well where the pieces came from."

"And where was that?" Chapman asked.

"The necklace had been commissioned by King Wilhelm of Prussia for his queen. And the figurine as well. Sold at auction in Geneva several years ago. Can't remember the price they brought, but it was quite high."

"And Lowell bought them for Deni?"

"No, no." Mattox seemed bothered that we hadn't followed his point. "Deni only *said* she had gotten them from Lowell. Actually, they were a gift to her from a friend."

"You know who he was?"

"*She,* Detective. From a woman called Marina Sette."

"Pretty nice stocking stuffer," Mike said.

It seemed even more curious that Deni would relinquish something that her closest friend had given to her. I still had every note card and silly souvenir that Nina or Joan had ever sent me, not to mention the more serious gifts. "But why would she get rid of something so precious, from someone she liked so much?"

Preston Mattox looked at me with a curious glance. "Liked so much? They hadn't talked to each other in a long time."

Chapman spoke before I did. "I thought they were best pals."

"I don't know what gave you that idea. They used to be quite close, but they had a terrible falling-out this spring. I don't think Deni had returned Marina's calls in months."

"What was that about, do you know?"

"The only person who thought she had a greater entitlement to Lowell Caxton's fortune than Denise did was Marina Sette. Deni came to believe that the primary reason Marina had befriended her in the first place was to work herself back into the inheritance—the fortune that would have been

Marina's had her mother not abandoned her when she married Lowell. There was nothing logical about Marina's position. I doubt she has a leg to stand on in a court of law. But I think it was more of an emotional attempt to regain some connection to the mother she never knew, by claiming that she had a right to some of the masterpieces acquired during the period her mother was married to Lowell Caxton."

"Seems to me there was more than enough money to go around," Chapman murmured.

"But they'd never argued about that before?" I asked.

"It never was an issue with Deni before this spring. But then, once she suspected that Marina Sette had been sleeping with Frank Wrenley, it became more than an issue. It was the end of the friendship. The worm turned."

27

Mercer Wallace lifted his head off the pile of pillows as we entered the room and gave us a weak but warm greeting. The nurse who helped feed him his dinner—still a liquid diet—was moving the tray off the bedside table as we settled in around the patient.

Chapman grabbed the television remote control panel dangling from a cord on Mercer's bed railing and pointed it at the small set that was hanging from a support in the corner.

"Too early," Mercer said, laughing. It was only six thirty-five, and he thought that Mike was looking for the *Jeopardy!* channel. "Let me hear what's going on."

Mike kept clicking until the screen was set on NBC and the

national news report. "Don't you want to see Cooper's guy? Has he got a live shoot tonight, kid? Whoops, looks like Brian Williams has the anchor spot." He muted the sound and asked Mercer how he felt.

"I don't remember much about yesterday. Pain's under control, and they even had me out of bed for an hour this afternoon. One lap around the hallway."

"There he is!" Mike said, rising from his armchair and walking to stand directly under the television set. "Gimme volume, Mercer."

Jake was standing on First Avenue, in front of the United Nations building, and he was midsentence when I heard his voice: ". . . after the secretary of state and the delegate from . . ."

Mike's pen was in his right hand, held up against the screen and tapping at Jake's chest. "Here's the thing, Mercer. The reason you and I will never get to first base with Ms. Cooper is that we don't have these ties that all her beaux wear, know what I mean? Every one of 'em has these itsy-bitsy, teeny-weeny little friggin' animals all over 'em. Grown men, and they got little squirrels runnin' around with nuts in their cheeks, sheep jumping over fences, monkeys swingin' on vines, giraffes standing on tippy-toe. I would be mortified to be here on national television, talkin' about sending troops to the Middle East, decked out in some French necktie—what do you call them, Coop? Hermies or Hermans or Ermies—something like that. Anyway, the thing is, Mercer, that it *works.* 'Cause whatever it is about those ties, every one of the goofballs who shows up wearing one of 'em gets laid.

"Am I right, blondie? Ever do a simple guy with a striped tie? I doubt it. I'm telling you, if Alex Trebek walked in with one of these on, she'd go down on him like a pelican, wouldn't you, kid? You wanna predict who Cooper's gonna get up close and personal with, you check out the tie. That, my good friend, is my Dick Tracy crimestopper clue of the day."

Mercer was holding his hand over his chest. "Don't make me laugh, Mike. Somebody want to tell me what's going on with the case?"

"First of all, forget that you ever saw Alex tonight. Pat McKinney's riding her pretty hard. Doesn't want her to visit with you, so you don't talk about the facts of the case together."

Mercer looked across at me to see if Mike was still kidding. "It's true. He's afraid we're going to conspire and rearrange the events if we talk to each other. I spent three hours last night giving my statement. I'm sure they got one from you today, as soon as you opened your eyes. I don't know what he's so worried about."

"They were here. Two guys from Major Case, first thing this morning. They said they're taking you back over to the scene later in the week."

"Yes," I said, hoping that my involuntary shudder at the thought of revisiting the gallery hadn't been visible to Mike or Mercer.

"That is one spooky exhibit," Mike said. "I stopped there this morning on my way to the hospital the first time. Kind of reminds me of that great Orson Welles scene in *Lady From Shanghai*—the shoot-out in the fun house? Only thing missing was the mirrors. Listen to this."

Mike pulled a wrinkled piece of paper from his pants pocket. "They're already moving a new show into Caxton Due. Somebody probably needed all that friggin' yarn to make a sweater. I'm reading right from the description Bryan Daughtry wrote. It's in *New York* magazine. 'The artist affixes hardened blobs of paint and scraps of paper, hair, and other scavenged materials to her monochromatic canvases.' I'm looking forward to wrapping this case up so I can go back to working something real, like a pickpocket detail."

Mercer winced as he tried to push himself up in bed. I

327

moved to his side to adjust the pillows behind his back and beneath his head. I grabbed one of his enormous arms and pulled on it as gently as I could, but was unable to move him. Mike got on the other side, and together we raised Mercer so that his head rested in a more comfortable position.

"Watch out for the tubes," I said to Mike, lifting the IV drip from where it was caught under a roll of bedsheet.

"Else you'll get *strangulated* on all those concoctions, Mr. Wallace. That's a word for the *S* section of my dictionary. I got to jot that one down. 'Fixiated'—that goes with the *F*'s, not the *A*'s—and 'strangulated' are two very popular causes of death among perps."

"Have mercy, will you please, Mr. Chapman? I'm supposed to be lying here very still. Don't make me get up and have to hurt you."

We spent the next half hour telling Mercer what we had learned from Don Cannon and Preston Mattox. "Who do you like in all this?" he asked.

Mike shrugged his shoulders. "Nothing and nobody is like what you'd think they'd be. Me, I always thought the international art world was for the elegant and elite. Classy, calm, sedate, cultured. I'm tellin' you, there are more lowlifes in *this* business than all the Hannibal Lecter wanna-bes in the world."

"Between the fakes and the frauds, and centuries of thefts and misrepresentations, I can't imagine now how anyone sets a value that can be trusted on any painting," I added. It was odd that for so many of the people we had encountered, their passions had become obsessions, and their lives as illusory as their art.

Mike reached for the clicker and raised the volume again. "Okay, the Final Jeopardy topic is Sports. Way to go. I'm in for fifty dollars. Partners, Mercer?" Mike gave him a thumbs-up and got a wink in response. "Get your money up, Coop."

I opened my pocketbook and reached in to dig around. Even though I had just taken another handbag from the apartment late last night to replace the one that I had lost in the shooting, I had already filled it with more than any reasonable person would cart around. The heavy wallet, laden with a checkbook, credit cards, business cards, and assorted notes, had sunk to the bottom of the deep tote. On Mercer's tray table I unloaded house keys, car keys, office keys, and Jake's apartment keys. A lipstick case and blusher came out next. Handkerchief, pens, hairbrush, Post-it pads, and my official badge piled on top.

"How the hell do you ever find anything in there? It's really one of life's great mysteries.

"Okay, the answer is: First major league athlete to play all nine positions in the same baseball season. You got sixty seconds, blondie. Mercer and I got this one locked up . . . What the hell is that?"

As I pulled out my wallet, with it came a small plastic bag that had snagged on its clasp, holding an old-fashioned razor and set of double-edge platinum blades, along with a toothbrush and tube of paste.

"I brought a little supply kit for Mercer. Jake has dozens of those travel cases so he can just pack them and go when he gets sent on assignment. Thought maybe you'd be able to use some of this stuff while you're here," I said, holding it up so Mercer could see.

He pointed to his drawer and told me that his dad had brought him everything he needed, so I replaced all my belongings in the bag.

"Enough with the Clara Barton imitation. You either give us a name or just drop the money in my pocket."

I had no idea that anyone had ever accomplished that feat. I took out a fifty-dollar bill and handed it to Mike, at the same time as I said, "Who was Whitey Ford?" As far as I was concerned, if it hadn't been done by a Yankee, then it hadn't ever happened.

Trebek was just consoling the three contestants, none of whom had delivered the correct answer. Before he revealed it on the game board, Mike announced, "Oakland. Who is Bert Campaneris?"

The television echoed the same question: "Who is Bert Campaneris?"

"I can't believe you knew that."

He'd pocketed the cash before I finished the sentence. "You don't mind if I don't spend it on flowers or candy, do you, m'man? I got some informants who need a little monkey grease to make 'em sing to me."

The phone rang and I picked it up. "Could I speak with Detective Chapman?"

I stepped back and Mike squeezed around the side of the bed and took the receiver. "K.D.? Whaddaya got?" Mike raised his left shoulder to hold the phone in place against his ear while he reached into his pocket for a pen and paper. He listened to Jimmy Halloran for several minutes, occasionally punctuating the conversation with a "When?" or a "Who?" while I held a straw to Mercer's lips and helped him drink some of the water that the nurse had directed him to finish. "No, it's not everything," Mike said before hanging up, "but it's not a bad start. Thanks."

Mike began his narrative for us. "Anthony Bailor. Gainesville, Florida. He's forty-two years old now, but back when he was eighteen, he burglarized an apartment. Raped a college student who was living there. Knifepoint. Also I.D.'d in three other cases in town within six months."

"And did less than twenty years?" I asked.

"Three of the victims were too scared to press charges. Hey, it was almost twenty-five years ago. Nothing unusual about that back then."

It was only within the last ten to fifteen years that victims of sexual assault were treated with any dignity in the courtroom. The bad laws that had prevented women from having access to the system had begun to be revised throughout the seventies, but public attitudes about this category of crime had been even slower to change. For centuries, rape was the only crime for which the victim was blamed, and the stigma that attached itself to women who had been forced to experience such an intimate violation kept many of them from seeking justice.

"What didn't show on his sheet was his youth record. Again, Florida. Did time in a juvenile facility, also for rape. Carjacked a woman in a supermarket parking lot."

"So we got a sexual predator on our hands."

"Served his felony sentence in Raiford. They got a prison there, Coop, makes Attica look like a beauty school. Bailor did hard time. *Real* hard time. I'm talking chain gangs and leg irons. Must've been one of the first guys to get himself into the DNA data bank. Even though they didn't exist when he was convicted, by the time he was eligible for parole, no one was let out until his genetic fingerprint was on file."

Mike looked back at his pad and flipped the page. "When he got out of jail, he moved right out of Florida. Can't say as I blame him. If you're gonna foul up again, might as well come north to one of our country club prisons. Be my guest, Mr. Bailor. I love New York.

"Ready for the larceny arrest?" Mike asked. "The original charge was grand larceny, but he pleaded out to possession of stolen property. That's how come he did so little time. Prosecutor had to drop the top count and take the lesser plea 'cause the theft actually occurred in Massachusetts. Anton Bailey was stopped on the New York State Thruway for speeding. When they searched his car, the troopers found a couple of oil paintings. Valuable ones. Seems Anton hadn't saved his sales receipts."

"Massachusetts? From the Gardner?"

"Nope. Right state, wrong museum. Something called the Mead Art Museum, in Amherst. Couldn't pin the actual burglary on Anton. His alibi back in Buffalo held up pretty well. So all they had him for was possession of the goods. They even offered him a deal of no jail time if he gave up his accomplice. But he hung tough. Shit, after the stretch he did in Florida, he must have done this sentence standing on his head."

It was an interesting development. Somewhere along the way, Bailor had connected with art criminals and had perhaps lent his break-in talent to their undertakings. A simple calculation confirmed that he was still in a Florida prison when the Gardner theft had occurred, but he must have more recently marketed his skills to this murky underground world of thieves.

"Do you think he knew Omar Sheffield before they wound up in the same cell?"

"No sign of that yet. We'll have to talk to some of the other prisoners. So far, what K.D. got is only from the paperwork in the warden's files. Could be just dumb luck. Omar's doing his usual scam. Tells Anton about Denise Caxton, maybe even shows him the clippings from the *Law Journal* about the Caxton divorce, which lists every one of their assets and describes all of their dealings in the art business. Anton has bigger plans. Passes off the information to . . ."

"Whom?" I asked. "That's all we've got to figure. He must have been in this with someone else, someone who had his own scam in mind for Denise."

"Or for Lowell," Mike reminded me. "I'm not sure who was out to get which one first."

"You don't really think Lowell was intended to be a victim in all this, do you?"

Mercer had been listening to us without joining the conversation, as he struggled against dozing off. "You said you spoke

332

to that Sette woman out in Santa Fe yesterday, Mike? That she really was back there?"

Mike paused before answering. "It was actually her house-keeper who answered the phone and told me she expected Sette back in an hour or so. She was Mexican, with a thick accent, and hard to understand. No, I didn't speak to Sette directly. And I forgot to check the airline manifest afterward to see if she really flew out there. Sorry, Mercer. I'll get on that tonight."

It was Marina Sette's message—or one that had been left for us using her name—that had resulted in my trip to the Focus gallery with Mercer yesterday and that had set us up to be shot. For good reason, Mike was concentrating more on that intrigue at the moment than on piecing together the puzzle of Deni Caxton's death.

The phone rang again and I answered it. "Alexandra? It's Rose Malone. I thought you might be there with Mercer. I wanted you to know that Mr. Battaglia is on his way home. He's going to stop in at the hospital."

Thank goodness for Rose. She was better than a radar detector. I'd say good night to Mercer before Battaglia arrived, and let the squad detectives take me back to Jake's apartment for the night.

"And one other thing. The police have arrested that Wake-field man who was here at the office looking for you earlier."

"Did he come back?" I asked, alarmed at his persistence.

"No. But that young girl who was in your office—was it Ruth?"

"Yes."

"She showed up at his apartment this afternoon, to try to get together with him again. He beat her up pretty seriously. For admitting to you that she'd been sleeping with his room-mate."

"Oh, no." I closed my eyes and gritted my teeth at the

thought of the anger that Wakefield must have unleashed at that child. I thanked Rose for the call and hung up the phone.

"You're running on fumes, Coop," Mike said. "I'll sit with Mercer tonight. Let me take you downstairs and send you off. Get a good night's sleep and we'll talk in the morning. Put a double rush on those prison phone records when you get to the office. We gotta figure out who Bailey's connected with, okay? And I think we need to find Marina Sette as soon as possible."

I sat in the back of the unmarked car, looking out at the dark streets as we drove uptown and making small talk with the detectives about the usual office gossip. They discharged me in front of Jake's building, watching as the doorman let me in and then parking at the curb, where they would sit out their shift before they were replaced by the midnight team in a couple of hours.

I turned the key in the lock and entered the apartment. A small lamp was lighted on the vestibule table, where I saw a handwritten note addressed to me.

"Dearest A— My turn to disappear. Running for the last shuttle to Washington. Have a 7 A.M. interview with the secretary of defense. Sweet dreams, see you tomorrow. Love, J."

I groped the walls in the semidarkness of the unfamiliar layout to turn on a light switch in the hallway leading to the bedroom. Once I found my way, I reached for the suitcase I had packed the evening before and laid out some of the clothes for the next day.

The silence and the emptiness made me uncomfortable. I wanted the comfort of my own home, and the warmth of Jake's caress.

28

I couldn't find the coffee beans in Jake's kitchen when I got out of bed, shortly before seven o'clock. I showered and dressed, joining the team in the department car for the ride down to 1 Hogan Place. They let me out right in front of the building, and I bought us each some breakfast at the cart on the corner before going up to my office. Now that Wakim had been arrested I felt at least somewhat more secure.

The pile of unanswered correspondence on my desk was growing out of control. There was a stack of indictments on sex crimes cases that needed to be proofread and approved before the end of the August term, which was a week away. Phone messages from friends were taped to the computer screen; a request from Elaine to set a time to come into the Escada store to have the clothes I ordered from the fall collection shortened had been ignored; and solicitations for charitable fund-raisers collected dust on the far corner of the desk. It was still too early to find most people at their offices, so I busied myself in the review of grand jury proceedings to make sure the lawyers in the unit met their filing deadlines.

The first call was from Bob Thaler, the chief serologist at the Medical Examiner's Office. It was not even eight thirty, and I was answering my own phones because Laura would not arrive for another hour.

"Sorry it took me so long for the tox on Omar Sheffield." While autopsy results were available to us quickly, it frequently took weeks to run all the toxicological tests looking for foreign substances in the deceased's brain, liver, tissue, or lungs.

"Find anything?"

"Just about everything. Omar might have been breathing when that train ran over him, but he wouldn't have been aware of very much. He was loaded up with speedballs, more than enough to kill himself with if he'd been attempting to O.D."

"And if someone else was trying to kill him?" Speedballs were a deadly combination of heroin and cocaine, usually mainlined right into the system.

"It'd work like a charm. Just keep pumping it into his arm."

"But the cause of death, what have you put down for that?"

"Gross internal trauma. I mean, he died at the moment the train ran over his body, Alex. But in all likelihood the drugs could have done the trick by themselves. Somebody finds you in a hotel room in a coma, they can still get you to a hospital and try to pump the stuff out of you. Slim chance, with this amount of poison in his veins, but it might have been possible for him to survive. Run a few railroad cars over this perfectly inert body, it's a sure thing he's gone to meet his maker."

"Thanks, Bob. Would you fax over a copy of the report to me?"

Lawyers were beginning to dribble into the office. I had my door open, listening for Pat McKinney's arrival. The click of high heels on the tiles of the deserted hallway caught my attention. Pat's office, like Rod Squires', was at the far end of my corridor. But there were no other women assigned to this executive wing of the Trial Division, so I stepped out to Laura's desk to see who was walking by.

I recognized Ellen Gunsher from the back. She was junior to me, having been in the office for almost eight years. Bright enough and quite aggressive, she had taken to all of the duties of a prosecutor fairly well—except for the one that counted most. She had never grown comfortable in the courtroom and backed away from trying cases. Her surname lent itself to the unfortunate alias "Gun-shy," and her colleagues teased her mercilessly about her retreat from the kind of professional battle that most of us relished.

Ellen had found a protector in Pat McKinney. As deputy chief of the division, he had taken her out of her trial bureau and created a special unit for her to supervise. Most of us recognized that it was a make-work kind of assignment—to serve as a contact with the NYPD's Warrant Squad, to initiate and oversee active searches for the most dangerous of the thousands of defendants who failed to appear on their cases after bail had been granted. Many of the prisoners for whom Wanted cards had been issued were petty offenders who would turn up in the system before too long on charges of shoplifting or jumping a turnstile. Ellen's job consisted of sifting through court papers and targeting the more violent offenders, then assigning Warrant Squad officers to make an active search for their return.

I believed that McKinney had manufactured that niche because Ellen was a decent lawyer and a nice person who was not otherwise a fit in our division. For two years I had ignored office gossip that they had been having an affair, but now the amount of time they spent together behind closed doors seemed inordinate for the nonessential nature of Ellen's work.

I went back to my desk to gather the notes I planned to take in to McKinney to discuss the latest interviews Mike and I had done on the Caxton investigation. McKinney waved at me as he passed by my doorway. "We gotta talk."

The case papers had outgrown a single folder. I pulled out the sheaf of reports we had worked from yesterday, took my thick legal pad including my to-do list, and headed down to the deputy's office. I knocked on the heavy metal door.

"Come in," Ellen called out to me. Not exactly the welcome I wanted.

She was standing by a hot plate at the far end of the room, boiling water for tea. She had opened a jar of honey and was holding two mugs. McKinney had his back to me and was talking on the phone. It was all a bit too domestic for my taste.

"How's Mercer?" Ellen asked.

"He's in rough shape. It was a very close call."

"You must feel awful. I can't imagine how you handled watching him get shot."

I slowly moved my head back and forth, biting my lip. I had no intention of telling her anything about how I felt, and was boring my eyes through the back of McKinney's sweaty T-shirt as though it would somehow get him off the phone faster.

"Want some tea?" she asked, holding up a third mug with a photo of McKinney's kids under a Christmas tree emblazoned on its ceramic side.

"No thanks," I said, raising my cardboard coffee cup at her.

"Any new leads?"

"I'll wait until Pat gets off the phone."

"Been up to the Vineyard at all?"

"Uh huh." When you're ready for full disclosure on your personal life, I'll be happy to give you an update on my own.

"You really look whipped. Ought to try a little concealer for those circles under your eyes. Maybe you should take the next couple of weeks off. Stay up there until after Labor Day."

Women in the workplace, I sighed to myself. Why is it that Mike Chapman could tell me how bad I looked and I could acknowledge it, but when Ellen eyeballed me and said the same thing, it sounded bitchy? Maybe I could take two weeks in the country if I was as expendable around here as you are, I thought. "I'm fine. I'll take it easy next weekend."

McKinney finished his conversation and sat down opposite me at his small conference table. "I want to talk to you about the case, Alex—I mean, the whole matter. I've been thinking that maybe the best thing—"

"Pat, would you mind if we just do this one-on-one?"

Ellen had poured the water and was squeezing the tea bags now.

"You mean Ellen? She's a unit chief in the division. What's the problem?"

"This discussion is between you and me. I know you've called a meeting for ten o'clock this morning to which I wasn't invited. I'm planning to be there."

"That's a stupid idea, Alex. In fact, I'm not even sure it makes any sense for you to stay on the Caxton investigation."

"Ellen, would you mind leaving the room, please?"

She placed the mugs on the table, and instead of answering me, she looked at Pat, who was looking directly in my eyes.

"I'm *not* having this conversation in Ellen's presence. Last I knew," I said, trying not to let my temper take over my response, "no one in this case had jumped bail, failed to appear, warranted out on a misdemeanor, or otherwise done anything to invoke the awesome power of Ellen Gunsher's irrelevant little unit. This is between the two of us, Pat. You have *no* business talking about it with Ellen. And don't you dare even think about taking me off the Caxton murder. I'll go right to Battaglia and—"

"I've already done that, Alex."

Ellen's head was snapping back and forth between us like it was on a spring. I was infuriated that Pat had spoken to the district attorney about removing me from the investigation.

"I'll bet he told you to stick it. He has absolutely no problem with the work I've been doing."

It was a bluff, but a successful one. McKinney's moment of hesitation revealed to me that although he had raised the issue with Battaglia, he had not been given a green light to take the case away from me.

I pushed my chair back and walked to the door. "I'll be in Battaglia's office. When you and the Lipton Tea lady finish your morning tête-à-tête, feel free to come in, by yourself, to get a bulletin on the case. Meanwhile, I'll leave you to the important matter of how many of yesterday's token suckers failed to show up in AP17."

I doubled back past my office, across the main corridor, and used my magnetized identification badge to buzz myself into the executive wing. Secretaries to the administrative assistant, the first assistant, and the chief assistant were setting up their desks for the day and greeted me with interest and concern.

Rose Malone was already at her word processor when I approached her desk. She was the last to leave the building most nights—sometimes with Paul Battaglia, but never before him. And she was always the first one in place the next day.

She didn't even turn her head to speak to me. "He's not here yet, Alex. There's a community board breakfast meeting in East Harlem."

"Do you expect him before ten?"

"No. He's going from that one directly to the Midtown

Court. There's going to be a press release about the new computer system that will track bench warrants in all the borough courthouses and police precincts."

Great. A new technology that will make Ellen Gunsher completely obsolete. "Will he call in from the car?"

"I expect so. Shall I transfer him over to you?"

"Please. Especially if you get him within the hour, okay?"

"Anything wrong?"

"Was Pat McKinney alone with him for any period of time yesterday?"

Rose stopped typing and looked back at Battaglia's date book, as though trying to find a way to remind herself of the day's meetings.

"I know he called and asked if the boss would see him. They may have spoken for a minute or two, but Paul was tied up most of the afternoon with the accountants who've been working on that welfare fraud case. It couldn't have been much of a conversation."

I thanked her and walked back to my office. As much as McKinney may have wanted me off the Caxton case, I was still alive. I needed to sit down and go over what the rest of the week might produce for us, knowing that any kind of evidentiary break would help cement my position on the team.

I could hear Chapman serenading Laura as I went back to my office. What had probably started as a cross-examination of what she knew about my relationship with Jacob Tyler had segued into an impromptu version of Paul Simon's "Fifty Ways to Leave Your Lover." As I turned the corner he grinned at me and continued singing. "Don't make a mistake, Jake. Just let yourself go."

"To what do I owe this unexpected pleasure?" I growled.

"People to talk to, places to go, subpoenas to get. Let's start with the latter. What happened to your manners? What about 'Good morning, Mr. Chapman. How are you today? Thank you for bringing me another cup of coffee,' huh? I'm even going out on a limb for a 'Don't *you* look lovely today, Miss Cooper. Could be you had a good night's rest at long last.' "

"Thanks. But I've already been told by Ellen Gunsher that even makeup can't help me in my current condition. Pat's trying to knock me off your investigation."

"What kind of suicide mission is *he* on?"

"There's a meeting at ten to assign one of the senior trial counsel to Mercer's shooting. And since I'm a witness to that, he wants to take me off the whole thing and set one of his pets up to handle it, before Rod Squires returns from vacation." My back was to the door as I reached across my desk to replace the case papers on top of the folder. "I'm trying to get a call into Battaglia before this morning's caucus on the subject."

"Speaking of carcass, what's up, McKinney?"

Mike warned me that Pat had appeared in the doorway, and I spun around.

"Now I'd like to talk to *you* alone, Alex. Why don't you wait down the hall, Mike?"

"Battaglia gave me strict orders that she's to have police protection around the clock, Pat. No can do." Mike sat behind the desk in my chair and lifted his feet up on my desktop, one at a time, making the statement that he was not about to move. "We got some breaking developments on Caxton you might want to know about."

"Take a walk, Chapman. C'mon."

Mike checked with me before he slowly removed his legs, then stood up and started for the exit. "Be sure to give my best to your wife and kids, Pat."

The intercom buzzed and I could hear Laura calling my name.

"Yes?"

"There's a gentleman downstairs who wants to talk to you. His name is Frank Wrenley. Can he come up?"

I exchanged glances with Chapman, who had stopped in the doorway, and he nodded at me in response. "Keep him down there for ten minutes while I make a few calls. Maybe he can clear up some of this business about his relationship with Marina Sette. I'd like to find out exactly where she is right now."

I told Laura to have security hold him there until Mike could go to the lobby to escort him in. "This isn't a very good time to talk, Pat. Might as well go ahead with your ten o'clock meeting. I can't make it anyway."

29

"I just woke up the housekeeper in Santa Fe. She doesn't expect Ms. Sette back there for another week. Laid on a heavy Spanish accent, says I must have misunderstood her when I called on Sunday. I'm telling you, Alex, I swear that woman told me Sette had just flown back home the other day. This is Mercer's life, for chrissakes. It's not anything I would have made a mistake about. Today when I press her about where I can get in touch with Sette, all I get is that the housekeeper doesn't know. '*La Señora*' is traveling." Mike was fuming.

"All right, relax. Let's just make a plan."

"You know why I like it better when I'm working on something where everybody's poor? 'Cause the friggin' perps can't go too far. One guy's maybe got a mother in Queens, next one chills out at his brother's place in the Bronx, another sleeps on the rooftop. None of this Airborne Express crap that the rich can pull. That mope I locked up for the triple homicide in the Polo Grounds project two weeks ago? Gave me more trouble than any of 'em. His sister told me he lived in a mobile home. In New York City? No way—we don't have 'em here. Took me days to figure out she meant the A train. He just moved his plastic bag of worldly goods into the subway and rode from one end of the system to the other and then back, night after night. It should happen to these people. What if it actually *was* Marina Sette who left the message for you and Mercer to meet her?"

"Then she either has something to do with the killings or she's on the run because she's truly terrified of something or someone."

"When are you gonna get results on all the subpoenas for telephone records?" His impatience was palpable.

"I call every day, and every day they tell me that the volume is tremendous and I'll have what I need as soon as possible. The only ones back were in yesterday's mail. Omar Sheffield's phone calls made while he was in jail. I had Maxine and one of the other paralegals go through them to check for calls to Denise Caxton. Not a one."

"How can that be?"

"I checked with the warden. You'll love this one. There's a foolproof way for inmates to place untraceable calls now. They buy those prepaid telephone cards and then use the cards to make the calls from prison pay phones. All you're left with is a record of a call to the company that issued the card, but no link at all to the number actually dialed. Max says Omar's phone-privilege time slots—you know, the half hour each day he had access to the booth—show lots of activity in the period that would fit with the dates after Deni started to get letters from him, but all the outgoing ones he made just reflect the number of the calling card company in Brooklyn."

"Damn. And no word on when you'll have the incoming calls to the Caxton house or the galleries?"

"That takes longer. I'd guess we're at least a week away from that stuff."

"Let me go downstairs and get Wrenley. After he tells us why he's here, I'll move it to talk about Marina Sette, okay?"

I walked to my desk to find my file notes on the antiques dealer and review them. Laura stuck her head in the doorway and asked if she could borrow an emery board. I pointed to my handbag, which I had left on the leather armchair in front of the desk. "Just fish around in there. I know I've got a few on the bottom."

"Would you mind if I take the day off tomorrow?" she asked tentatively.

I guessed that was the real reason she had come into the room in the first place. "As long as you can get someone to cover the phones. They've been wild since this started. And help Mike with the subpoenas he needs you to type up this morning." We were short staffed because of the normal summer vacation schedule, but the pace of the investigation didn't correspond with the seasonal slowdown. "Any luck in finding Rod Squires?"

"Rose says he's on a sailboat off the coast of Maine. If he contacts Paul, she'll flip him over to you."

For the moment, Frank Wrenley's unexpected appearance gave me a reprieve from McKinney's plan to boot me off the case.

Mike came back into my office with Wrenley and I rose to shake his hand across the desk. This time he was head-to-toe in slate gray, a slight contrast to his jet black hair and almost a match for the cloud-filled sky that hugged the city with its humidity.

"Why don't you have a seat and tell us what brings you down here?"

Wrenley turned to sit and I saw my bag in his way. "Just put it on the floor. Sorry."

He lifted it and sat it down next to the row of file cabinets. "Must have your whole arsenal in there, Miss Cooper."

Chapman laughed. "She would if we'd let her. Temper like hers, Mr. Wrenley, Cooper couldn't get a permit to carry a pointed pencil."

Wrenley looked directly at me. "I wasn't sure who to talk to about this, but perhaps you ought to know. And you might be able to help me, too."

It was getting harder and harder to find anyone to talk to us who didn't want something in return. "What is it?"

"Last evening I found out that Lowell Caxton is going to be closing his gallery."

He stopped speaking and both Mike and I waited for him to continue.

"I mean, this week. Abruptly. Doesn't that surprise you?"

"Elephants flying? Monkeys tap-dancing? Those things might surprise me. The people in this case, the pals you've been running with who've been scamming each other and the public for most of their adult lives? Very little they do could surprise me at this point."

Wrenley ignored Chapman and talked to me. "Caxton's had one of the most substantial businesses in this city for longer than I can remember. It would be one thing for him to announce a closing and wind down his affairs over the next few months. But to pull a few moving vans up to the front of the building and start loading them like a gypsy in the middle of the night, well, it's more than a bit odd."

"Last night?" I asked. "Who told you about it?"

"Bryan Daughtry called me. He still has a lot of contacts who work in the Fuller Building."

Wrenley's statement reminded me that before Daughtry went to jail on the tax case, his original gallery had been on Fifty-seventh Street, several floors below Caxton's suite.

"What else did he say?"

"One of the custodians, a fellow who runs the freight elevator, figured he could make a few dollars by passing the information to Daughtry. It worked. Bryan went right up there and gave the guy a hundred bucks. Saw what was going on himself. Paintings and sculptures being loaded onto a truck at eleven last night, complete with a cadre of security guards. But Caxton's employees wouldn't spill the beans. Not a word about where they were taking the stuff, or why. I'm sure he paid them well enough to ensure their loyalty."

"I guess I'm missing the reason why either you or Daughtry think any of this is your business," Chapman said.

"Understandable. That's why, as I said a few minutes ago, I wasn't sure what to do about it when Daughtry called me in the middle of the night. Both Bryan and I were involved in a number of art deals with Deni. She and I recently bought some paintings at auction together," he said, switching his attention to Mike. "You're the skeptic, Detective. Check with Christie's. Back in May we were partners on some minor Impressionist works that sold pretty reasonably."

"Lowell's in on this, too?"

"Oh, no. Not at all. But a lot of the things we bought— well, it just made more sense for Deni to keep them for us, to store them until we decided whether we were going to hang on to them or sell them to clients. I mean, Lowell had warehouses and guards and insurance. Even their apartment was a safer place to keep artworks than any temporary facility she and I could arrange. We were lovers, after all, Detective. I didn't have to get a signed pledge from Deni when I agreed to let her hold on to something we bought as partners. She wasn't trying to screw me out of anything, if you'll forgive the expression."

"So you think some of the art you own is being spirited away by Lowell?"

"Possibly. And I don't even mean intentionally. Lowell doesn't have any reason to know the details about Deni's latest acquisitions. I just think there should be some way for me to have a look at what he's got before he ships it out of town or abroad. I have papers and sales receipts for everything. I'm not asking you to get in the middle of deciding what's mine and what isn't. My lawyer will handle all that. He wanted me to, well, to exaggerate to you a bit."

"What do you mean?"

Wrenley was fidgeting now. "I called my lawyer to ask him to get involved this morning. The problem is, of course, that Lowell won't let me inside to look, neither at the gallery nor the apartment—still their home, certainly. It was my lawyer's idea to come to you, Miss Cooper. Look, I don't want to lie to you, but he suggested I swear to you that I know Lowell Caxton has got property in the gallery that belongs to Deni and to me. That perhaps then you could intercede and go in with a warrant to search for things." He tapped his fingers on the arm of the chair. "Frankly, I have no idea what Deni did with some of the paintings. I can't 'swear' where they are—that would simply be a logical guess, but not necessarily true. Bryan Daughtry's been very helpful. I'm going to go through his warehouse, too. Perhaps some of the things I'm looking for are stored with him."

"Can you give me an inventory, a list of the works you have a claim to?" I asked.

"I don't have one prepared right now, but I can have it drawn up within a day or two." Wrenley's hands were on his knees, and he looked down at the floor before he spoke again. "When you're in love with a woman as young and healthy as Deni, you just never think that she's going to walk out the door and . . . never, never come back. The business side of our partnership was the last thing it occurred to me to worry about during this past week. That afternoon, I just waited and waited for her to meet me for lunch—"

"The day she disappeared? She was on her way to meet you?" Chapman asked.

"Perhaps I have surprised you after all, Detective. I assumed you'd know that, from the housekeeper or someone you'd interviewed. Didn't you ask me that the first time we met? I was sure you had."

Chapman seemed embarrassed that he didn't know one of the fairly basic facts about Denise Caxton's last day. "The guys who work in her garage have her going out with the car early in the morning. No one else we talked to seemed to know much about her plans for the day. What did you do when she didn't show up for lunch?"

"I waited half an hour. Tried her at home, in the car, at the gallery. No luck. Check with the maître d' at Jean-Georges—I thought you would have done that by now. I must have tied up his phone for twenty minutes calling around to find Deni."

"Were you upset? Call the police to look for her?"

"No, I suppose the maître d' would also tell you I wasn't very upset, so there's no point pretending. Nothing from which a couple of martinis couldn't distract me. I'd half expected she might stand me up that day. We'd had a bit of a tiff the week before."

"Business?"

"Not business at all. And in retrospect, not exactly pleasure, either." Wrenley looked me in the eye. "I told you when I met you the first time that Deni and I dated other people. Well, I ran into someone in Paris, a woman who'd been recently widowed and was doing the grand tour to announce that her mourning period was officially over. We spent a weekend together, which there was no need for Deni to find out about. Unfortunate coincidence, she turned out to be a friend of Deni's."

"Marina Sette?" Chapman asked.

"*Bravo*, Detective! Forty-eight hours in a small hotel on the Left Bank, and *tout* New York seems to know all about it. I know Marina told Deni, and that's what had her so mad at me. Deni didn't mind what she didn't know about, but Marina really pushed her nose into it."

"Was it over between you and Deni?"

"Of course not. But it was cool, to say the least. She made a point of letting me know that she was spending a lot of time with Preston Mattox. But that was just to get back at me."

"You don't think she was in love with him?"

"Deni was an intensely physical creature, Ms. Cooper. She'd once made the mistake of telling me, when she was unusually giddy in the middle of a rather vigorous round of lovemaking, that there wasn't enough Viagra in all the laboratories in the country to get Preston through another month of his relationship with Deni."

Every time I was on the verge of liking her a bit more, I'd hear something that would cause me to take three mental giant steps in reverse. No point in exploring with Wrenley whether his rival had other redeeming features.

"When she didn't show up at the restaurant for lunch and I couldn't find out where she was, I thought that all she needed was some time to get over what I had done with Marina. She'd only graced me with the luncheon meeting because we had some business decisions to make and because she wouldn't accept an evening date with me. She already had dinner plans with Mattox." I didn't think I had displayed any expression, but Wrenley looked from me to Mike. "Surely you knew that, didn't you? Preston would have had more to worry about than I did when she didn't show up for that date.

"I guess my trip down here wasn't altogether useless," Wrenley said. "I do hope you'll give some thought to looking into why Lowell Caxton is in such a hurry to close his gallery."

I had no intention of telling Wrenley what we would do next. "I'd suggest you let your lawyer go ahead with whatever action he thinks will protect your business interests as well." I stood up to see him out. "Thanks for letting us know about it."

"Do you still have any contact with Marina Sette?" Mike asked.

"Nothing directly. But I hear about her from time to time."

"When's the last time you saw her?"

"Couple of months ago."

"She call you when she came to New York?"

"You mean yesterday?"

Chapman didn't hesitate for a moment. "Yeah, yesterday."

"No, but she called Bryan Daughtry. He told me that last night when he telephoned to let me know about Lowell Caxton. Bryan said that Marina had stopped by the new gallery on Twenty-second Street to see him. Probably to find out if he'd heard any rumors about whether Deni had left a will, or any instructions about who was to get which paintings."

I thought she had told us she detested Daughtry. "Why did she go to him?"

"She could hardly go to Lowell, considering their relationship, and she wasn't talking to me."

"What did Bryan tell her?"

"That the only will he knew of was the original one Lowell's lawyers had prepared for Deni when they first married. Like so many people her age, Deni thought she'd have all the time in the world to amend it. But Marina was still looking for her piece of the rock, what she thought was her 'entitlement.' She really believed, when their friendship was in full bloom, that she had convinced Deni to give her some of the Caxton heirlooms."

"So Lowell gets it all?"

"I suppose. I mean—except for the handful of things that Deni bought with either Bryan or me. Her fortune all started with Lowell, didn't it? In any event, Bryan just wanted me to know that Marina was bad-mouthing me, blaming me for her falling-out with Deni. And that she seemed frantic, out of control. Very hyper about something. That I should stay out of her way if she tried to see me."

"Will you let me know if Marina Sette calls you?" I asked.

"Certainly, Miss Cooper. Thanks for your time."

Chapman waited several seconds after Wrenley shook our hands and walked out the door. "Saddle up, blondie. Let's see why Caxton's heading for the hills."

30

Mike parked the unmarked car illegally and threw his laminated police identification plate in the windshield. The Fuller Building was on the northeast corner of the intersection, with entrances on both Madison Avenue and Fifty-seventh Street. An eighteen-wheeler was parked in front of the side door in a large space protected by a red sign that announced NO STANDING EXCEPT TRUCKS LOADING AND UNLOADING.

The lettering on the vehicle said *Long Island Baking Potatoes, Bridgehampton, New York*. It was definitely loading, and the cargo was not spuds.

There was a fine mist and I hurried to get inside the lobby. In addition to the two men standing at the rear of the truck, there was another person stationed inside the double doors whom I assumed to be part of Caxton's security team.

"Recognize any of them?" I asked Chapman, hoping to get lucky and discover that some retired cops were on the payroll.

"Too ugly. Must've been Feds."

The building was familiar to me because I'd been coming to the hairdresser there for almost ten years. With the exception of the Stella salon on the second floor and a handful of dental and medical offices, the structure was almost entirely leased by gallery owners. I knew that the eastern bank of elevators I used once a month went up only eighteen stories, so I led Mike to the western bank and pressed 35 to get to the top floor and the Caxton Gallery.

We stepped off onto an empty hallway. The glass doors of the space were covered by some kind of makeshift screening, and a note that said the gallery was closed. There was a telephone number to call for people making inquiries about exhibits and purchases.

Mike tried the brass handles on the entrance behind the temporary partitions, but they didn't give. He knocked several times on the panels and the door was eventually opened by an unsmiling man in a dark suit.

"Lowell Caxton's expecting us," Mike said.

That brought a smile to one half of the man's mouth. "Mr. Caxton is not here."

"That's strange." Mike looked at me as though surprised and asked, "Didn't he say today, at eleven o'clock?"

The man didn't wait for me to answer. "He's been called out of town unexpectedly. You can leave a message for him at this number." He pointed to the paper that we had just seen.

"I'd like to leave a note for him. May I come in and—"

Mike had started to walk inside but was blocked by our somber gateman.

"Don't make it difficult for me, will ya?" He took the

leather case from his pants pocket and held up the gold shield, expecting to be let through the doorway.

"Let's see your warrant, Detective."

"Very good, very good. So, you probably finished at the academy, huh? Must have worked your way right up to the top, ironing Mr. Hoover's dresses, to get yourself a plum job like this one when you left the Bureau. Can you at least call Caxton now and tell him that it's urgent we talk to him today?"

"I just told you how to leave him a message."

"Suppose I told you his life may be in danger. You realize there've been a series of killings since his wife was murdered, and we're the ones working on that case. It might behoove him to let us tell him what's been going on with—"

"Mr. Caxton is not in any danger. If he's interested in talking to you, he'll give you a call. He's a bit bored with being looked at as a suspect in Mrs. Caxton's death. He'll get back to you when he's ready."

"You know where he is right now?"

The man stared back at Mike without answering.

Mike took my arm and started to lead me away before turning back to his nemesis. "I'd rather have my balls cut off by a great white shark than end up doing bullshit security work for some billionaire dirtbag. Have a nice day."

On the way back down to the lobby, we talked about whether or not it was worthwhile to hang out there for a while to see who was coming and going from the thirty-fifth floor.

"Can't you get someone from your squad to sit on the place this afternoon and evening?" I asked.

"Let me call and find out who's around. Maybe the lieutenant can get the precinct to send some Anticrime guys over. We haven't got the manpower to do this stuff."

"Come up to my hairdresser. Elsa'll let us use the kitchen to make calls."

"Don't you have your cell phone with you?"

"Yes, but let's see what the girls know about what's happening in the gallery. When Daughtry had his business here, there wasn't much they hadn't heard about him. They had better sources than the Westchester District Attorney's Office. Sooner or later someone from the staff in just about every place in the Fuller Building uses Stella for color or cuts. Besides, wait till you see how adorable Elsa is."

We switched elevator banks and rode up to the second floor. Pat, the manager, was surprised to see me walk in without an appointment in the middle of the week. Her eyes went directly to my hairline, looking at the state of my roots.

"You're not due till Saturday morning, week after next, right?"

"That's some welcome. Just came by to gossip with Elsa and use the kitchen to make a few phone calls."

I introduced her to Mike and she led us past the reception desk into the rear of the busy salon. Elsa, my colorist, was wrapping foil around a client's hair strands while Mike watched in bewilderment. I signaled to her that we were going into the back room, and she mouthed to me that she'd join us as soon as she was finished.

Mike called to explain the situation, and the boss told him that he would try to arrange for coverage from the local precinct as soon as possible. Mike also asked that a car be sent to sit on Caxton's residence, check with the doormen, and monitor the movement of traffic in and out of that location, too. We helped ourselves to coffee and tried to figure out how we could find Caxton quickly and learn what had prompted this sudden move.

Elsa came into the kitchen, removed her rubber gloves, and washed her hands so that I could introduce her to Mike. I had spent so much time talking to each of them about the other over the years that it was hard to believe they had never met. Elsa had long been my friend, and in addition to restoring the blonde to my naturally light hair, as a devotee of the opera and ballet she alerted me to theater and art events that I had neglected to read about. I knew, also, that when there was a rare lull between clients, she explored the galleries throughout the building and collected catalogues of the shows.

"This is a nice surprise. Are you here to see Louis or Nana for a haircut," she said to me, then looking over at Mike, "or do you have a new customer for some streaks?"

"We were in the building trying to get into the Caxton Gallery, so I thought I'd come by and see if you had any scoops for us."

"About the move? Nobody knows what's going on. It's all so sudden."

"Didn't you have any connections there?"

"No, one of the other girls here did highlights for the receptionist, though. Her name was Genevieve. She called yesterday and canceled her appointment. Said she'd been laid off and wouldn't be working here anymore."

"Got a full name on her, and a home phone number?" Mike asked.

"Let me check with Pat. She's got a file on every client. I can get it for you before you leave."

"Have you ever spent time at Caxton's?"

"Browsing, sure. They always had fabulous things, stunning exhibits."

"D'you know either of them?"

"Not more than to say hello to. He knew I worked here—I usually walk around with my smock on during the day—so he didn't waste any time on me. He realized I wasn't a buyer. But Mrs. Caxton had a good sense of humor and was always very nice to me. She wasn't in the building all that much the last couple of years, but before that she'd often talk to me about what she'd picked up at auction or how much she'd sold something for. I didn't know her well, but I liked her."

Elsa was petite and thin, with short dark hair and creamy porcelain skin. She worked in a black painter's jacket, black slacks, and thick black clogs, exuding style and a quiet intensity. She took in everything that her surroundings—and her chatting customers—gave out. And as Joan Stafford always said, you could trust her like a grave to keep a confidence.

"What else have you heard?" I asked.

"Rumors. Nothing reliable."

"About her death?" I was incredulous, expecting that if she had heard anything, however unreliable, Elsa might have called me before our unplanned visit today.

"No, no, no. There was a commotion a couple of weeks ago, maybe a day or two before Mrs. Caxton disappeared. Genevieve's the one who told us about it. Sort of a row in the gallery."

"Between Denise and Lowell?"

"No, I don't think he was even in town, from what we were told."

That fit with what we knew of Lowell's movements.

"What was it?"

"Denise showed up in the gallery one afternoon carrying lots of bags, as though she had just been on a Madison Avenue shopping spree. Genevieve told me that most of the staff had remained loyal to her, but the guy who managed the place for Lowell wasn't a fan of hers. She did whatever business she had come in to do, and then left. The manager literally ran out of the gallery five minutes later, trying to stop Mrs. Caxton before she got into a cab. Genevieve says he accused her of making off with a painting—something small but valuable."

"Was there a scene on the street?" I asked.

"Actually, it was in the lobby. He reached the ground floor before she did. Stopped Mrs. Caxton in front of that clerk at the building's information booth and forced her to let him look through all her bags."

"Did she make a fuss?"

"Nope. Knowing her sense of humor as I did, I expect she enjoyed the commotion. He pulled out all her purchases—lingerie, a peignoir set, a teddy—intimate items like that were flying out of his hands while everyone watched."

"And the painting?"

"No painting. Off she went. At least, that's the version we got down here."

Mike rested his elbow on the counter and looked at Elsa. "So, where did Mrs. Caxton stop on her way downstairs, so that he got to the lobby before she did, even though she had a good head start, huh?"

"Maybe she popped into one of the other galleries, to see a friend?"

"I'll follow up on that. See if I can get the date of the squabble from this Genevieve, when we find her." He paused. "But if Mrs. Caxton didn't pay a social call, and just supposing for the moment that she was trying to take a valuable item out of the building, can you think of any likely place to hide something between the thirty-fifth floor and the lobby?"

Elsa had worked in the salon for more than fifteen years. She had probably inspected every exhibit and office and nook of the Fuller Building during that time, shunning the elevators in favor of the back staircases, as she often told me, for exercise and to relieve the tedium of standing all day at a stationary place behind her work chair.

"I know where Denise used to go to sneak a cigarette," she said softly.

"Whaddaya mean?"

"Even before the city passed laws about smoking, Lowell never let anyone light a cigarette in the gallery. He had all kinds of special air controls for the maintenance of the art, especially because he had so many old paintings. Most of the staff would go all the way down to the ground floor and stand out in front on the sidewalk to smoke. Denise wouldn't bother to go that far. She'd mooch a cigarette—I don't think she did it very often—and she found my secret hideout. That's where we ran into each other from time to time."

"You smoke?" Mike asked, like he was interviewing her as a prospect for a date.

"No. But I like to clear my head every now and then. The fumes of these hair dyes can get to you after a few hours. I just go up there for a breath of air, some peace and quiet, and a great view of the city."

"What is it, like a balcony?"

"Not even close. In fact," she said, giving Mike the once-over, "I'm not certain you'll fit. I'll show you if you'd like."

We left the salon and Elsa pressed the button to go to the eighteenth floor, which was the highest level we could reach from the eastern bank of elevators. She led us to the large gray fire door and pressed her weight against the long metal bar that opened it onto the staircase. Together we walked up to the nineteenth floor, which was basically a darkened hall-way connecting the two sides of the building.

The only illumination came from the glare of the cherry red neon exit sign above the doorway we had just entered. My eyes tried to adjust to the gloomy corridor as I followed behind Elsa, with Mike bringing up the rear.

Two-thirds of the way to the far end, there was a pocket in the wall on our right. Had Elsa not turned toward it, I doubt I would have noticed it at all. She moved surely in that direction and cautioned me to watch the two steps that she climbed, coming face-to-face with another, smaller fire door. As she turned the knob and pushed outward, the door gave way and a sliver of the gray midday sky appeared over her head.

Beyond where Elsa stood was a perch, no more than two feet wide and three feet long. It extended like a small lip, high above the street and out from the side of the building, completely open except for a small iron railing that stretched across it at chest height. My delicate friend stepped onto the ledge, held the bar, and leaned forward to look over the rooftops below.

Then she stepped back and suggested I do the same. "Vertigo," I said. "Not for me." I held on to her arm and tried to stand close to the rail with my eyes open, but I couldn't bear to stay out there. There didn't seem to be enough barriers between me and the sidewalk, nineteen stories down. I offered the post to Mike but he declined, crouching on the floor with his fingers outstretched, trying to measure the size of this exterior shelf.

"What are you doing?"

He stood up. "Great place to stash a painting, then come back to pick it up later on. Does the building stay open after the galleries close?"

"Sure. Our salon has much later appointments than the businesses do. Same for the dental offices. The only other office on this floor is the Malaysian Travel Bureau. It keeps regular hours but I've never seen much traffic there."

"Not that many people knocking each other down to get to Malaysia," Mike said.

Elsa smiled. "I guess not. Of course, lots of the dealers see people by private arrangements, anytime that's convenient. That's why there's always someone at the booth in the main lobby. Denise Caxton was well known to everyone here. She could walk in and out of this building whenever she wanted, without a problem. I just can't imagine her stealing a painting, or anything else for that matter. That's why I didn't think the story was anything serious. The way Genevieve told it, the manager was either simply trying to embarrass Mrs. Caxton or he was making a fool of himself."

"Suppose she wasn't 'stealing' anything," Mike suggested. "Maybe it was something that was hers, a painting Lowell didn't know about that she had warehoused at the gallery. Or that she had hidden up there in one of his storage areas."

Elsa didn't know anything about the Caxton business dealings, so now Mike was talking to me. "Maybe it was something that she felt she had every right to take, but Deni knew that Lowell's people wouldn't let her leave his place with anything. She goes in with lots of bags, makes her rounds, gets what she's after, and walks out before his manager can check what she's got. Then she stops by the little ledge and leaves this package—which I expect is wrapped in something protective. Am I safe in guessing this spot isn't very well trafficked?"

"I've never seen anyone here except Denise Caxton. I'd be willing to bet that ninety-nine percent of the people who work in this building don't even know it exists."

"She makes the drop and continues on to the lobby. Lowell's guy is waiting for her there. He either assumes, or she tells him, that she stopped off to see someone else in another gallery. Gives her a perfectly valid excuse for a short detour on her way downstairs.

"Then she comes back that same night or the next day to pick up her painting. Hell, she could even have circled the block in the cab and gone right back for it ten minutes later. Everyone says she was a risk taker."

Elsa looked concerned. "I hope this has nothing to do with her death. It was such a silly story—it didn't seem worth repeating when I heard about it. I never connected the two things."

"No reason for you to have thought anything about it," I assured her. Mike squinted to look at the number displayed on his beeper, which must have been vibrating on his waistband, while I went on talking. "At this point, we're just grasping at anything. It's good to know about this."

"Let's get back to the phone. The lieutenant's looking for me. This'll go over big when I tell him I'm at your hairdresser's."

We retraced our path back to the kitchen, where I had left my handbag. Mike called the squad while I asked Elsa to keep her eyes and ears open for information about the Caxton Gallery's closing and move.

Mike started singing the opening bars of Willie Nelson's "On the Road Again" as he hung up the phone. "Either make yourself comfortable and let Elsa lighten up your silken tresses, or I'll get you some escorts from Midtown North to take you back to work. I'm off to beautiful downtown Piscataway."

"What's there?"

"Man checked himself into the local hospital this morning. He's got an infected wound in his groin that's festering away. Told the E.R. staff that he had an accident on a construction site, but the X rays show there's a bullet inside. Right now the Jersey troopers are holding him. Could be that Mercer hit the bull's-eye after all. Patient matches the description of Anthony Bailor."

31

It pained me to admit that Pat McKinney might be right about anything, but there was no point in my asking Mike to go along with him on the ride to New Jersey. If Anthony Bailor was the person under guard in a hospital, then it was likely that he had been the gunman who had aimed at me, shot Mercer, and killed the young receptionist in Chelsea on Sunday. I had no business being anywhere near him.

"What's your plan?"

"To get my ass down there to Piscataway before that pair of clowns from Major Case find out about it."

Physicians were required by law to report gunshot wounds,

and some clever detective in the town where Bailor sought treatment, recognizing that there were no open cases in his jurisdiction in which anyone had claimed to have injured an assailant, had the great sense to notify police in the tristate area about the suspect's appearance.

"It looks good?"

"Yeah, the guy's a transient, a walk-in. Used a common name but has no I.D. to back it up, and gave a phony address— a street that doesn't exist, in a neighboring town. Fits the physical scrip of Bailor. Elsa, she's all yours for the next fifteen minutes. Loo got a uniformed detail from the North to ferry you around and keep you safe till I come back this evening."

There was no point arguing. Mike wasn't going to undercut Battaglia's direction that someone escort me from place to place. "Should I keep working on trying to find Caxton?" I asked.

"Yeah, as long as you do it from behind your desk. If you get a lead on where he is, we can confront him tonight or tomorrow morning. What you could do, in the meanwhile, is let these cops take you to Denise's new gallery on your way downtown. See if you can charm Daughtry into telling you what he found out last night about Lowell Caxton's exodus from the city. You may do better with him if I'm over the border, Coop. Maybe you could coax him into letting you look around the storage area."

"Remind me what I'm looking for, exactly. The Vermeer? The Rembrandt?"

"Maybe I'll have a better idea of that after I talk to Bailor." He looked at his watch. "Give me an hour to get out to Piscataway, and another hour to talk to him, then I'll either beep you or call Caxton Due looking for you."

"Meet you at Mercer's room when you get back tonight?"

Mike was distracted. "Suppose you were Deni and you had

something—a painting, in all likelihood—that someone else wanted. Where would you hide it?"

"Let's begin by recognizing that she had more options than most of us could even imagine. And who's she hiding it *from*? I mean, if it's Lowell, then I doubt she'd have it at home or anyplace they use together. If it's Daughtry, then she wouldn't hide it at their gallery. Depends, in part, on who she's avoiding, don't you think? It would help to know that first."

"Forget who it is. What *I'm* thinking is, if it's any kind of artwork, she could have hidden it in plain view, if you know what I mean. She could have had Marco Varelli undo any restoration. He could re-create the cover of a restored painting, or obscure a masterpiece. She could hide something like that in a warehouse, and if she treated it casually, maybe nobody would pay it any attention. You'd need *her* eye, *her* knowledge, *her* tutor. Maybe Deni could even carry it around in a shopping bag and nobody'd think twice of it. Maybe what's at the heart of this case is one giant optical illusion, Coop." Mike's idea wasn't altogether crazy.

"So I'll crank up the search for Lowell, stop in to schmooze with Brian Daughtry and scan the gallery's warehouse at the same time. Will I jinx things for you if I buy a bottle of champagne to open at Mercer's bedside when you come back from checking out Anthony Bailor?"

"Dom Pérignon. But you gotta promise that I can be the one to break the news to him. If you get over there before I do, don't even raise his hopes. I'd hate for this to be a false alarm. If it's the real deal, I want to tell Mercer myself."

Mike was ready to take off. "Great to meet you, Elsa. Keep an eye on blondie till the precinct cops get here."

I called Laura to check my messages. There was a note from McKinney, who wanted to talk to me as soon as I got back to the office. I had a couple of hours to kill until I could expect to hear from Chapman about the identity of the man with the gunshot wound, and I had no intention of returning to Hogan Place until I knew whether this new development could turn the investigation around.

The more urgent message was from the sergeant at the Special Victims Squad, about a new case that had come in several hours ago. I phoned him immediately.

"What have you got?"

"Victim's at New York Hospital. Twenty-six-year-old businesswoman from Georgia, staying at a hotel in town. She's being treated for an inner ear disorder, comes to town to see a specialist. Woke up this morning but blacked out on her way out of the bathroom. She was able to call her husband back home, and he phoned the manager. Two hotel security guards got into the room and radioed for an ambulance. Then the older one told the second guy to go downstairs and wait for the EMS crew. He assumed the woman was unconscious, but she was just too weak to respond. In any event, he ripped her pajama top off and started to molest her. Finally she came around and was able to tell him to stop. Reported it to the ambulance driver as soon as she got inside and they closed the doors."

"What hotel?"

"Would you believe the Sussex House?"

"On Central Park South?"

"You got it. She paid six hundred fifty-three dollars for the privilege of being abused by a member of the staff."

"What do you need?"

"Her husband's flying up from Georgia this afternoon. Can you get her interviewed and set up the grand jury, so she can get back home when the doctor releases her?"

"Absolutely." I checked my watch. "I'll go over and talk to her now—I'm just ten blocks away from the hospital. I'll assign somebody senior to handle it. Need any help at the hotel? Are they being cooperative?"

"One of her girlfriends met us there to pack up her belongings. She's the one who found the two buttons on the floor—ripped off the shirt of the pajamas."

"Did you get the guy?"

"Yeah, but he's not talking. Ponied up with a lawyer right away. Just doing his job."

I called Catherine Dashfer to tell her about the case.

"I'm doing a hearing this afternoon in front of Judge Wetzel," she told me. "But I'm free the rest of the week. If she's released in the morning, just have her be in my office at ten, and I'll put it right in the jury. We can have her at the airport by this time tomorrow."

"Thanks a million. Would you do me another favor? Call McKinney for me and tell him I just got called out on a new case, and that I won't be back until late in the day, okay?"

Elsa had ordered two salads from the local deli, and we were eating our lunch when a policewoman in uniform presented herself at the reception desk. I finished up before saying good-bye and heading off on my rounds.

Police Officers Brigid Brannigan and Harry Lazarro had been told that their assignment was to take me wherever I needed to go until they were relieved later this evening by another unit. On the short ride to New York Hospital I gave them a brief rundown on what had been happening in the Caxton case. The rest of the story they knew from newspaper accounts. One of *them* had been gravely wounded, and there was no more serious situation than that to a cop.

Brannigan got out of the car at the Sixty-eighth Street entrance to the large facility. "Want me to take you in?"

"I'm fine, thanks. This stop was just added to the itinerary, so I'm not expecting any trouble."

From the information booth I called the emergency room, but Callie Emerson had already been treated and had been admitted for observation and tests concerning her inner ear imbalance. She was on 6 North, and the volunteer worker directed me to that wing.

When I reached her room, Callie was sitting in an armchair dressed in a hospital gown and answering questions from a physician and a resident. I explained who I was and why I was there. My purpose was not to question her in depth about the assault—since Catherine would do that in the morning—but rather to explain the proceedings to her and engage her cooperation. Witnesses and their families were always surprised to learn how much gentler the process had become with a specialized unit like ours, and how comfortable we could make the person who had been victimized.

I stepped back outside the room and waited for the doctors to finish their examination. When they were through, I returned and sat with Callie, telling her what would happen the next day and answering all her questions about the system. She and her husband should go to Catherine's office, where the questioning would take place. The grand jury presentation would take less than ten minutes and the assailant would not be present for it, so she did not have to see him again or tell the story in front of him. After that, Catherine would be responsible for the motion practice in the case—presenting the court with information responding to defense requests for facts to which they were entitled. Three or four months thereafter, we would bring Callie back to New York for the trial, and with any luck Catherine would be working again in front of a jurist as sensitive and knowledgeable as Wetzel.

She seemed grateful for the overview and willing to participate.

"Were you examined in the emergency room?"

"Fortunately, I wasn't raped. So they didn't do an internal exam. They were more worried about my physical condition—that my blood pressure had dropped so dramatically and my vital signs were weak."

I knew from my conversation with the sergeant that the attacker had put his mouth on Callie's breast and sucked on it.

"Did anyone look at your chest?"

"I'm not sure. There was so much going on when we got here—I just don't know."

"Would you mind going into the bathroom and looking at yourself in the mirror?"

When she emerged, she was nodding her head. "There's a large discoloration on my skin, where his mouth was. And there are a few scratches on my breastbone, which might have happened when he was ripping at the buttons."

"I'm going to ask one of the nurses to come and look at you again, if you don't mind. I'd like her to note those marks on your medical chart. And Laura, who's one of our photographers, will take a few pictures of them tomorrow morning."

"They seem so minor."

"Even so, Callie, they corroborate exactly what you said this man did to you. It will be very useful for you at the trial."

We talked for a while longer before I thanked Callie, reassured her about what a good witness she would be, and left the hospital.

The patrol car was waiting for me in the parking circle off York Avenue.

"What's next, Miss Cooper?"

I checked my watch. It was almost an hour and a half since Mike had left for Jersey, and I was trying to control my curiosity about his encounter with the man who might be Bailor.

"Before we go to Chelsea, why don't you just swing by 890 Fifth Avenue? It's not too far out of the way. I want to check with the team that's watching an apartment there."

In ten minutes we were in front of Lowell Caxton's building. There was an unmarked detective car parked next to the awning. I got out to talk to the men sitting inside, both of whom were eating hot dogs and drinking root beer. They worked with Mike at the Homicide Squad and were annoyed at being stuck on such an uninteresting post.

"Nothin' happening here. Doorman says it's business as usual with Caxton. This guy only does days, so he don't know what time Lowell came home last night. But his chauffeur picked him up a little before eight this morning. I had him call up to the maid, too. She says Caxton's due home sometime after seven o'clock this evening. You and Chapman planning to come over then?"

"Yes, unless you see something else we should know about earlier. Have you got my beeper number?"

"No, but I got Mike's."

"He's not with me today, so why don't you write mine down, too?"

The surly fat one in the driver's seat took another bite from his tube steak and handed me the paper napkin that had been draped over his knee. I tore off the corner with the mustard stain on it and wrote down the number to hand back to him. He was as likely to call a D.A. with a hot lead as he was to run in the next marathon.

"Any other traffic in or out we should know about?"

"If you know a Mrs. Cadwalader on three, she's either turning tricks on the side or she's runnin' a halfway house for retired hockey players. She's got action comin' and goin' every twenty minutes, and most of her company's sportin' half their teeth and bowlegs. And there's a schnauzer on five with a very weak bladder, so he's out here peeing on my front tire once an hour, courtesy of his housekeeper, who's carrying a pooper scooper looks like it's made outta sterling silver. And she's got a great ass—the housekeeper, not the schnauzer. Now, are you gonna sit here and watch us watching them, or are you gonna find some way to make yourself useful to Mr. Battaglia?"

Brigid Brannigan was leaning against the patrol car and opened the door for me to get in the backseat. She looked crisp and cool in the police uniform, and her neat auburn ponytail set off her fine features handsomely. "I used to think *I* had a hard time, breaking in as a prosecutor with all these tough old dinosaurs in my department who thought handling homicides was only a man's prerogative. I bump into a guy like that one, and I bet you could tell me stories about what it was like for you to come onto this job that would make my experience seem like a cakewalk."

She got in the car laughing and started to talk about her rookie adventures with some of the hairbags—the stiff old-timers who never made it out of uniform—that she'd encountered in the four years she'd been on the force.

"Why don't you take the Sixty-sixth Street drive through the park and head down Ninth Avenue? I'm going to a gallery called Caxton Due, on Twenty-second Street, between Tenth and Eleventh."

Brigid continued to amuse me with her anecdotes while her partner weaved in and out of the midafternoon traffic on the approach to the Lincoln Tunnel. Once that cleared, Lazarro drove down to Twenty-first Street and came up Tenth Avenue, about to make the turn into the one-way westbound block on which the gallery entrance was located.

We could all see that it would be impossible to drive into the narrow street. In addition to the cars parked at meters on each side, there were three enormous trucks lined up in a row right in the middle of the pavement. Wooden stanchions were spread from the north corner of the curb to the south.

There didn't seem to be anyone directing this operation. Officer Lazarro gave off a few whelps, and two men in T-shirts and jeans poked their heads out of the cab of one of the trucks. Since they weren't moving, Brannigan got out of the car and walked over to them.

She came back and leaned in the window. "They've got a permit to block the street off for the afternoon. There's a place farther down the way called the Dia Center for the Arts. They're installing a major exhibition today, so this is legal while they're unloading sculpture for the new show. Want me to walk you into your gallery?"

"This might work even better. There's a rear door on Twenty-third Street, through the warehouse of the gallery. We saw the sign for it, like a service entrance, the first day we came here. Maybe Daughtry'll let me in that way. As Chapman said then, Daughtry might even prefer we use it." Again, I checked the time. "Chapman should be calling soon. C'mon, let's go around the corner."

We drove up to Twenty-third and Lazarro signaled left, then made a U-turn to pull up to the curb in front of the spot I pointed out as the garage entrance to Deni's gallery. Brigid got out of the car when I did and walked with me over to the rusty-colored door frame, which had an intercom system with two buzzers next to a small enamel plate. One was marked CAXTON DUE—SERVICE, and the other said CAXTON DUE—GALLERY.

I pressed the second bell and waited a couple of minutes.

"Any idea how long we'll be here?" Brigid asked.

"With some luck, if he lets me poke around the warehouse, I might be an hour or more. If Chapman turns up anything important, be ready to fly out of here with me, okay?"

The gray haze seemed to be lifting, as the forecasters had promised, and the sun was beginning to filter through. I was hot and looked forward to being received in the cool of the air-conditioned art display space.

We both heard the sound of the intercom click.

"Yes?" Judging from the crackling quality of its sound, the system was as old as the building.

"Alexandra Cooper. From the District Attorney's Office," I identified myself to Daughtry.

"I'll buzz you in. Come on up—is not—but I'll—top—"

The entrance led directly up an old iron staircase, which bypassed the storage area to lead into the gallery itself. Before the door swung shut behind us, I heard Lazarro calling Brigid's name.

"Sergeant Danz wants to talk to you. Needs an idea of how long we're going be tied up here. Wanna take it?"

Brigid looked at me. "Do you mind?"

"Of course not. I do the same thing when my boss calls."

"Can you wait down here a few minutes while I report in? The sergeant's gonna have to get permission for us to work over the end of the shift at three thirty."

I pointed up. "You know right where I am. I'll be out as soon as Chapman calls."

As I climbed the steps, I could see scores of paintings arrayed in bins beneath, most of them covered in bubble wrap or kraft paper, and all labeled by the artist's name and some kind of numerical code. They varied in size from tiny objects, not larger than four by six inches, to giant canvases that were best suited for museum walls.

I rang at the door at the top of the stairs and the buzzer sounded to unlock the way into the small lift, which descended to this ground floor area to take me up to the top of the atrium, where Daughtry awaited my arrival. When the door slid back, I was again overwhelmed by the beauty of the open atrium space. Emerging from the elevator on the north side of the building, I was facing the glass wall of the southern exposure and its great view of the city sky.

As I stepped off into the room, I felt the relief of the cold surge of air that I had anticipated. It contrasted with the unexpected brightness of the afternoon sun at the end of a gloomy day, which lit up the gallery space and beamed down on the tracks of the deserted Hi-Line Railroad.

I took my sunglasses out of my jacket pocket for the first time that day.

"Over here," called a voice that was familiar to me, but it was not Daughtry's.

I looked around and saw Frank Wrenley sitting on one of the couches in the exhibition area one flight below me.

"Welcome, Ms. Cooper. I'm baby-sitting the art for Bryan. He should be back anytime now. May I offer you a cold drink?"

I remembered that this morning, in my office, Wrenley had told us that Daughtry was going to allow him to look through Denise's belongings to see whether any of his property was included there. He was holding a sheaf of papers in one hand and a tall glass in the other.

"Shall I come down?"

"Please."

I followed the catwalk around the bend until I arrived at the metal staircase that led to the level below. I walked down, shook Wrenley's hand, and accepted his offer to sit on the couch. I could see the documents he had laid out on the glass-topped table between us. He had a red pen and appeared to be going through lists that he was checking against his own.

"Will you join me in a Bloody Mary?"

"No thanks."

"Ah, the constable doesn't drink on duty, does she?"

"I'm so exhausted, Mr. Wrenley, that I'd probably curl up and take a nap if I so much as smelled a whiff of the vodka. Your inventory?"

"Bryan's off trying to solve the mystery of Lowell Caxton's hasty retreat. He's been good enough to let me attempt to reconcile some of my records with Deni's things before I return to Palm Beach." He waved his receipts in my direction as though to convince me that he had proof of title for anything he needed. "Where's your sidekick? I was beginning to think you and Detective Chapman were joined at the hip."

"He'll be along soon. We were— I was hoping to get Mr.

Daughtry's permission to look around a bit at some of Denise's things."

"I thought that first day I met you here you'd gone all through this place with warrants and everything short of commando troops. Bryan was sure he was going back to prison."

I smiled at his exaggerated description. "That's one of the problems when you do a search before you know just what it is you're looking for."

"But now you *do* know?"

Not really. But I saw no reason to tell that to Wrenley. We'd try again with some of the information we had picked up after Varelli's murder and during our conversation with Don Cannon. "Do you have any idea when Mr. Daughtry is due to return?" I didn't know whether to try to wait it out or get down to my office and face the music with McKinney.

"Pretty soon, I should think. He's got to lock the place up for the night."

It was now going on three hours since Mike had left the city. I reached in my bag to get the cell phone to try to beep him. When I turned it on, the failure of the three green icons to light up reminded me that the battery must have run down. I kept the charger set up on my desk at home and plugged the phone into it every evening as a matter of habit, but since I had spent the last two nights at Jake's apartment, I had neglected to recharge it.

"Would you mind if I use the telephone for a moment?"

Wrenley pointed to the portable unit on the table next to his papers. "Help yourself."

I picked it up and dialed Chapman's beeper, punching in the number of the gallery as I read it off the plate on the receiver. Then I set it back down, knowing he would return the call to the unfamiliar number only when he was ready to take a break.

"I can't give you access to the storage area, but I don't

imagine Bryan would mind if you look through the gallery and the office while you're waiting. After all, you've done that once already, haven't you?"

I was feeling even more foolish as I stood up and glanced around. There was nothing in the midst of this thoroughly modern exhibit that I could connect by my wildest stretch to the art treasures that I associated with Deni Caxton's troubles. I started to work my way about the place, reading the descriptions and trying to make sense of the works.

Within several minutes the phone rang and I hurried back to the area where Wrenley was sitting. He had answered it by saying, "Galleria Caxton Due," and passed it off to me when I approached the table.

Instinctively, I turned my back to him and started to walk a few steps off. I was aware that it was rude, but I also wanted whatever privacy might be necessary. "No, that was Wrenley. Frank Wrenley," I said, responding to Mike's question about whether the man who had spoken was Bryan Daughtry.

"Can you talk?"

"About what?"

"Never mind. You'll explain where Daughtry is later, I guess."

"Sure. No big deal. Is it our guy?" I whispered into the receiver.

"Order a magnum of the champagne, Coop. Anthony Bailor is about to have an incurable case of gangrenous balls. He's not talking, but he's the man."

"What do you mean he's not talking?"

"He still denies everything, including his name. But I've got his mug shots, and the Jersey police ran his prints this morning."

"Have you arrested him?"

"Why? You gonna give your pal Jake a scoop for the nightly news? No leaks on this one till we know who's behind it. Bailor

380

took the fall for someone in that last theft he was involved in. There's got to be a link to somebody in this investigation."

"Don't be ridiculous. I just want to know what to do next. Should I go down to the office and draw up a complaint on Deni's homicide? You're going to have to lodge a warrant so we can start extradition proceedings from New Jersey."

"Take it easy. I haven't even told the lieutenant yet. Let me see how the boss wants me to handle it and what the Jersey cops want to hold him on out here. You find out anything useful about Caxton?"

"Not a thing. Where do you want to meet?"

"I'll call you back as soon as I sort this out. I'll pick you up at Hogan Place and take you to Saint Vincent's."

I hung up and walked the phone back to Wrenley, who seemed absorbed in his checklist.

"Good news? You look a lot happier now than you did ten minutes ago."

"Please tell Mr. Daughtry I was here. Perhaps he could give me a call tomorrow, and I'll set up a time to see him."

"You've decided not to wait?" Wrenley stood up, looking at me and shielding his eyes with his right hand. He was facing directly into the sun, which had now saturated the atrium. "Must have some new developments on the case. Have you found Lowell Caxton?"

"No, it's another matter altogether. Nothing to do with the Caxtons. You'll probably hear it on the news tonight—an assault in a midtown hotel. I've got to get some things started on that one before morning." No point giving him any information on Anthony Bailor.

"Well, good luck with this. For Deni's sake I sure hope you get a break soon. I'll be back up from Florida next week, if you need me for anything." The late-August sun was like a ball of fire, coming over the tops of the low buildings across the street and sparkling through the wall of glass. I lifted my sunglasses off the top of my head and replaced them on my nose.

My heart was pounding as my mind pieced the clues together at precisely the wrong place and time. Like Anthony Bailor, Frank Wrenley had been raised in Florida. I picked up my bag to leave and did an involuntary double take at Wrenley, who was squinting back at me without benefit of sunglasses.

32

"You look as if you've seen an apparition, Ms. Cooper."

"Sorry, I'm just very tired. I don't feel well. I'll see myself out." I was backing away from the area around the two sofas, thinking of the sunglasses that had been vouchered at the scene of Marco Varelli's murder a week earlier. How many coincidences does it take to make a fact?

Wrenley was walking toward me. I quickened my pace, knowing that Brannigan and Lazarro were waiting for me right outside the warehouse door.

"I suppose Detective Chapman has managed to get his hands on Anthony Bailor. Is that what put you in such a good mood, Ms. Cooper?"

I was holding on to the railing now, two levels above the obsolete train tracks cutting through the center of the gallery, dizzy from the combination of vertigo and the question that Wrenley had just asked me.

He broke into a run before I did, and was upon me in a second, grabbing my free arm and spinning me around to face him. He was holding a small-caliber revolver in his right hand, the kind that was probably used to put a hole through the brain behind Marco Varelli's ear.

"Did Anthony's wound get worse? Is that how you found him? I couldn't come up with a physician anywhere to treat him. He's not exactly John Wilkes Booth. Just couldn't find a taker. And all I needed was another day or two to tie up loose ends so I could get myself out of town for good. I didn't want this to happen." His grip tightened on my wrist.

"So you, Ms. Cooper, will have to be the sacrificial lamb. You might take a terrible fall, say, from the level above us." He prodded me in the ribs with the gun.

"You can't get out of this building without me—alive and well." My voice must have been trembling as I tried to construct a reasonable bluff. "If you kill—" I stopped, unable to complete a sentence that held the implication of my own death. "If you try to hurt me, you won't be able to walk out the door. There are police officers stationed in the front and back of the building. They have orders not to let anyone in or out without my approval."

Wrenley stood still, not knowing whether to believe me or not. With the gun held against me, he lifted the glasses off my nose and placed them on himself. Now I blinked as I tried to avoid the direct glare. "Why should I think that's true? Have you seen the trucks unloading out front for the Dia exhibit? Not even a police car could get through that block."

"There are two men in plain clothes standing at the entrance of the gallery," I lied, "and a patrol car with two oth-

384

ers out in back. You have yourself to thank for that. It all started after your efforts to kill me the first time, didn't it? There have been bodyguards taking me everywhere since your attempts on my life."

I remembered the day I had met Chapman and Wallace here to interview Bryan Daughtry. We had interrupted his meeting with Wrenley. My Jeep had been parked directly in front of the gallery, with my identification plate in the windshield. It was he who must have had me followed from Twenty-second Street to the garage at Lincoln Center. He'd had plenty of time to alert Bailor to try to run me down that night, after the ballet. Wrenley must have thought I'd known more than I did. Maybe he had relied on Mickey Diamond's made-up headline.

He was considering his options. "I can offer you a livelier proposition, then. You're going to be my passport out of town."

Anything that would get me away from this unlikely mausoleum. "What do you mean?"

"Take me downstairs with you and have them drive us wherever I decide to go."

My panic heightened at the thought of putting another police officer within range of a man with a loaded gun, of exposing Brannigan and Lazarro to this murderous thief. "That might not work," I said. "If they don't know you, they won't fall for that."

"It can't be your friend Chapman down there, can it? He just called you from somewhere else. So it must be some uniformed cops who pulled this duty. I'm sure they don't know you and all your colleagues, do they?"

I couldn't figure where he was going with this, so I gave an honest answer instead of trying to outguess him. "They're precinct cops. They don't know me well."

"And tell me how well *you* know Charlie Rosenberg?"

My head was spinning. I couldn't follow him. The name sounded vaguely familiar but I couldn't think of who or what he meant. "Who?"

He reached into his left pants pocket and pulled out the gray security badge issued by my office, which dangled from a silver-colored metal chain. With one hand, Wrenley slipped it over his head and let it hang around his neck, like I wear mine at the office. Now it clicked. Charlie was a young assistant who worked in one of the trial bureaus. Like McKinney, he was a morning jogger.

"I picked this up at the front desk today when I came down to your office to see you. Tsk, tsk, tsk—they ought to be much more careful with those I.D. tags when you people leave them lying around. I actually had other plans for this, in case we needed to get past the doormen at your apartment building. But it will do fine for you to introduce me to your bodyguards. You can say I was here working on the case when you arrived. Charlie Rosenberg. Shit, some of my best friends are Jewish."

"But the photograph—"

"Can't even make it out with all the use the badge has had—dark hair, pleasant smile. I'll pass."

I thought of the morning two weeks ago, right after Deni's body had been found, when Mike and I came back from Compstat and McKinney's tag had been mislaid in the pile at the front desk. I was so pleased at the time that he had trouble getting back into the building that I hadn't raised a stink about the lax security.

Wrenley poked me again. "Where's your tag? Put it on."

"It's in my bag."

With his free hand he reached inside my oversized tote, never taking his eyes off me. It was hopeless that he'd find anything in it. He gave out a quick laugh. "I guess Chapman gave you away. Since he told me there's no gun in your bag, why don't you get the I.D. badge out yourself? And leave the sharp pencils inside there."

I set the bag on the floor and knelt down, riffling through it to feel for the chain and pull it out. It snagged on something and I grabbed at it. Now I could feel the plastic bag in which I had placed the toilet articles for Mercer. I pulled up the small plastic razor blade case and palmed it, bringing the chain and gray tag with my name on it out of the handbag. Still crouching, I hung the chain around my neck and pocketed the slim blade holder as I reached my hand to the floor to stand up again.

Wrenley jabbed at me to move toward the staircase. We were closer to it than to the lift in the far corner. There was no point making a dash to the elevator with a gun at my back. "Down the steps, Ms. Cooper. Let's try the back door, where you say the car is waiting."

I descended the stairs slowly, my hand shaking as I tried to grip the banister. We had gone from the fifth level to the fourth. I turned on the landing and went down to the third floor, where the old Hi-Line tracks ran through the length of the building.

"Hold it right there," he said sharply, drawing up by my side as I reached the bottom step. He rested a foot on top of the nearest railroad tie. "You've got to get this quivering under control, Alex. It's Alex, isn't it? These cops have to think we're partners, too, don't they?"

Wrenley didn't realize Battaglia was running the Children's Crusade. Most of my colleagues were kids right out of law school, staying in public service only as long as they could resist the lure of the high-paying private sector. Someone Wrenley's age would be an executive or supervisor, and not likely to be out in the field working cases or taking orders from me. Even if I could calm myself down, Brannigan was bright enough to know that something was wrong with this picture. I would put us all in grave danger.

He lowered his right arm, his gun to his side but still visible. "Never send a rapist to do a man's job."

"What?" I asked.

"Deni wasn't supposed to be murdered. Maybe I can make you more comfortable if you understand that I'm not a killer. Well, I didn't set out to be one. You just need to get me safe passage out of here, and then I'll simply disappear, leaving you unharmed. But we can't go anywhere until you settle down and stop shaking so badly."

I didn't believe him for a moment, but it was clear that he wasn't letting me move until he saw my tremors subside. "Tell me what you mean. If you want me to stop shivering, explain to me why Deni had to die."

"Two words: Anthony Bailor." Wrenley braced his back against the banister.

"You knew him in Florida?"

"Much to my father's regret. Wrong side of the tracks and all that. I met Anthony during my brief stay in a juvenile home, back when I was a delinquent. A quaint term you don't hear much of these days, do you, Alex?"

I was certain we had run a rap sheet on Wrenley and it had come up clean.

"You look puzzled. I was fifteen at the time. My father's lawyer was good. Had the case sealed because of my age. Knew enough to get the fingerprints and photos back. Most of them are too lazy to follow through on that, as you probably know. But then, it wasn't all bad. After I met Anthony I never had to do second-story work again.

"I've had an eye for nice things all my life. Couldn't always afford them. But I was able to get myself invited into the right homes for cocktails and dinner. Called Anthony a week or two later, gave him the layout and a schedule, arranged myself an alibi for the time of the burglary, and I built myself up a very nice little collection of antiques. The Keys were a bit confining for me, so we eventually set up shop further north. By the time Anthony got sent away big-time, I was flourishing in Palm Beach. The old ladies loved me."

"The Gardner heist. You—"

"Don't be stupid. I'd never have dared an operation like that one. Besides, Anthony was tucked away in prison ten years ago."

"But he did the theft from the museum at Amherst. That's what he went to jail for in New York."

"Exactly. One of the guys responsible for the Gardner masterminded the break-in at the Mead. Anthony took the weight for him when he got caught with some of the art."

"But never gave him up?"

"He's good at that. I'll bet your man Chapman is having a hard time."

"And Denise Caxton?"

"I'm sure you know by now that Anthony and Omar spent some time together in jail. Omar had that lamebrained scam of writing threatening letters to wealthy divorcées. He began to brag about it to Anthony. Told him about the Caxtons and their art connections. Bailor got in touch with me. I knew Deni and Lowell—everyone in the business knew them. We used Omar to stay close to Deni."

"Did she really hire him to kill Lowell?"

"She didn't want her husband dead. She just wanted him frightened a bit."

I'd say a bullet creasing his skull could do the trick. "Omar shot him?"

"No, he subcontracted that out to Anthony. Far more capable with a gun. You're doing much better, Alex. You're almost ready to go." He was watching my hands, which I had clasped together to keep from shaking as much.

"But the paintings from the Gardner, this all has to do with them, doesn't it?"

Wrenley paused.

"I know you showed one of them to Marco Varelli."

He looked me in the eye to see whether I was just testing him.

"Those paintings have been out of circulation for almost ten years, since the date of the theft. Everyone knows, Alex—well, everyone in *my circle*—that the thieves have had trouble unloading them. Some of the minor things have sold, of course—"

"But not the Rembrandt or the Vermeer."

"So Anthony was asked to get in touch with me long before he met Omar."

"By the thieves?"

"I prefer to call them the custodians. I have no idea who the Philistines were who actually broke into the building. Couldn't have been art lovers—I think they left the most valuable painting behind, in their ignorance."

Titian's *Rape of Europa,* wall-sized and worth even more than the Rembrandt and the Vermeer.

"I'd been trying to find a way to sell them, collect a broker's fee. I had heard about Lowell's fantastic private collection, and I knew Deni was supposed to be a bit of a wild card. They were still together at the time, of course. I thought I might interest her in buying one of the great pieces for their own collection. Discretion advised. It happens more often than you'd think with stolen art."

"And you called her shortly before she was supposed to travel to England with Lowell. That's why she didn't go on that trip with him, isn't it?" Sooner or later our subpoenaed phone records would show the incoming call to Deni from Frank Wrenley. If only those records had arrived before now.

"She was wild with excitement when I told her about the paintings. Funny thing is, she wanted to buy them for Lowell.

It was to be the greatest coup of her life, to give him something he didn't have and couldn't have found anywhere else in the world. She sent him on ahead to England with the best intentions."

"And she took the Vermeer to Marco Varelli, to make sure it was the original?" I asked. I thought of our conversation with Don Cannon, who had witnessed the meeting.

"I never expected to become personally involved with Mrs. Caxton. That wasn't part of the grand design. But it was icing on the cake. She developed a serious case of cold feet once Varelli threw his tantrum, so she decided to catch up with Lowell in Bath. She'd been planning the surprise of a lifetime for him, and he's in bed with the young English girl. Drove Deni right back home, into my waiting arms."

"You convinced her to keep playing with the paintings, even though she knew they were stolen?"

"Let's say it was the free spirit in her. Once she and Lowell decided to split, she became more carnivorous, more worried about how she could maintain the lifestyle to which she'd become accustomed. Every now and then she'd get a little crazy on me. You know about the reward?"

"Five million dollars tax-free from the Feds, for the return of the art."

"Deni would occasionally try to convince me to turn in the paintings, in exchange for immunity from prosecution for possession of stolen property. Take the five million and run off with her—well, I can't tell you where, exactly. I'm still hoping to be there by tomorrow. Beyond your jurisdiction, Miss D.A. And no extradition policy, either."

"But the other man she was dating? Preston Mattox."

"Why is it women like you always enjoy a sad love story? I did have some competition. Deni wasn't quite ready to make a commitment after what happened with Lowell. Her self-confidence had skyrocketed after our first few months together."

The story was becoming clearer all the time. I stretched out the fingers of both hands, to see whether they trembled. Wrenley watched me. "Very good, Alex. Getting better."

I balled them into fists and looked back at Wrenley. "Then why was she killed? She had the paintings, didn't she? You were afraid you'd lose everything if she walked away from you?"

"Correction. One painting. We were going to be partners, so I let her hold on to the Vermeer. Less valuable than the Rembrandt, but she loved that domestic little scene. I favored the seascape.

"I called to tell her I thought she was right. That we ought to return the paintings to the museum and collect the reward. Her name wouldn't be connected to the scandal, and I'd give her half the proceeds. We had been doing other deals together, so it made perfect business sense. To prove my bona fides, I offered to take her to lunch so she could give me the painting—wrapped up, of course—at Jean-Georges. In public. Neat and clean. She could carry it to the table in a Bergdorf shopping bag and just pass it to me with a peck on the cheek. A check would eventually follow for two and a half million."

"But you must have concocted a way to get all five million?"

"Well, minus a slight commission for Anthony."

"Did you know where she kept the painting?"

"If I knew that I wouldn't have had to offer her a two-hundred-dollar lunch, would I? Anthony was to follow Deni from home. He had borrowed Omar's station wagon. He was to abduct Deni, drive her to a fairly remote spot, and steal her purse and whatever else was in the car. He knew he was after a painting, but the painting was supposed to look incidental to the usual money, jewelry, fancy-car theft."

I closed my eyes and my right hand covered my mouth, trying to keep the words inside. "But you knew he was a rapist. How could you let him near Deni?"

"I didn't know that Anthony had been convicted of rape. It's not a popular category of criminal acts among inmates. He always described himself as an armed robber. True, naturally. And a carjacker. True as well. He just neglected to tell me that he'd also raped his victims.

"All he was supposed to do was steal the Vermeer. Obviously, Deni wouldn't be able to report the crime to the police. That was the bottom line of my plan. She would have undermined her whole divorce settlement with Lowell if she had gone to the police. No judge would give her a nickel of Lowell's fortune, or any of his art, if she was caught with stolen paintings. A Vermeer that had been missing for a decade? How do you walk into a police station and tell them that you were just carrying it around when you went to meet a friend for lunch? Then, there'd be me to deal with. She'd feel badly about my loss, and I'd be sure to make her feel guilty, and there she'd be, owing me more than two and a half million dollars, just because she'd been careless and lost our painting."

"Plus, you'd still have the painting. Or both paintings?"

"*Voilà!*"

"Where did the plan go wrong?"

"Denise made Anthony angry." Wrenley's indifference was chilling. "First of all, he tells me that Denise didn't have the painting with her in the car. Lots of cash, enough jewelry to make a splash at our lunch—he was entitled to keep those things, under our agreement—but no Vermeer. Now, between you and me, Ms. Cooper, this is still a point of contention between me and my old pal Anthony. He's not beyond pulling a sting on me, either.

"So he was angry with her. And then—well—you know this better than I do. What makes a man decide to rape a woman? Anger? Lust? Control? Or the Willie Sutton theory of robbing banks—just because she's there?"

I had been doing this work for more than ten years and I

had never seen or heard any satisfactory explanation of what motivates a human being to force another into an act of sexual intercourse, the most intimate contact two people can experience. The only factors that were the same in every case were the vulnerability of the victim at a particular moment in time and the opportunity that this presented to the assailant.

Wrenley stepped forward and moved closer to me, passing behind me and putting his left arm around my back, ready to lead me to the staircase going down to the street level.

"Bailor denied assaulting Deni at first. Made up a whole story about Omar being along for the ride, and blaming the rape on him. That's actually why he killed poor Omar—so that dumb con artist couldn't tell me otherwise. Worked fine with me until I read the newspaper story about the DNA eliminating Omar. Not so tense, Alex. C'mon. I'm telling you all this so that you don't waste the government's money trying to hunt me down. I don't have the damn paintings after all. I got screwed out of the Vermeer, and the Rembrandt was never actually in my control."

I pulled away from Wrenley and walked alongside him.

"So Anthony and I had another meeting. That's when he told me about getting mad at Deni for not having the painting. He knew I'd understand that, since I wanted it so badly. What he couldn't make me understand is why he made her get in the back of the station wagon and, well . . . He said he never meant to get rough with her. He just didn't expect her to resist, especially since he had a gun. Thought just the threat of it would make her tell him where the Vermeer was. But he couldn't scare it out of her. Said she fought like a tiger. Claimed he had to hit her in the back of the head with the gun to shut her up."

I was biting the inside of my cheek so hard that I tore through the thin membrane and could taste blood in my mouth. I put my right hand in my jacket pocket and began to play with the case of Jake's razor blades, sliding one out the open end of the container and squeezing it between two fingers. I thought of Preston Mattox's description of Deni, so feminine looking but such a fighter, and his sorrowful certainty that she would have struggled against her attacker. For some women, resistance saves them from the completion of the assault, but for others it causes the attacker to use even more force to accomplish his goal.

"There's an object lesson in all this, Ms. Cooper." Wrenley held his revolver up for a moment for me to see, as a reminder. "I'm going to tuck this back in my waistband during my short freedom ride, but I know you're clever enough to understand that it's not smart to make me angry."

Frank Wrenley was standing at the top of the stairwell, lowering his arm from in front of my face as I took my fingers out of my pocket. With a single stroke, I sliced at his hand with one of the sharp cutting edges of the razor blade. The gun fell onto the steps beneath him and clattered to the floor below. Wrenley grabbed his wrist and howled in pain.

33

I ran as fast as I could go, in the direction of the double glass doors that surrounded the Hi-Line Railroad ties and opened out onto the antiquated structure leading downtown, several stories high above the streets of Chelsea. Wrenley had been at the top of the stairs, blocking my way to the patrol car in the rear of the building. I didn't waste time; he might have reached the gun before I did, which would have been deadly. I knew I had temporarily disarmed him, but I also guessed the wound had not disabled him completely.

The bolt affixed to the exit yielded easily to a twist of my hand. I yanked it back and was met by a blast of the hot August air as I escaped onto the tracks. For once—I prayed silently—don't let Chapman's stories be full of their usual exaggeration. I was trusting his brief oral history of the neighborhood to make my dash away from this callous killer, and I needed Chapman's facts to be right.

The rusted iron frame of the deserted railway rose on thick beams over Twenty-second Street and stretched out ahead, cutting through the center of the buildings opposite me. The track bed was wider across than most small tenements in the city. Looking down at the littered ground, I chose a path directly between the parallel lines that were vestiges of old track, hoping to avoid tripping over pieces of wood and steel that were obscured by weeds and garbage of all sorts.

I screamed for help. I was headed south, and Brannigan and Lazarro were parked on the north side of Caxton Due. I knew they couldn't see or hear me as I ran, but I was sure I could attract the attention of someone who would call for assistance. "HELP! POLICE!" I yelled as I crossed to the far side of Twenty-second Street, looking down for signs of life amidst the vans that had congested the entire block since before I had arrived at the gallery. I gasped for breath, holding on to the edge of the building adjacent to the tracks, but could see no people on the pavement below. Wrenley was charging at me from the open glass doors of Caxton Due.

I started jogging again, slowing somewhat as I zigzagged around holes in the skeleton of the trail, afraid I would catch my foot and wedge myself in a crevice from which I'd be unable to retreat. There were shards of broken glass and dirty hypodermic needles, discarded sneakers and dead pigeons, and I danced around objects on the obstacle course, wanting none of them to bring me down in flight.

Racing through the valley of warehouses that rose above the tracks on either side of me, I emerged onto Twenty-first Street, stopping to peer down and repeat my cries for help. Kids were playing ball at the far end of the block, near

Eleventh Avenue, and they stopped to look as one of them heard and pointed up at me. "POLICE!" I shouted to them, not knowing if they could make out my words. I glanced back to see Wrenley gaining on me, so I ran again.

There was open iron grillwork on the side of the guardrail at the next intersection. I gave a fleeting thought to climbing over and trying to lower myself down from it. I was still too high off the street to jump, but perhaps I could cling to a ledge until police arrived. Then I saw the rolls of barbed-wire fencing directly below me, spitting their jagged edges upward, so I propelled myself on.

Wrenley was getting closer. His route was a more reckless one than mine, straightforward and relentless in pursuit. Taller buildings rose around me as I followed the next strip of tracks, the intense glare of the sun briefly lost to the shade of the brick walls.

I heard a grunt from behind me and ignored my own directive not to look back. Wrenley had tripped on something and fallen to the ground. Taking a deep breath, I surged ahead and ran on past the giant warehouses, onto a long open stretch of track. I must have been below Nineteenth Street by now. In the distance I could hear the faint wail of sirens. I had no idea how remote they were, or any hope that they would reach me in the maze of one-way streets.

Lowering my eyes to the pavement below in search of the blue-and-white patrol cars that might be on their way, I saw only the tall traffic signs on the nearest corner, their bright red flashers urging me on. DON'T WALK.

The length of the run had not been enough to slow me down, but the dense humidity and August heat were oppressive. I was gasping for air and felt like my body was running on fumes, trying to find oxygen in the stillness of the stale afternoon.

Wrenley was closing in again. I didn't have to turn my head

to see him, but I could hear his labored panting over the noise coming from my own chest. We were somewhere below Seventeenth Street, and the entire structure of the railroad lay out before me, curving slowly around to the east, away from the surrounding buildings.

I felt the tug on the tail of my jacket a split second before Wrenley pushed me down from the rear, landing with me in a tangle of legs and arms. My knees slammed against the metal tracks as I tried hopelessly to break the fall. The palms of my hands stung as they landed on pieces of rusted metal, rocks, and debris I couldn't identify. I pushed up and kicked one leg out back behind me, smacking it against Wrenley's chin or chest—I couldn't see which—drawing a groan as his head snapped back.

As I raised myself up on my feet, I grabbed at one of the empty beer bottles scattered along the path and carried it in my hand as I resumed my gallop, heading to the section of the Hi-Line that crossed out over Tenth Avenue.

I was hugging the left side of the railing as the elevation passed over the piece of sidewalk edging the wide thoroughfare. I knew the danger that slowing down would bring Wrenley closer to me, but I also knew that this main artery running below me, four lanes wide, would be my most obvious chance to get help. I had no idea how much farther the tracks ran before they would corner me at the dead end of a brick wall on some abandoned tenement.

As I looked down I could see the mesh fencing and barbed wire that bordered a parking lot directly below me. Beyond that, for the first time since I began my run from the gallery, I was free of the prickly metal underpass that would have ripped my skin apart had I landed on it.

I was even with the curb of the sidewalk below me as I looked up the broad avenue. Moving against the sparse flow of uptown traffic were two patrol cars coming at us, lights spinning furiously atop them and sirens screaming their appearance.

I stopped at that point and stuck one foot in the iron gridwork of the side rail, lifting my other leg over the top, half dangling above the street, hoping to make it easier for the cops to see me as they approached, and harder for Wrenley to get to me. My right hand was still clutching the bottle, and with my left I tried to balance against the top of a billboard frame that was posted along the rail.

Wrenley was on me now, coming directly at me with his arms outstretched. His right hand looked like a road map, trickles of blood forming streets and highways. As he prepared to lunge at my neck, I shattered the bottle against the steel frame of the Hi-Line and screamed at him to keep back.

His right hand landed on my shoulder. I anchored my foot in the open grille of the banister and pivoted out of his grip, my pants leg ripping as it twisted against the steel trim. He grasped again and caught a hunk of my hair, trying to pull me toward him, back onto the tracks. Gripping the billboard top to stay in place, I swung my right arm at Wrenley's head, slashing him with the fractured end of the broken brown bottle.

This time his screams were louder than mine, as I opened up a gaping hole between his ear and forehead, with blood erupting from the gash and spilling down into his eye.

He staggered back for a step or two, then vaulted at me like a wild animal that had been mortally wounded in a hunt. His hands still wanted my neck, and as he charged toward me I shifted my weight and swung my leg onto the track, flattening myself against the back of the billboard.

Blinded by the blood, Wrenley hurtled himself over the guardrail headfirst, onto the street below.

I bent over to see his body crumpled against the blacktop like a deer on a dark country road, with cars screeching to a halt to try to avoid him.

Within seconds the two police cars pulled up from the north, directly under the tracks. From above I watched Brigid Brannigan's ponytail swinging as she yelled to Lazarro to check the body, while she ran in my direction, looking up to see whether I was the woman slumped over the railing, staring down at the corpse of Frank Wrenley.

"Are you hurt?"

I shook my head from side to side, not daring to try to speak. More sirens, and the large square shape of an ambulance lumbered into view. Too late to be of any use for Wrenley. What had Chapman called this street? I thought to myself. Death Avenue.

"Can you stay up there till I get the Fire Department here with a ladder?"

I nodded to her, then turned my back and sat down on the ground. I leaned against the railing, rubbing my calves with my scraped hands and trying to breathe at regular intervals.

Fifteen minutes later, after the body had been removed from the scene, I heard Brannigan calling my name again. I stood and looked down at the long red engine that had been summoned, watching as the ladder was hoisted into place. Two of the firemen climbed up it and over onto the Hi-Line tracks, introducing themselves and shaking my hand.

"Can you make it down?"

"I hate heights." I gave them as much of a smile as I could muster, not able to explain to them what it had taken for me to be poised on the edge of the railing when Wrenley had come at me just a little while ago.

"Nothing to it. I'll be one rung below you, guiding you down. Harry'll stay on top and load you on. Just close your eyes and trust me."

When I opened them again, I was on the street. The ad on the billboard plastered above my head was visible for the first time. It was a six-foot-tall vodka bottle in the shape of the fuselage of a jet airplane, with words beneath it in bold yellow paint: ABSOLUT ESCAPE.

The cluster of uniforms around me, all meaning to be helpful, was stifling. Police and firemen were having a cordial turf battle over who would take me into their care—cops as first on the scene, or firemen as my rescuers.

I pulled Brigid Brannigan aside. "Tell them I'd like to ride with you."

"Will you go to Saint Vincent's so they can check you out?"

"Yes. I think I'd like a tetanus shot." I wasn't sure what my knees and hands had been raked against. "But I want to make a stop on the way there."

She explained to the others that I was going with her. I got in the front seat of the RMP. Someone handed me my bag, which I had dropped in the gallery. The beeper was going off, so I removed it and saw that it was my office number. Brannigan began driving up Tenth Avenue, about to turn east to loop around downtown to the hospital. "Would you just go straight a few blocks, to the corner of Twenty-first Street?"

I called Laura from Brannigan's cell phone. She sounded concerned. "Mike's been beeping you. He's probably through the tunnel now, back in Manhattan. Says he hasn't been able to find you. Are you okay?"

"I guess I didn't hear it. Would you call him back and tell him to meet me in Chelsea, the northwest corner of Twenty-first and Tenth, okay? I'll wait for him till he gets there." She'd know the rest of the details soon enough.

The car came to a stop just past the traffic light. "Here?"

"Yes."

Brannigan looked at the small graceful building that I had noticed when we circled the block earlier today. "Want me to come in with you?"

"No thanks. I just want to wait there for Chapman. Think anyone would mind?"

She smiled back at me and simply said, "No."

I got out and walked up the four steps of the Church of the Guardian Angel. Its lovely Romanesque facade is bordered by two slim columns and a round stained-glass window. I pulled on the wooden door and walked inside, sitting down in the cool silence. I didn't know where the nearest synagogue was, but I needed to be in a place where I could be alone and pray. Somehow the name of this lovely church lent itself to the circumstances of the day.

Twenty minutes later I heard the door open and close, and the noise of a pair of footsteps walking toward me. I didn't turn my head.

Mike Chapman slipped into the pew beside me and looked at me, grimacing as he shook his head back and forth. He started to say something.

"Not right now."

He put his arm around my shoulder instead. I closed my eyes and rested my head against him until I was ready to leave.

34

Mike was singing background for Willie Nelson and Julio Iglesias—"To All the Girls I've Loved Before"—when Jake and I walked through the door at Rao's a week later. He got off the bar stool when he saw us come in. "They're playing my song. Best jukebox in the world."

Joey Palomino came out of the kitchen to greet us. "You got the first booth, Jake. Good to see you. Nice to have you back, Alex."

The tiny restaurant on the corner of 114th Street and Pleasant Avenue was like a private club. An unknown caller might hope for a reservation six months ahead, but the handful of tables were filled by regulars who came on a steady basis when

Joey gave them their dates. Once in, since there is no second seating, you could sit for the night and feast on luscious Italian food and wine for hours, to the accompaniment of great music from the fifties and sixties. Mike and I had been guests there a couple of times over the years, but Jake had worked his way up to a weekly berth after he hit the national news desk. Mike had asked Jake to set up a dinner to get me out of my dismal mood and to mark Mercer's move from intensive care to a regular hospital room. It looked like he'd be released in another ten days.

We settled into the booth as Vic, the bartender, came over with the first round of drinks. He forgot names from time to time, but never faces or beverage favorites. *"Salute."*

"To Mercer's recovery," Jake said, clicking glasses with us.

"So now you know why Caxton was packing up," Mike began.

"Let's not talk about the case tonight, please?" I looked from one to the other.

"You gotta face the music sooner or later, blondie."

I had avoided most discussions of the whole matter for the last week, immersing myself in the case folders that had been buried on my desktop since the evening I had learned of Denise Caxton's death. Jake hadn't pushed me, letting me ease back into my own apartment and assure family and friends that everything was fine.

Frankie Palomino, Joey's son, came to sit at the table and take our order. Mike was distracted for the moment. He'd obviously been thinking about what he'd eat from the moment I told him we'd be coming here for dinner.

"I gotta have the roasted peppers, clams *oreganate,* and the seafood salad to start. For pasta I want the fusilli with sausage and cabbage. Then some lemon chicken, veal parmigiana, and whatever else Coop wants. And a bottle of red wine. Tell Vic to make it a good one."

Mike had picked all the best things from the kitchen. Frankie laughed and asked if Jake and I wanted to add any choices of our own. The food was served family style, in portions large enough to feed half the guys back at the squad.

"Where was I? Oh, so you heard about Caxton?"

Jake looked at me and gave my hand a squeeze. "He's right. You've got to deal with this."

I played with the ice in my glass, drew in a breath, and answered Mike. "Kim McFadden called me at home this weekend, before the story broke in the papers on Monday." The U.S. Attorney's Office had brought down the first indictments in the auction bid–rigging case. Although Lowell Caxton was not among the defendants named, it had already been rumored that one of the dealers was cooperating and about to testify against others in the ring. Lowell had been moving his assets out of New York to some of his other properties, probably trying to get them out of the country before they could be seized by the government.

"Has Anthony Bailor talked?" Jake asked Mike.

"He's not exactly singing. The first time I saw him at the hospital, he wouldn't give up Wrenley for anything. Once he heard Frank was dead, he confirmed that's who he was working for. Still won't admit he did the hit on Deni, but we don't need his confession. We've got the DNA to make that case."

"Bailor was the guy in the garage after Alex?"

"Yeah. Seems Wrenley panicked at Mickey Diamond's story in the paper that we were close to solving the case. He followed Alex to Lincoln Center, then called Bailor to run her down. Same for the attempt on Mercer and Alex. Wrenley was the one who hired the receptionist to freelance for him on Sunday morning. She called to leave the message, at his direction, pretending to be Marina Sette. He also paid her to let you into the gallery. Bailor was told to kill her on his way in, and then shoot both of you."

"What does Bailor say about the paintings?" I asked.

"Back to square one. Holds to his story that he doesn't know anything about the art. And now, with Wrenley dead, we'll never know if he really had the Rembrandt, too."

I knew that cops as well as F.B.I. agents had gone through Wrenley's apartments in New York and Florida in painstaking searches. The possibility that after a decade these priceless treasures would be restored to public view again had been dashed with the murder of Denise Caxton and the death of Frank Wrenley. Both paintings were still missing. Was I responsible for the fact that Wrenley's secret died with him in his fall from the railroad track?

"I know what you're thinking, Coop. He was a mutt who didn't deserve to live."

"But if he had some of the stolen paintings, and we could have found out . . ."

"Hey, the friggin' Feebies couldn't find the stuff for ten years. They're probably just sitting on the floor under somebody's bed, collecting dust. Or in some storage case left in a warehouse that won't get opened for another fifty years, and then they'll get discovered by accident. These thieves have been scamming off each other for so long now, the art could be anywhere. A lot of dead bodies left behind for this loot."

I thought of Marco Varelli and why the old man wasn't allowed to die a natural death, simply because he might connect Wrenley and Caxton to the stolen Vermeer.

"The Feds got nothin' better to do than look for counterfeit money and seize illegal Cuban cigars. This gives 'em a mission, Coop. It ain't all bad."

Mike was tucking his napkin into the collar of his shirt. "Hey, Jake, better stick that tie in your shirt. You get sauce on that thing it'll ruin the design completely. What's he got on this one, blondie? Gerbils? Wait'll I tell Mercer you got little rodents running around on your necktie."

Frankie came over to make sure everything was okay. "See the group at that table for six? It's the CEO of one of the big ad agencies, with a few of his models. One of the girls saw you on TV the other night and wants to meet you."

I turned to look around, assuming that Frankie was talking about Jake.

"Relax, it's not me for a change. It's Chapman."

The tall redhead was beaming at Mike. She must have seen him on the news, being interviewed about the close of the Caxton murder investigation.

"Tell her I'll be over as soon as I finish my dinner, will you, Frankie?" He wiped the empty pasta bowl with a piece of bread and winked at his admirer. "So, either of you guys hear the question tonight?"

We had been in the car on our way to the restaurant when *Jeopardy!* aired. "No."

"Easy one. Would have been a split."

"What was the category?"

"Religion."

"I never bet against you on that."

"Yeah, but since you spent some time in church last week, I thought you'd give it a shot. The answer was: Seventeenth-century cleric who created the most famous sparkling white wine."

I laughed. "That religious I am. Dom Pérignon, the monk who discovered champagne."

Mike got up from the booth and called over to the bar. "Hey, Vic, you got any champagne on ice? I'll be back over when they bring out the chicken. I'm gonna go introduce myself to my fans. You know how that is, Mr. Tyler, don't you?" He winked at me and put his napkin on his seat.

Jake turned to ask if I was all right. I smiled and nodded, reaching up to kiss him on the side of his neck. "Thanks for your patience. I'll be fine."

He held my face and pressed his mouth gently against mine. Then he sat back. "There's a follow-up question to the one about Dom Pérignon. I feel just like that lucky old monk. Know what he said when he took his first sip of champagne?"

"I have no idea."

" 'I'm tasting stars!' " Jake said, pulling me toward him and kissing me again.

I heard the sound of the cork popping out of the bottle and flying up against the ceiling. The Temptations were singing "My Girl," Mike had come back to the booth to await the next course, and Vic was pouring champagne for everyone. The events since the night I met Mike at Spuyten Duyvil would be less raw in a few weeks, we'd catch the West Side rapist soon, and new cases would draw me back into the work I loved.

We lifted our glasses to toast our missing partner once more, with Mike extracting a promise from us to bring Mercer to dinner here as soon as he was able. We would be a team again, in spite of the devil.

Acknowledgments

For almost thirty-five years, Alexandra Denman has taught me everything there is to know about friendship. Her love, her loyalty, her humor, and her intelligence have enriched my life beyond measure. Ben Stein, Alex's husband, is right to call her "the goddess."

My fictional heroine draws her name as well from Alexander Cooper—artist, book lover, and devoted friend to Justin and me. This book owes much to Alex and Karen Cooper, who introduced me to the galleries of Chelsea, the brilliance of Richard Serra, and the existence of the Hi-Line Railroad. They advanced the plot over wonderful meals and lots of good wine.

Susan and Michael Goldberg give new meaning to the word "generosity." Along with the crew of the *Twilight*—Captain Cutter, Todd, Wes, Kelly, and Stephens—they have given us a paradise to which to retreat, calm seas for sailing, and a safe haven for dreaming. Their book parties make all the lonely hours at the keyboard worthwhile.

Although my beloved pal Jane Stanton Hitchcock lives a

shuttle flight away from me now, her fictional counterpart is ever present on the pages of this book. It was more reliable to research the art world capers with a phone call to Jane than through the texts.

I am deeply grateful to Vineyard friends, who help sustain and encourage me through long summer days, when writing novels seems to be the least likely way to pass the time. To Ann and Vernon Jordan, with enormous respect and boundless affection; and Louise and Henry Grunwald, with great admiration and eternal gratitude. Their morning phone calls boost my spirits and dinners together nourish my soul.

My prosecutorial patron saint remains Bob Morgenthau. I have been fortunate to have had the benefit of his guidance, his integrity, and his wisdom for a quarter of a century. The women and men of the Manhattan District Attorney's Office—and especially my devoted friends and colleagues in the Sex Crimes Prosecution Unit—are the best in the business. Along with our counterparts in the New York Police Department and the Office of the Chief Medical Examiner, they continue to work on the side of the angels. Survivors of violent crimes who come forward with courage and fortitude, and trust our ability to do justice for them, have my profound esteem.

Last year I lost two friends, each of great spirit and heart. Whenever Alex Cooper goes to the ballet—as she does here with Natalie Moody—she will be watching the dancers at American Ballet Theatre and honoring Howard Gilman, an extraordinary man whose spirit lives on in all of those—man and beast—whom he embraced.

And my young protégée, Maxine Pfeffer, who lost her valiant struggle with cancer, will always be Coop's paralegal, Max. Thinking of her will forever bring a smile to my face.

Some of my Vassar classmates asked me to create a character in memory of one of our dear friends, the actress Marilyn

Swartz Seven, who also died too young. She is here as a woman of mystery—a role I hope she would have enjoyed performing.

The crews at Scribner and at Pocket Books have been a delight. I am especially grateful to Susan Moldow, for her support; John Fontana, for his stunning design; Giulia Melucci, for her relentless and enthusiastic efforts on my behalf; and Sunshine Lucas, for her patience and efficiency.

My thanks to all the booksellers and librarians who continue to put this series in the hands of readers, and to readers who wait for more.

The collaboration with Susanne Kirk, friend and editor, has been one of the blessings of this business. She has helped me make this a better book.

I have seen so many books dedicated to Esther Newberg in the last year that I have run out of superlatives for her. The best thing my husband ever did for me, other than ask me to marry him, was to introduce me to Esther—brilliant agent, brilliant friend.

My family remains my most precious gift. My only regret is that my father—the gentlest man I've ever known, who introduced me to this genre when I was a child—did not live long enough to see the joy this career has given me. But I thank my amazing mother, Alice, and all the Fairsteins—Guy, Marisa, Lisa, and Marc—for their support, and the Feldmans and Zavislans—Diane, Jane, Jan, Matthew, and Alexander—for theirs as well.

Most of all, I am constantly inspired by the love of the most wonderful continuing character in this series—and in my life—Justin Feldman. He has made all my dreams come true.

The Deadhouse

Acknowledgments

I never asked permission of Alex Cooper—the real one—when I purloined his name for my heroine several years ago. He and Karen have been dearest friends, perfect traveling companions, great readers, and part of the family since Justin and I first met. I treasure their friendship.

A very special credit is due to Judy Berdy, who shares my passion for Renwick's stunning skeleton, and who helped enormously with my research about Blackwells Island. To Judy and the Roosevelt Island Historical Society, I am enormously grateful.

I was fortunate to find a wealth of material, in the form of old institutional records and reports, at the superb library of the New York Historical Society. My thanks to Betsy Gotbaum, and the librarians who take such fine care of the antique documents.

The archives of *The New York Times* and the microfiche files of the New York *Herald Tribune* were also invaluable. And two books, *Gotham* by Edwin Burrows and Mike Wallace, and *The Other Islands of New York City* by Sharon Seitz and Stuart Miller, provided wonderful vignettes of the crime scene.

Several characters take their names from real individuals. That is because a number of very generous people contributed to a variety of charitable causes and public service auctions in exchange for the opportunity to have a figure named for them in an Alexandra Cooper novel. Some are good guys, some are suspects, some are perps—that's the chance they take. They all have my thanks for their good cheer and benevolence.

Robert Morgenthau remains the professional patron saint of prosecutors, and I am always mindful of my great fortune in working for him for a quarter of a century. My friends in the New York County District Attorney's Office Sex Crimes Prosecution Unit are the very best in the business. They prove it every day of the year. The men and women of the NYPD who risk their lives for all of us on a daily basis have my most sincere gratitude, and our colleagues at the Office of the Chief Medical Examiner continue to amaze me, giving us cold hits and solutions to major cases with increasing frequency.

Everyone at Scribner has made this experience a real joy. That starts at the top, with the generous support of Susan Moldow, which I appreciate tremendously. Giulia Melucci is the best publicist in a tough business and a delightful friend.

Susanne Kirk, my beloved editor, started me on this path a few books back. She has been with me every step of the way, and her reputation as the finest in this field is well deserved. Her heart is in these books, along with my own, and that means the world to me. Thanks, also, to her assistant, Erik Wasson, for his good cheer and attention to detail.

My agent and pal, Esther Newberg, is beyond simple acknowledgments. She has changed my life. How did I ever get so lucky?

Family and friends make all this possible. My incredible mother, Alice—and all the Fairsteins, Feldmans, and Zavislans—continue to give me joy and encouragement.

And most of all, my husband, Justin Feldman, remains my devoted coach, most loyal fan, and constant inspiration.

Roosevelt Island

MANHATTAN

East River — West Channel

Island

MAIN STREET

East River — East Channel

QUEENS

ROOSEVELT ISLAND
BRIDGE

AERIAL
TRAMWAY

EAST
59 STREET
BRIDGE

Roosevelt

QUEENSBORO
BRIDGE

EAST 86 STREET

1. United Nations building
2. Smallpox Hospital ruins
3. Strecker Laboratory ruins
4. Pepsi-Cola Factory sign
5. Tram dock
6. Subway station Q & B
7. Meditation Steps
8. Blackwell farmhouse
9. Chapel of the Good Shepherd
10. Octagon Park
11. Octagon
12. Lighthouse Park
13. Lighthouse
14. Gracie Mansion

0   miles   1/2

1

It was hard not to smile as I watched Lola Dakota die.

I clicked the remote control button and listened to the commentary again on another network.

"New Jersey police officers have released a portion of these dramatic videotapes to the media this evening. We're going to play for you the actual recordings the three hit men hired by her husband to kill Ms. Dakota made to prove to him that they had accomplished their mission."

The local reporter was posed in front of a large mansion in the town of Summit, less than an hour's drive from where I was sitting, in the video technicians' office of the New York County District Attorney. Snowflakes drifted and swirled around her head as she pointed a gloved hand at the darkened facade of a house, ringed with strands of tiny white Christmas lights that outlined the roof, the windows, and the enormous wreath on the front door.

LINDA FAIRSTEIN

"Earlier this afternoon, before the sun went down, Hugh," the woman addressed the news channel's anchorman, "those of us who gathered here for word of Ms. Dakota's condition could see pools of blood, left in the snow during the early morning shooting. It will be a grim holiday season for this forty-two-year-old university professor's family. Let's take you back over the story that led to this morning's tragic events."

Mike Chapman grabbed the clicker from my hand and pressed the mute button, then jabbed at my back with it. "How come the Jersey prosecutors got to do this caper? Too big for you to handle, blondie?"

As the bureau chief in charge of sex crimes for the New York County District Attorney's Office for more than a decade, sexual assault cases—as well as domestic violence and stalking crimes—fell under my jurisdiction. The district attorney, Paul Battaglia, ran an office with a legal staff of more than six hundred lawyers, but he had taken a particular interest in the investigation of the professor's perilous marital entanglement.

"Battaglia didn't like the whole idea—the risk, the melodrama, and . . . well, the emotional instability of Lola Dakota. He probably didn't know the story would look this good on the late news broadcast or he might have reconsidered."

Chapman lifted his foot to the edge of my chair and swiveled it around so that I faced him. "Had you worked with Lola for a long time?"

"I guess it's been almost two years since the first day I met her. Someone called Battaglia from the president's office at Columbia University. Said there was a matter that needed to be handled discreetly." I reached for a cup of coffee. "One of their professors had split from her husband, and he was stalking her. The usual domestic. She didn't want to have him arrested, didn't want any publicity that would embarrass the administration—just wanted him to leave her alone. The DA kicked it over to me to try to make it happen. That's how I met Lola Dakota. And became aware of her miserable husband."

"What'd you do for her?"

Chapman worked homicides, most of the time relying on sophisticated forensic technology and reliable medical evidence to solve his cases. He rarely dealt with breathing witnesses, and although he was the best detective in the Manhattan North Squad when he came face-to-face with a corpse, Chapman was always intrigued by how the rest of us in law enforcement managed to untangle and resolve the delicate problems of the living.

"Met with her several times, trying to convince her that we could make a prosecution stick and gain her trust to let me bring charges. I explained that filing a criminal complaint was the only way I could get a judge to put some muscle behind our actions." Lola was like most of our victims. She wanted the violence to stop, but she did not want to face her spouse in a court of law.

"It worked?"

"No better than usual. When reasoning with her failed, we relocated her to a temporary apartment, arranged for counseling, and sent a couple of our detectives to talk to her husband informally and explain that Lola was giving him a break."

"Happy to see the local constables, was he?"

"Elated. They told him that she didn't want us to lock him up, but if he kept harassing her, that wasn't a choice I would allow her to make the next time he darkened her doorway. So he behaved . . . for a while."

"Until she moved back in with him?"

"Right. Just in time for Valentine's Day."

"Hearts and flowers, happily ever after?"

"Eight months." I turned back to glance at the screen, motioning to Mike to give us sound again. Flakes were caking up on the reporter's eyelids as she continued to tell her story, reminding me that undoubtedly snow was piling up on my Jeep as well, which was parked in front of the building. A picture of Ivan Kralovic, Lola's husband, appeared as an insert on the bottom right corner of the screen.

"We've got to take a short break," the reporter said, repeating the euphemistic phrase that signaled a commercial interruption, "then we'll show you the dramatic footage that led to Mr. Kralovic's arrest today."

Mike got rid of the noise. "And at the end of those eight months, what happened? Did you lock him up the second time?"

"No. She wouldn't even give me a clue about what he had done. Called me that October to ask how to get an order of protection. After I greased the wheels to expedite it for her in family court, she told me she had rented an apartment on Riverside Drive, moved to a new office away from the campus, and settled her problems with Ivan the Terrible."

"Don't disappoint me, Coop. Tell me he lived up to his name."

"Predictably. It was in January of this year that he cut her with a corkscrew, while they were enjoying a quiet dinner for two. Must have mistaken her for a good Burgundy. Sliced open her forearm. He raced her to St. Luke's and it took twenty-seven stitches to close her up."

"They were together for just that one evening?"

"No, he had coaxed her back for the holidays a month earlier. A seasonal reconciliation."

Chapman shook his head. "Yeah, I guess most accidents happen close to home. You nail his ass for that one?"

"Once again, Lola refused to prosecute. Told the doctors in the ER—while Ivan was standing at her bedside—that she'd done it herself. By the time I heard about it through the university and got her down to my office, she was completely uncooperative. Said that if I had Ivan locked up, she would never tell the true story in a courtroom. She had learned her lesson by trying to reunite with him, she assured me, and wasn't going to have anything further to do with him."

"Guess he didn't get the picture."

"He stalked Lola on and off. That's what led her to hide out in New Jersey, at her sister's house, sometime in the spring. She called me every now and then, after Ivan threatened her or when she thought she was being followed. But her sister got spooked—worried about her own safety—and brought Lola to the local prosecutors over there."

"Let's go to the videotape," Mike said, spinning my chair back to the television screen and hitting the sound button on the clicker. The film was rolling and the reporter's voice-over was providing the narrative. The scene appeared to be the same large suburban house, earlier in the day.

". . . and you can see the white delivery van parked at the side of the road. The two men walked up the steps in front of the home, which is owned by Ms. Dakota's sister, carrying the cases of wine. When the professor opened the door and came outside to accept the gift bottles, both men put their packages on the ground. The one on the left presented a receipt that Dakota leaned over to sign, while the man on the right—there he goes now—pulled a revolver from beneath his jacket and fired five times, at point-blank range."

I leaned forward and watched again as Lola clutched at her chest, her body pushed backward by the force of the impact. Her eyes opened wide for an instant, seeming to stare directly at the lens of the camera, before they closed, as she fell to the ground, blood oozing from her clothing onto the clean white cover provided by the preceding day's dusting of snow.

Then, the camera, held by a third accomplice in the van, zoomed in for a close-up, and the man seemed to lose control of the equipment as it apparently dropped from his fingers.

"When the killers played their tape for Ivan Kralovic in his office at noon today, after the Summit Police Department released the news of Ms. Dakota's death to the wire services, they were rewarded with a payment of one hundred thousand dollars in cash."

Back to a live shot of the chilled reporter, wrapping up her story for the night. "Unfortunately for Kralovic, the gunmen he had hired to kill his estranged wife were actually undercover detectives from the county sheriff's office here in New Jersey, who staged the shooting with the enthusiastic participation of the intended victim."

The tape rolled again and showed the supposedly deceased Dakota now sitting upright against the front door of the house and smiling for the camera as she removed the outer jacket that had concealed the packets of "blood" that had spurted and flowed so convincingly moments before.

"We've been waiting here, Hugh, hoping this brave woman would tell us how she feels now that she has taken such dramatic steps to end years of spousal abuse and bring to justice the man who wanted to kill her. But sources tell us that she left the house here this afternoon, after Kralovic's arrest, and has not yet returned." The reporter glanced down at her notes to read a comment from the local prosecutor. "The district attorney, however, wants us to express his gratitude to the county sheriff for this 'innovative plan that put an end to Ivan's reign of terror, something that prosecutors from Paul Battaglia's office and the New York Police Department across the Hudson River have been unable to do for two years.' Back to the studio—"

I pulled the remote away from Chapman and slammed it onto the desktop after shutting off the set. "Let's go back to my office and close up for the night."

"Temper, temper, Ms. Cooper. Dakota's not likely to win the Oscar for her performance. You peeved 'cause you didn't get a chance to do the film direction?"

I turned off the light and closed the door behind us. "I don't begrudge her anything. But why did the Jersey DA have to take a shot at us? He knows it hasn't been our choice to let this thing drag on as long as it did." There wasn't a seasoned prosecutor anywhere who didn't know that the most frustrating dynamic in an abusive marriage was the love-hate relationship that persisted between victim and offender, even after the violence escalated.

My heels clicked on the tiles of the quiet corridor as we snaked our way down the long, dark hallway from Video to my eighth-floor office. It was almost eleven-thirty at night, and the tapping of an occasional computer keyboard was the only noise I heard to suggest that any of my colleagues were still at their desks.

Only a handful of cases went to trial this time of year, in the middle of December, with lawyers, judges, and jurors all anticipating the two-week court hiatus for the holiday season. I had been working late—reviewing indictments for the end-of-the-term filing deadline, and preparing to conduct a sex offender registration hearing after the weekend—when Detective Michael Chapman came over to tell me the eleven o'clock news was leading with the Dakota story. He had been down the street at headquarters to drop off some evidence at the Property Clerk's Office and called to see if I wanted a drink before knocking off for the night.

"C'mon, I'll buy you dinner," he now said. "Can't expect me to last the midnight shift on an empty stomach. Not with all the dead bodies I'm likely to encounter."

"It's too late to eat."

"That means you got a better offer. Jake must be home, cooking up some exotic—"

"Wrong. He's in Washington. Got the assignment on that story of the ambassador who was assassinated in Uganda, at the economic conference." I'd been dating an NBC News correspondent since early summer, and the rare nights he was free in time for dinner took me away from my usual haunts and habits.

"How come they keep giving him all that Third World stuff to cover when he seems like such a First World guy?"

The phone was ringing as I opened the door to my office.

"Alex?" Jake's voice sounded brusque and businesslike. "I'm at the NBC studio in D.C."

"How's your story coming?"

"Lola Dakota is dead."

"I know," I said, sitting down in my chair and turning away from Chapman for some privacy. "Mike and I just watched the whole bit on the local news. I think she's got a real future on the stage. Hard to believe she went for all that phony ketchup and—"

"Listen to me, Alex. She was killed tonight."

I turned back to look at Mike, rolling my eyes to suggest that Jake clearly had not seen the entire story yet and didn't understand that the shooting was a setup. "We know all that, and we also know that Paul Battaglia is not going to be thrilled when the tabloids point the finger at me for not putting this mess to bed a couple of—"

"This isn't about *you,* Alex. I've heard the whole story with the Jersey prosecutors and their sting operation. But there's a later headline that just came over the newsroom wires a few minutes ago, probably while you and Mike were watching the story run on the air. Some kids found Lola Dakota's body tonight—her dead body—in the basement of an apartment building in Manhattan, crushed to death at the bottom of an elevator shaft."

My eyes shut tight and I rested my head on the back of my chair as Jake lowered his voice to make his point. "Trust me, darling. Lola Dakota is dead."

2

"I'm sorry, Miss Cooper, but Lily doesn't want to talk with you just now. It's almost midnight, and our doctor is about to sedate her to let her get some rest. She thinks Lola would still be alive if you prosecutors hadn't talked her into this ridiculous scheme and exposed her to so much risk by faking her death."

My first impulse had been to call the victim's family, despite the late hour, to offer our assistance in the aftermath of this tragic turn of events. I knew they were unlikely to accept my help. It was her brother-in-law who answered the call. "I'm sure you must be aware that my office didn't think it was wise to—"

"It's all the same to us. None of you was able to protect Lola from this insanity of Ivan's."

Chapman had taken over my phone and I had moved to the alcove to use the one on my secretary's desk. My conversation ended abruptly and I stared at the calendar hanging on the wall in front of me.

"Snuggle into your snowsuit and mittens, kid. We're going to the two-six." He hung up the receiver and called out to me as I tried again to get through to the sheriff's office in New Jersey. The line was still busy, so I put on my coat, gloves, and boots and followed Mike to the elevator. "Leave your car here. I'll drop you at home when we're done."

The snow had tapered off to a flurry as we walked around to the rear of the courthouse and got into the black Crown Vic that was Mike's duty car. "Body's already been taken down to the morgue. Thought you'd like to grab a look at the scene with me."

"Why didn't Peterson beep me about Lola? Nobody reached out for me . . ."

"Don't take it personally, Coop. The lieutenant didn't even get this one till an hour ago. Seems that as soon as Dakota heard the ex had been arrested, she told her sister she needed a break. She'd been cooped up in the burbs for three weeks and wanted to go home for a few hours. Nothing to worry about with Ivan in custody, so those schmucks from the Jersey office let her drive off into the sunset. Alone. Four seventeen Riverside Drive—must be somewhere near 116th Street. Peterson says it's one of those old prewar apartment houses, in the process of going co-op. Scaffolding out in front 'cause they're repointing the building, and lots of repairs under way inside, too."

"Jake said some kids found her. Did the lieutenant mention anything about that?"

"Yep. Just around dinnertime, some of the boys from the 'hood came into the basement from Riverside Park to hang out. Get warm and get high, probably in reverse order. When they pressed for the elevator to come down, the doors didn't open completely, since the cab couldn't get all the way even on the bottom."

Mike was driving north to Canal Street, then heading over to the West Side Highway for the ride uptown. Tacky aluminum holiday decorations bordered the closed stalls on this dismal downtown shopping strip, where every kind of counterfeit designer product would be back on sale, out on the crowded sidewalks, by daybreak.

"The super heard a commotion and started to chase the kids outside. He thought they'd screwed up the equipment by playing around with it. So they offered to help him raise the cab a few feet to see whether something was stuck beneath it. When they looked into the shaft, they saw the body."

"Did they know—?"

"Whether she was dead? Fuggedaboutit."

"No, did they know that it was Lola?"

"You know what happens when you step on a cockroach? Any idea if it was Willie or Milton? The one that was crawling on your desk, or the one that was living in your file cabinet? The super hadn't even seen her in the building for months. Emergency Services responded to help get the remains up, and she was carted off to the ME's office."

"But they didn't treat it as a homicide?"

"Everyone involved assumed, up to that point, that it was all an accident. The elevator's been on the fritz, stopping between floors when it wasn't quitting altogether. The super told the first cops on the scene that some broad—probably just visiting in the building— must have stepped off into the black hole without even noticing that the elevator wasn't there."

"No one had any reason to know what she had been going through," I mumbled aloud as I struggled to recall whether I could have pushed Lola any harder when I had wanted her to press charges.

"Hell, it wasn't till one of the morgue attendants found a few papers in the pocket of her blouse that anyone even knew the identity of the deceased. Called back up to the Twenty-sixth Precinct, and they passed the news on to the lieutenant. Could still easily be an accident, according to what the super's been telling the cops. But then, in light of all the other bad news in her life, I'd have to think Ms. Dakota had outlived her string of lousy luck and was due to win the lottery."

Mike hit the brakes and I jerked forward, restrained by the seat belt. He had tried to pass a Yellow Cab at the entrance to the highway, and the turbaned driver gestured obscenely and cursed at us as he fishtailed on an icy patch of road.

"Move it, Mohammed!" Chapman yelled back, blasting the words into my ear as he aimed them across me toward the cabbie. "Those camel-humpers can guide a herd across the burning sands of the Sahara, but there oughtta be a law to keep them off the snow."

"I thought we had a deal for the new year?"

"I got a couple of weeks to go, kid. Don't expect any mouthpiece miracles overnight."

The New York City skyline glittered against the cobalt ceiling stretched out above and beyond it. From the Chelsea Piers, outlined against the water off to our left, to the red-and-green-lighted spire of the Empire State Building, across the middle of town in the distance, everything was gaily dressed for Christmas. I stared out at the assortment of blinking lights while Mike dialed up the numbers on his cell phone to check the whereabouts of his team.

I had known Chapman for more than ten years, and accepted the fact that he was no more likely to change his ways than I was able to explain the nature of our friendship, intensely close and completely trusting, despite the vast differences in our backgrounds. It had been almost twelve years since I joined Battaglia's office, and I smiled, remembering my father's prophecy that I wouldn't last there much past the three-year commitment required by the district attorney when I signed on. No one in my family believed that my training at Wellesley College and the University of Virginia School of Law would prepare me for the grim realities of life in an urban prosecutor's office.

My father, Benjamin Cooper, was a cardiologist who

had revolutionized surgical procedures when he and his partner invented a plastic valve that was used in virtually every heart operation in the country for more than fifteen years following its introduction to the field. To this day, he and my mother, while aware of the great personal satisfaction I derive from my work, worry about my ability to separate myself from its constant emotional drain—and its occasional dangers.

"Tell Peterson I'm on the way." Chapman turned to me and winked. "I'm bringing the lieutenant a little surprise." He clicked off the phone and was quiet for a few minutes. "I just assumed you'd want to come with me tonight. If I'm wrong, I can cross over to the East Side and drop you at your apartment."

Mike knew me well enough to know that I wouldn't have missed the opportunity to go with him to Lola Dakota's home and see for myself, firsthand, what the police were about to learn. It was logical for onlookers to presume some kind of freak accident, but the odds should truly have been in Lola's favor at this point, and the lieutenant was not going to let go of someone who had met an unnatural death on what he would consider his watch.

"Did you like this Dakota dame, blondie?"

I rolled my head back away from Mike, staring at the vista as we drove up onto the elevated portion of the highway.

"She was a tough character to like. Admire, maybe, but hard to warm up to. Very smart. And even more arrogant than brilliant. But she was willful and shrill, rode herself really hard, and from what I understood, rode her students even harder."

"And the husband? What made him so irresistible?"

"Who knows what goes on inside anyone else's marriage? I'll pull my files together in the morning and check my notes. I've got all kinds of details from our conversations and meetings about the case." I remembered again the many hours I had spent with Lola throughout the past two years, trying to convince her that we could make the criminal justice system work for her, and to let me take Ivan to trial for assault.

Chapman came from another direction altogether. His father, Brian, had been a second-generation Irish immigrant, who worked as a cop for twenty-six years and then died of a massive coronary two days after turning in his gun and shield. Mike was in his third year at Fordham when he lost his father, and although he completed his degree the following spring, he immediately took the exam and enrolled at the police academy, in honor of the man he most admired and respected. He was half a year older than I, and had recently celebrated his thirty-sixth birthday. Mike was one of the few people I knew who was thoroughly comfortable in his own skin, doing exactly what he most wanted to do in the world. That was simply to come to work every day at the Manhattan North Homicide Squad, with the best detectives in the city of New York, and spend all his waking hours restoring some dignity and a bit of justice to victims who had been murdered on what he liked to think of as his half of the island.

"Maybe we can stop by Mercer's house over the weekend. He's got some case folders on this one, too," I added. "And probably some good insight about Lola."

We had both been counting the days until Mercer Wallace would come off sick leave and back to the department on limited duty. Four months had passed since the attack that had almost taken his life, and it still took my breath away to think how close I had come to losing one of my dearest friends. Mike and Mercer had been partners in Homicide for several years, until Mercer was transferred to the Special Victims Unit, where he carried the lead role in some of the most complex rape investigations in the city.

Grand old apartment houses lined up along Riverside Drive, to our east, and Mike took the Ninety-sixth Street exit to wind his way up the quiet streets till we saw the array of NYPD cars and trucks that blanketed the intersection and rested on the snowy slopes of the park entrance opposite Lola's building. "Must be the place, kid."

Two uniformed cops were stationed on either side of the front door, and one nodded at Mike as he flashed his badge and asked the way down to the basement. "Press hasn't crawled all over this yet?" he asked, puzzled by the lack of interest from the media.

"Been and gone," the younger guy answered, jiggling one foot at a time and flexing his fingers, trying to keep warm. "They pulled out after a few shots of the body bag."

"Is there a doorman?"

"Not all day. Just came on at midnight. The entrance is only covered from twelve till eight A.M. And I think we're cramping this guy's style already. He likes to hang on to his flask pretty tight, and he's really spooked out by this. You gotta use the stairs or the north elevator to get down to where they found her. The south car has been shut off altogether. That's where the body was."

A couple in formal dress glanced at the police officers and brushed past Chapman on their way inside. They were still in the rear of the lobby as we entered, standing in the recessed area off to the right, by the mailboxes, trying to find out from the confused doorman what the commotion was about. Two elderly women in flannel bathrobes and one grad student type with purple-streaked hair had beaten them to the old guy for a chat, and I expected that by dawn, most of the tenants would have some version of a rumor from one of these sources.

Chapman pulled open the heavy service door that led to the fire stairs. There was no lightbulb at the top of the landing, and I followed him slowly down the two flights of steps.

Lieutenant Peterson was sitting at a bare desk in what I assumed was the super's office at the foot of the staircase. His cigarette dangled from his lips as he clutched the phone receiver with one hand and held up his other in our direction, palm outward, signaling Chapman to be quiet.

When he finished the conversation, he rose to his feet to greet us. "Alexandra, how've you been? That was the deputy commissioner, Mike. Can I talk to you alone for a minute?"

"Jeez, and I brought Sonja Henie all the way up here just to see you, Loo."

Peterson wasn't amused. He motioned Mike into the small room and closed the door. I turned the corner and said hello to the rest of the team from the Homicide Squad. Four of them were standing in front of the open space of the elevator shaft, and the bottom of the deadly cab was posed eerily above their heads and behind them, like a huge weight ready to drop again. They were talking about the squad's Christmas party, planned for the next evening, with no mention of the gruesome death that had brought them to this filthy room.

"You in on the pool?" Hector Corrado asked me.

"Only if you make sure I don't win. Battaglia thinks it's in such bad taste that we shouldn't humor you guys by chipping in."

"Pick a number, Alex. It'll only run you twenty bucks, and it's a big pot this year. You wanna lose, go low. Man, things always get crazy around the holidays, and this one's starting off wild. You're too young to remember, but it's beginning to look like the eighties around here."

Homicide cops had a tradition of betting on the number of murder cases they expected to occur before the end of the year. Hector kept track of the field, since choices had to be made by late summer. If there were open slots left, prosecutors were invited to kick in before the night of the party.

"So far, we've only had three hundred sixty-two in Manhattan this year. I just missed by six bodies back in eighty-eight. Total was seven sixty-four, can you believe it? And these wimps think they're overworked now when they're carrying a handful of investigations."

Chapman had left his overcoat in the super's office and emerged holding an oversize flashlight. He held out his right hand to Hector and asked the guys if the Crime Scene Unit had finished its work.

"Hard to make this a crime scene. Super was selling it to the first guys who responded as an accident. Peterson pulled in every chit he could think of to get Crime Scene to come over and give it a look, sort of unofficially. They're treating it as a suspicious death, not a homicide yet. Not every day you get a broad who lays down and rolls out her front door into an elevator shaft just hours after somebody else paid a lot of money to have her knocked off," Hector opined. "They took some photos of the body before she was scooped out. You could look. All you're gonna see is some dark stains."

Lieutenant Peterson, the veteran detective who ran the Homicide Squad, could get the Crime Scene Unit to do almost anything he requested. He had the best instincts in the business when it came to death investigation, and the finest track record in the department for solving cases. When he asked for backup, men knew he wouldn't be wasting their efforts.

Mike squatted and pointed the beam into the dark shaft. I rested one hand on his shoulder and looked in over his head. "You want to step aside, blondie? I know you think you give off quite a glow yourself, but you're blocking the little bit of help that seventy-five-watter is shining down at me from over your head."

I straightened up and stepped back.

"Hector, anybody get down here and scrape some of this crap up? It's impossible to tell what's blood and what's oil from the works, just by looking." Mike was standing, too.

"Yeah, that's all been done."

"They dust for prints?" I asked.

"Nobody even knew what parts of the building to include in the scene, Alex. We don't know if she had been dead for one hour or four by the time she was found. In the meantime, one super, two handymen, and a bunch of teenagers had been all over this area. They didn't know who she was, so they couldn't figure out which floor she'd dropped from or which elevator button she'd pushed. Sure, they went up and down all twenty-two landings, dusting for latents, looking for signs of a struggle, canvassing to see if anyone was at home who heard any noise. Pretty futile runaround so far. You go try that other elevator bank. It's not impossible that she just missed her footing and went off into a swan dive. You'll see, these things are on their last legs."

"Anyone been inside her apartment yet?"

"Waiting on that now. Peterson sent someone down to the morgue to get the keys they found on the body. Emergency Services is on their way back with a ram. Whoever gets here first, that's how we're going in."

"Super doesn't have a key?"

"Nope. She didn't trust nobody with nothin', is what he says."

That would be Lola. Chapman motioned to me to follow him back up the staircase to the lobby. There was a pair of stuffed armchairs against the wall, covered in a dreary tapestry fabric, sorely in need of reupholstering, and we sat opposite each other in them while he told me about his conversation with the lieutenant.

"Loo's really ripped. The commissioner's sticking with the accident story. It certainly can't be Ivan who had anything to do with this, they figure, since he was already under. That's what Peterson took me inside to tell me. That, and to get you off the premises pronto. If the mayor says this is an accident, then there's no need to have an assistant district attorney meddling in it."

For the moment, we both ignored that point. "They

never heard of backup? What if Kralovic didn't trust the guys he hired in Jersey and wanted a little security, some extra insurance, to make sure his plan to kill Lola worked?"

"I don't need convincing. City Hall does. The first day of Christmas my true love gave to me, a shove in the back and a trip to the morgue, right? The mayor doesn't want to add to the murder tally for the end of the year. And he's getting additional pressure from the powers that be at Columbia University."

"But Lola didn't even work there anymore."

"They farmed her out to a new, experimental school—King's College. It's got an entirely separate administration, but it bought some of the old Columbia buildings, so it's adjacent to the Columbia-Barnard campus. Somebody up there's got a direct pipeline to the mayor's office. The school officials don't want to open the whole can of worms about the history of their own tortured relationship with Lola Dakota, so they'd like this shoved under the carpet as well."

"They're leaving out a great big stumbling block, in the oversize form of the rotund, thick-skulled, and honorable Vinny Sinnelesi, the Jersey prosecutor who put together this clever sting operation. Battaglia thinks the entire plan was to snag some visibility to launch Sinnelesi's bid for the gubernatorial race next year. Vinny had no qualms about getting attention on the back of Ms. Dakota while she was alive, so I doubt he'll lose a minute's sleep about doing it over her dead body."

Mike laughed at my description of Sinnelesi, and at my obvious state of agitation. "Calm it, Coop."

I was too wound up to stop. "Easy for him to sit tight in his own little fiefdom and point his fat finger at us, calling this a murder—whether it is or isn't—knowing he can't screw up *this* investigation 'cause it will be in Battaglia's jurisdiction."

The front door of the building opened and, with the frigid air, in walked Lieutenant Peterson. Chapman got up and his trademark grin vanished in a flash. "I thought you'd gone home, Loo."

Without breaking stride as he moved toward the elevator, Peterson barked back, "I told you to get Ms. Cooper out of this building, Chapman. She's got nothing further to do with this matter. This, this, . . . accident."

3

I sat in Chapman's car, shivering against the chill of the night air, which kept me wide-awake despite the late hour. Peterson's unexpected reappearance in the lobby had been due to the arrival of the detective who had been sent to the morgue to fetch Dakota's keys. The two had crossed paths as Peterson was about to close his car door, so the lieutenant doubled back to see whether they could gain entry to Lola's fifteenth-floor apartment.

Chapman knew that it wasn't Peterson's style to examine the woman's home himself. He wasn't a micromanager in that sense, and would rely on the intelligence of his men—and the photographs they would bring back—to highlight any information of significance. "Loo'll give it a once-over just to satisfy himself, somebody'll snap some pictures, and then I'll come down to get you," he said as he led me to his car and unlocked the door. "Just slink down in the seat so

27

he doesn't see you when he's leaving—no heater, no radio. He'll be gone in twenty minutes."

"You know he'll kill us if we get caught."

"Can't happen, kid. It'll just be you, me, and George Zotos. Who's gonna squeal?"

Zotos was one of the guys on Mike's team in the squad, and I had worked well with him over the years. "There's no downside to this for you. Battaglia doesn't even know you're here, and Peterson gave orders to me, not to you."

Shortly before one-thirty in the morning, Peterson walked out on the sidewalk and his driver swung around in front of the building to pick him up. Ten minutes later, Chapman came out the same way, said something to the uniformed cops still posted next to the entrance, and crossed the street to the car to help me maneuver the icy road. We walked down to 115th Street and into the alley that led to the rear of the building. The heavy iron door was wedged ajar by the flashlight that Chapman had been holding earlier. He picked it up from the ground as he pulled open the door and took me inside through the basement. We rode to the fifteenth floor on the one elevator that was still in service, which creaked its way upward, slowly and noisily, then crossed over to the south side of the building to get to 15A. When Chapman tapped lightly on the door, Zotos opened it immediately and we joined him inside the apartment.

Mike passed me a pair of rubber gloves, in exchange

for the black leather pair I'd been wearing all evening. "Don't touch anything without showing it to me first. Just poke around and see what strikes you as interesting."

"Some kind of slob, eh?" George was shaking his head, not knowing where to begin. "You think it was ransacked, or she just liked to live this way?"

I had been to Lola's office several times to discuss her case and to try to pressure her supervisors into supporting her during the process. "I think this is her natural habitat. It's pretty consistent with what I saw on campus."

We were standing in the living room, which appeared to have been decorated with the remains of a Salvation Army used-furniture sale. The classic bones of a prewar six-room apartment were practically obscured by the bizarre accumulation of odd-shaped chairs, a pair of Victorian love seats covered in faded burgundy velvet, a beige Naugahyde lounger, and cardboard boxes piled everywhere, with strapping tape still in place. Whenever she had moved them in, Lola had not yet opened or unpacked them.

I walked through the other rooms to get a sense of the layout. The small kitchen, still decorated in the drab avocado tones of the sixties, was quite bare, which fit with the fact that she had been living in New Jersey for almost a month. The dining room featured an old oak table, pushed up against the window, overlooking a glorious view of the park and river. It, too, was stacked with boxes, with the word BOOKS scrawled on the sides of almost every one.

The master bedroom had the same view, outside and within. Here, some of the cartons had been opened and the volumes were spread around the floor and partially scattered on shelves.

"What'd she teach?" Mike asked, moving into the room with me.

"Political science. When I first got the case and met her, she was still on the faculty at Columbia. Had a spectacular reputation as a scholar and a teacher. Lola was a brilliant lecturer."

I glanced at a small stack of books on her nightstand. They were all novels rather than textbooks. I wondered whether they were favorites she kept at hand to reread. A bookmark stuck out from the pages of the one on top of the pile—an early Le Carré, one that Lola would never finish.

"Students loved her because she brought the classroom alive. I remember one day last winter, I was going up to the school for a meeting with her. She said I could catch part of her class. Municipal institutions in the early part of the twentieth century—the mayoralty, the corrupt officials of Tammany Hall, the city jails and courthouses. Of course I was intrigued, so I made a point of getting there in time to walk in and sit in the back of the classroom."

"Busman's holiday," Mike said, opening drawers and examining their contents.

"Lola lured me right into that one." I smiled, remembering the day. "She'd spent the week on the politics of Gentleman Jimmy Walker, the mayor of New York City in the late 1920s. But she had a unique method of showing the students the tone of the period. She was parading around the podium, doing a perfect imitation of Mae West, describing the actress's arrest and prosecution for the stage perform-ance of her play—called *Sex*—in 1926. She was reading from West's autobiography, describing the condition of the prison cell in the Tombs, and how the confused, diseased women were herded inside like animals."

"A bleeding heart, under all that flesh, you're gonna tell me."

I ran my finger across the spines of a row of books, checking the titles and noting that most in that section were treatises about nineteenth- and twentieth-century government in New York City, which was her specialty. "She ended by describing how the jail system was run by greedy and stupid civil servants, worse than the pris-oners. She looked over the heads of her students and quoted West right to me. 'Humanity had parked its ideals outside.'"

"Staged just for you?"

"I was there to make her understand how important it was to prosecute Ivan, and she wanted me to know that she wasn't about to see him stuck in a jail cell. The typical ambivalence of a survivor of domestic abuse."

Chapman lifted the dust ruffle to look under the bed and continued to poke around the room.

"Doesn't sound like scholarship to me. Sounds like two-bit, second-class theatrics. Same kind she went for with those Jersey jerk-off prosecutors yesterday."

"She was capable of both. I'll give you some of her published articles to read. You'll like her writings about the Civil War period and the Draft Riots." Mike knew more about military history than anyone I had ever met and read extensively on the subject.

"Save 1863 for another day and transport yourself back to the twenty-first century."

Mike was impatient with my diversion, with good reason, and I turned away from the bookshelves and moved on to the desk. "The computer?"

"Leave it alone. Jimmy Boyle's coming to pick it up tomorrow."

Boyle headed our cybercop squad and was a genius at retrieving files and information that literally, to my view, were lost in space.

The rest of the desktop was a maze of spiral notepads, computer disks, phone messages dated three and four months earlier, which detectives would scour in the days to come, and small framed photographs. I recognized a young Lola in her cap and gown, at what must have been her graduation from Barnard, and then a Dakota family shot of more current vintage, taken in front of her sister Lily's home in Summit.

There was a black knit cardigan sweater over the

back of the desk chair. "Any idea what she was wearing today?" I asked.

Mike called to George, but he hadn't seen the body either, so Mike added that question to the list he had started in the memo pad he kept inside his blazer. "They'll have it inventoried at the ME's office in the morning. Then I've got to check with the sister to see if the clothes she had on when she died are the same ones she left Jersey with."

I used my forefinger to pull at the pocket on the chest of the sweater. "Hey, Mike, want to take out this piece of paper?"

I didn't want to be responsible for touching anything that might raise an issue of chain of custody. For all intents and purposes, I wasn't there tonight. He slid his gloved fingers in and came up with a folded page from a telephone pad printed with the words KING'S COLLEGE at the top, and beneath that, the single handwritten notation, in bold print:

THE DEADHOUSE

Below the words was a list of four numbers: 14 46 63 85.

Mike read the words aloud. "Mean anything to you? A person? A place?"

I shook my head.

"Probably what the other tenants will start calling this building," George said.

"Is that her writing?"

I had seen enough of her correspondence to recognize it at once. "Yes. Any date on it?"

"Nah. I'll voucher the note and the clothing. When we go to Jersey, remember to ask the sister if she can tell us whether Lola had this sweater there with her yesterday."

I opened the closet door and we poked around the contents. An ordinary mix of skirts and slacks, dresses and blouses, sizes consistent with Lola's large chest and slim hips.

"What do you know about a boyfriend?" George called out to me from the second bedroom.

"News to me." I closed the closet and went into the smaller room.

There was a couch and a chair, and George was standing in front of a chest of drawers, having pulled open each of the three levels. He was dangling a pair of Jockey shorts on the end of his pen. "Get me some bags from the kitchen. Let's see if we can find out who Mr. Size 40, Briefs-Not-Boxers, might be."

Mike noticed the end of a striped sheet sticking out below the edge of the couch. He threw the cushions onto the floor and rolled out the metal frame of the sleep sofa. He stripped the sheets off the narrow mattress and folded the top and bottom ones separately. "Let's see if the lab comes up with any love juice." He wrapped each one in an ordinary brown paper bag, to avoid contamination from one surface to another, and

34

because sealing damp materials in plastic could cause them to deteriorate.

George chuckled. "So much for the mayor's theory that she threw herself in the elevator shaft 'cause she was so despondent about having Ivan arrested. Peterson told me the first thing I had to look for in here was a suicide note. Damn, seems like she squeezed in one last fling before it was lights out."

"Let's just leave this all here and send a team in for the morning with an Evidence Recovery Unit. Someone needs to go through this stuff," Chapman said, waving his hand at the several pieces of men's clothing hanging in this room's closet. "Got to check the labels, look for ID. It'll take hours. We'll just seal off the apartment now and have them put a uniformed post outside the door for the night."

"Any mail here?" I was taking one more look around as I put on my coat.

"No. The brother-in-law said all her mail was being forwarded to her office at school, then she went through it there. We'll have to pick it up tomorrow."

"Fat chance. I've had dealings with the legal departments, both at Columbia and at King's. I can only tell you that if Sylvia Foote gets to Lola's office first, everything will be so sanitized that you'll think it had been swept by a CIA operative. Never a trace of Professor Dakota."

Foote was the general counsel of King's College, having served in the same post at Columbia for more than a quarter of a century. She would opt for protecting the institution every chance she had.

"You know her personally?"

"Yeah. And she's like fingernails on a chalkboard. 'Don't disturb the students' is her mantra, but what she really means is that the university's golden rule is not to scare the parents. Nobody paying those tuition rates wants his kids to go to a school where there might be a hint of scandal. We'd better try to get in there as fast as we can."

Chapman called the two-six and asked the desk sergeant for an extra body to sit on the door of 15A. Then we said good night to George and retraced our steps downstairs and out the rear door of the building, around to Riverside Drive, where the car was parked.

As we let the engine warm up, I reached for the radio and moved the dial to 1010 WINS, the all-news station, to see when this arctic front would pass through the city. I caught the tail end of the traffic cycle, warning about icy patches on the bridges leading in and out of town, and shivered again at the top of the early morning news.

"This just in: the body of a Yale University senior, missing from her New Haven dormitory since the day after Thanksgiving, was found shortly after midnight, floating in the Hudson River, near the promenade off Battery Park City. The content of the letters left behind by Gina Norton have not been released to the press, but police sources say that there are no signs of foul play."

"So much for my mother's theory that the school yard was a safer place to be than the streets—one more corpse tonight, we'll have a hat trick. And how handy for Hizzoner. No foul play declared before she's even been dried off, thawed out, and taken apart by the medical examiner," said Chapman, flipping off the radio, turning on the headlights, and easing out of the parking space to take me home.

4

I heard *The New York Times* slam against my apartment door at six-thirty, flung there by the porter who distributed the papers throughout the building every morning. Drops of water from my hair, still wet from the shower, dripped onto the front page as I leaned over to pick it up and check the headlines for the story of Lola Dakota's death.

Three pages back in the Metro section was a photo of Lola, standing at a lectern in full academic dress, mortarboard atop her head. The caption read "University Professor Dies in Bizarre Accident," above a subheading printed in smaller type describing her as a "Witness for the Prosecution." The reporter had managed to incorporate every stereotypical expression of reaction into his brief story. The administration was shocked and saddened by news of the beloved professor's death, students were puzzled by the ironic twists of fate in Dakota's final days, and her husband's family was outraged at charges that he was alleged to have been involved in the thwarted plot to kill her.

The phone rang and Chapman gave me the morning weather report. "You're gonna need a dogsled to get downtown this morning. The streets are coated with ice and the windchill brings it down to about five degrees. I'm on my way home to catch a few hours' sleep."

"Anything develop during the rest of the tour?"

"Nope. Made the usual notifications, took care of all the paperwork, got the preliminary reports down on the chief of detectives' desk so he's in the know first thing he walks in. Subway's the only way to go today, kid, much as you hate it. The driving is treacherous. See you around lunchtime."

I finished dressing and reluctantly headed for the Sixty-eighth Street Lexington Avenue station, anxious to beat the rush hour crowds. Once settled into my seat, I scoped out the other passengers and sat back to read the rest of the newspaper. It was early enough so that most of my companions appeared to be people going to their jobs and offices. A bit later and too many of the riders who stayed on board south of Forty-second Street would also be on their way to the courthouse, to make appearances for their criminal cases. On those occasional days that I got on the train at nine o'clock, it was an eerie feeling as we looked each other over for the last ten minutes of the ride, knowing at a glance—the closer we all got to the

Canal Street station—that we were combatants on opposite sides of the battle. Usually, I preferred to drive to work.

The cold air bit at my cheeks as I reached the top step of the subway exit and turned south for the short walk to Hogan Place, fighting the strong wind as I walked carefully around icy patches on the sidewalk. The guy inside the small pushcart on the corner closest to the office saw me coming and readied a bag with two large black coffees.

I scanned my identification tag into the turnstile, greeted the uniformed cop who sat at the security desk, and got on the elevator with a few other lawyers from the staff. I stuck my head in at the press office around the corner from my own desk to remind the assistant to include Dakota's story and obituary in the clips she was preparing for the district attorney to read. Each morning, Brenda Whitney's aides combed the *Times* and the tabloids, the local and national papers, cutting and compiling all the stories related to our cases or to crime stories that might be of interest to Paul Battaglia and his executive staff.

Before I could remove my coat and boots, Pat McKinney stood in the doorway, resting a hand on the back of my secretary's, Laura's, empty chair. "Lost a big one last night, huh?"

I tried not to let my intense dislike for McKinney, who was deputy chief of the trial division and one of the supervisors to whom I answered, affect my response. "After all that woman had been through, you might think about putting it in terms of *her* life, not mine."

"Lucky for us it didn't happen on *your* turf. Pretty clever sting they pulled off in New Jersey with the fake hit. How come you weren't so creative with the case?"

"It was Paul's decision not to be involved in such a risky plan, and I think he was entirely right about it."

"That's what you get for not going up the chain of command, Alex. I would have backed you on that one. Our squad wouldn't have let her walk away yesterday afternoon without taking better care of her, tucking her in at home, making sure she was safe and sound. Next time, check with me first. I can often be more flexible than Battaglia. And Lola Dakota would be alive." He slapped his hand against the back of Laura's chair and walked away toward his office at the end of the hall.

The phone rang and I picked it up as I sat down to turn on my computer. Rose Malone, Battaglia's executive assistant, was calling to tell me that he was on his way downtown and wanted to see me as soon as he got in. That gave me half an hour to try to get the Jersey prosecutors to bring me up to speed on what they had learned during the night. The one answer Battaglia didn't like getting too often was "I don't know, boss."

I dialed the number for my counterpart in Sinnelesi's office and left a message in his voice mail to call me back as soon as possible. How did the case against

Kralovic look? Exactly what time did Dakota leave her sister's home? How did she travel into Manhattan? What kind of mood was she in? Who saw her last? Battaglia was likely to ask me what she'd had for breakfast, too, and whether or not she had cleaned her plate. There wasn't anything about her last days on earth that he wouldn't expect me to detail for him as soon as he got into the office.

"Have a minute for me?" Jody Soellner was standing tentatively in my doorway, and I waved her in. Her arms were loaded with notepads, a copy of the penal law, and what looked like an NYPD evidence envelope. "I'm on my way to the grand jury to put in that case I picked up last weekend. The guy who broke into the apartment on West Twenty-third Street and raped the baby-sitter who was watching the three kids. Remember the facts?"

I told her I did.

"The victim just showed me two of her fingers. When the perp put down his knife on the bed, she tried to roll off, away from him. But he pulled her by the arm and bit down hard." Jody held up her left hand and grabbed her own middle and ring fingers. "She was back at Roosevelt Hospital for her follow-up yesterday and the doctor confirmed that she had two severed nerves. Can I charge an extra assault count—you know, that the perp's teeth are a dangerous instrument?"

"Good try. Unfortunately, the court of appeals disagrees with you. I think the case is *People* versus

Owusu, a couple of years back. The distinguished jurists said it's different from upping the ante by bringing a weapon along to assist the bad guy in his criminal endeavor. His teeth come with him naturally—they're not 'dangerous instruments' and you can't get the extra charge, even though I like your creative thinking. What's in the brown folder?"

Jody unclasped the catch and withdrew a plastic package covered in black ink with a voucher number and case identification. When she flipped it over to the clear side and held it up to show me, I could see the carving knife with the ten-inch blade. This victim was lucky. The jurors wouldn't even need to wait to hear the definition of forcible compulsion before they voted a true bill.

"Be sure and give Laura a copy of the indictment as soon as you file it."

I e-mailed instructions to Maxine, my paralegal, to pull the Dakota papers as soon as she got in. Reporters would soon be calling to get whichever facts about the case history were public record in order to reconstruct the story behind yesterday's events. I pushed aside the notes on the hearing for which I was trying to prepare, jotting down a Post-it reminder to take the whole file home for the weekend and work on it there, when I could better concentrate on the issues.

Battaglia had a speed-dial number that rang directly on my console, bypassing both of our secretaries. Usually, I jumped out of my seat when I heard its distinctive ring, but this morning Rose had helped me with an estimate of his arrival time. I greeted him and told him that I would be in immediately to brief him on the Dakota case.

"Save it till this afternoon. The governor just called. He's on his way to the Mayor's office and wants to stop in to talk about the DAs' Association proposed legislation package for the January session. You got anything that can't wait, or is it as straightforward as the papers make it appear?"

"I've made all the calls to get details on what happened during the last twenty-four hours, and I'm waiting for Jersey to get back to me. Chapman and I were both pretty skeptical about the accidental death theory last night, but I've got nothing unusual to give you yet."

"Keep it that way, if you can. The last thing I want for Christmas is a high-profile case that sets me up as Sinnelesi's whipping boy."

"No problem," I promised him, and kept my word for almost two hours.

Chapman sounded groggy when Laura put through his eleven o'clock phone call. "The news from both ends is bad."

"Hey, you're supposed to be sleeping. How can anything bad have happened?"

"Peterson just woke me up with the results of the inventory that some of the guys have been doing. You know all those shoe boxes in Lola's apartment? Well, she didn't share your fetish for high heels, slinky sandals, and velvet slippers. A few of those cardboards have some worn-down leather pumps, most are crammed with index cards that look like notes or research for a project, and two tired old boxes are stuffed full of cash."

"Like savings for a rainy day?"

"Like a stash for the monsoon season, Coop. Not kosher."

"Glad I wasn't on the scene for that discovery. What else?"

"And then there's the latest word from the ME's office. Autopsy won't happen until the end of the day, but Dr. Kestenbaum has already noted a few things that don't make him happy. Like some hairs—not Lola's—that she had gripped in her tight little fist, and, more to the point, lots of petechial hemorrhages in her eyes."

I knew the significance of the findings before Chapman went on. The tiny red pinpoints were the classic forensic hallmarks of strangulation.

"Kestenbaum thinks she actually struggled with her attacker while he choked her to death. Then he rolled her into the elevator shaft to make it look accidental. Fasten your seat belt, Coop, while he takes a close look at Lola's innards. He's just getting ready to declare this case a homicide."

5

I called Sylvia Foote. She was not an easy person to reach.

"She'll be in meetings all afternoon," her secretary said. "I don't think she'll be returning any calls until the beginning of the week."

"Tell her it's about Lola Dakota. About the murder of Lola Dakota."

"Murder?" she asked, taking down my number.

By the time I had left a similar message with Rose Malone for Battaglia, Sylvia Foote was on the line.

"Miss Cooper, my secretary just repeated your conversation to me." Foote was in her late sixties—humorless, rigid, and entirely protective of the administration's concerns. "I need to tell my president about this immediately. I'd like you to answer some questions for me."

"And I'd like *you* to answer some questions for us."

"Perhaps we can schedule an appointment for the end of next week."

I knew that the Jersey prosecutors would move in as quickly as possible, looking for clues that would connect Ivan Kralovic to Lola's death. If, in fact, Dakota had been murdered in Manhattan, then Sinnelesi would have no jurisdiction here. But if he wanted to keep his name in the headlines, as Battaglia figured, Sinnelesi would argue that he had a duty to investigate whether Lola had been kidnapped from his side of the river and follow the trail to our doorstep.

By Monday, New Jersey police might already be swarming around the King's College campus and Lola's apartment building, scouring students and neighbors for information, gossip, and potential witnesses.

"I think we need to talk this afternoon. One of the detectives can bring me up to your office."

"I simply don't have time to do that."

"Don't have time?" A prominent member of the university family was dead, and I was only hours away from formal confirmation that we were dealing with a homicide, but Sylvia Foote was stonewalling me already. "I'll be up at your office by two o'clock."

"I'm sorry I won't be here to discuss this with you today."

"In that case, I'll start with the students over in the political—"

"We'd prefer that the students are not involved in this."

Where was Chapman when I needed him? He'd be

telling Foote that either she could play hardball with him or do this the nice way. He'd be up there with grand jury subpoenas that she could ignore at her own risk, or she could cooperate and be treated like a lady. And the first time she looked down her long crooked nose at him and attempted to dismiss him with an arrogant order to leave, he'd stick out the subpoena and tell the sour old bag to take it.

"Not involved? It would be lovely if nobody had to be involved, and even nicer if Lola Dakota was alive. That's simply not one of your choices. We're going to have to sit down with you and go over everything that will need to be done, identify every individual we'll need to interview and each document we'll need to access."

Laura walked into my office and placed a slip of paper on my desk as I listened to Foote drone on: *Mickey Diamond is on your other line. He's looking for confirmation that Dakota's death has been declared a homicide by the ME.* I shook my head in the negative and mouthed back to her to get rid of him.

"I've already got the *Post* calling me," I tell Sylvia. "Somebody's leaked the story to the press and the autopsy hasn't even been started yet. You'd better give some thought to how the students—and their parents back home in Missouri and Montana—are going to react to news of a murder in your comfortable little community. It's going to get their attention a lot more quickly than the obituary page did." How would

Chapman punctuate that point? "Especially if word gets out that the president's office is stalling our investigation."

Foote was silent. I expected that she was balancing the reality of what I was saying against the bet that her old friend Paul Battaglia would not approve of my heavy-handed style. But she was also smart enough to know that he would back me in my effort to get to the campus before Sinnelesi's troops arrived on the scene.

"My office is in the new King's College building on Claremont Avenue, half a block in from 116th Street. Did you say you could be here by two?"

I phoned Chapman and told him that since I'd left my Jeep at the office the night before, I would swing by to get him in front of his place and head uptown to interview Foote. I told Laura to beep me if any urgent calls came in, and that I would check with her for messages when the meeting was over. The ice was still caked thick on the windshield, and I struggled with the scraper as the defroster worked slowly to melt it.

Chapman was standing in front of the coffee shop next to his apartment building on First Avenue. His only concession to the bitter cold was the fact that he wore a trench coat over the navy blazer that he had adopted as his uniform once he had been assigned to the detective bureau. His black hair was blowing wildly in the wind, and he kept reaching up with his hand to chase it. He opened the passenger door and got in. "So what else do I need to know about Columbia beside the fact that its football team sucks?"

"You'll drive Foote crazy if you don't keep it straight that Dakota was teaching at King's College when she died, not at Columbia. They'll be very jumpy about that. They use some of the same facilities, and students enrolled in either school can take courses at the other, but they are entirely separate institutions."

I had spent a lot of time in Manhattan during my undergraduate years. My best friend and roommate at Wellesley, Nina Baum, met her husband, Gabe, when we were sophomores. He was a junior at Columbia, and I had often accompanied Nina when she came to the city to spend a weekend with Gabe.

As we drove uptown, I tried to fill Mike in on the bits of college history that I remembered. Columbia was founded in 1754, by royal charter of King George II of England, and its original name was King's College—the name recently adopted by the experimental school that carved out a piece of the neighborhood for itself at the start of the new millennium. The university's first building was situated adjacent to Trinity Church on lower Broadway, and some of its earliest students included the first chief justice of the United States, John Jay, and the first secretary of the treasury, Alexander Hamilton. The institution closed down during the American Revolution, and when it reopened eight years later, it had shed its imperial name in favor of "Columbia," the personification of the American determination for independence.

By 1850, the college had moved to Madison Avenue at Forty-ninth Street, shaping itself into a modern university by the addition of a law school to its undergraduate and medical faculties. In 1897, the campus was moved to its current site in Morningside Heights at Broadway and 116th Street; this academic village—modeled on the idea of an Athenian agora—represented the largest single collection of buildings designed by the great architectural firm of McKim, Mead and White.

"What's with this experimental school thing?"

"I only know what I've read in the news. King's is an effort to set up an alternative educational model, drawing from a few of the stars of the Columbia teaching staff, but trying to structure a fresh view of the process. It borrows some of the stature of the Ivy League reputation, but it's been spun off on its own, free and clear of the mother university."

"Who's in charge?"

"We're about to find out. Foote said she'd have the acting president at the meeting."

"Wanna take Third Avenue uptown? Stop for a minute at the corner of Seventieth Street."

I pulled up in front of P. J. Bernstein's.

"Hungry?"

"No, thanks. Had a salad at my desk."

Chapman got out of the car while I double-parked

and waited for him. In a slight nod to Christmas, Bernstein's window displayed a few large smiling Santa faces. But there was also a huge menorah with electric candles on the countertop, while blue, gold, and white-fringed streamers declared a Happy Hanukkah to the deli's customers.

Mike returned in a few minutes with two hot dogs wrapped in a napkin, overflowing with sauerkraut and relish, and a can of root beer. "I know the rules. No droppings on the floor mat. No sucking the sauerkraut out of my teeth in public." He chewed on his lunch as I continued driving and cut through Central Park at Ninety-seventh Street, taking Amsterdam Avenue the rest of the way north to the campus.

"Had any cases out of King's College yet?" Mike asked, licking the mustard off his fingers and swigging from the can of root beer.

"Not one."

"Must be the only school in the country with no reported crimes. Wait till these kids find Cannon's and the West End." Those two bars were magnets for the collegiate community and havens for the binge-drinking students who found their way to our offices with every kind of problem that alcohol abuse created.

Mike displayed his badge to the expressionless, square-tinned security guard who sat inside the small gatehouse at the entrance to College Walk on 116th Street, barely looking up from the skin magazine he was holding in his bony hand. "Okay if we park this inside for a couple of hours? I'm taking my niece here for an interview, see if I can get her back into school. A mind is a terrible thing to waste."

The guard waved us in without looking up. I found a space in front of the Graduate School of Journalism, on the corner of Broadway, and Chapman locked his arm in mine as I lowered myself out of the Jeep; we jogged together across the double-wide street and headed down to Claremont, fighting against the strong wind as we ran.

Sylvia Foote's secretary was expecting us. She took our coats and led us into Foote's small office, which overlooked the avenue and Barnard Hall directly opposite. Foote extended a hand to both of us, and made the introductions to Paolo Recantati, explaining that he was the acting president of King's College, and formerly a history professor at Princeton.

Recantati invited us to sit in a pair of black leather seats with our backs against the large bay window, while he moved across from us to a straight-backed wooden armchair and Foote remained behind her desk. They offered nothing, and waited for me to speak.

"As you know, Sylvia, I'd been working with Lola Dakota on the case against Ivan for almost two years. And I'm sure she made you aware of what the New Jersey prosecutors were doing. Despite their best efforts, it's doubtful that Lola's death was an accident after all. Detective Chapman and I are here to try to get your help in finding out what was going on in her life and who else, besides Ivan, might have wanted her dead."

Recantati spoke to me before Foote even opened her lips to form a response. "I know what your area of expertise is, Miss Cooper. Are you telling me that someone sexually assaulted Lola and then killed her?"

"There's no reason to believe that at—"

"Then exactly why are you involved? Shouldn't we be working with Mr. Sinnelesi's office on this? Lola's case was being handled by his people."

"The Dakota matter has been my investigation for close to two years. I supervise the domestic abuse cases as well as sex crimes. The issues, the sensitivity concerns, the needs of survivors going through the system—many of the problems overlap in these situations. I know the background of Lola and Ivan's relationship, most of her history, a lot of the intimate details of her private life. If she was the victim of an attack—a murder—in New York, I will be the person in charge of the prosecution."

Recantati pursed his lips and looked off to his left, as though to take a cue from Foote. He was tall and lean, and for a few moments, the crossing and uncrossing of his long legs was the only obvious sign of his discomfort. He'd probably never dealt with anything quite like this in his idyllic ivory tower, before coming to Manhattan.

Chapman pushed himself to the edge of his seat and eyeballed Recantati. "You think if you don't give us what we need, we'll just fold up our tents in the night and slip off to the next unsolved crime? You got how many students here?"

"Almost three thousand at King's," he said softly.

"And how many next door at Columbia?"

"Close to thirty thousand," he murmured.

"So start out with something like sixty-six thousand mothers and fathers picking this up on the evening news, half of 'em spread out around the country, who didn't want their kids coming to this city of perverts and potheads to begin with."

Foote and Recantati exchanged scowls.

"Best view of it is, you had a little marital discord that got out of hand, off campus, so nobody else here is at risk," Chapman said, brushing his hands against each other as though to wipe away the problem. "Worst view of it is that you got somebody roaming this neighborhood, making all these darling scholars and social saviors of the future vulnerable to violence. And exactly what are *you* two doing to make little Jennifer and little Jason safe at school?"

"Believe me, Detective, this is an entirely new problem for us here on campus."

"You must be frigging nuts if you think I buy that one. We're not talking 'animal house' and student pranks. This is a college in the middle of a neighborhood that used to boast one of the highest homicide rates in the city. Just look next door at Columbia—they've had students murdered in their dorm rooms and apartments, kids who've been robbed and raped by other students, as well as by strangers from the street."

Recantati opened his mouth to speak but Chapman wouldn't be interrupted. "There's been more drugs used in some of these halls than Keith Richards and Puff Daddy have seen in their combined lifetimes. This isn't the time to hide behind your cap and gown, pal."

Foote broke in to relieve the president. Chapman's directness didn't make her happy. "Alex, for the moment, since Lola had personal contact with you, can't we just discuss this one-on-one? The police don't have to be included until we get official word that this wasn't an accident. After all, that's our understanding of the findings at her apartment last night."

Chapman got up and walked to the phone on Foote's desk. "Mind if I call the morgue? I'd hate to waste your time if the docs can step away from the table in the middle of sawing Lola in half to assure you this was only a slip and fall."

Recantati's stunned gaze moved back and forth between Chapman's face and Foote's hand, which she had clamped over the telephone receiver. He seemed caught in the glare of the headlights and longing to be back in the library instead. "Have you and Ms. Cooper worked together on this kind of thing before?"

Chapman laughed. "Seventy years."

Recantati's brow furrowed more deeply. "But—?"

"I count 'em in dog years. Every one I spend with Coop feels like seven."

Recantati was responding to Mike in a way Sylvia Foote never would, looking as though he hoped the police would help him out and take the entire matter off his hands. "So, what is it you need from us?"

Foote cleared her throat. "Not that we can promise you anything before the middle of next week. We've got to clear this administratively."

"How about a command decision, Mr. President?" Chapman ignored Foote completely and spoke only to Recantati. "Next week's gonna be too late. I'd like to get into Ms. Dakota's office this weekend, start checking her files, her correspondence, her computer records. I'd like to find out who knew her best, which students were in her classes, what faculty members worked with her, who liked her and hated her, who slept with her . . ."

Recantati's face reddened at the mere thought, it seemed, that we would be exploring such intimate aspects of Dakota's life. He was silent.

"We could walk right over to her office now, with both of you. That way you can make sure that Ms. Cooper and I don't do anything to cause trouble here."

Time to soften the approach while we had him on the line. "You understand, sir, that not everything

Detective Chapman is talking about may be necessary," I said. "It's entirely possible that Lola's death
will prove to be related to her husband's efforts to get
rid of her, and not to the campus community at all.
We're exploring that angle first, of course. Nobody
wants to involve the school or the kids, except as a
last resort."

Foote was harder to fool. "Suppose I can gather
together some of the political science faculty for you
on Monday morning. We'll make the library available
to you for interviews, so our staff members don't have
to be carted downtown. Then we'll move on to talk
with the students, but only if we must."

Not a bad compromise. "I've got to be in court for a
hearing at nine-thirty on Monday. So if we can say two
o'clock for you to have some people lined up, that will
give you the morning to contact whoever you haven't
been able to reach over the weekend. Shall we take a
look at Lola's office while we're here?"

Foote buzzed the secretary and asked her to have the
head of security bring the passkey up to us as quickly
as possible. Within minutes, Frankie Shayson knocked
on the door and came into the room. "Hey, Mike. Alex.
Haven't seen either of you guys since that racket they
threw when me and Harry left the job. Never dull, is
it?" The former detective from the two-six squad, the
neighborhood precinct, crossed the room and grabbed
Chapman's hand as he greeted us warmly. "Want me to
take 'em downstairs, Ms. Foote?"

She was obviously unhappy that we had an independent connection to the college, and she wasn't about to let him take us to Dakota's office alone. "If you give me the key, I'll return it to you later today." She reached out her hand to take the ring from Shayson, motioning to Recantati to come along.

The three of us marched down the hallway behind Sylvia Foote and up two flights of stairs to a turreted corner office. On the wall next to the door, instead of a nameplate, there was an ink and pen drawing, two inches by three inches, of a small piece of the U.S. map, with the word BADLANDS written in the middle. The Badlands of Dakota.

Foote unlocked the door and entered first, followed by Chapman.

"Jesus, the feng shui in here is for shit."

Recantati continued to look lost and overwhelmed. "Sorry, Detective?"

"Don't you know anything about the principles of negative energy? This place is a hellhole, just like her apartment. First of all," Chapman said, kicking a box of books out of his path into the room, "all entrances should be free from obstruction. You need a generous flow into the working environment. And she's got too much black fabric in here. Bad karma—symbolizes death."

Chapman worked his way around the room, looking at books and papers that were piled on the floor, careful not to touch or disturb surface items. Foote had taken Recantati aside and was whispering something to him. I took the moment to stifle a smile and ask Chapman a question. "When did you become an expert in the Chinese art of feng shui?"

"Attila's been shtupping an interior decorator for the last six months. That's all you hear about when you work a tour with him. The office is beginning to look like a Jewish princess's idea of a Chinese whorehouse. 'Don't leave your toilet seat up 'cause your fortune will flow down into the sewer.' See, dried flowers like this?" Mike pointed at the dusty arrangement on Dakota's windowsill. "Lousy idea. Represents the world of the dead. Gotta use fresh ones."

Marty Hun was one of the guys in the Homicide Squad. Mike had nicknamed him Attila.

"We'll get Crime Scene over here this afternoon. I'd like them to process the room for prints and take some pictures. Okay with you two?"

Mike moved behind Lola's desk, noting in his steno pad what lay on top of it and sketching a general outline of the office. The smile was erased from his face, and with his pen he shifted some of the papers on top of the blotter. "Who's been in here since last night?"

"No one," answered Foote.

"I'll betcha my paycheck you're wrong on that count."

Foote approached the desk from the opposite side and placed her palm on a stack of books as she leaned over to see what had caught Mike's attention.

"You wanna get your hand off there?"

She straightened up and brought her arm down to her side.

Mike pulled open the top middle desk drawer by putting his pen into the brass handle. "It's too neat. Way too shipshape, both on top of the desk and in this first drawer. Right where you'd keep whatever it was you'd been working on most recently, or something that was pretty important. Every other pile is sloppy and out of line. Even the stack of mail is too fastidious. Somebody went through some of this stuff and couldn't resist just patting these papers into order. Nothing major, but it's just not in keeping with Lola's messy style. Maybe a careful once-over can come up with a print or something. She chew gum?"

Recantati looked to Foote and then shrugged. "Not that I ever noticed."

It was Chapman's turn to whisper now, leaning over and speaking only to me. "Let's lock up the office and get Crime Scene over here immediately. There's a wad of Wrigley's in the wastebasket. It's great for getting DNA. All that juicy saliva will tell us exactly who's been messing around in here."

Mike turned back to face the others. "Ever hear Ms. Dakota talk about a deadhouse?"

Foote glanced at Recantati before both of them looked at us blankly. "Sounds more like your line of work than ours."

As Mike walked from behind the desk, he stared at

a small corkboard affixed to the wall by the window. "You know who any of these people are?" he asked.

Foote moved in next to him, and Recantati looked over his shoulder. "That's a photograph of Franklin Roosevelt, of course, and this one's Mae West. I believe that woman in the corner, in period dress, is Nellie Bly. I can't place the other man."

"Charles Dickens, I think." My undergraduate major in English literature kicked in.

Foote stepped back and turned away, but continued speaking. "I'm not sure who the people are in the photos with Lola herself, but I assume they're friends and relatives. That other snapshot is one of the young women Lola taught last semester, in the spring."

Mike must have thought, as I did, that it was unusual for one student's picture to be singled out to be on the board. He asked the obvious question. "Know her name?"

Foote hesitated before she spoke. "Charlotte Voight."

"Any idea why Lola would have her picture up here?"

Dead silence.

"Can we talk to her?"

"Detective Chapman," Foote answered, sinking onto the cushion of the sofa against the far wall, "Charlotte disappeared from the school—from New York—altogether. We have no idea where she is."

Mike's anger was palpable. "When did this happen?"

"She went missing last spring. April tenth. Left her room early one evening, in the midst of a bout of depression. No one here has seen her since."

6

Chapman wanted to preserve the integrity of Dakota's office for the Crime Scene team to photograph and fingerprint, so he led the unhappy pair of administrators back down to Foote's quarters to finish the conversation.

"And now we're gonna play 'I've Got a Secret' and hope the dumb cop doesn't figure out what kind of problems we got here at school, right? Who was this Voight kid and what do you think really happened to her?"

Foote picked up the story. "Mr. Recantati wasn't appointed until this fall semester, so he's not to blame for not remembering to bring up Charlotte's disappearance." The osteoporosis that had stooped Foote's shoulders seemed even more pronounced as she sat hunched in her chair, calling up facts about the missing girl.

"Charlotte was a junior—twenty years old. Came to

64

us with a very troubled background. She was raised in Peru, actually. Her father's American, working down there for a large corporation. Her mother was Peruvian. Died while Charlotte was finishing high school. The girl was extremely bright, but had had a long battle with depression and eating disorders."

Mike was taking notes as Sylvia Foote talked.

"We didn't know until she got here, of course, that she had a history of substance abuse as well. I doubt that she would have been better adjusted at any other college in the States. There were no relatives anywhere in this country, and when one of those black moods overtook Charlotte, she'd just disappear for days at a time."

"Surely someone found out where she'd been, once she returned?" I asked.

"She was never very open or direct about it. Freshman year she dated a Columbia student who lived in an apartment off campus, and she'd spend time with him. Then she got involved with some Latinos from the neighborhood, the source of her drug supply, we believe."

"What did her roommates think?"

"She didn't have any. Charlotte requested a single when she applied to King's, and she lived a pretty solitary existence. She didn't number many of the girls among her friends. D'you know the kind? She preferred the company of men. Not boys, and generally not other students. She was restless and isolated from most

65

of the school social life. Thought herself much too worldly for most of the kids she met here."

"Didn't you get the police involved when she disappeared?"

"Certainly we did. You must know how it is. They won't even consider a missing person's report until forty-eight hours have elapsed. Nobody noticed Charlotte was gone for most of that time. The girls in the dorm assumed that she'd gone off to party with her drug crowd, and the professors had grown used to her cutting classes. The Twenty-sixth Precinct has a record of the report we filed. I made the notification myself, after I called her father."

Chapman looked up. "What'd he have to say about all this?"

Foote lowered her head. "He didn't even come to New York. Not then, or later. He had just remarried, which engaged most of his emotional interest, and seemed to believe that Charlotte would show up eventually, when she needed his money or his help. He thought it was just a gimmick to get his attention."

"Anybody check out her room?"

"Yes, the detectives from the precinct. Undisturbed and unremarkable. Her credit cards were never used, her bank account was never tampered with—"

"Make a list, Coop, when you do your subpoenas for Dakota. Let's get bank records, credit card information, and phone records for Voight, too. Her computer still around?"

Foote shrugged. "I imagine when the semester ended

in June that all of her belongings were shipped back to her father in Peru, but I'll check that for you."

"And line up some of her classmates for Monday, some of the kids that she lived near in the dorm or hung out with in class. The former boyfriend, too."

Recantati knew that he was in over his head. "Can we slow this down? I think you're making some quantum leaps here that will serve no good."

"Welcome to the real world, Professor. Wake up these it-can't-happen-here nerds and make them get involved in all this. You do it, or I will." Chapman slapped his steno pad against the palm of his hand to drive home his point.

The sharp buzz of the intercom startled me. Foote's secretary's voice came through the speakerphone intercom. "Professor Lockhart is here for his four o'clock meeting with you. He thinks you might want him to join you now."

"No, no. Tell him I'll leave him a message and reschedule for early next week." She turned her attention back to us. "What else do you need by Monday?"

I spoke before Mike could. "Every detail about every criminal incident that has occurred on this campus and to your students, whether here or wherever they're living in the city."

"That's hard to put together quickly. There's no, well . . ." Recantati was stammering.

"I guess you're not familiar with the Cleary Act, Professor?" I asked.

This was Sylvia Foote's territory, and she stepped in to spare Recantati the embarrassment of his ignorance about an important administrative function. "We're in the process of putting together that information now, Alex. I can certainly give you whatever reports and referrals we have."

"Then we'll see you here, on Monday. We've each got a beeper," I said, handing my business card to both Foote and Recantati. "If you need us for anything at all, or want to bring something to my attention, just give a call."

As we walked out of Foote's office, her secretary told us that Detective Sherman and his partner from the Crime Scene Unit were on their way up to Dakota's office. Mike nodded to me to follow him up the staircase to watch them get to work.

"So what's the Cleary Act?"

"About fifteen years ago, a student named Jeanne Cleary was raped and strangled to death in her dormitory at Lehigh University in Pennsylvania. The bastard who killed her was also enrolled at the school. He was a drug addict with a history of deviant behavior who had broken into her room to burglarize it while she was sleeping. Her parents fought a long, tough battle to get federal legislation to make it mandatory for every campus official to report the statistics of criminal occurrences at their schools."

"At least it gives the applicants an idea of what the problems are at each college."

"That's the point. It's got to be in all the admissions literature, so families making decisions about where they're sending their kids can assess the risks. What kind of security measures the school has, how it handles crime reporting, what kind of disciplinary measures the administration enforces—all that sort of thing."

"Does it work? Do any good?"

"It's a great idea, but I haven't seen one school anywhere near this jurisdiction that reports it accurately. Not Columbia, not NYU, not Fordham, not FIT. Do you know there are more than twenty college campuses in Manhattan alone, from those large universities down to small commercial colleges that just have a single building? I can give you ten criminal complaints a year taken from students who report to the local precinct or to my office for every one you'll see in the numbers supplied to the government—and to the parents—by the schools. They all want to fudge it."

The door to Dakota's office was open and Sherman was beginning to document everything in sight with his camera and flash.

"Get a shot of that bulletin board on the wall by the window, Hal. And watch your mouth—I got Cooper with me."

"Hey, Alex, how goes it? Understand Kestenbaum's got a hush-hush preliminary finding of a homicide on this broad. So much for the accidental death theory they were floating last night, I guess. Tough break on that verdict last week in the case from the bus station. Sorry the stuff we came up with wasn't too helpful. Helen took the loss pretty hard."

One of my assistants had just had a not guilty verdict the previous Thursday. Her victim had been beaten in the face so badly that she was unable to identify her attacker. The fact that thousands of people a day passed through the Port Authority terminal made it impossible to get a clean set of fingerprints from the corridor in which the attack occurred, and the circumstantial case had been too weak for a jury to believe in.

"Cooper trains her troops not to look at an acquittal as a loss, Hal. Just figure Helen came in second place . . . right behind the defense attorney. Most other jobs, that gets you the silver medal. No harm in that."

"What do you want me to do after I dust these surfaces?"

"I want copies of as much of the paper as you can give me. Originals if it's not worth trying to lift prints off this stuff."

Sherman removed the gum from the wastebasket with a pair of tweezers, slipping it into a small manila envelope and labeling it with the date and number of the Crime Scene run. "I'll drop the copies off at your office. Gotta get to midtown. Just had a double homicide called in. Guy in a Santa suit did a stickup at a doughnut shop, using a ten-year-old customer as a shield. The owner had a licensed pistol. Plugged Santa and one of his aging elves before they could make it back into their getaway sleigh."

"Best of all possible dispositions, eh, blondie? Case abated by death. Perps blasted into the great hereafter—God's own Alcatraz—by a law-abiding citizen just trying to make a living. Give the doughnut man a kiss for me. You gonna make it to the party later, Hal?"

"Depends on whether the good guys or the bad guys are winning. Have one on me."

It was the night of the Homicide Squad's annual Christmas party, and although our moods were not festive, Chapman and I wanted to be there for a while to wish our colleagues some holiday cheer. Darkness had enveloped the city early, and the temperature had dropped substantially during our hours at Foote's office. I pulled on my long gloves and raised the collar of my coat as Chapman held open the front door of the building and we trudged uphill toward Broadway to get the car. Tiny white lights decorated the trees on College Walk and candles rested on windowsills in some of the dorm rooms.

As the motor idled, I watched the groups of college kids, seemingly oblivious to the bitter cold, making their way from classrooms to living halls to dining facilities. There were bunches talking on the great steps of Low Memorial Library, which was festively adorned with a giant wreath, and I imagined they were making plans to meet at parties or nearby bars and apartments. It wasn't much of a stretch to recall the feeling of invincibility in that period of my life, the sense of security the academic community offered—the endless possibilities of youth, fueled by intelligence and energy.

Yet one year ago, the Columbia campus had been rocked by the death of a talented and popular athlete, found in her dorm room with her throat slashed, killed by another student she had been dating, who threw himself in front of a subway car hours later. That followed the similar killing of a brilliant law student the preceding year, also by a former boyfriend who had stabbed her repeatedly.

I began to think of all the cases I had handled with students from schools throughout the city and to make a mental list of what the relationship was between victim and offender, so I could pull the files and examine the facts. For the students at King's, the illusion of the sanctity of the university setting was about to be shattered.

"Want to stop by my place and relax for a bit before we head to the soiree?" The party was held at the Park Avenue Armory, on Sixty-sixth Street, just a few blocks from my home.

"Sure. Is Jake gonna be there tonight?"

"No. He doesn't get back to New York until Sunday." The schedule Jake Tyler had as a political correspondent and stand-in anchor for Brian Williams on *NBC Nightly News* made his life even less predictable than my own. It was a pleasure, for a change, to be involved with a lover who had no complaints about my unavailability when I was called out on a major case.

I parked the car and we went upstairs. As soon as I put the key in the door, I could smell the delicious scent of the Douglas fir that I had bought two nights ago on my way home to serve as a Christmas tree. I had been raised as a Jew and was observant in the Reform tradition, but my mother's religious upbringing was entirely different. Her ancestors were Finnish, and she had converted to Judaism when she married my father. Our family tradition combined elements from both of their backgrounds, and although I had lighted the candles on a Hanukkah menorah earlier in the month, I always looked forward to decorating a tree and rediscovering the boxes of antique ornaments that my mother had collected throughout her life.

"I'm going to freshen up. Make yourself useful. Pour us a drink."

"Mind if I use the phone? I was gonna meet some of the guys down the street at Lumi's for a drink before the party."

"Of course. Anybody I know? Invite them over here. And while you're calling, check with your office to see whether there's a final on the autopsy results. Then you can start putting some of those bulbs on the top branches of the tree that I can't reach. Don't peek at the pile of presents. I haven't finished wrapping yours yet."

I went inside to wash my face, add a colorful scarf

to my black suit, slip into a pair of higher heels, and spritz some Caleche on my neck. I played back the messages on my answering machine. The usual freeway greeting from Nina Baum in L.A., a callback from one of my sisters-in-law in response to my question about what the kids wanted for Christmas, and the persistent voice of *Post* reporter Mickey Diamond begging me to give him any kind of scoop about the Dakota investigation. I held my finger down on the delete button.

Chapman had rested my Dewar's and his Ketel One on the coffee table while he hooked and hung some of the fragile old ornaments. "That one belonged to my grandmother. She landed at Ellis Island when she was an infant, just before Christmas in 1900, a century ago. It's a glass bird, hand painted, that her father bought for her that year."

"Think she'd approve of the way you make a living?"

"She would have liked me to have gotten married by the time I was twenty and had six kids in pretty short order. Made her crazy that I never learned her recipes for Finnish icebox pudding or blueberry pie."

I thought of the time I had almost made her happiest. In my grandmother's last years, when she was living as an invalid in my parents' home, I had come up from Virginia during my final semester of law school to tell my family that I was going to marry Adam Nyman, a young medical student with whom I had fallen in love. Although in her nineties and quite infirm, Idie had insisted on coming to the Vineyard to be with us at the wedding. I know it hastened her death and literally broke her heart, as it did mine, when she learned that Adam had been killed on the turnpike the night before the wedding.

"Wipe that frown off your puss and stay with me, Coop. My Granny Annie wanted me to go back to the old sod as the ambassador to Ireland. Live in Phoenix Park. Ride to the hounds. If she ever thought for a minute I'd be sniffing around dead bodies like my pop, she'd have locked up all the liquor and never let me watch *Dragnet* or read Dick Tracy in the Sunday funnies. Ready for the latest?"

I sipped at my scotch and nodded my head.

Mike glanced at his steno pad to read the notes of his conversation. "The ME spoke to Lieutenant Peterson an hour ago. Lola's death was asphyxial. No question she was strangled, probably with a ligature. Kestenbaum will do some more tests on the pattern of injury, but he thinks the killer used her own woolen scarf. Thrown overboard just for show. The elevator cab certainly crushed the body, which was designed to disguise the homicide. But somebody made sure she took that header without any air in her lungs."

"Any semen?"

"Nope. Not in the body. He hasn't checked the bed linens yet. That takes more time. But there were two strands of hair—just loose, no roots. Kestenbaum can't say for sure that they were in her hand, like she'd grabbed at anybody. Could be they just transferred from someone's clothing earlier in the day—or from the first cops who came to the crime scene. They're not going to be of much value at the moment.

"The other news is from the building inspector, who was at Lola's apartment with Lieutenant Peterson. He's confirmed that the elevator's been out of whack for weeks. First of all, it was under repair, and wasn't even supposed to be in operation yesterday. The out-of-order sign that had been posted in the lobby had been taken down at some point, which could easily lend itself to an accident theory. Besides, people had complained that the cab was stopping between floors all the time, so it wouldn't have been tough to catch it a foot off the ground on the fifteenth floor and roll the body in."

Chapman glanced at his watch and walked into the den to click on the television. A series of commercials preceded Alex Trebek's close-up, announcing the subject of the *Final Jeopardy!* answer. Mike and I had a long-standing habit of betting on the last question. The rest of the show didn't interest us, but I had seen him ferret out a television screen at crime scenes, sports bars, and the morgue. Once, outside a concert at Madison Square Garden, he even commandeered Tina Turner's chauffeur to let him watch the end of the show in the back of her stretch limo while she was in her dressing room warming up for the big performance.

"Tonight's category is Famous Quotes," Trebek said, pointing up at the card displayed on the screen.

"Twenty bucks," Mike said, taking the bill out of his pocket and dropping it on top of the coffee table. "I'm feeling lucky. Jake's out of town, I've got a new murder on my hands, and there's no reason for Santa to put coal in my stocking this year."

I laughed and told him to make it thirty, pulling the bills from my wallet.

"Pretty cocky, blondie." He withdrew another ten and tossed it on the pile. We knew each other's strengths and weaknesses inside out after a decade of this trivia exercise. My four years of major concentration in English literature before going to law school raised my expectation of taking the evening's pot.

"Well, gentlemen," Trebek enthused, turning to the three contestants poised at their buzzers. "The answer is, the majestic leader who urged his troops to battle with the phrase: 'Soldiers, forty centuries are looking down on you.'"

Dead meat. Chapman had not only studied military history at Fordham, but the subject had become a passion for him: he read about it voraciously and visited battlefields whenever the opportunity presented itself. The butcher from Kansas City and the ophthalmologist from Louisville seemed as clueless as I was, neither one writing anything on his electronic screen.

"Belly up, blondie. What's your best guess? Double or nothing?"

"Not a prayer." I watched the pastry chef from Baltimore record his answer with furious determination, as I tried to think of a civilization with that long a heritage. "Who was . . . Genghis Khan?"

Chapman gloated as he picked up the sixty dollars, giving the correct response while Trebek was telling the chef he had guessed incorrectly. "Napoleon, 1798. Rallying his men to fight the Egyptians at the foot of the great pyramids of Giza. Enjoying a brief success, actually, like ten days, before m'man Horatio Nelson arrived in time to destroy the entire French fleet."

I sidled up next to him and reached my fingers into his pants pocket, pulling out the wad of money. "But you forgot to put it in the form of a question, so—"

As he slapped my hand away, the doorbell rang.

"And one more surprise for the night," Mike added. "Hope you don't mind, I told the doorman your guest didn't have to be announced." I walked behind him as he went to the entrance, and gasped with delight to see Mercer Wallace.

He towered over both of us, six feet six inches tall with dark black skin and a rock-solid chest that had stopped a bullet just four months ago. Mercer grabbed me in an embrace as we swayed each other back and forth. "This is the very best of Christmas presents," I said, pulling his face down to mine and planting a kiss on the top of his head.

"So this was the date you were meeting at Lumi's, huh?" I said to Mike. "And not planning to invite *me*?

Santa may have to rethink whether that was naughty or nice."

"Well, if you hadn't suggested stopping here, I was going to take you there. But they don't have a TV and I didn't want to miss the chance to score a few bucks off you, Coop. You allowed to drink yet, Detective Wallace, or does it still pour out through that mean-looking exit wound in your back?" He headed back to the bar to fix a club soda for Mercer.

I had visited Mercer at his home at least once a week since the shooting last summer, and I knew his recovery from the chest wound that had threatened to rip him apart had progressed well. He was due to come back to work on modified duty early in the new year, but I thought it would take more than a holiday party to bring him to my doorstep.

Chapman was in the den pouring drinks against the background noise of *Win Ben Stein's Money* on the Comedy Central channel. The brainiac host was, as usual, about to knock off all the contestants with a string of good answers to tough questions, while I watched Mercer—still limping slightly—walk ahead of me and sit down. "Just took enough money off Coop to buy you a Kwanza present, Detective Wallace."

Mercer raised his glass and we all clinked. "To a better year for each of us. And to Lola Dakota, may she rest in peace."

"Mercer started beeping me this morning with a million things he wanted to know. Said he was coming into the office to bring his case folder and notes for us, so I figured he might as well make a guest appearance at the armory."

We spent close to an hour talking about all the facts Mercer remembered from handling the domestic assault investigation that was part of Lola's original complaint. She had loved the quiet calm and dignified manner of the detective, which had made him such an outstanding member of the Special Victims Unit, the police department's companion unit to my bureau. Lola had called him often when she was indecisive or frightened, and he had talked her through some of the toughest moments of her ordeal with Ivan. I could tell how it pained him that, in the end, nothing he could do had saved her.

"Time to bundle up and boogie." Mike was on his feet, taking our coats out of the closet and getting ready to leave. "Who gets the first dance, Chief Allee or Inspector Cutter?"

"What are you doing tomorrow night, Alex?" Mercer asked.

"No plans. I had been thinking about going to D.C. to meet Jake, just for Saturday night, until Mike got that preliminary report from the ME this morning telling him this was probably going to be declared a homicide. I called Lola's sister, Lily, right after I got the news, to see whether we could go out to her house to talk with her. It's not a very smart time for me to leave town."

"Come out to my place for dinner. Mike'll drive you. I'm having some friends over to do my tree. Seven o'clock."

"Sounds good."

"Still nice to get a crack at Miss Lonelyhearts when her own personal talking head is out of town, isn't it, Mercer? Just like old times."

I rode with Mike and Mercer to the Seventh Regimental Armory, an enormous fortress on Park Avenue, built in 1879, which took up an entire city block. The interior was a throwback to another era, its vast halls—designed by Louis Comfort Tiffany—lined with plaques honoring war dead from the last century, and its rooms decorated with moose heads and other dusty antlered animals whose glass eyes stared down at the festivities. The original function of its drill hall had given way to use as rental space for endless rounds of weekend antique shows and the occasional rubber-chicken dinner meetings of organizations too penny-wise to engage private salons at real restaurants.

As we entered the fourth-floor room in which the squad party was being held, we were swamped by detectives and cops who had not seen Mercer since the shooting. I stepped back and walked over to greet the chief of detectives before I made the rest of the rounds.

"Heard you and Chapman were up at King's College this afternoon. Any headway?"

"They're beginning to see the light."

We talked for several minutes until I felt my beeper

vibrating on my waistband. There was a phone booth on the main floor and I excused myself to go downstairs to return the call. I recognized the number displayed as the main line from ECAB—the Early Case Assessment Bureau—which was the intake unit through which every arrest in Manhattan entered our office. The expediter answered.

"Hey, it's Alex Cooper. Any idea who beeped me?"

"Ryan Blackmer's looking for you, Alex. Hold on a minute."

"Sorry to bother you, but I figured you'd want a heads-up," Ryan said. He was one of the brightest and best lawyers in the division, and had drawn the Friday night supervising position in ECAB. "Uniformed guys in the Sixth Precinct just collared a mope for sex abuse tonight."

"You got the facts yet?"

"The complaining witness was walking home from a friend's house, right along Washington Square Park—on the north side near the Arch—when this clown grabbed her from behind and started to rub against her, trying to drag her into the park. She was able to break away and get home. Called nine-one-one from her apartment. Cops drove her around for almost an hour and she ID'ed him a few blocks from the square."

"Make any statements?"

"Yeah, claims he's gay. Not guilty."

"Anything I can do to be useful?"

"No. Just didn't want you to read about it in the

morning papers. The victim's a graduate student at NYU. It's probably not related to what you're working on, but I thought you ought to know about it. Seems like it's open season on college campuses this week."

I hung up and took the elevator back to the fourth floor. Lieutenant Peterson had just arrived and was talking to the chief, who summoned me to them with his forefinger.

"I'm surprised you and Chapman didn't stay for the service."

"What service?"

"Peterson's just telling me that President Recantati called for a prayer session and candlelight vigil tonight, then canceled all the classes and exams next week, and dismissed the students for the Christmas recess."

I was livid. Recantati and Foote must have made those plans before we saw them in the early afternoon, and they had chosen not to tell us. I thanked Chief Allee for the news and worked my way through the crowd to find Chapman, who was in the middle of the dance floor with one of the assistant DAs from my unit, Patti Rinaldi.

"You can have the next tango with him, I just need him for a few minutes." I took Mike's hand and led him to the side of the room, explaining the news to him. "You realize that means we're not going to have any kids there to interview by Monday afternoon, and possibly not any faculty members? They'll all scatter home over the weekend."

"Relax, blondie. I"ll pay Foote a visit first thing tomorrow morning and get some names and numbers. We'll do the best we can." He shuffled back to the dance floor without missing a step, calling out to Patti, to the Motown beat: *"Rescue me! Take me in your arms . . ."*

I fumed on the sidelines, annoyed that Chapman didn't seem as distressed as I was by Sylvia Foote's duplicity.

7

"Just once, I'd like to read an obituary of a murdered woman who hasn't been canonized overnight." It was Chapman, my Saturday morning 6:45 wake-up call. "Doesn't anybody wicked and ugly ever get blown away? I picked up the tabs on my way home."

Home from where? Patti's apartment? I wondered.

"'King's and Columbia Mourn Death of Beloved Professor.' Who beloved her? Mercer says she was a real ball breaker. 'Raven-haired Prof Slain After Spousal Sting.' The *Post*, of course. The broad is dead—what frigging difference does her hair color matter? D'you ever read a man's obit that says he was balding or blond? Someday I'm going to write the death notices for all of my victims. Truthfully. 'The despicable SOB, whose face could stop a clock, finally got what she deserved after years of being miserable to everyone who crossed her path.' That kind of thing. So what's the plan for the day? What time is Lola's sister expecting us?"

"When I spoke with her yesterday, she suggested one o'clock. Is that okay with you?"

"Rise and shine, twinkle toes. I'll pick you up at Fifty-seventh and Madison at noon."

Mike knew that my Saturday routine began with an eight o'clock ballet class, the one constant in an exercise schedule that had long ago been abandoned to the unforeseeable nature of the prosecutorial job. I had been studying with William for years, and relied on the stretches, pliés, and barre work of the studio to distract me from the tension of my daily dose of violent crime. From there, I was due at Elsa's, my hairdresser at the Stella salon, for a touch-up on my blonde highlights, for what I had expected to be a cheerful holiday season.

I picked up the paper from my doorstep, took the elevator down, and waited in the lobby until someone pulled up in a Yellow Cab, not anxious to stand on the corner trying to hail one in the frigid early morning air. On the ride across town, I read the *Times* coverage of the Dakota story. The reclassification of her death as a homicide bumped the news from the second section to the front page, above the fold: "Academic Community Stunned by Scholar's Death."

The piece led with the achievements, publications, and awards that the professor had garnered in her relatively short career. A second feature described the reaction of college officials. "Morningside Heights Mourns Neighbor," it began, explaining the decision of both Columbia University and King's College to suspend classes on the eve of the holiday week, while police tried to determine whether the killing was the work of someone stalking Dakota, or a threat to the schools' population at large.

Another sidebar item traced the course of the case against Ivan Kralovic, questioning the wisdom of the Jersey prosecutor's choice of techniques to cement the evidence against Lola's estranged husband. Each of the articles wove in quotes from a variety of sources close to the deceased, and referenced the eloquent words of King's chaplain, Willetta Heising, Sr., who spoke of the loss of her friend and also urged the students to remain calm in the face of this menace to their general sense of security. A photograph of the throngs pouring out of Riverside Church after the service, slim ecru tapers in every hand and a tissue dabbing the occasional eye, filled the rest of the page on which the stories concluded.

I folded the paper inside my tote, hoping to find time later to do the crossword puzzle, and paid the driver. I raced in the door and down the steps to William's studio, leaving my coat in the dressing room and joining a few other friends who were limbering up in the center of the floor. The warm smiles and routine complaints about stiff joints and unnoticeable weight gains signaled to me that none of the dancers had connected me to the bad news in today's headlines. It was a relief to be spared the questions and concerns that accompanied my involvement in the tragedies of others' lives, and I continued my stretches in silence.

Each time I picked my head up, I looked around the room to see whether Nan Rothschild had arrived. I knew that she was on the faculty at Barnard College and remembered that we had talked about Lola Dakota on several occasions a year earlier. I thought I could pick Nan's brain for some insights about how to handle her colleagues during this sensitive investigation, but there was no sign of her this morning.

I finished my knee bends as William entered the room, clapped the class to attention, and moved us to the barre to begin the session.

He started with a series of deep, measured pliés, counting for us to set a tempo. The recording, he explained, was Tchaikovsky's symphonic fantasy "The Tempest." I let my mind wander with the music, enjoying the fact that if I concentrated hard enough on holding my position correctly, I stopped thinking about the things I needed to do for the Dakota investigation.

"Head higher, Alexandra. Pull straight up when you do the relevés." He ran his pointer down the legs of the woman in front of me, showing me the perfect lines of her elevated pose. By the time we were ready for floor exercises, I had worked up a good sweat and loosened my limbs completely. I sat on the hardwood and extended my legs into a wide V-shaped wedge, my ballet shoes coming toe to toe with the elegantly arched foot of Julie Kent.

"What are you doing for Christmas? Going to the Vineyard?" she whispered.

I nodded. "A really quick trip. You and Victor?"

William put his finger to his lips and "ssshed" us to silence, tapping me on the shoulder with his wooden stick. Julie beamed at me and mouthed the word "later."

At the end of the class, we chatted about the holidays as we showered and dressed against the wintry day. I slogged for several blocks through slush made gray by traffic and filthy car exhaust without sighting a taxi, and finally reached the crosstown bus to take me to the hairdresser. My friend Elsa had read the morning paper, and we talked quietly about the bizarre events of the preceding day while she painted streaks in my pale blonde hair.

When I went down to the lobby of the building shortly before noon, Mike was parked directly in front, on Fifty-seventh Street, with his flashers blinking. We drove to the West Side and down to the Lincoln Tunnel for the ride to New Jersey. Typical for this time of year, most of the traffic was heading into Manhattan, not in our outbound direction. Suburbanites were coming to shop for Christmas, view the elaborate window displays at the Fifth Avenue department stores, skate, and enjoy the mammoth tree at the Rockefeller Center rink. We had much more sobering business before us.

Mike had called Lola's brother-in-law while I was at class in the morning to tell him and Lily that the medical examiner had officially declared Lola's death a homicide, something the morning papers had broadcast to the entire metropolitan area. Now the family seemed quite anxious to meet with us.

We pulled up in front of the house at one-thirty, and it was instantly recognizable from Thursday night's broadcast of the footage of Kralovic's hired hit. The wreath was gone now, and signs of seasonal joy were overshadowed by the gloom of the postvideo events.

As Mike lifted the brass knocker, the door swung open. A portly man in his fifties greeted us and introduced himself as Lily's husband, Neil Pompian. "My wife's in the kitchen. Why don't you come inside."

We wiped our feet on the bristled mat and followed Pompian through the entry hall and past the great room, which was dominated by a large tree surrounded by dozens of wrapped packages. Three women, who identified themselves to us as neighbors, rose from their seats around the table, took turns hugging Lily, made sure platters of pastry were fully packed for our choosing, and offered us food and drink as they let themselves out the back door.

I poured two cups of coffee and we joined Lily at the kitchen table, in a bright corner of the room, facing a large backyard with a swimming pool all covered up for winter. Lily was sitting on a window seat, her legs tucked up beneath her, and a glass of white wine in front of her.

"That bastard was determined to get Lola one way or

another, wasn't he?" She lifted the drink and sipped at it as we each introduced ourselves. "I know you didn't think we were right to do what Vinny Sinnelesi suggested, Ms. Cooper. My sister told me about her conversations with you. But she was really at her wits' end, and she liked the idea of an undercover sting to get Ivan once and for all. She thought it was a much more aggressive way to keep him behind bars, once she decided that's where he belonged."

"Here's what we'd like to do, Mrs. Pompian. I'm a detective with the Homicide Squad. I know how you feel about Ivan Kralovic, but he was in custody when Lola was mur—"

"This whole case is about control, Mr. Chapman. Ivan liked to control everything. Everybody. All the time. He needed to control Lola the way most people need to eat and sleep. That's what his fights with my sister were about. It would be an understatement to call Lola independent. Once she got it in her head to disagree with you, or to disapprove of something Ivan was doing, there was no bringing her back into the fold."

"I understand that, but I don't want to jump to—"

"I'm not jumping to any conclusions. These are facts, Detective. Ivan wanted my sister dead. He put the word out. Unfortunately for him, the cops are the ones who got the word. He paid handsomely to have these cops pretend to kill Lola."

"That's my point. That's why he's in jail."

"Yeah? Well, suppose he was smarter than they are? Suppose he didn't trust them? Let's say he caught on to their scam and just wanted to lull us all into thinking Lola would be safe the moment that Sinnelesi's cop team pretended to shoot her? Then he one-ups all of you, and sends the real killer to her apartment." She shook her head back and forth and reached for her wineglass again.

"That's one of the possibilities we're looking at, Mrs. Pompian."

"*One* of them? I suggest you look a little harder, Mr. Chapman. And faster, this time." She glanced in my direction. "Where's Ivan now? He's not loose is he, just because Lola can't testify against him?"

"He's locked up over here on the attempted murder charge. He's being held without bail." Mike had gotten through to the sheriff's office before he picked me up. "Who's the prosecutor you've been working with? We'd like to talk to him, too."

"Her name is Anne Reininger. She was very good to Lola. You think Ivan isn't capable of controlling this thing from inside the jailhouse? He's got money, he's got connections to every scumbag on both sides of the river, and he wanted Lola dead."

"Do you know why?" I asked. It was one thing to attack her himself, in the middle of a fight when they were alone together. But a hired killing, after they were separated and living out of each other's way, suggested another kind of problem. Avoidance of alimony payments? Something that Lola knew about Ivan that she threatened to expose, personally or professionally? A matter, perhaps, that was connected to the cash she kept hidden in a shoe box? I was willing to consider that it might be an issue less obvious than marital discord.

Lily Pompian thought my question was a stupid one. She had already explained why. It was becoming obvious to me that this was going to be Chapman's interview. I was being dismissed without an answer, and the repeated hits of Chablis, as Lily refilled her glass, were making Mike look like the warm and fuzzy one on our team. She shifted her weight on the bench and leaned in on her elbow to talk directly to Mike.

He took advantage of that dynamic and, armed with his most sensitive gaze, responded to her approach. "Let's start with Ivan. I think Alex knows a lot about him, from the earlier incidents, but why don't you tell me what kind of business he's involved in?"

"Yesterday or today?" Lily laughed at what she thought was her own joke. "Ivan started out with an MBA from Columbia. Worked on Wall Street for twenty years. Left his company after a merger and went out, quite comfortably, on his own. Then he got involved in all kinds of penny-stock deals. Stuff I didn't understand at all."

"Did you and your husband invest with him?"

"Not for a minute. He was always trying to get us to pour money into his deals, but we've got two kids in

93

college and my husband wasn't falling for any of Ivan's tricks. You'll have to talk with Ms. Reininger. Maybe she can tell you who he was scamming lately."

Lily got up from her bench to open another bottle of wine. "You comfortable there?" she asked, gesturing toward the table. "Either of you want to join me in something stronger?"

We both thanked her for the offer and Mike stood to refill our coffee cups.

"Tell us about Lola. I mean, from your perspective, as family. Before Ivan. And after him."

She closed the refrigerator door and leaned her back against it, pausing before she motioned to us to follow her into the adjoining room, a wood-paneled library. Two walls were stacked with bookshelves and the one behind the sofa was lined from floor to ceiling with family photographs.

"To understand any of us, you'd probably have to start with my mother, Ceci Dakota. Ever hear of her?" Before we could answer, she went on. "That's your problem, Detective. You're too damn young." One of her hands clutched the glass firmly, while the other rested on Mike's broad shoulder. "Mother was a Broadway showgirl, a hoofer, really. Better dancer than she was a vocalist, but in the days of the great American musicals, those girls had to be able to do it all."

I moved behind Lily to examine the early black-and-white pictures. "Cecile—she hated that name—made her debut in *South Pacific,* playing one of the nurses in the chorus. April seventh, 1949, Majestic Theatre on Broadway. Ask me anything about those days, and I can tell you more than you'll ever want to know, just from listening to Ceci. That show played one thousand nine hundred twenty-five performances—five years—and she stayed with it for two full seasons. How many times do you think anybody can wash a man right out of her hair and never get beyond the chorus line? She actually understudied Mary Martin for a few weeks, but the woman was never sick a single day, so Ceci moved on.

"Bottom line was that each of us kids was named for a character from one of the shows. For some reason she got hooked on the *L*'s. I got Lily, from *Kiss Me, Kate,* which isn't at all bad. My middle sister wound up with Liat, from *South Pacific.* Bloody Mary's daughter, y'know? It's not easy to grow up Tonkinese in Totowa, New Jersey." She took another drink. "And then came Lola."

The memories had made her smile, but her own mention of Lola's name brought Lily up short. "Ceci was still dancing." She aimed her glass toward a still of her mother, dressed in a pinstriped shirt over black fishnet tights, hands on her hips and mouth wide open. "Closest she ever got to a lead. Three performances subbing for Gwen Verdon in *Damn Yankees.* Stayed with it most of the run, from opening night on May 5, 1955, through another one thousand and nineteen shows. Even got a part in the movie, in fifty-eight.

Then took some time off to have another kid. That gave us my baby sister, Lola."

Mike was staring at a photo of three long-legged little girls in tutus standing around a basinet draped with blue ribbon. "A younger brother?"

"Yeah, he'll be over later, if you want to talk to him."

"Lemme guess, *Guys and Dolls*?"

"He should have been so lucky. Might have had a tough guy's name. Louie or Lefty or Lucky. Maybe missed out on a few school yard fights. But it was the sixties, and Ceci was madly in love with Robert Goulet. Try *Camelot*. Lance, she named him. Lancelot Dakota." Lily sunk down into a tapestry-covered sofa and put her feet up on the glass-topped table that faced it.

"So your mother was a Broadway gypsy, and your father?"

"Taught history at the local high school. Let Mother go her own way, take us to dance classes and sneak us into town to go to Saturday matinees if she knew some of the girls in the chorus line. Dad thoroughly immersed himself in local politics when he wasn't reading history books. Liat and I wanted to go the show biz route. Endless auditions and the deafening sound of tap shoes all over the house, day and night. Lance was my dad's clone. Very serious, very studious. His favorite place was the public library, in part to escape the constant screeching sound of Ceci making us sing 'Let Me Entertain You' to the milkman, the mailman, and anyone else who made the mistake of knocking on our door, and in part because he loved all the things he could learn from books."

"And Lola?"

"Like a perfect combination of their genes. She was smart as a whip. Couldn't keep her nose out of my father's history texts. Adored going with him to listen to the wheeling and dealing at the political clubhouses in town. But give her a sequined costume and a stage to dance on and she'd drop her schoolbooks, as long as there was an audience for her. No chorus line for Lola, and no understudy roles. She was the star or she didn't play. Being second banana to anyone wasn't acceptable to her.

"By high school, when she realized she didn't have the talent to make it to the big time, she threw herself into her studies. Got a full scholarship to Barnard. Majored in political science, with a minor in history. Got her master's and her Ph.D. at Penn. Never looked back. Liked every minute of what she was doing with her life. Her professional life, not her marriage."

Mike's wheels were turning. "Was there another woman in Ivan's life? Competition for Lola?"

"We didn't know about it if there was one. I believed my sister when she said she was rid of him for good. At this point, I think she would have welcomed the fact that he could focus his attention—and his rage—on someone else."

"How about *her* love life? Did she confide in you about that?"

"There was nothing to tell. Lola didn't have the time or the interest to get involved in a relationship at this point. She was all tied up in a new project at the college, and she had no desire to pique Ivan's anger by letting him find her with another man, until the divorce was final."

I sat in a chair opposite Lily and tried to ease my way into the conversation. "Perhaps you can take a look at some of the shirts and sweaters we found at Lola's apartment. It would help us to know how she was dressed when she left here on Thursday afternoon. And then, well, some of the things in the new place were men's clothing. You might recognize them, too."

"They must have been Ivan's. Or maybe one of her faculty friends. Sure, you can show them to me, but it's not very likely they'll be familiar to me. I signed a power of attorney yesterday, giving Vinny's office the right to go in and take any of her property they needed to help their investigation."

I grimaced at Chapman, sorry that Lily was still in the hands of the Jersey prosecutors, and thankful that the NYPD had declared apartment 15A a crime scene. Cops guarding the door, still blocked off with bright yellow tape, would be unlikely to let anyone step into it without the express permission of the chief of detectives.

"Do you know what kind of special project Lola was working on up at King's?"

"You know, it's a bit embarrassing for me. For the last few weeks, we used to sit here most nights after dinner, long after my husband went to sleep. We'd open more wine, talk to each other about everything from our childhood to our marriages to the Broadway theater. Revivals. Ever notice that's all it is these days, revivals? We talked about how we both loved Christmas. I used to be a Rockette, did I tell you that? Did the Christmas show for six seasons, till my first kid was born. Ceci loved it, seeing her own Lily Dakota on that big stage.

"Anyhow, I just lost it when Lola started talking about her job. I couldn't tell you the first thing about New York City, its history or its politics. North, south, or east of the Great White Way just doesn't exist for me. She said something about a multidisciplinary program that she was terribly excited about—digs and dead people—"

I interrupted her. "A deadhouse? Did she talk about that?"

"I said dead *people*," she responded with a pout. "That's all that comes to mind. Maybe it's the alcohol."

Maybe it was, but she showed no signs of slowing down. I kept my fingers crossed that she wasn't going to stand up and show Mike her best kick and her great extension. Wooden soldier number forty-four. Rockette Lily Dakota.

"Lily, do you know what Lola was wearing the last time you saw her?"

"My clothes. That's mostly what she wore the whole time she was with me. Black is all I remember. She wanted to wear black, for her phony funeral. She laughed about it, too."

Mike's nose was six inches from Lily's at this point, side by side on the sofa. "On Thursday, when the cops faked the scene with Lola's shooting, were any of them here with you in the house?"

"Are you kidding? We had a basement full of them. Anne Reininger was back in this room with us, explaining things to me step by step and trying to keep me calm. There were detectives and DAs all over the place, basement to attic, making sure everything went according to plan."

"And when it was over, did any of them stay behind with you?"

She stopped to think for a minute. "I know I asked for a sedative, to take a nap. I'd been extremely worried about this, and not being able to tell the neighbors it was all a fake. Lola and I sat up practically the entire night before, just trying to reassure ourselves that if the whole thing worked, she'd be rid of Ivan forever. I remember Lola and Anne giving me something to help me sleep that afternoon, once Lola was done with the shooting, but that's about all. I don't know when any of them left here."

"And Lola," Mike asked. "Did you know she was going back to her apartment?"

"Yeah. Yeah, sure. She made me promise not to tell

Anne. Anne left the room, then Lola kissed me, thanked me, and put the throw over my bedspread 'cause I was cold."

"She just told you she was going to walk out the door?"

Lily nodded.

"Did she ask to borrow your car?"

Lily's brow creased. She was working against the wine to remember what had happened. "No, of course not. She told me a car service was picking her up. At least, that's who I assumed she was talking to. She used the phone next to my bed to make a call. Told whoever it was not to come to the front door. Lola said she'd slip out the back, cross over Tess Bolton's yard—that's one of the neighbors you met—and wait next to their garage, on Arlington Street. She told me she'd be fine. Someone was taking her home, she said, where she'd be safe."

8

An hour later I was sitting at my secretary's typewriter, pounding out subpoenas for Mike to serve as soon as possible.

"What's first?"

"Verizon telephone services in New Jersey. MUDS and LUDS. I want every outgoing call made from Lily's phone on Thursday—in fact, all of last week. I suppose you should try each of the cab companies in Summit, too, but I think there's a good chance that she reached out to someone she knew—and trusted—to drive her to Manhattan. After the emotional drain of enacting her own murder, I assume she'd pick her traveling companion carefully."

"How about phone records for the apartment and her office?"

"I'm working on them. Give me your notepad. You've got all the relevant numbers written there, don't you?" We both knew the value of a paper trail, and started to think of any electronic or written means of communication that might have left a connection or a clue.

When I had finished looking for every possible link to Lola Dakota, I reached for another blank subpoena in my drawer. I flipped through Mike's pages until I found his references to Charlotte Voight, the student who had disappeared in April. There would be King's College records that could tell us which credit card she used at the school bookstore, and from there, we could get the company's vouchers to tell us what businesses she frequented and perhaps where she ate. As I took the subpoenas out of the typewriter, I signed them beneath the printed space with Battaglia's name in it, and passed them to Mike.

"What's this one for? King's College Student Health Services?"

"Long shot. We've got absolutely nothing to give us a control sample for Voight's DNA. None of her belongings are at school—no clothes, no toothbrush, no hairbrush. Nothing to let the lab develop a genetic fingerprint. What if we come across evidence or—worst-case scenario—a body? Once they work up a profile from that, we'd have zilch with which to compare it."

"What do you think she left at the doctor's office, a DNA sample in case of emergency?" Mike was growing impatient and was ready to leave.

"I'm willing to bet you that a sexually active college

student made at least one trip to that office, had one gynecological checkup during her time at the school. Needed birth control, or maybe—with Voight's lifestyle—a test for sexually transmitted diseases or pregnancy. And if she was examined there, most doctors would have done a routine Pap smear as part of the process. The cells scraped off during that procedure are more than enough to give us a control.

"So my guess is that sitting in a lab somewhere not too far away is all we need to get started on a DNA print of Charlotte Voight."

Mike nodded his approval. "C'mon, blondie. Nothing I can do with these papers till Monday morning. None of these business offices will be open at this hour on a Saturday. I'll drop you off at home. Then I'll be back at seven tonight to drive out to Mercer's."

I stopped in the lobby to pick up my mail, an assortment of Christmas cards from friends scattered across the country mixed in with the usual bills. There were two messages on the answering machine. One was my mother, hoping I could change my schedule and join the rest of the family at their Caribbean island home for Christmas. She hadn't heard the news of my latest case, so I would plan to spend some time with her on the phone tomorrow. The other call was from Jake, and I dialed his cell phone number.

"Still at the studio?"

"Trying to wrap up the piece for tomorrow. Brian's going to lead with the Ugandan story on Sunday's

Nightly News. We found some background information that puts a whole new spin on the assassination, and so far, it's an exclusive. How about you?"

"Wish I could say we were that far along. No spin, no leads. This is going to be a slow one. The administration closed down the school early for the holidays, so we're just treading water. Mercer's having a bunch of us over for a party tonight."

"Then you can hold out for a few more days till I get home?"

I was stretched out on the bed, phone to my ear, patting the empty space next to me. "Pretty lonely on your side of the mattress. Don't think I have any choice in the matter, do I? See if you can nab the assignment to do local traffic up here. Something unexciting that keeps you in my neighborhood all the time, okay?"

After we hung up, I called a few of my friends to say hello, wrapped some of the gifts I planned to take to the office on Monday, and dressed for the evening.

When Mike and I arrived at Mercer's house in Queens, the door was open and there were fifteen or twenty people clustered around the bar in his den. The first person to greet us was Vickee Eaton, a second-grade detective who worked at One Police Plaza, in the office of the deputy commissioner for public information.

Mike and Vickee were the same age and had gone through the academy together. He had introduced her to Mercer when the latter's brief marriage to a girl he'd grown up with had ended. Vickee and Mercer dated for almost five years, and were married for less than two when she walked out on him without any reason that he could articulate to us. When I saw her once thereafter, at a press event the commissioner held at headquarters to which Battaglia and I had been invited, she told me she just couldn't deal with the kind of danger Mercer was exposed to in the field. Vickee's father had been a cop, and had been killed on the job when she was fifteen. He was the reason she had gone into the department, and even more, the reason she feared how being a cop could be a death warrant as well.

I thought I had masked my surprise at seeing Vickee, but she read me clearly. "You haven't heard?"

I looked at Mike, who shrugged his shoulders.

"I didn't go to visit Mercer in the hospital—too many of you guys around for me to get down on my knees and apologize for how stupid I'd been." She was talking about the shooting in August, when the three of us had been investigating the murder of an art dealer, and Mercer had almost been killed as a result. "But I went over to Spencer's house immediately and kind of sat vigil with him that whole first week."

"That old dog really kept it under his vest." Mike and I had been in constant contact with Mercer's widowed father, Spencer Wallace, who lived for his only son. He never told us Vickee had reentered their lives.

Mercer had seen us come in and was making his way across the room with two glasses of champagne in his hands. He gave one to each of us, and Mike turned to pass his off to Vickee. She waved a finger at him and picked up a soft drink she'd been working on when we came in. "No alcohol for me. Not quite my third month yet."

Mike grabbed her in a bear hug, champagne sloshing from the flute and covering his lapel. "You mean that doctor got Mercer's plumbing back in order? Damn, you *are* my idol, m'man. Here I'm thinking you need all this bed rest and you're going to get out on three-quarters 'cause some asshole disabled you, and if you can ever be lucky enough to shoot at all again you'd be shooting blanks. While the whole time you're just practicing on Vickee, making love—"

I hadn't seen Mercer this happy in more than a year. He was trying to talk over Mike and explain that he and Vickee had decided to get married. "It's just going to be my dad, and her mother and two sisters this time. And both of you. New Year's Day, in Judge Carter's chambers. Will you be there?"

"Sure, we'll be there. Long as you don't do it during any of the bowl games, okay?"

The house was filled with friends and family. Mercer's team from Special Victims had all come to celebrate, and we tried not to talk cases as we ate and danced and drank. By eleven o'clock, I could see that Vickee was tired and trying to stay off her feet. I pried the third helping of lasagna out of Mike's hand and suggested we get on the road.

"The *Final Jeopardy!* category is Astronomy. Any takers?" Silence. "Blondie, make a stab at it? Could be something in it for you." I laughed and tugged at his jacket sleeve. "What is December twenty-first?" Mike asked aloud to no one in particular as I tried to pull him toward the door. "The winter solstice, ladies and gentleman. Shortest day of the year, but the longest night. Make good use of it—*I* certainly intend to."

Mercer walked us to the door and held it open as we said good night. "If your reputation wasn't shot before, Ms. Cooper, it's gone now. What are you doing for the solstice? You need Jake up here—enough of this toughin' it out alone. We've all been doing that too long."

"If I stopped to worry about every time Mike opened his mouth, they'd have to institutionalize me. I'm so happy for both of you. What a lucky little baby that's going to be."

We walked down the path and up the street to Mike's car. For most of the ride back to the city, I was quiet. We came through the Thirty-fourth Street tunnel, then Mike swung onto the FDR Drive going uptown. The cold spell seemed to be interminable, and I stared over at the sparkling lights of the bridges crossing the East River.

Off to the right, the forbidding outline of a ruined

building loomed against the dark sky, covered with frozen snow and icicles hanging from empty window frames.

"What are you thinking about? Where'd you go?"

"Just daydreaming. Thinking that's the most beautiful building in New York."

"Which one?"

"That abandoned hospital." I pointed to the southern tip of the island in the river. "It's the only landmarked ruin in the city. Built by the same guy who designed St. Patrick's Cathedral, James Renwick."

"Y'know, you can change the subject and create a distraction better than anyone on earth."

"I didn't know we had a subject. The solstice?"

"I know why you're brooding, Coop." Mike exited the Drive at Sixty-first Street and stopped at the first light. "You're thinking about Mercer and Vickee. And the baby."

"I'm not brooding."

"Makes you think about the direction of your own life, doesn't it? Family, careers, sort of what the purpose of—"

"Don't go getting all Hamlet on me tonight, Mikey. I'm thrilled for them. He's always been in love with Vickee and I think it's perfect that they've gotten back together. I really wasn't doing any heavy thinking."

"Well, you ought to do some." We were getting closer to my apartment now, and I was shifting my weight in the seat. "How much longer you gonna stay at this, Coop? Run around playing cops and robbers with us in the middle of the night? Now you've got a guy who's mad for you, plus you could name your own price at a law firm, or start one up, for that matter. Shit, you could hang it all up and have some kids. Little news jocks."

"This is all about *you*, Mr. Chapman." I tensed and fidgeted as we neared the driveway. "Sounds like Mercer's lifestyle changes appeal to you more than they do to me. He was getting anxious to settle down. I doubt he ever got over Vickee walking out the first time. Besides, he's forty—I'm only thirty-five—"

"And ticking."

"He loves kids. Always has. I watch him on the child abuse cases and he's great with kids."

"You are, too."

"Yeah, but he likes all of them. Me, I like the ones I know and love. I worship my nieces and nephews. I cherish my friends' kids. But I don't sit in an airport lounge listening to the whining toddlers, watching them wipe their noses on their sleeves, see the parents fighting with their petulant adolescents, thinking there's some great hole in my life. I'd choose a dog every time."

"People think you're nuts for staying in this job. Most of 'em think there's something screwy in your head, that you like it so much."

"I learned a long time ago not to worry about what other people think. Unless they're people I care about.

You love what you do. You don't understand why I like my end of it?"

"Different thing."

"What are you talking about? You're sniffing around dead bodies day and night. I get to help people. Live ones. People who've survived the trauma, who recover from it, who get to see a bit of justice restored because we *make* the system work for them."

I realized I had raised my voice in answering Mike, so I said more calmly, "Twenty years ago, prosecutors couldn't get convictions in these cases in a court of law. Now, the guys in my unit do it every day. Different thing? According to who? To *you*? 'Cause your narrow-minded, parochial upbringing wants you to think that women shouldn't do this kind of work, right?"

My pitch had gone up again. There was no point trying to explain what he already knew.

We were stopped in the middle of the driveway at my building, the doorman standing at the passenger side to let me out, but waiting till our argument stopped before daring to approach the car. I was sure he could hear my agitated voice through the window.

Mike lowered his tone a notch and spoke to me softly. "'Cause I think you've got to start thinking about the rest of your life, Coop."

"I think about it every day. Know what my thoughts are? That if a fraction of the people I knew did something that was as emotionally rewarding as what I do, they'd be a pretty satisfied bunch. I've got loyal friends who happen to have a great time working together, with one another and with the good cops like you and Mercer."

"And you're going home, by yourself, to an empty apartment. With nothing to eat in the refrigerator, nobody to keep you warm when the heat goes off, and no way for anyone to know if you're dead or alive until it's time to show up for work on Monday. It's pathetic. You should have been on the last shuttle to Washington, slippin' into Jake's hotel room—"

I stepped out of the car and slammed the door behind me. "When you straighten out your own love life, instead of going home and playing with yourself every night, then you can start giving advice to the lovelorn."

He accelerated over the speed bumps and raced out of the driveway.

"Sorry." I nodded to the doorman. "Thanks for waiting."

"Miss Cooper? There was someone here an hour or two ago asking questions about you."

I shivered. "Do you know who he was?"

"No, it wasn't a man. It was a young woman, actually. Wanted to know if you lived here."

"What did you say?"

"Well, it was the new guy she spoke to, the one covering for the holiday break. He thought she looked harmless enough. He told her that you did live in the building before he even thought about why she might be asking."

Great security. Must be why my rent is so high. "What else did she say?"

"She wanted to know if anybody else lived with you. She wanted to know if you usually came home alone at night."

9

The light was flashing on my answering machine when I walked in my bedroom at midnight. Jake said he and the film crew had gone out for dinner, but he was back in his hotel room and would wait up awhile for my call. The second caller was an unfamiliar voice.

"Miss Cooper? Hello? This is, um, Joan Ryan. I'm one of the counselors in the Witness Aid Unit at the DA's office. We haven't met yet, and this isn't exactly the way I, uh, wanted to introduce myself. But I need to tell you about a problem on one of your cases.

"I've been counseling one of your victims, Shirley Denzig, you know the one who claims the delivery guy attacked her? She was flirting with him in the deli when she bought her dinner, and then she paid him to bring up the dessert half an hour later?" Ryan was rambling now, in that way people do on answering machines so it seems to the listener that the story will be interminable. *What's the point, Joan?*

"I, um—I probably should have given you a heads-up about this yesterday, when she showed up at my office. But then, you know, whatever she tells me is privileged, 'cause I'm a social worker and she's a victim. It was only when she showed up again tonight that the supervisor called me. She really seemed out of control, asking all kinds of questions about you. Anyway, if you want to call me at home, here's my number. You'll probably want to know what Shirley was saying. My supervisor thinks I have to tell you."

I cut off her confessional narrative and dialed the number.

"Joan? It's Alex Cooper. Sounds like I woke you up."

"That's okay. This is really my fault."

I knew who Denzig was, so there was no need to go through the story again. It was during her second interview with me a couple of weeks ago, in our discussion of her psychiatric history, that I had set her off on a tirade. While I was asking the routine pedigree questions, Denzig had told me she was a student at Columbia College. Considering the other information she had provided, I was skeptical of her claim and asked to see her identification. She had presented me with a photo ID that had expired two years earlier. It looked fairly generic, with no Columbia crest, or any of the characteristic blue-and-white university markings.

When I pressed further, Shirley admitted that she had never attended the college, and had purchased the phony card on Forty-second Street, where just about any kind of counterfeit document is available for a price. I clipped the fake ID to her case file and continued asking questions.

From then on, she avoided eye contact while staring at the file. Once the interview about the alleged attack was completed, she asked for her ID back. I refused, explaining that it was forged and had no legal validity. I had steered her down to Witness Aid, where she could get help with her counseling needs and the problems with her landlord, who was trying to evict her because she was four months in arrears in her rent. The next day I learned she was wanted for shoplifting at a store near her parents' home in Maryland.

"What stirred her up yesterday?"

"Well, when she read about the professor who was murdered—the Dakota woman—she said it made her think about you again, and how mad she was that you took her ID."

"Did she tell you what made her angry?"

"You'll think it's crazy. But then, you know she's got an extensive psych history, right? She's been on medication for two years. Says she's gained more than eighty pounds. Shirley says that ID has the only pretty picture of her that she's got, and she wants it back."

"And you didn't call to tell me that she wanted it?" It would have been easy to deal with. I could have given her the photo without the bogus identification card.

"Well, Ms. Cooper, I know I learned it in graduate

school, but I forgot completely about the whole 'duty to warn' doctrine. I mean, everybody says you're so independent, it never occurred to me that poor little Shirley Denzig could really get to you."

My heart was beating faster. I was standing at the side of my bed, with my coat and gloves still on, listening to this conversation about the unhinged young woman who had apparently just shown up at my door. "Warn me about *what*?"

"The law says that it's not betraying the privilege for me to tell you if a patient threatens your—"

"I know what the case law says, Joan. The patient's privilege ends when the public peril begins. I want to know what Shirley said."

"She told me that she wanted to see you dead, just like the professor. She asked me how you got to work every day, and what time you left for home."

So far, I wasn't worried. The answers were that my travel route and hours were never the same two days in a row. This outpatient on a heavy diet of psychotropic drugs might be interested in making me unhappy, but she hadn't seemed the least bit dangerous to me.

"Actually, Ms. Cooper, I didn't know whether to believe her or not, but she told me she had a gun. Stole it from her father's house last weekend when she went home to Baltimore."

That racheted up my attention a notch. "And tonight? What happened tonight?"

"She showed up at Witness Aid. Told one of my

colleagues that she was a victim in a case of yours. That you had given her your home number. That she'd been thrown out of her apartment for not paying rent, and wanted to leave a small gift for you with your doorman. They know you give witnesses your number from time to time."

Yeah, but generally not to lunatics, if I can help it.

"She acted so upset and all that they gave her the information. They didn't know how she really felt about you. I'm the only one she told that to. I just wanted to give you a little warning tonight in case she shows up. She's very, very mad at you."

"Thanks, Joan. I'm going to have one of the guys from the DA's squad make a report about this on Monday morning, okay? I'll send him down to your office. Just tell him what you told me."

I walked to the hall closet and hung up my coat and scarf. I was too wired to sleep and didn't need any more to drink, so I tried settling into bed with *The Great Gatsby*. I had embarked on a plan to reread all of Fitzgerald's novels, but this wasn't the time to begin. I went back to the living room to find my tote and fished out the crossword puzzle. The bottom left corner stumped me completely but I was determined not to go to the encyclopedia to find the four-letter name of a Tasmanian Indian tribe. I worked around the blank spaces.

At 1 A.M., I called Mike's number to apologize to him for my remarks at the end of the evening. The phone rang five times before his outgoing message kicked in. I guess he did have better things to do with himself than I had suggested.

"Just me. Sorry I snapped at you. Hope you're having a good time, wherever you are." No point telling him about my disgruntled victim. He'd hear soon enough. "And you're right about one thing. I should have taken the shuttle tonight."

I slept fitfully and got out of bed at six-thirty, when I heard the thud of the Sunday *Times* landing against my door.

I poured coffee beans into the machine and opened the paper while they ground and the brew began to drip, looking for stories about local crimes in the Metro section, before turning to the national and international news.

Mike was right about the food supply in my home, too. There were three English muffins left in my freezer, so I defrosted one and popped it into the toaster. I sat at the table and made a shopping list of groceries to order, figuring that there were some new leaves easier to turn over in my life than others. Filling the bare cupboards was one of them.

When the phone rang at seven-thirty, I was sure it was Jake, and I picked it up, eager to make our plans for the holiday week.

"Alex? It's Ned Tacchi. Sorry to hit you so early on a Sunday, but we picked one up during the night that you'll want to know about."

Tacchi and his partner, Alan Vandomir, were two of my favorite detectives at Special Victims. Smart, sensitive, and good-humored, they got victims through the investigative process with kid gloves. When they called me, I knew it was something I needed to hear.

"Sure. What did you get?"

"Push-in sodomy. East Sixty-fourth Street, right off York Avenue. Fifty-five-year-old woman coming home from a Christmas party at three this morning."

"How is she?"

"Seems to be doing okay. She's in the ER now. We'll pick her up as soon as she's released and do a more thorough interview."

"Injuries?"

"Nope. In fact, she called nine-one-one to report it, but didn't want to go to the hospital. The perp pushed in behind her when she opened the vestibule door. A bit tipsy."

"Him or her?"

"She was. A little too much holiday cheer. He knew exactly what he wanted. Told her to get down on her knees, right there in the hallway. First he lifted her sweater, opened her bra, and put his mouth on her breasts. Then he exposed himself and made her put her mouth on his penis."

"Did he ejaculate?"

"Yeah. But she went right upstairs and brushed her teeth. Doubt we'll get anything for DNA, but she still said she had an awful taste in her mouth. That's probably more psychological than anything else. We asked the nurse examiner to do the swabs anyway. We're also having them swab her breasts."

"Good thinking." Even the microscopic amounts of saliva that might be found on the victim's torso would yield enough material for the newer kind of DNA process—STR testing—in which "short tandem repeats" of the genetic fingerprint are multiplied millions of times to yield the unique, identifiable patterns.

"Get her toothbrush, too. You may get lucky. Did he take anything?"

"Yeah. Left with her pocketbook. Didn't get much. She was holding her keys in her hand the whole time. Just had thirty bucks in her purse, along with some business cards and her cell phone. Schmuck dumped the bag in a trash basket a block away. Cell phone is gone, but we've got the purse. I'm sending the cards over to latent prints, hoping they can lift something off the surfaces, if he touched them."

"Has she canceled the cell phone yet?"

"No. We told her not to for twenty-four hours."

"Great. When I get to the office in the morning, I'll fax you up a subpoena." Most of the guys who stole cell phones during robberies were stupid enough to make calls on them until the phones were cut off or the batteries went dead. With records from the companies available in three or four days, we could often track down the offenders through the calls they placed to friends or relatives.

"Thought Battaglia might want to know that the commissioner is looking over a bunch of cases in the Nineteenth Precinct. They're probably going to declare this as part of a pattern."

"I didn't know we had anything else like this going on."

"Not up at our shop. But the precinct has about four other push-in robberies between Sixtieth and Sixty-eighth Streets, Second Avenue to the river, since the beginning of November. Mostly weekends. All the victims are women. This is the first time the perp has forced a sexual assault, but the MO is pretty much the same. Then he snatches the bag every time and he always runs south."

"Same 'scrip?"

"Pretty close. Most describe him as a male black, five-ten to six feet, stocky. Well dressed, clean-cut, very articulate. Has a slight accent, but nobody can place exactly what it is. Some say islands, some say French. Hard to know."

"Can you get all the paperwork down to me in the morning so I can assign it? I'm jammed up with the Dakota case. I'll probably give it to Marisa Bourges or Catherine Dashfer, okay? But keep me posted on any developments. Are they going to beef up patrol in that area on the midnight tour, Friday to Sunday?"

"The boss in the Nineteenth wants them to saturate it, but we've still got Savino and his gang running the task force on the West Side Rapist, so we're stripped of manpower as it is." For almost three years, an attacker had been operating on the Upper West Side of Manhattan, and despite an extensive manhunt and a genetic profile that had been entered in local, state, and national data banks, he continued to elude us. "We'll call you later if we break anything else on this today."

I crunched on the cold muffin and poured a second cup of coffee. Shortly before I started at the district attorney's office more than ten years ago, not a court in the United States accepted DNA technology as a valid forensic technique. By the late eighties, as the methodology was refined in the handful of laboratories that performed the testing, Frye hearings were held in criminal courtrooms around the country. Every prosecutor, case by case and state by state, had to convince the judge—before the evidence could be used at a trial—that the kind of genetic testing at issue had been deemed reliable by the scientific community.

By the time this groundbreaking investigative tool had gained general acceptance in the criminal justice system, it roared into the headlines in the O. J. Simpson trial, and skeptics everywhere attacked the soundness of its findings. As a result, standards in lab procedures were instituted and accreditation practices were firmly established to reassure investigators of the value and accuracy of this innovative technique.

Even more important, the actual method of testing improved and changed dramatically. The original means of performing the exams was referred to as

RFLP, for restriction fragment length polymorphism. It required large amounts of body fluid, in good condition, to yield a result. By the late nineties, the transfer to PCR-based technology—polymerase chain reaction—and the use of short tandem repeats, almost like photocopying the minuscule particles, expanded the horizons enormously. It is a method that requires just a minute amount of material from which to test, and is even successful with old and degraded samples. DNA technology had revolutionized the nature of our work in the short time that I had come to the practice of law, and was making possible solutions to crimes that had not been dreamed of a short decade before.

Within a week's time, the swabs taken from a victim's body hours earlier might supply us with a secret code, unique in all the world to the man who forced himself upon her this morning. It would be analyzed and mapped, serologists detailing at least thirteen distinctive loci, or places on the assailant's genetic fingerprint that matched no other human being's on earth. They would feed it to the medical examiner's crime scene computer database to see whether this offender had committed a similar offense anywhere in New York City. Within the month, his profile would be uploaded to the state's files in Albany, and the FBI's system in Washington, in hopes that one of those sources would have this suspect on record in an unrelated arrest, and solve this latest case with a computer-generated cold hit.

The phone rang again at nine-thirty. "Only three shopping days left till Christmas. Where shall we meet? Everything in town is open late today. I need to get Jim's gift, and then pick out something for you to tell him that I want, just in case he hasn't done that yet."

One of my closest pals, Joan Stafford, was in town for the weekend, and we had planned to spend the day together finishing our lists. "He's already got it wrapped and in your stocking, kiddo. I know exactly what it is and you're going to be very happy with Santa. You've got to help me with Jake's. I've thought of almost everybody but him. I'm ready anytime you are."

"Okay. I've set an itinerary for us. Your time is too precious to screw around with. We start at James II. Best antique cuff links in town. Across the street to Turnbull. You must get Jake some more of those great striped shirts with the white collars. He'll never out-dress Brian Williams, but you can keep trying." A wonderful respite from the week behind and the week ahead. Joan could make me laugh about anything. "We skim past Escada. Make sure Elaine has something in mind for Jake to take you to the Washington Press Club dinner in style. A quick peek at Asprey. Then a triumphal march up Madison Avenue, in and out of all the little boutiques. Do you have things for les deux divine detectives, messieurs Chapman and Wallace? We've got to take care of those guys—they're so good to you. Lunch at Swifty's, with a spicy Bloody Mary,

125

and dinner at Lumi's. Dewar's for you and some kind of delicious red wine for me. You can help me concoct a menu for my New Year's Eve dinner party. Are we broke yet?"

"Credit cards will be totally maxed out and it will be a perfect diversion for me."

"And you'll turn the damn beeper off, right?"

"I'll switch it to the vibrate mode. You'll never know it's there." Even my best friends had to deal with the fact that my days often started with an assault or were punctuated by a murder.

"Heat wave, Alex. It may actually get up to twenty-eight degrees today. See you in an hour."

The day went exactly as planned. Bundled up against the cold, we shopped ourselves into a state of exhaustion. Most of my family's gifts had been mailed out of town so they would arrive in time for the holiday. I could scatter the rest to my friends throughout the week, take a carload to the office for everyone there, and save Jake's for Christmas Eve.

We were savoring our last cup of espresso after dinner when the small device attached to my waist-band began to buzz and wriggle against me. I pulled it off and saw the lighted notice declaring that I had one page. I depressed the button and it displayed Mike's home number.

"You call him back. He always asks how you are." I handed Joan the phone, knowing she would break the ice between Mike and me.

She dialed the number and spoke into the receiver, affecting her best French accent. "Can I interest you in a brandy, Detective Chapman?"

"Who's—?"

"Surely a flic as brilliant as you should be able to—"

"Mademoiselle Stafford! Your place or mine?"

"I'm afraid that I'm not alone. I've got that blonde with me. Don't forget, I'm expecting some little Christmas trinket from you."

"Well, I've got Coop's all picked out."

"What are you getting her? I'm green with envy already."

"You know those LoJack things you install in cars so the cops can track them in case they're stolen? I'm gonna do the first human LoJack insertion. I spend more time hunting down this broad around town, trying to figure out where she is when I need her. I'm gonna stick a needle with that computer chip deep into the buttocks of her cute little right—you've probably seen 'em bare, Joanie. Which one's cuter? The right or the left cheek?"

"Neither one's that appealing, Mike. They're both a bit scrawny. Drinks on me. Please come join us. We're at—"

"No can do. Somebody beat you to it. Put blondie on."

I put the phone back to my ear. "Did you get my message?" I asked sheepishly.

"Yeah. Had to run right out and get myself a date last night. Didn't want you checking my hand for blisters."

"I'm sorry for——"

"There's more important stuff to talk about. Just got a call from the captain over in the two-six. One of the custodians was going through the dorms at King's College today. Making sure everybody was out 'cause they're closing the building down till after the first of the year.

"The guy had to break open the door to one of the bedroom suites that was locked and bolted from the inside. Found a kid from Philly, a twenty-one-year-old senior, swinging from the railing in his closet. Hung himself with the drawstring from a pair of sweatpants. Suicide."

I thought first of the boy's family, and how their lives would be shattered by this news they might not even know yet. Mike talked on.

"Criminal justice major. Julian Gariano."

"In Lola Dakota's classes?"

"No connection to her that anyone can make. Seems your office was about to bust Gariano next week. Six-month investigation with an indictment that was supposed to be unsealed for his arraignment, by the Special Narcotics Bureau. Kid and his accomplice have been importing huge quantities of Ecstasy for a couple of years. His codefendant was arrested at the airport, coming in from Amsterdam with more than a hundred thousand tablets. Rolled over and gave up Gariano in a flash."

"So what's this got to do—"

"Guess who he lived with a year ago, his main squeeze? Charlotte Voight, the girl who's been missing since April."

10

Planning anything this particular Monday morning was a futile race against time. Every agency and business from which I needed records and information would be shutting down, some for just the period surrounding Christmas, and others for more than a week until after the New Year's holiday. Lab scientists, cops, prosecutors, and witnesses would be taking days off for traditional celebrations and trips to be with family out of town. I took a cab to the office at 7 A.M. and reviewed the file for the short hearing I had to conduct at nine-thirty.

Then I blasted out a list of e-mails on the in-house network. I had to find one of my senior attorneys to handle the new pattern in the Nineteenth Precinct, and to put a rush on the subpoena for the victim's stolen cell phone records. I drafted a list of things for Laura to work on while I was in court, and wrote memos about case developments that she needed to type and get to the district attorney.

We had our own NYPD branch, a squad detail of about fifty officers, based one flight above me, so I called the voice mail of Detective Joe Roman and told him to do a complaint report with the statements Shirley Denzig had made to the Witness Aid workers. I also asked him to run a pistol permit check on Denzig's father, in Maryland, and to determine whether his gun had in fact been stolen.

Laura had just reached her desk at nine, and before she could sit down she was buzzing me on the intercom. "It's Howard Kramer."

"I'll take it. But if Chapman calls, put him right through. I thought he'd be here by now."

I picked up the phone to greet Kramer, a litigator and managing partner at one of the premier law firms in the city, Sullivan and Cromwell. Although I knew Howard through his work, we had become better acquainted after his marriage to Nan Rothschild, the Barnard professor who was also my ballet class companion.

"How've you been?"

"Fine. Everybody's well. I know how busy you are, but I thought you might want to see Nan sometime this week. She's flying in from London this afternoon, on her way back from a conference at Oxford. I read in the *Times* that you're involved in the Professor Dakota mess. Nan was working with Lola on a project that the college was sponsoring, and she may have some insights for you."

I knew that Rothschild was one of the most prominent urban anthropologists in the country. A professor at Barnard College, she had led and participated in some of the most extraordinary excavations in America, including several in the heart of New York City that had unearthed Colonial burial grounds and artifacts of early settlements.

"I was talking to Nan at class a few weeks ago and she described the dig she was supervising in Central Park. Seneca Village. Is that what Dakota was involved in?" The village was a community of several hundred people who were moved from their mid-Manhattan homes in the 1850s to make way for the creation of the Great Lawn in the park. Nan had captivated me with stories of the most current high-tech means of exploring the city's past.

"I don't think Lola had anything to do with that one. Nan was brought in as a consultant by King's College on something brandnew. The head of their anthropology department, a guy named Winston Shreve, asked her to head up a small project for them. Shreve had this idea to take a significant urban structure with an interesting architectural history, let Nan lead the excavation, and then combine the students' physical dig with courses about the political and cultural history. Lola was one of four teachers heading up the operation. It's attracted a lot of attention in academia—very substantive, but at the same time very lively for the students. You'd be amazed at some of the things they've found."

"Where are they working?"

"The Octagon Tower. Do you know it?"

"Never heard of it."

"You'll have to let Nan take you over to see it—it's quite extraordinary. It was New York's first lunatic asylum. Of course, that's what they called it then, back in the early nineteenth century. It's on Roosevelt Island, the northern end, just south of the lighthouse."

"Not part of that great-looking ruin you see from the Drive?" The one I pointed out to Chapman on Saturday night.

"No, not the hospital. You can't see the Octagon from this side of the river. Tell you what. Come over to the house for drinks tomorrow night, and Nan will tell you everything she knows about Lola. Then, when you have a chance, I want her to promise she'll take you out to the Octagon so you can watch what's going on."

We agreed to meet at seven on Tuesday just as Chapman walked in the door, taped a sprig of green plastic mistletoe on the bookshelf overhanging Laura's chair, and kissed her on the back of the neck. "I'll be bringing a detective with me, if that's okay. See you then."

"Where are we going?" Chapman asked.

"Right now, we're going to Part Seventy-four for my

hearing. Can you believe that the dig Lola was working on was an old lunatic asylum? I'm afraid if the two of us make a site visit, they're likely to keep us. My friend's wife is going to tell us what Lola was up to if we stop by their house tomorrow. This hearing will be short. As soon as I'm finished we can scoot out of here, up to the college."

Pat McKinney was standing in the doorway, mug in hand, as I gathered my papers and white legal pad. "Guess I don't need to worry about the direction of your investigation anymore, Alex. They're giving you the big guns to work the case. Detective I've-got-a-ninety-three-percent-clearance-rate-on-my-homicides himself." These two despised each other. McKinney took any shot he could at Mike, and Chapman felt a constant need to cover my back against McKinney's double dealings.

"Don't dally too long, Pat. You'll be missing your Mensa meeting," Mike said just as snidely. Over McKinney's shoulder, we could see Ellen Gunsher and Pedro de Jesus on their way down the hall to his office for their daily ritual of coffee behind closed doors.

"I want to be sure you sit down with us before I head upstate for Christmas, Alex. Pedro has some ideas about the trial you're starting in January. The blood-spatter evidence. I think it would be useful to hear him on it."

"Pedro hasn't tried a case since I was in the academy. He's giving advice to Coop? You two ought to start your own Web site. Www.I-used-to-be-a-contender dot com. Sit in your corner office telling war stories to Little Miss Gun Shy about what it was like in the days when you didn't have to turn over Rosario material, and scientific evidence meant proving someone was blood type A or O. She probably even buys into your baloney. Thinks you were a trial dog once upon a time. Gunsher wouldn't know the difference between the inside of a courtroom and the Spring Street Bar. We got work to do, buddy. And you, Ms. Moneypenny," Mike said, winking at Laura, "I expect you to tell me whether you've been good or bad this year. Don't let McKinney under my mistletoe. His breath's funny. See you later."

We brushed past Pat and trotted down the staircase across the seventh-floor corridor to take the elevators up to the sixteenth-floor courtrooms. "How come you were late? I thought you were going to be in my office by eight o'clock."

"Forgot I had to make a stop at the hospital. See a friend."

"Sorry. Who's sick?"

"Nobody you know. Just promised to be there for some blood tests. I'll tell you later."

It was unlike Mike not to respond directly to my questions, so I left it alone for the moment. "Anything more on the student who killed himself?"

"He was one of the kids that the dean had lined up to talk to us this afternoon. So far, that's all I know about him. People are dying to get out of your way, Coop."

Truly, a sobering thought. "The narcotics assistant who has the file wasn't in yet. I left a message for him to call as soon as possible and get a copy of all the police reports over to me." I pushed through the courtroom door and walked forward into the well.

The judge, defense attorney, and court officers were all waiting for me to appear. I apologized for keeping them waiting as Judge Zavin ordered the defendant produced from the pens. Behind each courtroom was a small holding cell to which incarcerated offenders were delivered from the correction department, brought to the building from the nearby Tombs or the longer bus ride from Rikers Island.

From her desk in the far corner, the court clerk called the case for the record. "Calendar number four. People against Harold Suggs. Indictment number 4362 of 1994. Matter is on for a hearing under the Sex Offender Registration Act. Counsel, state your appearances, please."

"For the People, Alexandra Cooper."

"Bobby Abramson for Mr. Suggs."

Since the murder of six-year-old Megan Kanka in a small New Jersey township several years earlier, every state in the country had responded with legislation mandating that convicted sex offenders be required to register their addresses upon release with a local police agency. In New York, before they could be paroled from prison, a hearing had to be held to establish a level of offender responsibility, which would determine how often that individual would have to report for monitoring of his home and work situations. It would also decide whether the public could be informed that Mr. Suggs had moved into the neighborhood.

These Megan's Laws, as they have come to be called, arose from the facts in that little girl's case. Her killer was a convicted child molester who settled in a home across the street from Megan's house, although no one in her family was aware of his background. After luring her into his yard with the promise that he would show her a puppy, the "rehabilitated" parolee molested and murdered the child.

"Ms. Cooper, Mr. Abramson—have you each had an opportunity to examine the recommendations made by the review board?"

"Yes, Your Honor," we answered at the same time.

"Do either of you wish to challenge the findings?"

Again, we each said, "Yes."

Of the three possible ratings, Suggs had been evaluated a 2 by the board. I had done a thorough background workup of him and wanted to argue that he was eligible for the most serious monitoring level, or a 3, while my adversary was fighting to reduce his exposure and take him down to a 1.

"I intend to call witnesses, Judge," Abramson said.

I glanced over to the row of benches behind him and

saw a middle-aged woman with a scowl on her face, sitting beside a stack of folders. Just what I needed. An unanticipated witness for the defense to drag out the morning's proceedings.

"I'll hear Ms. Cooper first. Are you personally familiar with this matter?"

"Yes, Your Honor. I tried the case for our office in ninety-four."

"Perhaps you can give me more detail than the court file has."

It was always an odd experience to appear before Frances Zavin on a sex crime. She was a very stern jurist, nearing retirement age, who had chosen to decorate her courtroom with two oversize canvases that hung on either side of her raised chair. Both were modern paintings in bold colors, and the one situated above the witness box portrayed a large, mangy dog with an exposed, erect penis. It was our practice to warn rape victims not to look up at it as they took the stand for fear that it would unnerve them, and we often wondered what jurors thought as they listened to graphic testimony and stared at the aroused mutt.

I talked to Zavin, framed as she was by her artwork. "Mr. Suggs was fifty-eight at the time he committed these acts. He is what I would call a classic pedophile, which is the reason—"

"Objection, Judge. That's a prejudicial and conclusory—"

"Mr. Abramson, hold your objections until Ms. Cooper completes her statement. There's no jury here, so you won't impress me with your interruptions."

"In the instant case, the defendant was convicted of sexually abusing two girls, who were five and six years old at the time." The court officer standing at my back groaned softly. Score extra points for multiple victims. Score triple miles for children under the age of eleven.

"Any force?"

"Absolutely none, Your Honor," Abramson interjected. "There's no allegation of force or the use of any weapons."

Like the five-year-old was *willing* to be fondled? "Most pedophiles don't use knives and guns, Judge. They don't need to. We never charged him under the forcible compulsion theory. These are statutory cases. Sexual abuse in the first degree, the same level of felony as if he had been armed. These babies were clearly unable to consent, in fact, and under the law."

"Oh, please," Abramson whined. "*Babies?* Can she call them something else?"

"Surely they are babies, sir. What do you think is more appropriate, 'young women'? Go on, Ms. Cooper."

I laid out the facts of the case, which involved allegations that Suggs, who was living with the mother of the children, regularly carried them into his bed when she left for work three nights a week as a nurse's aide at Metropolitan Hospital.

"Any priors?"

"Actually, yes, Judge. Although no convictions. Mr. Suggs was arrested several times throughout the eighties for similar offenses. None of those charges resulted in indictments. I pulled the papers on the cases, and because of the corroboration requirements still in place for child victims, the prosecution was not able to prove those matters at the time."

"The witness I have here today can speak to the defendant's efforts to control his own impulses." Abramson pointed at the woman seated behind him. "Dr. Hoppins with the MAC treatment program."

I turned to catch Chapman's eye. "Everybody's got a frigging acronym," he mouthed to me. We knew this one well. The Modality Alteration Center on East Ninth Street, right off Lower Broadway, a private clinic with psychologists who specialized in counseling for admitted offenders. Half of our convicted felons went to that office as a condition of their parole, and I had yet to see any of them rehabilitated. The shrinks working there were some of the same geniuses who had declared Megan's killer ready to rejoin society.

"Dr. Hoppins will tell you that Mr. Suggs was already in therapy when he was arrested in ninety-four. He was trying to do something about his problem, without the intervention of the court."

"What Dr. Hoppins, and perhaps counsel himself, may not be aware of—since Mr. Suggs was represented by Legal Aid at that time—is that when the defendant was apprehended for these charges, he had just left Dr. Hoppins's office. Suggs was picked up for public lewdness directly across the street from the clinic, standing against the wire fence. That's the playground at the Grace Church School, where he had exposed himself while watching the kindergarten class playing kickball in the yard. Unfortunately, the center is a magnet for all sorts of sex offenders."

"Judge, my client is sixty-four years old now. He's hardly able, well—hardly likely—"

"The crimes Mr. Suggs has been charged with are not assaults that require the use of Viagra for a perpetrator to commit them. We're not claiming that he's completing sexual assaults like rape, which require penetration. No matter how old and how infirm he gets, these are acts he'll still be able to perform. This is a man who should never be allowed in the unsupervised presence of children." I knew the NYPD's monitoring unit had designated Megan-mappers, officers who worked with parole and probation to make sure pedophiles did not move out of jail and into apartments on the same blocks as elementary schools and day-care centers.

"Mr. Suggs has been a model prisoner during the term of his incarceration. No disciplinary infractions, no positive drug testing."

"I spoke with the warden at Fishkill last week, Judge. He told me that when they moved Mr. Suggs down here for this hearing on Wednesday, they conducted a routine search of his cell. There were more than five hundred photographs of naked children under the mattress of his bed.

"And one more thing on that point." Abramson and Suggs both glared at me as I spoke. "Mr. Suggs has his own Web site."

Zavin was about to turn against me. "I'm well aware, Ms. Cooper, that no prison in this country allows inmates access to the Internet. Don't undermine your entire case by making claims you can't support."

I slipped a downloaded series of papers from my folder and handed copies to the court officer to deliver to counsel and the judge. "There's a woman in Missouri who operates a third-party Internet service for prisoners. Ten dollars bought Harry Suggs his own biographical sketch, his photo, and the opportunity to have this woman forward to him—by regular U.S. mail—any responses he gets to his inquiries. I'd like to read this into the record:

Hi, I'm Harry. I'm caring, honest, and lonely. I'm sixty-four years old, looking for a home with someone who shares my love for kids and animals. I've got a few grandchildren of my own, and there's room in my heart for you and yours. I've been traveling a lot these last

few years, but I'm ready to settle down. Write
anytime. Send family photos. I'm a good correspondent.

"I think this goes directly to his behavior while
incarcerated." Add ten points, I thought. There aren't
many other ways to act out your interest in child abuse
from behind bars.

"What I would like to do, Your Honor," I went on,
"is to keep this defendant in state prison for another
twenty years. Unfortunately, he has served the maximum sentence that the court was able to impose for
these crimes, and with his good time factored in, he
will be eligible for parole by February tenth. It is
imperative, I think, that he be re-rated as a Level Three
offender, with all the attendant consequences."

"If you're done, Ms. Cooper, I think I would like to
hear from Dr. Hoppins. Would you please call your witness to the stand, sir?"

Suggs was trying to get Abramson's attention. He
was angered by my remarks and clearly agitated.
Abramson ignored his client. "I'd like a few minutes
to talk with my witness." He turned and walked out
of the well, as the judge announced a five-minute
break and stepped off the bench to go to her robing
room.

I reached for my pad to draw up a list of questions
for cross-examination. With a deafening crash, Suggs
lifted the massive oak counsel table off the floor in

front of him and heaved it on its side. At the same time, he charged across the well and threw himself at me with outstretched arms, screaming my name and spitting as he came flying through the air. Court officers rushed from every direction to grab for a piece of the prisoner and subdue him, while the captain of the team picked me up from the floor, where I had landed when Suggs's body collided with my own.

Chapman vaulted over the railing and helped the guys lead the laughing pedophile back into the holding pens.

"You okay? Did he hit you?"

I sat at the table and tried to will myself to stop shaking. "I'm fine. He just bounced himself off me."

"And here I thought you were way too old to be *my* type, no less his. You're safer in the field with me and my murderers than with these pervs of yours. Let's go, blondie."

Mike picked up my folders and we started out of the courtroom, while Abramson and Hoppins followed us down the aisle.

"Hey, Alex. Don't hold that flying tackle against *me*," Bobby urged. "I'll just adjourn the case till the middle of next month. Have Ryan or Rich stand up on it for you next time. They won't collapse like a house of cards."

"Thanks, Bobby, I'll be sure to do that."

"Ms. Cooper? May I have a word with you?" Hoppins asked.

"Some other time, doc," Mike said as he prodded me toward the door, away from her.

"It has to do with King's College, Detective. You both might want to hear it."

11

Hoppins followed us into the hallway to an alcove near the elevator bank.

"You handled a case several years back, Ms. Cooper. David Fillian, do you remember him?"

"Of course." Fillian was a street kid from Manhattan with a serious cocaine habit who supported himself by selling drugs to the rich prep school students of Carnegie Hill and upscale collegians. One night, after delivering a load of blow to a senior in one of the Columbia College dorms, he partied with his customer, who let him sleep over. When everyone had fallen asleep, Fillian prowled the dormitory halls, looking for things to steal. In one suite, he accidentally awakened a girl during the theft, who resisted and struggled when he tried to assault her. Fillian stabbed her in the chest, leaving her for dead. A roommate's quick response and the surgical team at St. Luke's saved her life.

"I've been doing some of the offender counseling in state prison. Fillian's in my program. You probably know that he wants to become a CI for the department."

Confidential informants—CIs—were a staple of narcotics investigations. Fillian had been hammered by the judge at his sentence, as we requested, and had been trying everything possible to reduce the time he spent in jail. I hoped no power on earth could speed his release.

"Hard to be useful to cops with current street news when you're as far north as Dannemora." He was incarcerated just miles away from the Canadian border.

"Some of the kids he ran with still keep in touch with him. He thinks he's in the know. Anyway, he's been telling me that one of the King's College professors has been selling drugs to the students—a regular candy shop. You ask for it, the prof's got it."

"Who is it? What's the guy's name?" Chapman asked.

"I don't have a name for you. There was no point in my asking him for the information, since I couldn't do anything with it professionally, and it has nothing to do with the treatment program. David was just complaining to me that nobody in the correction department seemed to be interested in the fact. I see from the papers that you've got this murder case, and also that one of the students with—shall we say, an alternative lifestyle?—disappeared last spring."

"How often do you see Fillian?"

"I'm not due to see him again until the end of January. I spend one week a month traveling around to the maximum-security jails, supervising the sex offender groups. I thought that if, perhaps, David had some valuable information to help you on the King's College cases, you could support his request for an early release to parole."

It was my devout wish that Fillian's parole officer had not yet been born. And I doubted that an occasional session, up close and personal, exchanging techniques with other convicted rapists had "cured" him of his habits. I was anxious to dismiss Hoppins and get on to our more immediate work. "We'll see if we can get him produced at a prison downstate to interview him. If he doesn't have any more details than this, he won't be much use to us."

We thanked her and walked away. I'm sure she detected the chill in my voice, as I questioned the sincerity of her patient's bona fides.

Joe Roman was waiting for us when we reached my office. "You still have that photo of the Denzig girl?" he asked.

"Sure. It's attached to her folder, on my desk."

"Talk about archaeological digs," Mike said, shaking Joe's hand. "That's what the pile on your desk looks like."

I flipped through the manila case jackets till I found Shirley Denzig's file. "What did you learn from the Baltimore cops?"

"That her papa has a licensed handgun. Kept it in a locked storage box in his garage. Sometime during the week he noticed it had been taken, so he reported it to the local detectives. I'm going to have copies of this photo made to give to Security downstairs here and to keep with the doormen at your building. Bad news is, she finally was evicted from her apartment. Captain's going to let Frankie and me work on it. See if we can find her and tell her what a lovely person you really are."

"Remember that Shirley's not wrong about herself. She doesn't look that good anymore. Tell them to add seventy or eighty pounds to that image, okay?"

"You're doing something wrong, Alex. It's supposed to be the bad guys who are after us, not the victims," Joe said, shaking his finger at me as he walked out of the room.

"Wanna fill me in?" Mike asked.

"I'll tell you later. Just an old complainant resurfacing when I need her least."

I dialed Ryan Blackmer's number. I needed more information about the assault near Washington Square Park. "Hey, I wanted to catch you before I go up to the college. Did your NYU graduate student show up for her interview?"

"Not only did she come in, but she recanted the entire story. Hope it's okay with you, but I locked her up. Filing a false report."

"What's the deal?"

"The girl was frantic when she got here. She had made the whole thing up. Her last exam was supposed to be this morning, and she had two major papers due before the winter recess. She just couldn't cope, so she figured if she told the dean she'd been accosted on the street and was too traumatized to finish the semester, she wouldn't flunk the courses. They'd let her make up the work in January."

"And for *that* she identified somebody out of the blue and actually had him locked in jail overnight?" The fabricated reports of assault were the most pernicious actions I could imagine women taking.

"Yeah. Claims she never expected the police to take her seriously, and by the time they had driven around for almost an hour, she felt like she owed it to them to pick out somebody."

"How's the poor guy doing?"

"I released him without bail the other night. The cops thought she was flaky from the get-go, and they called his employer, who backed him one hundred percent. Did I do the right thing by having her arrested?"

"You always do the right thing. See you later."

Laura buzzed me on the intercom. "There's someone named Gloria Reitman on the phone. Says to tell you she knew Professor Dakota, and she's supposed to meet with you at school."

"This is Alexandra Cooper. Ms. Reitman?"

"Thanks for taking my call. Ms. Foote asked me to

talk to you. I was just wondering if you'd mind meeting with me at the law school building, over at Columbia? I'm a first-year there. But I knew Professor Dakota. I'd just be more comfortable alone, not being asked questions in front of all the administrative types at King's. Can you do that?"

"No problem. We were supposed to be in Ms. Foote's office at two."

"If you come a little earlier, I can meet you at one-thirty. I'll be in the Drapkin Lounge. We can talk privately there."

The scene on College Walk was a lot calmer now than it had been last week. The campus seemed almost deserted, emptied of the students who had moved so briskly down the library steps and between buildings the last time we were here. Mike and I entered the law school and asked the guard for the meeting room that had been named, undoubtedly, in honor of some fat-cat generous alumnus.

Gloria walked toward us and introduced herself. "We've actually met before. Not that I expect you to remember, but I heard you speak at the public service lecture you did here last year." She smiled at Mike as she shook his hand, then looked back at me, blushing slightly with embarrassment. Brunette ringlets framed her narrow face. "The reason I came to law school is because I've always wanted to be a prosecutor. In your office."

She had arranged some chairs in a corner of the

room, and we sat together to talk. "The dean went through the lists of Professor Dakota's classes from the last two years and picked a few of us to talk to you. Of course, lots of the students have already gone home. I don't know how many are still here."

Gloria took a deep breath, apparently having difficulty saying what came next.

"The easiest way for me to start off is to tell you straight out that I hated Professor Dakota. Despised her. Shall I go on, or are there specific questions you want to ask me?"

I tried not to show my surprise. I didn't want to stifle what might be a candid portrait from an intelligent source. "Why don't you just tell us everything you think we should know, and we'll take it from there."

"Professor Dakota joined the faculty at King's during my junior year, from Columbia. All my friends who'd studied with her there thought the world of her. Brilliant scholar, great instructor. Told me not to miss the chance to get to know her. I even sat in the back of her classroom once or twice the first semester 'cause everyone raved about how she brought the past to life. I had a double major at King's—history and poli-sci—so it was a natural for me to sign up for her courses. It almost cost me admission to law school."

That was about the same time that I, too, had first met Lola Dakota. Maybe her domestic problems had created a change in her nature. I knew that kind of stress could alter a victim's entire personality.

"Second semester, junior year. 'Gotham Government—New York City, 1850 to 1950.' Sounded good to me, and I needed it for my major credits. I worked like a dog on my research paper. It may seem immodest, Miss Cooper, but I hadn't had a grade below A-minus since I started college. I was terrified about getting into a good law school, coming from King's, since it's so experimental, without any record of achievement by its students. All I could do was try to get as close to a four-point-oh grade average as possible, and study hard for my law boards.

"Dakota gave me a D. Only one I'd ever had in my life."

"Shit. I used to go home with one of those every semester. Stood for Damn Good, I told my old man." Chapman was giving her the full press now, putting her at ease, so he could ferret out whatever she had to tell us.

How could I measure her complaint? Every disgruntled student who'd ever fallen short wanted to blame the teacher for the grade. "Did you appeal it?"

"The dean of students almost drowned in appeals from Dakota's classes. She'd pick one or two pets for the semester—usually guys—and the rest of us would struggle to stay on board. We used to joke that she had a twenty-four-character alphabet, which began with the letter C."

Mike leaned forward, one elbow on his knee, supporting his chin in his hand. "Did you know she was in the middle of a pretty ugly marital situation at the time? That her husband had—"

"I didn't know she was still married till I read the story in the obituary. We thought she was having an affair with another faculty member."

Mike stayed focused on Gloria's face. "Who was that?"

"Oh, no one in particular. You know how college students are. Anytime we saw two of them together in the faculty lounge, or she showed up five minutes late for class, rumors would spread. Goofy stuff, and we knew it."

"Like what kind of rumors? What names do you remember?"

"One week it might have been Professor Lockhart—he teaches American history. Then it was one of the science guys—biochem, I think. I can picture his nerdy little face—wire-rimmed glasses with urine-colored lenses. When Recantati showed up this fall to take the temporary presidency, some of my friends thought she was slobbering all over him. Every now and then someone tossed a student's name into the mix."

"But did you hate her as much before you got the lousy grade?"

"There was something very mean-spirited about her. In the classroom, actually. She loved performing, so we'd be mesmerized during lectures. All the detail she had and her willingness to give it to us so openly. But then she'd snap into a rage for no reason at all, especially on the days that we had to make presentations. Maybe some of the kids weren't as smart as her students used to be at Columbia. Maybe she took out on us the fact that she'd been asked to leave that faculty and start up a program at King's.

"But there was no excuse for the way Professor Dakota made fools out of us. Made students stand up for ten or fifteen minutes at a clip, firing questions at us about obscure political events of 1893. Questions nobody could answer unless you'd gone beyond the course materials and guessed correctly which year she might focus on that particular day. She reduced a couple of my classmates to tears, and she seemed to enjoy doing that. That sign on Dakota's door—BAD-LANDS? She relished that reputation."

"Was Charlotte Voight one of those students? Was she in your class?"

"Who?"

"A junior, the one who disappeared from school last April."

"Never heard of her."

"What do you know about the drug scene there?"

"Like every other college campus, it was huge. Just happens not to be my thing, but you can find plenty of people to talk to about that."

"D'you have anything to do with the dig that Professor Dakota was working on, on Roosevelt Island?"

"No, but Skip knows about that. Professor Lockhart."

Gloria blushed again, this time as though she had slipped in a too familiar reference.

"The one you said Dakota was rumored to be involved with?"

She twisted the ringlets behind her right ear. "Well, that's one rumor I know wasn't true. I mean, *I* was involved with Skip, junior year. We were sort of having an affair."

That helped account for the A in American history, I guessed. "Mind telling us about him?"

"I mean, he was single. There wasn't anything wrong with it." Gloria was looking at Mike for approval now. She seemed proud of herself, in that foolish way that girls sometimes are when they take a lover under inappropriate circumstances. "But I'd been seeing him since the summer after my sophomore year. That's why I confronted him about the stories that he and Professor Dakota were involved." She looked so earnest. "I guess I was jealous."

"What did he tell you?"

"Not to be ridiculous. Skip told me that he used to spend a lot of time with her, because their intellectual interests were the same. But he said she was a real gold digger. Not his type at all."

"What did he mean, gold digger? Was that his word for her, or yours?" From what I had learned during my initial investigation of Lola's marital situation, she seemed to have a very comfortable nest egg of her own. She had invested her money intelligently, with Ivan's professional assistance at first, through all the years of their marriage. She didn't seem to have a penchant for jewelry or fancy clothes, as I had observed in our many meetings, and it was obvious that she hadn't spent big dollars on decorating her new apartment.

"It was something like that. Treasure hunter. Gold digger. That's all I could get out of him, really. You can ask Skip yourself. I'm sure you'll be speaking with him. He's part of that multidisciplinary project they were working on at some old loony bin. Just don't tell him I told you about our relationship, okay? The administration wouldn't approve."

"So what was the buzz on campus before everyone left town? Who killed Lola Dakota?"

"I went to the service on Friday night. Not 'cause I was heartbroken about the professor. But a lot of my old friends were going to be there, so we figured we'd go out together before everybody split town.

"By midnight, after a few drinks, we all began to look guilty to each other." Gloria laughed. "A few of my friends—the ones who'd done well in class— defended her. The rest of us had gripes to air and stories to tell. A lot of guys figure it's just some bum from the neighborhood who knocked her off. Everybody worries about getting mugged up here. It's a constant problem, on campus and off. One guy was a suitemate of that kid who hanged himself the next night. Julian? You know who he is? That's how I heard about Lola and her crazy husband."

"Heard what?"

"Apparently Julian used to brag about being on Ivan Kralovic's payroll. That the husband paid him for information about Professor Dakota—what her hours were, when she was at her office, where she had moved, when she was out in the field on her new project. In fact, that's the reason some of the guys think Julian hanged himself. That he didn't realize Kralovic wanted the information so he could kill his wife. Julian just thought he was harassing her. And believe me, there were plenty of people on campus who wanted her harassed."

I was thinking out loud, directing my question to Mike. "Where in the world do you think Julian Gariano would have crossed the path of Ivan Kralovic?"

"Not hard to figure," Gloria responded. "My friend was there the day they met. Julian's dad had just hired a lawyer to handle his drug case. Turned out to be Ivan Kralovic's defense attorney, too. They met in the waiting room at the lawyer's office. Julian was wearing a King's College sweatshirt. Said Kralovic started asking him a million questions. That same night, back in the dorm room, Professor Dakota's husband called to talk to Julian again. Offered him a ton of money to rat on his wife. There was nothing Julian wouldn't do for money. He didn't think anyone would get hurt."

Mike gave Gloria his card. "Call me if you hear anything else." We thanked her and walked back across

Amsterdam Avenue, passing the car and continuing on to keep our appointment with Sylvia Foote at the King's building on Claremont Avenue.

This time, she was expecting us. I suspected it gave her a good deal of pleasure to tell us that she had been unable to comply with our request to have students lined up ready to talk with us. "You know what this season means to so many families. Despite my best efforts, most of the young people from out of town wanted to keep to their plans and get home to their folks. I've got a few local students here, and you're welcome to use my deputy counsel's office now."

She smiled wanly and I guessed she had sanitized their stories pretty well.

Mike had opened his notepad and was ticking off his new requests. "We'll move on to the permanent residents, Ms. Foote, faculty and administration. Here's a list of the people I'd like to see tomorrow. At *my* office. Let's start with the acting president, Mr. Recantati. I'd like Professor Lockhart—he's the historian, right?—and Professor Shreve, from anthropology, and the heads of each department involved in the project Professor Dakota was working on. I want—"

"I'm just not certain of the availability of these people on such short notice."

"Coop, have you got any paper with you?"

I opened my folder and removed several grand jury subpoenas. Foote knew exactly what that meant. "They can be in Detective Chapman's office in the morning, or they can come directly to the courthouse at the end of the week and be questioned by me, under oath, before the grand jury. Their call, Sylvia." I scribbled in the names and dates while Chapman kept talking.

Foote ushered us into a small room adjacent to her own. For the rest of the afternoon, we saw a stream of young adults who attended King's College and lived in the five boroughs or surrounding suburbs. Most of them acted as though they would rather be boarding the *Titanic* than talking to a detective and prosecutor. Not one of them admitted to having any personal knowledge about Lola Dakota or Charlotte Voight. Drugs were everywhere on campus, they seemed to agree, but none of these kids had ever inhaled and didn't know who the dealers or steerers were.

One of the last to straggle in was a senior who had lived on the same floor as Charlotte during the spring semester. Kristin Baymer was also twenty. Her home was a Fifth Avenue apartment, where her father and stepmother were raising her infant half brother. She parked herself on the sofa opposite the desk at which I had been working and curled up with her knees underneath her, stifling a yawn as she greeted us.

"I'm not gonna get in trouble for this, am I?"

"Depends what you did," Mike said, trying to apply his charm, along with his best grin and most collegiate affect.

"Drugs. You probably know that I was on academic

probation sophomore year. Got caught with some pills. Amphetamines, tranquilizers. That kind of stuff."

"We're not here on a drug bust, Kristin. We've got a murder to solve and a girl to find. Hey, I'd like it if nobody stuck needles in their arms or snorted coke, but I'm not the Vice Squad. What you say to us about any of that stays right in this room."

Foote hadn't given us the student files, so we hadn't known Kristin's background. She looked too wasted and too tired to worry about whom she could trust. She just started talking.

"Charlotte and I had a lot in common. Both loners, both stubborn, both enjoyed getting high. My mom died a few years ago, like hers. And my father married my big brother's girlfriend. My stepmother's two years older than I am, and now I've got an eight-month-old brother. Classy, huh? And they call *me* dysfunctional."

"Did you and Charlotte spend a lot of time together?"

"Only when we were doing drugs. Otherwise, neither one of us was very sociable."

"Did she have a favorite? Not person. I mean drug of choice."

"Charlotte? She'd try almost anything. Pills were nothing for her. She'd take ups when she was depressed. Then she'd get so manic she needed something to bring her down. She liked cocaine a lot. And heroin."

Heroin had ravaged the drug users in urban America

throughout the sixties and seventies. It had rarely appealed to young women, experts thought, because so many of them were averse to injecting themselves in the arm and developing track marks. The late nineties saw a surge of heroin use, with a new and potent strain that could be snorted and smoked, just like the more fashionable cocaine.

Kristin was biting at a hangnail now, twisting the torn skin between her teeth. "And Ecstasy. That girl loved her Ecstasy." She said it like an endorsement for cornflakes. Good old wholesome Ecstasy.

The pills, originally patented by the E. Merck pharmaceutical company in Germany, in 1914, were now made in Holland, Belgium, and Israel. They were being smuggled into the States in enormous quantities and had taken over the drug scene faster than any substance tracked before. The euphoric condition Ecstasy produces, along with its reputation for enhancing sexual enjoyment, made it hugely popular among young adults. The tablets stimulate the nervous system like speed, but at the same time create a sense of well-being and an almost hallucinogenic haze. So new on the scene that it wasn't even a controlled substance in New York until 1997, it was now a staple on high school and college campuses.

"Where'd you get it? The Ecstasy, I mean."

"Are you kidding? It's easier than getting a pack of Marlboros. Kids need proof of age for cigarettes these days. Ecstasy's everywhere." Kristin smiled.

"It's expensive, isn't it?" I thought the pills went for at least thirty dollars a pop. Fine for models and stockbrokers, but tough on a college allowance.

"Charlotte used to call my prep school friends 'Trustafarians.' No shortage of funds for a good time. My dad would rather send me money to keep me away from home than have me bitching about his wife all the time." She looked Mike up and down, then switched her scrutiny to me. "I don't know when either of you was last in a bar in Manhattan. But a Cosmopolitan costs nine bucks per drink. I can get the same buzz off one Ecstasy that it takes me five cocktails to match. Do the math.

"Besides, Charlotte was sleeping with Julian for the better part of a year. When you're putting out for the guy who's dealing the pills, there's an endless supply."

"Were you close to Julian, too?"

Now she was picking at her lavender nail polish. "Never slept with him. Didn't have to. Like I said, I could afford to buy most things that I wanted."

"What was he like?"

Kristin shrugged her shoulders and went on flaking off the chips. "He was an okay guy. He actually seemed to care about Charlotte. Maybe that's why she dumped him. I don't think she liked anybody getting that close to her."

"Did she leave him for someone else?" Mike asked.

"What's the difference?"

"'Cause maybe she's still alive. Maybe someone can help us find her."

"Some of us figure she doesn't want to be found. Just went off to lead her own life." Kristin's cavalier attitude about Charlotte's disappearance was disturbing.

"Did you know Professor Dakota?"

"Only by reputation."

"But Charlotte was a friend of the professor's, wasn't she?"

"No way," Kristin said, looking at me as if I were crazy.

"What makes you so sure?"

"Fall semester, last year, okay? Charlotte flunked Dakota's class. Capital F in some bullshit course about the mayoralty in New York, La Guardia to Lindsay. Set her off in a complete funk. It was one thing for her to sweet-talk a guy like Julian into feeding her pills, but if she was kicked out of King's, then she'd have no choice but to go home to South America. Tuition was the only thing her father would pay for. No frills. If she wasn't at college, hasta la vista, sweet Charlotte. You two look surprised."

"I am a bit surprised," Mike led off. "Lola Dakota kept a bulletin board behind her desk. Had some pictures of her relatives, had some snapshots of famous people. But she also had a photograph of Charlotte Voight. Like something from a freshman mug book. We just assumed it meant she took an interest in the girl. Cared about her. Missed her."

Kristin nipped at her raw skin again. "Julian would

have keeled over at that one. He used to tell Charlotte that Dakota would get what was coming to her someday. I just thought he was being macho for her sake. Never thought anyone would kill the SOB. Must be some other reason that Charlotte's picture's on her board."

"Who else can we talk to about Charlotte?" I asked. "There must have been other people she confided in about her plans. You don't just disappear into thin air."

"Can't think of a soul. I was the last person to see her alive, far as I know."

"Where was that?"

"I was coming into the lobby of the dorm about eight-thirty at night. She was on her way out, going to Julian's. She never got there. Must have changed her mind. Found another source."

"Did she seem to be in distress? Unhappy? De—"

"Nope. She seemed just fine. Cheerful almost. I asked her if she wanted to come up to my room to do a few lines with me. Charlotte laughed and said she had a better offer. She was going to the lab."

"Where's that?"

"That's what she used to call Julian's room. If he didn't have what you wanted, just wait ten minutes and he'd cook it up for you," Kristin said, obviously pleased by the memory. "He was wasting his time in the criminal justice department. He should have been a science major."

Chapman was disgusted. "Better living through chemistry," he said, looking at his watch.

"Anyway, Charlotte walked out the door and I never saw her again. I just assumed she was partying over at the lab."

12

I rang the bell at the Kramer-Rothschild town house shortly before 7:30 p.m. Nan opened the door and I introduced her to Mike Chapman.

"We might as well go upstairs to my study. All the information about our project is there. I've lost my husband to a new client this evening. He's working late." We declined her offer of a drink and followed her up to the second floor.

"Could I trouble you for a television, ma'am?"

"Let's stop in the den first, then," she said, leading us around the corner and clicking on the set. "Something breaking on the news about your case?"

"No. Alex and I have a standing bet on the *Final Jeopardy!* question. It'll only take a few minutes."

We caught up on small talk while we waited for Mike to find the station and then for the commercial to end. Trebek was reminding the three players that tonight's category was Famous Firsts.

"Twenty bucks, Coop. Could be anything."

"Be generous, in the spirit of Christmas. Make it forty."

Trebek stepped aside and the answer was revealed on the screen. "First woman in America to receive a medical degree."

"I'm toast, blondie. I can never beat her on this feminist trivia, Nan. Probably right up your alley, too."

Neither Chapman nor the flight attendant from Wisconsin even ventured a guess. "Who was Elizabeth Blackwell?" I asked, before the Maine fisherwoman or the Virginia enologist gave their wrong answers.

"Sorry, sorry, sorry, folks," Trebek said, chiding the three contestants for their failure to come up with the right answer. "Born in England, Elizabeth Blackwell immigrated to this country and in 1849, she became the first woman in the United States to get a medical degree, at Geneva Medical College in New York. So let's see how much money that leaves—"

"The Blackwell family settled on Martha's Vineyard after that. Right near my place in Chilmark."

"Not a bad lead-in to my story," Nan said, as Mike clicked off the television and we walked down the hall to her home office. "This dig we're working at is over on Roosevelt Island. But it wasn't given that name until 1973. Before that it was Welfare Island, and in the period we're studying, it was called Blackwells Island. Different Blackwells, of course. This piece of land was owned by a colonial merchant named Robert

Blackwell, whose family lived there in the 1680s. Their original wooden farmhouse is still standing."

"And before that," Mike interrupted, "the Dutch called it Hog Island. It was a pig farm in the early 1600s. Covered with swine."

"You two will be light-years ahead of me," I explained to Nan. "Mike knows more about American history than anyone I've ever met. The fact that he's familiar with the island probably means it had some significance in military life. That's his real specialty."

Nan shrugged her shoulders. "Not that I'm aware of."

Mike lifted a ruler from Nan's desk and pointed to the southern tip of Manhattan on the huge map of the city she had pinned to the wall. "In 1673, when the British and Dutch were still at war, the sheriff of New York was a guy named Manning. The Brits put him in charge of the fort down at this end, the entrance to New York Harbor. The Dutch launched a naval assault to regain control of what had once been their colony, New Amsterdam. Manning surrendered without a battle. So King Charles court-martialed the disgraced commander and banished him rather than put him to death." He moved the pointer up to a place in the East River, halfway between Manhattan and Queens. "He was exiled to your little island to live the rest of his life."

Nan responded, "It's always been a place for exiles. For outcasts. That's part of its tragic background. Do you know much about it?"

"Nothing at all. I look at it just about every day, on my way up and down the Drive. It can't be more than the length of a football field away from Manhattan, and yet I've never set foot there. When you see it at night, there's a hauntingly romantic look to it."

"It's got a wonderfully romantic aura, I agree with you completely. It's a bit like the Ile de la Cité, in the heart of Paris. A sliver of land, in a river, right in the midst of a great city. And a quiet, small-town pace that makes you think you're in a private enclave, not an urban neighborhood. It's even more dramatic from the heart of the island. You get to see the magnificent skyline of Manhattan from every angle, and then off to the other side, there's the industrial backdrop of Queens that lines the river's edge—factories, smokestacks, and barges.

"Let me tell you what the project is, and what Lola Dakota's involvement was with us."

Nan took the pointer from Mike's hand and began her description of the river-bound fragment of land. "The island is two miles long and just eight hundred feet wide. See? It parallels Manhattan from Eighty-fifth Street, on its northern tip, to Forty-eighth Street in the south. That lower border of land is directly opposite the United Nations. Great views.

"Today, it's got several high-rise residential structures, parks, two hospitals for the chronically ill, a tramway that connects it to Manhattan, and a footbridge that links it to Queens. But what fascinates some of us most are its bones."

"Skeletons?," Chapman asked.

"Not human ones. The remnants of the unusual buildings that dominated the landscape here a hundred years ago—well, almost two hundred years ago. As New York grew into a metropolis, it experienced all the social problems and ills that we connect with urban America today—crime, poverty, disease, mental illness. By 1800, the city fathers came up with the idea of walled institutions to confine the sources of trouble. The compound at Bellevue housed contagious yellow-fever patients and syphilitics, and Newgate Prison, in Greenwich Village, was home to rapists and highway robbers."

"My kind of town." Chapman was riveted.

"And did you know that 116th Street and Broadway was the original site of the Bloomingdale Asylum for the Insane?"

"A nuthouse, right where Columbia stands today?" Mike asked. "Now why doesn't *that* surprise me?"

"Then it occurred to these urban planners that they didn't need to use the valuable real estate of Manhattan to segregate their untouchables. There were a number of small islands that would relieve the growing city of its criminals and its crazies. So they looked to the river for property to acquire—to Wards and Randall Islands, to North and South Brother Islands, to Rikers and Hart Islands"—her pointer moved across the riverscape—"and the very first one the city purchased, in 1828, was Blackwells.

"From a bucolic family farm, the island was immediately transformed into a village of institutions. Enormous structures, forbidding and secure. A penitentiary, an almshouse for the poor, a charity hospital—"

"That wonderful Gothic building that you see from Manhattan? The one that looks like a castle?"

"No, Alex. That one came a bit later, for a different purpose. And then, of course, there's *my* pet. The Octagon—the lunatic asylum that was built to replace Bloomingdale's."

Nan walked to her desk chair and opened a drawer, removing from it an oversize notebook with sepia-toned blowups of old photographs. "The asylum was designed to be the largest in the country. It had arteries stretching out in every direction—one to house the most violent of the patients, another for females, a third for the foreign insane."

"Wasn't everyone a foreigner?" Mike asked.

"I think it's always the case, Detective, that some are more alien than others. Did you know that whenever an immigrant was found alone in the streets, unable to communicate because of the language barrier, our benign forefathers just placed him in the asylum until someone could make out what he was saying?

"The other discouraging thing about this place was that there was a very small medical staff. The patients were actually cared for by prisoners from the penitentiaries. I can only imagine the abuses."

"Is the asylum still there?" I asked, studying the photo images of the primitive outbuildings.

"All those wings are gone. What remains today are the ruins of the Octagon Tower. It's a stunning rotunda, built in the Greek Revival style, with an elegant winding staircase, all columned and pedestaled." She showed me the interior photographs, which looked like a shot up five spiraling flights of cast-iron steps. "It was once considered the most elegant staircase in New York. Now that broken frame climbs up to the open sky. Completely deteriorated and neglected."

"I guess the theory of the day was to treat the inmates like animals, but do it with charm."

"Exactly. There were vegetable gardens and willow trees and an ice-skating pond so that the external appearance seemed like an oasis of calm and care. But within the walls, it was truly a madhouse."

"What interests you about it? Why the dig?"

"It's everything an urban anthropologist craves. There aren't many places to burrow into in Manhattan these days, much as I'd like to. This offers a very confined site with a fair amount of known history. We've got records of an early Indian settlement there, before the Colonials came to America. We're already finding those artifacts—tools, pottery, weapons. Then you have the agricultural community which existed there for another century.

"And, of course, the asylum years, for most of the nineteenth century. Remember, many of these patients who were not indigent went there with all their possessions. They were served on china plates, not the tin cups of their almshouse neighbors. When these buildings were all abandoned, much of this stuff got left behind, buried in place. Scores of dignitaries visited the island to see this innovative social welfare setup, and some of them, including de Tocqueville, wrote about it extensively.

"You really must—both of you—come out to see how we work and what we've found. The dig is at a bit of a standstill with this frigid weather we're having, but I can have one of the students tour you around the Octagon. The whole island, if you like."

"We'll take you up on that offer. But we'd also like to talk to you about Lola Dakota, Nan."

"I'll tell you the little that I know," she said, sitting down at her desk and motioning us to take seats opposite her. "Of course, I first met Lola when she was on the Columbia faculty. Bit of a wild card, personally, but a talented scholar."

"Did you socialize with her?"

"Not much. Without even knowing about their marital problems, Howard never trusted Ivan very much. He always seemed to be hustling people. Looking for the quick score. We were occasionally invited to the same dinner party, but the four of us never spent any time together."

There was something different about the tone of Nan's responses when she talked about Lola. She did not seem quite as open as she had when discussing the history of New York.

"Were you here for the funeral?"

"No. No, I left for London on Friday evening. That was the day she was killed, wasn't it? I didn't learn of her death until one of Howard's phone calls." She fumbled with paper clips in the top drawer of her desk.

"We've only spoken to one of her sisters and a couple of students. What was she like as a colleague or peer?"

"Well, her style was a lot flashier than my own. I wouldn't say that we had much in common." Nan was a brilliant scholar, nationally renowned in her field, and as modest as she was good. "But one-on-one, she was perfectly pleasant to work with. She never confided in me, if that's what you mean. I don't think I had seen her in more than a year after she moved to King's College. It was the Blackwells Island project that brought me into contact with her again."

"How did that get started?" Mike asked.

Nan looked at the ceiling and laughed. "Several years of wishful thinking on my part. Hard to remember which of us pushed the idea forward first. Let's see. Winston Shreve helped to organize the plan. He's the head of the anthropology department at King's."

"Have you known him long?"

"Fifteen years. Very impressive credentials, which is why they recruited him for the school. Undergrad and graduate degrees are both Ivy League, if I remember correctly. Spent some time at the Sorbonne. Helped with the excavations at Petra. He's wanted to do something on the island for as long as I have. Like me, one of those New Yorkers in our profession who's always wanted to get his hands in some local dirt, but just keeps watching apartments and office towers get planted on top of every square inch of historical soil that we covet.

"Yes, Winston and I have been talking about digging on the island for as long as I've known him."

"And the others?"

"It was a four-department program. Multidisciplinary, as they like to call it these days. Something for everybody. We each seem to have a special place on the island that attracts us for a different reason. Winston and I run the anthropological courses. My favorite site is the northern tip, from the lighthouse to what remains of the Octagon Tower. Skip Lockhart chairs the American history segment. His heart seems to be attached to the people who passed through here, their stories and what became of them. Thomas Grenier is in charge of the biology students."

That's a name we hadn't heard yet. "Who's Grenier?" Mike asked.

"King's College. Head of the biology department there. Out of UCLA, if I remember correctly. Haven't seen him around in weeks, but I think it's because he's been on sabbatical this semester. Might not even be in town." Mike was writing the name in his notepad.

"Why biology?" I asked.

"The scientific piece is as important as all the digging we're doing. Maybe more so. By the 1870s there were almost a dozen medical facilities here. Every 'incurable' patient from the city was sent to a hospital or clinic on Blackwells. One was for scarlet fever, another for epilepsy, a separate place for cripples, for cholera and typhus sufferers. There were tuberculosis facilities, and a special building for lepers. It even had the first pathology laboratory in the country.

"Then there came your ruin, Alex. Eighteen fifty-six, to be exact. Smallpox continued to be a societal scourge throughout the nineteenth century."

"What about Jenner? I thought there was already a smallpox vaccine by that time."

"Yes, the vaccine was being used in America by then, but the constant influx of poor immigrants who had been infected in their own countries brought the disease here from all over the world. Because it was so wildly contagious, patients in New York City had always been quarantined away from the population. They were generally sent to live in wooden shacks on the banks of the two rivers, until it became even safer to ship them off to the island of undesirables."

"Blackwells?"

She nodded. "Renwick designed a stunning home for those latest outcasts. The Smallpox Hospital. You see it lighted up so dramatically at night from Manhattan, with its pointed, arched windows and crenellated roofline. A great gray monument to disease. Small wonder the biologists want to study the place."

Nan moved to the giant map and ran her finger up the narrow piece of waterway that separated Manhattan from the grim institutions of the old Blackwells Island. "How are you on Greek mythology?" she asked. "The River Styx, Lola used to say this was. Souls crossing over from the realm of the living on their way to hell. To what she called the deadhouse."

13

"What *was* the deadhouse?"

"Just Lola's name for Blackwells Island, I guess. It was a nineteenth-century expression that meant a place for dead bodies."

"Did she refer to it that way?"

"I know you had met her, Alex. She had this tremendous flair for the dramatic. Used it to great advantage in the classroom whenever things got dull. We were all brainstorming about the dig one night—I think we were downstairs in my own dining room—going through a pretty good case of red wine—and that's when I heard Lola use the expression for the first time."

"Was it an actual place on the island?"

"Not on any map that I've ever come across. Imagine the scene, as Lola used to say. There you were, raging with fever and blistering with pustulant sores, as epidemics swept through communities in the crowded city dwellings. Smallpox was spread both by direct contact and by airborne virus, as you probably know. Public-health workers separated out the ill and infected—rich and poor alike—to isolate them from the able-bodied."

The image of a plague-ridden city was chilling.

"Then, Lola would describe the bedlam on the piers in the East River as the afflicted were loaded onto boats to bring them over to the hospital. Most of them knew that for the diseased, it was a sentence of death. Some tried to escape from the officials at the docks. From time to time, one or two dared to jump in the water and brave the fierce currents of the East River rather than be ferried to hell. The once tranquil farmland had become a zone for the dead and dying. Boats went out loaded with contagious patients. As these untouchables neared the shore, their first sight was the stacks of wooden coffins piled by the edge to be loaded on for the ride home. Chances were good that if your destination was Blackwells Island, as Lola said, you were going to the deadhouse."

We were silent until Mike spoke.

"So she had the fourth piece of the project? Government, political science."

"Exactly."

"Any particular interests, like some of you others?"

"Lola had a special preoccupation, I'd say, with the prison and the madhouse. Disease and the hospital conditions revolted her, she said. But a lot of famous people passed in and out of both the asylum and the penitentiary, and she loved to learn their stories. I've never seen anyone do research about these places the way she did. Lola read all the books, she devoured letters and diaries of the time that were original source material, she even found some old survivors who had lived or worked on the island in the 1920s and thirties."

"Do you know who they were?"

"No, but surely someone in the department must have catalogued names. I'm too busy belowground to talk to people. We left that to Lola. As long as this place was mentioned, she didn't care whether it was the notebook of a nurse or the autobiography of Mae West—"

"I saw her do that bit in her classroom once. I thought that West was locked up in Manhattan, in the Tombs."

"One night there. Then a ten-day sentence to the workhouse on the island. Mae had it pretty cushy, for a prisoner. The warden agreed that the inmate underwear was too rough for her delicate skin and let her wear her own silk teddies and white stockings. He even took her out for horse rides in the evening.

"Lola knew all their stories. Boss Tweed, Dutch Schultz, lots of corrupt New Yorkers wound up there."

"Damn, I'd love to hear some of those tales," Mike said.

"Talk to Professor Lockhart in the history department. Or even to Paolo Recantati. The historians were tracking that kind of thing. I've got my own tales of woe from the asylum."

"What kind of guy is Recantati?" I asked.

"He was new to King's this semester. Quiet, very aloof. He was a history scholar, too, so Lola tried to engage him in our cabal, get his support for continued funding. Our goal was not only to complete the dig, but to try to get the money needed to restore these unique buildings. She brought Recantati in on a few of our meetings to hear what we were up to. I've talked with him about it several times, and he seemed quite interested."

"Were you and Lola the only two women running the show?"

Nan paused for a moment. "Yes, we were."

"Any sense of Lola's personal life? Was she involved with any of these other professors?"

"I'd probably be the last one to know. The students always seemed to be more interested in that kind of information than I was."

I showed Nan a photograph of Charlotte Voight, a copy of the one on Lola's board, which Sylvia Foote had given to me earlier in the day. "Did you know this girl, one of Lola's students? Ever see her on the island?"

Nan studied the picture and handed it back. "No help to you there. I supervised the Barnard and Columbia kids. If she went to King's College, then any one of the group we've talked about would have been working with her."

"It's puzzling why Dakota would have cared about the kid enough to hang her picture in the office. Along with Franklin Roosevelt—"

"The Roosevelt piece I can answer," Nan interjected. "FDR was one of Lola's heroes, for whom Blackwells was renamed in 1973."

"Charles Dickens?"

"No idea."

"Nellie Bly?"

"She's one of *my* inmates. Your office helped, Alex."

"We did?"

"Assistant District Attorney Henry D. Macdona, 1887. Nellie Bly was a young reporter, working for *The World,* Joseph Pulitzer's scandal-loving newspaper. Some editor had a brainstorm to expose the hideous condition of the patients in Blackwells insane asylum, and Nellie Bly volunteered for the job. Undercover, you'd call it. She actually went to the district attorney for advice, and for the promise that they would begin a grand jury investigation if she found abuses.

"So Bly checked into a women's boardinghouse, claiming to be a Cuban immigrant called Nellie Moreno. Within days of her arrival, feigning insanity and babbling in an incomprehensible tongue, she was escorted to the police station and then to court. First stop was Bellevue, where doctors ruled out the delirium of belladonna, the deadly nightshade poisoning of so many nineteenth-century mysteries, and actually declared her to be insane. On to Blackwells."

"Committed to the asylum?"

"Spent ten days there, documenting everything from the filthy ferry that brought her over, to the vicious prison attendants from the penitentiary who choked and beat their patients, to the baths that consisted of buckets of ice water being thrown on her head, to the descriptions of the perfectly sane women who were just sent away because they couldn't be understood. 'Inside the Madhouse' made a pretty compelling story in the *World,* and then your office exposed the whole operation."

"Did that close the asylum down as a result?"

"Certainly helped make it happen. All the mental patients were moved away from the island at the turn of the last century. My building became the first incarnation of Metropolitan Hospital."

"The one that's now on the Upper East Side?"

"Exactly right."

Mike had checked off Bly's name from his list in the steno pad. "About Lola, would you know why someone would call her a treasure seeker or gold digger?"

"That's what we all are on this project, of course." Nan smiled. "Each of us is looking for a different kind of mother lode. For me, the treasure is as simple as a stone ax or a porcelain teacup, coal boxes or ox yokes. One of my interns actually found a handful of pearls last fall."

"Pearls?"

"In those days, men were able to discipline insubordinate wives by committing them to the asylum for a spell."

Chapman winked at me, nodding his head in approval.

"Some of the well-to-do women sewed jewels in the hems of their skirts when they were sent to Blackwells, hoping to buy favors from their keepers. Or perhaps their escape. I've got one volunteer on the project, Efrem Zavislan, who dreams of stumbling across Captain Kidd's buried gold. No one's ever found the million-dollar lode the pirate was bringing back from Madagascar to New York, before his capture. Talk to Efrem, he spent lots of time with Lola. She sure wasn't interested in my kind of booty.

"My view of it is that if all those prisoners were digging for years, and they didn't come up with any treasure, then there's none here to be found."

"What were the prisoners digging?"

"Every inch of the place. The island's bedrock is gneiss. Fordham gneiss. And there's lots of granite, too. From the time the penitentiary opened in 1835, until it was shut down a hundred years later, the healthier prisoners were forced to do hard labor. All of the stone for these many buildings on the island was quarried from its own land. No rock had to be brought in.

"The granite was used to build a seawall around the entire circumference. And the gneiss is what they mined to create the exteriors of the notorious Blackwells institutions. If there were treasure to be found, some miscreant would have dug it up long before now."

"This gives us a great head start, Nan. We're hoping to meet with some of the faculty members tomorrow. At least we'll have an idea about what has had all of you so absorbed."

Nan walked us down to the front door, retrieved my coat and gloves, and waved us off into the cold night air.

We made the short drive down Second Avenue and Mike stuck his laminated police department parking permit on top of his dashboard as he left the car illegally positioned in front of a bus stop near the corner of Sixty-fourth Street. "C'mon, Coop. There's not a brownie in town who'd brave this weather to stick a ticket on my wreck."

We weaved our way across the late-hour Christmas shopping traffic that was blocking the intersection and pressed through the crowd around the bar at Primola, hoping that Giuliano had not given away my eight-thirty reservation.

"*Buona sera,* Signorina Cooper. Your table will be ready in a minute. Have a drink on me, please. Fenton," he called over to the bartender, "a Dewar's on the rocks and a Ketel One, *subito.*"

People were five-deep waiting to be seated at my favorite restaurant. Most had drinks in one hand and shopping bags in the other, adding to the volume of the pack. It was too noisy to talk murder in their midst, so we relaxed with our cocktails till the maître d', Adolfo, led us to a corner table in the front of the room.

I didn't hear the chirping sound of my cell phone ringing until I had lowered myself into the chair and hung my bag over the armrest.

"Alex, can you hear me? It's Bob Thaler." The chief serologist usually started his day in the lab at 6 A.M. That he was still working at 9 P.M. meant that he had pulled out all the stops to do the testing on the Lola Dakota case. "Am I catching you at a bad time?"

"Never. Any results?" The DNA testing that had routinely taken six months to yield information when I first submitted samples to the FBI ten years ago now came back to us from the medical examiner's office in less than seventy-two hours.

"Dr. Braun and I worked on your evidence all through the weekend. I've got some preliminary answers you might want to get going with. All I'll need from you are some suspect controls, when you come up with them."

"That's Chapman's end of the deal. He's working on it."

"Dakota's vaginal swab was negative for the presence of semen. But we did find some seminal fluid on the sheets the cops sent in for testing. From a sofa bed, is what the voucher says. I worked that up and got a profile from it for you.

"The wad of gum Chapman pulled from the wastebasket in the deceased's office? Dr. Braun handled that piece. He also got a DNA sample from it. Just thought you'd like to know as soon as we confirmed them that it's a match. Whoever was sleeping in Dakota's bed is the same guy who paid a visit to her office. Does that help you?"

14

"Anybody out there blowing bubbles?" I asked, greeting Mike at the office of the Manhattan North Homicide Squad at eight-thirty Tuesday morning. I had walked up the stairs and in the rear door, near the Special Victims Unit, to avoid any members of the King's College faculty who had responded to Sylvia Foote's directive to appear to answer questions.

"It wasn't bubble gum. It was Wrigley's Spearmint. Just keep that in mind if you see any of those jaws masticating." He motioned me to sit at the table that was back-to-back with his own.

"Won't Iggy need it when she gets in?"

"Nope. Gone to Miami for Christmas."

Ignacia Bliss was one of the only women in the squad. They had tried to team her with Mike when she first arrived from the Career Criminal Apprehension Unit, but her humorless nature and plodding investigative technique were not suited to his style. The banner

189

he had hung over her desk more than a year ago was still tacked to the windowsill: IGNORANCE IS BLISS.

"Who's here to chat with us?"

"Only got three. The rest of them seem to have scattered to the north and south poles." Mike's jacket was hanging from the back of his chair. He swung around and put his feet on the top of my desk, reading from his pad. "Skip Lockhart, the project's history professor, is out of town till the end of the week. Grenier's the biologist who's had the semester off. He's due back in the middle of January. May have to hunt those two down.

"Here with us for bagels and brew are Mr. Recantati, Professor Shreve, and Foote herself."

"Let's begin with Shreve. Nan puts him back at the beginning of all this. Why don't we see how helpful he is?"

Mike walked past the lieutenant's empty office and returned with a man I guessed to be in his late forties and dressed, like Mike, in jeans and a crewneck sweater, carrying a cardboard container of coffee that had been set out in the waiting area for our guests from King's College. Before we could be introduced, he reached for my hand. "Good morning. I'm Winston Shreve. You must be Ms. Cooper."

I pointed to one of the chairs usually occupied by the hapless or homeless who were being interviewed by Mike on a murder case. The stuffing was hanging out of the seat pad and two of the four rollers on the chair legs were missing, so it scraped unevenly along the floor as Shreve moved it forward to rest his folded elbows on the desk.

About all I knew was that he was an anthropologist. "Would you mind telling us a bit about yourself, Professor? We're trying to get a picture of the group of people who worked most closely with Lola Dakota."

"Anything you'd like to hear." He started with his credentials, which had been cited to us the previous evening by Nan Rothschild. His accent sounded vaguely foreign. Shreve's responses to my questions were quite direct. "No, I was born on Long Island. Oyster Bay. But you've got a good ear. My family took me abroad when I was an adolescent. I did what you would call high school in England, before coming back here for university. Harvard."

His eyes moved back and forth between us. "You seem to know some of this already. Shall I go on?"

"Till we stop you," Chapman said with a grin. "From Paris to King's College? Sounds like a downhill run to me."

"I'm young enough to take chances, Detective. There's something quite exciting about an experimental school, about the opportunity to build an entire department and all the programming from scratch. They've already attracted quite a bit of intellectual talent, wouldn't you agree?"

"Can't say I'd recognize it. I'm the beauty of this operation. Coop's the brains. If she tells me you guys are smart, I'll accept it. Talk to me about Lola."

191

"You knew her?" Shreve asked, surprised by the familiarity of Chapman's first-name reference.

"Coop's actually the one who worked with her. I'm in charge of the homicide investigation. How well did you know her?"

"Well enough to recruit her for King's. And to consider her a good friend. Lance and Lily, they're her—"

"Yeah, we know."

"They asked me to say a few words at the service yesterday. I guess I was as close to her as anyone at the college."

"Have you known her long?"

"I'd say almost ten years. I'm forty-six now, a few years older than Lola was. Met her the first time at the Aspen Institute. We were each delivering a paper at one of those summer panels. Seemed we had a lot of the same interests, professionally."

"How about personally?" Chapman jumped ahead, trying to speed the process of getting some body fluid to Bob Thaler's office. It wasn't subtle.

"Were we ever intimate, Detective? Yes, but it's been quite a while. The summer we first met, Lola and Ivan were separated. She had walked out on him the first time he lifted a hand to her."

I tried to recall the history of her marriage, as Lola had detailed it to me during our first few meetings. She had never mentioned any formal separation, but all the statistics about domestic violence supported the probability that several had occurred. In most abusive situations, there are seven failed elopements—seven unsuccessful efforts to split from the abuser—before a woman completes the move.

"How long did your relationship last?"

"The better part of a year. Long distance and infrequent, at that. I had returned to Paris to work on a project that just opened to the public last year. Are you familiar with it? There were extensive ruins that had been built on top of several times throughout the centuries, right at the front of the plaza where Notre Dame stands. Lutetia, it was called. The original Roman village that was settled on the Ile de la Cité in medieval times."

Interesting, I thought. Nan had likened Blackwells' midriver positioning to the Ile de la Cité, too.

"Lola was teaching at Columbia then. Used to find any excuse she could to fly over to France. Field trips, student holidays, academic seminars on international government. Boondoggles of every kind. I had a charming flat on the Left Bank, near the university, between Luxembourg Gardens and those amazing bookshops along the Seine. We spent some great weekends there."

"Ah, we'll always have Paris, right, Shreve?" Doing his best Bogie, Mike couldn't help taking a shot at the romantic reverie. The professor didn't catch the reference. "What broke it up?"

"Lola and Ivan had gotten back together. And I'd fallen madly in love with a Frenchwoman, from

Toulouse. Six months later I was married. I'm a French citizen now, in fact."

"So your wife lives here with you?"

"No, she doesn't. Giselle's in France. The marriage lasted eight years. But our divorce is quite amicable, and you're very welcome to talk to her, if that's what you mean. We have two young children, whom Giselle wanted to raise in her country. And she wanted to finish her degree at the Sorbonne, too. She was my student when we married, so that meant she had to drop out of the classes. She'll finish her studies and graduate in the spring."

"But she knew Lola Dakota?"

"Certainly. Whenever Ivan and Lola traveled to Europe, the four of us spent time together. It was no problem for Giselle. I'd been single when I hooked up with Lola. But I don't think Ivan ever knew anything about our relationship. Open-mindedness is not his strong suit.

"She and I always remained close. I'm to blame, if you will, for inviting her to come to King's to teach. I assumed she would have a much greater opportunity to become a department head here. Fewer entrenched alumni to battle with over her unorthodox or, shall I say, more innovative ideas, less heritage to have to embrace than back at Columbia. Lola could rub some of the traditionalists the wrong way."

"How about you? D'you ever battle with her? Get on the receiving end of her tough streak?"

"I take it you've been talking to some of the students. Lola Dakota—the professor—was a perfectionist. If these kids weren't applying themselves according to her standards, she was ruthless." He was somber now. "My department had little to do with hers, in general. But because of the Blackwells project, many of the interns from King's worked under our joint supervision. We planned a number of courses that we cotaught, combining the anthropological features of the island with the politics of the period.

"But I can't remember fighting with Lola about anything significant. On which end of the project should the dig begin? Should a student be graded a B, or did we throw in a plus or minus? How much time should be spent talking to descendants of some of the inhabitants?"

"When's the last time you slept with her?"

"She'd admire your directness, Detective," Shreve said with some hesitation. "More than I do. Eight years ago, to be exact. In her cheap hotel room on Boulevard St-Germain-des-Prés. "And it was good for *me*, if you want to know that, too."

I tried to get us back on course. "Did you know a girl named Charlotte Voight, Professor?"

He straightened in his chair and put both hands on the back of his neck. "Sad case, Charlotte. She was in one of my classes last spring, when she suddenly walked away from all this." He looked back at me. "Now, *she* was a source of disagreement between Lola and me. I thought the girl had a lot of intelligence to be channeled, and a creative imagination."

"With or without the aid of hallucinogens?"

"Her drug use was no secret, Detective. But when she was clearheaded and engaged, as I think she was in my classwork, I thought we had a chance of saving Charlotte. Lola didn't see it that way. Came down on her hard. Some of us thought that helped drive the child off, send her over the edge, emotionally speaking."

"What do you think happened to Charlotte?"

"I just assume she went home to South America. Probably wandered around Manhattan until she ran out of contacts to keep her high, then packed her bags and went home." He brightened as he spoke his next thought. "Charlotte will come back round, Ms. Cooper. I'm sure of it. Hungry to learn, anxious to be accepted, though she didn't like to show that side to people. She's not the first college girl to take a breather."

Mike was back to Lola Dakota. "Lola must have told you what went wrong with her marriage, didn't she?"

"Ivan's right hand, so far as I know. And occasionally his left. He beat her, Detective. And once she realized there could be life without him, and that his rages weren't confined to days of the month that she could predict and avoid, she was ready to walk away from it."

"Another man?"

"I hope so."

"Any guesses?"

"I'll let you know if I come up with any. Skip Lockhart, maybe. Lola seemed to be spending a lot of time with him. Perhaps even President Recantati," Shreve said, finishing his cup of coffee and recapping the empty container with its plastic lid. He laughed, adding, "But Lola would have been on top in that arrangement. He seems a bit passive for my old friend. She was vying for his attention from the moment he arrived, so I wouldn't put anything past her. Still waters and all that."

"What do you know about Ivan's business dealings?"

"That I wanted to be at arm's length from them, Detective. I don't know what he was up to, but Lola thought he'd end up in jail."

"Was she still getting money from him?" Chapman was thinking, like I was, of the shoe boxes full of cash that had been stashed in her closet.

"I don't think he'd give her a nickel, and I doubt she would have accepted anything from him. She wanted out. Over and out."

"What attracted you to the Blackwells Island project, Professor? Seems that some of you who were involved have favorite parts of the place that were of particular interest." I was curious about what drew Shreve to this site.

"Like Lola, I was attached to the work planned on the southern end, everything from the original mansion, which is about midpoint, down to the lower tip."

"The Smallpox Hospital, the City Penitentiary? That area?"

"Precisely. It was Lola who first brought me to the island, the same summer we met in Aspen. I was on my way back to Paris, and New York was hosting one of those parades of tall ships. The harbor was filled with magnificent old sailing vessels that evening. Lola packed a picnic and we took the tram over. She told me it would be the very best vantage point from which to see the schooners sailing up and down the East River, and the fireworks exploding above the cables of the Brooklyn Bridge. In those days, you could traipse on foot right down to the southern end.

"Do you know du Maurier, Ms. Cooper? That's how Lola introduced me to Blackwells. Ever the actress—would have made her mother proud. 'Last night I dreamt I went to Manderley again,' she said, laying a blanket below the blackened windows of the old facade."

"That's exactly what the old hospital looks like. No wonder it's always attracted me." I turned to Mike. "That's the opening line of the novel *Rebecca*."

"Same as the movie," he snapped back at me. I may not be as well read as you, he was telling me, but don't push me.

"The most startling thing that night was looking

back at the incredible view of the Manhattan skyline. We were spread out on the ground, drinking warm white wine from paper cups, and staring directly across the water at River House. It's where my father lived before I was born, and I'd never seen it from that angle."

So Winston Shreve came from money. The fabled apartment building, east of First Avenue on Fifty-second Street, was constructed in 1931 as a palatial cooperative apartment, complete with squash and tennis courts, an interior swimming pool, and even a ballroom. It boasted a private dock, right on the spot where the FDR Drive was later built, at which Vincent Astor kept his famous white yacht called *Nourmahal*. Lived in then by the rich and the royal, today it was home to world-famous personalities like Henry Kissinger and the great international beauty Lady Lynn de Forrest.

"Can't you do that now? Walk down to that vista, I mean?" I asked.

"Not till we've finished our dig, Ms. Cooper. And not unless the money is raised to reconstruct Renwick's fabulous building. Now the hospital's completely in ruins, like an old Gothic castle. No floorboards to speak of, crumbling walls, falling granite blocks. That portion of the island is blocked off from public access by metal fencing across the entire plot, east to west. Topped by razor wire. It's far too dangerous to let people near it."

Chapman poked at me with his pen. "If you're nice to me, blondie, I'll get you a pass for Christmas. The

114th patrols there." Present-day Roosevelt Island had its very rare criminal statistics tallied as part of Manhattan's Nineteenth Precinct, the same Upper East Side neighborhood in which I lived. But patrol duty fell to the auto-accessible Queens cops, and I didn't know any of the guys assigned to that precinct. "I'll get you in for an up-close-and-personal."

Shreve's territorial grip took hold and he spoke, brusquely, over Mike's words. "I'll take you myself, anytime you'd like to see it."

"You got a key?"

"All of us supervising the project have access, Detective. We've got security clearance to come and go as we please for the duration of the study. The grounds are a bit more inviting in the spring, but as soon as some of this ice melts I'll take you both over."

"Did you ever hear Lola refer to 'the deadhouse,' Professor?"

"All the time, Mr. Chapman. You know the island wasn't a very inviting place, even into the twentieth century. When the city finally abandoned these properties, the officials just walked out and closed the doors behind them. Things were left exactly as they were on the last days in use. Sheets were made up on the hospital beds, stretchers stood in hallways, wheelchairs and crutches were propped in doorways and against walls. People were afraid to go there for years, frightened that some of the contagion still lurked in the empty corridors or beneath the eaves.

"Lola liked it that way. When she called the place a 'deadhouse,' it conjured up ghosts of the people who perished there. Kept the amateurs away, which suited her fine."

"I hadn't seen her in months, Professor. She had chosen to work with the prosecutors in New Jersey rather than my office, as you certainly know now. My boss thought their plan to stage her murder was absurd. Can you tell us, had she been worried about Ivan lately?"

"Constantly. Fear consumed her, wherever she was. Somehow, he seemed to know just how to spook her, whether she was walking on Broadway to meet a friend for lunch or getting off the tram when she came to the island. He always kept tabs on her whereabouts. Lola was certain that she was being followed and didn't know whom to trust. I think that's why old friends were so important to her, in the end."

"Was she afraid, even when she went to the island?" I thought immediately of Julian Gariano, and of the thought that he had been hired by Ivan Kralovic to sell information about her comings and goings.

"That's what she told me. I had no reason to disbelieve her. You see," Shreve said, his elbow resting on one knee, "she really did have a phobia that Ivan would finish her off. She was awfully prescient, Detective, wasn't she?"

"So you think that whoever killed Lola was working for Ivan?"

"As opposed to doing the job for Sylvia Foote, Ms. Cooper?" Shreve chuckled. "That's an idea I hadn't thought of until this moment. A King's College cabal? Possible, I guess, but most unlikely. You'd have to give me a pretty good reason."

"Anything else?" I said to Mike.

"I'm not going to let you go without asking a few things about Petra, Professor. D'you mind?"

Shreve rose to his feet and stretched. "If you know of it, I can only tell you that it's as spectacular as everything you've ever heard." He spoke directly to me, quoting the Burgon poem. "'A rose-red city half as old as time.' Have you ever been?"

Chapman answered in place of me. "*I'll* get there before the princess ever will. Can you still see the citadel?"

"Not much of it left. Seven centuries older than these local ruins of ours."

"Built during the Crusades. Part of Jordan now," Mike explained to me, turning to walk Shreve out toward the exit. "You still have to go into the plains over that narrow pass, on horseback? I'm definitely gonna do that someday."

As Shreve nodded his head, Mike shook his hand, continued to chat, and then took the empty coffee cup from the professor. "Thanks for coming in. I'll throw that in the trash for you."

He walked back to his desk after ushering Shreve out. "How come everyone figures right off the bat that you're so couth and cultured, and they all make me out to be such a frigging Philippine?"

"Philistine?"

"Philistine. Whatever. I know more about the Crusaders and the sack of Zara than that egghead anthropologist will figure out in six lifetimes.

"And what he was also too stupid to know was that I generously provided them with these coffee cups so that he could leave me just a little bit of saliva on the rim, in order for Bob Thaler to tell me all the unique things in his double helix that make him such a special guy." Mike was holding Shreve's container in the air, spinning it around in his hand. "Put his initials on the bottom, Coop, and stick it in this paper bag. Attila can take them down to the lab when we're done."

Pleased with his coup, he went back into the waiting area and returned with Paolo Recantati. The timid-looking historian was still clutching his cup, so Mike refilled it from the hot plate in the squad room and gave me a thumbs-up.

"Sit down and relax, sir. Might not be as bad as you think."

"I can't imagine it can get much worse, Mr. Chapman. I left Princeton to come into this nest of vipers. Whatever for? I'm an academic, you understand. Never really been involved in administrative work. The last thing I needed to end my first semester here was a murdered colleague. It's the coldest day of the year and I'm sweating as though it were the middle of July."

It always interested me how people close to murder victims put their own woes ahead of concerns about the deceased. Somehow, I expected each of these interviews to begin with some expression of solicitude about the departed soul of the late Lola Dakota.

"Had you known Ms. Dakota very long?"

"I didn't meet her until I came to the college in September. She has—had, I guess—a wonderful reputation in her field, and I was well aware of her scholarship in twentieth-century New York City government affairs long before we met. I was counting on her to continue to be one of our more productive faculty members. She didn't disappoint in that regard. Lola's next book was scheduled for publication in the spring, with a small university press. And she had already placed several articles about Blackwells, both in academic and commercial journals."

"Published *and* perished? These times are cruel."

Chapman's humor wasn't for everyone. I made a note to try to get a manuscript of Dakota's forthcoming work. Perhaps there was something in her research that would relate to the investigation. "Was she ever accused of plagiarism, or stealing another professor's intellectual property?"

"I think everyone would agree that Lola was an original. That wasn't one of her problems."

"What were they, Mr. Recantati? What were her problems?"

He stammered a bit. "Well—well, certainly, you

could start with the marriage. With that crazy husband of hers. That was an issue for all of us at the college."

"How do you mean?"

"Lola brought the marriage to campus with her every day. I don't mean physically, of course. But she was always terrified that Ivan would appear at school, following an argument or after a meeting with their matrimonial attorneys. She was just as frightened for her students and for us as she was about herself. Talked about it to Sylvia and to me quite often. Afraid that Ivan would show up—or worse still, send some hired gun to the school who would kill anyone that got in the way when he targeted Lola. Thank goodness she was alone when it happened."

I winced at the man's selfishness. What must her last moments have been like? Confronted by her killer at the portal of her own home. Had he been in the apartment with her? Had he waited outside, knowing she planned to go somewhere? Or was it a chance encounter with a stranger, and were Chapman and I wasting our time talking to her cronies while a rapist or robber—an opportunist—was at large in the neighborhood?

Recantati rubbed his forefinger back and forth across his lower lip. "That sounds kind of cold, doesn't it?" His speech halted again. "And, and I—uh—we're just assuming she was alone when she was killed, I guess. Do you know anything else about it yet? How she died, I mean?"

Mike ignored the questions. He wanted answers to his own first. "You're a historian, right? Give us your background before getting to King's."

"My credentials? I did my undergraduate work at Princeton. Master's and Ph.D. at the University of Chicago. I'd been in charge of the history department at Princeton, until I came here to take the position as acting president while the search committee is finding someone for the permanent position. I'm, uh—I'll be fifty years old in March. I live just outside of Princeton, although King's has given me an apartment on campus while I'm here."

"Married?"

"Yes. My wife teaches math at a private school near our home. We've got four young—"

"She know anything about your relationship—your sexual relationship—with Lola?"

Recantati rubbed his lip furiously now. "I didn't— we didn't have any such thing."

He had hesitated a few moments too many to be credible. I had the sense that he was trying to figure out whether there was anyone who could possibly know the truth, before he had to commit himself to an honest answer.

"That's not what your colleagues tell me."

"What, Shreve? I suppose he told you that he and Lola were just friends, also. That's a laugh. Do you have any idea what it's like in a closed community like a small college? You have dinner at the faculty club with someone who's not in your department and therefore you must be in bed with her. A student stays fifteen minutes too long in your office, and you're making a pass at her. If it's a male student, you must not be out of the closet yet.

"I'll help with your investigation in any way that I can, but I won't sit here and be insulted."

Chapman leaned back and opened his desk drawer. He placed a box of Q-Tips on top of the blotter and pointed to it. "How about giving me a buccal swab, Professor?"

"What? I've never been in a station house before. I'm afraid I'm not familiar with your language, your question."

"I didn't learn the word from J. Edgar Hoover. It's science, not police lingo." Mike slowly drew open the sliding lid from the box and removed one of the cotton-tipped wooden applicators. "That's buccal—from the Latin *bucca*. Your mouth, in the old country.

"If you'd be kind enough to just run this down the inside of your cheek, then Cooper's heartthrobs, those serologists over at the lab who solve all her rape cases and make her look so damn good, they'll tell me if it matches any of the DNA we found on things in Ms. Dakota's little apartment."

"B-but you need blood, surely, or s-s-s—"

He couldn't bring himself to say the word "semen."

"I need a buccal swab, is all. The same little bit of spit that's kind of frothing on your lips, sir."

Recantati repeated his nervous habit of stroking his mouth. He stood up. "This is not what I came in here to discuss with you today. You can't make me do that."

"I got a four-year-old nephew who says that to me, too. Stamps his foot at the same time. You should add that touch, for more emphasis. *I* can't make you do it, today, is a fact. But watch out for blondie, here. She's hell with a grand jury."

"If I can be useful with serious information that might actually help your investigation, please call me. I'll be in Princeton until the beginning of next week." He walked to the exit before either of us could see him out.

Chapman smiled, picking up Recantati's relinquished coffee container and marking it with the professor's initials on the bottom. "Got him anyway."

"Well, you may have won a minor skirmish, but in my book you lost the war. Whether he's sleeping with her or not may play a role in this, but you gave up the opportunity to ask all the other questions about things I wanted to know." I tossed my pad onto the desktop.

"Look, we get these cups down to Thaler's office before three o'clock and he promised to run them for us over the holiday. By the weekend, we'll know whether or not any of these academic marvels were anywhere they shouldn't have been. I didn't mean to play with him, but it was irresistible, once he started to squirm."

"But that could be something as simple as having

had a fling with Lola and being mortified that his wife will find out. Now we don't even know why she was after him for money and whether he had a hand in her project."

"You can go at him again more gently next week. I'll have other things to do. Let's get Ma Kettle in here." He bagged the empty container, separate from the one he took from Shreve, and walked to the door to bring in Sylvia Foote.

Stooped and sour-faced, Foote shuffled in behind Chapman with a slim briefcase in one hand. He led her to the broken chair and steadied it for her as she sat. "Coffee?" he asked.

"I don't drink it."

"There's one in every crowd," Mike mumbled as he resumed his seat.

"What did you do to my president?" Sylvia glared at me. "He left in a huff. Wouldn't even tell me why."

"I think he's just rattled by all this going on during his tenure."

"I'm beginning to think my faculty shouldn't be talking to you without legal representation."

If Sylvia was looking for a signal from me that none of her employees was going to come under our microscope, I wasn't willing to give it. She realized that by my silence.

"In that case, Alex, I'll have Justin Feldman get in touch with you."

That would mean trouble for us. A friend and a

brilliant litigator, Justin would brook none of Mike's tactics. They had clashed in the past. He'd be cordial but tough, and we'd be likely to lose direct access to the entire King's College academic staff.

"Why would you bring in the big guns? Coop tells me you're the legal eagle." He smiled at her. "Save those administrators some money. Feldman's hourly rates are sky-high."

"There could obviously be a conflict of interest between the college and some of the individual employees you'll be talking with. I'm sure we could get him to do this pro bono. Justin's a Columbia man— college and law school."

"Boola boola."

"That's the wrong—"

"I know that, Ms. Foote. But the only academic tunes I know the lyrics to are that one and 'Be True to Your School.'" He sang her a few bars of the Beach Boys classic while she opened her briefcase and put her glasses on, then he settled in with his notepad.

"Let's see how far we get without resorting to outside counsel, Sylvia, shall we?" I tried to keep the beginning of this conversation on course. "Why don't you tell me what concerns you have, and then we'll ask you for the things we need."

She looked over her shoulder as though Paolo Recantati would reappear at any moment.

"I didn't think it's my business to tell you what's been going on with the grant money that's been disappearing from the college, but Recantati's in charge and he has directed me to be candid with you about it."

Foote fidgeted with her papers, having mistakenly made the assumption that the subject she was about to disclose was what had rattled the acting president and caused him to storm out. "He's not responsible for this, Alex, I can assure you. We've been trying to look into this ourselves since the federal investigation started in the spring.

"Why the missing cash from the anthropology department would have anything to do with Lola Dakota's death is beyond me, but I did come prepared to discuss it with you this morning."

15

Neither Shreve nor Recantati had mentioned any financial improprieties at the college. Mike and I were both thinking of Lola's shoe boxes, and whether this would be a connection to the unexplained cash.

"Have either of you heard of Dr. Lavery? Claude Lavery?"

Neither one of us answered.

"He was thought to be a trailblazing anthropologist. We hired him away from John Jay." John Jay was New York City's college of criminal justice. "The administration convinced me, at the time, that it was quite a coup for us.

"Lavery's expertise was urban drug use." She extracted several clippings from her leather case. One of them was a John Jay alumni magazine, several years old, featuring a cover photo of Lavery and heralding an article on his inner-city work. He sported a colorful dashiki, unkempt dreadlocks, and a tangled beard. He was holding a crack pipe in his hand.

"I'm upping my contribution to the Jebbies this year. The closest this guy could get to the faculty of a Jesuit college like Fordham would be the service entrance."

Foote narrowed her eyes and examined Mike more closely. If she thought he was crossing the limits of political correctness, she hadn't seen anything yet.

"What came with Dr. Lavery to King's College was a grant of three million dollars, courtesy of the National Institute on Drug Abuse. That's a branch of the Department of Health and Human Services. It made him even more attractive to us than his résumé.

"The first problem we faced was where to put him. Winston Shreve was running the anthropology department and, quite frankly, didn't want a thing to do with Lavery's study. Shreve is a classicist, really. He has very little experience with modern urban culture and certainly not this kind of thing. He wanted us to put Lavery in the sciences, or with sociology."

"Anybody want him?"

"Actually, yes. There was a bit of competition to get him. Professor Grenier runs the biology department and was very interested in carving a position out for Lavery because of the potential for health-related studies of drug use. Long-term physical problems of heroin addicts, everything from HIV infection to dental deterioration. It fit nicely with their premed courses, overlapped with the chemistry curriculum, and linked them more tightly to the social sciences.

"And poli-sci wanted him as well. Lola staged quite a campaign to convince us. She thought it was a wonderful basis to study the city, everything from the criminal justice reaction to the drug issue, the competition for funding between prison facilities and treatment programs, and the political response to substance abuse in society."

"What was your solution?"

"It was one of the few battles that Winston Shreve has lost here. Dr. Lavery calls himself an anthropologist, and that's the department in which we saw fit to place him. Much like the Blackwells Island project—"

"Is Lavery involved in that?"

"Not that I know. But it's a similar situation in that Lavery created a multidisciplinary approach to his issue, so the other departments could each get a piece of his very large and quite delicious pie. Money for everyone."

"What's the problem, Sylvia?"

"A complaint was initiated by the government a few months ago. Not in your office, but with the feds. Southern District of New York. It seems that a substantial sum of the money he was awarded is missing and unaccounted for.

"The grant came with a discretionary fund. It

made one hundred thousand dollars available annually for Lavery to use as he saw fit. Related to the research, of course." She was thumbing through documents that appeared to be spreadsheets and accounting records.

"Lavery claims that he purchased computer equipment and office supplies and gave cash to student interns who researched short-term matters for him. There don't seem to be records to support him, but most academics wouldn't be surprised by that."

"What's the theory?"

Sylvia Foote studied a point on the floor between her shoes and Mike's desk. "Drugs, Detective. Sort of everyone's worst fear about this grant from the outset. That the cash was being used to buy drugs—illegal street drugs—to keep his worker bees happy. Perhaps to use for his own pleasure. The investigation is still ongoing."

"But how—?"

"Claude Lavery is a unique character. Kind of a Pied Piper in a college setting. Smart and creative, but gave the impression of being the anti-academic at the same time. He has a very laid-back style, and early on, right out of the London School of Economics, Lavery would venture into the bleakest parts of the city. Central Harlem, Bed-Stuy, East New York, Washington Heights. He bonded with street characters, the kind who would never let outsiders into their world. That's why his research was unique.

"He wrote about phenomena that made him the darling of scholars in urban studies—both the hard government types and the more 'touchy-feely' sociologists. And then, all the major newspapers picked up his theories as though they were gospel."

"Like what?"

Foote pulled a copy of a *Washington Post* front-page story from her briefcase. "Citing data from Lavery's studies, the story backs his claim that it was the federal government's strict interdiction policies about marijuana back in the seventies and eighties that created the market for international cocaine trafficking to fill the void.

"The students were wildly enthusiastic whenever they came under his spell. They would walk into a neighborhood with Claude—the kind of place these middle-class kids wouldn't dare to go on their own—and find that he had established this wonderful rapport with the locals. That led him, and them, to the addicts and, finally, to the dealers."

"You thought maybe by bringing this guy to the college he was gonna be hanging around on Sesame Street? What's the surprise here?"

"Frankly, Detective, you're right. That's why some of my colleagues aren't the least bit shocked. They expected no less. I presume," she said with great resignation, "that some of them are the people who sparked this formal complaint. Caribbean vacations to study island sources and native drug use, major foundations pouring money in on top of the government grant—things quite likely to make other serious academics a bit envious. And then you have the real distress. What if Claude Lavery was literally putting money into the hands of these students to enable them to buy drugs themselves?"

I wondered if this could be the story that had reached David Fillian in state prison. Perhaps Lavery was the professor Dr. Hoppins was referring to when she stopped me in the courtroom to tell me the news that Fillian was trying to barter for an early release. Was he the person selling drugs to students?

"The kid who hanged himself the other day—any connection to Lavery?"

"Not that we can tell. Julian Gariano was more involved with what they call designer drugs—speed, Ecstasy, some cocaine. Claude's work was primarily with street drugs, but as you know, those lines have been increasingly blurred the last few years. They had certainly met, and Julian was in one of Lavery's classes. No one puts them together outside the lecture hall."

"The missing girl?"

"No link at all."

"Lola Dakota. Connect those dots for me."

Sylvia looked at her files. "As soon as the federal allegation was filed, we suspended Lavery. Quite frankly, we were trying to mount a case to revoke his tenure, which is not an easy thing to do. Professor

Dakota led the opposition to the administration. Backed Claude with all her strength. Even turned Winston Shreve around and had him barking at us to wait and see, allow Claude the presumption of innocence."

"Why?"

"Well, we don't know exactly why. She claimed it was strictly for professional reasons. He bucked the system, just as she did. If anyone admired his unorthodox techniques, it would have been a maverick like Lola.

"Then, there's a more malevolent view. Some people were worried that there was something more in it for Lola. Money, to be exact. That she had been using some of Claude Lavery's funds for her own purposes."

"For drugs?"

Sylvia Foote frowned. "No one's ever made that claim. There's not even the hint of a rumor that Lola would have anything to do with drugs. Nor would she tolerate that in her students. But her own projects were quite costly to run. And she was dreadfully competitive. If she could buy an edge for herself, there are those on our faculty who are convinced she would have done it."

"Do you believe it?"

"Lola was a thorn in my side. Constantly. If someone could create trouble for my staff any day of the week, it would be Lola, pushing the envelope every time. I didn't like her alliance with Lavery, and the reason for it is still a mystery to me. She wasn't a particularly materialistic person, and I don't understand what she would have wanted with the money. But the fact remains that a substantial sum has vanished, and before you saw that story in the headlines or heard it from your federal counterparts, Paolo thought I ought to tell you that it was under investigation."

"But other than the fact that Lola was backing Dr. Lavery, was there anything else to suggest an attachment between them?"

Sylvia gave it a few moments' thought. "Nothing unusual. Good friends, neighbors—"

"Whaddaya mean, neighbors?" Mike asked.

"Claude lived in the same building that Lola did: 417 Riverside Drive. He lived one flight above her. Directly overhead, if I'm not mistaken."

I looked at Mike and could tell that our wheels were spinning in the same direction. I did a mental runthrough of the police reports of the canvass of the apartment house that detectives had conducted the day after the body was found. I couldn't call up a memory of any particular names, but it should have been obvious that a building that close to the King's College campus would have been full of residents who were faculty members or staff. Had the cops talked to anyone named Lavery? Had they accounted for his whereabouts the afternoon Lola Dakota was killed?

Had they cross-checked names of tenants with Lola's family or friends to see what her relationships were with others in the building?

Chapman's impatience was more obvious than my own. "Where's Lavery now?"

"I have no idea, Detective. The last time I saw him was at the vigil on Friday evening. So many people have gone out of—"

"Who can tell me where he is this very minute? Today." Chapman was standing now, ready to be unleashed from the polite tether of administrative interviews and get his hands into the dirt.

"He has been suspended from the college. He doesn't have to report to us or tell us his whereabouts. Dr. Lavery continues to receive a paycheck from us until this is resolved, and if the feds come down with an indictment, I assume the rules may be somewhat different for him."

"How about this other guy, the biologist?"

"Professor Grenier? What about him?"

"He's another one I'd like to talk to."

Sylvia pushed some more papers around. "Grenier's on sabbatical until the beginning of the new year. Can you be patient another week or two, Detective?"

"Frankly, Ms. Foote, I can't be patient another damn minute." He towered over her, shaking his pen in her face as he talked. "You get a forty-eight-hour reprieve 'cause Santa's coming to town and there's nothing I can do about that. These guys are on your payroll; you just said that. Lola Dakota is colder than a stone and six feet under. *Find* these guys, understand me? I want to see Skip Lockhart, Thomas Grenier, and Claude Lavery by the weekend. Move heaven, earth, and unlock your unsmiling frozen jaw to make it happen."

Sylvia's papers were sliding off her lap as she listened to Chapman's booming voice. They scattered to the floor, and I helped her organize them while he continued to list instructions. By the time she left us, she was walking so unsteadily that I had to hold her arm all the way out to the reception area.

"When are you coming back from the country?" Mike asked as I walked toward his desk. I looked at his calendar. This was Tuesday and tomorrow was Christmas Day. "I'll be back on Thursday, unless you want me to change our plans."

"Don't bother. Nobody's here to work with. Just figure we'll be scrambling all next weekend on this, if Foote rounds up her troops and if the lab is good with any test results." He picked up the phone that was ringing on his desk. "It's Laura, for you."

"The superintendent of your building just called, Alex. There's a problem."

"What kind of problem?"

"Seems like there are two workmen who were found in your apartment. The super needs you to come home right away and see if anything's missing."

I slammed down the phone and told Mike I had to go home.

"Not without me. I'm driving."

"You've got things to do. I'll grab a cab."

"Not with that chubby little whackjob whose ID you glommed running around looking for you. You live twenty floors up, with two doormen on every shift. How the hell did anyone fly into your little love nest? I can't get there on my best day, best behavior."

We drove downtown and parked in the garage in my building. The woman from the apartment below me was standing in the lobby, with her Boston terrier, when we walked in.

"The management's security guys are upstairs, along with a detective from the precinct," Jesse said, following us into the elevator.

"What happened?"

"You know the guys who've been working on the scaffolding? Well, you don't see them much, 'cause you're at work all day. But once my kids leave for school, I'm around the house in the morning, and then I'm in and out all day. It's been really creepy to have them around. They seem to be looking in the windows all the time."

For the past six weeks, scaffolding had been erected around the entire high-rise apartment building as it was undergoing repairs to the brickwork and the replacement of some of the windows. Workmen arrived early and spent most of their days hanging off the roof, being raised up and down by a series of pulleys as they went about their business.

"This morning," Jesse continued, "I left about an hour ago to do some errands. Got all the way up to the avenue and realized I had forgotten something, so I turned and went back. When I got inside, the first thing I noticed was that the windows in the living room were wide open and my dog was barking. Then I could see the scaffolding platform rising on the ropes. I grabbed the dog and ran down to the door.

"I told one of the guys on duty what had happened, and Vinny took a run up to check your apartment, since it's right above mine. He must have your passkey."

"He does."

"He opened the door, and the two workmen were standing in the middle of your living room."

We stopped on twenty and got off. My apartment door was ajar and I could hear the loud arguing between the detective and one of the workmen as the three of us walked in.

"Not the traditional way to enter someone's home, but thanks for having us, Alex." The guys from the Nineteenth greeted us as they sat in my living room, trying to talk to the two interlopers. "You heard the story?" one asked, looking over at Jesse.

"Yeah. What's their version?"

"They say the wind was so bad that they had to get inside, or they were afraid they'd be blown off." It was the first thing I had heard that seemed logical. "They kicked the window in and came through that way," Detective Powell said, pointing to the marble-topped counter on my cabinets behind the dining table. "Looks like they broke some of your china."

I glanced over to see that several of the decorative antique plates that were displayed on the sideboard had fallen to the floor, splintered into pieces.

"So how come, if they were so terrified, they broke the window downstairs but didn't go in?" Mike asked. "Doesn't make sense if all they were worried about was saving their asses."

"The story they're giving us is that when the dog started barking, they backed out."

Jesse wasn't buying it. "They were more frightened of a weeny terrier than of being blown off the side of the building? That one's hard to swallow. I think they saw me returning and just panicked. Why'd they go *up* and not down?"

Powell answered again. "Their boss says that when it's windy, it's actually more dangerous to be lowered than to go up higher. If they drop, it means they have to let out more rope, and that causes them to swing more, and that makes it riskier for them."

He put his arm around my shoulders and guided me off into the den. "I don't want to make a scene in front of your neighbor, but you gotta know that since the scaffolding went up, there have been three burglaries in the building."

I turned to look at Powell, surprised by the news. "Nobody's mentioned it to me."

"Needless to say, management would rather not

have it known. There's no forced entry, so we've been looking at them as inside jobs. We actually started with the house staff as suspects—"

"Hey, I'd start with these guys on the outside. I'd go to the mat for the men who work in the building. Every single one of them."

"Well, today seems to prove the point. You want to look around for me and tell us if anything's missing? I patted them down, and they've got nothing on them. Of course, since your neighbor was so quick to act, these guys never got out of your apartment. So if they didn't drop stuff out the window, they probably didn't have a chance to take anything.

"And you might want to know, just for your comfort level, that these mopes who've been staring in everyone's window the past few weeks? They've both got sheets a mile long. The short one standing near the kitchen door, he's on parole in the Bronx for armed robbery. The taller one, who pretends he don't understand English? He's had four collars for larceny.

"One of your neighbors in the C line moved in on a Monday night, and woke up the next morning to see him standing in her bedroom doorway. She screamed her guts out."

"And he's still working here?"

"The guy backed right out. Said he thought the apartment was still empty, didn't know she'd moved in. He'd been using the bathroom as his Porta Potti all month. Apologized and left. Hard to know what to do about him."

"Would you mind getting these guys out of here while I check around for you?"

"We're taking 'em over to the precinct. Gonna print both of them, to compare against the other cases. I won't charge 'em with anything here unless you tell me something's gone, okay?"

The two detectives walked the men out of the apartment while Mike, the super, and I surveyed the damage. Broken glass was everywhere, mixed in with the shattered china.

"Is Powell locking them up?"

"I can't see it, for this. What if their lives really were at risk and they had to come inside? I'm not going to second-guess anybody on that. They don't seem to have gotten out of here with anything. All they did was make a mess." We were standing by the window, and even though there didn't seem to be much wind today, the frigid air streamed into the room.

"Yeah, well, I think it's bullshit and they're lucky they landed where they did. Nice to know you're so forgiving about guys who crash into your pad. I may bank on that. What are you gonna do about this mess?" In one corner of the room stood my cheerful little Christmas tree, while here at my feet was a pile of debris.

The super spoke. "We'll take care of it for you, Ms. Cooper. We'll clean all this up by the end of the day.

Just make a list for us of the things that were broken and we'll submit it to the insurance company."

He looked at the giant hole in the glass. "I doubt I can get the window replaced before tonight. Were you planning on being here for Christmas?"

I shook my head.

"Then you'll have a new one by Thursday, I promise."

When everyone left, Mike and I knelt on the floor to pick up some of the porcelain pieces. "Now I've got something new to worry about. I can't think of many places I've felt safer than behind the doors of this apartment, once I get inside at night and turn the locks. No fire escape, no back entrance, no way in unless I open the dead bolt." I tried to laugh. "Now I've got to worry about men climbing in off scaffolding twenty stories above the street?"

"These guys were trying to give you the same message I was the other night. Time to settle down and develop a more stable lifesty—"

"Don't go there, Mr. Chapman. Get up off your knees. There's nothing to salvage in this pile. I'm just going to check with the office and then I'll take a cab out to the airport."

"But they wrecked the joint."

"Puts things in perspective, though, doesn't it? Lola Dakota is dead, and all I've got to complain about is some broken china. Want to open your Christmas present?"

"Nope. Let's celebrate when you come back. Maybe we can get Mercer in for dinner one night and have our own little holiday, okay?"

"Pick the date. That's fine with me."

I dialed my office number and checked with Laura to see if there were any messages that had come in since we last spoke. She told me no and patched my call through to Catherine Dashfer, who was supervising the unit while I was uptown. "Thanks for covering for me. Anything going on today?"

"A new case just came into the complaint room. Looks like we're going to have to do a hospital hearing at the end of the week, to hold the perp in. Do you think you can get Leemie or Maxine to cover it on Friday? Paul and I are still planning to be at my sister's house through the weekend."

"Sure. Let me make some calls. Why a hospital hearing, though?" There could be several reasons the proceeding would be held in an institution and not at the courtroom. It was frequently done when the defendant was confined with an injury or an illness, or if he had a mental condition that required detention at a long-term-care facility. In that case, the judge, lawyers for both sides, court officers, and an official stenographer trouped to the site to conduct the arraignment or probable-cause hearing. "What hospital?"

"Bird S. Coler. The one on Roosevelt Island."

"Even better. I'll do this one myself. Tell Laura to

have the file messengered to Jake's doorman." That way it would be waiting for me when we came home from the Vineyard on Thursday evening. "What's the case?"

Catherine repeated the facts that the officer had told her. "Perp's name is Chester Rubiera. He's a paranoid schizophrenic with a history of substance abuse. Assaulted one of the other patients. I'll get a facilitator for her, too. The victim has a severe mental disability. You may need someone to help the court understand her testimony. Friday at ten, okay?"

I turned to Chapman and explained the situation. "How about if I ask Nan to show us around Roosevelt Island on Friday afternoon? I've never been there. The new case happened at Coler." A chronic-care facility located on the north end of the island, the hospital was home to many patients with physical ailments, and had a large psychiatric unit as well. "I can do the hearing in the morning, and you can meet me over there at lunchtime. Maybe we can get a sense of the place."

"You're living in the past, blondie. Your fascination is with Blackwells Island. There's no such thing anymore, and there's no evidence, at the moment, to think that Lola's death is connected to what's going on over there today."

"You're right. But I'm just interested in what had Lola so engaged in that project. If there's something more important to be done on Friday, I'll skip it. If not, I'll exorcise my curiosity."

"You know what curiosity did to the cat, Coop."

"It's a perfect place to be, under those circumstances," I said, smiling. "At the deadhouse."

16

Jake Tyler was waiting for me when the shuttle landed at Logan Airport. I dropped my bags and threw my arms around his neck. "I was so afraid that something would happen to get in the way of these forty-eight hours. More murder and mayhem. Or a snowstorm."

He picked up my tote and we started walking to the Cape Air counter. "You got lucky on the first two. There's a front coming through Boston in about three hours, headed for the Cape and islands. So if we don't get out of here soon, we're likely to be stranded."

The gray sky was thick with clouds, and had dimmed to charcoal before we boarded the five o'clock flight to Martha's Vineyard. The nine-passenger, twin-engine Cessna took off after a long runway delay, and the heavy chop in the air slowed the usual thirty-three-minute passage to almost forty-five. The wind bounced us around in our narrow seats in the rear of the plane, and we circled out over Nantucket Sound until the tower cleared us for landing. The pilot lowered us out of the fog to see the white-capped surf pounding the island's southern shore and guided us into the airport, surrounded by the tall pines of the state forest.

I had been talking throughout most of the ride about the case—Lola Dakota's life and the tragic circumstances of her death. Jake had listened carefully, and interrupted from time to time with the skilled cross-examination of a good investigative reporter. "I'm letting you get this out of your system now," he chided me. "I'm putting a two-day moratorium on all autopsy results, serological reports, and police investigations. World crises, too."

He leaned over and kissed my lips as we taxied to the small terminal, and then the pilot stepped out on the wing to come around, open the door, and lower the exit stairs. "Is that acceptable to the People, Ms. Cooper?"

"Yes, Your Honor."

I had asked my caretaker and his wife to set up the house for us—turn on heat, make up the bed, arrange flowers that were delivered a day earlier, stock the groceries that I had ordered, put champagne on ice, and lay a stack of logs in the fireplace. He had also left my car at the airport lot so that we could drive ourselves home whenever we arrived.

A thin dusting of snow coated the parked cars. We let the engine warm up and put the defroster on to melt the ice that had formed on the windshield. I had dressed warmly in slacks and a sweater, topped by my ski jacket, but the bitter cold worked at my nose and ears and within seconds gave both of our cheeks a ruddy glow. The local radio station played generous helpings of the island's musical treasures, James Taylor and Carly Simon, and I tuned in as she was singing the chorus to "Anticipation." Like Carly, I was thinking about how right tonight might be.

The twenty-minute ride up island was quick and quiet. There were no reminders of the traffic of the summer people, who poured onto the Vineyard between Memorial Day and Labor Day, renting beach houses, filling the small inns, and crowding the tiny streets in town. My old farmhouse, way out on a hill-top, overlooking an endless expanse of sea and sky, was one of the most peaceful places I had ever known. Whatever the horrors that crossed my desk every day, this was where I came to be restored.

South Road's wintry darkness gave way to the high beam of my headlights. Without the leafy fullness of the summer foliage, houses set back from the road were visible this time of year. Many were lighted for the holiday season, decorated with garlands of greens, ribbons of red and white velvet, and candles set on windowsills in the traditional New England fashion. I had bought this home with Adam, in the months before our wedding was to have been celebrated. For almost ten years thereafter, it had been impossible for me to think of it as my own. Then, with the tragic shooting of my friend Isabella Lascar, I had questioned whether I could actually come back here at all. I renovated and redecorated, knowing those changes were merely cosmetic and couldn't reach the soul of my trepidation. But since the summer, the great joy I had found with Jake had renewed my excitement and my love for this unique place.

I made the last turn at Beetlebung Corner and pulled into a parking space in front of the Chilmark Store. Nothing else was open at my end of the island, so the general store was our lifeline to all essentials. I ran up the steps, clogged in summer with beachgoers, cyclists, joggers, workmen—tourists and regulars—who sat and gossiped over morning coffee and *The New York Times*, came from miles away for a slice of Primo's pizza at lunchtime, and bought everything from iced cappuccino to batteries to fresh blueberry pie before the doors closed at sunset. A sign on the door announced that they were closed for Christmas week, so I crossed my fingers that all the supplies we needed were at the house.

My driveway was only two miles farther up the road. Wind began to howl around us as I drove up the last hill before the house. As always, my heartbeat quickened with delight at the prospect of coming home. I slowed the car as we approached the familiar stand of mailboxes on the side of the road, then drove in through the granite gateposts, startling a doe and her two fawns, who were foraging on the snowy ground for something to eat. They darted off and I drove up next to the door. Upon each arrival, I drank in the beauty of my view. Headlights off, we sat in the car without speaking as I gazed off at the dim lights in the distance, till Jake caressed my neck and again brought my mouth to his.

"C'mon, Mrs. Claus. We've got work to do. Aren't you hungry?"

I looked at my watch and saw that it was almost eight o'clock, as we took our bags from the car and went inside the house. "I've got the whole evening scheduled. You're not allowed to be hungry yet. Dinner is going to be at eleven, so that we can begin our official celebration at midnight."

"Mind if I nibble on an earlobe or a collarbone till then?" Jake was following in my footsteps as I went from room to room, turning on lamps and illuminating the scented candles. "There's got to be something unplanned, every now and then, that I can slip into your demanding schedule."

A small tree, not even two feet high, had been set up beside the stone hearth. There was a giant box, gift-wrapped and ribboned, from the great toy store FAO Schwarz. "I hope none of my wires got crossed. That's probably something that was supposed to be shipped to my niece."

"You're not the only one with a Christmas list, Goldilocks."

I unpacked two red stockings from my tote and laid them across the back of the sofa. My mother had needlepointed them for each of us, our names stitched in white and green on the cuff. "Why don't you put some music on while I clean up?"

I went into the bedroom and undressed. I stared out my window over acres of land ringed by ancient stone walls, secure that the problems against which I protected myself in the city couldn't reach me here. The fishing village of Menemsha was no longer visible across the pond through the haze as the first soft flakes of snow began to blow against the panes of the French doors and melt. This was my sanctuary.

I set the timer for the steam shower at ten minutes and the temperature to ninety-five degrees, stepped inside, and reclined on the wooden bench. The room filled with mist and I began to sweat. Memories of Lola Dakota's videoed faux shooting swirled and mixed with visions of the actual bloodstained elevator shaft. I wanted the toxins to be removed from my body and my mind to be cleared of all thoughts of death and violence. The physical cleansing worked, but the opportunity to do nothing except think made it impossible for me to erase the mental images.

After six or seven minutes, I shut off the steam and turned on the nozzle, holding my face up to the twelve-inch showerhead that cascaded hot water all over me. I washed my body and shampooed my hair. Jake was outside the steam room when I emerged, standing naked and holding a bath sheet to wrap me in. We kissed again, long this time, and tasted each other lovingly, until I rested my head against his shoulder blade. He stroked my wet curls and pressed his lips against the nape of my neck.

I led him over to the bed. "What makes you think this was *un*scheduled? You never give me credit for anything."

Jake's mouth moved along the lines of my body, kissing my arms first, and then up and down the length of my back. I rolled over to face him, bringing his face up to meet mine and inviting him to be inside me.

"Not so fast," he whispered.

"There's time for slower later. I've missed you so badly this week. I've needed you, Jake."

We both stopped talking and lost ourselves in making love to each other. When we had finished, I nestled against his lean body and rested my head on his outstretched arm. I closed my eyes, and when I opened them again I realized that I had actually fallen asleep for almost an hour.

"I'm sorry. I must—"

"You must have needed it, darling. Relax."

Jake had already showered and dressed for the evening, in jeans and a cashmere crewneck sweater. I showered again and this time when I walked into the bedroom, there was a long red shiny box wrapped with a gauzy silver ribbon on the bed.

"I'm such a baby. I'm going to wait till midnight."

"No, this one's a gift for *me,* and I want you to open it now."

I pulled at the ribbon and opened the lid. Beneath the tissue paper was a pair of lady's silk lounging pajamas in the most delicate shade of aqua. "It's the color you're wearing when I dream about you. When you have clothes on, that is." He held the top up against my skin. "Would you wear it for me, please, tonight? For dinner?"

I dressed in the pale, smooth outfit, brushed my hair, and dabbed some Caleche behind both ears, on my throat and wrists. Jake was in the living room, where he had started the fire, while Ella Fitzgerald was singing Cole Porter to him. He had poured us each a scotch and was standing by the window, watching the flakes pile up on one another.

"I understand that dinner is part of my holiday surprise, but a hungry guy tends to get nervous when the woman he loves can barely boil water. Do you need help in the kitchen?"

"The ladies who feed you so well all summer have helped me put together this wonderful feast. You'll simply have to trust them, not me. It's all island food." I disappeared into the kitchen and opened the refrigerator, where everything had been stored for my arrival, along with explicit instructions. My first task was the hardest—to open a dozen Tisbury Pond oysters.

I had learned after many summers here how to use an oyster knife to pry the lids apart without drawing blood on both my hands. Fifteen minutes of lifting, twisting, and scooping the delicious creatures out of their shells, and I returned to the living room with one of Jake's favorite treats. The fresh, briny oysters tasted as though they had been pulled from the water just hours ago.

"You're off to a winning debut, darling. What's next?"

"You open the wine. I'll set out the first course in the dining room."

There was a smaller fireplace in my dining room, as well. And I started that, after I lighted the six candles in the chandelier above the table. Jake found a bottle of Corton Charlemagne, *grand cru*, and worked on drawing out the cork.

"The first course, Monsieur Tyler, is compliments of the Homeport." Jake loved the chowder at the lobster house in nearby Menemsha, which—like every other restaurant on our end of the island—closes in the fall. "I actually had the good sense to freeze a quart of it. Cheers!"

When we'd finished the soup and I had cleared the dishes, I sent Jake back into the living room. "The next one is trickier." There was a tiny wooden shack in Menemsha called the Bite. And for years, the Quinn sisters, who owned the business, had been cooking and selling the world's absolutely most delicious fried clams. Jake detoured to the Bite, straight from the airport, on every trip to the house. He had even convinced NBC to have the *Today* show do a summer feature on the tasty little enterprise.

Before they closed in October, I had urged Karen

and Jackie Quinn to sell me a batch of the batter in which they roll the morsels before deep-frying them. I bought clams to store in the freezer, and a Fry Daddy in which to attempt to concoct their magic recipe. When I was done with the effort, I carried a trayful into the living room.

"Not even close." Jake laughed. "Tell the girls they've got nothing to worry about. Must have something to do with their shack and its ambience."

The main course was the easiest. Chris and Betsy Larsen kept one of the family fish markets open in town all year long. They had boiled two three-pound lobsters for me in the afternoon, and the caretaker had brought them up to the house. I reheated them in the oven, melted some butter, and we feasted for an hour on the meaty tails and claws.

Jake added logs to the fire, and I stretched out on the living room floor while he opened a bottle of champagne. "Merry Christmas, Alexandra," he said, joining me in front of the hearth and filling a flute for each of us. I rested my head against his knee and wished him the same. We clinked our glasses together and I watched the bubbles rise and burst before I began to sip.

"Where are you?"

"Just thinking."

"About what?"

I rolled onto my back, a pillow from the sofa beneath my head, and stared into the flames. "How much my life has changed this year. What a sense of stability you've given me, in the middle of all the turbulence I see on the professional side every day."

"Can't you look me in the eye when you tell me these things?"

I slowly turned my head to glance at Jake, smiling. "I wasn't planning on saying them. I'm not sure that I've even stopped to reflect on them before now. I just know how very differently I feel about everything I do and think. If I hadn't been able to talk to you when Mercer was shot, I can't imagine what—"

"You don't let people in easily." He was stroking my hair and placing tender kisses on my nose and forehead. "You've got to be more trusting."

"The problem is that at the beginning I trust everyone. That's what's so damn disappointing. It seems as though every time I open the door to something new, the odds are twice as likely that it will slam shut on my fingers."

"Let's try to come up with solutions. For example, darling, think about this. Here's two of us, each with a ridiculously overpriced, way too large for one person who's hardly ever home, Manhattan apartment. Same general neighborhood—same proximity to your favorite restaurants, delis, liquor store, and Grace's Marketplace. Critical factors in a relationship."

I had been drinking enough to know that whatever Jake said, I wasn't going to have the appropriate answer. I could feel my pulse quickening and knew the silken pajama top couldn't muffle the sound of my pounding heartbeat. I shifted back to watch the flames dance in the fireplace.

"I think this morning's broken window and bumbling scaffolders were an omen, Alex. Why don't you give up that place and move in with me? I'm not even in town enough to get in your way very often." Jake had rested his glass on the floor and was massaging my neck. "Imagine that every single night could be like this one."

He couldn't see the tears that had welled up in my eyes. My head was swimming with conflicted feelings. It had been so long since the heartbreak of my fiancé's death, and I had struggled for years to keep free of emotional attachments, fearing that I would lose whomever I let get close to me. For the first time, I had someone to come home to who listened to me talk about my passion for my work, the failures when I couldn't solve a victim's case and the triumphs when justice was actually achieved. Jake never carped when something kept me late at the office or when the phone rang in the middle of the night.

"I know what you're thinking now. You can't make this kind of decision yourself, without consulting your friends. This move will take a summit meeting. All the major powers have to be assembled. No problem, darling. I've covered summits for years. The Middle East, the former Soviet Union, the Pacific Rim, Camp David. How difficult can it be to move one five-foot-ten-inch, hundred-and-fifteen-pound prosecutor less than ten city blocks? Even a stubborn one? We'll bring Joan in from Washington and Nina from Los Angeles. We'll import Susan and Michael. Louise and Henry, are they on the island for the holiday? With Duane?"

I nodded my head, licking the tear that had dripped to the corner of my mouth and smiling despite myself as he ticked off the names of my friends.

"Well, I'll start with them at the crack of dawn. Take a dog sleigh up Herring Creek Road to get to them through the snow, if you insist. If I can't win you over myself, then I'll bring in all the allies I need to persuade you that it's the only sensible thing to do. Get Esther on the line. Get me Lesley Latham. Where are Ann and Vernon?"

I wanted to speak but knew that I would break the spell of the moment. Nothing Jake could say would convince me to move in with anyone, without being married. And he wasn't any closer to thinking about that permanent kind of commitment than I was. I knew him well enough to know that. I cherished my freedom and my independence. As much as I loved being with him and around him, it had only been half a year since we met, and we both had such frenetic lifestyles that it was impossible to know whether we could sustain the intensity of our relationship.

Jake put on his best anchorman's voice. "News flash. Ladies and gentlemen, this bulletin just in to our desk. Exclusive from Liz Smith. We take you live to

Chilmark, on Martha's Vineyard, where former prosecutor Alexandra—"

"*Former* prosecutor?" I rose on one elbow and faced Jake, sure that the tip of my nose must be red, betraying my tears.

"—Cooper has announced that, after a conference with her college roommate and dearest friend, Nina Baum, and with the encouragement and support of a bevy of other loyal Cooperites, she is going to vacate apartment number 20A at—"

"Can we get back to this 'former' business?"

"I needed to do something to get your attention, didn't I? You seemed positively spellbound by the flames. How about it, darling? Of course you can bring your clothes. Yes, all your clothes. I'll get rid of my own, and the golf clubs and tennis rackets cluttering up the hall closet. You look bleary-eyed." He paused to kiss my damp eyelids. "I swear I'll make plenty of room for all the boxes of Stuart Weitzman shoes. What am I forgetting?"

"You're forgetting that anything I say at this glorious moment—my brain soaked in scotch and wine, topped off with a touch of champers—in the state of Massachusetts, lying off the coast of North America somewhere in the middle of the Atlantic Ocean, is not binding on me when we get back into the jurisdiction of New York. So even were I to acquiesce to your generous offer—"

"You can say anything except the word 'no.' You can

tell me you're flattered, that you'll think about it, that the movers will be there on Thursday, that you had them come in earlier today because you hoped I'd ask you, or that you'll leave all your worldly goods behind and come, barefoot, with just the silk pajamas on your back. Any of those answers is fine. The only thing I want for Christmas is that you do not turn me down tonight."

"That's a deal. It's a wonderful offer and you make me very, very happy, just for wanting me to be there."

Jake took a minute to reflect. "Didn't you always hate it when you were a kid and you asked your parents if you could do something wonderful or exciting the next weekend—go to the fair or get a new bicycle or buy a puppy—and they answered, 'Maybe'? I think that's what I just got. A big, fat 'maybe.' Think about my offer, Ms. Cooper. I hope it keeps you awake all night tonight, and every night hereafter until you give in and throw up your hands and knock on my door, begging me to let you in."

"In the meanwhile, why don't you open your presents."

"Ah, bribery. Try and divert me with material things."

I reached for the package under the tree and handed it to Jake. He unwrapped it slowly and dropped the paper next to him. "Where did you find them? Now *I'll* be up all night."

Three leather-bound volumes, all first editions of

works he loved. Jake collected books, like I did, and was always searching out rare finds to add to his shelves. He handled the covers carefully, reading the names imprinted on the spines. "Faulkner, Hammett, Keats. Eclectic, and all favorites. What a perfect gift."

I slipped a smaller box out of the stocking with his name on it. "Something else?" This time he ripped at the red bow tied around the shiny white paper to reveal a black leather case. Inside was a pair of antique Edwardian cuff links, powder-blue enamel baked over eighteen-karat gold. "They're so handsome."

"I thought they'd show nicely when you're on air. When you're traveling without me and you wear them to do a story, I'll know you're thinking of me."

"Move in and you can stick them in my cuffs every morning yourself, just to make sure I do."

"You are hopelessly persistent." I poured another glass of champagne.

Jake walked to the tree and came back with the toy store package. "This one's for you."

I sat up and crossed my legs, undoing the green ribbon. When I got the box open, I lifted a giant stuffed teddy bear out and sat him next to me on the floor. I grinned. "Now why would I even need you when I've got a cuddly guy like this to come home to? I'm sure he's a much better listener than you are. No cross-examinations about my day, no complaints about the competition."

I turned to the bear and opened my mouth to speak.

The words stuck in my throat when I saw what was gleaming on his furry chest. Pinned right where his heart should be was a magnificent sparkling diamond bird perched atop a large aquamarine stone. "That's just breathtaking, Jake." I threw my arms around his neck and hugged him to me.

"Let go of me and put it on."

"I'd rather let the bear wear it. That way I can look at it all the time."

"Bird on a rock. Your friend at the Schlumberger salon said you've been eyeing it for years. Hold still." He unhooked it from the animal's plush stuffing and attached it to my pale silk pajama shirt. "That's why I had to get this outfit to go with the brooch."

I stood up and headed for the bedroom. "I've got to see how it looks. It's the most beautiful thing I've ever owned." Jake followed me in and watched me preen in front of the full-length mirror. "I'm never taking it off."

"Except when you go to work every day, and right at this very moment." He unbuttoned my top and laid it carefully across the chaise at the foot of the bed, the facets of my elegant bird catching every glimmer of light from the candles on the bedside tables. "That's how I want you to think of us, always. You're the exquisite, delicate bird, and you've always got me to land on, to be your bedrock. Merry Christmas, my angel."

We finished undressing and got under the covers, making love again before we drifted off in each other's arms.

Our internal alarm clocks each went off as usual at about six-thirty, as the morning sky was attempting to brighten. We ignored the signals and decided to sleep late, reveling in the fact that neither of us had a deadline or a decision to make the entire day. It was eleven o'clock by the time I was up and dressed and had brewed the first pot of coffee. After calling our families and friends, we bundled up in thermal underwear and heavy jackets and set out on a hike to Squibnocket Beach. For more than a mile, packed snow crunching beneath our boots, we walked along the ocean, hand in gloved hand, talking about things we had never explored with each other before.

Jake asked me questions about my relationship with Adam, and about my slow recovery from the nightmare of his death. He spoke about his broken engagement, when the woman he had dated for four years moved out and married one of his closest friends, tired of the instability of his life on the road and anxious to start a family.

The only people we passed were several of my neighbors, walking dogs along the vast expanse of Atlantic beachfront. Back at the house, we converted the remains of our dinner into a lobster salad, and then spent the afternoon in front of the fireplace with our books. My Fitzgerald novel was constantly interrupted by Jake's discovery of something in his new Keats that he wanted to read aloud to me.

After a simple supper of chowder and some greens,

we watched a DVD of *The Thirty-Nine Steps* and put ourselves to bed early. We were up before dawn, on a seven o'clock flight to Boston, connected to an eight-thirty shuttle back to La Guardia. Jake's car service picked us up in front of the terminal and we drove into Manhattan. I dropped him at the NBC studios at Rockefeller Center and we kissed good-bye.

"I'm expecting you at my apartment tonight. Till you get confirmation that your window has been replaced and that your pistol-packing victim isn't waiting by the front door, we're doing a test run of my proposition. See you later."

The driver took me down to Hogan Place and let me off in front of the entrance. It was after ten, and the place seemed like a ghost town. Only a skeleton staff would be at work today and tomorrow, and I expected to be able to get a lot done.

Laura had taken the day off, so I signed for the packet myself when the FedEx deliveryman appeared with an overnight letter from the New Jersey telephone company.

I opened the envelope to study the jumble of digits that comprised the incoming and outgoing calls made to and from Lola Dakota's temporary shelter at her sister Lily's. It could take hours for a detective, using a reverse directory, to put the numbers together with the subscriber to whose home or office the calls had been placed. Each was coded with the date, hour, and minute the connection was made, as well as its duration.

I scanned the pages until I found the day, one week earlier, of Lola's murder. I ran my finger down the rows of figures. There had been dozens of calls in the morning, when people had been coming and going to arrange the faked homicide performance. Then the activity had slowed to a standstill.

Lily had heard Lola make the call presumably to be picked up by a cab company. And then Lily had medicated herself and gone to bed.

I stopped at 1:36 P.M. A single call, made to a local Jersey number from Lily's home. Maybe I wouldn't need a detective to help decipher and track the telephone connection. The number looked familiar. What if Lily hadn't called a stranger to transport her safely to Manhattan, but had reached out for a friend instead?

I dialed the exchange and waited while the phone rang three times.

An operator answered. "Office of the District Attorney, may I help you?"

I swallowed hard. "Perhaps you can. I'm not sure if I dialed the right number. Is this Mr. Sinnelesi's office?"

"It's his office. But it's not his direct line."

"The extension I dialed," I said, looking down at the printed record, "is 8484. Can you tell me whose number that is?"

"Who are you trying to reach, ma'am?"

The last person to see Lola Dakota alive, I thought to myself. I stammered. "I, uh, I've got a message to call this number. I just can't make out the name my secretary took down."

"Oh, okay. This is Bartholomew Frankel's office. He's the executive assistant district attorney, Mr. Sinnelesi's number two man. Mr. Frankel stepped away for a bit. Shall I put you through to his secretary?"

17

"You saved me from a miserable afternoon with my mother." Mike had been at his desk in the squad when I called, and instantly agreed that we should drive out to Sinnelesi's office to confront Bart Frankel with our new information. The secretary had assured me he would be around all afternoon, so we were soon on our way through the Holland Tunnel.

"Mom's been begging me to help her plan her funeral. Pick out the coffin, go to—"

"Has she been ill?" I had known his mother for years and had no idea that anything was wrong. Perhaps that's why Mike had been delayed at the hospital on Monday morning.

"Fit as a horse. But at Midnight Mass on Christmas Eve, she got me to promise I would take her to get everything arranged. Peace of mind and all that. She's so excited you'd think she was going to Disney World with John Elway, for chrissakes. Told her I was breaking the date 'cause of you. That's the only way I could get a reprieve."

"Tell her that when we solve this one, we'll both come out and take her to lunch. . . . Does it bother you as much as it does me that Frankel's the guy who got Lola's call?"

"Hey, if the escort was strictly professional, they would have had detectives taking her out of Lily's home and making sure she got inside her apartment safely. Your big guns in the Manhattan DA's office do witness escort and protection? I can just see Battaglia asking Pat McKinney to run somebody uptown to Harlem. Not a chance. You know Frankel?"

"I've only met him once, when Sinnelesi sent a delegation to talk to us about helping them stage this shooting of Lola. Anne Reininger was doing a very professional job with the investigation. She had some really good ideas about wiring an undercover cop and proving the case just through incriminating admissions from Kralovic. But the district attorney thought this sting would be great press for him, just in time for his reelection campaign. Battaglia and I disagreed. The plan was over-the-top hokey, dangerous, and unnecessary. Frankel came to our office to try to get me to change my mind."

"Any sense of what he's like?"

"I heard he's a law school buddy of Sinnelesi's, so he's probably the same age. About fifty. They were at NYU together. Frankel started with the Brooklyn district attorney, right out of school—"

"Which means he was rejected by your office, no doubt."

"He did six or seven years there, before my time. Then went into private practice, doing criminal defense work in New Jersey. When Sinnelesi was elected, he brought Bart in as his right-hand man. He really runs the shop."

"Did Lola ever mention him to you?"

"No. But we really weren't in contact often once Jersey got involved in the case. And when Bart came to see me with Anne, he was just acting like a supervisor. I never imagined he had any hands-on connection to the case."

"Hands *on*? How about private parts *in*? Can't wait to hear his explanation for this."

We parked behind the civic center and found our way up to Sinnelesi's office a bit after one o'clock. The receptionist was startled to see visitors on this quiet, postholiday afternoon.

"We're here for Mr. Frankel," Mike announced.

"Is he expecting you?"

Mike jerked his head in my direction. "She's an old friend of Bart's. Passing through town. I think we'd just like to surprise him."

"How nice," she said, smiling in my direction. "I'm sure he'll be pleased. He called to say he'd be stopping for a sandwich on his way back here, so he should be in any minute."

I took off my coat and hung it on the rack in the

waiting room. "What the hell is that frigging glob you got stuck on your suit?" Mike was staring at the gift Jake had given me for Christmas.

"Well, I didn't stop at the apartment, and I was afraid to leave it in my office with the suitcase."

Self-consciously, I unpinned the bird and wrapped it in my handkerchief, putting it inside my shoulder bag.

"Guess Mr. NBC went to the well for that one. Don't let me cramp your style, blondie. You could probably wipe out the entire national debt of Sri Lanka if you—"

"Alex? How nice to see you."

Bart Frankel came through the front door and approached me to shake hands. I introduced him to Mike. "Are you here to meet with the district attorney?"

"No, Bart. We want to speak with you."

A large brown paper bag in one hand, Frankel pushed open the entrance to his wing with the other. "Come on in. I still can't get over what happened to Lola. Such a tragedy." He ushered us into his corner suite, removing his backpack and his coat. This prosecutor's small modern office complex in a suburban corporate park was far more gracious and comfortable than ours. Two chairs faced Frankel's desk. Mike and I seated ourselves while he unwrapped his lunch and put it to the side.

I couldn't help but notice that he was chewing gum.

"Can I order something in for you?"

"No, thanks."

"What can you tell me about how the investigation is going?" He took a tissue, swiveled in his chair, removed the gum, and threw it in his wastebasket. Mike gave me a thumbs-up.

"It's actually going really well, Bart. Faster than I expected. We've had some lucky breaks."

"What do you mean?" He glanced back and forth between Mike's stone face and mine. He laughed nervously, or so it seemed to me. "I get it. Need to know. Tell me and you'll have to shoot me." He nodded his head up and down. "Maybe it's sour grapes 'cause Battaglia wouldn't let you buy into our sting plan. Well, he was right, Alex. Tell him from me, off the record, that once again he made the right choice. Vinny's getting lots of heat from everybody. Starting with Lola's family. The dancing Dakotas, he calls them. A whole chorus line of whining siblings, waiting for their fifteen minutes of fame. That's what their mama primed them for." Bart was talking nonstop, tapping the fingers of both hands on his desktop.

"I got the governor on my back, too. She's big on domestic violence and all that political garbage. Then we got victims' rights groups. You name it, we got it. And you know the drill, Alex. When the shit hits the fan, the number one man is always unavailable for comment. Mr. Sinnelesi had to leave town. Family emergency down in Boca. Vinny, I tell him—Vinny, first I take a huge pay cut to come work for you and do public service, instead of making a real living for me and my family. Now I got to have my balls on the chopping block, too?"

"You wanna come up for air, Mr. Frankel, or you wanna just babble on?"

"Sorry, Mike. It's Mike, isn't it? Exactly what can I help you with?"

I answered, trying to set a pace for the conversation. "I hadn't spoken with Lola in months, as I think I told you when you and Anne Reininger came to my office. I'd really like to get a sense of what her life was like those last six weeks. How she was spending her time, who she was in touch with, what your contact was with her."

"Me? *My* contact with Lola?"

"Hey, who do you think she's talking to? You got somebody under your desk we can't see?"

"No, it's just, I mean—well, Anne's the prosecutor assigned to the case. I had to meet with Lola on a few occasions, just to oversee what was happening with the sting. Anne's the one who spoke to her almost every day. She can answer your questions."

"I'd like to begin with you, as long as we're here. Why don't you give us an idea of how many times you met with her? Where and when."

Frankel thought for a moment and opened his large red desk calendar. "All of my business appointments are logged in this. Let me just see." He opened the book about midway, to June, and began to flip through the pages. "I guess the first time I met Lola was in the early fall. September twenty-third, to be exact. Anne brought her up to me to introduce us. High-profile case and all that. Vinny likes me to keep an eye on things."

The intercom buzzed. "Excuse me, Mr. Frankel. I've got your daughter on line two. She wants to know if she can use the car tonight after you get home. Would you like to speak with her now?"

"Hold my calls, will you? Tell her yes, and try not to interrupt us till I'm through here, okay?"

"How many meetings after that?"

"Skimming through here, it looks like six, at the most."

"Where were they?"

"That was the only one in my office. The other times I went down to the second floor, to Anne's bureau. Family Violence Unit."

"Did you ever meet with her anywhere else, outside the office?"

"Yes. I was at her sister's house—Lily's—the day we staged the shooting. We went over, Anne and I, with the detectives just to make sure we approved the setup and to stroke the rest of the family. Pump Lola up."

Frankel was on his feet now, adjusting the blinds on his window as the sunlight bounced its glare off the icy surface of the parked cars in the lot below.

"Must have been a very tense morning. Were you there when the scam went down?"

He did the "me" thing again. "Me?"

"Yeah."

"No, I did what I had to do and got out of there. Had stuff to work on back at the office."

"What stuff?"

"Had to meet with one of the guys on a home-invasion case. Had to help him draft a bill of particulars."

"Got that in your big red book?" Mike asked.

"Got what?"

"Your meeting on the case you just told us about."

"That, um, that came up kind of unexpectedly. It's probably not in here." Frankel patted the cover of the book.

"Mind if I take a look through those entries?"

"I just told you, I doubt that one's in here."

"I mean the references to Lola. Mind if I jot down those dates?"

Frankel opened the book to the first September date and passed it across to Chapman. "Help yourself, Detective."

Mike rested his notepad on the desk. He turned the pages and copied the dates and times of the Dakota-Reininger-Frankel appointments. When he got to the day of the shooting, he paused and read aloud: "'Thursday morning, December nineteenth. Nine A.M. Meet Reininger at Dakota scene. Sting preparation. Noon. Lunch with Vinny. Two P.M. In the field.'

"Strangest thing. When my partner uses that expression—'in the field'—it means he took the rest of his tour off to get laid. But then, we're just cops. What does it mean to you, Mr. Frankel? What kind of home invasion were you working on?"

"Who's in control of this operation, Alex, you or this rude—?"

"Mike and I want to know exactly the same information. How did you spend that afternoon?"

"I, uh, I must have gone . . . I guess I left here early. I probably did some holiday shopping."

"Like Ms. Cooper tells the street mopes that sit in her office and lie to her all day, 'probably' and 'I guess' and 'I must have' don't cut it. This ain't ancient history, Mr. Frankel. It's one week ago this very day. When you and Fat Vinny pushed back from the lunch table, where did you go and what did you do?"

"My daughter was coming home from college the next day. I went over to the mall to pick up a few gifts for my kids."

"What stores? I assume you can tell me what you bought and give me receipts for the things."

"You know, Detective, I'm the executive assistant district attorney for this county. You blow in here like you're auditioning for a bit part as a wise guy on *The Sopranos*. All bluff and bluster and bullshit, and I actually let you rattle me, like I have something to worry about. Well, you came to the wrong place this time. I supervised this investigation. I'm not the subject of it. Why don't you two just crawl back through the tunnel, or however you dragged yourselves here, and go solve your case like professionals, okay?"

"Did you drive Lola back to Manhattan with your own wheels, or did you use a government car to take her home?"

Frankel strode to the door of his office and opened it wide. Mike got up from his chair as though to leave, then walked behind the desk. He leaned over and reached into the trash, removing from it the Kleenex-wrapped piece of gum that had been discarded when Frankel first brought us into the room. He held it up to the light and admired it as though it were a trophy.

"What the f—?"

"I'm sorry. Would you prefer that I have the office sealed off while Ms. Cooper gets us a search warrant to take your droppings? You a Wrigley's man? Or would you suggest we compare your underwear to the things we found in Lola's apartment? I'd say those size-forty shorts would fit him pretty well, don't you think, blondie?"

Frankel walked over to Chapman and grabbed the tissue from his hand without meeting any resistance. "You two must have lost your minds."

He was like an animal trapped in his own lair. He was patently unhappy with our presence, but afraid that we would walk out without telling him what we knew. Then he put his hand to his eyes and shook his head. "Or maybe I have."

He walked to the windowsill and sat on its edge. "Lola was desperately lonely. She was looking for somebody to cling to, some kind of safety net. I took her out a few times. Never here, in New Jersey, where anyone could see us. In the city, up near the college. I'm not married, if that's what you're thinking. I've been divorced for a couple of years."

"That wasn't my first thought," I said. "I actually wondered how you could get involved with a victim while her case was pending in your office."

"My shrink wants to know the same thing." He sat at his desk and again his fingers tapped steadily against the wooden top. "I had thought about calling you, Alex. I just couldn't pick up the phone to do it. I realize that it's selfish, but if I get myself in the middle of all this, I obviously have to walk out the door here. Give up my job. Make waves for the district attorney."

I was waiting for him to invoke his right to counsel. Like most lawyers, he was loath to do it, figuring—I was certain—that he was smarter than any young prosecutor and the average cop, alone or in combination. I was trying to stay calm, wondering how Frankel could explain being with Lola in her apartment last Thursday afternoon, and how much we should consider him a suspect in her death.

He retraced his steps to his September meeting with Lola and filled in more of the blanks. She had called him again, he said, in October, and invited him to a presentation she was making at an academic convention at the New York Hilton. Her speech was magnificent, Frankel told us, and despite all the professional prohibitions, he began to come into the city to see her from time to time, becoming intimate with her before Thanksgiving.

"Does Vinny know?"

"He'd break my neck. I suspect this could cost him a few votes in the next election, and that's the bottom line."

Chapman worked him a bit more, and then I tried to move things along to the day of the murder. "After Lola called you, what happened that afternoon?"

"I was the only one who knew she was going to leave her sister's house. Lily was driving her crazy. The histrionics, the crying, the busybody nature of her personality. We had all we could do—Anne did, really—to keep Lola there long enough to execute the plan. I had promised to drive her home afterward. She didn't want detectives sitting around her apartment. She was tired of being watched and waited on. She just wanted to go home and get back to work."

"So she called you here at the office."

He looked at me quizzically. "Surveillance?"

"Even easier. Telephone records."

"I went back to Lily's neighborhood and waited around the corner. Lola was in great spirits. Felt she'd helped us nail Ivan, and that she would begin to regain a bit of control over her life. We drove into town and I took her up to Riverside Drive. She had some things she wanted to do at home, and then she was going to meet me, at seven o'clock, for dinner at a Chinese place on Amsterdam Avenue. She never showed up. I called and called, and when I finally decided to drive back to the apartment to see what the problem was, cops were swarming all over the place. The last time I saw her was when I let her out of my car in front of her building."

We were all silent. Frankel had taken us halfway there, but I didn't believe that he was telling the truth about how he left Lola. I was thinking of the semen-stained sheets, and I'm sure Mike was, too.

"Where did you go? How'd you spend the rest of the afternoon?"

Frankel was fidgeting again. "Let me think a minute. Um, I—I drove down to, um—there are a couple of bookstores on Broadway. I wandered in and out of those. I had some coffee and read a newspaper."

Mike took the pencil he'd been writing with and snapped it in half. "I hate it when people lie to me."

"I don't remember exactly what I did that afternoon. But you don't want me to say I don't remember, so I'm telling you what I would have done. I was wandering around Columbia, I was walking in and out of shops, trying to keep warm and pass the time. It had no significance at the moment because I had no idea anything was wrong. I was just killing time—"

"Or Lola."

"Don't be a horse's ass, Detective. Don't sit in *my* office and even presume to treat me like I did something wrong." His voice was raised now, shrill and strident. "I never went inside Lola Dakota's apartment last Thursday." Frankel spit each word at us, slowly and angrily.

"Then how come there's seminal fluid all over the sheets on her sofa bed? And how come if you just spit over at me one more time, I'm gonna have enough of your goddamn body fluid from this slobbering saliva all over the new tie my aunt Bridget gave me for Christmas to let the lab match it up before your kid gets home with the car tonight."

"*If* there's semen on those sheets, and *if* it happens to be mine, Detective . . . let me stop right there. That's a really big 'if,' 'cause Lola and I did not exactly have what I would call an exclusive relationship."

"Maybe we can narrow it down a bit. Coop, how much you wanna bet that Mr. Frankel here has a pack of gum, white wrapper with that distinctive green arrow, right in his pants pocket?"

"I'm not betting against you, Mr. Chapman."

"What's the point of that?" Bart was furious.

"We've got DNA from the sheets, and DNA from the gum. You know where the bed linens were, and the two of us happen to know exactly where we found your chewed-up ball of saliva. Now all you have to do is remember how many places you were when you tossed your gum. Was it in Lola's bedroom? In the kitchen? For a guy with a regular habit like yours, it's gonna be hard to single out every stick you got rid of. Leave out an important stop, and I'll nail your ass to the wall. The easiest thing for you to do is just to retrace your steps for us, honestly this time. We know damn well that you're leaving something out."

"Well, I sure as hell wasn't in the elevator shaft when she was murdered. Alex, please. You've got to believe that I was never, *never* inside Lola's building the day she was killed. Of course I won't deny that we'd been intimate. But whatever you found on the sheets must be there from two or three weeks ago. We slipped away from Lily's one afternoon, and I took Lola to run some of the errands she needed to get done around school. Then we stopped by at her apartment and yes, we made love. She never spent another night there, so she obviously didn't have any time to do the laundry.

"And the gum? Yeah, I chew gum all the time. It's probably in every wastebasket in the apartment. It's a nervous habit. Started when I gave up cigarettes, and now I do it all the time."

Chapman fisted both hands and leaned his knuckles on the desk, bending toward Frankel. "If you didn't go into Lola's building that day, where else did you go? Help me. Tell me one other stop you made that I can verify."

Bart twisted and squirmed. Mike tried to nudge him in the right direction. "Start with the campus. Did you go anywhere near the college?"

"Columbia?"

"Or King's."

"I'm not familiar with King's. Didn't exist in my day. So I walked around Columbia a bit. But it was too cold.

I got in my car and drove down Broadway. Manhattan has a bunch of these great little mystery bookstores. Four or five of them, all over town. It took me a while to find one. Just took a book into a coffee shop and read for a while. I told you that before, and it's true. I'll check at home and see if I can find a receipt."

Both of us knew, from the gum that Mike had spotted in the trash basket, that Bart had made a stop in Lola's office. I wondered if he had done that because she had asked him to pick something up, or if he had gone there on his own. Why wouldn't he give that to us? Why did he continue to lie about it? And what else did it mean he was lying about?

"Was there a reason Lola didn't want you to come upstairs with her?" I asked.

Bart reached into his pocket and stripped the wrapper off another stick of Wrigley's spearmint.

"Not really." He rolled his head in a circle and pressed his hand against the back of his neck. "I mean, what we had originally planned was to spend a few hours there. But when we pulled up in front of the building, one of her friends was on his way inside. We just decided that I should get lost for a few hours and come back later. Lola didn't want anyone asking questions, didn't want anything to happen to screw up the case. Like for Ivan to find out she was sleeping with a prosecutor. Shit, was I stupid."

"How the hell would Ivan find that out, just 'cause you were driving her home?"

"And staying overnight? He had eyes everywhere. Lola was paranoid. Thought he was paying people to find out information. Just figured it would get back to Ivan if we were caught together. She told me to stay loose and she'd give me a call later that afternoon on my cell phone." He looked pained. "The call that never came."

"And the friend, the guy who was going in when you pulled up to the building? What's his name?"

"Her friend, not mine. I never saw the guy before in my life. I think he teaches with her. Black guy with dreads and a kind of wild-looking beard."

Lavery, I thought. "Claude? Claude Lavery?"

"Yeah. That's the guy. Held the door for her and they walked in. I never saw her again after that."

18

Chapman was itching to get out of Frankel's office. Bart followed us past the receptionist's desk and into the hallway. "What do you think, Alex, do I have to tell Vinny about this?"

"Hey, schmuck. Get real. You're now a permanent part of my files on the case, and we're not even out of the box. Coop and me have a few dozen questions for you we haven't even thought of yet. We haven't talked about Ivan, we haven't asked you about the work Lola was doing, we haven't asked whether you know anything about a load of cash she was hiding. Or about drugs."

Mike gave up on the elevator and tugged on the strap of my bag as he turned to trot down the three flights of stairs to the exit. "Next stop for you is my office. Pick a day. Make it easy for yourself, Counselor. And try telling Vinny the truth. Might be a new thing for you. Or, you can tell him you're in the field. That seems to have worked for you before."

"Let's try and schedule an appointment for the beginning of the week, Bart," I said. "You know how this is going to break, so why don't you tell the district attorney about it before Battaglia gives him a call?"

Frankel was leaning over the banister, calling down to us as quietly as he could. "Do you think I'm going to need a lawyer?"

"Line up a good proctologist first, Mr. Frankel. It's rough in those maximum-security pens."

Mike started the engine and we sat in the lot while it took its time warming up. "Born loser. Knew it the minute I saw him. Know how I could tell? Grown man with a backpack. There's just no excuse for it. Half of those twerps in your office use 'em, too. I get on the elevator at Hogan Place, one of those guys from Appeals gets in after me and turns around. Bam! I get smacked right in the puss with nine pounds of law books. By the time you get out of high school, you should figure out some other way to carry stuff around. What are you thinking about?"

"The position Frankel put himself in. That he'll be out of a job before New Year's. Whatever his involvement is in Lola's death, he was terribly indiscreet to be sleeping with her. And we'll have to tell Sinnelesi that he withheld evidence from us. Not to tell us that he had been with Lola after she left Lily's, and that he actually saw her go into her building with a witness who we didn't even know about before this? Irresponsible and unethical."

"There's some reason that Bart wouldn't give up the fact that he went to Lola Dakota's office," Mike said. "Before we have him back over to interview, let's be sure and examine the inventory of stuff that was there, and get the photos Hal Sherman took at the college. It's even creepier to think that he might have gone there *after* he found out she was dead.

"Want to swing by the county jail and see if Ivan has anything to tell us? Talk to him about his student snitch, Julian Gariano? See what kind of mood he's in?"

"I'd love to, but his lawyer called on Tuesday while I was up at your office. Said Anne Reininger gave him my name and number. Left me a message telling me who he was and how to get in touch with him. And that under no circumstances was anyone to attempt to speak with his client out of his presence. Does Ivan still bother you, too?"

"Sure does. It's too neat to assume he didn't have something to do with Lola's murder, when he had already gone to such lengths to get rid of his wife. Suppose he figured out or got tipped off that the hit men were part of a government sting operation? It's too late to remove his voice from the tapes and get out of trouble completely. But say he sets up some kind of defense that proves he—what do you call it in legalese?—that he had withdrawn from the plan and he just let these mopes go ahead with it to show what grandstanders they were.

"Meantime, he makes a backup plan to kill Lola. Paying someone in the city to let him know when she's returned to Manhattan. Lola gets knocked off . . . splat, all over the bottom of the elevator. So even if you don't believe it's an accident, Ivan the Terrible's got a rock-solid alibi for the rest of last Thursday, sitting behind bars, waiting to be arraigned in a Jersey courtroom. And Fat Vinny looks like the incompetent that he is."

People like to think of domestic violence as an issue of the underclass, as something that occurs in minority communities, among the poor and uneducated, as something personal that is not "our problem." Both Mike and I, just like every cop and prosecutor in this country, have investigated and charged doctors, lawyers, judges, businessmen, and clergy with beating, raping, abusing, and murdering their spouses. I was not about to ignore Ivan Kralovic, who had already proved that he was at best abusive, and at worst a potential killer.

"Am I dropping you at your office?"

"Let me check my messages. It was slated to be a slow day. There's no point going there if I don't have to." I used my cell phone to dial into my voice mail. The mechanical voice told me that I had four new messages. I played them back and the first two were from assistants in the unit, telling me about the new cases that had come in over the holiday. The third call was from Sylvia Foote.

"Your pal Sylvia called an hour ago," I told Mike. "About Professor Lockhart, from the history department—"

"The guy who was, shall we say, 'tutoring' the law student we interviewed?"

"Yes. He's returning to town tomorrow afternoon. She left his number. He's agreed to speak to us over the weekend anytime we like. Sylvia says Lockhart is willing to cooperate. Was very fond of Lola. That's the gist of it. She's still looking for Grenier and Lavery." I hit the prompt to save the message so that I could retrieve Lockhart's number and call him when he reached New York.

Message four. Three twenty-six P.M. I looked at my watch. It had been only ten minutes since that message was recorded. *Hey, Alex. It's Teague. I'm up at Special Victims with a new complaining witness. Just reaching out to see whether anyone could interview her before she heads back out to L.A. tonight.*

The Special Victims Unit occupied space in the same office building to which Manhattan North Homicide had been transferred more than two years ago. Just above 125th Street, in an unlikely-looking brick structure that faced the elevated subway tracks on the West Side, the two squads were on the same busy corridor. I dialed the number and the civilian aide who answered passed me along to Teague Ryner, another bright young detective who often teamed with Mercer.

"Thanks for calling back so quickly. I was hoping you'd make a decision on this one before she hops on a plane. I don't want to make an arrest unless you think we've got something. Want me to give you the facts?"

"Sure."

"Girl's name is Corinne. Twenty-eight years old. Lives in Santa Monica, says she works in the music business. It all started after she had a few Brain Tumors—"

"Brain tumors? How awful. Is she—"

Teague laughed. "Not *that* kind. It's a drink. A pretty lethal one."

"What's in it?"

I had seen women's vulnerability increase dramatically after downing multiple Tequila Sunrises, Long Island Iced Teas, Sex on the Beach, and other creations that bartenders invented with every new season. They woke up in strangers' apartments, on the backseats of taxicabs, beneath trees in Riverside Park, and on sidewalks in midtown. "It's my right," they would often tell me, "to drink whatever I want, and as much of it as I want." Detectives, prosecutors, advocates, and jurors were supposed to deal with the aftermath. This was my first Brain Tumor.

"About six different liqueurs mixed together," Teague told me. "She can't remember how many of them she drank. In fact, that's the trouble. She can't remember much of anything."

"Did she drink them voluntarily? I mean, she's not

claiming someone drugged her, is she?" Two different kinds of problems, under the law.

"Voluntarily? She was chugging them like they were root beer."

"Tell you what. I'm with Chapman, on our way back from an interview in New Jersey. Since he's got to go up to the squad, I'll just come with him to your office and we'll figure it out together." No point spoiling the end of another colleague's day, as long as I was working.

"I'll check with you before I leave, okay?" I said to Mike as he let me out in front of the building. I headed upstairs while he parked the car.

The day tour had just ended, and the teams working four to twelve had come on duty. Teague had caught the case in the morning, when the victim had called the police from the emergency room at New York Hospital to make an official report. Even though many of the cops took vacation leave during Christmas week, sexual assaults continued to occur at an alarming rate. Despite the drastic reduction in street-crime statistics, the volume of acquaintance-rape cases remained steady. Women were far more likely to be attacked by men who were known to them rather than strangers—not the public perception but a well-documented fact. And the alcohol that fueled so many of the holiday parties, at people's offices as well as their homes, led to an alarming number of new incidents.

"Hey, Sarge, how've you been?"

"We can hardly keep up with everything. What a wild week."

"Where's Teague?"

The sergeant led me to a small cubicle in the back of the squad room. Ryner and his witness were talking quietly, as he took notes while she recalled more events of the night before. "Corinne, this is Alexandra Cooper. She's the prosecutor who can answer your questions."

Before I could be seated, Corinne asked the first one. "What kind of case do you think I have? I mean, like, I really don't want to go through, like, all the hassle if nothing's going to happen to this guy."

"I'll try to give you an answer, but I'm going to have to get a lot more detail from you about everything that went on during the evening."

"Well, that's part of the problem. I don't remember much of the night. I met this guy at a party. He told me he's a vocalist. Sings with the Baby Namzoos."

"Who?" Whatever happened to rock and roll?

"They're kind of a hot group now." She could barely disguise her disdain for my ignorance. "Anyway, I started drinking with him. Next thing I know it's ten o'clock in the morning, and I wake up in his hotel room. Naked. There's no way I would have done that unless he forced me to be there."

"Did he have sex with you?"

"Why else would I be naked and in bed with him? He must have. That's what I went to the hospital to find out."

"I'm going to have to start at the beginning with you, Corinne." No one was going to be charged with rape in this jurisdiction because a woman *assumed* that a crime must have occurred. The doctor or nurse who examined Corinne may have been able to find evidence that recent intercourse took place, but they would be unlikely to know whether it was with or without her consent.

"Any medical findings of significance?" I asked Teague.

"Nothing."

"Lacerations, abrasions, discoloration, swelling?" He shook his head in the negative.

I elicited background information from Corinne about her education and employment. I questioned her about the medications she took regularly and her alcohol consumption habits.

"Have you ever had so much to drink before that you couldn't remember things the next day?"

"Yeah. It happens to me every now and then. I've had some blackouts, too. Not passing out completely, but just carrying on with my friends, and then having no memory of it the next day. My doctor tells me I'm not supposed to mix my antidepressants with liquor, but most of the time it doesn't really bother me. . . . I haven't had anything to eat since last night. Do you think you could send out for a sandwich for me?"

"No problem," Teague replied. "There's a sandwich shop that delivers, or there's a guy on the corner with a hot dog stand. I can run down and get one for you, whichever you'd prefer."

Corinne's face screwed up in disgust. "You mean those New York City hot dogs that sit in that dirty water in those pushcarts all day? I couldn't possibly eat that stuff."

No, but she could drink a six-pack of some liquid concoction without a clue about what was in it or how it would mix with her medication, and never even blink. Teague left the room to call in an order for Corinne and a few cups of coffee to keep us all going.

Corinne rested her head, cushioned on her crossed arms, on the table in front of her. "Would you like to tell me about the evening, or as much of it as you can remember?" I asked.

She had met Craig at the party at about midnight, and they were really getting along well together. After a few vodka and cranberry juice cocktails, they left to go to a bar somewhere in the East Nineties. That's where she had the Brain Tumors. Maybe three of them. Maybe five.

"Was he coming on to you at all?"

"Like, what do you mean?"

"Did he seem to be interested in you physically? Did he ever touch you or kiss you?"

"Oh, yeah. We were dancing, I remember that. The jukebox was playing music and I asked him to dance with me."

"Fast or slow?"

"Slow stuff, mostly. He was kissing me, you could say."

"Were you kissing each other?"

"Sure. But I know what you're gonna say. And that doesn't give him any right to have sex with me, especially if he didn't use a condom."

"Did you see anybody else that you know at the bar?"

"No. He's the one who decided where to go drinking. I didn't know another soul."

"How about the bartender? Were you talking to him?"

Corinne thought for a minute. "Yeah. After we'd been there for a while, most of the place kind of cleared out. He and Craig were having a long talk about something—movies, I think it was. They both liked the same kind of movies. Science fiction, stuff I don't know about."

"So there's a good chance, if Teague stops over there tonight, that the bartender can help put together some of the things you don't remember when it came time to leave the bar?"

"Like, what do you mean?"

"How you two were acting toward each other. He might recall some of your conversation, if you had any in his presence at the bar. How many drinks he served you and how drunk you were. Or what kind of physical interaction there was between you and Craig." It was often useful to remind a witness that other people we could talk to might actually be able to help us reconstruct some of the things she had been too wasted to think about clearly.

"You're really going to speak with that bartender?"

"Don't you want us to? After all, part of what you claim is that you didn't go to Craig's hotel room willingly, under your own steam."

She extended one arm out on the table in front of her and rested her head back down on it. "What if he tells you, like, that Craig and I were making out while we were in the bar?"

"That still doesn't give him the right to force you to have sex with him, or to take advantage of you if you weren't participating." I fed her back the line she had tried to use earlier to get me to act on her complaint. If Craig had engaged in a sexual act with her after she had passed out, we might be able to establish the occurrence of a crime.

"Yeah, well, what if the bartender tells you that we both went into the men's room for a while? What's that gonna do to my case?"

"That depends on what you tell me happened in the men's room, doesn't it?"

"You're gonna be all judgmental about it." Corinne focused her eyes on a spot on the ceiling, above my head, and looked even more sullen than she had when I arrived.

"I have no reason to be judgmental. You tell me what the facts are, I'll tell you whether we've got evidence that proves a crime was committed."

"But it's only my word against his?" She was whimpering now.

"That's all we need—your word—in any case. It used to be different, twenty years ago. There had to be more proof than the story of the woman who brings the charge. But now, rape is like every other crime. Your testimony—your *credible* testimony—is what I present to the jury. Then you're cross-examined by Craig's lawyer. After that, Craig tells him everything he remembers."

I paused to let that fact sink in. "Corinne, what happened in the bathroom at the bar? Did you have sex with him?"

Her eyes returned to the spot on the ceiling. "Not sex. I gave him a blow job. I didn't let him touch me."

I had told her I did not have to make judgments about people. That didn't stop me from wondering about her definition of sexual acts. Maybe it was a generational thing, although she was only ten years younger than I. I had heard it enough times that I had learned to train the young lawyers in my unit never to accept a victim's characterization of the encounter when she said there was "no sex." Ask, I taught them, exactly which body parts made contact with the other person. Most of us make too many assumptions about what other people call sexual acts.

Now she was rubbing her eyes and yawning. "You know, Miss Cooper, I never wanted to call the police about this. It wasn't my idea. That woman at the hospital made me do it. The only reason I went to the emergency room was to get a morning-after pill. I mean, like what if he had sex with me, didn't use a condom, and I find out I'm pregnant?"

"Do you think that's what happened?"

This time she groaned. "I don't know. I just don't know what happened. Don't you get it? That's exactly what I told the doctor who examined me. And after he told me he couldn't see anything unusual, that's when the counselor told me that maybe I was raped."

"*Maybe?* We don't charge people with felonies, Corinne, 'cause 'maybe' they did something bad. I have to believe a serious crime was committed before I authorize the police to make an arrest. And I have to persuade a jury, beyond a reasonable doubt, that the person charged committed that crime. I can't ask them to guess. I can't ask them to fill in the blanks that you don't remember. If Craig had intercourse with you when you were unconscious, that's another thing— that's a crime. But nobody goes to state prison for twenty-five years because you got drunk and then don't like the way the night ended for you.

"And Teague and I will have to spend a lot of time trying to figure out which of those things is what actually happened."

"But how can you do that?"

"Maybe we won't be able to. But we'll start with the bartender. We'll see if there's a desk clerk at the hotel who saw you coming in with Craig. Maybe even a security surveillance tape that will show you walking with him. It might suggest whether or not you were in any distress—or instead, that you were laughing, having a good time. I'll get the records of all the charges from his bill. See if there was any room service, any minibar use, any pay-TV movies charged to Craig's room during the time you were—"

"Oh, jeez, let's just forget about it then." Now she was moving from apathy to anger.

"You don't have to do all that work. That's Teague's job. Did I remind you of something you had forgotten? Did you have more to drink in the hotel room? Get into bed with the guy to watch a movie?" It wouldn't be the first time.

"Where's the detective? Can I talk to him a minute? I mean, like I have a plane to catch."

"Teague and I are here because you wanted our help. We'll get you to the airport. Please try and answer my questions. One call to the hotel and we'll have some of this information anyway. It's all part of the record that goes on the guest's bill."

Corinne was fuming. She wouldn't look at me for almost a minute, and then she spoke.

"All right, so we had some more to drink. He ordered up a bottle of champagne. Is that against the law? I had a couple of sips of champagne."

Nice nightcap for a bunch of Brain Tumors. The chances were good that there would be a charge for an X-rated movie on Craig's bill, shortly after room service arrived with the chilled bucket of bubbly.

"How about the movie, Corinne?"

"It was so gross I couldn't even watch it after the first ten minutes. Like group sex in a hot tub or something. *He* was into that shit. Not me. Look, let's just forget about this. I don't think I have much of a case." She twisted her watch around on her wrist to see the time. "If I don't go now, I'll never make this flight." She stood up and opened the door.

"This morning, when you woke up, did you ask Craig what had happened?"

"Yeah, I asked him. He was like all surprised I didn't remember. He said we—um—we like made love. That he thought I was having a really good time. I just know I wouldn't have done that if I had been sober. Not without a condom."

"But you weren't sober, Corinne. That's what alcohol does, that's what drugs do to us. They change the way we act, they loosen us up. Sometimes we say and do things we wouldn't have done otherwise. Sometimes it makes us more vulnerable to many kinds of danger."

"Well, I'm just too hungover and tired to deal with this now. I didn't want him arrested. I just wanted to teach him a lesson anyway. Please, can I go home?"

Teague had paid the delivery boy and returned to the interview room with Corinne's sandwich. I left them alone so that he could try to soothe her and get her to go over the more complete version of her story, which she had neatly trimmed for him on the first telling. The hot coffee tasted good at the end of a long day, and I walked back to sit with the sergeant and talk about the rash of holiday assaults.

The door to the squad room opened and Mike Chapman burst through before I could finish the cup. "Yo, Sarge. Be sure you get blondie delivered right to the door of Walter Cronkite's apartment when she leaves here. The most trusted man in television can take care of her for the night. Gotta run."

I stood up, holding my finger in the air to signal that I'd be ready in a minute. "Teague doesn't need me anymore. I can—"

"Sorry, kid. Just got a call from the boss at the Nineteenth Precinct. Seems like little miss Annie Oakley made an attempt to get into your building through the garage. Tried to get one of the attendants to let her in with his key. Slipped him twenty bucks. I'm meeting the cops over at P. J. Bernstein's. See if we can pick her off the street before she starts target practice. You and lover boy are grounded for the night, understand?"

I didn't have time to protest. Mike turned to leave, but stuck his head back into the room. "And by the way, I checked with Freddie Figueroa, the detective who canvassed Lola's building the day after the murder. Remember Claude Lavery, 'Professor Ganja-R-Us,' Coop? The upstairs neighbor? On the DD5, all Figueroa had written for his interview with Lavery was that he was in his apartment, working on a research paper and listening to classical music. Didn't see or hear anything unusual on Thursday afternoon. Freddie asked Lavery if he knew the deceased. Said he did, but that he hadn't spoken to her in over a month."

19

Jake dropped me off at the Roosevelt Island tram station at Second Avenue and Fifty-ninth Street on his way to La Guardia in a cab at 8 a.m. Friday morning. He was back off to Washington to cover the end-of-the-year resignation of the secretary of agriculture. I climbed the three-tiered staircase and watched one of the two cable cars pull out of the station as the second arrived and unloaded its crew of daily commuters.

With a few minutes to kill, I called Mike and found him still at home.

"I assume that you would have phoned me last night if you had any luck finding my friend, Miss Denzig."

"We rode around the neighborhood for almost two hours. Nowhere to be seen."

"I'm on my way over to Bird Coler Hospital to do that hearing. Jake won't be home in time for dinner tonight. Why don't you see if you can lure Mercer into town for our Christmas celebration? I'll think of some-place lively to go, okay?"

"Let me see what's cooking. You still planning to take a scenic tour of the island when you're done?"

"Yes. Nan asked one of the students who stayed in town during the holidays to show me the dig site. I'm headed out there now, so I may poke around a bit before I come back. Can you still meet me after I finish at Coler?"

"I'll beep you if I can get there."

There were only seven other people going to the island at that hour on this cold December morning. Two of them had tennis rackets and were clearly headed for the bubble in the sports complex at the foot of the tram station. I wondered what the business of each of the others could be. The young conductor opened the doors of the car and we all boarded. There was a bench at each end, with four large poles to hang on to at various points on the floor, and straps with metal handles hanging from the roof's interior.

Like a cable car at a ski resort, the doors closed and the heavy tram lumbered off, rising on thick steel wires as it lifted off above the city streets. I could see the people in the automobiles that were cruising down the Fifty-ninth Street Bridge ramp. Powerful winds rocked my massive carriage and it shuddered mildly as its sev-eral sets of wheels rolled over the stanchion at the first tower.

In the sky beyond, I watched a steady stream of takeoffs and landings heading to and from the La Guardia Airport runways, and below that, three gray stacks belching smoke from some unidentifiable factory in Queens. The crossing took less than four minutes, and I snaked my way out behind the other passengers, who all seemed familiar with the routine. A bus waited at the exit path, and I fished a quarter out of my bag to pay the fare.

The second stop, just beyond the original Blackwell farmhouse, would put me on Main Street. When I stepped down from the bus, I was struck at once by the feeling that I was in a small town, millions of miles from Manhattan. The streets were lined with cobblestones, and the handful of new high-rise buildings stood alongside the redbrick facade of the Chapel of the Good Shepherd, constructed more than a century earlier for island residents.

I walked north, following the winding street the equivalent of a handful of city blocks, to the lighthouse at the island's tip, just beyond the hospital. The sweeping view of Manhattan from that point was the most spectacular panorama I had ever seen.

It was after nine o'clock when I presented my identification to the security guard at the desk at Coler Hospital. He directed me to the psychiatric ward on the second floor, where I was met by a slender young woman in a white lab coat. "Miss Cooper? I'm Sandie Herron. I'm the physician in charge of this wing of the hospital. We've got one of the arts-and-crafts rooms cleared and set up for your hearing today."

"Fine. Would you have a private place for me to interview the victim?"

"Yes. That's what I'm here to help you with." She asked me to follow her down the hallway to her office. "You're going to need some help with Tina. It's difficult to understand her unless you've worked with her for a while."

"Will she talk with me?"

"You won't be able to get her to stop talking. Problem is that because her mental disability is so severe, I don't think you'll be able to understand her without help from me or one of my staff."

"What's her history?"

"Tina's thirty years old. She's spent most of her adult life here at the hospital. She has some congenital brain damage, as well as being bipolar. Her developmental level is about that of an eight-year-old's. She has dramatic mood swings, from extreme emotional highs to very profound depression. She's on a number of medications, including Depakote and Neurontin."

I was trying to take down everything Herron was saying. "Don't worry, I've had a copy of Tina's chart made for you. All of the meds are listed in that. The problem . . . may I call you Alex? The problem is that her speech and language are particularly immature.

She's incapable of normal verbal communication, and a lot of what she tries to express is incomprehensible to an outsider's untrained ear."

"Have you ever testified at a preliminary hearing, Doctor?"

"About a patient's condition? A diagnosis or finding?"

"No. I think I'd like you to stay with me while I try to ask Tina to tell me what happened. If she isn't able to make it clear to me, or to the judge, I'd like you to act as an interpreter."

"That's fine. Why don't we bring her in and let you get started." Herron called the nurses' station and asked one of the attendants to bring Tina to her office. "One thing you need to understand, Alex, is that Tina exhibits an unusual preoccupation with sex. She's what we call on the ward a chronic public masturbator. We have a companion assigned to be with her most of the day, so she doesn't interact sexually with the other patients."

My luck to draw this complication at a preliminary hearing. The best I could hope for would be to get a good judge who would appreciate the issues here. My witness would be an unintelligible thirty-year-old, with all the sexual interest and curiosity appropriate for a woman that age, but with the mental capacity of a child. The law presumed that she was incapable of consenting to whatever sexual act had occurred.

This must have been an "up" day for Tina, who did not yet have a clue that she was about to appear in a court proceeding in front of a judge, a defense attorney, and her assailant. She walked in holding the hand of her attendant, neatly dressed in a clean white sweatshirt and khaki slacks. She smiled at me when we were introduced, and said something that sounded like "pleased to meet you."

For more than an hour, I struggled to get a narrative from the young woman. Her companion sat by her side, stroking her arm gently when my most basic questions seemed to confuse Tina. If I failed to understand a response, Dr. Herron told me what the patient had said. Whenever I mentioned Chester's name, Tina became visibly agitated.

Somehow, despite all the precautions that had been taken at the hospital, a male patient named Jose had encountered Tina in the hallway after breakfast one morning and had invited her into his room. She liked Jose and accompanied him willingly. Dr. Herron interrupted softly to mention that Jose was a paranoid schizophrenic, with some confusion about his sexual orientation. Tina told us that Jose was always kind to her, and she had sex with him because she thought she was screaming. Her mouth widened and her tongue protruded as she tried to get it to move around the word "screaming" a second time.

"Screaming? Why were you—?"

"No, no, Alex. Tina said she thought she was dreaming

when she did it." The patient smiled as Dr. Herron corrected me. "Tina's aware that we don't approve of her . . . well—she usually tries to account for her activity by saying she didn't think it was really happening. That she just imagined it or dreamed about it, isn't that right, Tina?"

She nodded her head in agreement with Herron. It was obvious to me that I would not be able to conduct the hearing unless the judge allowed me to use the doctor as an interpreter. "What happened after that?"

Tina explained that Jose left her to go to the bathroom. That's when Chester came in and found her in the room. He asked if he could get into bed and make love to her. She was scared because she knew that he had a terrible temper, but she told him it was okay.

"Were you afraid of Chester?" No answer.

"Did he say anything to threaten you?" I was wondering if I could raise the level of the felony crime, if Chester had used any force.

Tina answered clearly when she said, "No."

"Jose came back to the room, Alex. When he saw Chester in bed with Tina, he went to get one of the nurses. That's the reason we know for sure that intercourse occurred. The nurse actually witnessed it."

"Fine. I can spare Tina having to testify at the hearing if I can use the nurse as a witness."

"I'm afraid she went back home to Montana for Christmas."

"What's Chester's ability to understand right from wrong?"

"He certainly knows the difference, and he knows that what he did with Tina was wrong. His psychiatrist can give you all that. His problem has to do with control of his temper and the explosive outbursts from which he suffers. Chester's twenty years old. He's been in and out of hospitals for most of his life, but was homeless at the time of his last arrest."

"What was the charge?"

"He beat up an old man who tried to stop him from getting on a bus without paying."

I continued to prepare Tina for the preliminary hearing, which had to be held before the end of the week in order to keep Chester in on bail. The hospital authorities wanted him removed from their facility, while our purpose would be to have him hospitalized in a prison psych ward during the pretrial period. I did not want to see him released, on the street, with no home to go to and no one to supervise the taking of his antipsychotic medication.

"Excuse me, Dr. Herron?" We all looked up as another nurse entered the room. "There's a call from a judge's clerk who's downstairs. He wants to know when this hearing is going to start."

It was after twelve. "I need another half hour, at least. Why don't we say one o'clock?"

"That's good for me, too, Alex. Tell them where we're setting up, and that we'll be ready at one. And let's be sure Tina has some lunch before you get going. She really slows down with all those meds unless she eats at regular intervals."

"There's a message for you, Ms. Cooper. Detective Chapman said he can meet you after the hearing, unless you call to tell him otherwise."

An hour later, I entered the arts-and-crafts center of the psych ward. Much like the walls of a kindergarten class, this room was lined with pictures, crayoned and painted by the patients, all of whom were adults. A makeshift judicial bench had been fashioned out of several of the tables, and the stark black of the judge's robes was in sharp contrast to the brightly colored, childlike illustrations that would be our background for this sad proceeding.

"Ms. Cooper? I was expecting Assistant District Attorney Dashfer to be here today."

"And I was expecting Judge Hayes, Your Honor." We each forced a smile.

The judge was probably as crestfallen as I appeared to be. I had mistakenly relied on the tentative schedule distributed earlier for the week's arraignment part, not figuring on holiday substitutions. Instead of Roger Hayes, one of the smartest and most sensitive jurists in our jurisdiction, I had been saddled with Bentley Vexter. I knew this would prove to be a more difficult experience for Tina, with a judge not long on patience or understanding.

My adversary was a young lawyer from the Legal

Aid Society. He had met his client for the first time just minutes ago, when he arrived at the hospital. They conferred briefly while we waited for Sandie Herron to come to the room.

"Are the People ready to proceed?"

"Yes, Your Honor."

"Call your first witness." He held the criminal court complaint up to his nose and lifted his glasses to examine the typed accusation.

"I would like to make an application to the court before I do that."

The judge put the glasses back in place and met my statement with a frown. "We've wasted half a day out here while you got your witness ready for this. What is it now?"

I launched into a description of Tina's condition, both physical and mental, while she and Dr. Herron waited in the corridor. "The request I'm making is that the court allow the victim's physician to appear with her in the courtroom, to serve as a facilitator, should that become necessary during the taking of testimony."

"I'm going to have to object to that, Your Honor."

"Hold it a minute, Mr. Shirker. What, this woman doesn't speak the language? What kind of interpreter do you need? Nobody told my clerk we—"

"Not a foreign language interpreter, sir." I repeated the nature of Tina's difficulties and explained Dr. Herron's relationship with her.

"Objection."

"On what grounds, Counselor?" It was clear the judge had no idea whether he should grant my somewhat unusual request, so he was hoping the defense attorney would provide him with a legal basis to make Tina's task more arduous.

Mr. Shirker had nothing more than a gut feeling and a knee-jerk reaction. "Um, uh—due process, Your Honor."

"He's right, Ms. Cooper. This is a very peculiar step you're asking me to take."

"The fact that it is unconventional doesn't mean that it doesn't have a valid purpose in a legal proceeding. Our courts are supposed to be accessible to everyone. The fact that this witness has a severe impairment should not deprive her of her day in—"

The judge held his arm straight out in front of him to stop me. Then he lowered it, pointing his finger at the official stenographer. "We're off-the-record here, understand?"

I stood up to object. Vexter was most pernicious when he could clean up the official language of his hearings. His finger pointed back at me, telling me not to dare to stop him. "Look, Alex. You got a retard here who doesn't mind a roll in the hay. She hops into bed with Jose, so who's to say Chester can't have a date, too?"

"I'd like all of this to be *on* the record, Judge. I'd like the opportunity to respond to it." I wanted an official transcript reflecting his ignorance in black-and-white print that an appellate court and a judiciary committee could examine. Vexter's views were as limited as his intelligence.

The stenographer's hands were poised over her machine. She was waiting for the judge to give her the signal to resume working, while glancing back at me with a shrug of her shoulders, knowing that she was helpless to do as I asked. Vexter was in charge of the courtroom.

Vexter put his glasses on the tip of his nose and motioned to me and my adversary with his forefinger. "Why don't you approach the bench?"

"No, thank you, sir. I want all of this on the record. My witness is developmentally disabled, with severe mental and physical handicaps. But she knows what happened to her and she is entitled to tell her story in this forum."

Chester Rubiera was digging his fingers into the palm of his hand as he watched the goings-on around him. I expected him to draw blood at any moment.

"And I'm telling you that this whole thing is a waste of the court's goddamn time."

"Is that what you and Mr. Shirker mean by due process, Your Honor? Would you like me to talk about the law on this issue, or doesn't that particularly interest you?" Vexter knew as much about rules of evidence as I knew about NASA.

"You got cases on this?"

Catherine had sent the file on the matter to Jake's apartment. She had researched the issue and I had read the opinions last night. I nodded to the judge and started to cite opinions. "There's a Second Department case, *In the Matter of Luz P.*" I handed copies of the decision to the court officer to give to the judge and my adversary. "And the *People Against Dorothy Miller.*" I described the facts and holdings as the stenographer urged me to slow down.

"Yeah, I knew that," Vexter said, tossing the pages aside without reading them.

"The unaided testimony of this witness is likely to be meaningless without our ability to have Dr. Herron interpret her responses. Counsel is welcome to cross-examine and ask whatever appropriate questions he chooses. As previous courts have ruled, this is simply a pragmatic question, not a legal or scientific one."

The three of us continued to argue while the defendant became more irritated, and my witness no doubt grew more anxious out in the hallway. When the judge finally reversed himself and let us go forward, Dr. Herron guided Tina in and sat beside her. The patient's pleasant smile faded when she saw Chester sitting on the opposite side of the long worktable. She clung to Herron's hand and wriggled in her seat.

For the better part of the next two hours, we went through the encounter between Chester and Tina, with Herron clarifying the language whenever Tina's verbal utterances were incomprehensible. By the end of the cross-examination, the patient had exhausted herself by the combination of her concentration on the retelling of the story, and her apprehension about being close to Chester.

When Vexter ruled that there was sufficient evidence to hold the matter for the action of the grand jury, he released Tina from the room and dealt with the business of finding an appropriate facility in which to secure the defendant, away from Coler Hospital.

At four-fifteen, I thanked the doctor and retraced my steps to the lobby of the building, where Chapman was waiting. "Proud of yourself, blondie? Chester the Molester moving on to a better place? Can't believe they actually got a psychobabble disorder named for a bad disposition."

"Yeah. 'Intermittent explosive disorder'—temper tantrums that the perp's unable to control."

"And a medication that works for them?"

I nodded.

"Get a double dose and I'll keep it in my desk drawer, to have on hand for those days you lose it with me. C'mon, that student who was supposed to meet you had to leave for the day. One of the guys from the one-fourteen is going to cruise us around for ten minutes. Will that do?"

We went outside, where the sky was already darkening and the wind had picked up force. A blue and white

RMP—radio motor patrol car—sat in front of the hospital. The two uniformed cops in the front seat looked less than thrilled to be chauffeuring us around the quiet little island.

They pointed out the landmarks as we wound our way south, past the remains of the Octagon, the apartment houses, the meditation steps, the observation pier. Near the southern tip, we came flat up against the heavy metal fencing that blocked off the ruins of the Smallpox Hospital.

"Can we get in there to see it?"

The driver flashed his annoyance at his partner, who answered more politely. "Nothing to see, really. You can't go inside the building 'cause it's all crumbled and full of falling blocks of granite. And broken glass. And then there's the rats."

I got the point. "Can we just drive up closer so I can take a look?"

With some hesitation, the driver started the car again and drove us to the locked fence. He got out of the RMP, inserted his card in the automated locking device, and watched as the gate slid open. He stepped back into the car and drove slowly through the entrance. In the wintry darkness of the late afternoon, I could barely make out the shapes of the large boulders on the darkened landscape. "You won't see much, and I can't let you out to walk around. Last guy I took in needed a tetanus shot from tripping and cutting himself open on some old can or bottle."

"What are these huge rocks?"

"The walls of the old City Penitentiary. That's what it all was, once. Came down in the 1940s. It's just been sitting here ever since. Kids used to really get hurt on this stuff. That's why they finally fenced it off."

He drove south until he stopped at the abandoned ruin of the Smallpox Hospital. Chapman and I stepped out of the car and walked to the waist-high wooden fence that kept trespassers at bay.

"Isn't it glorious?" The facade looked like an old castle, the dark gray stone porch of the entry now draped in icicles and bare of all the ivy that cascaded down its sides in summer. Through its paneless window frames, the enormous bright red neon letters of the bottling factory's Pepsi-Cola sign lighted the black sky above the river. On the Manhattan side, the glitter of the United Nations complex sparkled with the outline of its distinctive shape.

"This all that's here?" I could see Mike's breath forming the words in the chilled air.

The driver of the RMP nodded in response.

"Now you've seen it, kid. Let's hoof it back to the mainland. Must be like a girl thing. The place doesn't do anything for me. Mercer's gonna meet us at your place at seven-thirty."

The cops dropped us at the station and we waited with two other passengers until the cable car landed and disgorged its returning commuters.

Mike and I stood in the front of the tram, hanging

on to the overhead straps, as the red behemoth lurched from its berth and lifted toward the first tower. For just a few moments we were below the roadway of the Fifty-ninth Street Bridge, and then we reached the height that put us almost at eye level with the huge girders that spanned the river. The wind was fiercer now, and I could feel the play in the tension of the steel wires.

Mike turned to say something to me when a burst of shots resounded on the side of the moving cab. They pinged and smacked against the steel sidings and the thick glass of the upper body of the tram. Before the second volley was fired off, and without a word between us, Mike had tackled me to the ground and covered my body with his own.

The window had shattered as the hail of gunfire continued, a second round and then a third. The car swayed and frigid air rushed in to fill the small heated space of the wounded tram. The remaining two minutes of the crossing seemed endless, and my mind flashed to those desperate moments almost five months earlier when Mercer had taken a bullet meant for me.

My face was pressed against the muddy tiled floor of the cab. I could hardly breathe from the combination of terror and the weight of Mike's body flattened against my back. I closed my eyes to keep the glass particles from blowing into them, and heard the sound of Mike's gun scraping against the floor of the tram as he positioned it alongside my ear to cover the opening of the door as we docked.

20

Startled commuters awaiting the short ride home gasped at the spectacle of the four of us, crawling on the bottom of the cable car, and a gun in the hand of Mike Chapman, who had been unable to reach into his pocket to display his badge.

"I'm a cop. It's okay," he said. He stood up and went to check on the older couple who had been sitting on the bench in the rear of the tram before they had dropped to the floor. "You two all right? I'm a police officer."

The elderly woman was clutching her chest and began to cry as Mike helped her to her feet. "He's got a heart condition," she said, pointing at her husband. "Is he—?"

Mike was assisting her husband onto the bench and restoring the cane to his hand. "You wanna call for an ambulance?" he shouted to no one in particular, as the trembling man assured Mike that he was fine.

A bystander said that someone had already called 911 after the first shots were heard.

"How's your wife?" the old gent asked, pointing to me. I was standing up, brushing the slivers of glass off my knees and trying to maintain my composure.

"Nothing a six-pack of Dewar's won't fix in a minute. She takes a flop like that every couple of days, just to keep me on my toes." Mike was doing his best to defuse the situation, to keep everyone calm until he could sort out what fears were appropriate.

Within minutes, six cops bounded up the steps to the departure platform. Two of them recognized me and one of them had known Mike for years. They helped the older couple make their way down the staircase to an ambulance, and put me in the back of one of the patrol cars. One cop stayed with me to take the details for a police report, while Mike and the others examined the inside of the cab.

By the time Mike got back to the car, the uniformed sergeant had arrived and introduced himself to me. "They're doing stops at both ends of the bridge, Mike. What do you think it was?"

"I left 'em up there for Crime Scene to photo, but it's pellets of some kind. Meant to kill somebody? I doubt it. But you could send a loud message that way. Could be somebody just goofing around with a shotgun, could be somebody looking to break windows and scare the shit out of people, could be somebody thinks you're running a shooting gallery in the Nineteenth. I'll leave it to you to figure out."

"There's been a dingbat on the loose after Miss Cooper, hasn't there? Saw a scratch on it back at the house."

"Yeah, but this was definitely not a handgun. Besides, nobody knew it was going to be us on that tram. Maybe it's just some loose cannon, warming up for New Year's Eve."

I thought of Lola Dakota. Was I getting to be as paranoid as she had been? "Remember the kid who hanged himself last weekend? Lola wasn't so crazy. He *was* selling information to Kralovic about where she was and what she was doing. Maybe someone snitched that I was out on the island today, and this attack really was aimed at you and me."

"She's just out on a day pass, Sarge. I'm taking her back to Bellevue right now." Mike stepped out of the car to talk with the sergeant before he left, then slid back onto the seat beside me, closing the door behind him. "You want people to think you're nuts? That was just some carful of kids from Long Island being frisky on the ride home after an outing in the Big Apple. Don't start seeing your cases in every odd thing that happens."

He was running his fingers through his thick black hair, a sure sign that he was more upset than he was willing to acknowledge. Mike didn't believe this was random mischief any more than I did. "They'll beep me if their search turns up any goofballs with shot-guns. My guess is that whoever did it was off the bridge before the nine-one-one call went through."

A couple of the cops returned to the patrol car and asked where we wanted to be dropped off.

"Let's go to my place to meet Mercer." This unex-pected event had chewed up more than an hour of our time. "I'd like to put on some sliver-free, clean clothes for dinner, okay? Wash my face and hands."

"Dab some perfume on, too, Coop. You didn't smell so sweet when I was breathing down your neck."

Mercer was already waiting in the lobby of my building. The doorman stopped me as I crossed to the seating area to greet him. "Miss Cooper? The super asked me to tell you, if I saw you, that your window still hasn't been replaced. The glazier they use is on vacation, so it can't be fixed until January second. Is that okay?"

I didn't have much of an alternative. "As soon as they can get it done, I'd appreciate it."

On the way upstairs in the elevator, we told the story of our harrowing tram ride. Perhaps it was a result of his own recent attack, but when I left them in the living room to go change, Mercer was insisting to Mike that we make the cops work to identify the shooters.

Despite the tarp on the empty window frame, the apartment was as cold as the inside of a refrigerator. I changed into a casual outfit, packed some more clothes to take to Jake's place for the weekend, and returned to find Mercer and Mike pouring drinks in the den, the pocket doors closed in an effort to keep out the cold.

"Here's to our own little Christmas. Looks like it'll be the last one for this trio without significant others, spouses, offspring. Chokes me all up inside." Mike lifted his glass and we clinked together. "Too bad you didn't have your hardware on your chest today. This thing Jake gave her, Mercer? It must be like kryptonite. Probably could have melted that buckshot on the spot. We can't top it, blondie, but we have some trinkets—"

Mike interrupted himself and hit the television remote to eliminate the mute function. Alex Trebek announced that the *Final Jeopardy!* category was an audio question, and the topic was the Oscars. "How much, guys?"

Mercer and I smiled at each other. There were categories in which we didn't stand a chance against Mike, but we could both hold our own at the movies. "Fifty bucks."

"I'm in," I said to Mercer.

Mike was reluctant. "Probably some dumbass song from a Disney flick. Make it twenty."

Mercer held his ground and Mike yielded.

"Here's the music," Trebek said. The introduction to the song played, and the Main Ingredient did the opening lines of "Everybody Plays the Fool." Mercer took my hand and started to dance with me as Trebek gave the clue.

"Tonight's answer is, the Oscar-winning actor whose father was the lead singer in this group."

Mike protested as Mercer and I danced around him. "That's a really misleading category. What did the guy win the award for?"

Mercer and I answered at the same time. "Supporting actor."

"We'll split the pot on this one, Ms. Cooper, okay?"

Mike, like the three contestants, did not know the right question. "That's not cricket. You two know more about Motown than I know about the Civil War."

Mercer told Trebek that the question was "'Who is Cuba Gooding Junior?' Now," he continued, turning to Mike, "Mr. Chapman, show us the money." We each took twenty-five from Chapman and began to open our presents.

"For you, Detective Wallace," I said, passing a wrapped package to him. He ripped at the paper and smiled when he lifted the cover off the box to reveal a photograph in an antique sterling-silver frame. I had asked the mayor to inscribe the picture of himself with Mercer and his father taken at City Hall, when Mercer had received an award for his work on a prominent art dealer's murder. It had been taken the week he had gotten out of a wheelchair and was walking without assistance, and the expression on Spencer's face told the whole story.

I gave Mike his gifts. First was a complete set of

Alfred Hitchcock videos accompanied by gift certificates for two tickets to his local movie theater good every month of the coming year.

For each, I had sketched an IOU for a plane ticket to the Vineyard, with dinners at the Outermost and the Beach Plum Inns, so we could all go up for a long weekend in the spring.

They had a bag full of surprises for me, including a little red voodoo doll, with a set of pins, labeled with Pat McKinney's name. They had wrapped a complete collection of Smokey Robinson CDs and had somehow managed to get Derek Jeter and Andy Pettitte to sign a note inviting me to the dugout after the opening game at Yankee Stadium in the spring, for which we all had tickets.

The last box was a tiny one, wrapped in shiny gold foil with white ribbon, with a card that read, *For our favorite partner.* Inside was a pair of cuff links. Each was a miniature blue and gold NYPD detective shield, one bearing Mike's number and the other Mercer's. I took the navy silk knots out of the French-cuffed shirt I was wearing with my blazer and jeans and replaced them with their gift.

Mercer drove us across town to West Forty-ninth Street, where I had reserved an eight-thirty table at Baldoria's. The bouncer held open the door and we were greeted inside by Frank. Since the chic downtown offshoot of Rao's had opened last year, it was one of the hottest tables in town. The great buzz, the classy brown and white decor, the same superb jukebox selections, and the outstanding food combined to make the place an instant success.

Bo Dietl was at the bar. He had retired from the police department after solving the Palm Sunday Massacre in Brooklyn several years back, but he was a dogged private investigator who seemed to keep tabs on every crime that went down in Manhattan.

"Buy them a round," he told the bartender. He had Mike corralled in a bear hug as he got off his stool to offer it to me. "What are you drinking?"

"Make it doubles all around. We had a rocky ride this afternoon." The story of the tram shooting became more embellished with each telling. Bo was chewing on his cigar as Mike described how he knocked me to the ground and had to cover my mouth because I was screaming so frantically.

"I didn't scream. I was so terrified, I think the words froze in my throat."

Bo asked what we were working on and Mike explained where we were in the Dakota case. "Did you remember to call Professor Lockhart this afternoon?" he was reminded to ask, turning to me.

"Yes, from the hospital, when the hearing was over. He lives just north of the city, in White Plains. If we drive up there tomorrow morning, he'll be happy to talk with us."

Bo kept looking over my shoulder, at the table closest to the end of the bar. "Guess the case they had in Jersey is falling apart."

"Not that I'm aware of—"

"Hey, Alex. The Bo reads the newspapers, y'know." He had a Bob Doleish way of talking about himself in the third person. "That guy, sitting with the broad with all the hair poofed up on top of her head? That's Ivan Kralovic, isn't it?"

My head snapped in the direction Bo's cigar was pointing. The face of the man in the booth was obscured by an upswept bouffant hairdo, but the retired detective kept talking. "Heard it in the car on the radio when I was on my way over here. Sinnelesi's number two man was putting the wood to the dead professor. Sleeping with her in the middle of the investigation. I'm telling you, it would take a prosecutor to be that friggin' stupid. Sorry, Alex. Kralovic's lawyer made a bail application this afternoon. Seems the defense team had known about the affair for weeks. The judge was ripped about it, and granted the application today. Looks like old Ivan knew where to get his first good meal."

I could see Kralovic clearly now as he leaned in to cut the thick veal chop on the plate in front of him. Ivan's mourning period for Lola had ended.

21

"We'll be back another time," I said, kissing Frank good-bye and trailing out of the restaurant behind Mercer and Mike. "It's not the food, it's the company." The last thing I needed was Kralovic telling his lawyer I tried to talk to him when I ran into him at dinner.

"I had a real craving for Peking duck, anyway," Mike said, opening the rear door of Mercer's car to let me in. We drove across town to Shun Lee Palace, and I stopped in the phone booth to try to reach Paul Battaglia to tell him what had happened.

After eight rings, I remembered that he was out of town until New Year's Day. Reluctantly, I dialed Pat McKinney's home number. "Thanks, Alex. I actually knew a few hours ago. Sinnelesi called me when he couldn't find the boss."

It would have been courteous, not to mention useful, for McKinney to have beeped me to tell me about Kralovic's release on bail. I hated having to learn it from an outside source, late on a Friday evening when it was impossible to get accurate details. "Did he tell you anything else?"

"Yeah, he fired Bart Frankel today. It'll be all over the papers tomorrow morning. Ivan's lawyer made a pretty compelling argument to the judge this afternoon that his client only went along with the sting because he knew in advance exactly what was happening, and wanted to be able to argue entrapment to the court."

"You mean entrapment as a defense to hiring someone to kill his wife?"

"Yeah. He's saying the tapes will prove the whole operation was Sinnelesi's idea. They're going to argue that Kralovic had himself wired up for months, every time he met with or spoke to the undercovers. And that if the two sets of tapes aren't the same, he'll prove the New Jersey prosecutor was corrupt and simply out to get him."

It had never occurred to me that Lola's husband might have any kind of viable defense to the charge of trying to kill her. But Sinnelesi's reputation was not beyond question, as Battaglia's was. Perhaps Paul's nose had been even more accurate than usual in detecting a good reason not to participate in the Jersey plan. If our counterparts across the Hudson had been unable to nail Kralovic squarely for his penny-stock fraud, then maybe they had stretched procedure and undermined the attempted murder case.

All that was certain is that Ivan the Terrible had exactly what he had wanted. Lola was dead, and the evidence pointing to him as the prime mover in her killing was looking muddier and muddier.

We settled in for the meal. The little bit of appetite that remained after the tram ride had evaporated with our sighting of Kralovic dining at an elegant restaurant. I watched Mike and Mercer go through steamed dumplings and chicken soong and a deliciously crispy duck, but I even refused my fortune cookie for fear that its prophecy would depress me.

They had dropped me at Jake's apartment by eleven. I called him at the Watergate Hotel to let him know that I had been delivered home safely. Unable to sleep, I drew a steaming-hot bath and tried to escape with the latest issues of *In Style* and *Architectural Digest*. When they failed to make me sleepy, I immersed myself in an interminable *New Yorker* piece on a lost Tibetan temple that had been rediscovered by a group of British trekkers. Midway through the story I was ready to turn out the light.

Mike was waiting for me outside the building at eight-fifteen. We stopped for coffee on our way north to Westchester County, to the suburban home where Professor Lockhart was staying. The car stops on the Fifty-ninth Street Bridge the night before had been unsuccessful, and the ballistics lab confirmed that the pellets had come from some kind of shotgun, not a pistol. I tried to buy into Mike's theory that it was simply pranksters with an early burst of holiday fireworks.

It was almost nine-thirty when I rang the bell at the neo-Victorian home on a quiet dead-end street in White Plains. The sandy-haired man who opened the door to us looked no older than Mike. He had fine, chiseled features and an athletic build. "I'm Skip Lockhart. Why don't you come inside and warm up?"

The large living room was filled with antique furniture and decorated in a very formal style. There were pictures on all the tabletops, which I tried to scan as he led us into a study.

"Thanks for coming up here. I'm kind of stuck for the next week."

"We just assumed that you lived here."

"It's my parents' home, actually. They've gone out to Scottsdale to visit my sister for the week, and I promised I'd come up here after Christmas to keep an eye on my grandfather, who lives with them. He's ninety, and as much as he thinks he can take care of himself, we need to keep an eye on him. I was a friend of Lola's. Anything I can do to be helpful, I'd like to try."

"Where's home?"

"In the city."

"Near campus? Near Lola's apartment?"

"A few blocks away."

Lockhart told us that he was thirty-eight years old, single, and an assistant professor of American history at King's College. He had known Lola for five or six years, and had never been romantically involved with her. Yes, he admitted that he had dated several students at the school, despite the fact that it was against the administrative guidelines. But he had never known Charlotte Voight and never given any thought to her disappearance.

"How much time did you spend with Dakota, on campus or off?"

"Very little, until she got me involved in the Blackwells Island project."

"What was your interest in that?"

"Two things, really," Lockhart answered, sitting back in his leather armchair and crossing one leg over the other knee. "Obviously, being a student of Americana, I'm quite familiar with the history of the area. An astounding number of well-known people have spent time there, and as a social phenomenon, it's a great resource for teaching students how we've dealt with society's outcasts throughout time."

He cleared his throat several times as he talked, looking us over and trying to get comfortable with us, it seemed to me.

"But I've always had a personal reason to be fascinated with that little strip of land. You see, my grandfather used to work on the island."

Mike was engaged now, both because of the investigation and because of his own love for historical nuggets. "What do you mean?"

"You probably know that the place was once covered by institutions—hospitals, asylums, jailhouses. And the New York Penitentiary."

"We were over there yesterday. That building doesn't exist at all anymore, does it? Just a pile of rubble and rocks."

"You're right. It used to stand directly to the north of the Smallpox Hospital, but it was demolished before the Second World War. It was the gloomiest place on the island, which is saying quite a lot. Unless you've made a study of it, as I have, there'd be no reason for you to know about the terrible scandal that took place there shortly before it was closed."

"What kind of scandal?"

"During the Tammany Hall days, the prison was a cesspool of corruption and graft. The place was actually dominated by mob members who were inmates. You'd have to see photographs to believe the way they lived."

"You mean how awful it was?"

"Not for the top dogs. They had quite a luxurious lifestyle, with personal pets and private gardens, food and liquor that was smuggled in to them. A few even dealt drugs inside."

"That piece of it hasn't changed too much," Chapman said.

"Finally, when Fiorello La Guardia was elected to the mayoralty and Tammany Hall fell, he named a new commissioner of correction. A gentleman named

Austin MacCormick. My grandfather was a young lawyer at the time, hired out of your office, Miss Cooper."

Lockhart leaned over and handed me one of the old photographs from the side table. "He wasn't even thirty years old. MacCormick hired him to work on the cleanup of the penitentiary. He and his cronies planned a huge surprise raid of the prison—a very successful one, which ended up shutting it down. It was quite a big deal. Gramps still has all the clippings to prove it."

Lockhart stood to adjust the thermostat in the room and check on the heat.

"Did Lola Dakota ever meet your grandfather?"

"Meet him? I thought she was going to elope with him." He laughed as he said it. "Once she found out that he had actually spent time on the island, there was no keeping her away from this house. And it was a god-send for my folks to have someone who took a real interest in the old guy, who could listen to his stories day in and day out."

"What did they talk about?"

"Everything he could remember. She listened to him describe the raid itself, she looked at his photo albums and read his diaries. In fact, I think she may still have had some of the volumes. I suppose someone will sort that all out and get them back to us. Seems rather irrelevant in light of what happened to Lola."

I made a note to look for the diaries among the inventory of Lola's books and papers.

"Were you there for those conversations?"

"Two or three times, at the outset. But I grew up on these stories and I've heard them all my life. I don't suppose there was anything he told her that I didn't already know. She'd just take the train up here, have lunch with my grandfather, spell my mother for a couple of hours. I don't think any great revelations came of it, Miss Cooper."

"Can you think of any reason, any motive for someone to kill Lola?"

"Is Ivan too obvious a choice? I've only met him a couple of times, but I know she was very frightened of him. There are plenty of students who hold her responsible for their not making the dean's list or bringing down their averages, but I don't think we had any homicidal maniacs among them."

"Did you ever accuse her of being a gold digger or a treasure seeker?"

Lockhart blushed. "That's what I get for being out of town when all this started. You've clearly covered some territory." He looked down at his Top-Siders and back up at Chapman. "Not in a literal sense. She wasn't after Ivan's money—if he really had any. It's just that she would latch onto people and use them for whatever she could suck out of them. Then she'd just discard them when they couldn't give her anything else. It wasn't a nice thing to watch."

"What do you know about Claude Lavery?"

Lockhart was slow to answer. "More than I ever

wanted to. I can't tell you I objected to his activities at the college. I can't say he was selling drugs to kids, exactly, but he introduced so many of them to a culture in which there was a general acceptance of substance abuse. There are so many rumors about his misappropriation of funds—well, it just makes me furious. We've been struggling awfully hard to get King's off the ground, and Lavery did everything he could to allow intellectuals at the better schools to think we were just all about street jive."

"What do you know about the missing money?"

"Not a thing. I'm on a tenure track myself, trying to keep my hands clean and mind my own business."

"Lavery and Lola?"

"I didn't meddle with it. They were pals. Nothing intimate, of course. She was working on something else with him, and I just put up a Chinese wall between us."

"Would you mind if we talked with your grandfather, as long as we're here?" I asked.

"Not at all. I'm sure he'd be delighted, too. Hope you don't have to be anywhere very soon. You get him going on the MacCormick raid and he'll bend your ear off."

Lockhart stood up to lead us out of the room, then turned back, biting the corner of his lip.

"Something wrong?"

"I doubt he'll realize that Lola is dead. I've told him about it, naturally, and I've read him the newspaper stories. It's just that he's got a bit of a problem with his memory. Long-term, it's quite remarkable. Doesn't forget a thing. But ask him what I gave him for breakfast, or the fact that Lola was murdered last week, and he won't know a thing about it. Some of the doctors believe it's an early stage of Alzheimer's, while others assume it's just part of his aging process."

Mike and I followed the young professor through the length of the rambling house, beyond the enormous kitchen to a cheerful solarium, where Lockhart's grandfather was sitting on a chintz sofa, washed in the sunlight that was streaming through the glass-walled room.

"Gramps, these are some people who are trying to help Lola. They'd like to talk to you."

"Lola? What's wrong with Lola?" The tall, lean man with an elegant mane of white hair raised himself to his feet and shook hands with Mike. "Orlyn Lockhart, sir. Who might you be?"

"I'm Michael Chapman. I'm a New York City detective. This is Alexandra Cooper. She works in the district attorney's office."

He checked behind himself to be sure the sofa cushion was in place, and as he lowered himself down, his grandson reached an arm out to steady his descent. "Did young Orlyn tell you I used to work there myself?"

"He certainly did." I smiled at Skip, who held up three fingers to indicate to me that he was the third Orlyn Lockhart.

"What service do you perform there? Are you a secretary?"

"No, sir. I'm an assistant district attorney in Mr. Battaglia's office. I run the Sex Crimes Prosecution Unit there."

"Still can't get used to the fact that women practice in the criminal courts." The old gent was shaking his head back and forth. "Wouldn't have seen one anywhere near the well of the courtroom in my day. Not a lawyer, not even allowed to serve on the jury. Where'd you go to school?"

"University of Virginia."

"Mr. Jefferson's university? My alma mater, too, young lady. They've come to let women in these days? I'm shocked. The whole damn school was men only back then, and a great place. Came out and went right to work in the best law office in the country. New York County district attorney. Joab Banton—I was one of Banton's boys. Blame all these women in the courtroom on Kate Hepburn. She started the whole damn thing with her movies. And wearing pants, no less. Who's the DA now? It's not still Dewey, is it?"

Not since 1941, when he left to run for election as the governor of New York, before two unsuccessful attempts at the presidency. "No, sir. Paul Battaglia." I was beginning to question how reliable a conversation with this man could be.

"Where's Lola?" The man's eyes were alive with interest, the fine light blue color coated with a thin layer of glaucoma-like haze.

Mike mumbled under his breath. "On ice."

"You say you were with Lola?"

"I told you they were Lola's friends, Gramps." Skip tried again to explain our connection to Lola without mentioning her death. The old man didn't get it. As they talked I could see the yellowed front page of the New York *Herald Tribune,* framed on the table at his elbow, with its banner headlines proclaiming the top news story of January 24, 1934: GANGSTER RULE OF ISLAND SMASHED BY MACCORMICK. "Worst Prison in World Recaptured from Control of Prison Mob Bosses."

The lead article, with its photograph of MacCormick and the young, good-looking former prosecutor at his side, appeared just above the news that the notorious John Dillinger had been taken into custody in Tucson, Arizona.

I seated myself on an ottoman facing Orlyn Lockhart, our knees practically touching as we spoke. "Someone tried to hurt Lola, so we thought we should find out why. We're talking to all her friends."

"Seems to *me* you should talk to her enemies. That's what I would have done."

Mike winked at me as he sat next to Skip's grandfather. "Score that one for Banton's boys, blondie. Bet he never lost his touch."

"What did Lola like to talk about with you? Can you tell me?"

He kept it all in the present tense. "We don't have to wait for her. She's heard most of my tales. Loves to hear me talk about the island."

The telephone rang and Skip stood up to walk to the kitchen. "Will you call me if you would like something to drink or eat? Gramps, you okay? I've got some phoning to do."

Orlyn kept talking right over Skip's announcement. "Biggest thugs in New York, and they were the ones running the penitentiary—from inside, no less. It started with Boss Tweed, back before I was born. You know he stole millions from the City of New York, and when they finally caught up with him, they sentenced him to twelve years on Blackwells Island.

"Want to know how he was treated? Tweed was given a furnished apartment in the penitentiary. Never locked. Had his own library and even a private secretary who came in to do his work. Wore his own suits and fancy clothes. Even had his lady friends in to visit. Died there before he could serve out his sentence."

"How did you get involved?"

"I'd done my prosecutorial work in the Rackets Bureau, trying to bust organized criminals who were taking over the town. Did I hear you say you're a detective, young man?"

Mike explained his assignment to Lockhart. At the same time, I tried to remember what my father had told me about the workings of neurons and the degeneration of brain tissue, how some contemporary memories become completely inaccessible but events deep in the past could be as distinct as if they had occurred the day before.

"Perhaps you've heard stories about the island in my day?" he asked.

"Not really."

"First thing they did, turn of the last century, was change its name. Not to Roosevelt, mind you. That didn't happen until after the Second World War. But for a brief time they called it Welfare Island.

"Most people thought Blackwells was cursed. The city closed down most of the hospitals and moved the sick and insane to more benign places. All shut down, except for the penitentiary. Ever hear of Dutch Schultz?"

"Sure," Mike answered. "Arthur Flegenheimer. Legendary mobster. Controlled a lot of business in the city."

Orlyn Lockhart zoned out on me. He had found a responsive audience in Mike and was playing to him. "I put his right-hand man away." He was tapping his forefinger against his chest. "I tried the case myself. Joseph Reggio. Know that name, too?"

"Harlem racketeer. Probably the number two guy in the mob at the time."

"Convicted him of extortion, ran the beer and soda water trade. Word got back to us, down at the district attorney's office, that Reggio had set himself up in prison like a king. He'd bribed all the authorities to get the inmates in the jail's clinic moved out to the general population. Reggio took over and made that infirmary his home. Dressed in silk robes and used lavender cologne. Cultivated a nice garden, kept a pet cow to get his own milk. Dined on the finest steaks and wines in his own apartment."

"In the *penitentiary*?"

"Two of them, there were, took over the prison hospital. Reggio ran his men, and the Irish hoodlums were led by a guy called Edward Cleary. That's the guy who kept his German shepherd with him in his room. Named it Screw Hater. 'Screws' are what they used to call the guards. Both of these toughs kept homing pigeons with them. Actual cotes of birds that carried notes—and probably narcotics—in and out of the jail."

"These two mobsters swaggered around while the regular crooks waited on them like slaves. Sad part is that the men who really needed medical treatment were just dumped into the general population. All the boys with social diseases—that's what we used to call it back then—they were mixing freely with the healthy ones. The whole place was a sea of misery. Full of degenerates. Faded tigers."

"Excuse me?"

"Didn't you ever read Dickens, young lady? When he visited New York, he asked to be taken to see old Blackwells."

I thought I had plowed through most of him in my undergraduate days, but the phrase didn't sound at all familiar. Perhaps that explained why Dickens's sketch was on Lola Dakota's bulletin board. Just one more notable figure who had connected with this island that so fascinated her. Now what we still needed to know was why Charlotte Voight's picture was there.

Lockhart was mumbling on about Dickens's visit to the prison, inmates dressed in the black-and-buff garb that the Englishman likened to faded tigers.

"Tell me about the raid," Mike said. Skip came back into the room with chamomile tea for his grandfather and mugs of coffee for us. He put them on the table, smiling at Mike's enthusiasm for the tales he had heard so many times and walking back to the kitchen. "Did you actually go along?"

"Go along, sir? MacCormick and I led the whole thing ourselves. I handpicked the detectives and wardens to come with us, but we led the very charge into the pens. First one to fall was a deputy warden who'd been on the take the whole time. Placed him right under arrest."

"I'd like to have been at your side," Mike said, egging him on.

"MacCormick had this planned to the minute. Closed down the prison switchboard so no one could call out while the raid was on. He dispatched the first men to the hospital ward to drag out Reggio and Cleary." Lockhart was chortling as he sipped his tea. "Guess he was afraid to let us get at each other. So he had them taken out of their luxurious quarters and thrown into solitary confinement."

"But you, did you go into the prison itself?"

"My boy, I can still smell it today. Most of the prisoners had been turned into dope fiends."

"After they went inside the walls?"

"Reggio and Cleary were running a drug smuggling business in the jailhouse. That's how they got all their lackeys to keep them in style, and segregated. First thing I saw were rows of men, shivering on benches, pleading with us to let them take their drugs. Most of them were covered with needle scars, all up and down their arms. Word spread that Commissioner MacCormick was walking through the three-tiered cell block himself."

"Never happen today. They'd just show for the photo op."

"All of a sudden we heard lots of clanging and things being thrown about. I went running to see what it was. Turns out prisoners were throwing their weapons, and their drug paraphernalia, out from between their bars. Nobody wanted to be caught with contraband in their cells. I leaned over and picked up some blackened spoons, what they cooked the drugs in. Spikes they used to shoot up. Whole sets of hypodermics. Cloths soaked in a heroin solution."

"Did you find what you expected?"

"Worse than that. Far worse. Drugs of every sort. And then the weapons started coming. We took out meat cleavers, hatchets, stilettos, butcher knives. I've got pictures, missy, front page of every newspaper in the country. Skip'll show you my scrapbooks.

"These gorillas had a real pecking order. The two at the top had their henchmen. There were at least twenty-five of them who kept the lowlifes in line, living in the worst conditions, waiting on Reggio and Cleary, and doing it all to get narcotics. Meanwhile, the goon squad who helped the bosses lived off the fat of the land. Taken off by van every day to work at the warden's home and eat pretty well themselves."

"Did you actually see where Reggio lived?"

"You wouldn't believe the sight. Hell, I wouldn't have, unless I'd been there in the flesh. After he'd been taken out, MacCormick and I went up to see his lavish digs, just to find out whether the reports we'd gotten had been exaggerated. Hah! Not a bit. He had a large suite of rooms in the old hospital wing, all laid out with his finery. A maroon cashmere lounging robe was spread across the foot of his bed, with two pairs of shoes, shoe trees neatly in them, lined up underneath."

Lockhart was shaking his head and wringing his hands as though he were right in the middle of the scene he was describing.

"There was a locker below the window and I got one of the boys to break it open. Inside there were a dozen boxes of expensive cigars, bars of perfumed soap, monogrammed stationery, face cream, kid gloves, linen handkerchiefs." He shook his head. "Here I thought I'd condemned him to purgatory when he was sentenced to jail, and he was living far better than most folks I knew. That was before I saw his kitchen and his garden."

"His own kitchen?"

"Well, Reggio and Cleary shared a private one. The men downstairs were eating slop and gruel, just like the old days. These guys had gallons of fresh milk, crates of cranberries, fresh meat, pickled herrings, bags of potatoes. They had a pretty nice stash of liquor, too.

"Cleary, his room was a little less refined. Where Reggio had a crucifix over the bed and rosary beads beside it, Cleary had a dagger stuck in the wall over his head. I guess we'd interrupted him. There was an unplayed hand of pinochle on the table, some device up on the rafters that was concocting a home brew, and an empty pint bottle of whiskey. Screw Hater, the dog, was sitting next to the bed, trembling till we took him down and fed him one of his master's steaks. Then there was a little lounging area next to it where Cleary and his thugs spent the day, when he didn't choose to be out wandering the grounds."

"What grounds?"

"Behind the penitentiary. Reggio paid the other inmates to build him a garden. That's where he kept his milking cow and his pet goat. Beautiful spot it was, looking back over to Manhattan. He'd set up park benches and exquisite flowers, though they weren't in bloom that day. And he controlled who could enter the place. Kept the riffraff out.

"The pigeon cote was up in the roof above Cleary's room. Each of them had about two hundred birds, cooing themselves up a storm. MacCormick truly thought that's how they got messages in and out. Hell, it wouldn't have made a bit of difference. Once they'd bought the wardens, bribed them with all the mob money that Dutch Schultz could muster, they carried anything they wanted in and out the front door of the joint. Easy as that."

"So it must have been a great day for you." Mike had picked up the framed clipping and was reading the text of the story. "I've closed down a lot of joints in my time, Mr. Lockhart, but not quite the way you did. I'm impressed."

"Shut it tight. Demolished the entire building. A fortress, it was, and now it's just a pile of old stones." He pushed himself up and walked to the window at the side of the house, looking for signs of movement in the driveway. "Where's my Lola? Always brings me licorice. Those little bits of black licorice. She likes the part about the man who was killed."

"In the raid?"

"Only one hurt in the whole damn thing. Could have cost me my job."

"Why does Lola like that part?" I asked.

"Ask Lola." He shuffled back to his seat and eased himself down.

"One of the mobsters was killed?" Mike wanted to know.

"No, no. A gentleman. One of the cosseted prisoners who lived there like a lord. Paid Reggio a fortune to be mollycoddled in his own private prison aerie. That's

333

probably why Lola liked him. He was a real gentleman. I knew him too, before he wound up in the penitentiary."

"Who was he?"

"Freeland Jennings, Detective. Wasn't half bad. Do they still talk about him?"

Mike and I exchanged glances. Neither of us had ever heard the name.

"Talk about the stooges like Dutch Schultz and Edward Cleary and everyone knows the tales, but nobody remembers the men who built the city. Freeland Jennings was a merchant, a friend of Pierre Cartier's. Cartier put him into the diamond trade and Jennings made himself a fortune. Spent half his life on ocean liners, crossing back and forth to London and Antwerp. But he was a great philanthropist, mind you. Helped Vanderbilt pay for the new opera house. Gave money to the public library and created the historical society."

"How'd he wind up inside the walls of the penitentiary?"

"Shot his wife. And I have to say, young lady"— Lockhart fixed his gaze on me and wagged his finger—"I have to say that it's a case I myself would never have prosecuted. Ariana, she was. Jennings married a foreigner. Clever, good-looking girl who had just about anything you could want. He showered her with jewels, of course, and showed her off everywhere. She'd have never been in the *Social Register*, being

Italian and all, if she hadn't married Freeland. I used to play cards with him once a week, over at the University Club. Saw him just two days before the murder.

"Ariana became restless while he was abroad so much. Took up with a lover, a real rogue. It wasn't unheard of in my time, but most people kept quiet about it. Not Ariana—she flaunted it so's it was all over town. Took him to Jennings's box at the Metropolitan Opera, danced with him in public, some even say he was the father of her child."

The old man was tiring now. He'd been talking with great animation and was slowly losing steam in the process.

"It's names I have trouble remembering. Not the ones I put in jail, or the fellows I knew well, but some of these other characters. Forgive me. Anyway, Jennings was called back unexpectedly from Europe one time, and I guess he'd just had one embarrassment too many. Ariana wasn't home to greet him, but when he went out that evening, he ran into her with her beau, just strolling through the Grand Army Plaza. He made the assumption that they were just coming out of the Plaza Hotel after a rendezvous. Words were exchanged between the two men—I'm not exactly clear on what was said. But Ariana defended her lover. Right there on the street, nice people parading all around and minding their own business.

"Plain and simple, Jennings pulled a pistol and threatened his rival. The man taunted him—called him all kinds of names. Insulted his manhood. Freeland just went berserk and fired the gun. But he killed Ariana instead of her lover. Shot her once through the chest."

Lockhart thought about it for a minute. "Justifiable, is what *I* would have argued. 'Twas Ariana the cause of the whole damn mess. If she hadn't been such a loose woman—well . . . In any event, he was convicted of manslaughter."

Views about spousal murder had not changed very much over time. It was neither a new phenomenon nor a well-understood one. But that might have been enough of a reason for Lola's interest in the Freeland Jennings saga.

"And he was sentenced to the penitentiary?"

"Very same one, of course. And those convicts who weren't protected by the mob did some hard labor. Quarrying island stone and things that weren't fit for a gentleman to do. Fortunately for him, Freeland had the means to pay Reggio and Cleary for a finer lifestyle.

"That was actually their downfall. It was Freeland who complained to me about the narcotics problem. Wrote me a letter and explained to me how everything was for sale on the island. Liked his jailhouse apartment fine, he did, under the circumstances. Had a small turret in the prison, looking right out across the East River to his home on Manhattan. Paid dearly for it. He was allowed to keep some cases of wine with him and all his favorite clothes. Had a radio and headset so he could stay current on the news."

Lockhart's voice was giving out a bit. I leaned closer to hear him. "Freeland just couldn't tolerate the addiction, and what was happening to the lowest class of prisoners. Felt all those drugs coming in were making the situation dangerous for everyone. They were a scurvy bunch, desperate and violent."

"Was he killed when your cops went in with MacCormick? Did he resist—"

"Thank goodness, we had nothing to do with it. It was the thugs that got him. One of them rammed a shiv right between his ribs. Went like a stuck pig."

"Was it because he squealed about the narcotics in the penitentiary?"

Orlyn Lockhart paused. He rubbed his right eye with his hand and seemed exasperated when he spoke to me. "You're just as impatient as she is. It's Freeland's diamonds you want, just like Lola. Do you believe they're buried on Blackwells Island, too?"

22

The old man wanted to tell the story his way.

"MacCormick was right. He knew that Freeland Jennings was my friend, so he didn't think I ought to be anywhere near his quarters during the raid. As soon as my deputies seized Reggio and Cleary, their hoodlums scattered pretty quickly. Mind you, the mob lieutenants weren't even under lock and key at the time. There were a couple of dozen of them scrambling around, knowing they were about to get shipped up the river for real. These were their last moments of freedom before their corrupt world collapsed.

"Two of the most vicious broke into Jennings's apartment and cornered him there. He wasn't part of the rackets, of course, so he wasn't one of their own. They'd been treating him special only because he was paying the two top dogs for his privileges."

"They wanted his money, I guess."

"They wanted everything he had. And so a legend

had grown up around my old acquaintance." He glanced back over at me. "This is the part you girls like. Story goes that what Joseph Reggio had demanded from Freeland Jennings was diamonds. Sparkling pieces of ice that could be smuggled out with ease. Forget about needing a pocket or pouch to hold them. You might actually come across an honest warden who would search in those things. Why, these'd fit inside a shoe without anybody noticing. Sneaked out in the folds of a hem when a lady visitor passed through. The most perfect currency for an imprisoned privateer."

"Did Jennings really keep diamonds in the penitentiary?"

"Well, he certainly hinted to me that he had. Did what he needed to do to stay alive."

"Did he have them right in his room?"

"This is the stuff of legends, now, son. I'm telling you what the boys told Commissioner MacCormick and me, not what I saw for myself. They said Jennings was the wily type and didn't trust any of these goons around him. Most he ever kept in his apartment were two or three gems, 'cause one of them went a long way at that time. It would have been a lot easier to hide a small stone than it was to try to conceal a stack of bills or enough gold to keep Reggio happy.

"But there were other places on the island, see, to keep his jewels."

"I realize they had the run of the penitentiary, Mr.

339

Lockhart," Mike said, "but not access to the rest of the land beyond the jail walls."

"Ah, but you're forgetting what most of the prisoners did every day."

"Some of them had to work as caretakers in the other hospitals and asylums," I offered, still chilled by that startling fact.

"But most of them, missy, were doing hard labor. The island abounded with rich deposits of stone. Desirable building material, granite and gneiss. Most of the convicts were sent out in their striped uniforms to spend their days excavating the rock.

"And some of Reggio's men believed that Jennings had bought the services of a laborer to dig him a secure place in one of the quarries. A concealed lair in which he could secrete his cache of precious gems. That way, he didn't have to be afraid that if the thugs found everything he had in his room and robbed him of it, he'd lose his means to pay Reggio."

"So someone would smuggle the diamonds in to Mr. Jennings, and he'd use them as he needed them?"

"I suspect it was his lawyer who brought in the jewels. You know, since ancient times, there's been a universal method of carrying loose stones. You just fold them into a paper pouch, smaller than the palm of one's hand, and you can pretty much go anywhere you want, unmolested."

Lockhart was right. To this day, throughout the diamond district in midtown Manhattan and in the gem trade all over the world, the most incredibly valuable stones were carried this way—wrapped only in a thin slip of paper—in the pockets of pants and jackets of the most unlikely-looking couriers.

"Were any found during the raid?"

"Just two. Saw them myself, right in the warden's office, when one of the detectives carried them in to us. There was a rose-colored one, about the size of a pigeon's egg, sewed right into the cuff of a pair of pants. And then a crystal-clear diamond with more brilliance than the brightest star I've ever seen. It was just a small one, and it was stuffed in a tiny slit inside the leather cover of Freeland's mother's Bible that he kept next to the bed." He laughed to himself. "Guess it wouldn't occur to the thugs to look in the Lord's book.

"Problem was that one of Reggio's men—believe his name might have been Kennelly, but can't be sure—thought he could strong-arm Jennings right at the start of the raid. Knew it was his only chance to get the diamonds, and so he stormed the apartment with a cohort and demanded the gems." Lockhart was flagging now, and something had made him sad. "Blame myself, in some ways, for the fact that he died."

"How so?"

"If there really were other diamonds, well—the reason poor Freeland didn't yield to the bastards was because he thought he'd be perfectly safe during the raid."

"He knew that you and MacCormick were coming?"

"Let me say this, young man. I never betrayed a confidence of the commissioner's, but I was the one to whom Jennings was sending the letters. I certainly wanted to give his lawyer an assurance that we had heeded his message."

Lockhart stiffened in his chair and bored his eyes into Chapman's. "I wanted Jennings to understand that we believed the stories he was sending out. We should have made him safe the instant we got in. I argued with MacCormick about it, but he was all consumed with nailing the door shut on Reggio and Cleary. Just didn't figure that anything could go so very wrong."

"What happened to Jennings?"

"Kennelly and some other tough started roughing him about. They knew he had been assigned a couple of laborers to do his dirty work, but if he had actually trusted one of them to go out and bury his gems, my friend wasn't talking." He shook his head from side to side. "Might even have been smug about it because he was confident I'd be coming along.

"Whatever it was, Jennings was up against men who didn't know how to play by the rules. When they threatened him with a meat cleaver from Reggio's private kitchen, so the story goes, he picked up a sharpened knife he kept next to his bed. Beside the Bible, actually. He tried to use it to repel Kennelly, but he was no match for that animal. The two of them overpowered poor Jennings and one of them shoved the knife right between his ribs. Killed him instantly."

"And the diamonds?"

"My detectives were on these two fellows pretty quickly. Mind you, at the time, no one knew the men were in Jennings's room to find jewels. That's the story that other prisoners began to tell long after the dust settled. They both were examined quite thoroughly since we were all looking for contraband and drugs, small things that could be concealed. No jewels, my dear."

"Was the island searched?"

"By the time these stories surfaced, the penitentiary had long been abandoned and the quarries on the island had been mined of their riches. People have scoured it and fools will continue to do so well after I'm gone, if you ask me.

"Course, if I didn't have this tale to tell, probably wouldn't get a single visitor anymore. That's why Lola comes." He lifted his left arm and squinted to see the time. "She's late."

"Was Lola looking for Jennings's diamonds?"

"She may guess that I'm stupid and senile, but if Lola thinks I believe there's any other reason she's been here to visit me, she's mistaken. She's been all through my diaries, too. I suspect she's looking for clues that she thinks I've forgotten by now. Probably knows more about all my lady friends and some of the crooks I represented in my practice than she does about any buried treasure"—he smiled broadly now—"but if it keeps her coming back here to chat with me, she's welcome to them. Hell, I've answered to more important people than Lola about that."

"What do you mean?"

"Old MacCormick himself called me on the carpet many years after the raid. Thought I was living mighty high on the hog and had heard all the rumors by then. Looked me straight in the eye and asked whether Jennings had paid me off before the raid, or had I known where his stash was hidden. Even the mayor bought me a drink one night. Fiorella La Guardia. Over at the 21 Club it was. Had to know about the diamonds, he said, and whether I thought they were really there."

"What did—?"

"And Jennings's son. He was going off to Europe to fight. Middle of the Second World War. I call him Jennings's son, but all I know for sure is that his mother was Ariana. Hard to figure whether Freeland had been cuckolded by that tart before the kid was born. The boy had run through most of his old man's money and felt the diamonds were his due. He wasn't just curious. He accused me of stealing the damn things out from under my dead friend. Angry with me, he was. But it didn't make any difference. Never saw him again after that."

"Did you ever look for the diamonds yourself?"

"I only set foot on the island once, the day of the raid. No reason to go back, in my book."

"Did Lola talk to you about the deadhouse?"

He snapped his head to look at me. "You damn well must be her friend. What is it? Where is it? Damned if I ever heard that word before she sat at my feet going at me. Doesn't mean a thing to me, young lady."

"May we come back and visit you sometime, Mr. Lockhart?" Mike was on his feet, hand on the shoulder of the old guy so he didn't feel the need to stand up with us.

"Certainly, certainly you must. Come to the party next week. Skip's having a little holiday party at the house." His eyes brightened and he looked up at me. "You'll bring me some licorice, will you? And you, miss, you'll send my best to Mr. Hogan?"

Frank Hogan had been one of America's great prosecutors, before Bob Morgenthau and Paul Battaglia. He had died in 1974 after twenty-eight years as Manhattan's district attorney. I wondered anew how much of what Orlyn Lockhart had been telling us was fact, and how much was lost in the confusion of time past. Perhaps I could get some articles from the microfiche newspaper files at the New York Public Library and research the story of Freeland Jennings and the penitentiary raid.

We made our way back through the kitchen, where the professor was working on his laptop computer. He looked up as we entered the room. "Thanks for listening to my grandfather. You've just spelled me for an hour and I've gotten some work done."

Chapman was annoyed. "When I asked you about whether you'd ever called Ms. Dakota a gold digger, you jerked me around. Seems pretty obvious to me that you know she's been nagging the old man about buried treasure. You gonna tell me you haven't been party to her diamond excavations?"

Skip Lockhart stood up to face Mike. "Look, half of the stuff the guy's talking about is just nonsense he makes up, I'm sure of it. He likes to have an audience, and quite frankly, it's worn most of the family pretty thin over the years."

"But it's his story that interested you in the Blackwells project in the first place."

"Sure it is. But that's on an intellectual level. The raid really happened. The prison conditions that he probably described to you are quite accurate. I've researched all that. But my grandfather doesn't know any more about missing diamonds than you do."

"Except that he actually eyeballed two gemstones the very day of the raid. That gives some credence to the whole story, doesn't it? When will you be back in your office in the city?"

"Next Thursday, January second."

"Expect me. Early and often. And I'll want to see the reports of all your trips over to the island with Lola Dakota—and anything else that might relate to the project. Have them ready. And a list of the students who've worked on the dig with both of you."

My beeper began to vibrate as I buttoned my coat

and walked out the door. I shuddered once against the cold and then a second time when I recognized Pat McKinney's home number. I opened the car door and dialed my cell phone.

"So what do you do for excitement when you and Chapman aren't making people's lives miserable?"

"That does seem to account for an inordinate amount of our time, Pat." It was clear he was about to unload some kind of bad news on me. "Want me to think about it and get back to you?"

"I figured if you had nothing better to do today you could get yourself back over to New Jersey, to the medical center near Hackensack. Bart Frankel's car was rear-ended early this morning by a Mack truck. The truck won."

23

"If we got three choices, the only one I can rule out is suicide. Pretty hard to count on killing yourself by letting the car behind you run you off the road. Ain't always a sure thing."

It was early Saturday afternoon and the detective from Sinnelesi's office, Tony Parisi, was talking to us in the visitors' lounge at the hospital.

"Between an accident and a homicide attempt, what's your guess?"

"Tough to prove it's anything but an accident. Old shitcan of a car moving along on Route Seventeen, and a trucker comes barreling down behind it at one of those treacherous curves in the road. The driver gets distracted, hits a patch of ice, and slams on the brakes too late. Schmuck behind him just whacks him off the road into a row of trees. Splinter pie, man.

"And let me tell you, Bart was really distracted. When the news got out after that bail application yesterday and Kralovic was released, Bart was ready to crawl into a hole. If the old will to live has anything to do with getting him off the life-support machine, he ain't gonna make it. He's toast."

"What do you know about the truck?"

"Not even sure that's what it was. Hit-and-run is all we know. Somebody wanted him out of that lane real bad and then didn't even stop to see what happened. Shit, if Vinny Sinnelesi was in town, I'd put my money on him. He'll be royally pissed if Bart blew the Kralovic case for him."

"Don't you think he'll live?" I asked tentatively.

"Not a prayer. Just hooked him up so his kids could say good-bye to a warm body. They're in with him now. His lawyer claims he did one of those living wills. 'Don't crank me up again once the pump shuts off.' I'd say, you want to make sure it's curtains for Bart? You two grim reapers walk in the room and hand him one of your bona fide New York County subpoenas. *Finito*."

At least I didn't have to be paranoid that Pat McKinney was the only person who blamed me for Bart Frankel's condition. Mike ran his fingers through his dark hair, clearly troubled. He started to speak. "What—?"

"Don't even ask what you think you can do for him, Chapman. We'll be taking care of this one all on our own. You know we got real cops here in Jersey, too?"

"Yeah, but you haven't solved a friggin' case since the Lindbergh baby was kidnapped."

"Bart's one of ours, whether you liked him or not. Poor slob was thinking with his penis instead of his brain. Gettin' in bed with that Dakota dame was a stupid thing to do, but you got a long way to go to convince me he'd whack a broad or throw a case."

"Tony, I appreciate your feelings for Bart. And I understand why you're unhappy with us. But there was information he had that we needed." I was trying to dance around the fact that the prosecutor had not told us the truth. This detective had no cause to know it, and I did not want to broadcast the fact, given Bart's medical condition.

While it was possible to believe he had dropped Lola off at her building's entrance as he had claimed, it seemed hard to deny that he had then gone on to her office at King's College. He may even have taken something of significance from her desk. Something, I had hoped, that would lead us to the reason for her murder.

"Look, you got no jurisdiction here, Miss Cooper. And besides that, I don't think nobody that knew Bart even wants you on this end of the tunnel."

"Alex is being polite, pal. She isn't telling you the half of it. Executive Assistant District Attorney Bart Frankel looked the two of us in the eye and lied to us."

Parisi was unmoved.

"He fibbed about things that happened the very afternoon that Lola was killed. Not just the fact that he was sleeping with her. Where he was at the moment she died, what he was doing. He even held back for an entire week the name of the guy she walked into the building with."

Parisi bit his lip, not wanting to trust Chapman. "What do you want from me?"

"I want the chance to go to *his* office, the way he went through Lo—"

"Are you nuts or what? Don't even finish that sentence. I'm gonna take you two over to Sinnelesi's office while his main man is sucking on an air tube in a hospital bed, sneak you inside, maybe get my balls cut off in the process if anybody catches me, just 'cause you think you're gonna find something you can use to sink Bart in this even worse? Not happening, baby."

"We'll be fast. You can stay with us the whole time."

"And who's gonna hire a gone-to-seed former investigator for Vinny Sinnelesi when I get thrown out on my ass? Chapman, you've pulled a lot of crap in your day, but you ain't calling the shots on this one."

"Just for once, why don't you do something useful for society?"

"Screw you. I recycle."

"Tony, when we were up at Lily's house—Lola's sister—she told us that she had signed a power of attorney so that Vinny could go into Lola's office and remove her belongings. All of them. Who actually went and did that? Was it Bart?"

Parisi fidgeted.

"You're looking at this with blinders on. Buy into my facts for a minute. Bart went to the campus the day

Lola was killed, maybe already knowing she was dead. He was searching for something. Alex and I can prove that. If he found what he wanted that day, or if he went back for it with legal authority to do so a few days later, maybe he got what he was after.

"And just suppose, for one minute, that what he discovered in Lola's office is what got him followed this morning. Got him killed."

"Suppose *you* start thinking that if there's any truth to what you're saying, I'm gonna be able to figure it out myself. It's what they pay me the big bucks to do." Parisi had given us all the time he was going to waste, so he turned on his heel and headed for the door.

"Tony, you know what to look for, right? You'll recognize all the players? Charlotte Voight, Skip Lockhart, Sylvia Foote, Freeland Jennings, the Blackwells project . . ."

Chapman was calling up every name he had heard in the past eight days, aware that none of them would ring a bell with the New Jersey detective. There was no reason for Parisi to have known them, but it worked perfectly to nag at his insecurity. His footsteps slowed.

"Twenty minutes, Tony. Just you and me. Blondie waits in the car."

My opportunity to participate in the search had just been sacrificed to the greater cause: male bonding.

"I must have a death wish. I'll meet you over at the office. Park a block away and leave her there." Parisi dismissed me with a heaving sigh and a look back over his shoulder. "Give me a ten-minute lead and I'll let you in the back door. Deal's off if any of the lawyers are in there working."

Mike checked his watch. "Saturday afternoon at three o'clock when it's eighteen degrees outside and we're in the middle of the holiday weekend? In Battaglia's office, even the cockroaches wouldn't be behind their desks."

He nudged me out of the waiting area. I walked to the nurses' station to inquire again about Bart Frankel's condition. A new face behind the desk asked me if I was family and I shook my head in the negative. "There's nothing I can tell you." Her grim expression spoke volumes.

We made the short drive to the prosecutor's office and this time, instead of using the rear parking lot, Mike stopped in front of the pizza shop at the far corner. He left the ignition on so that I could have the benefits of the heat and the radio.

"You mind?"

"I always knew I'd be the first thing to go. Come back with something good and I'll forgive you."

It was close to half an hour later when Mike returned to the car. The wind blew in with him as he opened the door and got back into the driver's seat. "I wouldn't say we hit the jackpot, but we got a few things to work with. This stuff would have sat in Sinnelesi's drawer till you started sprouting gray hair underneath that peroxide before anybody would have told us about it.

"First of all, Bart Frankel was—as a tribute to modern medicine, I'll say *is*—up to his ass in debt. Left his private practice, which wasn't exactly a thriving one, to come back to public service when the Fat Man called him. Paying a huge amount of alimony 'cause his ex has a serious medical problem. Three kids, two in college and one getting ready to go. And a slight penchant for the horses. The Meadowlands was his second home. Gambling debts running close to a quarter of a million."

Hard to do on a prosecutor's salary.

"What do you know about penny stocks, Coop? I mean the kinds that are bad schemes."

"The basics, why?"

"Explain 'em to me. I Xeroxed a file that was on top of Bart's desk, but I don't know anything about that business."

"They're generally really cheap stocks in small, sometimes dubious companies. A lot of them have involved investment scams. There are salesmen who make cold calls by telephone, just reading from a script. The guys behind the scam pump up the shares by fake trades and false publicity. When the stock soars, the promoters generally cash in and leave the other investors holding worthless shares."

"Ever hear of"—Mike looked down at the tab on the manila folder—"Jersey First Securities?"

"No."

"Seems like Sinnelesi's been investigating the company.

The two partners behind the business are about to declare bankruptcy, and it looks like the note on the file quotes the feds as saying this was a 'continuing massive fraud.' And one of the penny-meisters is—"

"Ivan Kralovic, of course."

"So it would seem. And who lost lots of nickels and dimes betting on Ivan's pot?"

"Bart?"

"So when Vinny gets back from the sunny south, maybe he can explain to you why he'd let Bart anywhere near this investigation. Hold on to the file. Now, exhibit number two. Here's a photocopy of a little envelope," Mike said, holding up an image of a tiny white packet that looked no longer than three inches. "You recognize the penmanship?"

I did. It was Dakota's.

"Can't say I'm as familiar with it as you are, but when I saw the little Post-it attached with the initials L.D., I took a wild guess."

I looked at the single word printed on the front by Lola: "Blackwells."

"I lifted the flap and guess what slipped into my hand?"

I shook my head at Mike, puzzled.

"A little gold key. No markings, no numbers."

"Was there anything else with this?"

"Nope. It was buried under a few personal notes in his top drawer. Now all we have to do is find out what it fits into. Get one of your clones started on a warrant."

He revved up the engine and made a U-turn on the quiet street. "And last but not least, we're going to meet Dr. Claude Lavery."

"Now? Is he back? Why—"

"Because that's who Bart Frankel was on his way to see this morning when he was so rudely interrupted."

24

_____

"Tony Parisi told you about Lavery?"

"No, he called over to Bart's house. I almost had
him convinced after a once-over of Bart's office that he
should walk me through his home to see if we could
find anything. You know that if Bart's life was as
screwed up as it sounds, he's probably got stuff there
that we should be looking at. Anyway, one of his kids
had taken a break from the hospital vigil and answered
the phone, which put the kibosh on that idea for the
moment."

I couldn't imagine what this was like for Bart's three
children.

"But when Tony asked the daughter why her dad
had left the house so early this morning, she said that
a man had called him last night and Bart had told her
that he had to go into the city to see him. There was a
pad next to the telephone that had Lavery's name and
number written on it."

"Not bad for a quick sweep through the office."

"Hey, easier than if I had to search your place for anything of value. You got four extra pairs of shoes under the desk, different-height heels for every occasion. Drawers filled with panty hose, nail polish, perfume, and Extra-Strength Tylenol. Somebody bumps you off and the first thing Battaglia has to do is run a tag sale to get rid of your beauty supplies."

Mike was enthused now. He had new directions in which to proceed and pieces of the puzzle to try to fit into place. "How do you even begin to figure out the significance of a key? And how do you know what door it fits?"

"Start with the fact that it's labeled 'Blackwells.'"

"Yeah, but there aren't a lot of buildings still standing on the island from those days. And the remnants that are there don't have doors."

"So it's something connected to the project, probably."

"I think even two hours' exposure to New Jersey has damaged your brain. No kidding, Coop. Like I needed your help to figure that one out."

"Were any of the things taken from Lola's office, after Lily gave Sinnelesi permission, listed and inventoried so we have a record of them?"

"Nope. Would it surprise you to learn that Bart Frankel picked two of his squad cops, drove over himself, and just sort of packed up the whole bundle to be sorted out at his convenience? In the privacy of his office. Somehow that stinks as bad as the rest of what he was doing."

"Where is the stuff now?"

"Parisi doesn't know. He'll have to find the guys who went with Bart and see what closet they dumped everything into."

"Sooner rather than later. We've got to see what he found."

"Give me credit for something, Coop. I do believe I've lit that fire under Parisi's ass."

"You think Lola knew, when she got into bed with Bart, that he had lost all his money in one of Ivan's deals?"

"Hard to imagine that it wouldn't have come up in conversation. Gave them both a reason to hate the guy. And it gave Bart an extra incentive to go after Ivan."

I thought for several minutes. "That's one way to look at it. But there's a darker side to that. Suppose Ivan's about to get jammed up by Sinnelesi's office. The number two man is up to his ears in debt, and Ivan knows why. What if he tried to buy his way out of the whole thing—two cases at the same time? I mean, how could Bart have screwed up Lola's undercover sting so badly? Bad enough that Ivan's back on the street. You'd have to try awfully hard to step on yourself that way."

Mike was with me. "So you go as far as having Bart getting paid off by Ivan. Bart maybe even delivering Lola right into the killer's hands. Dropping her off at her front door. *Ciao,* baby, see you later. Then he drives off into the sunset, stopping by the campus to pick up the key—the key to . . . ? That's sort of where the plan gets parked with me."

"I'm not saying that's what I think happened. I just know I'm praying for Bart's recovery for all the wrong reasons. I'd love him to answer some questions for us."

On the ride back to the city we thought aloud about all the possible links among Ivan's fraud investigation, the domestic violence complaints, and Lola's death.

The scene in front of 417 Riverside Drive was a much calmer one than the one the night of the murder. Mike rang the bell in the vestibule next to Lavery's name and within a minute, through the intercom, a voice said, "Yes?"

Mike muffled his mouth with his hand and spoke a single word: "Bart." "Bart" was a few hours late, but still welcome enough for Lavery to buzz us into the lobby. We entered together and walked to the elevator.

When we reached the sixteenth floor, the door to Lavery's apartment was ajar. I could hear someone speaking on the telephone, so I pushed it wider and Mike came inside behind me. The man whom we assumed to be Lavery was standing with his back to us. His conversation was ending, and he thanked his caller before he hung up and turned around, startled to see us.

"I'm Mike Chapman. NYPD Homicide," Mike said, flipping his gold shield out of its case. "This is Alexandra Cooper. Manhattan DA's Office. We've been—"

"Not exactly who I was expecting when I let you in, Detective." Lavery walked to the doorway behind us and stuck his head out in the hallway. "Is Bart coming along, too?"

I could sense that if Lavery did not yet know about Bart's accident, Mike wasn't going to tell him. "He's had a rough day. I doubt he's gonna make it."

Lavery was clearly puzzled. He walked to the CD player on the bookshelf along the far wall and lowered the volume. If Chapman had been expecting Bob Marley and the Wailers, with Lavery smoking weed through a wooden pipe, he must have been disappointed. A Beethoven adagio provided the soft background to our conversation. Lavery had apparently been sitting at a desk in front of his park-view window, working longhand on some piece of writing. He was dressed in African garb and still had his hair done in dreadlocks.

"Bart's been a friend of ours for a long time. He decided, after you two spoke on the phone, that he really didn't want to meet with you alone. He thinks it would be better if you say what you want to say to the two of us."

Lavery's expression gave nothing away, but he seemed too smart to trust the situation. Or the cop who was giving him the once-over.

He folded his arms across his chest and looked at me. "Aren't you the woman handling the investigation into Lola Dakota's death? I recognize your name from the news stories." His voice was a deep baritone, and he spoke in a measured cadence.

"Yes, we're both working on that case."

"Lola was a dear friend of mine. And a great supporter, in what have been some difficult days for me." He turned away to walk to a living area, motioning us to follow. "I suppose you've heard about that?" He asked it in the form of a question, not quite sure what to think.

"Yeah, we know a bit about it."

"Lola has stood by me from the outset. Taken my part with the administration. I shall miss her friendship terribly."

"Actually, that's what we'd like to talk to you about. We've been trying to reach you—"

"Would you mind if I called Bart, Detective? I'd prefer to—"

"Bart's out of the picture, Mr. Lavery. For the time—"

"Doctor. It's *Doctor* Lavery." He lowered himself into an armchair and we sat opposite him.

"You got a stethoscope, a prescription pad, and a license to practice medicine, then I'll call you 'doctor.' Every other ologist who writes a dissertation on some useless theoretical load of crap is just plain old 'mister' to me."

"Professor . . ." I tried to start anew.

"Ah, the diplomat on the team."

"Yeah, the Madeleine Albright of the Manhattan

District Attorney's Office. She wants to know the same thing I do. Bart was kind of surprised when you called. He didn't know you were back in New York."

"I arrived home last evening. Around eleven o'clock."

"We've been trying to interview all of Ms. Dakota's associates and friends. I hope you don't mind if we ask a few questions?" I tried smiling at him. "They're quite routine."

"If it will assist you in finding the beast who did this, I'm pleased to help."

"When did you leave town, Professor? I mean, where were you coming from last evening?"

"I flew to visit friends during Christmas week. Went to St. Thomas, in the Caribbean."

"When did you leave town exactly?"

"On December twenty-first, I've still got the ticket right here. I can show it to you, if that's necessary."

"That's two days after Lola was killed. Last Saturday, am I right?"

"I guess it was. I debated about staying for her funeral in New Jersey on Monday, but my friends were expecting me and I didn't think there was anything I could do to be useful. Many of our colleagues didn't share Lola's feelings about my work."

"The guys from my squad canvassed the building on Friday. Miss Cooper and I have read those reports. I understand you were here in the apartment on the afternoon of the murder."

"Yes, I talked to the police. Of course, I have no idea what time it was when all this happened to Lola."

"Don't worry about that. Why don't you just tell us what you were doing that day?"

"Thursday the nineteenth . . . let me think a moment. Most days, I work from my home instead of the office over at King's. As you must be aware, I've been suspended from the college while they examine this glitch with my grant."

A several-hundred-thousand-dollar glitch, I thought to myself.

"I seem to recall going out in the morning to pick up some things I needed for the trip. The drugstore, the bank, the film shop. That sort of thing. It was snowing, and I remember coming home to work on a study that I've had to write up for the government. Never went outside again. I sat right at this table and kept looking across as the snow covered the bare limbs of the trees in Riverside Park, thinking over and over again that I'd be swimming in turquoise waters in a matter of days.

"Frivolous thoughts, really, when I heard later what had been going on down below. With Lola, I mean. I didn't hear the slightest bit of disturbance. I think that's what will always torment me."

Lavery seemed to be sincerely troubled.

"No loud voices arguing? No screams? No sounds of a struggle?"

"Exactly what does a struggle sound like, Detective?"

Mike was stumped. There had been no furniture

overturned in Lola's apartment, no bruising to suggest a prolonged attack by her assailant. Just a wool scarf that had been pulled too tight for too long around her neck. It had caused her to be unable to breathe, and perhaps unable to scream as well.

"I have this tendency, you see, to sit here at my writing table, absorbed in my work no matter what kind of commotion is going on around me or outside on the street. It's a trait that has served me quite well in my career. And when I'm here at home, I've always got music playing. Sometimes a bit too loud, but then these old buildings were really built solid. They absorb the noise pretty well. Every now and then," Lavery said with a slight grin, "after a particularly booming crescendo, my friend Lola would bang on the pipes that ran up through her living room into mine.

"But the day she died," he said, somber again, "I can't say I heard anything at all."

"How well did you know Ms. Dakota?"

"Quite well, both professionally and socially. We were in different disciplines, of course, but she was a bit of a maverick, as I am, and she was interested in my approach to the urban drug problem. Away from the school, we spent some time together, too."

"Did you ever date?"

"Nothing like that. But we could sit up till the middle of the night, arguing about solutions for the homeless or the mentally ill. There was no off switch to Lola. She was always thinking and working and doing."

"Had you seen much of her in the days before her death?"

He took a long time to answer. "I have become so engulfed in my own legal entanglements, unfortunately, that I've tended to push most of my friends out of the way. I'm trying to recall the last time Lola and I had a good, long go-at-it together."

"How about a short one? How about a sighting?"

"I know I saw her the week of Thanksgiving. I remember coming in with a lot of groceries and stopping by to talk with her for a while on my way upstairs. Have a drink. Then she was off to her sister's home, and—I simply can't summon up any other time that I saw her."

Was he lying to us, or had Bart Frankel been mistaken when he told us he had left Lola at the door because she saw Lavery going into the building?

Chapman had nothing to lose at this point. "The day she died, like half an hour before she was killed, did you happen to run into her, right at the front door of the building?"

Lavery was biting the inside of his cheek, looking perplexed. "I may have gone down to the lobby once in the afternoon to get the mail, but after I came back from my errand that morning I'm absolutely certain I never went back outside. Where would you have heard something like that?"

"How do you know Bart Frankel?"

"He was in charge of her case, Ms. Cooper. He had

come to the apartment once or twice to bring Lola papers to sign. I think that's what she told me. And to help prepare her for their plan to build the case against her husband, Mr. Kerlovic."

"Kralovic."

"I didn't know the man. I'm not really sure what his name was. One time, I ran into Lola with Bart Frankel at a restaurant in the neighborhood. I guess she had come to rely on him in these last difficult weeks."

"How come you called Bart last night and asked him to meet with you?"

Now he was growing more wary. "Well, Detective, either Bart told you the answer to that question when he asked you to come here, or you've pulled one over on me." He walked to his desk and picked up the receiver, looking at a number on the piece of paper next to the phone. "Shall I just call him and clear this up?"

Mike stood up, too. "No, but Bart did tell us he saw you walk into this building, holding the door open for Lola, about half an hour before she was killed."

"And *I'm* telling you that statement is not true, Mr. Chapman." Lavery started to dial.

"We'll have to resolve this some other way, Mr. Lavery. All you're gonna get is a machine. Or maybe one of Bart's kids. He's in the hospital. His car ran off the road this morning on his way here to see you."

Lavery replaced the receiver. "Was he hurt badly?"

"Probably won't make it."

The professor winced and sat down at his desk.

"You wanna explain to us why you called him to come talk to you? Tell us what you were planning on telling him?"

He looked up at Chapman to answer. "I didn't have anything to say to him."

"But you called him. Even his daughter can confirm that."

"I got back from my trip last night and among the messages on my answering machine was one to call Bart Frankel. He reminded me what his connection to Lola had been, and he left his home phone number in New Jersey."

By the end of next week, telephone records might again resolve the issue for us, but at the moment I did not know whether to believe him.

"Did he say what he wanted?"

I sensed that Lavery thought he had regained the upper hand. His tone was cool once more, and almost arrogant as he talked to us. "Not at all. Just that he needed to see me. I assumed it was about Lola's case."

"He was taken off that investigation. He's—"

"And I've been out of the country, Detective. Staying at a beach house in the islands with no television and with newspapers that arrived about three days after they hit the stands in Miami. So I don't have the faintest idea what's been going on up here. Why was he taken off the case? Would you like to bring me up-to-date?"

Mike ignored his question. "Did Lola talk to you about the Blackwells project?"

"Of course she did. It had consumed her these past few months. We're a relatively small faculty, Detective, compared to those at large universities like Harvard and Yale. I'd had my enemies when I first came over to King's, but we've generally tried to work it out among ourselves. When I was hired, the head of the anthropology department didn't want me working under his watch."

"Winston Shreve?"

"Precisely. But then Lola went to work on Shreve, on my behalf. I wouldn't say he's my close friend, but he accepted me within his division and has been rather kind to me lately, with all the troubles I've had. And Grenier, he's in charge of the biology division. He was a bit more anxious to have me.

"Now, if you're spending any time with those three—Dakota, Shreve, and Grenier—you can be sure the subject of Blackwells will come up," he said. "That's what they've spent most of their time working on for the better part of the year. And Lockhart. I'd say he's their fourth Musketeer."

"Have you had anything to do with the project yourself?"

"I live in the present, Ms. Cooper. Oh, they talk to me about what they're doing, and they ask me plenty of questions about it."

"Like what?"

"I think when Lola first found out about the drug trade in the old penitentiary, three-quarters of a century ago, she was amazed at the scale of the problem. But it was quite a famous scandal, and of course, I'm familiar with the history of the drug culture in this city. So I was able to explain to her what the drugs of choice were in those days and how widespread the narcotics business was—even inside American penal institutions."

"And Grenier, what was his relationship with Lola?"

"I bet you've had a hard time getting him to come to the table, haven't you?" Lavery wasn't wrong. I was hoping that by Monday we would have word from Sylvia Foote that the biology professor was back and available to us.

"Why do you say that?"

"Because Thomas Grenier is a selfish son of a bitch and it would be quite out of character if he was any use in a matter like this."

"We've been told that Grenier was actually willing to bring you into his department, when Shreve and the others weren't all that interested in having you in anthropology."

"That's true, Detective. But not because he had any belief in what I was doing. He saw it as a business proposition. It put dollar signs in front of his eyes, not mortarboards."

Both Mike and I were lost. "I never knew that money was so much of an issue in academia," I said.

"Then I would guess that you've never met Thomas Grenier. And you have no idea what the Internet has done to the college campus. Not in the classroom alone, but as universities have tried to cash in on the commercial market."

"Would you mind telling us what you mean?"

"It used to be, Ms. Cooper, that the idea of an academic making money from his research was not acceptable at any university. I'm not talking about *my* situation, if that's what you're thinking. There has always been a perception that we scholars are outside the marketplace, and we've long benefited from that. We've been giving away our knowledge for generations. Now many of the large institutions are looking to get a fair return on their intellectual capital. Turn it into financial capital, like the rest of the world."

"And the Internet?"

"It's a gold mine. It provides a much larger payback, and a much faster one, too. There's a lot of competition in the dot-com community, and administrators everywhere are trying to foster various opportunities to let faculty members increase their income—through the expanded use of their research—and let the universities themselves share in the bounty. That's the big score. I'm surprised you haven't read about this. Front page of *The Times* a short while ago. Grenier was a key player."

"I just do the sports page, comics, horoscope, and 'Dear Abby.' Tell me about it."

"Columbia University has sort of led the field in this business. The vice provost there has promoted the efforts of some of his professors to joint-venture with Internet start-ups. They've partnered with an on-line company to do a human nutrition study. And made money by mating with that junk-bond character, Michael Milken, in a curriculum of serious college courses. They've already made millions from that."

"What's the flap?"

"Well, under the old rules, Mr. Chapman, we professors owned the rights to any books and articles that were published. The institution itself owned the patents from our research, and we were lucky to get a quarter of the revenue. Columbia started a new policy last year. It allows the university to retain rights to Internet projects that are supported by Columbia's funds, or make substantial use of its labor, but professors can get a greater share in the revenue."

"And Grenier's role?"

"A lot of these Internet companies with a significant amount of venture capital have been sniffing around the campuses. Biology is one of the fields in which they figure they can buy a lot of research rather cheaply. And turn it into gold. Grenier was sort of pushed out of the department at Columbia. Couldn't get along with some of the favorites there. A bit too heavy-handed. He came here and is trying to get the same kind of interest revved up on the King's College campus.

"These biotech companies are all looking for major drug studies. Think of the return on an investment when you have some brilliant graduate student, not costing you a dime in salary, toiling over his laboratory test tubes all day. Guided by a professor whose income is just a fraction of what the corporate executives make."

"What's the problem?"

"A major conflict with the new president here, Paolo Recantati. He'd like to have firmer control over decisions on what type of research the college should support. He's a purist. He thinks there can be terrible fallout when the faculty or the college has a stake in the financial result of its work."

"Did Lola and Thomas Grenier get along?"

"Until she found out that he was trying to use me. That he had not been very candid about why he was interested in me. It turned out not to be for the reasons he expressed to the administration."

Long-term studies of health problems connected to substance abuse, if I remembered what Sylvia Foote had told us. Lavery chuckled. "Lola turned on Grenier like a rattlesnake on its prey. Ready to strike in a flash. If he said something was black, Lola said it was white. You know what I mean, I'm sure."

"When was that?"

"Early this fall, a few months back."

"What is it he really wanted from you?"

Lavery laughed more heartily. "What do you know about Viagra, Detective?"

"Not enough."

"Viagra's main ingredient comes from the poppy.

The same seedpod that brings you opium and heroin. It works by increasing the blood flow directly to the penis. But it's had some disastrous side effects, as you're probably aware. It doesn't mix well with other medications.

"So a lot of pharmaceutical companies have been searching for a better fix, a healthier solution to an age-old problem. And nobody on the faculty knows the poppy as well as I do, in the professional sense. Grenier had made a deal with one of the large drug companies to lead the research team. He simply neglected to cut me in on any of the potential profit."

"Did you two have a falling-out?"

"We didn't come to blows with each other, but it hasn't been pretty. I don't like being taken advantage of."

"Where did Lola stand in this?"

"With me, Detective. I can't say she has any personal regard for Grenier."

"But they still worked together on the Blackwells business?"

"I'm not sure the sandbox was big enough for both of them, but she tried to make do."

"Did you know about the legend of Freeland Jennings's diamonds?"

Lavery pushed away from the desk and laughed again. "Of course I did. That's one of the things Lola and I used to argue about late into the night. Do this dig for whatever historical purposes interest you, I used to tell her. There's a lot of sorry history of this city on that island—a storehouse of human misery. But don't be wasting your energy on some far-fetched tale that may not even have been true."

"Is that what kept Thomas Grenier and Lola Dakota together?"

"Don't be ridiculous. The man is a scientist. He thought that Lola was foolish to have believed the diamonds were still in the ground. His interest in the island is strictly scientific."

"What's in it for him?"

"Grenier again expects to profit from the work the students will be doing when they study the Smallpox Hospital. There's enormous debate in the field of medical ethics about whether or not the smallpox virus should be completely eradicated when the disease is conquered worldwide. Since you need the actual virus to make the vaccine, does one save a small amount of it against the day that some form of the pox reappears in the world? And who is the keeper of the deadly virus? Whom do we trust not to engage in germ warfare?"

"And obviously, some biotech company would support this project, hoping that a study of all the plagues treated on Blackwells Island a century ago would be useful to scientists making determinations about the future," I reasoned.

"Exactly. It's hard to think of any other finite stretch of land, isolated from the population, which institutionalized, treated, and buried so many of society's untouchables. That's why Grenier loves it there."

"Does this venture of his have a name?"

Lavery paused for a few moments and then shook his head. "I should know it, but it's not coming to me right now. You'll have to ask him yourself. Some fairly gruesome pox-related thing. Lola used to joke and call it deadhouse dot com."

"Deadhouse?"

"That's how Lola referred to the island."

"Do you know why?" It appeared that the phrase was not as mysterious as it had seemed when we first encountered the word on a piece of paper in her apartment.

"You know that a lot of the interns who worked on the project refused to be involved with the plans at that old smallpox hospital? They're enthralled with the insane asylum and the penitentiary, but that abandoned hospital spooks the best of them. Many of those who aren't science majors believe that they might dig up things that are still germ infested, that contagion lurks even now in some of the objects that were buried a century ago. They simply don't want anything to do with all that deadly history."

"Did you ever go with her to Blackwells—I mean, to Roosevelt Island?"

"Only three or four times. She walked me through the area they call the Octagon, with that magnificent staircase. And of course we had to see the remains of the hospital. I'd always wondered what it was, from this side of the water."

"Would you mind, Professor, if I asked you about

the accusations concerning the misappropriation of the grant money?" It seemed unusual that Lola would be such an advocate for Lavery, under the circumstances that Sylvia Foote had described.

His mood changed again and he stiffened. "I have an attorney, Ms. Cooper, and I've been instructed not to discuss this matter with anyone out of his presence."

Chapman veered off in another direction. "You know anything about this kid Julian Gariano? The one who hanged himself last weekend?"

It was hard to discern whether Lavery had a good poker face or truly had never crossed paths with the campus drug dealer. "Gariano? The name doesn't sound familiar to me. Was he a King's student? It must have happened after I left for the Caribbean."

"One more thing, Professor. There's a young woman who was a junior at the college last year. I don't believe she was in any of your classes, but I understand she had a problem with drugs, and I thought perhaps you might have heard something about her disappearance. Her name is Voight. Charlotte Voight."

"I had heard that she had dropped out, although I didn't know her either. The administration always circulates a notice to the faculty if something unusual happens or if a student withdraws from classes without an official leave. These kids are often going through a tough time, and one of us might be a lifeline to them. Dropping out is nothing new for college students, is it?"

Lavery stopped speaking for a moment, then looked up at me. "But Charlotte Voight is back around, isn't she?"

Perhaps Lavery had information we didn't. "That's news to us. Any clue where she is?"

"No, I have no idea. But the last time I talked to Lola, that's what she told me. That she knew where the Voight girl was, and that she was going to see her."

25

Each time I thought we were about to take a step or two forward, we were thrown back five or six. Mike had pushed Lavery hard on when it was that Lola Dakota had told him she was going to see the missing girl. If the professor was being truthful, he had not seen his neighbor for almost one month. But if Bart had been honest, then Lavery might have heard that news from Lola within an hour of her death.

Either way, the effort before us grew larger rather than focused. Had Charlotte Voight returned to the King's College campus a few days before Christmas, ready to attempt to reenter school for the new semester? Did her reappearance have anything to do with the suicide of her former lover, Julian Gariano, who had supplied her with drugs? And who else other than Lola knew where the girl was?

There were significant discrepancies between the story told to us by Bart Frankel and the facts as reported by Claude Lavery. Each of them was undoubtedly lying about something. Lavery seemed to paint a flawed picture of each of his colleagues while underscoring the feuding world of academic politics. And why wouldn't Lavery admit that he had seen and spoken with Lola Dakota when she had returned to the building just a short time before she was killed?

"We've got to sit down on Monday morning and map out all these connections. I'm so tired and emotionally drained at this point. It's lucky that no one from Special Victims beeped me these last two days." The clock on the dashboard of Mike's car was slow, but it was already close to seven o'clock in the evening as we headed downtown from Lavery's apartment. "The last thing I need is a handful of new complaints."

"It's Fleet Week, isn't it?"

"Yes, and I'm delighted that everybody's so well behaved this season. That's usually good for five or six cases." From time to time, when a special event like the Fourth of July or New Year's called for it, a large contingent of warships would gather in New York's ports and harbor. There were festivities aboard as well as up and down the Hudson River. But sometimes, when the sailors who had been at sea for long stretches reached Gotham City, the parties got out of control.

"Maybe the guys don't even bother coming ashore anymore. Maybe 'don't ask, don't tell' is working better than anybody thinks."

"And maybe I'll just keep my fingers crossed for a

quiet evening. Jake's supposed to be back from D.C. by now. We'll probably run up to Butterfield 81 for a steak. Why don't you hang out with us?"

"'Cause I've got a date. I'm gonna drop you off and go over to her place for dinner."

"And she is . . . ?"

"A good cook."

"That's all you're telling me?"

"I'm not ready to go public." He grinned at me. "You're worse than my mother."

"Well, you've been much too secretive about what you're up to. Makes me suspect something more serious is going on. I hate to say the *i* word, but I'm beginning to believe that you're actually involved with someone. Especially after that heart-to-heart talk you had with me on our way home from Mercer's house."

"You'll be the first to know, blondie."

Mike dropped me at the entrance to Jake's building and the doorman helped me out of the car. "Mr. Tyler just came in himself a few minutes ago, ma'am. Asked if I'd seen you this evening."

"Thanks, Richard." I took the elevator upstairs and slipped my key in the lock. Jake was on the StairMaster in his den, a set of headphones linking him to yet another cycle of news on the television in front of him. He didn't see me come in. I took off my coat and gloves and sat in the leather chair behind him, waiting until he finished his exercise and stepped off the machine.

"I'm not so bad to come home to, am I?" he asked, walking over to kiss me on the nose. "Have you and Chapman solved this one yet? I've given you a week."

"My brain is spinning. Can we talk about *your* day?"

"I'll take a quick shower and then we can head out for dinner, okay?"

Despite the cold wind, we walked uptown to the restaurant, passing storefronts with their Christmas decorations and, now, all the signs for postholiday sales. We settled into a quiet corner banquette, and the dark, handsome decor of the room suited my mood. I was brooding about the week's events and the gloom that had enveloped this season that I so loved. Jake devoured his steak while I swiped a few of his perfect *pommes frites* to go along with my soup and salad, and we sipped a wonderful Burgundy.

By the time we were ready to go home, the temperature had dropped precipitously and we hailed a cab on Lexington Avenue to take us to the apartment. Once inside, I undressed and got into bed alongside Jake. I fell asleep with the lights still on and Jake still flipping the channels. When a nightmare awakened me at 3 A.M., I cradled myself against his body and tried to push out of my mind the autopsy photographs of Lola Dakota.

I had already bathed and dressed by the time he opened his eyes on Sunday morning. The coffee beans were ground and brewed, and I had taken the newspaper in from the doormat. Jake went into the kitchen and opened the refrigerator door.

"Scrambled? Sunny-side up? Omelette?"

"One egg over easy."

He looked over my shoulder at the paper. "Why do you start with the obituaries? Looking for business? Or are you just reading it, as my father used to say, to make sure your own name isn't in it?"

I put the section aside and set the table for breakfast. We lingered in the dining room for more than an hour, Jake working the Sunday crossword puzzle while I was determined to finish the tougher Saturday maze.

"What shall we do today?"

"How about the Frick? They've got an exhibition of Velázquez paintings. We can walk over there, spend an hour or two, and then come home and I can do some paperwork on the case."

"Are you all set for New Year's Eve? I mean, this won't get in the way, will it?"

"I expect it'll be fine." Joan Stafford was giving a dinner party for five couples in Washington. We were going to take a late afternoon shuttle down on Tuesday and spend the night with Joan and Jim, coming back early the next morning now that Mercer and Vickee had included us in their wedding plans.

This was the one holiday I hated. There was such an artificial air about the forced gaiety, and my favorite way of celebrating had always been to stay at home with friends. Joan was a superb hostess, and the idea of laughing and relaxing with her in front of a great fire, dining at her elegant table, then climbing the stairs to curl up for the night in the guest room of her Georgetown town house seemed a delightful way to welcome in another year.

"There's a winter storm warning for tomorrow evening. I guess we can always take the Metroliner."

I was rinsing the dishes when the phone rang for the first time. Jake came back into the kitchen and put his arms around me, embracing me from behind and pressing his mouth against the top of my head. "That was Mike, darling."

"I've been waiting for this call." Tears had already formed and I fought them back.

"Bart Frankel died. They disconnected the life support this morning." He tried to turn me around to face him, but I stood at the sink, staring out the window at the gray day while the hot water ran over my hands. "I just want to hold you for a minute, Alex."

I shook my head.

"You're going to have to let me in one of these days." Jake rubbed his hand across my back. "Mike said to tell you he's got the search warrant for Frankel's office. He's on his way to New Jersey to get it signed so he can pick up the evidence this afternoon." He was massaging my neck with his right hand, his left still holding my waist. "This isn't your fault."

I didn't blame myself for Bart's death, but I was pained by the unfortunate chain of events that had been created from the moment Lola placed herself in the hands of Vinny Sinnelesi. She had just wanted to extricate herself from the violent relationship with Ivan Kralovic, but instead had become a pawn in the prosecutor's efforts to stage a sensational vote-getting stunt. So often I had heard Paul Battaglia remind his senior staff that you can't play politics with people's lives. I admired his wisdom.

Bart had clearly been in greater turmoil than anyone knew. Now he had died under circumstances that were at best mysterious, with his reputation tarnished and his debts substantial. And the children, I suddenly remembered, squeezing my eyes shut. There were three children who had to cope with both loss and disgrace.

I leaned over the sink, cupping my hands and filling them with steaming water, holding them against my eyes. "Let's take a walk, okay?"

I held on to Jake's arm as we made our way uptown to the small museum at the corner of Fifth Avenue and Seventieth Street. I tried to explain my feelings, speaking as the frost grabbed at my breath and formed rings that rose in the icy air. The need to explore the lives of the people whose tragedies came our way took us to intimate places I had no more desire to enter than the deceased would have had to let me in. For me, it was impossible to do this work with a clinical remove. I could evaluate evidence dispassionately, and I could make judgments about witness credibility with precision, but there was an emotional pull that nagged at my heart with every life that was lost.

We strolled through the stunning exhibit, on loan from the Prado in Madrid. When we had seen our fill of royal portraits, we reclaimed our things from the cloakroom and walked around the corner to Madison Avenue for a cup of hot chocolate. We had almost reached home when my beeper went off.

I saw the complaint-room number and stopped in the doorway to take out my cell phone. The supervisor answered and I identified myself. "It's Alexandra Cooper. What's up?"

"There's a woman looking for you. Her name is Sylvia Foote. Says she's a lawyer for King's College. Claims she even has your home number but can't find you anywhere, so I thought you wouldn't mind the beep."

"Not at all." I had given Sylvia all my contact numbers before the window was broken at my apartment, and had forgotten to check my machine in two days. I could have kicked myself. "Did she say how long she's been trying to get me?"

"Just an hour or two. She left a number." I recognized her office phone. "While I have you, Alex, can I ask you something about a case that just came in?"

"Sure."

"Cops in Central Park made an arrest this morning around ten o'clock. Locked up a guy in one of the bathrooms for public lewdness and endangering the welfare of a child. Turns out he's a commercial pilot for an international carrier. Supposed to fly to Geneva at six tonight."

"Glad to know he's resting up for the long night ahead of him."

"Yeah, the cop told me his penis was on autopilot till they nabbed him. Anyway, the lawyer for the airline is down here kicking and screaming. Wants the case jumped ahead of all the other docketed matters so the Red Baron can be out of here and make the six o'clock flight. They're European-based so there's no backup for him; if he's not out of jail in time, they'll have to put all the passengers on other flights. Can I do it?"

"Does he have a residence here? Any roots, any reason to return?"

"Nope."

"Anybody interview the victim yet?"

"Only the cop. Says the kid is terrific, and that there's an adult witness, too. Strong case."

"Don't go through any hoops for the pilot. I hate to inconvenience all those people, but I imagine he won't be in very good shape to rocket that spaceship back home to Switzerland. A day in the pens and a few hours in the courtroom—"

"Not to mention that the press got hold of it already. Mickey Diamond's down here trying to get a photo for the *Post* to go with his headline story about the pilot and his juvenile joystick. Diamond's usual good taste."

"Just let it take its normal course. And ask for some

reasonable bail. If they reroute him to the Far East, we won't ever see this guy again."

I put my phone back in my shoulder bag. "Let's go home. I'll give Sylvia Foote a call." We went back to the apartment and Jake hung our coats, then followed me into the den while I returned Sylvia's message.

"I'm terribly sorry to hunt you down on a Sunday afternoon, Alex, but I knew you'd be displeased if I didn't respond to the requests you and Detective Chapman made."

"That's very gracious of you, Sylvia. I didn't expect you to give up your holiday weekend to get those things done."

"I'd like very much to clear this all up before we start a new year. I hadn't any plans for the day anyway. Now, I found out a few hours ago that Claude Lavery is back in—"

"Yes, Sylvia. We actually dropped by to see him yesterday afternoon."

"Oh." Her voice dropped and the enthusiasm she had mustered went with it. "I don't suppose you'll accept the fact that I *am* trying to cooperate with you. I came over to the school a while ago to write up some reports and I ran into Thomas Grenier, the biologist you've wanted to meet. So we've got almost everyone you need now, haven't we? I gave Grenier the detective's number and told him to call there on Monday."

"Where is he now? Right now?"

"I believe that he's in with the president."

"In Recantati's office?"

"Yes. They've been arguing with each other for the last ten minutes. I can hear them all the way down the hall."

"Can you hold them there for me? Ask them to stay until I get there?"

"Today?"

"Yes, Sylvia. I can hop in a cab and be there in twenty minutes." There was no point waiting until tomorrow to pin down Grenier. At the rate things were happening in the case, I would need all the time available to schedule interviews and examine any files that we might be able to get from Sinnelesi's office. Something had sparked the interest of a few of Lola's colleagues to have them back in the college building when I had not expected to find them there.

Sylvia was clearly annoyed. "They're grown men, Alex. I can't hold them here. I suppose if they want to talk to you, they'll wait."

"Well, will you tell them I'm coming?"

"Of course. I'll be here."

I turned around to look at Jake. "Do you mind terribly if I scoot up to the college for an hour or two?"

"I was just getting hooked on the domesticity of this scene. Reams of newspapers to read, sweat suits and slippers, me cooking, you doing the dishes, The Temptations singing 'My Girl.' I was even beginning to fantasize that one of my secret-recipe spicy Bloody Marys could lead to an afternoon nap that might turn into enough of a personal workout that I wouldn't have to get back on that damn machine for my daily exercise."

I went over and sat on his lap, my arms around his neck. "You do understand, don't you?"

"Absolutely. Want company? You're like a fish out of water without Mike and Mercer."

"Not necessary. I'm only going to the administration building. Recantati walked out on us the other day, so I'd love a few minutes with him, away from the presence of my not-so-gentle grand inquisitor, the ever-tactful Detective Chapman. And this Grenier guy has been completely unavailable to us until this very moment. Maybe that's just because of the holiday, but we do need to speak to him." I kissed his mouth and he kissed me back, deeply and lovingly.

"When you put it that way, I can't object to a thing you do. And the faster you get out of here to do it, the sooner you'll be back." Jake raised his knees to bump me off his lap and patted me on my bottom. "Dinner at home tonight."

"Radical idea." I was brushing my hair and putting on lipstick. "You're not expecting any help from me, are you?"

"Hey, I was thrilled to see you set up the Christmas tree stand the same way I do. Hot water in the pot to let the sap flow out. That's devotion, Alex. I was even set to invite you to move in with me before I was certain you could boil water."

"Just luck that you've got a whistling teapot. I'm not entirely sure how to know when it's boiling otherwise." I not only loved Jake's companionship, but also the fact that he never griped about my inability to cook anything more complicated than an English muffin.

"Eight o'clock. I picked up some salmon on my way in last night. I've got a delicious recipe stuck in the back of a cookbook somewhere. That'll keep me busy till you get home."

The doorman helped me hail a taxi and I huddled in the back of it while I tried to explain to the driver, whose Urdu was incomprehensible to me, that Claremont Avenue was a block west of Broadway, near the campus of Columbia University.

A security guard stared at my face to match it to the photograph on my DA's identification card. Grudgingly, he admitted me to the building and I ran up the staircase to Sylvia Foote's office. The usual crusty expression on her face summed up her attitude about my arrival.

"They're not pleased about your coming here today. Neither one of them. But it did stop them from screeching at each other." She slammed her door shut behind us as she pointed me down to President Recantati's suite of rooms.

"What were they arguing about?"

She flashed another sour look at me. "What we're all on a short tether about. Lola Dakota. Nobody wants to be dragged into this mess."

"You're her colleagues and—"

"That doesn't mean that we wanted to be involved with her dirty laundry."

Foote knocked when she reached his office. "Come in."

Recantati had appeared so mild-mannered when Mike and I first met him the day after Lola's death. Now he scowled to see me, as much because of what we had asked him as for the fact that I knew at least one thing about him that he wished to keep a secret.

"Thomas, this is Ms. Cooper, from the Manhattan District Attorney's Office."

"Good afternoon. I'm Thomas Grenier."

The biology professor was slightly built but rather wiry-looking. He had thinning dark hair and glasses that sat tightly on the bridge of his nose. He was no more anxious to shake my hand than was Recantati.

Foote turned to walk out of the room. I had one more question for her, which I wanted both of the men to hear. "Before you go, Sylvia, I was wondering if you had any recent contact with Charlotte Voight?"

"What?"

"A call that she wanted to register for class in the new semester, perhaps? Have any of the faculty or students heard from her, that she's back in town?"

Foote and Recantati exchanged glances. "Not a word. Why do you ask?"

"Her name came up in an interview we did yesterday. I just wondered whether anyone mentioned to you that they had seen her recently."

"I told you I'd let you know if I did. It's almost five o'clock, Alex. If you don't need me here, I'm going home." She pulled the door shut behind her and left the three of us standing in Recantati's office. He asked Grenier to step out into the anteroom while he had a few words alone with me, and I sat in the chair facing his large desk.

"Ms. Cooper, first I'd like to apologize for my walking out on you during our interview the other day. It must have created a terrible impression of me and I'm simply mortified—"

His voice broke off and he stopped talking.

"Nobody enjoys talking to the police, Professor."

"I don't really understand all about DNA and what kind of evidence it leaves behind. Thomas knows a lot more than I do. I learned from talking to him that a person can simply touch things—doorknobs and drinking glasses—and it can leave enough skin cells behind to develop a DNA pattern."

"That's quite true." There was enough genetic material in the skin cells that were sloughed off in just minutes of normal contact that it was becoming possible to solve even *non*violent crimes, like burglary, with the use of this technology.

I tried to put Recantati more at ease. "In England, they use DNA to solve property crimes, like car thefts. Detectives figured out that in order to jump-start a car, the thief usually touches some place on the steering column. So the Brits just wipe that part of the car down once they've recovered it, and put the profile in their computers. They solve cases they never used to be able to any other way. No blood or semen necessary."

He wasn't listening to my evidence-collection lecture. He was trying to find a way to convince me that he had never had a sexual relationship with Lola Dakota. "I don't want to deal with Detective Chapman anymore. But I'd like *you* to believe me, Ms. Cooper. I was not—I was never involved with Professor Dakota. She was a friend, she was a colleague"—he hesitated before he went on—"and she was also guaranteed to be trouble. I don't look for trouble."

"But you had spent time in her apartment, right? That's why you think we might have something with your DNA on it."

"I, uh—no, never alone. I had been to Lola's apartment, but only for coffee, or when she had a few of us in for cocktails. That's not what I'm concerned about.

"My position here is tentative. I'm just here in the role of acting president. And if I don't get the permanent appointment, then I'd like to be able to go back to my job at Princeton. Without a scandal. They won't take me back if there's any scandal."

"Then, I don't understand your concern."

"Ms. Cooper, I saw your Crime Scene Unit men when they came to Lola's office the day after the murder. I don't know what they're capable of determining with DNA, but they were processing the room for fingerprints, too. I've been a nervous wreck, that's why I walked out on you and the detective."

"Why? What are you afraid of?"

"The morning after Professor Dakota was killed I, uh—I went into her office. I didn't take anything, I swear to you. But I went in there quite early, before anyone else was in the building."

"How did you get in? Why—"

"I'm the president of the college, for the time being. When I asked the janitor to open her door for me, he would never have refused. I . . . um, I touched everything. I was a bit frantic. And then your policeman noticed that things seemed out of place, and the other men were called in to do all that scientific processing. I've just been beside myself."

"But *why* did you go in?"

He lowered his voice even more and bent his head in the direction of the door. "That's just it. I had been reluctant to tell you until I could talk to Thomas face-to-face. He's just back from the West Coast this morning, on the red-eye."

Why was he being so evasive?

"My wife called me from our home in Princeton at about one o'clock in the morning. I'm talking about the night after Lola was killed. She said that Thomas Grenier had called there from California, looking for me. Said he didn't have my number at the apartment in the city, which is just a sublet, so the phone isn't listed in my name. It all sounded so logical, I—I—I . . ."

"What did he tell her?"

"Thomas told her that it was urgent that she get a message to me. That I *must* get into Lola's office before the police did. That there was something in her desk that would, um, well—that it could prove to be an embarrassment to the college if anyone found it.

"Not illegal. Not anything that would be a crime for me to remove. I would never, never have participated in any such thing. But to avoid a scandal—"

"What kind of scandal?"

"We had several going already, Ms. Cooper. I didn't know what he was referring to at the time. He just told Elena—that's my wife—Grenier told her that he'd explain it all to me when he got back to New York. That I was just to take the envelope and slip it under *his* door."

"And that's what you did?"

"That's what I tried to do." He shook his head from side to side. "I stayed up half the night worrying about it, then got here at the crack of dawn. Actually, and perhaps this just goes to show my own naïveté—or, well, ignorance—it never occurred to me that the police would have any need to come to see Lola's office. I, uh, I've never had anything to do with a murder investigation. When I got that call from Elena, we all assumed that Ivan had killed Lola, and the school would have no reason to be involved."

Recantati was talking so quickly I thought he was going to run out of breath.

"I must have been in there for an hour. I started looking over her desk, neatly and calmly. When I couldn't find the envelope that Thomas had referred to, I practically panicked. I went through everything I could think of until I began to hear voices and footsteps in the corridor. I slipped out and went back up to my office."

Recantati rocked back and forth in his swiveling desk chair. "This will be the end of me with Sylvia Foote. She's so nauseatingly sanctimonious. And I was just doing what Thomas Grenier suggested to hold on to my job. It seemed perfectly harmless at the time. Besides that, I never found the damn thing."

"What kind of envelope was it?"

"A small one, very small. It had something to do with the project they were working on. The word 'Blackwells' was written on the front of it."

With the help of Mike's good instincts and a valid search warrant, I hoped that little envelope would be on my desk by the time I got there in the morning. When Recantati and Grenier were arguing before I arrived, it must have been about this.

"Did you and Grenier speak again during the week?"

"No, no. Not until today. He never called back, and I had no idea where in California he was staying. Since I 'failed' at his mission," Recantati said sarcastically, "I thought I'd just wait and tell him about it when I saw him. After I met you people last Friday, I knew I wasn't going back into Lola's office for a second try."

"I assume you were talking to Professor Grenier before I came in just now." I wanted to hear what the biologist had told Recantati before I interviewed him myself. "Did he explain to you why he wanted you to get the envelope, and what was in it that might possibly cause trouble for the school?"

"That's just it, Ms. Cooper. I'm afraid I snapped at Thomas, rather than talking with him. You see, he denies knowing anything about an envelope or a problem involving the Blackwells project. Thomas Grenier claims that he never made that telephone call to my wife."

26

"Shall I wait while you talk to Professor Grenier?"

"I'd prefer to speak with him alone, as we've done with each of you. Perhaps he and I can go down to his office, so I don't inconvenience you any longer. Will you be here at the college during this week?"

"The next two days. In fact, Sylvia and I were discussing the idea of rounding up some of the faculty tomorrow afternoon and having our own meeting about these events."

"I can't tell you how to run your institution, sir, but I hope you don't intend to conduct a private roundtable discussion about Lola Dakota's murder. If that's your plan, the detective and I would like to be present."

Recantati seemed hesitant to challenge any of Sylvia Foote's suggestions. "I, uh, I'll have to check with Sylvia. We were thinking more of housekeeping matters. Making sure that everyone knows we want them to assist you in any way they can." He bowed his head.

"I'm so ashamed of the fact that I might have done something to make your job harder. I probably ought to tell them all what I did."

"Please don't, Professor. For the moment, I take it only Grenier is aware of this. Am I right, or have you told anyone else?"

"He's the only one."

Grenier and the person who had actually made the telephone call, if there was such a person. "Let's leave it that way. I'd appreciate it if you let me know if you do decide to get a group of the faculty together.

"One other thing. What have you done with the books that were in Professor Dakota's office? Where are they now?"

"Her sister sent someone to pick up most of her personal effects—her papers and photographs, the knickknacks on her desk and the frames on her wall. But she didn't seem interested in Lola's books. Most of those have been packed away in boxes until we get word from the police that they're not needed for the investigation. Those things related to the Blackwells project will be distributed to other members of the faculty who are part of the team, and some of her research volumes will go to the library, of course."

"May I look through those cartons while I'm here?"

"Is that—? Well . . ."

"Is it legal? Yes, it's fine. I'll make a formal record of anything I take."

"I'll explain to Grenier where we've stored them,

and he can take you there when you and he are finished. It's just down the hall from his room."

Recantati stepped out to the anteroom to give
Grenier a few words of instruction, and then I followed
the biologist to his office one flight above.

In contrast to the stark decor of Recantati's temporary space, this was garnished with awards and
diplomas, a series of lithographs of Edward Jenner vac-
cinating his experimental population of village folk in
England, and a collection of cobalt-blue antique apoth-
ecary jars. They were lined up in alphabetical order, with
the one labeled "Arsenic" closest to my chair. A large
model of the double helix, with its ladderlike strands of
DNA in bright primary colors, sat before me on the
desk. Grenier expanded and closed it like an accordion
while I described my position and the nature of our
investigation. I had used the same exhibit in many of my
training lectures on the subject of genetic fingerprinting.

"Whatever Lola wants, eh? Lola gets." The biology
professor smiled as he spoke the words of the song.

"I don't think she wanted dead, Professor."

"No," he said slowly, stretching out the single syl-
lable. "But how she would have delighted in being the
cause of all this intrigue. I think what she would have
liked best is the air of suspicion that's been created
here and the pointing of fingers at those of us who
crossed her. If every one of us whom she disliked could
be suspects for even a nanosecond, I think Lola would
have left us behind without a second thought."

"Your concern for her is touching."

"Anything else would be pure charade, as you've probably heard. I once made the mistake of singing that song from *Damn Yankees* to her, the one about whatever Lola wants. I was jabbing at her, mocking her way of wheedling whatever she wanted out of the administration. Unfortunately she countered with the end of the refrain—'and little man, little Lola wants *you*.'" He pushed his glasses back against the bridge of his nose and squinted at me. "I hated being called a little man. She knew that. And she delighted in teasing me about not being able to get me. I'm gay, you see. Open, unashamed, perfectly content to take her humor. It was the 'little' business that used to drive me crazy.

"But she had a mean streak a mile long. And when she thought I had tried to deceive Dr. Lavery, she came after me like a man-eating shark."

"Would you tell me what that was all about?"

The helix twisted and turned in his hands. "I'm dead tired, Ms. Cooper. The flight in was extremely turbulent and I was awake the entire night. May we do this another time?"

"It would be helpful if I could get started now. The discussion you were just having with Professor Recantati, about the telephone call that was made to his home last week—?"

"I didn't make the damn call. I don't know anything about it. And quite frankly, the idea of that man going through the desk drawers of any one of us is frightening. Sylvia Foote probably cracked her big whip and Paolo jumped through the hoop for her. Just like her to want to know everything that each one of us is up to, and to use the acting president to do her bidding."

"How would you describe your relationship with Lola Dakota?"

The yawn he feigned to gain a few seconds to think about his answer was in direct contrast to the lively fidgeting of his bony hands. "Sorry, I'm so tired I can hardly think. Lola?

"We had gotten along just fine, most of the time. I assume that you've done your homework and know about the matter we were working on together?"

"On Roosevelt Island, the Blackwells project? Yes, I've learned a bit about it."

"We both shared a love for a particular building."

"The Smallpox Hospital?"

"Yes. Quite the most magnificent structure in New York City, in my view. And for me, of course, this program offered a rather dramatic study of the history of disease, as well as links to the future, like the potential of using these eradicated viruses for germ warfare. I'll have my hands full for years to come."

"And Lola's interest?"

"It started, appropriately enough, with her discipline—political science and the history of urban institutions. But the old island romanced her, Ms. Cooper."

"Interesting choice of words."

"Well, that ruin is a stunningly romantic building, don't you think?"

"I do, actually. But what do you mean about Lola?"

"For me, it's intellectually valuable to understand how all the infected populations of a large city were isolated in a single location. Typhus, cholera, ship fever. And then this glorious hospital, designed by one of America's greatest architects as though to disguise the fact that it was dedicated to the deadly smallpox.

"The city still has records of who these patients were, how they were treated, and how many—I should say how few—were cured and returned to their homes. I'm interested in documenting that information and using my students to put it together for the first time."

"What about Lola?"

"A lot of our interests overlapped—same records, same patients. For her studies of the culture, it was intriguing that the charity patients—mostly impoverished immigrants—were kept in a ward on the lower floors. The rich who were infected were banished to the same facility, but to private rooms on the upper floor. For *my* work, that's of no importance. But Lola liked that kind of cultural detail. She constructed entire fantasies about the people who passed through here."

"And Freeland Jennings's diamonds?"

"Hogwash, as far as I'm concerned. Those stories involved the penitentiary, not the hospital. Lola walked in both worlds, but my business was only with the medical aspects of the island."

"And you do have a business interest in the project, then?"

The helix was spinning wildly in Grenier's hands. "You've been listening to Claude Lavery. What we intend to do with this medical knowledge is to let society benefit from it. Hardly an evil motive, is it, Ms. Cooper? There are still places in this world where these diseases have not been wiped out. There still exist strains of these plagues that are resistant to current kinds of medication." The tone of his voice became more strident. "I guess you think I'm just supposed to let someone else profit from this when it's perfectly legal for me to do so myself?"

"But surely, Professor Lavery is also entitled—"

"We're into entitlements now, are we, Madam Prosecutor? Look, everyone's out there on that island digging around for a particular reason. Are you going to be the one to decide someone is more or less selfish than I am, more or less altruistic? Let's not be ridiculous.

"Recantati tells me he's going to get us all together tomorrow to discuss the late lamented Lola Dakota— Lavery, Shreve, Lockhart, Foote. Join us, Ms. Cooper. Come see the seamier side of academia."

"I'm hoping to be there. Professor Grenier, I wonder if you can tell me if there's an office, or a room, that's used as a base for the Blackwells project? Someplace that serves as a central headquarters for the work you've all been doing?" Someplace that needs a key to enter, I thought to myself.

"King's College is small enough and our offices are close together in this building, so there has not been a need for a dedicated space over here. And for the moment, until something comes of it, we've just got a rented room with a secretary as the sole staffer, which is over on Roosevelt Island, on Main Street. It's just a studio apartment that we're using until we need something larger to store any objects that we might find in the dig."

"Who has keys to that room?"

He yawned again. "We all do. Even a number of the students. No secrets in there, if that's what you're thinking. Just a desk, a phone, a few filing cabinets. You're welcome to go visit it anytime you like. What are you looking for?"

I wish I knew. "Something related to Blackwells that one might keep locked up."

Grenier placed the double helix on the corner of his desk. "One of Lola's little secrets, no doubt. I'll sleep on it, Ms. Cooper. Maybe one of my charming colleagues knows the answer." He rose to his feet. "I understand I'm to show you the packing boxes with her books?"

"That would be helpful." We walked a short distance from his office. The door was unlocked and he flipped on the light switch. Cardboard cartons lined the bare walls.

"Paolo says they've all been moved in here while I was away. Looking for something special?"

"Not really." *Not that I need to tell you.*

"He says there's an inventory taped to the wall over near the window. See it?"

I looked over the cartons and nodded to him.

"Can you let yourself out?"

"Yes, thanks."

Grenier said good night and I started to browse through the descriptions of the books. It was an eclectic collection, everything from Chernow's brilliant biographies of the titans of business through Wallace's definitive study of Gotham; nineteenth-century geological surveys to reports of the Department of Correction from the early twentieth century; stories of immigrants from every part of the world and tales of urban America. I couldn't imagine disliking anyone who had such a love of books and had preserved so many of them with such care.

My finger ran up and down the pages that were hanging on the wall above the boxes. I found the reference I had been looking for, listed with the items in carton eighteen.

The only noise in the empty corridor was the thud of the book crates as I unstacked and stacked them again to get to the one I wanted. The label on its top flap was marked "Blackwells Project—Penitentiary." I dragged it off to the side and sat on the floor to explore its contents.

The top volumes were years of annual reports from

the Board of Health, which supervised those prisoners who served as "nurses" in the other institutions. Below those were records of the Department of Correction, leading up to MacCormick's raid, which closed the penitentiary permanently. I piled up a few copies of each series and jotted down a note about which ones I was taking with me.

Three-quarters of the way down in the package was a set of matching black leather albums, their grainy finish frayed at the edges. The bottom right corner of each bore the stamped gold initials O.L. I opened the cover of the one on top and saw the elegant penmanship of the then-young man who had documented his life with such care.

I lifted the six volumes of Orlyn Lockhart's diaries from the box and added them to my stack of organizational reports. Now I could hear footsteps coming closer and resounding in the darkened corridor outside the small room. I stood to gather my night's reading material and put on my coat to leave.

When I opened the door I stood face-to-face with the night custodian. "Just coming to get you, miss. I'm supposed to lock up the main door at seven o'clock. Heat gets shut way low. The president asked me to be sure you got out okay."

I thanked him and we walked together down the staircase to the front door. The wind came howling off the river behind my back as I turned up to 116th Street and swept me up to Broadway in its wake. The air was heavy with moisture and the sky was an even shade of dark gray, clouds covering the tops of the tall buildings in the distance. It took me almost ten minutes and several blocks of walking south to find a taxi to take me back to Jake's.

"Smells heavenly." I dropped my books on the table in the entryway and walked into the kitchen, where he was putting a salad together.

"Worth the trip?"

"Definitely." I described the conversations and the two meetings.

"Mike called. Said he's got what you sent him for and he'll see you in the morning."

The table was already set and the candles were lighted. I went inside to slip into leggings and a warm sweater when the chef advised me that dinner would be ready in half an hour.

Back in the living room, I picked up the first volume of Lockhart's diaries. It was dated 1933, when he was still a prosecutor in the Manhattan District Attorney's Office. I read aloud to Jake, amused by the description of the work in those days. I browsed through the opening pages of the next three books, landing on the one that concerned the raid.

Jake had opened a report by the commissioner of correction and was reading selectively from it to me. "'January 11, 1934. The problem of the female offender is growing, due to her emancipation and tendency toward greater sexual freedom.' Are you listening?"

"Sorry. I'm looking for the part about Freeland Jennings." I skimmed quickly through Lockhart's recounting of the raid, and his personal pain when he learned of the death of his friend. There was no mention of diamonds or precious jewels, and I recalled that Lockhart had said those stories didn't surface until much later on.

"Slow down. You can read till your heart's content after dinner."

I came to the description of Jennings's fancy living quarters in the penitentiary. Then the entries stopped for several days. The narrative resumed after the funeral.

I should like to have something of Jennings's to keep for myself, something to remind me both of him and of this daring raid we conducted to weed out the evil on the island. The belonging that most intrigues me is his miniature secret garden, a detailed replica of all of the great buildings of Blackwells constructed in the last century.

It seems that Freeland befriended an indigent prisoner, a stonemason from Italy—same region as Ariana, actually—who was sentenced to the penitentiary because he was a grave robber. Broke into mausoleums and took precious objects that decorated private family crypts. A petty criminal but a gifted artisan nonetheless.

He created a meticulous tabletop copy of the island which my own friend kept in his prison room. An exceptional piece of artwork, really. Shows every edifice, every tree, and practically every rock on the whole place. I shall ask Commissioner MacCormick if I may claim the model as my souvenir of our endeavor.

Freeland wrote to me concerning his garden once. Said he would tell me more about it when I came to visit. He said it held the secret to his survival on the island.

27

"I've got to call Skip Lockhart."

"It's almost eight-fifteen. Can it wait until after dinner?"

I read the section about Jennings's secret model to Jake. "Maybe this miniature tableau of the island has something to do with Lola's murder. Why hasn't anyone mentioned it to me? Just five minutes and I'll be ready."

Jake looked annoyed. "Dinner will be on the table in three. Care to join me?"

I went into the den and opened one of my files. I dialed the number Skip Lockhart had given us for his apartment in Manhattan and got the answering machine. "It's Alexandra Cooper. Could you please call me first thing tomorrow morning? It's about your grandfather's diaries." There was no point being coy about this. I assumed he had read the volumes before letting Lola get her hands on them. "I'd like to talk to you about the model of Blackwells that Freeland Jennings kept in his jail cell."

Then I tried the Lockhart number in White Plains. A woman answered and when I told her who I was, she told me that Skip had gone back into town. "Would it be possible for me to have a few words with your father-in-law?"

"I'm sorry, dear. He ate his dinner at six o'clock and I'm afraid he's sound asleep now. Why don't you try him again tomorrow?"

I called Sylvia Foote's machine at the office to leave her a message, too. "It's Alex. I'm expecting to hear from you in the morning about the faculty meeting you may be planning later in the day. I'd like to be there for part of it, to explain to the group exactly what's going on and what I might need from them." As casually as I could, I dropped in an additional request. "And when you speak to them, Sylvia, tell them I'm interested in talking to them about the Lockhart diaries. You know, the ones kept by Skip's grandfather. And what any of them know about the model of his secret garden on Blackwells. Thanks a lot."

The old volumes had been kept in Lola Dakota's office, without any particular safeguarding. Even now, no one had claimed them or spirited them away. I assumed that any of the people with a particular interest in the project had already scoured the books for information anyway, and that there were likely to be dozens of photocopies floating around.

413

I didn't think the mention of the diaries would trigger any unusual response, but I was curious to see whether my inquiry about the miniature model of the island fueled a reaction.

Jake was seated at the dinner table when I returned to join him. The salmon and baby asparagus awaited me, and he had already begun eating. He was annoyed, and rightly so. Now, I wish I had put off those calls until after the meal, as he had suggested.

"I apologize. I'm sorry for getting so carried away with this investigation. Why don't you tell me about the rest of your afternoon. Any calls?"

"Joan called about New Year's Eve. Wants to know if you can bring some of that great caviar you served at her birthday party. I reminded her that we had to fly back first thing in the morning for Mercer's wedding. I lined up most of my plans for next week. Nothing as exciting as what you're in the middle of."

He was cool and removed now. Not the right moment to remind him that prepositions weren't good words with which to end sentences. I could usually tease him about grammar whenever he made an on-air slip.

"I'm going to have to pick up some things from my apartment after work tomorrow. I'll need an outfit for Joan's dinner and my travel kit."

"We're not even going to be away for twenty-four hours." Jake realized he was snapping at me and tried to bring it down a notch. "If Mike can't drive you by there after work, we can meet at my office and I'll take you over." We were both thinking about Shirley Denzig and whether she was still lurking in the neighborhood.

I reached over and put my hand on top of his, and he loosened up as we both ate and chatted. It was my fault that the fish was dry and overdone, so I finished all of it, so as not to be berated for that, too.

"Go ahead inside. I'll clean up." The job was quick and easy, and ten minutes later I joined him in the living room, where he was reading briefing papers for his next day's assignments. I sat on the far end of the sofa and entangled my legs in his while I carefully read the 1935 volume of the Lockhart diaries from cover to cover.

At 10:35 the phone rang.

"How've you been?" he asked the caller. Usually he mouthed to me the name of the person he was speaking to, if I could not recognize who it was from the context of the conversation. This time he did not.

"No, I don't remember ever meeting him. I've heard of him, of course. I think Tom did a feature piece about his firm, if I'm not mistaken."

The other party spoke.

"You're kidding." Jake sat bolt upright, both feet on the floor. "When?"

Presumably an answer.

"In Montauk? Where is he now? Where are the kids?"

Another brief reply.

"What makes you think it was murder?"

I put down the book and stared at Jake, who was looking straight ahead.

"Just hold on a minute, will you? I want to go into the den." He turned to me. "Darling, would you mind if I take this one inside?" He didn't wait for an answer. "Just hang it up for me when you hear me get on, okay?"

He walked toward the den and I held the receiver until I heard him ask if his caller was still there. She answered, "Yes."

For almost fifteen minutes while they talked, I sat in the living room and fumed. Less than a week ago Jake had invited me to move into his home. I had done so reluctantly, encouraged by the circumstances inside and outside my own apartment. The intimacies that had begun to make me savor our days and nights together were fragile enough to be shattered by one conversation he refused to have in my presence.

I got up to pour myself a drink.

"Don't I get one, too?" he asked as he came back into the living room.

"Sorry. I didn't know when you'd be off the phone." I returned to the bar and fixed him a scotch. The mood shift had been completed. Now I was cool and abrupt to Jake and he was fired up with the adrenaline rush created by an exclusive piece of breaking news.

He sensed my pout immediately. "You're not jealous, are you?"

"Of whom? I don't even know who called." He didn't offer to tell me her name.

"She's just an old friend. A paralegal at one of the big white-shoe firms."

"I wouldn't care if it was Gwyneth Paltrow or Emma Thompson. I am just stunned that there is something you can't talk about in my presence." I steered away from the sofa and sat in an armchair across the room. "You go through this whole big deal about *me* needing to let you more into my life and *me* needing to open up to you. You try to convince me that I should move in with you, and then the first time you get a serious telephone call you fly out of the room because there's a conversation that I'm not permitted to be privy to."

"There's your preposition, darling."

"I'm not amused, Jake. You can be damn sure"—I got up and walked in a circle around the chair as I talked—"*damn* sure that I'm not ever about to live with someone who takes private calls in a separate room. And especially when I hear the word 'murder.' Now, do you want to tell me what that was about?"

He leaned forward and rested his forearms on his thighs, his glass in one hand. He was smiling as he looked over at me. "Am I talking to my lover, or am I talking to a prosecutor?"

"When you say 'murder' and 'kids' in the space of a few minutes, I regret to inform you—*darling*—that I am a prosecutor."

He sat back. "That's the problem. My sources are privileged. I got this information in confidence, so don't ask me anything I can't tell you." He was too anxious to repeat the story not to go on. "She was working—"

"She?"

"The source. My friend. She was called in to assist a partner who had a business appointment with a client. Emergency meeting on a Sunday evening because the client's a stock analyst, specializing in foreign securities. He was supposed to be off to Europe in the morning. Very well-known guy in the financial community."

"What's his name?"

Jake looked at me. "Can't do that."

He paused. "They sit through half an hour of the meeting, then the senior partner takes a break to go to the men's room. Client follows him in and, standing next to him at the urinal, tells him that he killed his wife on Saturday and—"

Mike Chapman would have had an appropriate comment about the guy's timing, but the moment and its humor were lost on me. "In Manhattan?"

"They live here, but this happened somewhere between New York City and their beach home on Long Island. Nassau or Suffolk County, Madam Prosecutor. Not your jurisdiction."

He couldn't possibly think that I would fail to be appalled about a homicide that had occurred outside the confines of the city limits of my legal responsibility. "And the kids? What's the part about children?"

Jake paused slightly before answering. "This guy actually put his wife's remains in the trunk of his car. Then he got the two kids and drove upstate to dump the body."

"*Where?*"

"Where what?"

"Where is that woman's body right at this very moment? And where the hell are the children?"

"They're fine. She assures me that they're perfectly okay."

"And you're not going to tell me who this victim is and whether she's lying out in the woods or dumped in a lake or—?"

"Look, my informant's in a tough position, Alex. This is their client and the information he's giving them is privileged. They're trying to do the right thing and deal with getting him surrendered before he leaves the country, but right now he's resisting that idea. When there's more that I can tell you—"

The phone rang again and Jake answered. "Hey, that's fine. No problem. You can call me any hour of the night with a story like this. In the meantime, why don't we plan on lunch tomorrow? You can give me all the details then."

His caller clearly liked the idea.

"Michael's. Fifty-fifth Street between Fifth and

Sixth, at twelve-thirty. There's a great table in an alcove in the front. Very private. No overheards. I'll call in the morning and reserve it."

She had a suggestion for Jake.

"No, you're not disturbing anything. Sure, if you get something else, call right back." He hung up and turned back to me. "You can't solve all the world's problems, Alex."

"I'd like to think that even if I were not a prosecutor, this story would be so upsetting that it would make me get off my ass and do something about it. I can't understand how you can sit there and probably just think about whether you can scoop the other networks with some lurid personal detail about this woman's murder. I can't understand why calling the police isn't the first thing you do."

The phone rang again and this time, without asking my permission, Jake held up a finger as if to suggest that I wait a few minutes till he returned from the den to finish our conversation. He trotted off to the other room to take his call alone.

I walked to the window and looked out at the murky night sky. Three minutes of that did nothing to calm me. I picked up my cell phone, Jake's spare set of keys, the forty-seven dollars cash I had left until I hit the ATM in the morning, and I stuffed them in my shoulder bag. I had to get out of the apartment before my temper exploded. And I needed to find out who the dead woman might be.

Jake was still in the den when I put on my coat and walked out to the elevator.

I pushed the revolving door open before the doorman could get to his feet and reach out for it. A fine layer of sleet was falling as I turned the corner and tried to find a coffee shop where I could make some calls to local precincts to see whether any relatives or friends had reported a missing female in the past twenty-four hours.

After going three blocks, it was apparent that nothing in the area was open after eleven o'clock on a Sunday evening. Although I was less than five minutes from my own apartment, I knew it was foolish to go there. I did not want to risk an encounter with the unstable, stalking complainant, Shirley Denzig, and I had not received word that the window had been repaired.

I reached inside my coat and lifted my beeper when I felt it vibrating on my waistband. I held it up under the streetlight and saw it display Jake's number. I replaced it, tightened the collar of my coat, raised it against the sleet, and crossed the street.

If I walked another few blocks north, I would reach the Nineteenth Precinct station house on Sixty-seventh Street. If I went east instead, I could get to Mike's building just as quickly. He knew every homicide detective in a fifty-mile radius of the city. We could sit in his tiny studio apartment, which he had long ago nicknamed The Coffin, making calls all night if need be until we figured out who this killer was and locked him up before he fled the country.

I picked up my pace as I headed east to York Avenue. A coat of ice was forming on the sidewalks and streets and I took care not to slip as I walked briskly along. The only people outside were those who needed to be there. Dog walkers out for the last effort of the evening, hospital workers heading for the midnight shift at Cornell Medical Center, and the occasional homeless person huddled in a storefront or alleyway.

When I reached the entrance to the old tenement that stood dwarfed amid the surrounding high-rise condos, and upscale restaurants, I opened the outer door, shook the drops off my sleeves, and looked for the buzzer to Mike's apartment. It was marked with the number of his gold detective's shield rather than his name. As the beeper on my waistband went off a second time, I continued to ignore it and pressed the doorbell.

The several seconds it took for Mike's voice to come over the intercom seemed like an hour.

"Yeah?"

"I've got a problem. It's Alex. Buzz me in?"

The brass handle yielded to my grip as the signal to unlock it sounded in the small lobby. I grabbed at the banister in the dingy hallway and jogged up the staircase, flight after flight, to the fifth floor of the narrow building. I was huffing and puffing when I got to the landing and stopped to catch my breath.

I could hear Mike unlatch the dead bolt. He cracked the door about a foot wide and stood in the opening, his chest bare and a towel wrapped around him and knotted at his waist.

"Sorry, it never occurred to me you'd be asleep at this hour." I walked toward the door, expecting him to let me in. "Don't be modest, Mikey. I won't rip it off you. That could be the first thing I've had to laugh about all evening."

I reached my arm out to push at the door. I assumed he thought I'd want him to get dressed before I came into the small room. He held his ground as he gave me a once-over, as though looking from head to toe for an injury. "You okay?"

"Cold and wet. And furious. You've got to help me."

I brushed past him and stepped over the threshold as he started to speak. "Alex, just give me a minute to—"

I gasped as I stood beside him. There was a woman asleep in his bed, and I cringed as I realized how rude I had been to burst in and impose on his friendship so abruptly.

I put my right hand up in front of my face and tried to whisper an apology. "I'm mortified," I said, fighting off tears and backing out of the doorway. "It was so inconsiderate of me to rush up here without calling."

He grabbed for my wrist as I pulled away and turned toward the staircase. "Alex, don't be ridiculous. I just want to—"

"I'll call you in the morning," I said over my shoulder. "Don't worry. I'm on my way to Jake's. I'm fine." I was flying down the steps, calling up to him from two flights below. There was no way I'd go back to Jake's apartment now, but I didn't want Mike to worry about me heading for my own place. I ignored Mike's shouts to me to slow down and stop, and instead was planning the most direct route to the station house to get someone in the squad to help me.

There was very little traffic on the slick street so I dismissed the traffic light and dashed across York Avenue, moving west. If Mike had been dressed, I knew he would have been chasing me by now, so I broke into a trot and started running, in case he even thought about putting clothes on to follow me.

My mind was short-circuiting with irrelevancies. What would he do when he called Jake's apartment in five minutes and learned that I hadn't returned there? Maybe I should just suck up what had happened and go back to confront Jake, call the police in his presence. But if he objected to my doing so, I would be forced to walk out on him again anyway. Who was the woman in Mike's apartment, I wondered, and why had he been so close-mouthed about her? And how sorry I felt for her to have this madwoman burst in on her in her boyfriend's home at a most unsuitable time for a house call.

I stood on the corner of First Avenue to wait for a bus to pass, panting as I came to a halt. Maybe she slept through the whole thing, I thought to myself. And what would he say to explain the situation to her if she had not?

I reached the curb on the far side of the street and

practically lost my balance as I stepped on a slippery patch of black ice. Calm down, I tried to urge myself. Just a few blocks more and I could sit in the detectives' squad room making my calls, warm and secure.

Footsteps smacked at the pavement off in the distance behind me. Some other fool was out on this miserable night. I spun around to make sure that it was not Chapman coming after me, but saw only the dark figure of a man crossing the avenue against the traffic. If it were Mike, he would have called out to me by this point, and I assured myself that I would have stopped and explained to him the reason for my untimely visit.

I started loping along again, wiping the freezing rain from my eyelids and ducking my head to avoid the wind.

The running steps grew closer to me now and I turned again. This time the man was almost upon me and I could see him clearly. His face resembled the sketch of the young assailant who had been attacking women in this neighborhood for the past two months. My heart beat wildly as I tried to think of a way to get out of his path. Second Avenue was a long sprint from the middle of the block, but the brownstone buildings on either side of the quiet street required keys to get inside their front doors.

I accelerated and ran into the middle of the roadway, racing toward the busier thoroughfare ahead that would be bound to have taxi and bus traffic. Before I could reach the corner, the man had lapped me from the back. His muscular arms stabbed my shoulder blades and he tried to clutch at my mouth, muttering at me in a soft accented voice, repeatedly telling me to shut up.

I fell to the ground and my knees smashed against the concrete. My gloved hands flapped out in front of me and broke my fall. In a flash, my attacker ripped the strap of my bag off my arm and ran toward the avenue as I lay sprawled on the icy street.

28

"Hey, Quick Draw, wanna put out an APB for me?"

I was sitting inside the Nineteenth Precinct squad commander's office, shielded from the detectives' desks by the clouded glass window on the door, when I heard Chapman's voice, at top volume, calling across the room to Walter DeGraw.

"I'm looking for a dumb blonde. Big-time bad judgment written all over her. Put it out on the wires in case any of your guys see her skating around the city streets on the midnight tour. About five feet ten inches, too skinny for my taste, too stubborn to ask a cop for help, too vain to shed tears and run her mascara, too stupid to put a hat on her head in a snowstorm so her blonde hair's looking a little bedraggled from the sleet. But great wheels. And well dressed. They find her alive, she's likely to kill me if I didn't add those things. You seen her around or I oughtta try the psych ward down at Bellevue?"

DeGraw pushed open the door and Chapman reached out his arm to balance himself against the frame of it and stare down at me. I was sitting in the lieutenant's armchair, holding a steaming mug of coffee in both hands to warm them up, and wearing a turtleneck sweater that one of the guys had taken from his locker to put over my wet clothes.

"For a smart broad, sometimes you got the brains of a pigeon."

DeGraw started to excuse himself and get out of the room.

"Don't go, Walter," I implored him. He had begun to type the complaint report and the sooner I finished giving him the details, the faster I could get out of the cold station house.

Chapman stepped into the room and squatted in front of me. He placed his palms against my knees and realized when I jerked reflexively away from him that I had hurt them in my fall. He pried the coffee cup away from my clutches and pressed my hands between his own, rubbing them together gently but firmly.

"What's this all about, kid?"

I shook my head, not wanting to tell the whole story here and now, and DeGraw shuffled nervously, knowing that he was in the middle of something more personal. A uniformed cop knocked on the door, which was still ajar.

"Excuse me, Detective DeGraw? The desk sergeant sent me up." He was clutching my shoulder bag. "My partner found this on the sidewalk, about two blocks south of where she was hit. Nothing in it. Sarge wants to know if you can identify it, Counselor."

"There wasn't much in it anyway. Yes, it's mine."

DeGraw called over his shoulder to another detective in the squad room. "Hey, Guido. Wanna bring me a voucher for Ms. Cooper's bag?"

Now we were five, crowded into the tiny office, filling out police forms and documenting my thickheadedness.

"Word's out on the street, Coop. Even the perp knew it wasn't worth wasting his time to make you do it."

Don't bite, I urged myself. He's trying to make me laugh but I wasn't in the mood.

Chapman's grip on my hands was comforting, and it felt good to be with people who would care about finding the murdered woman Jake had been called about.

"What word?" Guido asked, suckered into Chapman's bait. "Make her do what?"

"The guy who mugged her's the one who's been chasing women around up here. Making them perform oral sodomy. But he didn't even slow down his pace for Cooper. Just took the money and ran. Must have heard she's no good at blow—"

"Why don't you back off, Chapman?" Lieutenant Grier had returned from his meal and walked upstairs to see what was causing such a late-night commotion. "There's a Mr. Tyler on the phone, Alex. Says he's a friend. Wants to know if he can come over here."

"Tell him no, please. Tell him I'll call him tomorrow." I pulled my hands away from Chapman and he stood up. I pressed my damp hair down and pulled the dangling strings of it behind my ears. "I don't know how he knew where I'd be. You either."

"You ran out of my place like a bat out of hell. Said you were going to Jake's. I waited five minutes and called him to make sure you got there." The men were listening to our conversation with interest, forgetting they had other things to do. "When he told me you'd had a fight and it had something to do with a missing woman, I just called over here, figuring that you had come to me to get information from the police. Next place you'd probably go was the precinct. I phoned and got Walter, who told me he had a hallucinating homeless woman, who looked like a vaguely familiar waterlogged prosecutor, dragging in a few minutes back with her tail between her legs. Told me what happened to you. Never dreamed you'd march in here as an aided case instead of an amateur dick."

"I'm not an aided case. I don't need an ambulance." I pulled my hands back and lowered them to my lap.

"Listen, Coop, you got less than forty-eight hours to turn your karma around before the New Year starts. Understand?"

Lieutenant Grier had walked away and returned from his own desk with a bottle of Glenfiddich. He chased the uniformed cop back downstairs, poured us each a shot into drinking glasses, and apologized to the three detectives as he served them in paper cups. "Happy New Year, everybody."

I drank the warm scotch and the rich single-malt stung as it went down my throat.

"Want to tell us about the call Jake got?" Mike asked.

I wasn't sure everyone in the room needed to hear the conversation.

"She gets real moody whenever she gets jealous, Loo," Chapman said, taking off his jacket and sitting on the edge of the desk. "Threw a tantrum 'cause she caught me with another broad. There probably isn't any missing woman at all. Just Coop trying to get my attention back."

"'Missing' isn't the operative word, Lieutenant. 'Murdered' is a bit more accurate." Maybe I had over-reacted when I saw that Mike had been in bed with a woman. I had run down the stairs without waiting for an introduction or an explanation, and now I was trying to convince myself that it was not jealousy that had sent me reeling back out to the treacherously icy street.

"See the extremes she goes to when the green mon-ster rears its ugly head? The lights were out, the candles were lit, my clothes were tidily stacked on a chair, and for once in a blue moon I'm in bed with a—"

"We ain't all that interested in your wishful think-ing, Chapman. Guido, Walter—why don't you go out and finish up what you need to do with the paperwork on Ms. Cooper's mugging." The two old-timers reluctantly picked up their cups and reports and shuffled off to the larger squad room. "Alex, you want to tell us what set off this whole thing?" Grier asked, closing the door behind him.

I explained to Lieutenant Grier who Jake Tyler was and why he had a professional obligation to protect his sources.

"Yeah, but not even to tell *you*? It don't make sense to me."

"Believe me, Loo. I understand the principle, but it doesn't make any sense to me, either. There's no question that the information Jake got from the legal assistant who called him is that their client had killed his wife—"

"In Manhattan?"

"I'm not sure, Mike."

"Where, then?"

"Maybe Suffolk County. Jake said something about a summerhouse on Long Island."

The lieutenant had less patience than I had expected. "Give me a place to start, Alex. There's five counties in the city and fifty-seven more in the rest of the state. You expect me to call every single one of them?"

He took a slug of his neat scotch and paced the floor. "What else do you know about these people? How old are they? How many children are we talking about? What does she do for—"

"I told you everything I know, Loo, and I realize it isn't much to go on. I just thought if we checked with a few of the precincts, maybe someone would have reported that a colleague hadn't shown up for work, or a sister didn't make it to a family birthday party, or that the baby-sitter was alarmed 'cause the kids were gone."

He looked at his watch as Mike walked behind me and stood at my back, rubbing my neck and shoulders. "More likely people would think the whole family's away for the weekend. I'll have the guys call around, but I wouldn't expect to hear nothing until tomorrow."

"Mind if we stay here awhile and use your phones?" Mike asked.

"Suit yourself. Seems like a shot in the dark to me." He walked out of the room.

"That's what you want to do, isn't it?"

I leaned forward, pushing the bottle out of my way, and rested my head on the desktop. "I just can't bear the thought that a woman's body is somewhere out there, exposed to this storm, while some member of my esteemed profession—for the right price—is probably arranging for the killer to get out of the jurisdiction."

"They can't do *that*, can they?"

"Not supposed to. But while the lawyer gets all his ducks in a row, hoping to bargain for a deal before the surrender, who knows where a financier with inter-national connections will wind up?"

Mike refreshed his drink and sat opposite me, trying

to make eye contact. "You and Jake going to be all right?"

I was silent.

"He hasn't got a choice in this, does he, Coop? He did what he had to do. You guys are good together."

"Looks like I'm the one who has a choice to make. It never occurred to me that he'd have to cover criminal cases until this happened. I'm not about to sit on the floor of the closet with the door closed and my hands over my ears when the phone rings and somebody confesses to homicide in the middle of the night."

"You want to come back up to my—?"

"I called David Mitchell as soon as I got here. He and Renee were still awake. David promised to take a spare key down to the doorman. I've slept on their couch dozens of times." Mike knew my neighbor, a prominent psychiatrist who had become a close friend over the years. He and his fiancée lived down the hall from me, and I had often spent the night, sharing the sofa with their dog, Prozac. "A wet nose snuggled up against my neck might be just what I need."

Chapman was dialing the phone as I spoke. "Mike Chapman, Manhattan North Homicide here. Who's this?" He paused to listen. "You got any missing persons reports in the last forty-eight hours? Yeah, I'll hold." A minute passed. "Fifteen-year-old runaway. Left home Thursday after a three-week correspondence with some guy she met on the Internet—"

I shook my head in the negative.

"—and a female black, topless dancer from a joint on Pine Street, last seen getting into a car with a Japanese businessman two nights ago. DWA oughtta be a crime, Sarge. Thanks."

Driving While Asian was one of Chapman's favorite legislative proposals for an amendment to the Penal Law. He could never resist running his mouth at a politically incorrect target.

"Nothing unusual in the First, blondie. You keep thinking about how to put your love life back on track and I'll—"

"I'm not thinking. I don't want to think anymore."

"I'm on the case." He dialed again, working from the list of precinct numbers in the department telephone book in the top drawer of the desk. From the lower end of Manhattan moving north, Mike called squad after squad. At some, the phone rang interminably and he never got a response. At most, the answers were predictable. The occasional missing adolescent, the husband not back from a weekend jaunt with his pals, the family of a mentally handicapped adult who had wandered away from a vocational training program and hadn't been seen since Friday.

I walked out among the maze of old wooden desks and found the rest room. By the time I came back, Mike was waiting for a detective to check the blotter in the Twenty-fourth Precinct, on the Upper West Side. I lifted my empty purse from the metal tray of the out box and looked in the zippered compartment, knowing the cash was gone.

"Hope you had the good sense to take your Christmas present when you blew out of Jake's place. We could hock that heap of glass and run off to the Keys, live the rest of our lives down there without ever working again. I could go bonefishing all day and you could drink margaritas and listen to Jimmy Buffett. D'you bring it?"

I smiled and shook my head. It was Mike's way of making sure that my pin hadn't been stolen in the mugging, knowing I would be too embarrassed to want to tell him.

"Boa constrictor? West Eighty-third Street? No thanks." He hung up and checked the number for the Twenty-sixth Precinct, talking as he dialed. "Woman moved into a sublet last week. In the middle of the night, an eight-foot boa comes slithering up on the pillow next to her, trying to give her a kiss. Last guy who lived in the place raised 'em. Seems he left one behind as a housewarming gift. Speckled band and all that . . .

"Who's this? Yo, Monty, it's Chapman. Looking for a missing broad." The guy who answered asked a few questions of Mike. "No, schmuck. If I knew who or where then she wouldn't be missing very long, would she?" Chapman listened. "Why'd they go up to King's College at this hour of the morning?" After a moment he placed the receiver back on the cradle.

"Time for forty winks, blondie. I'll look for your damsel in distress tomorrow. Somebody broke into the administration building at your favorite school after they locked up tonight. Must have gotten spooked in the middle of the getaway. Cartons of books were piled up next to the back door. The thief only made off with a few of them. They're the boxes marked with Lola Dakota's name on them."

29

Renee and I caught up over morning coffee. I had finally fallen asleep about 3 A.M., and had not even heard David slip out to walk the dog at seven o'clock. I borrowed her bathrobe and the spare key to my apartment. It was too cold to shower there, with the window still not repaired, but I needed a set of my thin silk thermal underwear to put on beneath my charcoal-gray pantsuit. For once the weatherman's prediction seemed to be on target, and just the news reports of the impending snowstorm chilled me again.

At eight-thirty I went downstairs to wait for Mike. All of the Christmas tips had been distributed to the building staff in the preceding weeks, and they remained unusually responsive to opening car doors, helping women with baby strollers into elevators, and ferrying packages from the entrance to the elevator banks. Poinsettias fringed the tables and glass windows of the marble-trimmed lobby, and everyone except for me seemed especially cheerful as they set out to work on this last week of the year.

"How's my little Nanook doing this morning?"

I had left my coat in the apartment and opted to wear my ski parka over the long johns and business suit. "Overkill, you think?" I asked Mike as I opened the car door.

"Not if you're planning to spend the night in an igloo. You get any sleep?"

"Took a steaming-hot shower and went out like a light. Listen, I really want to apologize for showing up on your doorstep last night. It was rude of me not—"

"Yeah, it was."

I turned to look at Mike's face, to see whether he was kidding. There was no smile. "I mean, it just wasn't like you at all. I didn't know who the hell was ringing the buzzer at that hour on a Sunday night. I just figured most people would have called first. You're the last person I expected to hear when I answered the intercom."

"But—"

"But what? You always get so grouchy when I show up in the middle of one of your romantic interludes, like it's gonna be the last time you'll ever get laid."

"How was I supposed to know I'd be interrupting a domestic vignette in your dark little lair if you never talk about your social life these days? I'm trying to apologize to you, if you let me get a word in. And to, to . . . ? Does she have a name, Detective?"

Mike concentrated on the slippery road surface as he steered the car onto the FDR Drive.

"Maybe I'll just refer to your guest as 'her.' That okay with you?" I barreled off a list of questions about the nameless figure in the bed. "Did I spoil your evening with her? Are you going to tell me how you met her? Have you given any thought to when you're going to bring her out of the closet and let your friends—"

"Valerie."

"That wasn't too tough, was it? Valerie. Nice name. Okay, tell me about Valerie, Mr. Chapman. Am I moving too fast for you? I'm trying to start with the easy things."

"She's an architect. Only woman partner in a pretty sizable firm. Does design work for large urban projects, everything from creating new sites adjacent to Battery Park City to planning the Miami Heat sports complex."

I guess the answer surprised me. I paused long enough between questions for Mike to sense my reaction.

"You were expecting a barmaid? Or maybe a peanut vendor from Yankee Stadium?"

I blushed as I protested, "I, uh, I wasn't expecting anything in particular." I had seen Mike through a number of casual relationships over the years, usually with women who had a lifestyle as uprooted as his— journalists, flight attendants, actresses—and rarely grounded at a serious stage in their professions.

"Thirty-two years old. Went to UCLA, majored in

medieval history. She can sit up all night talking to me about the rule of Saint Benedict and reciting lines from Havelock the Dane. Don't imagine it would turn *you* on, blondie, but it works like magic on me."

"She sounds—"

"Got so hooked on Gothic architecture—flying buttresses and Rayonnant design—she went on for her graduate degree at Stanford. Don't even toy with me on the subject, kid. I'll be murder on those *Jeopardy!* questions now."

"I'd love to—"

"Don't be patronizing with me. She's every bit as intelligent as your frigging pals."

"What are you getting so damn defensive about? I'm trying to tell you that I'd like to get to know her, to spend time with her."

"Jacobsen."

I slapped my hand on the dashboard. "That's what you're being so weird about." I laughed. "She's Jewish, too?"

"Like you're the only one I'm supposed to find interesting?"

"Like I'm delighted that you stepped out of your narrow-minded little world and—"

"You're only barking at me like this because you *are* jealous. I was right last night. You can't get beyond having me at your disposal, twenty-four-seven, then jerking me around when you set off on a jaunt with one of your fancy beaux."

"I can't believe that's the way you would characterize our friendship. There's nothing in the world I wouldn't do for you, and I know you've demonstrated that over and over again for me. Why wouldn't I want you to be happy?"

There was not a single reason for Mike to be sniping at me. I leaned back in the seat and pushed myself again to explore my feelings about our relationship. There was no question that I had never expected him to be seriously involved with someone who was not Catholic, and I had often wondered, despite his obvious intelligence, whether he was threatened by women of substantial professional accomplishment. Maybe we had both struggled against our mutual attraction from time to time. I hated the idea that I might be envious of his lover.

I shook off my concern and smiled over at Mike, hoping to soothe him with an effort at a joke. "What you don't realize is how flattering I find this whole thing."

"Right."

"Accomplished, interesting, smart, Jewish. Pat McKinney might even think I'm the one who opened your eyes to a different kind of woman."

Instead of responding with a clever dig, Mike snarled, "Val's nothing like you."

"Don't be such a Grinch. You know I'm just kidding about—"

"She's not lucky, Coop. You're the luckiest girl I

know, and Val is way overdue for a heavy dose of the good fortune you've been dealt." I had not seen Mike this intense since Mercer's shooting. There was no relieving his edge.

I didn't know in which direction to move the conversation. Every angle I started with met a dead end. I stared out the window as the wipers swished the soft flakes from side to side and waited for Mike to take this where he wanted.

We were in the underpass beneath the United Nations Building now, stuck in the middle lane behind three cars that had piled up in a fender bender. When Mike spoke, I couldn't see his face because of the darkness in the short tunnel.

"I guess Sloan-Kettering isn't the best place in the world to pick up a girl."

The superb cancer facility occupied a city block on York Avenue, midway between Mike's apartment and my own. Many of my friends had been treated and saved by the phenomenal medical staff that served its patient population. I looked at the shadow of Mike's profile while he talked to me.

"After Mercer was hit, I made it a point to donate blood, to replace all the pints that had been used in his surgery. All the guys did it. I decided to go to Sloan-Kettering. Just seemed like the best place to give. First time I was there, in the blood center, I saw her. She was resting on one of the recliners, like she was at the beach. Had a bright blue silk scarf tied around her head, knotted at the nape of her neck, with a big smile on her face while she chatted with the nurse. Just the most luminous skin I'd ever seen.

"We only talked for about fifteen minutes that day. She had to give some of her own blood to be tested for a kind of experimental treatment. She was finishing her juice, getting ready to leave, and they were prepping me to start. Long enough for me to find out what her name was and where she worked."

Mike maneuvered out from behind the stuck cars and into the right-hand lane, crawling back out onto the wet highway. "She wouldn't see me for more than a month. I hadn't realized that there was no hair under her scarf, and she was afraid to tell me. Afraid I wouldn't want to take the next step."

I thought back to my glimpse of the woman in Mike's bed. I had only seen the slender outline of her body beneath the sheet, and the short-cropped brunette hair against the pillow. "What kind of cancer does she have?"

"I'm using the past tense. Had. Val *had* breast cancer. A very aggressive kind, no family history. They did a mastectomy last year and some radical chemotherapy. She's healthy now."

He paused and looked away from me, out toward the river. "I'm betting on her, Coop."

"Of course you should be. You've got a whole built-in cheering section, for chrissakes. Why wouldn't you think Mercer and Vickee and Jake and I can't be part of this?"

He didn't answer me aloud but nodded his head in assent. Perhaps it had more to do with Mike exposing his own vulnerability to us than keeping Val away from his friends.

"How about next weekend, Jake and I can do a dinner party?"

Mike took his eyes off the road, looked over at me, and chuckled.

"See, I knew I could make you smile. Jake can cook, I'll do the dishes."

"You'll like her. You two can go on and on about Chaucer and Malory and the *Cursor Mundi*—all that Middle English literature you guys thrive on." The familiar grin was gone now. "She just gets tired easily. We'll make the first one an early night, if you don't mind."

I cursed myself for my glibness about Mike's mysterious woman. I knew and appreciated the blessings of good health and good genes. Last night, while Val was cradled safely in the arms of the man who adored her, I was tramping around the darkened streets of Manhattan in a petulant tantrum, thinking I could enlist Mike's aid like Guinevere summoning her knights. Why wasn't I content to stay at home and talk things through with Jake?

Mike let me out in front of the courthouse and I stopped to buy coffee for both of us before going upstairs to my office. There was a voice mail from Laura telling me that she wouldn't be in today from Staten Island because of the bad weather, and two messages from Jake, asking me to call. The earlier one was solicitous in tone, the second was stern and somber. I ignored both.

This would be a quiet week, with many assistants taking vacation leave during the court hiatus between Christmas and New Year's.

Sylvia Foote was the first to call, confirming the meeting she had set for one o'clock and asking whether I had heard about last night's burglary. Police were once again working their way through the King's College building, even as Foote's animosity toward me once again increased.

Mike walked in as I hung up the phone. He picked up the receiver and dialed Information, asking for Michael's restaurant. The automated voice connected him directly, at the additional cost of thirty cents to the district attorney.

"Good morning. This is Jake Tyler, NBC News. I called last night to book a table for lunch."

"He wanted that private table in the alcove, under the window," I reminded Mike in a whisper.

"That's right, that nice one up front. I won't be needing it after all. I'd appreciate it if you cancel my reservation." He hung up, then took off his trench coat and threw it on a chair. "Make you feel better? At least when he shows up with his secret source, they won't be holding a special place for him."

Mike picked up the phone when it rang again. "Hey, Jake." He looked at me for guidance.

I mouthed the word "no" as clearly as I could.

"Nope. Haven't seen her yet. Think she spent the night with David and Renee. You really put her in some kind of snit, man. Nothing that about three dozen yellow roses and the sight of you on your knees in the slush can't correct. Oh, and the whereabouts of that broad who got whacked this weekend. Call back when you got that, Jake. I'll tell her to give you a buzz when she gets down here."

He pressed the plastic button to end the call and stood with the receiver in his hand as the phone immediately rang again. "Ms. Cooper's office and she *really* doesn't want to talk to an asshole like you." Mike paused. "Whoops, sorry, Your Honor. I'm new here. Thought you were just another crank caller for the lovely prosecutor."

Mike passed the call to me. "Yes, sir, I do recognize the name. No, I think she's away for the week but I'll be right down. Yes, I'll handle it myself." I gave the phone back to Mike. "Make yourself useful. I've got to go down to AP3. There's a bit of a crisis on one of our old cases and the assistant has the week off."

I slipped the chain with my identification badge around my neck and went to the staircase to wind my way over to the elevator bank that descended to the misdemeanor courtrooms on the fourth floor of the building. My deputy, Sarah Brenner, had been on maternity leave since her baby was born in the middle of the summer, and it wouldn't be soon enough until she returned to the unit. It was impossible to stem the daily flow of incoming mayhem, even in the midst of an ongoing murder investigation.

I entered the rear of All-Purpose Part 3 through the double-swinging doors, and scanned the rows of benches for Juan Modesto. I couldn't spot him anywhere. Judge Fink had asked me to speak with the clerk, and the court officer guarding the entrance to the well of the courtroom unhooked the metal chain and let me through.

When I approached the clerk's desk, she motioned me to lean in so that she could speak to me without disturbing the judge during his plea negotiations with a defendant on a buy-and-bust case.

"Are you familiar with this one?"

"Pretty well," I said, trying to pull up the facts from my memory. "Modesto beat and raped his girlfriend. He's out on bail, pending the indictment. She's been uncooperative, claims he's been threatening her to drop charges or he'll kidnap the baby and take him back to the Dominican Republic. The judge issued an order of protection last time the case was on. I think we asked for an adjournment to late in January, figuring we might be able to change her mind after the holidays.

"Sorry, I didn't have instructions down here today. I honestly didn't know the case was on the calendar."

"It's not. Check this one out. You know what your victim looks like?"

"Yes. I've met her a couple of times." I had spent the better part of an afternoon with her at the beginning of the month, trying to convince her to prosecute. Together with my young colleague who was assigned to the matter, I had reminded her that Modesto's assaults were occurring with greater frequency and causing more serious injury.

"Why don't you take a slow walk back down the aisle. Second row, end seat on your left. Tell me who you think is hiding beneath the wig, sunglasses, and lady's overcoat?"

I made a cautious circle around the busy room, pretending to be in search of a witness, before returning to the clerk's desk. "It's not my victim, if that's what you mean."

"The judge just wanted to be sure. He thinks it's Juan Modesto himself. Marched right up to me, told me she was Lavinia Cabrinas, and that she wanted to ask Judge Fink to drop all the charges against Modesto and vacate the order of protection. We thought the five o'clock shadow and the falsetto voice were a little off for Ms. Cabrinas, so I told 'her' to have a seat. The judge just wants you to confirm it before we call the case."

I turned to check the audience again. "Not even close. I've seen lots of guys beat the rap, but never this way."

"Why don't you wait over here, behind me."

When the plea on the drug possession case was completed, the clerk nodded to the judge, who directed a recall on the Modesto matter, adding it to the day's calendar. The defendant moved to the railing behind the well and repeated his request, in his prissiest imitation of a soft-spoken Latina.

Four court officers surrounded him as Neal Fink, a no-nonsense jurist, ordered him to take off his glasses, which he did without hesitation. The next request was to remove his wig. Modesto froze, and again the judge told him to take off his hairpiece. When he refused to acknowledge the direction a fourth time, the judge told the officers to lift the jumble of black acrylic from the petitioner's head. Two held his arms while the others tugged at the phony curls, pulling them free from the bobby pins that had secured the wig to Modesto's own greasy pompadour.

"Your bail is revoked, Mr. Modesto. Put him in, gentlemen. You are remanded without bail, sir. Miss Cooper, I expect you'll be ready to advance this matter and move to the grand jury most expeditiously. And that you'll be adding the charges of hindering prosecuting and obstructing governmental administration. Can you get this done by the end of the week?"

"We'll do our best, Your Honor."

The last thing I needed now was any diversion from the Dakota investigation. Especially another domestic violence victim willing to give her man a break, ignoring the acute danger of her situation and the lengths to which he would go to escape prosecution.

Mike was playing solitaire at Laura's desk when I came back upstairs. "Battaglia's looking for you. He sounds completely pissed off. Sinnelesi called to complain about the stuff you had taken out of Bart Frankel's office. Battaglia wants a complete accounting of it. Says he's shocked you did that search warrant without running it past the front office first. Bad position to put him in with another elected official. You know the drill. You oughtta go on over and cool him down. I suggested maybe he should put you over his knee."

"Bet he passed on that one."

"Told me I could take the first shot, actually."

"This is one time he'll have to wait for me. No politics slowing down this train."

I opened the Dakota file folder to the sheet of information with all the case names and telephone numbers and dialed the Lockhart home in White Plains. Skip's mother passed me on to the grandfather, who was no doubt in his favorite chair in the solarium.

"Mr. Lockhart? It's Alexandra Cooper."

"He just left, Miss Cooper."

"Who just left?"

"Skip. That's who you're looking for, isn't it?"

"No, sir. I had a few more questions for you."

"What did you do to rile up the boy, Miss Cooper?"

"I haven't seen Skip today, or talked with him. I'm calling because when we met with you I hadn't read your diaries. I didn't know anything about Freeland Jennings's secret garden. But I was looking through your books last evening, and I'm interested in learning what became of Jennings's model of Blackwells. Do you still have it, Mr. Lockhart?"

"Don't be telling me you had nothing to do with firing up my grandson. He practically tore through the whole place today looking for that damn thing."

I took a breath. "Did Skip find it? Did he take it with him?"

"You know where it is?"

"I believed that you had it, sir."

"Skip's mad as a hornet with me. I told him to talk to Lola about it. Can't recall exactly the last time I saw it, but Lola knows. She's got it, maybe. Skip's coming back later to look through the garage. I'll tell him you were asking about it."

Back to square one. "Thanks, Mr. Lockhart. Sorry to trouble you."

I dialed Sylvia Foote's number again. "Check with your professors. Any of them have cars?" I thought for a moment about the weather. "Four-wheel drive? I think we should take a quick trip to White Plains this afternoon. Perhaps if all of us are together with the Lockharts, senior and junior, we can make some headway. I'd like to start the meeting in your office and make a run up to see if the old man is hiding more than he's telling any of us."

"But—"

"I'll explain when we get there. I think a field trip might help, Sylvia."

Maybe my phone message to Sylvia last evening, when I was reading the Lockhart diaries, had been a mistake. I thought it might alert the small group of faculty members that we were onto something that one of them might have concealed from us, but I had only meant to rattle the cages in preparation for our meeting today. I didn't want anyone making an end run around us.

Mike's feet were propped on Laura's desk when I hung up the phone and came out to intercept the kid from the mailroom who was distributing the Monday delivery.

"What have you got for me, Gilbert?"

"Just the usual, Miss C."

I sorted through the envelopes to see whether any subpoenaed information had been returned in the late-morning mail. The thicker-than-usual batch, rubber-banded together, consisted mainly of printed greeting cards from sleazy law firms and private investigators, complete with the tacky little calendars and wallet-size laminated business cards that served as clear reminders of whom *not* to call in case of emergency.

Halfway through the pack, I pulled out a legal-size

envelope with a return address scrawled in sloppy handwriting that was practically illegible. I squinted and looked again, then read the name to Mike. "Bart Frankel. Postmarked Saturday morning."

"Where from, blondie? Heaven or hell?"

"What a weird feeling, to get this today. He's not even buried yet."

"Think Shirley MacLaine. Think Dionne Warwick. Open the frigging thing, will you?"

I held the envelope in my fingertips by one corner, and used the letter opener on Laura's desk to slit a hole along the top. I withdrew the small slip of paper from inside and read the yellow Post-it that Bart had attached to the longer white page.

Alex—Everything in my life is out of control. I never meant to lie about any of it to you. I'll try and make it right next week, when we sit down at your office. Had a scare tonight. Thought I was followed to my home. I'm putting this in the mail when I walk the dog later. It's the paper I took from Lola's desk the day she was killed. I swear to you I had nothing to do with her murder. B. Frankel.

I lifted the note and looked at the enclosure. It was a hand-drawn map of Blackwells Island—circa 1925—meticulously crafted and perfectly scaled to dimension. Every building, every tree, every bench, and every boulder was assigned a number. On the bottom of the page was the signature of Freeland Jennings.

30

"Looks like the weatherman may give us a break."

It had taken us nearly an hour to drive from the courthouse to King's College. The radio continued to promise a winter storm, but was delaying its arrival until nightfall, and the wet flakes that deposited themselves limply on the windshield did not seem to be sticking.

Like any college community at Christmas break, the area around 116th Street and Broadway felt like a ghost town. The Barnard, Columbia, and King's students had scattered to their homes and families, and the normally lively sidewalks and footpaths were bare of young adults and earnest academics.

At one-fifteen, we knocked on the door of Sylvia Foote's office and were invited in. I glanced around the conference table, taking an informal inventory of the assembled guests. She ushered us to our seats, and I squeezed in between Chapman and Acting President

Recantati. As I placed my pocketbook on the floor behind me, my pager beeped loudly.

"Excuse me, please. I'll turn it off." I removed it and checked the number, worried that Battaglia might be tracking me down, annoyed that I had blown him off when he had requested that I come in to talk to him. Relieved to see that it was only Jake, beeping me for the third time since we had left downtown, I clicked the mechanism off and tossed it inside my bag.

"Unhappy boss?" Mike asked.

"Unhappy boyfriend."

Mike, in the meanwhile, was checking off the faces present against his list of names: Sylvia Foote, Paolo Recantati, Winston Shreve, Nan Rothschild, Skip Lockhart, and Thomas Grenier.

"As an aficionado of the detective story, Mr. Chapman, it appears to me that you've come here expecting one of us to stand up and announce that he—or she—is, in fact, Professor Plum, who killed Lola Dakota in the library with the lead pipe." It was Grenier who tried to break the ice with a bit of facetious humor.

"This isn't a board game." Mike glared at the biology professor, whom he was meeting for the first time. "But if any one of you wants to save us some effort, I'd welcome the admission."

"Are we waiting for Claude Lavery?" Grenier asked Foote, striking a more serious tone.

She turned to Mike. "Professor Lavery won't be

coming. He called an hour ago to say that since we've severed him from college affairs while he's under investigation for the grant impropriety, he doesn't feel obligated to participate."

I watched pairs of eyes find each other across the table, silently affirming alliances.

Winston Shreve, the anthropologist, looked back at me. "Perhaps that message you asked Sylvia to deliver to us last night unsettled him. About the diaries and the so-called secret garden."

"Why him in particular?"

"Claude Lavery and Lola Dakota confided in each other. They were neighbors, good friends." It was Paolo Recantati who picked up Shreve's lead. "I can't believe he didn't come here today. It's either arrogance, or it's exactly what Winston is suggesting. Claude won't discuss what he knows in front of the rest of us."

Sylvia Foote tried to regain control of her herd. "I thought it would be useful for those of us who worked with Lola to sit down together as a group and examine her professional circumstances. Most of us, of course, believe her death relates to her complicated personal situation. But perhaps if Miss Cooper and Mr. Chapman get a better sense of what was going on here at the college, they'll understand why we feel this way."

And they'll get out of our hair, she seemed to imply.

Sylvia asked Nan Rothschild to begin the conversation. If the severe general counsel meant to set herself a smooth sail, then she had chosen well. As the quiet anthropologist began her description of the Blackwells project, I tried to focus on her words and keep my imagination from divining the real dynamic between the two successful women, Rothschild and Dakota. Had I been too quick to eliminate Nan's interests and possible motives simply because I had known her as a casual acquaintance from the ballet studio?

Mike was making notes, and I jotted a reminder to myself to ask him whether he thought the tension between the female professors was something to explore.

Nan started with how the working teams came to be formed, then moved along to the technical aspects of the dig, which I found fascinating now, in light of the stories of old Mr. Lockhart. Wouldn't the high-tech equipment used by the interns and volunteers have uncovered any of the legendary treasures that had been concealed on the island? It didn't seem clear, though, that the team had actually done any work on the southern tip, where the prison had once stood.

Nan then turned the narrative over to Winston Shreve. With frequent punctuation by Lockhart and Grenier, Shreve led us through a much more congenial version of the academic staff relationships than we had been treated to during the one-on-one interviews. Any hopes that this gathering would help us disappeared by the end of the first hour.

I could tell that Mike wanted to take the meeting in another direction. While his pen jiggled up and down between the first two fingers of his right hand, he was brushing back his hair with the left.

"Let me ask you this, Ms. Foote. Is there any additional discipline the college could impose on Claude Lavery while his matter is pending a decision? Any other action to take against him?"

"I'm not sure I understand, Detective. What are you suggesting?"

"Suppose he lied. Supposed he lied about what Ms. Cooper here might call a material fact."

"Related to what?"

"To Dakota. Lola Dakota."

"Why don't you tell us the fact?" Recantati asked, trying, perhaps, to reclaim the position he had undermined by entering Lola's office after her death.

Mike looked over at me to see whether I agreed that we should reveal information, hoping to gain something in return. The slight nod of my head told him that I did.

"We've got a witness, an eyewitness," Mike began. He obviously didn't want to tell the assembled group that Bart Frankel was dead. "This guy observed Lola Dakota walking into her apartment building within an hour of her death."

No one spoke.

"Claude Lavery held the door open for Lola and walked inside with her."

Again, I tried to identify the allies. Recantati's eyes darted from Foote to Rothschild, Lockhart sought a reaction from Shreve, Grenier fixed on Mike Chapman.

"Problem for me is that when I interviewed Lavery, he denied seeing Dakota. Never mentioned it. Told me the last time he saw Dakota was around Thanksgiving, three weeks or so before she was killed."

"There's no reason to assume Claude's the one who's lying, Detective." Sylvia Foote was quick to take the supportive role. "It depends, doesn't it, on how reliable your eyewitness is. Someone who knew both of them? Some passerby who might be mistaken?"

"Solid as a rock," Mike answered, neglecting to add that he'd be as difficult as a rock to cross-examine at this point, too. "No mistake. I'm asking you to assume for the moment that Claude Lavery outright lied about something as important as that. Why? Does it put him in any worse situation with the college, or does it tell me something I need to know for my investigation?"

Eyelids raised, brows furrowed. I didn't know what Mike was digging for, but I was certain that this message was designed to get back to Lavery as soon as the meeting broke up. Stirring the pot, the lieutenant liked to call it. Seeing whether anyone could be flushed out or who would turn against whom.

"I thought from the outset that it was strange that Claude didn't report hearing any noise, living directly upstairs from Lola." Thomas Grenier wanted to get that off his chest. Nan Rothschild frowned, and I inferred from her expression that she disapproved of his candor.

"I'm a bit surprised, actually," said Shreve. "I don't know why Lavery said that to you. The morning after Lola's death—before he left for vacation—I called Claude to talk about her, about how sad it was. I sort of assumed he'd know more details, being a neighbor and all that. I *know* he told me that he had gone up in the elevator with her that same day. I'm positive about that. Maybe we can speak with him—"

"That's my job, Professor. I'd appreciate it if you let me do the interviews."

"If your question, Mr. Chapman, is whether Lavery faced administrative action of any other kind, then the answer is no. We'd leave that portion of the case up to you."

"You want to tell us, Mr. Lockhart, what you learned from your grandfather this morning, when you went there to ask him about Freeland Jennings's legacy? You find anything in the attic?"

The young instructor blushed as his colleagues all turned to follow Mike's jab. "I, uh, I had forgotten all about that model until Sylvia's message. Of course I tried to see if it was still at the house. Obviously, I would have brought it back here to the meeting. That's what Miss Cooper wanted to know about, wasn't it?

"I'm planning to drive back up to White Plains after this meeting. Sit down and try to have a lucid conversation with my grandfather, if you all think that would help." Skip Lockhart looked at the faces around the table.

"Maybe Ms. Foote told you, buddy. We're going to keep you company." Mike circled his hand in the air, drawing the group in the room into an imaginary ring.

"I'm game," Shreve said. "We're all interested in this, Skip."

"Well, we can't just pile in on him. The excitement would be too much." Lockhart fidgeted in his chair.

"We don't all have to talk to him at once," Shreve went on. "The detective and you can do the interview. We can wait in another room, so we can brainstorm if he remembers anything. After all, we've got a pretty good collective knowledge of Lola and her habits."

The phone rang and Sylvia answered it. "Just a minute. I'll have him pick up an extension." She motioned to Mike, who stepped out of the room.

"I don't think I need to go," Recantati said. "None of this has anything to do with me."

"Well then, Sylvia," Shreve said, "you can ride up in my car if you like. I've always wanted to meet your grandfather, Skip. Lola told me about his fascinating stories. I assume Miss Cooper and the detective will go together?"

"Yes, we'll meet you there."

Skip seemed reluctant. He had little choice but to offer to drive Nan Rothschild and Thomas Grenier with him.

The door opened and Mike waved me out to the

463

secretary's anteroom. "You mind grabbing a ride with one of them and trying to charm the pants off Grandpa?"

I started to ask him why but turned my head as I noticed that both Winston Shreve and Skip Lockhart had followed me out, looking for paper on the desk behind me to write directions.

"Listen up, blondie. You put the Rand McNally in a safe place, right?"

I was distracted again as Lockhart dropped his pen on the floor. "What?"

"The map."

I nodded that I had.

He looked at his watch and noted that it was almost three o'clock. "I can be in White Plains in an hour. I just got to swing over the bridge to Newark and take a peek in the Hertz parking lot by the airport."

The two professors reentered Sylvia Foote's office.

"How come?"

I was pleased to see his trademark grin. "Tony Parisi called. He's working round the clock on Bart Frankel's unexpected demise. Found out that one of the private investigators Ivan Kralovic had been using on Lola the last year may have a connection to Saturday morning's 'accident.'"

"What kind of connection?"

"A very direct one, apparently. Enough to make Parisi tell me the Jersey prosecutors think they can put the cuffs on Ivan the Terrible and lock him up before he has to shovel the snow out of his driveway tomorrow. Looks like the PI rented a van at the airport on Friday and brought it back in yesterday afternoon, claiming he'd had a fender bender on the turnpike."

"Any damage?"

"There's a big dent on the right front fender and it's covered with chipped paint and what looks like blood, so he's having it tested. Wants you to check the jerk's bank account for deposits from Kralovic when you get a free minute. And he wants me to eyeball it before they haul it off for repair."

31

I returned to Sylvia's office as the group was breaking up. "Mike has to make a slight detour," I explained to the academics. "Another case. He'll meet us in White Plains, if I can ride with you and Professor Shreve."

Sylvia deferred to Shreve, who confirmed that he had plenty of room. Nan was calling her husband to explain why she would not be back in the city until six or seven this evening as Sylvia and I walked down the hall to use the rest room.

On our way back, I noticed the lanky figure of a young man silhouetted against the wall beyond her door. "Efrem?" she asked.

"Yes, ma'am."

"Alex, this is the young man I told you about, Efrem Zavislan. He's one of Lola's brightest students. He called Nan this morning to ask her a question about the dig, and when I learned he was still in town, I thought you might want to meet him. Lola entrusted her most important research projects to Efrem. Everything all right? Any reason you didn't go home to Colorado for the break?"

"My folks came east to see my grandparents, so we're all in town. Miss Foote said you might have questions about Professor Dakota that I can answer," he said, turning to me.

Skip Lockhart came out of Sylvia's office with Winston Shreve, each buttoning his coat and lifting his collar against the brewing storm outside. "What's up, Efrem?"

"Nothing, Professor Lockhart. Just wanted to see if there was any progress in finding the guy who killed Professor Dakota."

"You're not working out on the island in this weather, are you?" asked Shreve.

"All closed down for a few weeks. Most of us weren't in the mood anyway."

"We'll be back in a few minutes with the cars. I'm parked in the garage over on Broadway. Sylvia, can I bring you a cup of coffee for the road? Miss Cooper?"

"Thank you, Winston," Sylvia answered. "How about some hot chocolate for me? Extra milk, if you would. Alex, coffee?"

"I've had enough caffeine to keep me wired for weeks. Chocolate sounds good."

I waited for the men to walk away before stepping aside with Efrem. "Do you mind, Sylvia, if I just have a few minutes with him?"

I led the student around the corner for a bit of privacy. Although I guessed he was not more than twenty years old, he towered over me, and seemed possessed of a maturity that most of the others I had met these past ten days lacked. He was eager to talk about Dakota, clearly sharing her passion for scholarship, and for the Blackwells project.

"Do you know anything about the miniature model of the island that one of the prisoners built for Freeland Jennings when he was in the penitentiary?"

Efrem's hands came out of his jeans pockets and he began to speak with great animation. "Have you seen it? It's amazing."

I wanted to keep our voices down. No need to alert the others that this kid might actually know the whereabouts of the mysterious piece. "No. But the police and I are quite interested in taking a look at it. Do you know where it is now?"

"Well, no. I mean, Professor Dakota had it. She let me see it a couple of times, but that was months ago."

"Where was it when you saw it?"

"At her office, right in this building. But she moved it out of here a while back."

"To?"

"I don't know. She told me she had to find another place for it. No room in her office."

"Do you know why it was so important?"

He looked puzzled. "I'm not sure it was. Least, not that she ever told me. I just thought it was beautiful.

Made with such painstaking devotion, accurate to the most minute detail."

Lola may have liked this kid a lot, but she didn't seem to have trusted anyone with the importance of her discovery.

"Would it help you guys if I poked around the island some more? There's lots of places to hide things over there. Places nobody goes to or looks in."

"I don't want you doing anything to get in trouble at school. How about you let the detectives do it with you?"

"Yeah, that's fine. You want me to take you around there tomorrow?"

"I don't want to screw up the visit with your family." I checked the time. "I'm going to see the detective I'm working with in another hour or so. Why don't you give him a call later on tonight and we can work out a way to do this together? Any day that it's convenient for you will work for us." I took out one of my business cards and wrote Mike's beeper number on the back. "In the meantime, just give some thought to where you think she would have stored the model for safekeeping, okay?"

If we weren't able to jog Orlyn Lockhart's memory, then maybe Mike and I could more thoroughly interrogate Efrem later tonight. I thanked him for coming by and rejoined the disgruntled-looking characters who were marching down the staircase to the lobby. This was not a good day for a ride in the country.

Lockhart pulled up in front of the building and honked his horn. Thomas Grenier held Nan by the arm and walked her to his SUV, closing the back door after he helped her inside, and then settling himself in the passenger seat.

Recantati waited several minutes with Sylvia and me until Winston Shreve arrived in a gray minivan. He slid back the door and I hoisted myself into the rear. Recantati boosted Sylvia up by the elbow and Shreve held her bag while she buckled up the seat belt, telling Recantati she would call him in the morning. He whispered something to her that I was unable to hear, then shut the door and walked away as the engine started up.

"Turn up the heat, Winston," she ordered with her usual display of charm. He angled the rearview mirror into place, and I could catch the corner of his smile as he then adjusted the temperature controls on the dashboard.

There was a steaming container of cocoa in the cup holder of each of our armrests. Shreve opened his and sipped at the hot drink.

"You know the way, do you?" Sylvia asked.

"Yes, Sylvia. Skip's given me directions," he said, holding up a slip of paper. "It's right off the Saw Mill River Parkway. Won't take long to get there. I just want to drink a bit of this before I start driving. Otherwise it will spill all over us."

"Good idea."

We uncapped the lids and I blew on the chocolate, warming my hands as I took a swallow. "Detective Chapman and I were up there the other day. The house is easy to find. I grew up not too far away."

"In White Plains?"

"No, in Harrison." I sipped a few more times before Shreve pulled away from the curb, making the west-bound turn to head over to Riverside Drive and the entrance to the West Side Highway. "Spent a lot of time there. I was a competitive swimmer in high school and they were our archrivals. Next town over."

"Just get us up there and back before this snow starts piling in," Sylvia said.

The liquid sloshed around the rim of the cardboard cup as Shreve accelerated past the yield sign, and I took another big gulp of hot chocolate, wiping the drops off my parka.

We were passing under the cloverleaf roadway that led up to the George Washington Bridge, following the signs to Westchester County, when I heard Sylvia make a gurgling sound. Her neck snapped forward and her chin dangled against her chest.

I reached for the headrest behind her seat to pull myself forward and yelled for Shreve to stop the car. "Are you all right, Sylvia?" is what I tried to say, but my tongue twisted around the words and they slurred as they came out.

My arms felt like leaden weights as I unbuckled my seat belt, pushed the strap out of the way, and attempted to reach toward Winston Shreve. Snowflakes swirled outside at a dizzying speed, blurring into one as I slid off the seat and onto the floor of the van.

32

My first sensation was of the cold, biting and urgent, piercing every pore of my body. The stinging pain that grated on my wrist and ankles was caused by bindings of some kind, although I could not see them as I lay facedown in the darkened space. A soft piece of cloth covered my mouth, tied behind my scalp.

Wind shrieked above my head and still the blur of white flakes fell around me. I was inside some structure, flattened against the remains of a wooden floorboard that had been partially destroyed by years of exposure to the elements. Whatever it had been, the draft and snow told me there was now no roof covering the walls.

I heard no sounds of a human presence. No inhalation or exhalation of breath. No footsteps. No words.

I shifted my weight and turned my body onto its side. Still, no response from anyone to the rustling sound made by my own movement.

Even this slight change of position charged the flashes of light that raced inside my brain, and the pounding waves of dizziness and nausea returned. I had been in my office, I remembered that. I was talking with Mike Chapman, and I was pretty certain that had happened. But now the crests and swells of wobbly images flooded my head again and I was sure of nothing.

Thoughts would not come clearly and my eyes closed, ceding to whatever it was that had overpowered all my senses.

I don't know for how long I lost consciousness this second time, but when I was able to see again, the inky surroundings were identical. I was dressed in my ski parka, and the lapel of a gray suit stuck out above the zipper. I pushed to order my thoughts, trying to recall when I had dressed this way to leave my home. There was a moth-eaten old plaid blanket stretched out down the length of my body, heavy now from the wet snow that it had absorbed.

My hands were gloved and boots were still on my feet. I could feel them. Only my face was exposed to the pelting drops of ice. I rolled it back onto the flooring. Think, I told myself over and over again. Think where you were today and who you were with. Think where you were going that brought you to this godforsaken place. But the neurons were short-circuiting and something had poisoned my brain's ability to connect the dots. All I knew for certain was that I was cold.

I drifted off again and wakened later still. Now I could see a brick wall a few feet away from my head, the side of whatever building I was in. I arched my back and saw, two or three feet above the floorboards, the empty frame of a window. Get to that, I directed myself. Get to that and find out where you are.

Turning back onto my side, I started to wriggle my feet, making sure I could control their movement. I bent my knees and drew them up toward my waist. Slowly, like some primitive, reptilian apoda, I extended my legs as far as possible and edged my body forward toward the wall. Repeating the motion eight or nine times, I worked myself across the splintered floor until my head touched the crumbling rows of brick.

I rested there for several minutes before trying to slide my body into an upright position. Sitting up would bring back the dizziness, since the oxygen would flow away from my brain. Expect that, I reminded myself. Mental and physical processes were all operating in slow motion. Don't fight it, I said, forming the words with my mouth.

Inch by inch, I righted my body and twisted to lean my back against the wall. It felt sturdier than its uneven surface appeared, and I knew it could support my weight. My head pounded as I forced it to remain erect. I settled there for several more minutes, adjusting my eyes to the darkness around me.

Something moved within the walls of my enclosure. I blinked and tried to clear my vision, tensing for the arrival of my captor. But these were scratching sounds, sharp and rapid, playing off the icy surface of the floor.

Rats. Two or three of them, chasing each other through an open portal and out the gaping hole where glass once fitted in a window.

For the first time, I had a reassuring thought. Large rodents terrified me, but I was relieved to think the odds were good that I was still somewhere in New York City.

Now I saw the outline of the building walls. The window beside me was on the ground level, but it looked as though there were two tiers of empty frames on flights above—three stories in all, though the flooring was missing from all but the foundation. The four sides, without a roof, seemed to be the entirety of the structure. Too small to be an institution, but too grim to have been a private home.

I dragged myself closer to the smooth orange brick that marked the window jamb closest to me. My left ear ached anew as the wind howled past. Straining my neck to look out the rough stone archway, I saw sharp icicles jutting down from every overhanging surface.

Cutting through the storm's gray haze was the glare of huge red neon letters. Read the words, I charged myself. Over my shoulder, the rats danced again, in and out of the asymmetrical cavities at the far end of the building.

I concentrated on the giant script sign, which was like trying to make out the object inside the dome when a snow globe has been turned upside down.

Pepsi-Cola. I read it four or five times to convince myself those were the words.

Why did I know that graphic? A huge red advertisement that I had seen more times than I could ever count, I thought. Focus on it, I urged myself. Make the pieces come together. The district attorney's office, my home, the skyline, the city. Make each image relate to another. Every night when I left the office and headed uptown on the FDR Drive, I saw the *Pepsi-Cola* sign, several stories high, shining across the East River from its enormous perch along the Queens side of the water.

I twisted farther to the left, an icy stalagmite gnawing at my chin as I tried to widen my view. Yes, there were the four great smokestacks of Big Allis, belching dense clouds into the night sky, blowing back at nature's offering.

So this must be the island in the middle of the river. Not Roosevelt, not the one I had visited several days ago. But Blackwells. Some gutted shell of a nineteenth-century building that had been abandoned and was waiting to be explored by scholars and students, historians and treasure seekers.

Now I began to reconstruct the puzzle. I remembered being at my office with Chapman. I had a clear recollection of our ride uptown to the King's College meeting with Sylvia Foote. But then everything turned hazy, and I couldn't figure whether I had sustained an injury to my head or ingested something that affected my memory.

It was difficult to move because of my restraints, but it was impossible for me to remain still. With my hands bracing my body behind my back, I pushed away from the window and propelled myself in the opposite direction, toward what looked like the gabled opening of the building entrance.

Wrenching myself back onto my knees, I tried to read an inscription that had mostly faded from a plaque on the wall. The bottom corner credited the Bible, and from what was left of the letters it looked like Hosea. Something about ransoming someone from the power of the grave and redeeming him from death. I didn't know the biblical context but I cherished the thought.

In the dim light, I could make out larger letters carved above the plaque into the terra-cotta panel that bordered the archway: STRECKER MEMORIAL LABORATORY.

I sank back to the floor as though I had been punched in the gut. This was the morgue.

What had Nan told us about it? One of the first pathology laboratories built in America, she had said. This must have been the place to which all the bodies on Blackwells Island had been taken. Why was I here? Who had bound me and left me in this frigid shell?

I could hear the screech of rats again, sprinting closer to the entryway. I half crawled, half pulled myself to the far side of the door, fearing that the filthy animals would find me in their path.

Another window sucked in frigid air from the night sky and I slithered past it, trying to get to one of the building's corners for a bit more shelter. My feet were tied so tightly together that I was unable to raise myself and stand on them. My back bumped against the contour of a wooden cabinet and I came to a stop. The top and edges had rotted completely and come loose from the support, jutting out into the room and making my passage more difficult.

I rested for a minute then pushed forward around this antique chamber, but my jacket snagged on a rusted metal strip that I had not seen, ripping a tear down the length of the sleeve.

I backpedaled to free the fabric and saw for the first time what had snared me. The mouths of the cabinets were agape as I turned to disengage my arm from the metal spike. Side by side were three drawers of morgue trays, each mounted in double rows, the wood decayed but the metal still intact.

The steel grooves were fixed in place, some rolled back into the drawers and others hanging partway into the room. This is where every plague-ridden patient on Blackwells had been stored, studied, and dissected.

As my bound hands ripped away, I jerked forward and bumped my head against the middle set of drawers. On the bottom tray I could see the profile of a small body, wrapped in a blanket of the same plaid design that had covered me. I was swept by another wave of nausea.

Beside the feet, closest to me, was a slim leather-bound book. I leaned my arms toward it and pulled it out onto the floor.

As quickly as I could, I pushed myself away from the gruesome cabinet, kicking the book before me with my knee. It spun around and I tipped back the cover, revealing the title page of the volume of García Lorca's poems, and the small print of the owner's name in the top corner.

I was here alone in the morgue with Charlotte Voight.

33

By the time Winston Shreve stepped through the old doorway, I had dragged myself back into the farthest corner of the deteriorated laboratory—away from the remains of Charlotte Voight, away from the rats, and away from the man who had kidnapped me.

He was dressed for the occasion—with a ski jacket, jeans, and heavy boots—and now I remembered I had seen him at the college, in Sylvia Foote's office during the afternoon, when he had worn a blazer and slacks. I still had no memory of how I had left the administration building and what had happened.

I shuddered when he spotted me in the dark recess into which I had crawled, but I had been shivering with cold for hours.

Shreve's tread crunched on the packed snow as he walked toward me, stopping to pick up the blanket that had fallen off my body as I'd moved myself around the room. He kneeled in front of me and replaced it around my shoulders.

"I'm not a killer. That's the first thing you've got to understand."

My eyes must have expressed my terror. He spoke to me again.

"I'm not going to hurt you, Alex. I've brought you here because I need your help tonight. I'm not a killer."

It was difficult to believe him with Charlotte's body between me and the front door.

"You've got something I need, I think, and we're going to have to trust each other for a while." He reached behind me and removed the binding from around my wrists. I could see that it was a man's necktie.

"I'm going to remove the gag from your mouth, too. Maybe that will help convince you that I'm not going to do anything extreme." He undid the knot in the handkerchief and then used it to wipe some of the moisture off my forehead and cheeks. I noted that his tools had been those of an amateur—spare pieces of clothing—rather than ropes and duct tape, and tried to draw hope from that fact.

I moved my jaw around, opening and closing my mouth. It was sore and stiff from the restraint. I was unconvinced by his removing the gag. Now that I knew my whereabouts, I assumed that there was not a living soul within a mile of us. Water surrounded us on three sides, and there was a wasteland of debris to the north that was gated off from the population of Roosevelt Island by metal fencing and razor wire. Even without the bluster of the fierce wind, there was no one to hear me scream.

I found my voice. "Is that Charlotte Voight?"

The anthropologist was standing in front of me, and he turned to look at the cabinet of steel morgue trays before he answered. "Yes. But I didn't kill her." He repeated his denial, slowly but firmly, as though it made a difference if I believed him.

"I was infatuated with Charlotte. There was nothing I would ever have done to hurt her."

I thought back to the students we had interviewed and their rumors about affairs between faculty members and undergraduates. It should have been obvious to me that Winston Shreve would be a likely offender. Hadn't he told us when we questioned him that his ex-wife, Giselle, had been one of his students when he taught in Paris? How typical to have repeated the pattern. He was probably a classic case of arrested development, fixated on twenty-year-old students and consummating that original love affair over and over again.

"This is one way you can help me, Alex," he said, squatting again and lifting the blanket off my shoulders to cover my head as well. "As a prosecutor, I mean. I can explain this to you and then you can tell them that I am innocent."

If he was waiting for a response, he got none.

"Charlotte and I had been having a relationship for months. Oh, there were boys now and then whom she got involved with, but she was as enamored of me, I think, as I was of her. She was nothing at all like most of the kids. She thought like a woman, not a child."

How many times had he used that bullshit line on some unsuspecting adolescent?

"I brought her over to the island to get her involved in the project. She didn't have much interest in the work here, but she loved the place itself. Not the new part," he said, waving his arm in the direction of the residential half of the island. "She liked my stories about the past, about the history. And she loved walking through the ruins."

Of course Charlotte Voight would have liked it here. She was an outcast herself, isolated from whatever home and family she had come to New York to escape, and alienated from many of the kids her age at the college. This, the centuries-old island of outcasts, had worked its spell on her, too.

"During last winter, there were many nights Charlotte had come to my apartment. It's easy to be disapproving, but I was a hell of a lot safer company than the hoodlums who were trying to keep her doped up all the time. But then, one night last April, she wanted to come here, to the island.

"It was a beautiful spring evening. She thought it would be romantic to make love out in the open, looking back at the city."

"That sounds more like *your* idea." It sounded exactly like what Shreve had told Mike and me he had done when Lola Dakota first introduced him to Roosevelt Island. "A romantic evening on a blanket in front of the ruins, watching the tall ships and the fireworks, drinking wine, looking back over at River House, where your father grew up."

Why could I remember last week's interviews so well and have no idea about what had hit me today?

"It hardly matters whose idea it was at this point, does it? The unfortunate part is that I couldn't get Charlotte to give up the drugs, no matter how hard I tried. She'd been using them back home in South America since she was thirteen, experimenting with anything that anyone offered to her. So on her way to meet me, she stopped to score some pills. But I didn't know it at the time, you've got to understand that."

"We spoke with her friends. She never got to Julian's. Is that what you mean, pills from what they called the 'lab'?"

Shreve sat in the window frame to answer me. "When Charlotte said she was going to the lab, *this* is what she meant."

How stupid of me. Strecker Memorial Laboratory. The pathology lab.

"Ghoulish, you'll say. But that was Charlotte's humor. She wanted to get high and wander around the lab and the old hospital. See what ghosts she could conjure. These things didn't scare or repulse her as they do most young people. She thought it was almost mystical, like a connection to another generation, another period of time."

"And that night?"

"We drove over here together. I've got a master key, of course, to get inside the gates. I'd brought a couple of bottles of wine. Charlotte got to explore all the hideaways she'd wanted to see, and we lay on the blanket for hours, looking at the constellations and talking about her life. But she became agitated, the more she drank. Got up and started climbing around the old buildings. I was afraid she was going to fall and hurt herself. I tried to slow her down, but she was euphoric, acting like she was hallucinating.

"That's when I realized she must have been taking pills, in addition to the alcohol."

"Did you ask her what?"

"Of course I did. She was behaving so irrationally that it was obviously something that had reacted badly with the alcohol. Ecstasy, she told me. Lots of Ecstasy."

Lessen her inhibitions. Enhance her sexual experience. Create a false euphoria. Turn an evening at the lab with Winston Shreve into a psychedelic delight.

I asked my question softly. "What happened to her?"

"A seizure of some sort. First she had a panic attack. I tried to grab her and convince her to get in the car so I could take her to a doctor. But she screamed at me and ran farther away. I chased after her, but she was breathless and agitated. I wasn't aware, at first, that it was some kind of overdose, but that must have been what happened. She was flailing wildly, twitching and shaking uncontrollably. And then she just collapsed in my arms."

"Didn't you try to get her to a hospital?"

"Charlotte was dead. What good would that have done? She'd had a massive paroxysm."

I'd seen cases like that related to my work. Kids who overdosed with what they considered a harmless drug at nightclubs and rave parties. Dead before the ambulance arrived. "I know that can happen, Mr. Shreve. Why didn't you call the police? Get help?"

"At the time, I didn't understand why she died. Now I've read about the drugs and realize they can be deadly, but I had no idea of that the night Charlotte OD'ed. I, I guess I just panicked. I saw my entire career wiped out. I sat on the far side of that wall," he said, and pointed to the entryway, "holding Charlotte's body in my arms, and I knew that everything I had worked for in my professional life had been destroyed."

"So you just left her here?" I looked around at the decaying rubble of the young girl's tomb.

Shreve was unhappy to be challenged. "I never planned to do that. I needed the night to think. I needed to figure out how I could walk into a medical center on a spring morning with this beautiful child in my arms and tell them that a terrible accident had occurred. I needed to find a way to explain her death to Sylvia Foote and the people at the college who believed in me."

All he was concerned with was his own predicament.

"This was, after all, a morgue," he went on. "I put my blanket around Charlotte, and I carried her inside here and put her down for the night." I filled in the blanks: on a rust-covered metal morgue tray in a rat-infested skeleton of a building, for the next eight months.

"And you never came back?"

"I thought I'd have a plan by the next morning, that I'd drive back over and—. And I couldn't do it, I couldn't bring myself to come back over here to see her. I knew that occasionally there would be workmen in this area, and I expected one of them to find the body long before now.

"In fact, I *wanted* them to find the body. But this part of the island spooks everyone. I never expected it would be this long before she could be taken out of here. If they autopsied Charlotte, everyone would know she wasn't murdered. Don't you think they can still tell that, I mean about the toxicology and how she died? There have been other cases like this in the city, haven't there?"

"Other deaths like that, yes." Other bodies left to rot by a brilliant self-centered anthropology professor? I doubt it.

"This building is actually designated to be converted into an equipment station for the new subway line. It will be renovated soon. Then they can give Charlotte a proper burial."

Had he lost his mind completely, that he could walk away from here and leave the girl behind another time?

I was certain, now, that I had left the administration building in the company of Sylvia Foote when this afternoon's meeting broke up. I forced myself to look in the direction of Charlotte's body, to see whether any of the other trays were occupied. The snow fell steadily and the shadows made it impossible for me to see.

"Sylvia Foote? Is she here, too, Mr. Shreve?" I thought of all my battles with her over the years and all the times I had wished her misery. "Is she dead?"

He pushed himself up from his windowsill seat and brushed his hands together to clean off his gloves. "Not at all, Alex. Sylvia's my alibi for this evening. I've spent hours with her at the hospital, since late this afternoon. Took her there myself, right into the emergency room. Stayed with her while they examined her and pumped her stomach. I was at Sylvia's side the whole time. Treated her with kid gloves until she was out of the woods and the resident cleared her to be admitted for the night, just to be safe.

"Some dreadful attack of food poisoning. Must have been something she drank."

34

"We're going to take a short walk," Shreve said, working to undo the knot on the piece of fabric that bound my ankles. "Perhaps it will calm you to get you away from Charlotte."

He placed his hand around my elbow and hoisted me onto my feet. The blanket slipped to the ground and he bent to lift it, then replaced the hood of my parka over my matted hair. I tried to steady myself without touching him for support, but my legs were numb from the combination of the cold and the hours of immobility.

Shreve guided my tentative steps past the cabinet of morgue trays and the frozen body of the young student toward the entrance arch and out of the ruined building.

A hundred yards away, to the south, stood the massive remains of the Smallpox Hospital. He led me that way on the slick footpaths, both of us bowing our heads against the ferocious gusts of wind that kicked up off the East River. When I lifted my eyes from time to time to check our course, I could see the crenellated parapets of the eerie giant looming before us.

I chided myself for the scores of times I had looked across from the FDR Drive at the elegant outline of this Gothic masterpiece and imagined it as a place of romance and intrigue. Now this hellhole where thousands of souls had perished before me might become my snowy tomb. What had Mike said to me on our drive to work? The luckiest girl he knew? The thought was almost enough to make me smile.

Wooden posts, like elongated stilts, supported the rear walls of the ancient granite structure. Shreve stepped around them, leaving our footsteps to be covered again by falling snow. When he stepped inside a doorway, he withdrew from his pocket a small flashlight and turned it on to ease his way through the littered flooring of the abandoned rooms. The light from the tiny plastic instrument was too dim and too concentrated to be seen across the river. Besides, I knew it would be masked completely by the floodlights that were focused on the great facade of the hospital from the ground outside, the ones that had made it possible for me to admire Renwick's skeleton as I drove home most nights.

As with the Strecker Laboratory, there was no roof left covering this building. Although abandoned for the better part of a century, its crumbling interior was clearly familiar to Shreve. Without hesitation, he led me through a maze of half-walled spaces that had once been patients' rooms.

Nan Rothschild had not exaggerated her description of how abruptly the city had abandoned these haunted properties. Old bedsteads were still in place, pairs of primitive crutches were scattered on the splintered floorboards, and glass-fronted cabinets with broken windowpanes held empty bottles on their dilapidated shelves.

We had crossed through what I assumed had once been the formal central hall of the hospital and continued on to a room in the very corner of the building. For the first time in hours, the precipitation seemed to have stopped. I looked up and saw, instead, that someone had fashioned a makeshift ceiling out of a thin layer of plywood.

Shreve moved forward and my eyes followed the track made by his light. Here was an alcove that had been transformed into a sort of shelter in this outpost of exposed ruins. On the floor in the corner was a slim mattress from one of the old hospital beds. Not even two inches thick, the mattress had faded ticking that barely showed from decades of wear and exposure. A small table sat beneath the long stretch of open space that had once been a window, and assorted pieces of rubble had been carried in to prop up the boards overhead.

"Sit there," Shreve said, pointing to a wooden seat

with a high back that had once been a wheelchair. He eased me onto the slats, which tilted backward and tottered as he knelt to retie my ankles. He stood behind me and reached around to place the handkerchief in my mouth again, tying it in back.

He walked out through the threshold of this small chamber and disappeared into the blackness of the adjacent rooms. What was he up to now? I wondered. Chills raced through my joints, my head still pounded, and my empty stomach ached and growled at me in the quiet of the very late night.

I stiffened my neck, shook off an array of grim thoughts, and pulled myself upright. Glancing out between the stone blocks, mitred at the top to form a pointed window frame, I could see from this direction the glitter of Manhattan's skyline muted by the endless flakes of falling snow. Straining my eyes, I could make out the spire of River House directly across the water from my corner seat.

Shreve must have made a call from his cell phone and left me alone so I would not overhear his conversation. But his voice echoed from within the thick gray walls of the neighboring area and I heard him ask for Detective Wallace. Why would he know anything about Mercer?

"Mr. Wallace? Winston Shreve here. Professor Shreve." Something about having just returned to his apartment and finding a message on his answering machine from Wallace. I had no idea what time it was now, whether it was still late Monday evening or the early hours of Tuesday morning, the very last day of the year.

Of course, if I had been missing for any period of time, even Mercer would have been brought in from home in the effort to find me.

Shreve, in his most professorial manner, was telling him that he didn't mind repeating something he had told Detective Chapman earlier in the evening. "The two ladies got into my car in front of the school and I headed onto the West Side Highway to go up to Westchester. Sylvia was complaining of nausea and dizziness. We thought perhaps it was something she had eaten for lunch that was making her sick. We'd just gone over that bridge into Riverdale when she sort of fainted, I guess you'd say."

Wallace must have asked a couple of questions and Shreve mumbled more answers that were inaudible to me. Flashbacks were coming to me now, just as drugged victims described as they emerged from the haze. I remembered being in the minivan and drinking the cocoa that the professor had bought for us.

"No, no. It was Ms. Cooper's idea. She suggested I get off and turn around. We drove immediately back to Columbia Presbyterian Hospital. Ms. Cooper knew where the emergency room was. Said she'd been there many times to see victims. I didn't want to waste time looking for a place to park, so she waited in the car and I carried Sylvia inside.

"Then when the doctor made the decision to admit her, I went back out to tell Ms. Cooper that I wasn't going to leave the hospital until I knew that Ms. Foote would be all right."

Wallace had questions. I rooted for him to break this goddamn alibi.

"Yes, Detective, Alex insisted on coming inside and waiting with me. I called the Lockhart house and told Skip's mother that we'd encountered a problem and wouldn't be able to keep the meeting after all. Alex came into the waiting room and—"

Shreve must have turned around and faced the other direction. It was more difficult to hear him but it sounded as though he was explaining how I'd passed the time while Sylvia was being treated by the medical team.

Whatever Shreve had drugged us with, I had no memory of the hours after the session in Sylvia's office broke up. It must have had amnesiac qualities. Is it possible that I actually had been inside the emergency room waiting area at Columbia Presbyterian? And if not, what a clever ruse. That place was a perpetual zoo. An endless procession of gunshot wounds, stabbings, car accidents, drug overdoses, women in labor, and miscellaneous misery of every sort. Most admissions were accompanied by strings of relatives and friends— whining, wheedling, bawling, and generally filling every inch of the enormous holding tank in which they waited for news of a loved one's condition.

The wind carried Shreve's words back to me. He must have shifted position again.

"For hours, Detective. She was there for hours. Watching television a bit, like everyone else. Making some phone calls."

Wallace was trying to figure out when I had left the hospital.

"Must have been close to nine o'clock. Yes, yes, of course. It was after they told us that Sylvia was awake and responding, but that they were going to keep her overnight for observation. I didn't want to leave without seeing her myself, but Ms. Cooper seemed impatient at that point. Told me she'd just grab a cab out on Broadway and get herself downtown."

Shreve hesitated before he threw in the next suggestion. "Seemed to be in a bad mood, Mr. Wallace. Something about a row with her boyfriend. Her beeper had been going off repeatedly and she paid it no attention. Rather willful, I'd say."

No one would argue with him on that point.

Shreve hadn't missed a detail. How stupid of me to have announced aloud to Mike that I had an unhappy boyfriend when my beeper had gone off at the beginning of the meeting in Sylvia's office.

"You mean come into the station house? Right now? But I've just told you everything that I know about—"

Break his balls, Mercer. Shreve'll never make it through a face-to-face encounter with you.

"Certainly, Mr. Wallace. No, no, thanks, I don't need a ride."

Shreve's footsteps crunched again on the packed snow as he walked closer to my little sanctuary and bent his head to come in under the plywood covering. He ungagged me and stood in front of me to explain that he was going to leave for a short while.

"What did you give me to knock me out? What did you do to Sylvia?"

"You needn't worry. Nothing with long-term effects. Just a sedative to make sure I could get you here and get her out of the way."

"A lot of a sedative. I can't remember anything."

Shreve smiled. "Gamma-hydroxybutyrate."

"GHB?" I knew it better than most. A colorless, odorless, tasteless designer drug, and I had quickly ingested it in my hot chocolate in a matter of minutes. Most ironic of all is that it was making the rounds as a date-rape drug, being slipped into drinks of unsuspecting women to render them unconscious for several hours.

"Amazing what you can buy on the Internet. I didn't know anything about these drugs until Charlotte died, but it's all there on the Web."

He wasn't exaggerating. Earlier in the year, a joint task force of city detectives and DEA agents had run a sting in which they bought two gallons of GHB from a Web site called www.DreamOn.com for several thousand dollars. It was simple to do.

497

"But surely the doctors will find traces of it when they test Sylvia." I didn't believe that he had really taken her to the hospital and was trying to challenge him to admit that.

"You should know better than that, Ms. Cooper. The ER admission is for a seventy-year-old woman who became ill after lunch while sitting in a car with a college professor and a prominent prosecutor. Why in the world would *anyone* suspect something like a date-rape drug to be the cause? They just pumped her stomach and were thankful when she came round. Keep her in overnight and she'll be released in the morning."

Shreve was right once again. Unlike cocaine and heroin, which leave trace material in the bloodstream for days, GHB doesn't even show up in blood. And it's evacuated from the urine within twenty-four hours of ingestion. No one would even think to look for it in Sylvia's case, and they would be likely to credit this brief physical disturbance in an elderly woman to a bad reaction to something in her last meal.

"I'm taking the tram over to talk to the police. I should be back in less than two hours."

That meant it could not be much later than midnight. The tram shut down at 2 A.M., and he was planning to return before it stopped operating.

Shreve wasn't telling me any more details about how he had gotten me here, but I was beginning to understand it. After Sylvia and I passed out, eagerly gulping down our potions, he must have driven across town and come onto the island with his van. It would already have been dark when he let himself into the deserted southern end and deposited my body in the Strecker Lab before taking Sylvia back to Columbia Presbyterian Hospital.

He would then have spent four or five hours making himself visible to the nurses and doctors in the waiting area, inquiring solicitously about his dear colleague. In the meantime, inches of snow would have completely obliterated the tire tracks that had taken me to the old morgue, and I would have been sleeping off the toxin that had felled me.

He must have redeposited his car safely in his garage so that it would be dry and warm if the police decided to examine it, and then returned by tram to begin his encounter with me. He obviously hadn't counted on a mandatory midnight visit to the detective squad.

"Don't worry, Ms. Cooper. I *am* coming back for you. You don't have to die, you know. If that were my intention, it would have happened already. As I said before, you can help me out of all this." Although Shreve had removed the gag, he left me tied in place. He had not wanted me to scream in the background while he had been on the telephone, but now there was no one to hear me.

"I just need to calm your colleagues," he went on. "Chapman's brought in this other fellow called Wallace. They're worried that they haven't heard from you."

"I can tell you an easy way to relax Chapman about me," I said to him softly.

Shreve looked back at me quizzically.

"I mean if that would get you back here faster so you'll let me go." I wasn't taking odds on the fact that he truly might release me at the end of this ordeal, but I was hoping to send a signal to my friends.

"What would you suggest, Ms. Cooper?"

I twisted in my seat and the old wooden slats creaked in response. "We watch *Jeopardy!* almost every night."

"You watch what?"

"It's a game show, on television. Do you know it?" Shreve had PBS written all over him and he stared at me blankly. I explained the final question to him and he laughed at me in disbelief.

I racked my brain for ideas, trying to make this work. I reminded him that Mike had known about Petra and discussed it with Shreve when we first met him. "You, uh . . . you could tell him we were watching the show together while we were waiting at the hospital for word about Sylvia. You could tell him that I insisted on watching the last question."

He was beginning to think about the idea.

"There'd be no other way for you to know that about me, and about Detective Chapman, unless you and I had been together at seven-thirty tonight. You know, we were just chatting and I was telling you about these silly bets we make against each other." I was trying not to sound too much as though I was pleading with him, but everything about me was on edge. "He'll be convinced I was all right while the two of us were together."

For God's sake let him go along with me on this one.

I took the next step. "I'll make up something for you. Mike was obviously much too busy to have been watching television tonight. He was probably talking to old Orlyn Lockhart, or had left White Plains on his way back to the city when the show was on. Just make it some category he doesn't know very well."

I furrowed my brow and pretended to come up with a question. "Like feminist stuff. Tell him—I know, tell him that the last answer was the name of the first woman doctor in America. And if you add that it stumped me, too, he'll buy right into it."

Please do exactly what I'm telling you and please let Chapman recall that we were together last week when that very subject came up: Who was Elizabeth Blackwell? I needed Chapman to remember that and then Chapman would know that Shreve was lying through his teeth. And with any luck he would also realize that I was somewhere on Blackwells Island.

"We'll see whether that helps things, Ms. Cooper. Then when I come back, I want you to think about how cooperative you're going to be about helping me find the diamonds that are buried on the island."

I was stunned. Winston Shreve believed that the diamonds were really still here? And what did he think I knew about how to find them?

"We'll talk about Lola later. Perhaps you're not even aware of the information you have," he said. I hadn't even thought about Lola Dakota since regaining consciousness. Shreve must be after something I had come across in the investigation. But what?

"I've got a legitimate right to those diamonds, Ms. Cooper. Not like those other fortune hunters. They belonged to my grandfather."

"Your grandfather?"

"Yes, Ms. Cooper. There were men like Orlyn Lockhart who were, shall we say, the gatekeepers of the island at the time. And then there were the men who spent their time here on the inside. The patients in this hospital, doomed as they were. And just a hundred yards away, the prisoners in the penitentiary.

"Freeland Jennings, Ms. Cooper. Freeland Jennings was my grandfather."

35

"Really, Ms. Cooper, you don't believe that all of us who grub around in the groves of academe have purely intellectual motives? Each of the scholars you've met has a selfish goal, whether it stems from the Blackwells project or his or her own special interests. Grenier stands to make a fortune from the drug companies for his research, Lavery's success would solve all his problems with the scandal, Lockhart gets on a fast track for tenure—" He interrupted himself when he mentioned that name.

"Do you have any idea how sick it made me to hear Skip pontificate about his grandfather leading the raid on the corrupt scum of the penitentiary? My grandfather died in that raid. My family was destroyed by those events."

"Did Professor Lockhart know that Freeland Jennings was your grandfather?"

"He's blinded by his own greed. And I had no

intention of telling him, anyway. It just would have made him and the others more intent on their own ends."

"I'm not sure I understand the connection either," I said. In fact, I couldn't make sense of anything any longer. Dizziness had yielded to simple exhaustion, and the cold was numbing.

"My grandmother was Ariana, Freeland Jennings's beautiful young wife. The *eye*-talian, as Orlyn Lockhart used to say. After my grandfather was convicted of killing Ariana, his sister took my father in. He was only seven years old. But once Granddad was murdered during the raid on the island, that sister and the rest of the Jennings family put my father in an orphanage."

He paused. "They weren't quite sure whether Freeland was really his father, after all. So why bother to split that lovely Jennings' fortune with a possible bastard? No one protested when it was decided to send the child out West. Out of sight, out of mind. Out of the will."

"And that's what became of your father?"

"That was the plan. But in the end, Ariana's lover took him off their hands. You see, it was the Church orphanage that was making all the arrangements to send the boy out West—very common in those days. Brandon Shreve apparently had reason to believe that he might be the father. Either that, or he loved Ariana enough to want to keep her child." He hesitated, then said what we both were thinking. "I suppose your DNA technology would answer all this for us today. But not in those times.

"So Brandon Shreve just gave the Church double the money the Jennings family had offered to lose every trace of the child, and both sides were happy. Shreve adopted my father and, of course, changed his name."

"But the boy remembered, didn't he?"

"Vividly. He talked to me about it all the time. Shreve was a good father, but my father's first seven years as a Jennings had instilled in him an interest in the Jennings birthright. Those diamonds were meant to be his, Ms. Cooper. Now they're meant to be mine.

"So I'm going to leave you for just a little while. If the snow breaks off, it's not a bad view. It's the same vista my grandfather had from his room in the penitentiary—straight across the water to his home in the River House. I'll be sure to give your regards to the gendarmes."

Shreve led himself out with the tiny flashlight and I was once again surrounded by darkness in my frigid quarters. Outside and on the ground just below the window frame, a spotlight beamed up at the brilliant architectural detail of the building's trim. If I could concentrate its aim just thirty feet lower, someone far away might be able to see the ghostly outline of a desperate woman and come to save me.

Dreaming about rescue didn't help. I tugged at my ties and squirmed to loosen the knots around my ankles. I told myself to slow down and make the attempts one at a time. I was far too rattled and weak to take on both tasks at once.

My efforts to work myself free were unsuccessful. I slumped against the back of the chair and closed my eyes. Think, I commanded myself. Do anything but give in to the paralyzing cold. Think. All I could think was why we should have smelled a rat in Winston Shreve.

Just looking at his résumé, Mike and I should have known the Blackwells project didn't suit his professional interests. This man had devoted his academic career to classic historical sites and digs on ancient civilizations like Petra and Lutetia. This little strip of land was too modern and too devoid of cultural importance to pique his interest.

And wasn't it Lola Dakota who had told him about the diamonds? She knew he was Freeland Jennings's descendant. She must have known. That night, so many years ago, when Lola brought him out to the island and made love to him while they watched the fireworks, they, too, had looked back at the fabled apartment building. What had he said to Mike and me in describing that romantic scene?—"Where my father lived before I was born"—not too far from the view that his grandfather had in the jail cell.

My weariness was fueled by my growing anger at myself. I wondered if Mike would remember the fit Shreve had thrown when we said that we'd be getting a tour of the island. How he had insisted that *he* wanted to be the one to bring the two of us here. What better control could a killer have? I could picture his demeanor and attitude. He would have let us in the security gate and driven us within spitting distance of the hospital and laboratory, cautioning us against the dangers of falling granite and broken glass. For the sake of our safety. All the time, he would have known that Charlotte Voight's body was under our noses.

It was probably Winston Shreve who had called Paolo Recantati's wife and pretended to be Professor Grenier. Shreve was smart enough to know that Recantati was thoroughly insecure about the growing scandal at the college. He could have been easily prodded into retrieving an envelope from Dakota's office—especially if such a harmless action could make all the trouble fade away. And Mrs. Recantati hadn't met any of them, so she wouldn't have known the difference between Shreve's voice and Grenier's.

For the first hour after regaining consciousness I had wanted to believe Winston Shreve. I wanted to believe that I would be safe and could trust him. He hadn't killed Charlotte Voight. But what crueler fate could he have masterminded than to leave her body in this desolate place?

And what about Lola Dakota? Why had Lola Dakota died? Her death, unlike Charlotte's, was not an accident.

And then I remembered what Claude Lavery had

told us. He had tried to convince us that he had not seen Lola since almost a month before her death. From Bart, we knew otherwise. But Claude was firm in his recollection that the last thing Lola had told him was that she knew where Charlotte Voight was, and that she was going to see the girl.

That statement had raised in Mike and me the false hope that Charlotte was still alive. Now my brain fought the sedatives that had slowed its normal processing and focused on the logical sequence of events.

If Bart had been right, then Lavery and Lola had encountered each other on their way into the building. Lavery was already facing a jail sentence from the feds. He didn't need to become a scapegoat in the murder investigation, the last person to see Lola Dakota alive.

But suppose she trusted him enough to tell him what she had finally figured out? That she knew where the Voight girl was, and she was going to see her, to find her. Like me, Lavery had assumed that meant that Charlotte was alive. Lola knew better. Did she confront Shreve with that fact, between the time she got to her apartment and the time she tried to leave, less than one hour later? Did she threaten to go out to the island to prove her theory? And was it Shreve who prevented her from doing that?

Now I was squirming again. Feet first, exerting every remaining ounce of my energy against the restraints. I couldn't tell if they truly felt looser or whether I just wanted to believe that they did.

I stopped to rest. Wind rushed in the oversize hole that had once been a window. It found every crevice around me, blowing in the sides of my parka's hood to sting my ears and whooshing up my sleeves to test the strength of my thermal underwear.

Homeless people survived this every winter night, I told myself. Older men and women, infirm and insane, were at this very moment hunkered down in cardboard boxes and storefront doorways all over the city streets and sidewalks. You can make it, little voices whispered to me. People know you're missing and they're looking for you. How many empty morgue trays were there on either side of Charlotte? What did I have to do so that I didn't wind up in one of them, waiting for the spring thaw?

I heard the footsteps packing down the thick snow before I saw the narrow sliver of light. Winston Shreve was back, carrying with him a six-foot-long piece of thick rope.

36

Shreve talked to me but I could not take my eyes off the rope. He crouched in front of me to remove my bindings, and they seemed like doll's clothes compared with the powerful weapon he had just dropped onto the fraying, stained mattress pad.

"That's only if things go terribly wrong, Ms. Cooper. Don't let it scare you."

I see. So far, things are right on schedule. Going really well. What had I unleashed when I'd stormed out of Jake's apartment on Sunday night? I shut my eyes tight and willed myself back on his living room sofa, thinking about how good it would feel to have him caress me and make love to me. What could go more terribly wrong than the events of the past twenty-four hours?

I played with my wrists and ankles, trying to limber them. My feet tingled from the deadening effect of pins and needles, from hours of restricted circulation.

Shreve had a plastic bag from some twenty-four-hour deli that he must have passed on his way back to the Second Avenue tram. He unwrapped sandwich halves from their aluminum foil and took the lids off two large Styrofoam cups of coffee.

"Here, perfectly safe." He took several sips from the container to show me that it had not been doctored. I drank the lukewarm liquid and it heated a few of the cold-restricted inches of my throat as I downed it. Maybe I didn't care if it was drugged. Sleep might be better than whatever I was facing in this urban igloo. I finished the entire container in three minutes. Something—either the caffeine or Shreve's return—had jolted me to full attention.

He passed the foil to me but I refused the sandwich. My hunger had been intense for hours, yet now I was gripped again by nausea and unable to look at solid food.

"What do you know about my grandfather's miniature garden of the island, Ms. Cooper?"

I didn't speak.

"You'll feel better if you put something in your stomach. You're going to fight me, aren't you?" He helped himself to some turkey while I watched in silence. "Trying to drag this out until daylight?"

I knew that Mike and Mercer would never have let Shreve walk out of the station house without putting a tail on him, especially once he came up with the phony line about the *Jeopardy!* question. If I could stall for a bit, I was certain that the homicide squad would find me.

"What did Detective Chapman say?"

"I'm sorry. I should have started with that. Mr. Chapman was nowhere to be seen tonight."

My right hand flew to my face to cover my mouth and I gnawed on the damp glove leather to mask my emotion. It wasn't possible that Mike hadn't been there to intercept the one clue I thought might lead him to me.

"Something about following a lead on another part of the investigation in New Jersey. A different fellow took all the information. An African-American gentleman, Mr. Wallace. He's getting married tomorrow, on New Year's Day. Everyone was quite cheerful there, actually. Bottles of whiskey out, toasting him and his bride. A bit distracted from the business of finding you, I would say.

"Wallace seemed to know about this television game, too. Said that sounded just like you. Always watching the final question."

Dammit. He was right. The information would have been reassuring to Mercer. The idea that I would have watched the quiz show in the hospital waiting room would have made perfect sense to him, and he had not been with Mike and me when the question about Elizabeth Blackwell had been aired last week. It would not set off any alarms in his mind. Would he even think to tell Mike about it when they next spoke?

"I believe Mr. Wallace understood my concern about your walking out of the emergency room at nine o'clock or so to find a taxicab by yourself. He said that neighborhood is plagued with drug dealers and youth gangs. I hope they double their efforts there to look for you. Seems they found an elderly woman in an alley just a few hours ago, beaten to a pulp by some young hoodlums, just to rob her of seven dollars and a crucifix on a gold chain. Brought her to the same emergency room where you and I waited for Sylvia."

Shreve paused. "And then another detective reminded Mr. Wallace that some woman had been harassing you as well. Some lady with a gun." He shook his head in mock dismay, and I thought how easily the detectives could be off on a red herring now, combing the East Seventies for my unhappy stalker.

I sank deeper into my frosted terror. What if Mike wasn't worried about me at all? What if he and Valerie were home together, enjoying each other's company like a normal couple? Maybe he'd gotten fed up with my repeated rituals of independence, believing that I'd walked out of Sylvia Foote's hospital scene just as I'd run away from Jake's conversation with an informant and run again from Mike's scene of domestic intimacy. Maybe I deserved to be marooned in an abandoned ruin with a killer.

"The miniature model that my grandfather had

built, Ms. Cooper. You seem to be as interested in it as I am. Shall we talk?"

Shreve had let me live so far because he thought I either knew something about the model's whereabouts or the key to its treasures. Now he was determined to get the answers.

"You've tried to convince me that you're not a killer, Professor. That Charlotte Voight was responsible for her own death." He looked at me but didn't speak. "But Lola Dakota is dead, too. And if you're going to tell me that was also an accident, then we've got nothing to discuss."

"It wasn't a murder, Ms. Cooper. Nothing was premeditated. I didn't go there to kill her."

Most lawyers didn't know the distinction between premeditation and intention, so why should Winston Shreve? He didn't have to plot the murder of his friend Lola before he went to see her that day, he simply had to form the intent to kill her in the moments before he executed the plan. Maybe it was a genetic thing, inherited from his grandfather.

All I knew is that I didn't want to be another notation in his agenda of women who had met their demise accidentally.

"In fact, it was Claude Lavery who caused her death."

"I don't believe that." As soon as I snapped those words at Shreve, I didn't know why I had said them. I was overwhelmed with confusion—from the sedatives, the situation, and the snow.

"I spoke to Lola often while she was out in New Jersey at her sister's house." He was standing again, swinging his arms as though to keep warm. "Both of us had been certain that the old laboratory—"

"Strecker?"

"Yes, that the Strecker building was the deadhouse. It's an old Scottish word meaning a morgue, or a place where dead bodies are kept."

How fitting that it has kept in character after all these years, I thought, not daring to imagine the condition of Charlotte Voight's remains.

"While Lola was hiding out at her sister's house she was also researching the island, using a lot of primary source material that student volunteers had come up with while assigned to the Blackwells project. Things they had found in the municipal archives, records from the Department of Health and Hospitals. Papers no one had touched for the better part of a century. Documents that explained exactly what the deadhouse was."

"And it wasn't the laboratory?" Could there have been a more ghastly place than Strecker?

"Its purpose was plain. It was just a theater for autopsies and a lab to examine the specimens. But there wasn't enough room to keep the bodies from all the plague-ridden institutions on Blackwells Island.

"Deadhouses were the wooden shacks they built all along the waterfront. Places to store and stack the corpses until they could be taken back home for burial."

The first sight from the Manhattan side of the water that patients bound for the island would see. The reason that some of them jumped into the deadly current to chance escape rather than a sure sentence of death by contagion. Deadhouses.

"Weren't they destroyed?"

"Moved, actually. Torn down and hauled to the other coast of Blackwells, to face the factories and mills on the Queens side of the river. No patients were shipped in from that direction, so the buildings were simply reerected out of sight of the arriving population. To give the patients hope, Ms. Cooper, to give them something to believe in."

Exactly what I needed at the moment. Something to make me believe that I could get off the island alive, too.

"But what did the deadhouses have to do with your grandfather?"

"It took Lola to figure that out. There was Freeland Jennings, a realist if one ever existed, stuck in a penitentiary with all of those lower-class criminals, most of them immigrants, full of their primitive superstitions. All of the papers make reference to the fact that none of the laborers would go anywhere near the wooden deadhouses."

"Those hospitals had all been closed years before your grandfather was sentenced to prison."

"Yes, but the buildings still stood there, much as you see them today. The Smallpox Hospital, Strecker, the Octagon Tower, and even the row of grim little shacks that had housed the dead. Freeland wrote about the circumstances in the letters he sent to his sister—the same one who was taking care of my father. First, his months of observations of the other inmates and their coarse manners and odd habits. Then his fascination with the way these seemingly fearless street thugs would avoid, like a ritual, the haunted remnants of all the places that had sheltered the terminally ill.

"It didn't take him long to figure out a safe place to hide his diamonds, the jewels he considered his life-line."

"Under the deadhouses." I thought of the map Bart Frankel had mailed to me shortly before he died, and how it diagrammed every inch of the island, signed by Freeland Jennings.

"Luigi Bennino was the prisoner who created my grandfather's model of the island. And it was Luigi he hired to dig the hiding places for his gems. No one would think to go where all that disease and pestilence might still lurk. Even today, lots of our students and faculty won't go near this building, fearful that they'll unearth some encapsulated germs that still bear their lethal poison."

"Bennino was an uneducated peasant, too. Why wasn't he just as superstitious about contamination?"

"Don't forget his crime, Ms. Cooper. He was a grave robber. Young Luigi had clearly overcome his concern about contact with the dear departed long before he reached Blackwells Island. He was the perfect hench-man for my grandfather's needs.

"It's just that Freeland had learned never to put all his trust in another human being. And although it's kind of veiled in his correspondence, it would appear that he paid a second prisoner to double-cross Bennino and move the diamonds. Still in the deadhouses, but in entirely different locations in the ground."

"Another grave robber?" How fortunate for him to find two such thieves.

"No. A murderer. A man who had killed a prostitute down at the Five Points," Shreve said, referring to a once notorious area of the city where our courthouse now stood. "Freeland talks about him in the letters, a much too solicitous concern for the man who was dying of syphilis. One last charitable thing that Granddad could do for him, so that his family would have enough money for a proper burial. And so that he would take Freeland's secret with him, well rewarded for his trouble."

"So three men knew about the diamonds and where they were buried."

"And all three died on the rock, as it were. My grand-father's death in the raid could not possibly have been anticipated. He never had time to retrieve his fortune. That's why I'd like the map, Ms. Cooper. The map and the model of the island." Shreve sat in the frame of the window, hands on his knees, and stared me in the eye.

"And Lola had them?"

"And Lola's dead."

"But if you hadn't killed her—"

His gloved hands slapped against his thighs as his temper flared. "Why would I have killed her without getting what I needed from her? It's Claude Lavery's fault that she's dead."

How could I evaluate what he was telling me? Maybe Chapman and I had given him an opportunity to blame Lavery by telling the group of professors that Lavery had been seen going into Lola's building with her the day she died. Maybe Shreve hadn't known that until we gave the fact away. And now he was just using it to make me think he wasn't the killer. Or perhaps both of them were involved, and they were both responsible for her death. How could I know?

I was more tentative now, talking softly to Shreve, aware that he might keep me alive as long as he thought I could give him what he wanted.

What had I done with the map before Mike and I had dashed out of the office on the way to King's College? Is it possible that it had been less than twenty-four hours since all that had happened? I bit my lip and took myself back one day. I had given my paralegal the map to copy, telling her to lock the original in one of the file cabinets until Mike could voucher it. And I had given one of the copies to him, then folded the other to slip in the pocket of my gray slacks, to examine later that night when I got home. Had Shreve overheard Mike ask me, in Sylvia Foote's office, whether I had secured Jennings's blueprint of the island?

I looked down at my pants leg to make certain that I was still wearing that same suit. My pocketbook and case folder were either in Shreve's van or his apartment. Perhaps he had gone through them in search of the map or any references to it, but if he hadn't thought to search my clothing, he would not have found the map.

The adrenaline pumped again and I swallowed hard. Now I knew that what Shreve wanted was here under his nose, and if he found the small slip of paper, there would be no reason to maintain our dialogue. I would be as good as dead.

"But Lola was telling you all these things while she was at Lily's house, doing the research. What did you two have to fight about the day she was killed?"

"I didn't go to see her to argue about anything. I was excited, thrilled that she might have solved the puzzle about my grandfather's fortune. I wanted to see the map for myself."

"Did she have it?"

"She was mad that I had come to her apartment. She stalled and tried to put me off. Told me she didn't have it with her. Told me the prosecutor from New Jersey was going to be arriving shortly and that she'd call me the next day. Of course, I didn't know at the time that she wasn't kidding about the prosecutor. He actually was coming over." Shreve sneered. "Not for Lola, but for his money."

"What money?"

"Apparently the guy had all kinds of financial problems. Lola was doling out cash to him to keep him afloat. Probably to keep him coming back to bed with her, which wasn't necessarily a pleasant place to be."

"How do you know that? I mean, about the cash?"

"After she died, Claude Lavery told me. That's what drove the two of them apart. Lola knew that Claude took an unorthodox view of his grant money. She pleaded with him to let her borrow some of it, claiming she needed it for the Blackwells project. Claude called me last week and asked me to return the money. I had to tell him she hadn't used a nickel of it for the dig. Then I remembered what she'd told me about the prosecutor and his financial problems. The money must have all been going to the deadbeat boyfriend."

Lola's shoe boxes full of cash. She had put the squeeze on Lavery to share some of his stash, pretending it was for her professional needs, but she was using it to solve Bart Frankel's personal problems.

I leaned forward and tried to look sincere when I asked the next question. I didn't believe what I was saying, but I wanted Shreve to think I did. "So why did Claude kill Lola? Was it about the money?"

He took too long to answer. I shivered again and put

my hand to my side, trying to feel the piece of paper through the layers of clothing. Was it there? I could not be sure.

"She had called me earlier in the week to tell me she would be home that afternoon. Not to worry about the news stories about Ivan's attempt on her life, if I should hear them. I stopped by the building—I was on the way to the college, actually. I tried her bell and she was home. Had just gotten there. She let me come up but was anxious to get rid of me."

"And Professor Lavery?"

A slight hesitation. Shreve wanted to tell a story that would weave Lavery into the murder, but he was not doing it convincingly. "Lola wouldn't let me in the door. Kept me in the hallway. Lavery was inside, although I didn't know it was him at the time. Lola told me that she was going over to the island."

"Then? Right then?"

"The next day. I wanted to go with her. She had no right to my grandfather's possessions."

The wind seemed less ferocious now, and my tone had lowered as well. "She had figured out about Charlotte, Mr. Shreve. Hadn't she? She was threatening to expose your—your accident." I tried not to choke on the last word. "She let you know that she'd just told Lavery that she'd figured out where Charlotte Voight was."

I remembered Lavery saying that to Mike and me, but Lavery had interpreted Lola's words to mean that

Charlotte was still alive. Shreve, on the other hand, must have panicked about Charlotte's body being found just as he was about to locate his grandfather's fortune.

"Lola wanted something in exchange for the map, didn't she?"

"She had no right to any of those diamonds, Ms. Cooper. She was trying to blackmail me, just like she had coaxed Claude Lavery out of his grant money."

Shreve was standing now, poised in the doorway of the small room. "Lola slammed the door on me, but I wouldn't leave. She came out later, maybe five, maybe ten minutes. I asked where she was going but she wouldn't answer me. I knew she was going to the island. To Strecker, to find Charlotte. I tried to stop her but she pushed past me and got on the elevator."

"Just the two of you?"

"Claude. That's when Claude came out of her apartment. I was shocked to see him there. The elevator lurched and I grabbed at Lola to pull her off. All I got was her scarf, her long woolen scarf.

"But the doors closed and caught the ends of the scarf as the cab started to move. I yelled at Claude to push the buttons and I pried the sides apart with my hands. There was Lola, completely blue in the face, flailing her arms and trying to fight for air or to catch her breath to scream. She thought I had done it on purpose."

Perhaps that part was true. He had painted such a

vivid picture of Lola, almost hanged to death by a piece of clothing caught in the elevator doors. A soft piece of woolen material, on top of the thick fabric of a winter coat collar, that would not even leave ligature marks.

"But she was still alive then?"

"Oh, yes. She couldn't speak, she couldn't loosen the scarf. 'It was an *accident*,' I said to her. I reached for the coat to undo it and she recoiled.

"That's when she started to scream."

I imagined that she did, also having figured that Shreve had somehow been responsible for Charlotte Voight's disappearance. I would have been shouting what I wanted to say to his face right at that moment. *Murderer!*

He stumbled now, stuttering instead of delivering a clear narrative. "It was Claude who did it. He wanted her to stop screaming, to make her be quiet."

It made no sense to me for Claude to want to kill Lola. But I had given Shreve the opening to insert an accomplice into his re-creation of the events.

"Claude grabbed at the scarf and pulled it tighter. He dragged her off the elevator and onto the floor of the hallway. He was calling her names, he was—"

It's not a fast death, strangulation. Not like a gunshot wound to the head or a knife in the chest. No doubt it had been hastened in this instance by the fact that she was almost hanged by the jaws of the elevator door. She was already weakened and had a compromised airway, so it would not have taken much effort to finish her off.

Shreve searched for words and actions to attribute to Lavery, but I knew better now.

"She, she didn't scream very loud. I, uh, I tried to pull Claude back but he wouldn't let go. He was so mad at her." He lowered his head and tried to add convincing facts. "That's when he told me that Lola had been blackmailing him for cash from his grant money."

"And Lola's body?"

"I wanted to call the police. I know you won't believe that, because of—" He broke off midsentence and nodded his head to the side, in the direction of the Strecker building. Toward Charlotte Voight's body. "This time it was Claude who refused. He was about to be indicted by the federal authorities for fraud. He, uh, he told me to leave. That he would handle this himself. And I did, assuming he would take care of things in an appropriate way.

"I never imagined that he'd roll her body into the elevator shaft. I mean, Claude's the one who lives there. I wasn't even aware anything was wrong in the building, that the elevators sometimes stopped between floors. How could I have possibly known that?"

He had me for a moment. It made sense for Lavery to know that fact. But any fool who had visited the old building and been on the elevator when it malfunctioned could have known it, too. It happened with the three elevators in our office building every day of the week.

"You put that map in my hands, Ms. Cooper, and when you prosecute Professor Lavery, I'll come back from Paris and testify at the trial. Now, who has the map? In what safe place did you leave it this morning?"

37

"You *do* know the piece of paper I mean?"

I tried to force myself to focus. Once he knew how to get his hands on the map, there was no need to keep me alive. I thought of the paper in my pocket and my hand unconsciously moved to stroke my throat, thinking of Lola's fate and imagining the many uses of the thick length of rope Shreve had brought back with him. There were two other copies, and I had to make him think I was indispensable in getting them into his possession.

"I didn't know about the significance of the map when we came across it, of course. I never knew the story of your grandfather's diamonds until just the other day. But I do know how to get it for you."

He was calm now, and talking to me as he squatted next to the chair.

"Look, Ms. Cooper. I'm a French citizen. You get me this map, and I'll find Freeland's ransom, go back to my home abroad, and donate half the money to the college or any cause you name."

I listened. Surely he would know we could extradite him from France. Or was he that certain that he could talk his way out of a murder charge?

"We're talking about millions of dollars." My head dropped to avoid his gaze. "Ah, ever the earnest prosecutor. Once you help convince all the authorities how Charlotte died, I'll be home free. And you'll still have Claude to blame for Lola Dakota's death."

"You'll need me to get the map, Mr. Shreve. The original is in the safe in Paul Battaglia's office."

"Your team is too efficient not to have made some copies. I took the liberty of looking through your file—the one that was in my car—but no map."

"One copy." I sucked in some frigid air and prayed that what I was about to say would not put Mike in harm's way. "Detective Chapman has that copy. And I can help you get it from him."

"How can you do that?"

I would have to think of something specific by daybreak, less than an hour or so away. "Because he'll do whatever I ask him to do."

"No wonder you've got some problems with your boyfriend. Rather confident of that, aren't you?"

"Chapman's a very intelligent man, Mr. Shreve. If you let me call him and arrange for him to meet us, you can tell him exactly what you've told me about Charlotte Voight and Lola Dakota."

"Surrender?"

"If Charlotte's death was accidental, and Lavery killed Lola, then you've got nothing to worry about."

I needed to talk myself out of this black abyss and into the open areas outside the building where someone might actually be able to see us once the morning came.

"I'd rather get back home to the Sixth Arrondissement and let *you* break the news to the NYPD. Where's the Blackwells Island miniature that my grandfather had Bennino make, Ms. Cooper? Do you know that, too?"

I moved my head up and down, slowly trying to think of a possible answer.

"Was that a 'yes'?"

"Yes, I do." Shreve himself had given me the idea when he had talked about Lola's weeks in hiding. "It's at Lily's house, Lola's sister." Why hadn't I thought of that possibility in all the days since the murder? Lola must have taken a lot of things with her to occupy her during the weeks in New Jersey. She was too much of a workhorse not to have done so. If that's where she was when she figured out Jennings's deadhouse scheme, that's probably where the model was concealed.

I went on weaving my tale, which seemed to interest Winston Shreve. "There's a key to a trunk that's in Lily's garage. It's where Lola left the miniature when she came back to the city. Chapman has that key. I'm supposed to meet him at nine o'clock this morning to go with him to pick up the model."

"And all that charade about old man Lockhart and going up to listen to his story?"

"To try to determine who else knew about the map and the diamonds. If you let me call Chapman now, on your cell phone, I know he'll agree to meet with us." And I know he'll get the tech unit to trace the call immediately. They could do amazing things with satellite systems, even pinpointing the location of the caller in a matter of seconds.

"I wouldn't want to alarm him in the middle of the night. He might be busy."

Shreve was right. Mike might be much too involved with Valerie to be giving me a second thought.

I didn't want to end my life in this godforsaken ruin like one more of the outcasts sent here and left to die. Slowly, I raised my head to meet his eyes. "I've studied your grandfather's map, Mr. Shreve. I believe I could recognize the shapes of some of the areas, the pieces of land where the wooden sheds once stood, if I saw them. If you want to walk outside with me, I can try to help you find the rocks that correspond with the locations noted on the map."

"That's a good way to start, Ms. Cooper." He turned to look out the hollowed window frame. It was still dark, and the storm had subsided. The precipitation had stopped and large wet flakes of snow blew lazily upward from the ground instead of falling in sheets. "The positions on the map, were they numbered?"

"Yes, yes, they were numbered." The first time I said that word aloud I recalled another set of numbers. In the pocket of the black sweater that we'd found in Lola Dakota's apartment just hours after her murder was the slip of paper that we had removed. The paper that bore the words THE DEADHOUSE, followed by a list of numbers. They meant nothing to us at the time, and now I realized they must have been the key to the map that Lola had deciphered while holed up at her sister's home.

Lola had come back from New Jersey wearing that sweater, but removed it at some point before she walked out of her apartment for the last time. Shreve had gone to intercept her, looking for the map and the numbers that might correspond to it and lead him to the diamonds.

"The numbers, Ms. Cooper. Tell me how they were ordered."

"I honestly can't remember that. I know that the lower numbers started at the southern tip of the island. I, uh, I could probably show you where some of the areas that were highlighted on the map are, if I could actually see the terrain."

"Nice try, Ms. Cooper. That's hardly the way it was half a century ago."

"But some of it is exactly the same. I, I—when I saw the map, I didn't even realize what the outline of the

Strecker building represented. But I know there were areas to the east of that, along the seawall, that were starred by Professor Dakota on her map." After Shreve's explanation this morning, it didn't take much else to figure out where the wooden sheds had been built, close to the morgue and out of view of patients arriving from Manhattan.

He was too smart to trust me entirely.

"You've got nothing to lose." I tried to say it casually, not to reveal how anxious I was to get out of this hellhole. "I can't get very far." Surrounded as we were on three sides by water that was so cold it would kill the strongest swimmer within minutes of submersion, even before the current could carry one away, and bounded on the fourth side by a razor-wire fence, Shreve could hardly disagree.

He picked up one of his neckties and rewound it around my hands, binding them in front of me—rather than behind—so I could move more easily. He carried the long piece of rope in his left hand, while lifting me to my feet with his right. "I'll call your bluff, Ms. Cooper. You've got a bit of time to see if you can find me a gem or two."

It took me several seconds on my feet before I was able to walk a few steps. The cold air had numbed them, and I was fearful of frostbite. That was a good thing, I reminded myself. It at least meant that I thought I was going to survive this ordeal if I was worried about losing a few toes.

Shreve led me through the shell of the building and out the rear door, the same way we had come in hours before. It was the only side of the structure that was not lit by floodlights, and so he knew he could guide me out to the shoreline without detection, in the event anyone had even thought to look for me in this unlikely place.

The city nightscape was more visible to me now. The gray-black sky had cleared to cobalt blue, in the final hour of predawn darkness on the last day of the year. Off in the distance on the Manhattan side, the Art Deco crown beneath the spire of the Chrysler Building was bathed in the red and green lights of the holiday season. Closer to me, in Queens, the Citicorp tower dominated the skyline, standing behind the Domino Sugar, Silvercup, and *Daily News* signs that stood atop the company plants that fronted the river.

Below the neon lights and factory smokestacks, on the streets and piers, I could not make out a single human being across the water.

Holding my elbow, Shreve walked me to the edge of the river. Rats the size of piglets scampered up and over the boulders that edged the seawall. There were boat docks farther north, on the populated part of the island, but no vessel could come close to this granite border without smashing its hull against the rocks.

I turned back to look at the two ghostlike structures. On my left, parallel with the front wall of the old hospital, was a giant elm tree, bare of her leaves and coated with icicles.

"That tree is one of the markers on the map. Behind us"—I swiveled and pointed with my bound forefingers locked together—"is where the island widens and curves north."

Shreve looked at the shape of the wall, following my direction. I went on, "That had to be the strip on which the deadhouses were built. It's close to the morgue, but still out of sight." That much was logical. I tried to sound just as convincing as I continued to speak. "The map had foundations of four old wooden buildings. The first one was a bit north of that bend in the seawall, if I remember it correctly."

He moved away from me and took a few steps to the edge of the wall, taking care not to slip on the icy boulders. He braced himself with one leg on a piece of granite closest to the water, and I saw it wobble beneath his foot. It must have given him a scare, because I heard him curse beneath his breath and back away from the edge. He decided to explore the loose boulder and got down onto his knees. The rock lifted easily and although it was dark where we were standing, there did not appear to be any treasure hidden beneath it. He scraped a gloved hand against the frozen ground, but the dirt wouldn't yield to such a soft probe. I assume that years of neglect had caused the seawall to decay, too.

"I don't think any of the rocks that close to the edge

were marked on the map," I cautioned. I wriggled my hands in the direction of a paved area that seemed to be composed of crumbling material. "This patch would have been under the base of one of the buildings," I suggested.

Again, Shreve dropped to his knees and began to dig his fingers into the crevices, moving anything loose out of his way but coming up empty. No long-buried treasure was going to be that close to the petrified surface of the land.

He was getting short with me now, figuring that I was leading him on a wild-goose chase to save my own neck. He pushed himself back to a standing position and picked up the rope from the ground beside him.

"It makes more sense if you just wait for me inside." Shreve took a step toward me and it was clear that he was ready to use the thick cable to restrain me. I knew he had less than an hour to decide whether it was safe to tie me up and leave me alive beside Charlotte Voight while he returned to Manhattan for the day, or if it was better to dispose of me in the icy current just ten feet away.

I slid my feet backward, one at a time, away from his outstretched arms. "Come on, Ms. Cooper," he said, extending the rope with one hand and trying to grab my wrists with the other. "I'll go over to the college and see what progress the police are making with your disappearance. Don't worry, I'll be here in the afternoon with something for you to eat, and another chance for you to cooperate."

I glided back in the direction of the footpath and Shreve tried to keep up with me, both of us slipping and sliding on the frosted rocks' glassy surface. I was not going back inside the morgue, to be a companion to the decomposed remains of Charlotte Voight.

"Don't be stupid, young lady. You've got nowhere to go."

"Take me with you," I pleaded, skating sideways as he fell on one knee and struggled to keep his balance.

As Shreve scrambled to get back on his feet, I could see over the top of his head that three police cars, red bubble lights flashing, were coming over the small bridge from Long Island City to the northern end, near Roosevelt Island's Main Street. My heartbeat quickened. Perhaps Mercer had given Mike the *Jeopardy!* message after all. Perhaps the motorcade was looking for me.

They were still miles away from this isolated strip of earth, and I needed to stall for as long as possible until they might find me.

I turned south, away from the ruins of Strecker, and headed for the southernmost tip of the island, the only point that could be seen from both Manhattan and Queens. It was treacherous going, and Shreve tried to overtake me as I balanced every tread on the slippery path. He was moving carefully, not racing, since it was as obvious to him as it was to me that I had no way to escape him.

When I was just several feet from the narrow end, I stopped and looked back at my pursuer. In the air, to my left, one of the giant red cabs of the tram had lumbered into view and was cruising down into its station. It was still too early for the system to be operating, and I prayed the movement meant that the police had pressed it into service. Shreve was bearing down on me and had not noticed the police cars or the tram that was traveling behind his back.

"I lied to you," I screamed out at him, my words blown off over the water by the fierce wind.

"What?" he answered, yelling back as he was still trying to make his way to me.

Off the very point of the island was a spit of rock, a huge boulder that was connected to the land by a series of smaller stones. Sometimes barely visible throughout the year, the stones now protruded through the water's surface because of the heavy buildup of snow and frost. Between and around them were patches of ice, thin coatings that endured defiantly during this cold spell against the constant pounding of the swift current.

Only a ten-foot-high beacon stood on the barren rock, useful in fog to guide ships around the island into the channels on either side.

"What did you say?" he shouted at me again as I scanned the horizon, hoping to see patrol cars careering onto the roadway that led to my lonely outpost.

He was not more than an arm's length away, and he

paused to catch his breath, winding and twisting the rope like a rodeo rider about to snare a calf. He was confident, and I was terrified, trying to buy time as he closed in on me.

"I said I lied to you before."

He laughed aloud at me. "And exactly which part was a lie?"

I checked over my shoulder and back to the very edge of the seawall. As I stood on top of an ancient fragment of granite, I pushed my jacket aside and poked my bound hands around the edges of my pants pockets.

Shreve's face screwed into a puzzled expression as he watched me fumble.

I strained to hear beyond the howl of the wind but could not make out the noise of any sirens. Where could the cops be? What was taking them so long to find us?

I stepped one foot down onto a flat rock that jutted out of the black water and was the first link to the boulder less than ten feet away. When I was standing securely with two legs in place, I glanced back at Shreve and pulled the paper from my pocket.

"It's the map, Mr. Shreve. I lied when I told you I had time to make copies. This is the original. It arrived in yesterday's mail, just before we went up to the meeting in Sylvia's office. This is what you want, Professor. It's the only one there is."

The wind whipped at the paper and tried to snatch

it from my hands and carry it away. I crammed it into the pocket of my parka, and continued on my hazardous journey.

It was *my* turn to be confident now. If I could navigate the seven or eight stones to get across to the large boulder, I would be safe. Shreve would not dare to follow me. The more than eighty pounds that separated what I guessed our weights to be would fracture the ice, should he attempt to step on it. And I could cling to the beacon, waiting out the sunrise, sure that the police were on their way to find me.

If I didn't make it, and I was keenly aware of that possibility, it would be an awful death. But faster, I assured myself, than anything Winston Shreve had in mind.

I hadn't counted on how badly he wanted to get his hands on the map.

I was on the fourth stone in the icy archipelago, straining to keep my feet from slipping, hindered by my inability to stretch out my arms and stabilize myself against the wind above and the slick surface below. Behind me, I heard the crackling noise of breaking ice.

I ignored the voice in my head that had been telling me not to look back. Shreve had followed my path and was on the first stone. He had stepped off to the second one, but his feet were longer than mine and the rocky incline could not hold his thick boots. His left leg had slid down and landed on the crust of ice, breaking it apart and allowing the black water tō bubble through.

"Give me the goddamn map," he screamed at me. He had frozen in place, it seemed, now aware of the dangerous trail he had undertaken. "Give me the paper!"

The wind played with him, too, and his words were lost somewhere over the roiling water.

My next two obstacles were relatively flat and elongated. I moved across them easily and counted only three more on my course to the big rock.

A glance back and it was clear that Shreve was consumed by his desire to get to the map. He had made the decision to come after me. His feet held on the third step, and he paused there to figure how to make it safely onto the next one.

The great buildings of the United Nations were directly across to my right now. Lights were going on in some of the offices as the sky began to brighten. The city was coming to life. Someone would find me.

My foot reached out to anchor itself on the next rock, but it was peaked and ragged, with no flat area on which to step. I leaned forward and grabbed its crest with my clasped hands, stretching out the toe of my right foot to find a hold on the slippery cover. It seemed secure, and so I pulled myself forward, balancing my one hundred fifteen pounds on either side of the crest. As fast as I could free my hands and move again, I teetered forward to the adjacent perch, almost at my goal.

As I stood on the next-to-the-last rock, I was ready to launch myself to safety. I grabbed at the naked shrub that was poised on the ledge in front of me and tried to pull myself onto the slick boulder. But the ice beneath my left foot ruptured sharply and my entire leg was submerged in the frigid water. I clung desperately to the small gray stubble of the branch that was supporting me and kicked my quickly benumbed leg furiously to get it out of the icy river.

Slowly and agonizingly, I hoisted myself onto solid ground. Shreve's scream pierced the air and the wind slammed its sound against my head.

I opened my eyes and saw him grasping for my leg, which was dangling over the side of the great boulder. He was trying to get me to save him, I thought, not to hurt me, although it hardly mattered at that point. As he had reached out for me, he slid off the peaked rock and collapsed through the slim coating of ice.

"The rope!" I yelled at him. "Throw me the rope."

But the wicked current tugged at him and swept him away from the rocks. I pulled myself up to a standing position using the sturdiest branch of the small bush, but with my hands still tied I was unable to extend my reach near the drowning man.

Shreve screamed once more as he struggled to keep his head above the waves. The turbulent inky water had claimed him, and he was dragged downriver at ferocious speed. He shouted something again, gurgling insensibly as he was pulled down by the paralyzing force of the raging flow.

I lowered myself onto the ground, wet and frozen. I rested my head against a low stump and gave up waiting for salvation. The Pepsi-Cola sign flashed and there seemed to be early morning traffic racing along the FDR Drive.

The little red snub-nosed tugboat of the New York City Fire Department seemed to be making a beeline for my deserted boulder. I tried to tell myself its crew would see me here, with dawn breaking through the night sky. As it neared me, on its prow I thought I could make out the figures of Mike Chapman and Mercer Wallace, standing beside two uniformed firemen. Mercer must have repeated the story I fed to Shreve about the Blackwell *Jeopardy!* clue, and Mike had made the connection.

Cold, exhaustion, and hunger overwhelmed me.

I closed my eyes.

When I came to, the first thing I saw was the pure white counterpane on my hospital bed. I felt warm and comforted for the first time in days. Looped around the upper rim of the metal railing was an intravenous tube. The IV pole was next to my headboard, and I could see that the glucose solution was almost empty. I must have been badly dehydrated.

I looked at the clock on the bedside table and it said 11:42. The shades were drawn three-quarters of the way down, open enough to reveal that it was night.

I rolled from my side onto my back, wiggling my

toes as I did so. I lifted each foot, one at a time, to reach my hands, and counted to make sure I had all my toes.

When I moved onto my other side, my cheek scraped against something hard. There, pinned against the corner of the pillow, was Jake's glittering little bird atop a rock.

Through the glass windows that separated my room from the nurses' station, I could see five people standing together. Jake Tyler and Mercer Wallace were leaning against the counter, watching Mike Chapman and laughing at him. He was gesturing with great animation, regaling two nurses with his war stories and adventures.

I knew it wouldn't take long for Mike and Mercer to coax me back to Blackwells, with the old map, to dig for diamonds with them. They would find my stalker, too. I was sure of that.

Outside the door to my room was another IV stand. Attached to it, hanging upside down, was a bottle of champagne. Tomorrow would begin a happier new year.

I smiled and closed my eyes.